THE DRAGON SHIFTER'S MATES

THE COMPLETE SERIES

EVA CHASE

The Dragon Shifter's Mates: The Complete Series

First Print Edition, 2021

Cover design: Covers by Juan

Case back cover illustration: Deden Supriatna

ISBN: 978-1-989096-97-0

DRAGON'S GUARD

THE DRAGON SHIFTER'S MATES #1

CHAPTER 1

Ren

"Are you waiting for someone, honey?" the bartender asked.

It was a reasonable question, considering that I'd been perched on one of the leather-cushioned seats at the bar for ten minutes without ordering anything. If the place had been any busier, he'd probably have pushed me a lot sooner. But there was only one other patron down the counter from me, a grizzled dude who was glued to his beer and the burble of the football game, and a handful of people scattered around the wooden tables in the rest of the room.

I'd picked this bar for exactly that reason. If she came, it'd be somewhere low key, not too noisy or crowded. At least, that had felt like the right idea. It wasn't as if she'd shown up anyway.

"Not exactly," I said to the bartender, leaning my elbows on the counter. The smell of wood varnish and booze tickled my nose. "And if you're going to call me anything, call me Ren." Most of the times I'd heard "honey" in the last seven years, it'd been followed by a leer and a grope.

The bartender didn't take offense, just grinned. "No problem, Ren. Can I get you anything, while you're 'not exactly' waiting?"

I was feeling too restless to want a drink for pleasure, but maybe that was why I should have one. It'd take the edge off my nerves. "I'll have a Bloody Mary."

"That I can do." His grin turned apologetic. "I do have to ask for ID. Take it as a compliment?"

I shrugged and pulled out my wallet. When I flashed the card at him, he chuckled. "Birthday girl, huh? It's an honor to serve your first drink." He raised an eyebrow. "Or at least your first legal drink."

Yeah, we wouldn't get into the amounts of cheap vodka and rum I'd gulped for a buzz over the last several years. When you were crashing on the streets, there was always someone passing around a bottle in a paper bag. But I was done with that part of my life now.

There was only one thing still missing.

"Make it extra bloody," I told the bartender. He saluted me and grabbed a glass. As he mixed the cocktail, I looked toward the door. Beyond the window, the headlights of Brooklyn traffic streaked by through the darkening evening. No one walked in.

My hand rose to the locket that dangled just below my collarbone. I traced the delicate vine pattern etched in the warm gold. My chest still tightened a little when I flicked the locket open, even though I'd done it already a dozen times today.

The necklace was the last thing my mother had given to me. Seven years ago, but I could remember so vividly the way her dark eyes had shimmered with a hint of tears as she'd pressed the locket into my hands. She'd clasped her fingers over mine and leaned close. The perfume she wore, like smoky roses, had filled my lungs.

"I have to go," she'd said. "If what I'm about to do works out the way I hope, I'll be back before you know it. But if I'm not... You hold onto this locket. Don't take it off for an instant. And keep it closed until your twenty-first birthday. Then, if I'm not here, you open it."

At the time, turning twenty-one had felt so distant I'd hardly processed what she was saying. She'd left before on her little trips, but she'd never been gone more than a week or two. When she'd pulled me into her arms, I'd hugged her back a little harder than usual, but I hadn't really believed she wouldn't come back. She was the one sure thing I'd always had.

But she hadn't come back. And here I was, twenty-one. I snapped the locket closed, nudged it open, snapped it closed again. There was nothing inside but another etching, this one a symbol like an upside-down flame at the heart of a spiraling line. It didn't mean anything to me. I wasn't sure if it was supposed to.

Somewhere in the back of my head, I'd had the idea that the second I'd open the locket, Mom would know. She'd know, and she'd come find me. Whatever had been stopping her before, it'd be over.

I'd braced myself and popped it open for the first time twelve hours ago. And here I was, still twenty-one, sitting alone in a half-empty bar on a Thursday night.

Not alone for long. The bartender set my Bloody Mary down in front of me, and a guy who'd been sitting at one of the tables ambled over. He plopped onto the stool next to mine, called to the bartender for a gin and tonic, and looked me up and down.

"You seem to be a little lonely tonight, sweetheart," he said.

His voice sounded as greasy as his hair looked. The armpits of his dress shirt were ringed with sweat stains. "Maybe I can help with that."

Hard pass on that one. "I'm good, actually," I said. "No assistance required."

He shuffled a little closer. He smelled like sweat too—sweat and the three to four drinks he'd already downed. Ugh. "Aw, come on. No harm in a little conversation."

I wouldn't be so sure about that, I thought. The truth was, even if he'd been remotely appealing, I'd have steered clear. Me and guys didn't seem to mix well. I'd had a few hook-ups over the years, but nothing that had gone past second base. As soon as things took a hot and heavy turn, a strange sensation rose up inside me. Like claws digging into my innards. And I'd suddenly feel as if I could rip the guy apart.

As if maybe I wanted to.

There's nothing like visions of gruesome murder to put a damper on your libido.

That wasn't the only time I felt the stirring of those claws inside me. The greasy guy tapped me on the shoulder with a smirk, and a prickle crept up over my ribs. The picture he was presenting snapped together into sudden focus. I could almost taste his bruised ego in its sauce of desperation.

"I'm not any more interested than your ex is," I said, and took a sip of my Bloody Mary. "So how about you leave both of us alone?"

The guy's face turned sallow. "Bitch," he muttered. He snatched his drink off the counter and stalked away.

I swallowed another mouthful of the spicy, tomatoey cocktail. The bartender had made sure it packed a good wallop, exactly the way I wanted. Enough to wash away most of the discomfort of that encounter.

My phone vibrated in my pocket. I pulled it out and smiled when I saw the name on the screen. "Hey, Kylie!" I said. "Are you really supposed to be making calls in the middle of your shift?"

"I made a deal with my supervisor that I'd cut out early tonight in exchange for an extra long shift tomorrow," my best friend said in her chirpy voice. "Birthday surprise! Where are you, Ren? We need to rock tonight, hard."

I laughed. Maybe this was what I really needed. Mom was long gone, doing whatever had been more important than sticking with her only kid, and of course no piece of jewelry was going to bring her back. But I didn't need her anymore. I'd gotten through the last seven years alive if not completely unscathed, and now Kylie and I had finally scrounged together enough money to put a down payment on an apartment.

It was a crappy apartment, on a street so seedy there were more weeds than concrete on the sidewalks, but it had four walls and a ceiling with no holes. It had a door with a lock, and only we had the keys. These days, that was heaven.

Kylie normally worked the evening and early night shift cashiering and stocking shelves at a rundown grocery store in the 'hood. I'd be back hauling boxes at my warehouse job tomorrow morning. No fun, but whatever paid the bills. And I could sleepwalk through the job, so I didn't need to worry about a hangover.

I turned around one of the coasters sitting on the counter to check the bar's name. "I'm at a place called Carmello's," I said. "It's on 5th Ave a few blocks from the park. But I can meet you wherever."

"No, no," Kylie said. "I'm coming to get you. And then I'm taking you on one epic adventure, little girl."

"I'll hold you to that promise," I said. Not that I had any

doubt Kylie would deliver. She was only a couple years older than me, but when I'd first run into her a few years back, that had seemed like a much bigger gap than it did now. She'd looked out for me as much a big sister as a friend.

Carmello's would definitely be too much of a snore for her to want to stick around here. I gulped some more of my Bloody Mary so I'd be finished before she showed up.

The door sighed open, too early for it to be Kylie already. My heart leapt despite the talking-to I'd given myself. But it definitely wasn't my mom walking in.

The guy looked young, maybe mid-twenties, but there was a confidence in the way he prowled into the bar that seemed to carry the weight of a lot more experience. His round face was broken by the jut of sharp cheekbones—not exactly handsome, but definitely memorable. His hazel eyes swept the room and came to rest on me.

I jerked my gaze away, realizing I'd been staring. And he wasn't at all the kind of person I wanted to be staring at. Living on the streets had given me a keen instinct for danger. This guy? He was not someone to mess with. A sense of purpose radiated off of him too. I figured it was better not to get in the way of whatever he was up to.

Just my luck, he sauntered up to the bar right beside me. "Give me the best thing you have on tap," he said to the bartender, and turned toward me. "Nice night to be out on the town."

"I suppose," I said noncommittally. How long was it going to take Kylie to get here and give me an easy exit?

Cheekbones cocked his head. "All the early summer energy in the air, it really brings the beast out."

What was *that* supposed to mean? I shrugged and acted fascinated by my Bloody Mary. He didn't take the hint.

"Maybe we could take a walk, get to know each other a little better."

I cut my eyes toward him. He *was* confident, wasn't he? My quick tongue got a little ahead of my better judgment. "Who says I'm looking to get to know you?"

Cheekbones grinned at me, looking unfazed. "I'm just saying, we clearly have a lot in common. This isn't our kind of place, is it? Why not come back to the fold, at least for a visit?"

A lot in common? The fold? Was this guy *on* something? No dilated pupils, no jerky movements, but you never knew what drugs were making the rounds these days.

I drained as much of my drink as I could in one swallow and set down the glass. The hit of spice and alcohol sharpened my inner claws. "I'm pretty sure we have exactly nothing in common," I said. "For one thing, I know how to take a 'No.'"

Before I had to find out how he was going to answer that, I hopped off my stool and made a beeline for the back hall with its *Restrooms* sign. He wasn't likely to follow me into the ladies'.

Washing my hands, I peered at my reflection. I hadn't put on anything other than my standard mascara and light maroon lipstick combo today. I was dressed casual in a faded Nine Inch Nails tee and jeans. I'd been blessed with a good hair day, my chocolate-brown waves drifting artfully across my shoulders the way I usually struggled and failed to style them, but otherwise nothing extra special was going on. So why were guys honing in on me like flies to a jar of sugar water?

It didn't matter. Cheekbones made me too uneasy. Either he was drugged out or partly insane, and neither would lead to a good outcome. I'd text Kylie to meet me at the all-ages club on the other side of town and grab a cab to be on my way.

I was reaching for my phone as I came out of the restroom, and a pair of arms slammed around me from behind. One clapped a damp cloth over my face. The other wrapped around my waist. A sickly sweet smell washed over me. I swung back my elbow—and the world went black.

CHAPTER 2

Ren

I WOKE up with a muddy feeling behind my eyes and velvety fabric against my cheek. Neither of those sensations felt right.

Blinking, I rubbed my forehead. The room around me came into focus. It still didn't make much sense.

I was lying on a four-poster bed in an elegantly decorated bedroom. Thin sunlight drifted in past the brocade curtains on either side of a wide window. The bedframe, as well as the dresser and the vanity by the walls, looked like mahogany, polished to a shine. Gold flower patterns glinted on the mint-green wallpaper.

The bedspread under me was actually velvet. The soft pile darkened under the pressure of my hands as I pushed myself upright. A sweet lilac scent drifted up from it.

Sweet. The memory rushed up of the arms catching me, the cloth over my nose and mouth. My pulse stuttered. I touched my face as if I could pull that moment out of my past. Make it not have happened.

But it had happened. Someone had grabbed me and knocked me out. And brought me here, wherever *here* was. Apparently my kidnapper had a lot of money and a decadent taste in furnishings.

I patted my pockets. My phone was gone. At least my clothes were all still on and in order. I didn't feel any unexpected aches or pains. No reason to think I'd been manhandled other than that initial assault.

At least so far. Who knew what my kidnapper had planned for me next?

Muscles tensed, I pushed myself off the bed. The window appeared to be at the front of the house. It looked out over a suburban street. A wide lawn led down to the road, and a large Victorian home stood on the far side, maybe a hundred feet away. There was another house in view to the left, beyond a thick hedge. I didn't see anyone moving in their windows or outside, but the sun had just risen over the horizon. I might get a chance to yell for help later.

In the meantime, I treaded across the floorboards to the vanity, looking for a letter opener or hairpin or anything else reasonably stabby. The drawers revealed only pots and tubes of various makeup powders and creams, a brush and a comb, and a mirror in a silver case that was smaller than my palm.

Footsteps sounded outside the door. My hand stuffed the mirror in my pocket automatically. Spend a few years thieving and it becomes an impulse. I shoved the drawer closed and backed toward the window.

The doorknob turned. There was no click of a key or scrape of a deadbolt. I hesitated despite my thudding heart. The door hadn't even been locked? I hadn't bothered to check, I'd been so sure it would be.

The door glided open. A guy I'd never seen before strolled

into the room. I was sure of that, because if I *had* seen him before, even years ago, I definitely would have remembered him. He was the most gorgeous human being I'd ever set eyes on.

A sleekly muscular body, at least a few inches taller than my five-foot-nine, filled out his fitted dress shirt and slacks. His face was sleek too, with deep indigo-blue eyes and a topping of spiky black hair. The only feature that marred its perfect symmetry was a small scar that nicked his left eyebrow, but somehow that only made him look more perfect. An earring gleamed in his right earlobe—a tiny sapphire stud that matched his eyes.

He stopped a couple steps into the room and offered me a crooked grin. A flutter raced through my chest.

Holy hell. I'd been knocked out and carted off into some stranger's house. This was not the time for melting panties, Ren.

And yet they were melting. My heart was still thumping, but it wasn't entirely fear now. The quiver running through my nerves felt more like eager anticipation.

What the hell was wrong with me?

And was it my imagination, or was the guy staring back at me just as avidly?

"Welcome to my home," he said in a jaunty, melodic voice. "I'm sorry we had to meet under these circumstances. I promise you, kidnapping isn't my usual style. I was hoping to speak with you in your own territory. My assistant got a little... overenthusiastic."

He cut a glance toward the doorway. I *had* seen the guy standing there before. It was Cheekbones, from the bar. My shoulders stiffened.

But after all his swaggering in the bar, he now looked totally deflated. He shuffled over the room's threshold and dropped to his knees, bowing his head.

"I am so sorry. I overstepped."

"By a *huge* margin," the first guy said dryly.

"By a huge margin," Cheekbones leapt to agree. "It was completely my fault. I wasn't even supposed to talk to you. I— Again, I'm sorry."

"All right," his boss said with a flick of his hand. "Get going. I'm sure she doesn't want to see your face any more than she has to. You can get started with your new job." He turned back to me with that slanted smile. "I've assigned him to cleaning duty for a month, which seemed to make sense, considering what a mess he made of things."

"I'm confused," I said. "I— So you didn't *mean* to kidnap me?" It was a little hard to wrap my head around that idea.

"Like I said, not my style. I'd have told Leonard to bring you back to your home if I'd known where that was. Since I didn't"—he motioned to the room—"I tried to make you as comfortable as possible in the meantime."

He hadn't come any closer, still giving me plenty of space. But he was standing between me and the doorway. I wet my lips.

"So, if I wanted to, I could go home right now?"

The guy's eyebrows lifted. "Well, of course. Be my guest to stop being my guest." He sidestepped to open the way to the door. "We're only a half hour from Brooklyn, and there's a train station a ten minute walk down the street. But maybe you'll consider accepting my hospitality for a little longer, now that you're here and all? I've been waiting a very long time to get the chance to talk to you."

I'd already crossed half the room. At that comment, my body froze up. I stared at him. "What do you mean? You said that before: that you wanted to talk to me. Talk to me about *what*? Who *are* you? Why were you—and your 'assistant'—poking around in my life at all?"

"Let's take those one at a time, starting with the simplest. My name is Marco. Pleased to meet you." He dipped his head in a playful half bow. "I'd like to talk to you about pretty much everything, but maybe starting with what you've been doing for the last sixteen years. And do you really have no idea why I'd be interested?"

Marco said the last bit lightly, but his indigo gaze held mine intently. That shiver of anticipation ran through my nerves again. Randomly I found myself wondering what one of those agile hands would feel like tracing over my skin—

Okay, Ren, mind out of the gutter. You've known this guy exactly five minutes, and you can't even be sure this whole kidnapping thing was really accidental.

Other than the fact that I *believed* him, right down in the core of me, for reasons I couldn't explain. *He wouldn't lie to me*, my gut said. How the hell could I know that?

None of those reactions answered his question, though. "No," I said. "I haven't got a clue. This isn't some kind of birthday prank that Kylie set up, is it?" It seemed awfully elaborate—and freaky—even for her.

Marco shook his head. "No. Definitely not a prank. I'm just trying to make things right."

"With *me*? But I've never met you before. I've never even seen you before."

"Haven't we met? Your name is Serenity, isn't it?"

I hadn't thought I could tense up any more than I already was. It turned out I was wrong. My back went completely rigid.

No one used that name. No one had used it except my mother, in the quietest whispers when I was sick or drifting off to sleep, in as long as I could remember.

"My name is Ren," I said. My voice came out in a rasp.

"Short for Serenity," Marco said. "You don't need to hide it with me. I'm not going to hurt you."

Why would he say that? My thoughts were spinning. I pressed my hand to my forehead. Marco stepped toward me.

"I don't understand any of this," I said. "I really don't."

His expression softened. As I dropped my hand, he raised his to touch my cheek. My pulse hiccupped, but with the urge to lean into his touch, not to pull away. My skin tingled beneath his fingers. A rich, spicy smell like cinnamon-spiked coffee wafted off of him. Delicious. My gaze dropped to his mouth.

His Adam's apple bobbed. "What did she do to you, my Princess of Flames?" he murmured. "How has she shut you away?"

"No one shut me away," I said. "I'm right here. Who are you talking about?"

"Your mother. It had to be her. To protect you, of course, but—"

I jerked back, my eyes widening. "What do you know about my mother? *How* do you know anything about her?"

Marco looked just as startled by my outburst as I felt. "You could say we ran in the same circles a long time ago. I've been looking for her just as much as you."

The hope that had started to bubble up inside me burst. "Then you don't know where she is now."

He frowned. "No. Don't you? Ren, I think you'd better—" He drew in a sharp breath and summoned his earlier jaunty tone. "I'm being a horrible host. All this talk over breakfast time and not offering you a single thing to eat. I'll bring something up for you. Why don't you take a moment to clear your head? It seems we have more to talk about than I realized."

He lifted my hand to give it a peck on the back. The brush of his lips left my skin burning. Then he swept out of the room without waiting for my response.

CHAPTER 3

Marco

LEONARD, the idiot, was hanging around in the hall. "What are you doing?" I snarled as I strode past him. "I told you to get started on your cleaning detail."

He hurried after me, looking bewildered. "I thought you were joking about that, Marco."

"Oh, really?" I spun on him at the top of the staircase. "Did you also think I was joking when I reamed you out for going up to my friend in there and trying to investigate on your own? Not to mention dragging her out here against her will? Or did that part, at least, sink in?"

Leonard cringed. With anyone else, he would have blustered back, but I knew he was a coward at heart. He crumbled in the face of a stronger authority.

Unfortunately I hadn't been around to exert that authority last night. *Track the source of the magic as closely as possible,* I'd told him. *I'll take over from there when I make it up from North*

Carolina. Apparently those instructions hadn't been clear enough. My New York lieutenant had gotten it into his head that I'd be impressed if he brought the girl in on his own. Because kidnapping was obviously the perfect way to rebuild the trust that had been so brutally lost.

But she didn't seem to remember there was anything to rebuild. She'd responded to me—I'd caught her reaction, that immediate draw toward one's mate. The same thing I'd felt the second I'd laid eyes on her. And, God, what a beauty of a mate I had. The smell of her, sweet and tart at the same time, when I'd leaned close to her... It'd taken all my self-control not to lower my lips to hers, to find out if she tasted just as good.

She wasn't ready for that. She wasn't ready for any of this. Her *body* had responded, but her confusion had been genuine. She didn't even recognize what I was, and I was pretty sure she didn't know what *she* was either. My Princess of Flames, without a clue she was anything other than an ordinary human being. You couldn't get much more absurd than that.

And now I had to try to explain it to her on top of justifying my lieutenant's unfortunate kidnapping tendencies.

I glowered at Leonard a little more, but really, the fault was at least half mine for picking him for the job.

"The other alphas will be on their way," I said. "They could arrive any minute. So now that you know I'm not joking, please find a lamp to dust or a toilet to scrub."

"Yes, sir. I'm sorry, sir." Leonard bobbed his head and loped away. Maybe he could learn. I didn't enjoy hearing my underlings simper, but it was better than them running around half-cocked—and fucking up the most important moment in my life so far.

I headed downstairs, picking up the scent of frying sausages and scrambled eggs from the kitchen. Lindy, who took care of this house during the long periods when I was situated elsewhere, had known we were going to need breakfast even if I'd forgotten. She was sharp enough that she'd probably already made enough for guests.

Under the sounds of sizzling oil and a spatula tapping the pans, a creaking reached my feline-sharp ears. I stopped, turning my head to zero in on the noise.

The back parlor. Someone was trying to jimmy open the window from outside.

First kidnapping and then breaking and entering. This really was shaping up to be a fantastic day. I sucked in a breath.

"Leonard!" I shouted, making for the front hall. "I've got another job for you after all."

~

Ren

What did she do to you, my Princess of Flames? How has she shut you away?

Marco's words echoed in my head. I leaned it into my hands where I was sitting on the edge of the bed. My mind hadn't stopped reeling since he'd walked out the door. Which he'd left open, so I guessed I *was* allowed to leave if I wanted to. I just didn't see how I could when there were so many questions *I* needed answered now.

How had he known my mother? Why did he think he knew me? How had he found out my full name? What was so important that he'd tracked me down—that his "assistant" had thought it was worth kidnapping me over?

Why did I feel the urge to walk into his arms every second I was near him?

A yelp from outside broke through my whirling thoughts. There was a thump and a grunt, sounds of a struggle. I was already on my feet hurrying to the window when a familiar chirpy voice, hardened with anger, carried through the glass.

"Let me go! And you'd better let Ren go too. I know you took her in there. You freaking assholes. I called the police! They'll be here any time now."

Kylie. What was she doing here? I dashed the rest of the way to the window.

Kylie's neon pink pixie cut flashed in the brightening sunlight. Marco's assistant Leonard had tackled her to the ground with her arms pinned behind her back. She squirmed against him, still yelling threats and insults even though her face was pressed against the grass. Marco stood over the two of them. His mouth moved, but I couldn't make out what he was saying to Leonard.

A chill washed over me. Marco had claimed the kidnapping was accidental, but he did at least hire guys who thought that kind of behavior was a-okay. What if he hurt Kylie—or worse?

I yanked up the window and kicked out the screen. Then, in a blink, I'd leapt onto the ledge and vaulted myself out into the air.

The wind rushed past me with the exhilaration a good jump always brought. Like a surge of power I could almost grasp hold of before it slipped through my fingers. My body hunched over, braced for impact. I hit the ground with a *thunk* that rattled my bones but didn't break any. I'd done worse.

When I scrambled to my feet, Marco was staring at me with those intoxicating indigo eyes. He glanced from me to the window and back again. Then he laughed. "If you wanted to come down, I do have a perfectly good staircase."

I ignored the quip. Leonard had frozen to watch what was

going on, but he still had Kylie jammed against the lawn. "Don't hurt her," I said. "Let her go. She's my best friend."

Marco arched an eyebrow at me. "I caught your best friend attempting to break into my home."

"Because I caught *you* dragging Ren off to do who knows what to her," Kylie snapped back. She managed to tip her head at an angle so she could meet my eyes. "Are you okay?"

"I'm fine," I said. Physically speaking, at least. Emotionally... My confusion had faded behind that sharp scrabbling feeling in my chest, which was getting stronger every second Kylie lay pinned on the ground. Leonard was only following orders. I glared at Marco. "I said, *Let her go*. She was only trying to help me. You can't blame her for that."

Something shifted in his eyes as he gazed back at me. A deeper heat than before collected between my legs. It *really* wasn't fair that this dude could make my panties melt with just one look, even when I was totally pissed off at him.

At least he listened. He raised his hand. "Leonard, that's enough."

He spoke smoothly and evenly, but his assistant jerked back as if Marco had barked the order. Kylie shoved herself upright, swiping at the bits of grass clinging to her tank top and bleached cutoffs. The second she was on her feet, she grabbed me in a hug. I squeezed her back, feeling steady for the first time since I'd woken up.

The sensation didn't last. Marco cleared his throat. "Can I ask your friend exactly how she found us?"

Kylie drew back, but she kept one arm slung around me protectively. She was half a foot shorter than me and wiry besides that, but I knew how fiercely she could fight if she had to.

"I was coming to the bar to meet up with Ren," she said. "And I saw your guy here stuffing her in the back of a car. She was obviously unconscious. He drove off before I caught up, but I got the license plate. From there..." Her lips curled into a smirk. "Let's just say I know people who know how to get into the right databases. And traffic cams are awesome."

Marco's gaze flicked to the traffic lights at the end of the long suburban block. He shook his head, looking almost amused. Kylie really did know people—lots of people. Pretty much anything you needed, she could find someone who could do it. She'd racked up a lot of favors over the years.

Believe me, I don't even like most of 'em, she'd said to me one time, halfway through a bottle of cheap wine. *But it's better getting in with people and knowing how far you can trust 'em than never knowing what they might be up to.*

"And are the police actually on their way?" Marco asked.

"Wouldn't you like to know," Kylie shot back, but I could tell from the twitch of her eyes that she was bluffing. Neither of us had a whole lot of faith in cops. She'd been trying to rescue me on her own.

It seemed Marco could read the lie too. "Well, you've found Ren, and you can see that she's all right," he said. "The situation is complicated. And it doesn't involve you. So as wonderful as it was that you dropped by, I'll have to ask you to leave now."

Kylie jutted out her chin. "Uh-uh. No way. There's obviously something sketchy going on here. Come on, Ren. Let's vamoose."

We could. Marco didn't make any move to stop me, just looked at me questioningly. Waiting to see what I would do. Seeing that strengthened my resolve.

"I can't go yet," I told Kylie. "I need to talk with Marco some more."

She tugged me around to face her. "Are you kidding me? The guy seems like a total scammer."

I swallowed hard. "He knows something about my mom," I said.

Kylie's eyes widened. I didn't talk about Mom very much with anyone, but my best friend had heard by far the most. And she was good at reading me even when I didn't want to show how I was feeling, so she probably had a better idea of how much my mother's disappearance haunted me than I'd have liked.

"Okay," she said. "I get that. But I don't want to leave you alone with these dudes either. If you're staying, I'm staying."

Of course she'd say that. My throat tightened. There wasn't any point in arguing with her. I turned to Marco. "Anything you're going to say to me, Kylie can hear it too. That's the deal."

We stared each other down for half a minute. Then Marco chuckled. "All right. This should be interesting. Come on in. We'll have a brunch party."

He sauntered back to the front door without even checking to see if we were going to follow. I made a face at his back, but I hurried along behind him. Kylie wrapped her hand around mine.

"You're sure he's legit?" she murmured to me.

"He knew things he couldn't otherwise." Like my full name, which I'd never told even Kylie. And that it'd been sixteen years since Mom and I had come to the city.

A memory swam up from my birthday just a couple days after we'd first arrived in our East Village apartment, the rooms still bare, a cake with five candles on the floor between Mom and me. *Make a wish. You can ask for anything you want. We're starting new.*

Marco led us into a sitting room on the first floor. Like the bedroom I'd woken up in, the furniture was all tasteful, expensive-looking antiques. Kylie and I sat next to each other on a velvet-cushioned settee.

A middle-aged woman with tightly curled gray-blond hair

glided into the room and set plates heaped with sausages, scrambled eggs, and buttered toast on the mahogany coffee table in front of us. The hearty smell set my mouth watering. I hadn't eaten since yesterday's mid-afternoon snack. I grabbed one of the plates and a fork that looked like actual *silver*ware and dug in.

Kylie eyed the spread. "Shit, that does look good." She picked up a plate and shoveled a forkful of eggs into her mouth. Her eyes rolled back with an ecstatic expression. Then she jabbed her fork toward Marco. He was leaning against the mantle of the empty fireplace, his arms casually crossed in front of him, watching us with a little smile.

"So what's your news about Ren's mom?" Kylie said. "We've got ears even if we're eating."

I lifted my head, gulping a piece of sausage. Marco ran his thumb over his perfect, firm lips. I was definitely not thinking about what it'd be like to kiss them while I waited on the edge of my seat for his answer. My heart had started thudding again.

"Maybe first I should ask what *you* know about her," he said in his usual light tone.

"Not much," Kylie said. "Only what Ren's told me. She was already out of the picture when I came into it."

"I'm getting the impression she's been 'out of the picture' for a while." Marco glanced at me for confirmation.

I nodded, hesitant to offer any details. I still didn't know enough about this guy to be sure how far I could trust him. "She took a lot of trips out of the city," I said. "The last time, she didn't come home."

"And how long ago was that?"

"Do you really need me to tell you that, or do you already know?"

The serious expression I'd only glimpsed once before came back, a brief shadow across his handsome face. "I promise you,

I'm not playing a game here. I want to understand what's happened as much as you do. I'm hoping that between the two of us we can put together enough pieces to see the entire picture."

He sounded sincere. I didn't sense any emotions in his stance other than concern and a little frustration, which I guessed was understandable. But he'd still told *me* barely anything.

"Why don't you—" I started.

Marco's head twitched to the side as if he'd heard a sound. A second later, it reached my ears too: the faint rumble of a car engine. He strode to the door.

"I'm sorry," he said. "Your friend is only the first of the guests coming to see you today. You're a popular girl."

He winked at me and slipped out into the hall.

CHAPTER 4

Ren

"You know this situation is totally wacko, right?" Kylie said, leaning back in the settee. She popped a folded piece of toast into her mouth and chewed vigorously. I'd never figured out how she could eat to rival a linebacker and keep that wiry frame.

"Yeah, that had occurred to me a few hundred times." I rubbed my forehead. "I'm so sorry I got you mixed up in it, Ky."

She gave me a gentle kick to the knee. "Don't be ridiculous. I'm glad I'm here. I can help you get out if things turn even more wacko. And I am kind of curious to find out the big mystery about your mom too."

"If Marco actually does know anything about her." It was starting to sound as if he hadn't seen her in even longer than I had. But the way he'd talked to me—the way he'd *looked* at me... There was something he knew, something big, that he hadn't told me yet.

Was that why my body was responding to his presence so

enthusiastically? I'd never had such an intense reaction to a guy before. Of course, I couldn't say I'd ever met a guy half that gorgeous before...

As if reading my mind, Kylie arched her eyebrows. "I've got to say, you have amazing luck in mysterious sort-of kidnappers. That guy is smokin'."

I had to laugh, even as my cheeks flushed. "Yeah, I noticed that too."

"Ooh." Kylie gave me another nudge with her foot. "Maybe Ren has ulterior motives for sticking around. I'm shocked. You never go gaga over guys."

"I've never seen a guy like that," I muttered.

On the other side of the house, the front door thumped shut. I strained my ears to make out Marco's voice or our new arrival's, but I couldn't hear either. What had he meant when he'd said people were coming to see *me*? How did these other "guests" fit in with whatever secret he hadn't spilled yet?

The uncertainty overwhelmed my hunger. I'd cleared half the plate anyway. I set it down on the coffee table. The growl of another car engine carried through the walls, stopping outside. I shifted on the seat. What were they talking about out there?

My hand rose to my locket. It'd been my touchstone for comfort over the last seven years. All those years of waiting until I was allowed to open it.

I'd opened it... and before the end of the day, Marco's assistant had shown up. I peered at the etched gold oval. That connection hadn't occurred to me before. But how could my opening the locket have brought Marco, or anyone else, my way?

I clicked it open and looked at the symbol inside. *What were you trying to tell me, Mom? Why did you make me wait to see this? I don't understand anything.*

"You opened it!" Kylie said, sitting up. Right. I hadn't seen her since I first had. She leaned over, and I held it up for her to inspect.

"I don't suppose that picture means anything to you," I said.

"Nope. Should it?"

"I don't know." Just one question on my rapidly growing list.

The necklace wasn't giving me any reassurance now. I reached to my pocket instead, feeling the hard circle of the mirror I'd pocketed upstairs. I pulled it out and ran my thumb over the cool, polished surface. My nerves settled a little.

I didn't like to think about all the minor thefts I'd carried out when I was younger, but being able to just *take* what I wanted, when I wanted, still gave me a sense of control. And I needed that sense badly right now.

A third car pulled up outside. My shoulders tensed. How many people were coming? When was Marco going to bring me into this gathering that was apparently all about me?

"You don't think this is some kind of organized crime thing, do you?" Kylie asked. "Did your mom ever seem like she was into anything shady?"

My stomach twisted at the thought. "I guess she could have been," I said. "We were almost always together, but she did take those trips, and she could have arranged jobs over the phone." She had always seemed tense, and a little sad, when she got back from the trips. More so with every one. "She was always super-careful about us keeping a low profile. Not doing anything that might attract attention. But she acted like she was more worried about *me* than herself."

And from what I could remember, she hadn't given off that jaded vibe I'd gotten from every criminal I'd ever met. The one I probably gave off at least a little now, even though I'd left that part of my life behind.

Voices filtered through the sitting room door. I stuffed the mirror back into my pocket. The hairs on the back of my neck stood up, but at the same time the thrum of anticipation I'd felt when I'd first seen Marco raced through me, even stronger than before.

It was time. It was finally time. For what, I couldn't have said. But that was what my body believed.

Marco opened the door. He dipped his head with a smile that looked apologetically self-deprecating. "The gang's all here." Then he stepped inside, leaving the door open for his guests to follow him in.

Just a few minutes ago I'd been commenting to Kylie that I'd never seen a guy as hot as Marco before. Now, suddenly, I was faced with *four* stunningly gorgeous men.

Marco ambled across the room and stopped behind an armchair, resting his muscular forearms on its arched back. The guy who came in after him was even more buff, with broad, well-built shoulders and a brawny chest that filled out his towering frame. His dark brown eyes were even more intense than the rich chestnut of his hair.

Mr. Buff's gaze shot straight to me, and a warm smile curled his lips. An electric tingle raced over my skin. He crossed the room in a few deliberate, powerful strides and stopped a few feet from Marco, his eyes still trained on me.

The next guy walked in at a faster clip. He was stockier, but with equally broad shoulders and a devastatingly strong jaw. The regal grace of his strides made him seem just as tall as the others. The sunlight streaming through the window made his pale hair gleam gold as a Disney prince's. He stopped in the middle of the room, fixing me with a crystal-clear blue gaze that felt hopeful and searching at the same time.

The last guy stalked in with a wary air that drew my eyes to him. What did *he* have to be worried about? He halted just inside and propped himself against the doorframe, crossing his arms over his leanly muscled chest. Even though he didn't look any older than the others, mid-to-late twenties at most, strands of silver streaked his light auburn hair, which fell to just below his earlobes. They gave a slightly mystical quality to his otherwise gritty good looks. When he finally looked at me, his forest-green eyes were so penetrating I felt pinned in place.

My heart beat even faster. They were here. I didn't know why that mattered, but every nerve in my body was jittering with exhilaration. I could hardly catch my breath.

Kylie shot me a glance that said, *Can you believe these guys?*

No. No, I couldn't. But here they were.

And they were *mine*.

Where had *that* bizarre thought come from? I frowned, but before I could sort out the whirlwind of thoughts and emotions rushing through me, Marco straightened up. He gave me a knowing look, as if he could tell exactly what was going through my head.

"Here we are," he said in his languid drawl. "Happy, Dopey, Doc, and Grumpy, at your service."

The wary guy by the door—who looked like he fit the title "Grumpy" just fine—turned his head to glare at Marco. Our host grinned back. "Excuse me. You already know my name, Ren. Let me introduce you to Nate, Aaron, and West."

"'Ren'?" Grumpy-West repeated in an incredulous tone. Even so, my name in his low, throaty voice sent a shiver of pleasure down my spine.

"As she would prefer to be called," Marco said.

Dopey-Nate nodded. "If that's what she wants to go by, that's what we'll call her." His deep baritone was just as warm as his smile. Which he aimed at me again. Damn. My chest was going all fluttery. All this hotness in one room was putting me on hormonal overload.

My Disney prince, Aaron, took a careful step toward me. I wasn't sure why Marco had assigned him Doc. Maybe because his bright blue gaze was so thoughtful I almost felt as if he was considering me through a pair of glasses.

"From what Marco's told us, there's a lot you're unsure of," he said. His voice was even and faintly but pleasantly raspy. "Maybe you could start by telling us what you do know. What has your life been like? What have you been doing with it?"

"I can think of a lot of things *I'd* like to know about now," Kylie mumbled. But somehow having the four guys in the room made me feel more at ease instead of less. I didn't know them—they were total strangers. Why did I feel as if there wasn't anywhere safer in the world I could be than right here with them?

That weird sense of belonging loosened my tongue.

"I've been living here—in New York, I mean—since I was five," I said. "Mostly... Mostly with my mother. It was really just the two of us. She home-schooled me, and we'd go out around the city, but we never really talked to anyone else."

"So you just ate, slept, learned, had a little fun here and there—nothing all that unusual?" Aaron said.

He was fishing for something specific, but I had no idea what. "Nothing except the whole keeping to ourselves part. At least not that I can think of."

"Don't worry about it then." He motioned for me to continue. "But at some point, that changed?"

"Well, like I told Marco, my mom took trips every now and then. When I was fourteen, she left on one, and she didn't come back."

I hesitated, my throat constricting. I'd had seven years to get over that loss, but it still stabbed just as deep. I didn't even know whether to be furious with Mom or to grieve. Had she abandoned me by choice, or had something happened to her out there, wherever she'd gone?

"You've been on your own for seven years?" Nate said. He shook his head. "That must have been tough."

I had the urge to go to him and let him wrap those brawny arms around me. But how had he known it'd been seven years since I was fourteen? Had Marco's assistant heard the twenty-first birthday talk in the bar?

"It was okay at first," I said, feeling the need to defend Mom, even though no one had criticized her directly. "My mother owned the apartment we lived in. We had a joint bank account with plenty of savings to cover food and the bills. I could handle myself. But then—the superintendent realized I was living there on my own. He called Child Services and the police. I couldn't stay. They started tracking the bank account, so I had to stop using it."

My voice faded. I looked down at my lap. I didn't want to talk about the rest of it. About the time on the streets, about the allegiances I'd had to form to stay alive. "*That* was tough. That's all you really need to know. But I found my way out. Kylie and I got an apartment of our own last month. I work in a warehouse. I'm good."

My hand had leapt to my necklace of its own accord. My thumb worried the latch, flicking the locket open and closed.

West's jaw twitched. Aaron's gaze jerked to my hand. "That necklace," he said. "Your mother gave that to you?"

"She did. Right before the last time she left." The strangest feeling crept up over me, that I didn't need to tell him I hadn't opened it until yesterday. Something about it—they all already knew.

"Aaron's a bit of a magpie," Marco teased. "An eye for the shinies."

Aaron ignored him. He took another step forward, as if to ask to see it. My fingers closed around the locket. Kylie grasped my other hand, squeezing it reassuringly.

"What *I'd* like to know," West said, his eyes still narrowed, "is what you remember from before you came to New York City."

Before. My pulse lurched, and my mouth went dry. I didn't know why. There was nothing so terrifying about it. Because the truth was: "I don't remember anything." My voice quavered. I paused to steady myself. "I know we moved here from someplace else, but... Everything before is a blank. My mom and I never talked about it."

I'd tried to ask, once, when I was ten. Mom's mouth had gone so tight and tense I'd been ashamed before the question had even finished coming out.

You don't need to think about that, she'd said. *Not for a long, long time.*

"So you haven't got the slightest clue," West started up. Before he could finish his thought, Nate swung around toward him.

"Leave her alone," he growled. "I know you can feel she's telling the truth just as well as I can. Do you really think it's fair to dump everything on her all at once?"

West shut up, but that didn't stop him from glowering at the beefier guy. Marco chuckled, as if he found their squabbling amusing.

"I don't get it," I said, sitting up a little straighter. "You keep talking as if you know more about this—about me, and my mom—than I do. What's really going on here? Why are you all even *here*?"

And why do you make me feel like I want to somehow jump all of you simultaneously? Yeah, I'd keep that question to myself.

Aaron's tone stayed calm and even. "We knew you a long time ago," he said. "Before you came to the city, when we were all children. The fact that you don't remember... My best guess is that your mother suppressed those memories to make it easier for you not to give yourself away."

"Give *what* away? And what do you mean, 'suppressed'? You're talking like she put a magic spell on me or something."

I laughed a little, but the guys didn't take it as a joke. They exchanged a glance. Aaron ran his hand over his golden-blond hair. "That is one way of putting it."

"Let's just say there's a *lot* your mother didn't tell you." Marco piped up.

Nate shifted toward me. The strong, protective energy of his presence washed over my body, settling my nerves. "There's something you need to know about what we are, and what you are," he said.

"Hold on," West interrupted. "If we have to handle her with kid gloves, fine. But that one doesn't need to hear this. She's got no place in this conversation." He pointed at Kylie.

My fingers tightened around Kylie's. "My best friend stays. That's non-negotiable."

"I don't think you'll get very far arguing the point," Marco said. "I already tried once."

"Yep," Kylie said. "I'm un-budge-able."

West grimaced, but Nate held up his hand. "If Ren trusts her, then we can trust her too. Ren's memory has nothing to do with her emotional awareness."

"It's against policy to break silence with non-kin," Aaron put in. "But I think just this once, we can make a reasonable exception."

"Would you all please stop talking about whether you can say it and get on with it?" I burst out. "What's the big secret? What are 'non-kin'? What the hell—"

I fell silent when Nate moved closer. He sat down on the chair Marco was standing by, kitty-corner around the coffee table from me. The closer he came, the closer I wanted to be to him, but I stayed frozen in place on the settee. His voice came out as warm as before, but his deep brown eyes were so solemn.

"Ren, your mother let you believe that the two of you were just ordinary people. But you're not. And neither are we. We're not human at all. We're shifters."

CHAPTER 5

Ren

For the first few seconds after Nate spoke, I could only gape at him. Finally, I relocated my tongue. "Shifters," I said. "What does that even mean? How am I not human? How are *you* not human? Look at us!"

"That's kind of the point, princess," Marco said lightly. "We *look* human, but when we're in the mood, we can shift. Into something else."

"Something like *what*?"

"Whatever animal essence is tied to your spirit," Aaron said. "It's different for each of us here. But our nature comes with additional powers even when we're in human form. I'm sure you'll have noticed you're stronger, faster, more agile than anyone else in comparable shape, for example."

My heart skipped. I'd become Fisher's best thief because my sticky fingers could snatch a valuable off a person so quickly they'd never notice. The warehouse manager had stared at me when I'd shown him how easily I could handle the heavy boxes. How did Aaron know?

Oh. Because if what he was saying was true, he and the other three guys before me were the exact same way.

"Oh my God!" Kylie said, cocking her head at me. "He's totally right. I know pro athletes who can't move like you do. I always thought it was just cool. But supernatural powers—that totally makes sense." An undercurrent of laughter ran through her words. She didn't totally believe it. She turned to Aaron, her gray eyes sparkling. "Is she supposed to be psychic too? I swear sometimes she knows things about people there's no way she should."

"Ky," I protested, but it was true. I'd known just what soft spot to hit to make that guy in the bar back off. I picked up on the flavor of people's emotions all the time.

"That'll be part of your animal side too," Nate said, but I was too keyed up for even his rich rumble of a voice to be soothing.

Aaron nodded. "Instincts for reading body language, pheromones in the air—our senses extend beyond what any ordinary human would pick up on. And we'd expect you to be particularly sensitive."

I held up my hands. "Okay. So maybe I'm a little weird in a few ways. But I definitely don't have an 'animal side.' I've never 'shifted' into anything. This is the only body I've ever had. I'm pretty sure I'd have noticed if it warped into something completely different."

"Hold up," Kylie said. "I forgot about that part. You shift into *animals*. You're talking, like, werewolves and shit then?" She cracked up, patting my shoulder. "Ren, you're a werewolf! This is awesome."

"Not a werewolf," West muttered where he was still skulking

by the door. "Human horror stories have no idea what they're talking about."

"Let's be fair," Marco said. "There are some similarities. But we come in a lot more forms than the garden-variety wolf. And the full moon doesn't really factor in. When we want to shift, we do." He snapped his fingers.

"You know how crazy this sounds, don't you?" I said to all of them. "Again, I repeat, I have never changed into any kind of animal. Not a wolf, not a goldfish, nada."

"There could be a couple of reasons for that," Aaron said. An academic-ish enthusiasm colored his measured voice. He rocked on his heels, looking even more the part of professor—a really, really hot professor. Explaining this stuff was obviously his wheelhouse. "If your memories of knowing you're a shifter have been locked away, you wouldn't have thought to try to exercise those powers. You might have felt an urge, but not known what it meant."

My back stiffened. That clawing sensation that came into my chest when I was caught up in anger—or other sorts of passion. As if there were something inside me trying to dig its way out...

"And," Aaron went on, "none of us come into our full powers until we turn twenty-one. Even if you'd been fully aware of who and what you are, the shift would have taken more effort and been difficult to hold for very long. So it makes sense that it wouldn't have happened automatically."

Nate leaned forward and set his large hand on the side of the settee, just inches from my arm. "Before she left, did your mother tell you anything about your twenty-first birthday? We found you because of a pulse of her magic we started sensing yesterday. I think she must have wanted you to return to your kind."

Kylie's eyes widened. "Your necklace."

I clutched the locket. "She gave me this right before she left. And told me not to open the locket until that birthday. You're saying *it's* some kind of magic?" After everything else they'd already said, that part no longer sounded particularly absurd. Well, actually, it all sounded equally absurd.

West must have heard the incredulity in my tone, maybe because he was so well versed in skepticism himself. "We're all here, aren't we?" he said. "Believe me, it'd have been a lot simpler if we'd found you earlier."

"No." I shook my head. "This is still crazy. Something weird is going on. I'll give you that. But people don't just change into animals. My mom wasn't some kind of witch."

Kylie glanced from one guy to the next, kicking her legs against the base of the settee. "It'd be pretty easy for you to prove it if what you're saying is true, wouldn't it? You said you don't need a full moon. Great! Let's have a shifter demonstration, right here, right now. Your eager audience is waiting." She smiled at them.

Aaron hesitated. "We don't generally reveal ourselves outside our kind."

I waved off his objection. "Oh, please. If you're telling the truth, you've already 'revealed' it. At least if Kylie's here, I can be sure I'm not hallucinating." Except there was such a thing as a group hallucination, wasn't there? Well, I could worry about that if these guys really did start morphing into animals in front of us.

"I'll do it," Nate said, standing up. "How else is she going to believe us?"

He pulled off his cotton tee, revealing a chest even more densely muscled than I'd imagined. Then he reached for the fly of his jeans. My jaw just about dropped to the floor.

"Oh. Um..." Heat flared across my face as Nate shucked off his pants.

Marco chuckled. "You'll find shifters don't have the same hang-ups about getting naked as your average human being. It comes with the territory."

The substantial bulge in Nate's boxers gave me a clear preview of the territory to come. I averted my eyes. I'd never seen a guy naked, not right in front of me. Not some stranger I'd only just met.

Kylie didn't have the same qualms. "You're missing the best part of the show, Ren!" she said, watching avidly. Then her expression froze. Her voice came out thin and tinny. "Holy shit."

My head jerked back around. I wouldn't have thought my jaw could go any more slack, but it did.

Before our eyes, Nate's body was... shifting. There really wasn't a better word for it. The rich brown hair on his head was rippling down to cover all of him in a thick pelt. His torso expanded, his haunches and neck thickening. His face had already lengthened with a narrow snout.

The entire transformation finished moving through his body in the time it took me to blink. I might have thought that kind of bodily change would have to be painful, but it had looked completely natural. Almost... beautiful. A twinge of longing shot through me from collarbone to gut.

Longing and recognition. Yes, that was what people like them were meant to do.

People like *us.*

And now a majestic grizzly bear loomed on its hind legs before me. Its head nearly brushed the light fixture overhead.

No, not *it—him*. Even as my pulse skittered, I knew it was Nate. He lowered himself onto his front legs so that we were at eye level. His deep brown gaze felt just the same as when it had looked at me from his rugged human face. Warm. Protective. The sense of recognition in my gut tugged me toward him. I raised my hand, my fingers curled and then extending.

The bear took a careful step toward me, dipping his head so I could touch the fur between his rounded ears. It was coarse but pleasantly thick to the touch. I had the sudden urge to bury my face in his neck, to drink in the sensation and the musky, peppery smell of him. To feel his protective warmth all around me.

He was a massive predator, but he would never hurt me. He would never let anyone else hurt me either. I knew that, as surely as I'd known the asshole in the bar last night was sore about his ex.

"There," West said. "You've gotten your demonstration."

"This is—" Kylie giggled, a little hysterically. I'd never seen her at a loss for words before. She opened and closed her mouth a few times before she managed to keep going. "Oh my God. It's real. You really—" She laughed again.

Why wasn't I just as shocked? That first glimpse had startled me, but now all I felt was awe and that deep sense of familiarity.

Maybe I'd known, deep down, that it was true, even when my mind had balked to accept it. I swallowed hard and looked up from Nate to the other guys.

"Nate's a bear. What are the rest of you?"

"Jaguar," Marco said. "Not quite as impressive as Nate in size, but I make up for it in other ways." He smirked.

"I'm an eagle shifter," Aaron said. He glanced at West. When the grouchy guy stayed silent, Aaron added, "And West *is* actually a wolf. Most shifters belong to one of four kin-groups. Canine, feline, avian, and, well, everything else." He gestured to West, Marco, himself, and Nate in turn, with a hint of a smile at the last. "We're the leaders of each of those kin-groups. The alphas, by our usual terminology."

"This is seriously the most amazing thing that has ever happened to me," Kylie said. "So when do we get to see the rest of you 'shift'?"

"I don't perform on command," West snapped. But seeing Nate had been enough. I was convinced. Of everything except the last, most important part. Nate nudged my arm with his muzzle, and I rubbed behind his ears automatically, searching for the courage to ask the question that I already knew would upend my life.

Could it really get that much more upended than it already was? I had to know.

I dragged in a breath. "All right. So we know all about you now. Maybe you can tell me—what am *I*?"

At the look Aaron and Marco exchanged, I braced myself. That didn't seem like a good sign. Marco's lips curved with his crooked grin.

"You, my Princess of Flames, put the rest of us to shame. You're a dragon shifter."

CHAPTER 6

West

The girl stared at Marco as if she couldn't wrap her head around a single word he'd said. Could she really be this ignorant? How could she have gone sixteen years without ever sensing the power inside her, even if her mother had meddled with her memories? I still found it hard to swallow.

"A *dragon*?" she sputtered. Nate, still in his bear form, shuffled backward as she pushed herself to her feet. "Are you kidding me?"

"As much as I enjoy joking around, at this particular moment I'm being totally serious," Marco said.

Ren—of all the things to be calling herself. It sounded like a fragile little bird—gestured vaguely with her hand. "At least bears and wolves and whatever are *real* animals. Dragons don't even exist."

Her disbelief, acted or real, was damn irritating. I pushed

myself off the doorframe and stalked a few paces toward her. "Look, you asked the question. You got the answer." I let my gaze travel over her slim but toned figure. "Although I've got to agree, right now you look like you have about as much fire in you as a puff of sparks."

She turned to glower at me, and I saw a hint of the power in her then. A flicker behind her bright brown eyes. It lit up every inch of my skin as if I'd been hit by a whole shower of sparks.

Damn it. The only thing more irritating than her bewildered human routine was how strongly my body responded to her no matter what I was thinking. I'd been waiting for her way too long.

But this wasn't how my mate was meant to be. She *was* meant to be powerful, stronger than any of us. Not the type to run away from danger and cower among humans for sixteen years. We hadn't known if there were any dragon shifters left. We hadn't known what might be keeping them away. From the sounds of things, it'd been nothing more than fear.

What had her mother been thinking, throwing her back to us now with no understanding of who she was or the role she was meant to fill?

Ren took a step closer to me, and her smell, sweet as strawberries and cream, wafted over me. Enough to make me half hard. Her expression was anything but sweet. She jabbed her finger at my chest, just shy of grazing the thin fabric of my henley.

"I'm trying my best, okay, tough guy?" she said, her eyes all but blazing now. "Try having your world turned completely upside down in the space of an hour sometime, and see how you handle it."

Technically, my world had been turned upside down in the

instant I'd felt that first tingle of dragon magic from afar. But I wasn't going to admit that to her. Especially not while her lips were curling with a hint of a smirk.

"And here's your watch back," she said. The thick metal band dangled from her fingers. What the hell? I glanced down at my wrist—which was in fact now bare. Had she just *stolen* that right off me?

Marco's melodic chuckle rang through the room, his dark blue eyes glinting. "Don't you know better than to poke a dragon?"

I grabbed the watch back from Ren, ignoring him. Feline-kin never knew how to mind their own business.

"*I* didn't even see her pull that off," Aaron said with his scholarly awe. He was probably getting a hard-on just from the chance to talk to a dragon up close instead of relying on all those old records he liked to pour over.

The theft had, maybe, been a tiny bit impressive. I refastened the watch around my wrist and eyed Ren. Now that she'd gathered a little more confidence, I could almost imagine a dragon's vitality in her. Her eyes were still shining, the deep brown waves of her hair flowing past her shoulders as if recently whipped by the wind. What kind of a dragon would she make after all?

The need to see it wrenched through me. I folded my arms over my chest. "All right, Sparks. You know a few tricks. You want to find out how real dragons are? Shift right now and you'll know."

Ren

West's dark green eyes flashed in challenge. The bravado I'd managed to call up faltered. "I don't know how. I have no idea about any of this. Haven't you been listening?"

I glanced toward Nate, the only person I'd ever seen "shift," and found he'd transformed back into his human self. He was just pulling up his jeans, his sculpted chest still bare. A fresh wave of heat coursed through me at the sight. But—if that was how you shifted—

My arms rose to hug myself, my fingers curling into the sides of my shirt.

"You wouldn't have to undress," Aaron said gently. "You're unlikely to make a full transition on your first try anyway. And if you're able to"—he tipped his head Marco's way—"I suspect our host has plenty of clothes around the house he could spare."

Marco shrugged. Under the jagged fringe of his black hair, his indigo eyes looked suddenly hungry. They gleamed more deeply than the sapphire stud in his ear. "My kin come and go from here. I keep the rooms well-stocked."

"Okay, okay," I said. "But what do I *do*?"

"Well, first, just in case," Marco said, "I think we should take this little party outside, dragons being the size they tend to be. I'd rather not turn this room into a pile of rubble."

"Fine." I wasn't sure what his neighbors would make of it if I did suddenly turn into a gigantic mythical creature, but I was still finding that possibility hard to believe in the first place.

Kylie sprang to her feet. "I'm not missing this!"

Marco swept through the room. We all tramped out back after him.

The second I stepped into the yard, I understood why he wasn't worried about privacy. The small grassy lawn was framed on all sides by tall pines.

I walked a little farther into the middle of the clearing. The guys spread out in a row to watch, Kylie bobbing on her feet beside them.

"Close your eyes," Aaron said. "Reach inside yourself. Try to feel the essence running through you. The core of your nature. Then grasp hold of it and pull it free. It'll want to come. It'll help you."

West had snorted in the middle of that set of instructions, but as mumbo-jumbo-y as they'd sounded, I thought I knew what Aaron meant. I *had* felt the essence running through me before—the flexing of those internal claws.

Like some kind of beast waiting to get out. But a dragon? Really?

I guessed I was going to find out. I inhaled deeply and closed my eyes like he'd said. There it was, waiting for me. That sharp tingle scraping over my ribs. It did want out. I focused my attention on the sensation. *Tell me what to do. Tell me what you need.*

A quiver tickled through my muscles. They flexed as if trying to open themselves up. My skin felt suddenly tight. The tingling inside swelled, as if to burst free—

And contracted, away from my encouragement. I frowned, squeezing my eyes tighter shut. *Come on. I know you want this.*

A full-out tremor rippled down my spine. I tried to grasp onto that stirring in my core the way Aaron had suggested, but it slipped right through my fingers.

My shoulders sagged. I wavered on my feet, exhaustion rolling over me. I rubbed my eyes before I opened them. How long had I worked at that for? It hadn't seemed like more than a few minutes, but I felt as if I'd just run a marathon.

The guys were still studying me, West with his usual cynical expression, Aaron looking puzzled, Marco considering, Nate concerned. "Are you all right, Ren?" the bear shifter said.

"Yeah," I said. "Yeah." But my legs were shaky when I took a step back toward them. Kylie dashed to my side. "I don't get it. I *felt* it, but it was like it didn't want to come..."

The furrow on Aaron's brow deepened. "Your mother may have suppressed not just your memories, but your powers as well. To make it less likely they'd emerge unexpectedly. But I can't believe she'd have done anything permanent. She must have left you a way of accessing them again."

"You haven't heard from her at all in those seven years?" West said. "Not even a message?"

I shook my head. "Nothing. I don't even know where she was going. All she gave me was the locket." I opened it up and looked at the flame-like symbol inside. "Does this mean anything to you?"

I held out the locket to show them. The other three took a quick glance and then looked toward Aaron, who I guessed they deferred to on topics requiring much in the way of research. He peered at the etching, but the confusion on his face didn't lift.

"No," he said. "I'm sorry."

"She wouldn't have put that symbol in the necklace if it wasn't important, would she?" Nate said. "It must be meant to tell us something."

"It could be something she'd hoped the last alphas would have told us." Marco's smile was more like a grimace this time.

"Maybe that's something I can help with," Kylie piped up. "I could take a picture and show it around. Out of all the people I know, there might be someone who recognizes it."

All of the guys looked skeptical at that suggestion, but they didn't know Kylie yet. "Sure," I said. "We might as well try."

I tilted the locket's interior to catch the sunlight so she could snap a picture with her phone. She tucked the phone back in her pocket and raked her fingers into her rumpled neon pink hair. "If I'm going to make the rounds, that means I have to go. Do you want to come with? You know you don't have to stay here with these guys if you're not sure about all this yet."

I wasn't sure about much, but the one thing I did know was that none of these four guys—shifters—however I was supposed to think about them—wanted to hurt me. And suddenly I wasn't so sure about the world beyond this house.

Why had Mom been so afraid? What had she been hiding us from?

I didn't think I wanted to find out on my own. And besides, between my short, drugged sleep last night, all the crazy news that had been heaped on me in the last hour, and my failed attempts at shifting, the only place I wanted to go right now was to a bed.

"I'll be okay here," I said. "There's obviously a lot more I need to learn—and I don't think anyone can help me with *that* except these guys. Text me if you find anything out." I turned to Marco. "I assume you've got my phone around here somewhere."

He snapped his fingers. "I knew I'd forgotten something. I thought it was better if we talked before I handed that over, considering the circumstances."

"Is that what you want to do now?" Nate asked. "To talk more with us? There is a lot more we can tell you."

A pressure was starting to build at the back of my skull. I rubbed my neck. "Actually, I think I'd like a little time to myself, if that's okay. To process everything I've already heard. And maybe to take a nap. Having your world tipped over is kind of exhausting."

"That room upstairs is yours for as long as you want it," Marco said. "I'll get Leonard to grab your phone for you."

As he ducked inside, Kylie enveloped me in a hug. "Promise me you're okay with this," she murmured by my ear.

I smiled tightly. I wasn't exactly *okay*, but that wasn't the fault of anyone here. "I just found out I have super powers," I said. "What's not to like?"

She laughed and gave me one last squeeze. "I'll check in with you soon, whether I've got news or not."

She slipped past the trees around the side of the house. The guys followed me back inside. West drew Aaron aside, muttering something to him I assumed was some new complaint about me. Nate came with me up the staircase. I skimmed my hand over the polished wood of the curving banister. Apparently being a shifter also meant being rich, at least for some people. Or maybe that came with being the "alpha."

"Do you have a place like this?" I asked the bear shifter.

Nate grinned. "Marco and I have pretty different senses of style. And our homes belong more to our position as alpha than to *us*. But I do have a few nice properties I'll be looking forward to showing you."

Upstairs, it took me a few tries before I found the bedroom I'd started this adventure in. I paused by the doorway, my awareness of Nate seeping into my skin. The memory rose up of just how much of himself he'd already shown me, and the warmth turned into heat.

Nate reached out and brushed a stray lock of hair back from my cheek. My heart thumped at his touch. "You'll be all right on your own?" he said.

What exactly was he going to propose if I said no? And did I want him to propose it? For a second, my body blared its answer: absolutely yes.

But I was more than just a body, and my mind was too full to be making any clear decisions right now.

"I will," I said. "Thank you."

He teased his fingers deeper into my hair and tipped my head toward him as he bowed his own. His lips grazed my forehead, and my breath caught. He stepped back, leaving me more flushed than I'd ever been before. I swallowed hard.

"Take whatever time you need," Nate said. He dipped his head. Marco came up from behind him, holding my phone.

"As promised," Marco said. He handed it to me as Nate ambled to the staircase. "Is there any other way your situation here is lacking?"

"I don't think so," I said. I walked into the room to give it a once-over, and Marco followed me. Well, why shouldn't he? It was his house, and he thought I might have something else to ask for. But his closeness beside me made my breath stutter all over again. Heat licked through my veins.

Dear lord, how could I be this horny—and for four guys all at once? Did shifters always provoke that response in other people? Kylie hadn't seemed anywhere near as affected. Maybe it was just between shifters.

If I was going to just accept that I definitely was one.

"No complaints?" Marco said.

"No," I said honestly. "This is the most gorgeous house I've ever seen."

I turned toward him at the same time, which maybe was a mistake. He smiled his slightly wicked smile, gazing back at me with the hunger I'd noticed earlier. An answering desire unfurled in my gut and tingled lower in my belly.

He raised his hand and traced his lithe fingers along the line of my jaw, tipping my face toward his. His languid voice dropped to a murmur. "And you have the most gorgeous eyes I've ever seen. So brilliant they're more amber than brown. Like fire. A person could fall right into them."

"Falling into fire?" I joked in a half-hearted attempt to diffuse the electricity between us. "That sounds pretty dangerous. You'd want to climb back out fast."

"Maybe not," Marco said. "I suspect it would be a very pleasant burning."

As if drawn up by his words, a rush of heat seared through me. Marco leaned his head a little closer. Before I caught control of myself, I'd pressed my lips to his.

He kissed me back with an encouraging growl. His mouth slid against mine, hot and teasing, coaxing my lips apart. His hand slipped back to tangle in the hair at the base of my neck. Everywhere he touched me, I felt as if I *had* caught on fire.

I gripped his shoulders as if I could pull our mouths even closer together. His tongue caressed mine, and I groaned into him. My hips arched toward his. His other hand trailed down my side, drawing a path of flames through my clothes.

I wanted those clothes off. I wanted him on the bed, over me, inside me. I wanted—

What the *hell* was I doing?

I wrenched myself away from Marco. My body protested so sharply it felt as if I'd literally torn us apart. Marco let his hand drop to his side. He watched me with heavy-lidded eyes, no judgment or accusation in them.

He was a stranger. I'd met him just a few hours ago. After he'd pretty much had me kidnapped. Obviously all this supernatural talk had addled my brain.

And *I* was the one who'd kissed *him*.

My face flushed again, with embarrassment this time. And maybe some lingering desire. It wasn't as if I'd stopped wanting him just because common sense had kicked in.

"I'm sorry," I said, my voice rough. "I didn't mean to— I

don't know if this is normal for shifters, but it's not normal for me."

"You draw the lines, Princess of Flames," he said. "I'm happy to take whatever you feel ready to give, but when you say stop, we stop." He tilted his head toward the bed. "Why don't you get that rest I'm sure you'll need? We've still got a long way to go."

CHAPTER 7

Ren

We were standing in a private cabin on a train—my mother and me. The floor hitched under my feet, and the window was rattling. We were racing far, far away. Far from the bad thing that still had my chest twisted tight, even as I tried not to think about it.

My mother knelt down to my eye level and cupped my cheek. Her eyes were wild as a stormy sky.

"Listen to me, Serenity," she said in a choked voice. "Somewhere deep down, where no one else can touch it, you need to remember you're a dragon. *Always* remember."

I blinked at her with a childish confusion. "Of course I'll remember, Mama. I can't *not* be a dragon."

A sad smile curved her lips. "Oh, darling. For a little while, I need you to forget. At least on the surface. But you're right. You'll never not be."

She raised her hands and pressed her palms to my temples.

Darkness swirled into my head. The scene pivoted.

I was running with my mother through a forest, her hand clasped tight around mine. So tight it hurt. My breath stung in my throat. My lungs ached. I tripped on a root, and she heaved me up in an instant. We ran and ran and—

I was crouched behind the big vase in the front hall, listening for girlish laughter. My heart thumped giddily. This time I'd be the last one found. This time I'd be the queen of hide-and-seek. They might be older than me, but I—

I was sitting in the grass, sweet clover scent filling my nose, laughter in my throat. A shape streaked by through the clear blue sky above me. Brilliant bronze scales, like her eyes. The flap of massive wings sending a comforting breeze over me. I clapped my hands together.

"Mama!"

My eyes popped open, back in the present. I stared at the wall across from me for a second as the dream faded and the real world came back into focus. Gold flowers winding through mint-green wallpaper. A velvet bedspread tucked under my chin. A sinfully soft mattress cradling my body.

Memories rushed in. Marco's house. The four shifters. Nate transforming into a bear. West's snarking. Aaron's careful explanations. All the things they'd told me. My failed attempt at shifting.

Nate's lips brushing my forehead. Marco's pressed hard against mine.

I sat up in the bed, heat washing over me. Yep, that had all been real. And I was still here.

My gaze shot to the window. The daylight was even paler than it had been in the morning, but it was streaming in at the same angle. As if it were morning again.

God, had I slept through half a day and then the entire night? All those dreams spinning me around...

I paused, my fingers curling into the bedspread. No, those hadn't been just dreams, had they? I felt the truth of them like an ache in the base of my throat. Those had been as real as this room. Real memories, from when I was a little girl. From before Mom and I had come to the city.

From when I'd known I was a dragon. When I'd seen her, soaring above me, like she was meant to.

The four alphas had been telling the truth. Mom had locked away my memories. She'd practically admitted to me she was going to do it before she had.

I was a dragon. I was a *dragon*.

I looked down at my hands, as if they might have sprouted scales and talons. Nope, those still looked like perfectly normal human fingers.

Had I ever shifted myself? I couldn't remember. Couldn't dredge up any fragments of my past other than the ones that had floated into my dreams. Aaron had suggested it'd have been more difficult when I was younger, and I'd only been five when Mom had locked those parts of me away.

Why had she done that? Why couldn't she have trusted me? At least before she'd wandered off wherever she'd gone...

Anger hit me, biting into my chest. But another ache closed around it. I missed her. So goddamn much. Not just the Mom I remembered clearly, either. The one I'd glimpsed, wild and powerful and more than human.

Was I ever going to get her back?

That question felt too big to sit with on my own. Especially when I'd apparently wasted half a day recovering from yesterday's revelations. I crawled out of the bed, stretched, and looked down at myself. I'd been wearing this tee and jeans for almost two days now. They were getting a little grimy feeling.

Marco had commented that he had lots of spare clothes around. I eased open the drawers of the dresser and found one full of lady-type clothing, although fancier than the stuff I'd normally have put on. I settled on a silky violet blouse and decided my jeans could hold up to another wearing as long as I got the rest of myself clean.

I'd seen a bathroom while searching for this bedroom yesterday. I crept down the hall and ducked inside. To my relief, there was a lock on the inside knob.

Tension seeped out of me as the shower streamed into my hair and down my back. I rubbed my hands over my body, letting the hot water carry away two days of sweat and uncertainty.

I was a dragon shifter. I still didn't totally understand what that entailed, but there were four guys waiting here in the house to help me figure it out. I was ready.

I dried myself with a towel so fluffy I was tempted to bury myself in it and never come out. The silk shirt clung to my figure a little more than I liked, but at least the scooped neckline showed minimal cleavage. I was having enough trouble keeping my hands off of Marco—and, let's be real, Nate too—without wearing clothes that screamed *Do me*.

Combing my fingers through my still-damp hair, I padded down the staircase to the first floor. A buttery smell was wafting from what I assumed was the direction of the kitchen.

Hunger twanged through my stomach. My last meal of sausage and eggs might as well have been a year ago. My feet pushed me faster of their own accord. I dashed around the bend in the staircase and careened over the edge of the next step.

Anyone looking on would have thought I'd slipped and

fallen. I guessed I sort of had. But the tumble gave me a jolt of excitement, not fear. I opened my arms as if to embrace the sensation—and brought them down to help me catch my landing at the base of the stairs. My knee jarred against the floor with a thump, but I hardly felt the impact. My spirit was still soaring.

Like the dragon in my memory. The dragon who'd been my mother.

Was that why I got off so much on jumps and falls? I'd always thought it was some random daredevil impulse, but maybe I simply missed the feeling of flight. Some part of me deep down had never completely forgotten it.

A figure appeared in the hall. Stocky, muscular, with a golden shine in his pale hair—Aaron. He was wearing a linen tunic with a slit neck that gave a glimpse of his impressive tanned chest. His expression relaxed when he saw me straightening up.

"I heard a thud," he said. "Did you fall down?"

I shrugged, smiling at him. I hadn't talked one-on-one with Aaron yet, but I appreciated the thoughtful approach he'd taken to my situation. Out of the four alphas who'd come to find me, he was the only one who didn't seem to have any specific expectations of who I'd be or what I'd do. He preferred to observe who I actually was.

"I've had worse," I said. I nodded to the spatula in his hand. "Are you the one cooking?"

He smiled back. "Hungry? No one's up yet, not even Marco's chef. I didn't want to hassle anyone else on my behalf. Most shifters are more on the nocturnal side, but I'm a bit of an early bird." His grin widened as if daring me to laugh.

"Ha, ha, Mr. Eagle. I just hope you're not cooking eggs."

He brandished the spatula. "Pancakes. Come on. I'd better get back to them before they burn."

"I definitely cannot be responsible for massacring your pancakes."

I followed Aaron into the kitchen. He strode straight to the stove where a huge frying pan was sizzling and grabbed another plate from a cupboard. I stopped on the threshold, gaping.

"Wow." The kitchen was as big as the entire open-concept common space in the apartment I was sharing with Kylie, with stainless steel appliances as far as the eye could see. "Now that's a kitchen."

"I don't think Marco knows how to do anything halfway," Aaron said. "It's all-out-luxury, or forget about it." He flipped the pancakes, sending a fresh waft of that buttery doughy smell to my nose.

My mouth started watering. I ambled up beside him to check whether his handiwork was close to done.

Aaron looked over at me. "Are you feeling more settled now that you've had time to think all this through?" His voice came out a little softer than usual, but still with that appealing rasp. My awareness of his presence snapped into focus with a warmth all down my side. We were standing close enough that I could smell him, a salty aquatic scent that reminded me of the ocean. I wanted to lick it off his skin.

Down, girl. Mind out of the gutter.

"Yeah," I said, my throat suddenly hoarse. Why did *every* one of these guys have this effect on me? "I guess I was kind of a pain in the ass yesterday, huh?"

Aaron chuckled. "Not at all. It was totally understandable. I like a girl who wants all the facts instead of just accepting whatever she's told."

So he liked *me* then? Oh, why did I even care? But I did. There I was peeking at him through my eyelashes while I tried to figure out the best response to make him laugh again.

"I like a man who has all the facts," I settled on.

That got me a grin. I'd take it. "Maybe not all of them," Aaron said. "But I do like to learn as much as I can about our people and our history. The way I see it, the only way you can avoid future mistakes is if you understand your past."

A sound theory. "That gets harder when you don't even remember your past," I muttered.

"I have to think those memories will start to come back now that you're back in the fold, so to speak. Your mother wouldn't have wanted you to be cut off from your powers permanently. She must have expected that we'd help you recover them."

He tossed the pancakes onto the waiting plates, two each, and drizzled them with maple syrup. My hands snatched up the first plate when he offered it to me, but there was one question I had to ask before I stuffed anything in my mouth.

"I still don't understand—how *did* my mother let you know to find me? I get that it had something to do with the locket, but other than that..."

Aaron led me out of the kitchen into a dining room that was way too big for the two of us. Fourteen chairs stood around a massive rosewood table. Aaron set his plate down at the foot of the table, but he turned to me instead of sitting. I put down my plate too and leaned my elbow on the top of the chair beside me, waiting for his answer.

"When we're named alpha, there's a full ceremony involved." Aaron held out his left hand, palm up, revealing a scar like a sunburst of lines in the middle of his palm. "This mark ties us to our kin-group, and to the dragons. The moment you opened that locket, whatever magic your mother worked on it activated. I felt it right there, in the middle of my hand, with a sense of direction. But I'd guess any shifter who was closer enough would have been able to feel it. From what I understand, that's how Marco sent his lieutenant ahead to track you down."

This time, I let my impulses take over. I took Aaron's hand in both of mine. "May I?" I said, abruptly breathless. He nodded, his clear blue eyes fixed on my face. I felt it then, with the thump of my pulse.

He might not *expect* anything from me, but he wanted things. The same kinds of things I found myself wanting when we stood this close together.

I dragged my gaze away from his to his palm. My thumb skimmed across it to trace the lines of his scar. He held still, but the muscles in his arm flexed. The breath he took sounded slightly ragged. I wondered how he'd react if I kissed that spot. Just the thought sent a pulse of heat between my legs.

I swallowed hard and yanked my mind back to our conversation. There was something he'd said...

"You said this mark ties you specifically to the dragons," I said. "Why? I mean, shouldn't we have our own alpha or something? Where *are* the other dragon shifters?" My heart leapt with a sudden hope. Did I have other family—grandparents or cousins or who knew what—that Mom and I had left behind?

Aaron turned his palm over, engulfing my slender hand in his larger one. He traced his thumb over the delicate skin on the back, sending a pleasant shiver up my arm.

"Dragons have always been the rarest of the shifters, as well as the most powerful," he said, even more quietly than before. Almost reverent. "To the best of our knowledge right now, you might be the last one."

"The *last*?" I repeated. The words struck a chord in me, but it was hard to think clearly with his careful thumb sliding back and forth over my skin.

Aaron nodded. "Which is why it was so important to your

mother that she protect you. As long as shifters have walked this earth, the dragons among us have played a special role, one no one else can fill."

"Great. No pressure there." My laugh came out shaky. "So what exactly does that mean?"

The corner of his lips curled up. "The dragon shifters are the core of all shifter-kind. They unite the kin-groups with one common tie, by taking all four alphas as their mates."

CHAPTER 8

Ren

AARON'S last comment was not the kind of revelation anyone should drop on a girl before she's even had breakfast. I stared at him, my fingers closing around his to stop the caress of his thumb—but not letting go. Because even as the shock rippled through me, some part of me leapt to accept the idea.

Yes. They were *mine*, all of them.

I shook that thought away. "Hold on. Just so I'm clear, you're saying that if I'm the last dragon shifter there is, my 'role' is to hook up with the four of you alphas?"

The corner of Aaron's lips crooked up. "Not just 'hook up with.' The mate-bonds shifters form are lifelong. You'd be partnered with all of us, 'til death do us part."

"That seems kind of... greedy, grabbing the four most important"—and hottest, I added silently—"guys around."

"Like I said, it's considered right because it unites the four kin-groups. I've looked back through the old records, as far back as shifters have kept them, and from what I've seen, our community has always worked that way. It's so natural it's woven into our beings."

He paused, studying my expression. His voice dropped to a pitch that sent eager shivers over my skin. "You've felt it, haven't you? That pull toward each of us—the same way we all feel toward you."

My breath caught. I couldn't look away from his brilliant blue eyes. I wet my lips, and his gaze dropped to them. Suddenly they felt as hot as if he'd already kissed them.

How could I lie to him when he was looking at me like that?

"I have felt it," I said. My voice came out in a murmur.

"Then you understand how innate it is. How meant-to-be."

He raised my hand to press a kiss to my knuckles. The heat of that touch flared down my arm and right through the core of me. I might have yanked him into a different sort of kiss if someone hadn't cleared his throat rather rudely at that exact moment.

I flinched back from Aaron, an embarrassed flush prickling over me. West was standing in the kitchen doorway, his arms crossed in his usual standoffish pose. His dark green eyes glowered at us.

"That might be how it's worked before, but that doesn't mean it's supposed to stay that way forever," he said in his low, throaty voice.

Aaron rested his hand reassuringly on the small of my back. My embarrassment didn't stop me from wanting to lean into him.

But the most infuriating thing was that neither that embarrassment nor West's jerk-ish demeanor stopped the pull drawing me toward the wolf shifter too. Even as I glared back at him, some part of me longed to see that handsome face soften with affection. A few strands of his silvery auburn hair had drifted across his angular cheekbones, and my hand itched to tuck it behind his ear. To linger on his cheek afterward.

I curled my fingers into my palm. Meant to be or not, West clearly wasn't mooning over me.

"We've got more reason to believe the arrangement should stay the same than that it should change," Aaron said. "That pattern of stability has held the kin-groups in balance for hundreds if not thousands of years."

"How do we know it's the arrangement that's kept us in balance?" West said. "Maybe we'd have been just fine without it too."

Aaron's mouth tightened. "That's a careless perspective to take. Throwing aside all that history could ruin us. Look at how things have gone even in sixteen years without the dragons present."

West shrugged. "Because we've been waiting and waffling, not knowing what to do, not letting ourselves make any decisions. Maybe it's time. Maybe all it'd take is for us to step up and pick a different path."

I didn't feel enough connection to these politics to try to argue on either side. And anyway, my mind had kept spinning with Aaron's revelation, which was bringing up all sorts of other questions.

"Wait," I said. "If this is how it always worked, with the dragon shifters and the alphas... My mother must have had four mates, right? One of them would be my father. Is he still—do you know who he is?"

I tried to keep my hopes in check, but excitement bubbled up inside me. Mom had never been willing to say much on the subject of my father, but I'd always wondered. Especially in the seven years since she'd left.

Then I noticed how West's expression had tensed. Aaron looped his hand right around my waist. "Every dragon shifter has four fathers," he said. "That's part of the unique structure of our rulership. A dragon can only be formed from the best qualities of all four kin-alphas: the loyalty of the wolves, the strength of the bears, the cunning of the wildcats, and the grace of the birds of prey. When all is at harmony between a dragon and her mates, a new dragon may be conceived."

I blinked. "*Four* dads." But the solemn note in his voice hadn't escaped me either. "What happened to them?"

He swallowed audibly. "The alphas before us, the ones who were your mother's mates, they passed away—passing on the responsibility to us... right before she left."

I turned to look him in the face. "Sixteen years ago? You must have been awfully young."

He waved aside my concern with the hand not resting on my waist. "Marco was ten, West and me eleven, and Nate twelve. Old enough that our mentors knew we'd grow into the roles. Every alpha has trusted advisors—the ones already in place worked alongside us almost like regents until we were of age to hold our own."

So they grew up like that, one generation after the next, dragons and alphas in unison. "You don't pass being alpha on to your kids," I said slowly, piecing what he'd said together. "I'm assuming? Do the alphas *only* mate with a dragon shifter—and only one? All of your kids would be dragon shifters, then?"

"And only one quarter ours," West put in from behind me.

Aaron frowned at him. "It isn't that less of us goes into helping make a dragon than any other child. It's that a dragon child is so much more than any other." He turned his attention back to me. "You're right, we don't pass on rule from parent to child, at least not that way. The alphas before us were your fathers. They picked us from the kin-group because they believed we'd be strong leaders—and the best mates for their daughter."

I didn't know how I felt about that. A few minutes ago, I hadn't known anything about my dad—or dads. I wasn't ready for them to suddenly be picking out my future partners-for-life.

"So the *daughters* never have any say in it?"

The corner of Aaron's lips twitched, I thought with amusement. "Oh, you can have a say. If a dragon feels one or more of her offered mates is unsuitable, she can reject him and wait for the kin-group to propose another. Or... Another shifter can fight to take the role of alpha from the one chosen. If the chosen alpha isn't strong enough to fend off the attack, then they weren't worthy of the honor anyway."

"Is that what happened to the alphas before you?" I said, and then realized that didn't make sense. If the previous alphas had been challenged and lost, then presumably the disciples they'd chosen would've been chucked aside as well. What the hell could have happened to all four of the last guys, all at once?

"No," Aaron said. His expression shuttered. "That was a more complicated situation. I think it'd be better if we waited to discuss that once more of your memories have returned."

He obviously took me for a much more patient person than I was. I opened my mouth to push for answers, but West raised his voice at the same moment.

"None of that matters anyway. Those decisions belonged to the old alphas—the ones before us and the ones before them. We're in charge now. We can make up our own minds about how we do things. And that includes whether we *do* you."

The edge in his voice made me grit my teeth. Some mate he was turning out to be. I swiveled around, my eyes narrowing. "Is that how you show the wolf 'loyalty' you're supposed to be known for?"

My jab hit the mark. I could tell from the way his shoulders stiffened. But his voice was firm when he bit out his reply.

"One more on the long list of things you need to learn, Sparks: Loyalty given blindly is worthless. I'm loyal first and always to my kin. To you? I haven't seen any reason to be so far."

"Well, you're not exactly inspiring a whole lot of confidence so far either," I snapped back.

"All right." Aaron held up his hands in a gesture for peace. "Let's table this discussion, all right? This is a strange situation for all of us. We've got a lot more getting to know each other to do before anyone decides anything."

He squeezed my shoulder. "Which is why I've been thinking we should see what we can do about activating your powers. Maybe once you have more of your dragon senses at your disposal, you'll find it easier to follow the path your mother seems to have left for you."

I jerked my gaze away from West's, willing my shoulders to come down from around my ears. "Okay. Something to actually *do* sounds good to me."

"Good. We'll eat, and then we'll see what we can unearth in there."

His smile settled my nerves a little. But as I pulled out my chair to sit down, the pancake smell trickling into my nose again, something else he'd said earlier twisted around my gut.

You might be the last one.

The last of the dragon shifters. That could only be true if Mom was no longer around. I'd known there might be a permanent reason she couldn't come back, but I'd never let myself follow that line of thought very far. The alphas had clearly thought it, though.

Maybe she hadn't come back because she was dead. Because something, wherever she'd gone, had killed her.

CHAPTER 9

Aaron

THE MUSCLES in Serenity's back flexed under my pressing fingers. I eased my hands in a slow line between her shoulder blades, fighting to focus only on the task at hand and not how much I wanted to touch every other part of her as well. She felt like a live wire beneath her silk shirt. So much power bottled in that slim frame. It was breathtaking.

"Picture the wings waiting there, folded tight, longing to unfurl," I said, keeping my voice quiet and even. I thought of the sensations my own body went through, as the only alpha who knew what it was like to transform into a winged creature. "Immerse yourself in that sensation. Send them the strength they need to break through."

My dragon shifter grimaced where she was kneeling on the back lawn. Her pale fingers had dug into the long grass. The rising summer sun was baking the yard, creating a warm green smell that mingled with the tartly sweet scent of her body.

"I'm trying," she said. "I'm trying everything you're saying. It just doesn't want to come." She let out a sound of frustration.

I couldn't imagine what it was like, having so much power coursing through your veins and not being able to release it. Maybe I was pushing her too hard. The thought made my chest constrict. At least West hadn't followed us outside. His constant criticism couldn't be helping things.

"Hey," I said. I sat down on the grass beside Serenity and slid my fingers up her jaw to turn her face toward me. She looked back at me, frustration shimmering in her amber eyes. Frustration and a heat that deepened when I let my thumb graze her cheek.

God, how could I not answer that longing? The same heat coursed through me. "It'll be okay," I told her. "You've got a lot of years of lost practice to make up for. It'll come."

Then I leaned in and kissed her.

I let my lips brush hers lightly at first. She'd only just found out the full truth about our connection. She hadn't seemed unwilling, but she hadn't leapt for joy either. It might be too soon.

No. She leaned into me, pressing her mouth harder against mine. The heat I'd felt before flared through me.

This was her. My dragon, my mate. I hadn't known for sure I'd ever get the chance to meet her, let alone get this close to her. Every inch of me, including the length hardening in my pants, clamored to make that true in every meaning of the word.

I tugged her a little closer, angling my lips in a way that drew a gasp from hers. I wasn't going to make a spectacle of us here on Marco's lawn, even though we were alone for the moment, but I wasn't going to let the other three get in the way of this partnership either. They could grumble or preen or hang back in chivalry all they wanted. Serenity needed a mate who was here for her right now, in every way she needed.

I'd never wanted anything more than to be that man.

Apparently I was making a spectacle of us despite my best intentions. The back door whispered open. Before I'd found the will to draw back from the kiss, Marco's familiar chuckle carried across the lawn.

"I'm thinking we need a recap on the differences between training and making out."

I eased away, tipping my forehead against Serenity's just for a moment. She sighed with what sounded like regret. We both looked up to see the other three alphas standing in a line.

"Sometimes a little of the latter can help guide the former," I said lightly, standing up.

~

Ren

I pushed myself onto my feet and gazed back at the assembled alphas. This time, only a flicker of embarrassment warmed my cheeks.

Why shouldn't I be kissing Aaron? Why shouldn't the rest of them see it? I was supposed to be kissing *all* of them at some point or another, from what he'd said. It was practically fated.

Apparently all I needed was one tiny excuse and I turned into a total exhibitionist. Who would have guessed? Not any of my ex-attempted-flings, that was for sure.

"If you've got some better idea for unlocking the dragon in there," I said, tapping my head, "I'm all ears."

Nate cocked his head, his expression pensive. I couldn't look at him without picturing the huge bear that had stood in his place for a little while yesterday. His chestnut hair gleamed exactly the same shade. But the way he'd behaved toward me so far had been more teddy bear than predator.

"If Aaron's strategies aren't working, I'm not sure any of us could come up with something better," he said. "But if there's anything you need me to do, just say so."

"Maybe we should leave the shifting aside for now and find out where we can get with the powers she's already showing," West said, with a skeptical glance over my body. "I'd like to see what she can do."

And what I couldn't, his tone implied.

I raised my chin. "Fine by me. Where do we start?"

"What were those qualities you mentioned?" West said, glancing at Aaron. "Speed, agility, and strength? Speed seems like an easy place to start."

"She's not really dressed for working out," Nate said.

"She's not going to get to call a time-out and go change every time she has to act."

I brushed my hands over the silky violet shirt. I'd worn jeans through most of my exploits in the city. They felt perfectly comfortable. The blouse was light and flexible enough, just fancier than I usually bothered with. "As long as Marco doesn't mind me possibly ruining his nice clothes, I'm good to go."

Marco smirked. "There's plenty to go around. I'm looking forward to seeing you in action, princess."

"We can start simple," West said, as if I needed coddling. "How fast can you run from one side of the yard to the other?"

"Faster than you, maybe," I said, but he glowered at me rather than responding to the challenge. I shrugged and ambled over to the line of trees that bordered the yard.

"You don't have to go along with this," Nate said.

"It's fine." I smiled at them all, with a little extra sharpness for West. "If it shuts him up for a few minutes, it's a win all around."

Marco raised his hand to his mouth as if trying to hold in his snicker—and failing. West turned his glare on the jaguar shifter. Marco just raised an eyebrow. "You asked for this."

"It *would* probably be useful for us to know exactly where your abilities are at," Aaron said calmly. "Are you ready?"

"On your marks, get set, go," I said, and pushed my feet off the lawn's spongy ground. I dashed for the stretch of trees across from me, pushing all my energy into my legs, as if there was a police officer chasing after me. Or a mark who'd caught on to a theft. Or some guy who really didn't want to take no as an answer.

All situations I'd experienced at least once.

My feet pounded the grass. The warming air rushed past me. I burst past the first few trees and caught myself, spinning around. A grin split my face. That had been kind of fun.

I walked back to the edge of the lawn, wiping my hands together. "All right, what've you got next?"

I must have done all right. Marco, Aaron, and Nate all looked pleased in their own ways. And West looked pissed, which meant I'd performed better than he liked. I gave him a pointed glance. I hadn't even broken a sweat yet.

"How long can you keep that up for?" he said. "A thirty-foot dash is nothing. You need endurance too."

"Do you have a longer track for me to take on?" I said. "Or are you suggesting I just run back and forth like a crazy person?"

He gave me a thin smile. "You'd better make do with what we have."

Oh, he'd like it if I backed down, wouldn't he? As if I hadn't been in situations ten times more humiliating than this in the last seven years. He had no idea what "endurance" meant. I wasn't going to let his arrogance get to me.

"No problem," I said, keeping my tone breezy. "I wouldn't mind giving my legs a good stretch anyway."

I took off without any preamble this time. I raced across the lawn to my starting point, pivoted on my feet, and zipped back the way I'd come. Once I fell into the rhythm of the thump of my feet and the heave of my breaths, the growing burn in my muscles was almost pleasant. I gave myself over to the sensation, not bothering to count repetitions. Just flying back and forth over the yard as if, if I pushed myself a tiny bit farther, I might actually leave the ground.

I had worked up a bit of a sweat, slick under the silky shirt, when West leapt forward in the middle of one of my dashes. He swung out his foot as if to trip me. But my instincts had taken over the second I'd seen him moving. I was already dodging out of the way. I slowed and swiveled, folding my arms over my chest.

"Really?"

"We're supposed to be testing agility too," he said, looking not even slightly guilty.

"And she's having no problem showing you up in that area too," Marco said.

"We're not done yet." West pointed to one of the tallest trees at the back of the yard. "How high can you climb?"

His smirk had come back. Probably thinking that in the city I hadn't gotten much experience with trees. And maybe I hadn't, but there'd been plenty of fences and buildings to clamber up.

"Would the top work for you?" I asked.

I marched over to the tree without waiting for an answer. All I got was an inarticulate mutter anyway.

The pine's lowest branches jutted from its narrow trunk

about a foot over my head. Low enough that I could still reach them with my arms extended, but I bent my knees and sprang up so I could hook my elbow right over one. Hugging it, I walked my feet up the trunk until I could swing my legs over the branch too. Then I scrambled up and reached for the next one.

Once I was in the tree, climbing was way easier than West must have realized. The branches were spaced so close together it was more like hefting myself up a ladder than any real challenge. I pulled myself along as quickly as I could without completely losing my breath. Sap was smearing the violet fabric of the shirt, but Marco had said not to worry about that. The pungent pine smell filled my nose. I drank it in with another grin.

As I got higher up, the branches grew thinner. So did the trunk. A hot breeze whipped past me, making the upper half of the tree sway. I gripped the rough bark tighter and kept going.

When my climbing material had pretty much run out, several feet from the tree's peak, I wrapped one arm around the trunk and glanced down. I'd come a little higher than the roof of Marco's house. In the yard below, Nate raised his hand to give me a thumbs-up. I couldn't see West's expression, but I'd bet it was even grouchier than usual.

And I could make him even more peeved. My grin widened as the urge came over me. The fall was twice my leap from the bedroom window yesterday, but a little extra risk just made it more exhilarating.

I stepped forward on the branch and jumped.

The air whistled past my ears. The blouse's sleeves billowed around my arms. For a second, I could imagine the wind catching them, lifting me up to soar toward the sky. My breath caught with a knot of longing beneath my sternum.

Someone let out a worried shout. Then I was hitting the ground, balls of my feet first. Pushing off them, I bent my knees into a roll. I tumbled over on my shoulder and flipped back onto my feet, straightening up in one smooth motion. My feet stung a little and my breath was still ragged, but damn, that had been a delicious sensation.

Aaron was giving me his usual quiet smile. "It looks to me like agility isn't a concern. And I think between all those tests, we've also covered strength pretty well."

West's jaw had clenched. Something flickered in his eyes, an emotion I couldn't quite put my finger on until he opened his mouth.

"In the real world, we don't pull stupid stunts like that unless our lives depend on it."

His tone was snarky, but my ears picked up a faint tremor underneath. I paused with a retort on my tongue.

He'd been a little scared for me, despite himself. And he hated that, didn't he? Hated it so much he needed me to snark back at him so he could go back to being pissed off with me.

Too bad. I wasn't going to give him what he wanted. I'd give him the exact opposite.

"I'm not going to argue with you about it," I said, keeping my voice soft and even. "You've got to trust I don't take risks without knowing what I can handle. And if you need to find some new reason to be angry with me, you'll have to come up with it on your own instead of trying to pick a fight."

West's lean body tensed. "Don't start thinking you can read people's minds, Sparks," he said, but he looked more unsettled than angry.

Nate rested his large hand on my shoulder. "Dragons see more than any of the rest of us can," he said approvingly.

I rubbed the back of my neck. I'd enjoyed the physical exertion while I was in the middle of it, but the effort was starting to catch up with me. Especially after all those failed attempts at shifting beforehand.

Sure I was quick and strong, and I could take a stab at people's emotions when I needed to. What good was any of that to the alphas if I couldn't make the full transformation into a dragon? I still didn't have a clue what Mom had been trying to tell me with the symbol in my locket.

How long would these guys stick with me before they gave up and—

A jolt of panic shot through me. I clamped down on that thought before my mind could finish it and pushed it away.

"I think our Princess of Flames has more than proven herself for the morning," Marco's smooth voice broke in. "As host to this party, I say we give her a break." He held out his hand to me with his crooked smile. Even with me tired and uncertain, it still provoked a flutter of attraction in my chest.

"There are a few parts of this house you haven't seen yet," he said. "One in particular I think you'll appreciate. Are you up for a quick tour?"

CHAPTER 10

Ren

As soon as I stepped into the house with just Marco beside me, a weight seemed to lift off my shoulders. All the pressure of having the four guys watching me, thinking about me... and me thinking about *them*. Some part of me might like the idea that they were all meant to be with me, but the feeling was still overwhelming sometimes.

How had Mom gone from that to having no male companionship at all for all those years, without ever showing she missed it? She must have. Maybe she'd just been too good at hiding it for me to notice.

Leonard was in the main hall, dusting the frame of an oil painting hanging on the wall. So Marco really had put his lieutenant on cleaning duty. Marco shooed him away, I guessed realizing I still might not be feeling super friendly toward the guy who'd grabbed me in the bar. That was fine with me.

"So what's this part of the house you're so eager to show off?" I asked Marco.

"You'll see." He guided me past the kitchen and down a hall toward the south side of the house with a hand on my back. The light contact sent a pulse of heat over my skin. My thoughts slipped back to yesterday. To that kiss in the bedroom. Just remembering it made my entire body flush.

Was the pull between us always going to feel this intense? Or did it ease off a little once the guys and I were officially mates? I had no idea how a relationship like that worked. But asking Marco directly felt way too awkward. He could probably already tell how much his presence affected me. The last thing I wanted to discuss with him was my out-of-control horniness.

"Here we are." He pushed open a door and ushered me through. The second I stepped inside, my jaw dropped. All thoughts of horniness went temporarily out the window.

Or window*s*, maybe would be more accurate. The room we'd stepped into was walled on three sides by enormous panes, like a massive greenhouse attached to the side of the house. The late morning sunlight streamed in from between the trees outside, warming the place with a comfortable glow. The floor space wasn't huge, maybe ten feet by ten, but the walls rose at least two stories into the air. Ledges and outcroppings in the shape of thick branches protruded from the walls at varying intervals. It was like looking up into a tiered jungle canopy.

"This house is a way station for any of my kin traveling through these parts," Marco said, looking pleased with my awed reaction. "There's not much room to run around in shifted form outside. This gives us a place to exercise our feline selves in privacy."

It was easy to imagine tigers and leopards—and jaguars—leaping from branch to branch or sunning themselves on one of those ledges. But all those windows... The trees didn't appear to provide total shelter. "Aren't you worried about someone wandering by and seeing you?"

Marco motioned to the walls. "That's one-way glass. On the outside, it's blank. We can see out, but no one can see in. We can get up to whatever we want without worrying about prying eyes." He arched a teasing eyebrow at me. The one with the scar through it.

How had he gotten that wound? A scuffle with another shifter? Or some other conflict I wouldn't have understood yet?

"Is it normal for shifters to live this close to a big city like New York?" I asked. "You must have to be really careful, even with a house like this."

Marco shook his head. "Maybe it's feline obstinacy, but my kin don't play so well by the rules. In theory, most of the country is divided up between the dominant supernatural groups. The cities are vampire territory, because they find it easiest to blend in —and they need a large supply of people to pick from for feeding." He grimaced. "Shifters mostly stick to small towns and countryside, the middle-ground between civilization and wilderness. But my kin's alphas have always liked to keep an eye on what's going on even in the places we're not supposed to be."

My eyes had widened. "Wait. There are *vampires* too? Living in New York?"

"Not a lot of them," Marco said, but his tone had turned more serious. "They like to keep their community rather... exclusive. But there are still more than enough of the bloodsuckers. If you're lucky, you'll never have to deal with them." He shuddered, and then gave me a more typical smile. "So let's not spend any more time talking about them. How would you like a proper climb?"

Now that I'd accepted the existence of shifters, my brain had obviously recalibrated its threshold for belief. If werewolves—and werebears and werejaguars and so on—existed, why the hell not vampires?

I looked up at the jungle gym above me, and my earlier fatigue fell away. Oh, yes. This was exactly what I needed.

I clambered up a protrusion shaped like a jutting rock. From there, it was only a bit of a stretch to jump onto one of the thick manmade branches. Marco followed me as I roamed higher, staying in human form himself. Maybe he thought it'd be impolite to shift when I couldn't? I was too busy exploring to care.

Here and there between the branches and ledges, objects like huge bowls were wedged, stuffed full of plush cushions. I poked at one of the pillows as I climbed past one. "Cat beds?" I said, shooting Marco an amused look.

He laughed. "Basically. We do enjoy our sleep."

He stopped on a ledge about halfway up the second story, watching me as I finished my ascent to the very top. The highest branch veered on an angle all the way to the vaulted glass roof. I scrambled up it and crouched where it bowed to take in my surroundings.

I could see over the roof of the rest of the house from here, to the tops of the pines on the other side. To the south, the suburban road was visible between the trees, stretching off into the distance. A car puttered by below me, the driver completely unaware of me perched there watching him. The view of the long drop to the ground below made my pulse thump faster.

If this was how cat shifters did things, I had to say I completely approved.

I couldn't jump through the window, but there were all sorts of possibilities for leaping my way down in here. I turned my gaze to the room beneath me. The shape and placement of the various protrusions made for their own sort of challenge. I fixed my gaze on a branch ahead of me and several feet below, bunched my muscles, and launched myself toward it.

My feet hit the artificial bark smack in the center. I grasped the sides of the branch to hold myself steady, exhilaration rushing through me. Without giving myself much time to think, I spotted an appropriate ledge and pushed off again.

The feeling of free-fall raced through me for an instant before I landed. So sharp and giddying. I glanced around and threw myself down toward one of those bowls of bedding. This time I let myself land on my hands and knees. I rolled onto my back and snuggled into the cushions.

"Okay," I said. "This *is* almost as good as the climbing part."

"And the jumping part?" Marco said, hopping onto a nearby branch. His indigo eyes glinted. "You're a pretty girl, my Princess of Flames, but you're spectacular when you come that close to flight. It lights you up."

The compliment lit me up in a totally different way. I pushed myself onto my feet. "Is this how you treat all the girls? Kidnap them and then seduce them with flattery and your awesome house?"

His eyelids lowered, his gaze turning more heated. "Not at all, princess. This is only for you."

His tone was serious enough beneath the flirting that my pulse skipped. I craved that intensity, but at the same time it sent my nerves jittering. How could I be that important to him, to anyone here, just like that?

I leapt away from those worries, up one of the other slanting branches. "Well, you haven't caught me yet," I called back to him.

I heard a laugh in his intake of breath. "Let's see if I can change that."

His feet scraped the outcroppings just beneath me. I threw myself forward faster, leaning over so I could pull myself along with my hands as well. As if I were an animal even if I still couldn't turn myself into one.

I sprang from one branch to another, dashed up that one to a ledge, and abruptly found I had no way to keep going up. I'd almost hit the roof again. Marco was halfway up the branch behind me, loping up it with perfect balance. He hadn't shifted either, but the feline in him showed in every movement.

"Ran yourself into a corner?" he teased, slowing a little to draw out his pursuit.

Oh, no. I wasn't letting him win yet. "No such thing," I informed him. Then, as he reached the edge of the platform, I flung myself off it toward a branch at least a full floor below.

The exhilaration of the fall burst through me—and tugged free a memory from long, long ago. Scrambling onto the roof of a wooden playhouse and launching myself into the air. Feeling my wings unfurl and catch the wind just for a second before my child's body hit the ground. Rolling in the grass and giggling, reveling in the glimpse of my future powers.

Mama! Mama, did you see that one?

My feet hit the branch hard. My knees jarred, and the vivid glimpse of my past slipped away. I held there, inhaling shakily, my fingers digging into the manufactured bark.

"Princess?" Marco said, lowering himself onto the branch just above me.

I shook myself, but my mind wouldn't quite settle. Where had I been in that memory? Somewhere with my mother, obviously. But not New York. That had been before New York. In a shifter community somewhere? Was that where I was supposed to go now?

I looked up at Marco. "You keep calling me 'princess.' Because my mother was pretty much queen of all the shifters."

He nodded, watching me curiously.

"She must have had some kind of official home, right?" I went on. "That people would know to come to, if they needed... I don't know, official guidance or something?"

"There are four houses that are the official property of the dragon shifter line," Marco said. "One near the center of each kin-group's main territory. She'd have moved from one to another periodically or as needs required, usually with at least one of her alpha mates. Why?"

I bit my lip. "I just wondered if maybe she might have gone back to one of those homes. When she left New York, I mean. I guess if that symbol had to do with any of them, you'd have recognized it, though, wouldn't you?"

"Most likely. And if she'd returned to prime shifter territory, she wouldn't have gone unnoticed."

So much for that lead. But that line of thinking tickled up another question. "Aaron said you all knew me back then. When I was a little kid, before Mom and I left. Were we, like, friends, or...?"

Marco's crooked smile looked softer than usual. "We saw you around, here and there. I don't think I ever spoke to you except a formal introduction after the last alpha chose me—which wasn't long before you and your mother vanished. You weren't much more than a toddler most of that time, you know."

I arched my eyebrows at him. "So you're not that much of a cradle robber?"

He laughed. "I was still a kid myself, remember. When I was ten, I was a hell of a lot more interested in climbing trees and winning races than thinking about future mates." The heat crept back into his gaze. "Of course, my interests have changed a lot since then."

"Oh, yeah?" I padded a little higher up the branch I was on, giving him a challenging glance. It was easier to turn my attention back to the present than to keep dwelling on everything I couldn't remember.

"Not convinced yet?" His grin widened. Then he sprang after me, so quickly I yelped.

Marco had obviously been holding back before. He knew this feline jungle gym a lot better than I did, after all. I clambered up the branch, jumped over another, and dashed along a ledge, but he caught up with me. Tucking his arm around me, he pulled us down into one of the bowl-like beds.

"Got you," he murmured, his face just inches from mine. He'd angled his body so it wasn't quite touching me, holding himself up by his elbow, but the warmth of him washed over me. It stirred up a wave of longing so intense I couldn't imagine fighting it.

I pushed up toward him, and he claimed my mouth with his.

The kiss radiated heat through my whole being. I looped my arm around Marco's neck, wanting him closer, harder, everywhere. He teased his teeth over my lip until I whimpered and then tipped his head to kiss me even more deeply. At my tug, his body settled against mine. My breath caught at the solid, muscular weight of him. My hips arched toward his instinctively, and he groaned.

"Yes, princess," he murmured. "That's the way."

His hand traveled up my side, sliding the silk of my blouse over my skin. He cupped my breast through my bra. His thumb swiveled over my nipple, and I gasped into his mouth. Marco smiled into the kiss, teasing that peak harder with steady, knowing strokes. My fingers traced over his cheek and tangled in his hair. The swell of pleasure inside me was rising so fast I didn't know how to rein it in, how to hold on to anything. It might just carry me away.

Marco dipped his head down to trail his lips across my jaw. His hand left my breast to slip under the hem of my shirt. His fingers eased up over my bare skin, and he nipped the tender skin of my throat. I moaned, my body trembling—and a sharp pain shot through my palm.

I stiffened, and Marco froze over me. He raised his head. The lust in his heavy-lidded eyes sent a fresh tingle through me, but the pain stopped me from getting swept up in it again.

"What's wrong?" he said.

My hand had balled into a fist. I uncurled my fingers from my palm and stared, bewildered, for a second before I understood what I was seeing.

A small blue gem shone darkly in the middle of my palm. Marco's sapphire earring. I'd nicked the stud off his ear without even realizing. And accidentally jabbed the pin into my hand. A small drop of blood was beading below it.

Marco laughed low in his throat. "My Princess of Flames and her sticky fingers." He sat back on the cushions, drawing me with him but leaving a little space between us. With his own nimble fingers, he plucked out the stud. Then he brought my hand to his mouth and slicked his tongue over the tiny wound. My heart stuttered.

But the desire coursing through me had dampened a little. I dragged in a breath. Maybe that was for the best. I still wanted him—*damn*, did I want him—but at least I felt in control again.

Marco tucked the earring into his pocket. He kept my hand in his, but he didn't pull me to him again. Could he sense my hesitation?

"This thieving habit of yours is a bit of a strange one," he remarked, with an easy smile. "Should I be worried you'll end up robbing me out of house and home before the end of the day?"

He spoke so lightly I couldn't help smiling back. "I, um, might also have pocketed a mirror from the guest bedroom. That's it so far. I'm sorry. It's kind of a nervous habit."

Marco cocked his head. "Can I ask how exactly one develops stealing as a habit?"

My chest tightened, but he was looking at me with so little judgment that a moment later I started to relax. The four guys here were sharing so much of themselves with me. Maybe it was only fair they had a better idea who they were letting into their lives.

"When I first lost my apartment, I didn't have anywhere to go," I said. The words stuck in my throat, but I pushed them out. "Mom had always warned me about the police and any kind of government authority, so they didn't seem safe. I ended up getting in with a group of street kids this guy named Fisher had sort of... hired on. He owned a building where he'd let us sleep as long as we'd bring him stuff we'd stolen every day. And he'd give us a small cut of what he got fencing the stuff, so we could buy food and all that. I didn't *like* doing it, because I know it's wrong, but I was good at it, because of how fast I can be. And I didn't know what else to do."

Marco stroked his fingertips over the back of my head soothingly. "I think we've all been in positions where we had to do things we'd rather not for our own survival. There's no shame in that, princess."

There was, though. The shame of it still burned my cheeks when I thought about it. "I didn't get away from Fisher until I was almost twenty. Kylie helped me. But it took a long time even after I met her, because he didn't want me to go. I was his best thief. I was scared of what he'd do... But I did get away, in the end, and I haven't *meant* to steal anything in more than a year."

I'd been looking at my hands through my entire confession. Finally I lifted my gaze to Marco's face. His eyes were gentle, but his tone was as dry and cocky as ever.

"So my princess is a tough girl. I can't say I have any complaints there."

The last of the tension inside me released. I gave his shoulder a playful shove. "It seems like you're a tough guy yourself. What's the story with that scar?"

I motioned to his eyebrow. The second the question came out, I knew I shouldn't have asked it. Marco's muscles tensed where his body was still aligned with mine. Shit. I opened my mouth to say never mind, and just then my butt vibrated.

Or rather, my phone vibrated against my butt. I squirmed a little farther away from Marco into the cushions and tugged it out. In the first instant I read the alert on the screen, every other concern faded from my mind.

"Kylie texted me," I said, springing to my feet. "She found someone who recognized the symbol from my locket."

CHAPTER 11

Ren

"It's right in the middle of vampire territory," Nate said, crossing his arms over his brawny chest where he stood by the arm of the sofa. "We can't just saunter on in there and expect them to give us a free pass."

"My scouts move through the city on a regular basis without any trouble whatsoever," Marco replied. He leaned back in the sitting room's armchair. "As long as we don't draw attention to ourselves, they'll never even realize we were there. I know stealth isn't your strong point, but you can manage not to lumber about like a total bear, can't you?"

Nate scowled at him. West paused where he'd been pacing back and forth near the door. "How do we know this information is even worth following up on? We're hearing it third hand."

My fingers tightened around my phone. I sat up straighter where I'd curled up at one end of the sofa. "Kylie knows the people she talks to. If she didn't think this guy was legit, she wouldn't have told me about it." She'd reported that a guy she played pool with sometimes did urban "explorations." He'd been pretty sure he'd seen the inverted flame image in a tunnel leading to one of New York City's abandoned subway stations.

"Why would anything to do with shifters be down in some abandoned subway tunnel?" Nate asked.

By the fireplace, Aaron raised his head. "The spot could have been chosen for exactly that reason, if the dragon shifters wanted to keep it hidden. No ordinary shifter would stumble across it there. But Nate is right. It'll be difficult for all four of us to enter the city together without any of the locals noticing. Which is why—"

"All *five* of us," I broke in.

He blinked at me, his clear blue eyes momentarily puzzled. "What?"

I gestured to the bunch of us. "You said 'all four of us.' But we're five. I'm coming too, obviously."

Apparently that fact wasn't so obvious. Aaron's mouth tensed, and Nate bristled as if his bear really were coming out.

"No," the bigger guy said. "It's dangerous enough with just us. Our job is to make sure you're protected, and that means you stay here."

"I was going to suggest that only one, or at most two, of the alphas should investigate," Aaron said in his light, even voice. "There's no need for even all four of us to go."

"Well, even if only one or two of you goes, I'm coming with." I waved my phone in the air. "I'm the one who got the information, remember? I'm the one it's *for*. The symbol was in my locket. It's some kind of message from my mother. If *anyone* goes, it should be me."

Nate shook his head. "If it wasn't vampire territory, I'd never argue with you. But you don't understand the full situation. It's not worth the risk, especially when the tip might not be reliable."

Marco's gaze darted between us, his expression somewhere between contemplative and amused. He wasn't telling me to stay home, but he wasn't leaping to support me either. The one voice in my favor was West's, although of course he had to say it in the most insulting way possible.

"If she's going to be head of all shifter-kin, she'd better be able to hold her own," he growled. "Let her come. It'll give her a taste of the supernatural world outside this ridiculous house."

Marco raised an eyebrow at that. "If you don't enjoy the comforts in here, you're welcome to sleep in the yard tonight."

"Who cares about the house?" I said. "If I *am* going to be head of all the shifters, I should get to make a few decisions for myself. And I say I'm going. You have no idea what we might be looking for. For all we know, my mom set it up so I'm the only one who can find it or figure out what to do with it. Won't making *one* trip *with* me draw a lot less attention than two trips when you realize you need me there after all?"

"You could stay nearby, ready to join us if we let you know your presence was needed," Aaron suggested.

"No. No way. I haven't had a say in *any* of this so far, but this could be my mother's last message to me. I have to see it for myself."

"Ren," Nate started, but West broke in.

"You're all too hung up on the past. This is a totally different scenario. Vampires had nothing to do with what happened before."

"If we *do* piss them off, vampires are plenty dangerous," Marco said. "We shouldn't completely dismiss them."

"Hold on," I said, setting down my phone. My fingers curled around the arm of the sofa. "What 'past scenario' are you talking about? Why *are* you so worried about protecting me? What—"

A splinter of a memory jabbed through my mind. Just a fragment, wavering and incomplete, but with a jolt of panic that brought a metallic flavor into my mouth.

I was huddled on the floor, clutching the arm of a girl a little older than me, pale with a head of blond ringlets. Her mouth was set in a thin, bloodless line. Another girl, even older, stood at my other side, black waves cascading down her trembling back. Her hand was braced against my head, too tense to really comfort.

The three of us were staring at my mother—my mother and the rugged, barrel-chested man who was arguing with her. I knew that low, hoarse voice had usually wrapped me up in comfort, but now it only made my pulse skitter.

"You have to go. Now."

"I have to stay and fight for what's mine," my mother insisted, her eyes flashing.

An agonized cry rang out. My mother flinched, and the man's expression shuttered. "There are too many of them. If you try to fight here, you'll lose your chance to fight your way out. Go. For them."

He swept his arm toward us—and the memory flicked away.

I slumped forward on the sofa, dropping my head into my hands. The immediacy of the moment was gone, but my sense of it was still trickling in. That man—he'd been one of my fathers. *Daddy*, some part of me called out with a pang. And the girls beside me...

I looked up, bracing my hands on either side of my neck. The guys had all fallen silent, watching me. My mouth was dry. I swallowed hard.

"I had sisters," I said in a ragged voice. "Two of them, older than me. Didn't I? Why did my mother run away with me and not them? What *happened* to them? What happened to my fathers?"

Nate and Aaron exchanged a glance. Marco opened his mouth and hesitated. West looked as if he'd swallowed his tongue, the one time I actually wanted him to let it loose.

"Tell me," I snapped. "Why do you keep trying to hide it? What are you all so afraid will happen to me?"

"Ren," Nate said roughly. He sank onto the sofa beside me. "It's not that we wanted to hide it from you. We just wanted to give you a chance to adjust before you had to deal with that too."

"With what?" I said, my voice suddenly small. It was horrible, whatever it was. I didn't need him to tell me that. The memory and their reactions stunk of it.

Aaron drew in a breath. "A band of rogue shifters attacked your family one night, sixteen years ago," he said quietly. "As far as anyone knows, their goal was to kill you, your mother, and your sisters—all of the dragon shifters—and the four alphas, who were there with you that night. Your fathers died trying to stop them from getting to you. The rogues caught your sisters and murdered them too. Your mother barely made it out alive with you."

I'd been braced for his explanation, but the words rocked me anyway. My stomach churned. Nate offered his arm, and I scooted closer to him, letting him pull me into an embrace. The reassurance of his strong body barely took the edge off my horror.

"And then she ran," I filled in. "All the way to New York City. She was afraid they'd try again." That was why she'd tried to keep us so invisible. Why she'd been so scared she'd felt she had to block my memories and my powers.

"From what you've told us, we have to assume that's the case," Aaron said.

"And I for one can't blame her," Marco put in. "She kept you safe—and hopefully herself too. She did what she had to do." He shot West a sharp look as if daring him to argue, but the wolf shifter had withdrawn to the doorway, his face shadowed.

"But *why*?" I burst out. "Why would anyone want to hurt us like that?" The remembered cry rang in my ears—the horrible pain in it. The image of my sisters' faces... Neither of them could have been older than ten. And these rogues had just *slaughtered* them?

"No one knows for sure," Nate said, rubbing my arm. "Your fathers and your mother killed a bunch of the rogues defending themselves, but of course the dead can't say anything. The ones who survived got out of there before anyone else realized what was going on. They were never caught."

"Most likely it was a power grab," Aaron said. "Most of the shifters who refuse to ally themselves with their kin-group are carrying a lot of bitterness and anger. They don't like the way the rules are made or who carries them out. Maybe they thought they could set themselves up as the new alphas. Maybe they just wanted to sow disorder. If we're lucky, we'll never encounter them again, so we'll never need to know."

"But if that group is still out there, and there's no reason to think they aren't, the first thing they'll want to do if they find out you're alive is finish the job they started," Marco said in a darker tone than usual. He lifted his chin toward Nate. "Which is why bear boy has gone into overprotective mode."

"I don't think there's anything *over* about it," Nate muttered. "Do you see why I'd rather you stayed here, Ren? No one except us and Marco's few people here know we've even found you yet.

The longer we can keep it that way, the more time we can buy before we might have to deal with the rogues again."

Right. More time for me to come into the powers that seemed stubbornly locked inside me, so I'd have any hope at all of defending myself.

A shiver ran through me. There were people out there who hated me so much they'd wanted to kill me when I'd been a helpless five-year-old.

And if they succeeded this time, what would happen to the shifters then? If I was the last dragon, and I died without passing on that line... My kind would be extinct. There'd be nothing left tying the kin-groups together.

My sense of shifter society was still vague, but that thought chilled me to the core. I wrapped my hand around Nate's. I did understand why he was so worried, why Aaron had argued in favor of caution too, why Marco hadn't spoken up for me. They needed me... and the alphas before them had already failed once.

I needed them too. I felt a connection to all four of the men around me, humming through the air. Even as the chill prickled through me, that connection steadied me.

I wasn't alone anymore. I had them now, like I was meant to. I couldn't keep running.

Mom had taken my memories, but not forever. I knew what I was now, and I needed to keep remembering.

I was a dragon.

I pushed myself away from Nate, with a squeeze of his hand to tell him it wasn't a rejection. "I get it," I said, standing up. "I don't blame you for worrying. But I'm still coming. It's the path my mother left for me to follow, and I'm not letting anyone stop me."

CHAPTER 12

Nate

OUR DRAGON SHIFTER was so strong. She sat squeezed between me and Marco in the back of Aaron's sedan as he drove the bunch of us into the city, her back straight and her jaw set. But I'd taken her hand a few minutes after we'd gotten in, and she hadn't let go of mine since. Her slim fingers stayed twined with mine, gripping tight.

They felt so fragile, but I knew the rest of her wasn't. The news about her family's murders had shocked her—that was obvious. I was never going to forget the way the blood had drained from her face as Aaron had told her the story, as if she were dying alongside her long-gone sisters and fathers. But she hadn't let her emotions hold her back. She wasn't letting anything stop her from being right here with us to face whatever waited ahead.

I had to admit, I *hated* that Ren was here. My hackles had

risen the second we'd crossed the city's boundaries. I hadn't scented a vampire yet, but the whole place stunk of metal and burnt gasoline. Even if there hadn't been any bloodsuckers around, this wasn't where shifters were meant to go. I had to admire Ren too, though. She might not have remembered much yet, but she was still every inch a dragon.

As soon as we'd figured out what had happened to her mother, we could get on with our proper lives. The way we'd all been waiting to for the last sixteen years. Alphas and dragon shifter, all the kin-groups growing in harmony.

As long as the other alphas didn't screw it up. West sat in the front passenger seat with that perpetual cloud over him, his expression grim. "Isn't there a way to avoid all this traffic?" he muttered to Aaron as we crept down a jammed street. He'd been so cold to Ren the entire time. How could he really think that pushing her aside, throwing away the legacy of the dragon shifters, was the right move?

And Marco... You could never really trust a cat. He lounged on the other side of the backseat with his elbow propped against the window. "Heel, doggie," he teased. "We'll get there when we get there." Which only made West's frown turn into a scowl. The feline alpha had welcomed Ren, sure, but he also took a little too much enjoyment from stirring up trouble.

"I can turn onto a street that should be less congested up here," Aaron said calmly. The avian alpha seemed steady enough, but the avians didn't mingle much with the rest of us anyway. I wasn't sure how to read him.

The bear-kin and those we ruled over had never wavered in our devotion to shifter law. *I* would stand by Ren no matter what happened. At least she could be sure of that.

I ran my thumb over the back of her hand, and she leaned a

little more of her weight on me. I resisted the urge to nuzzle her hair and take in her lovely scent. For now I had to stay focused on protecting her. All the other pleasures of having a mate could wait until our business here was finished.

But I was looking forward to them even more now that I'd met her.

Aaron drew the car to a stop. "From here, we need to go on foot," he said. Ren looked up at me with a smile that sent a bolt of desire through my chest. Resolve coiled around it.

She was leaving this city alive, or I'd die here too.

Ren

I braced my hand against the wall of the tunnel, and my fingers came away damp and gritty. My nose wrinkled at the sensation. The stairs we were tramping down were narrow, the air dank, and the space dark except for the bobbing beam of Aaron's flashlight as he led the way.

I'd never been really claustrophobic, but this place gave me the creeps. Nowhere to run or jump.

Nowhere to stretch the wings I couldn't convince to rise out of me yet.

At least I had my best friend with me again. Kylie squeezed my other hand where she was walking shoulder-to-shoulder with me and shot me a grin. *She* seemed more excited about this expedition than I was. Maybe because she hadn't just heard a story about practically her entire family being slaughtered.

"Do you have any idea what we're going to find down here?" she murmured. "I mean, why your mom wanted to send you to that symbol?"

I shook my head. "I don't know any more than you do at this point." About my mom's plans, at least. The second we'd met up by the subway entrance, Kylie had asked how I was, but I hadn't mentioned what I'd learned about my past. It seemed like a lot to dump on even my best friend. I was still processing the facts myself.

I must have seen more of the violence than the brief fragment of memory that had come to me, but none of the rest had come back yet, even after hearing the story. I wasn't sure if that was for the best or if I'd rather have had those images to examine. I could almost sense them, like sharks weaving by beneath water too dark to penetrate in my mind. They were going to surface sometime, and when they did, it was going to hurt.

"Quite an adventure," Kylie said, and nudged me with her elbow. "You looked like you were getting pretty close with the big guy. Now he's a hunk and a half."

She must have meant Nate. He was at the back of our procession, several feet behind us, making sure no unfriendly intruders snuck up on us. My face warmed a little. I was getting used to the idea that all four of these guys were meant to be my partners, but I knew it was going to sound kind of weird to anyone else. Anyone human, at least.

But it wasn't as if I'd be able to hide it from Kylie very long. I didn't want to.

"Actually..." I said. "I've been getting pretty close with all of them. Well, the three of them who don't spend the whole time glaring daggers at me." I glowered briefly at West's lean back where he was stalking along just behind Aaron. "It turns out that's the thing with dragon shifters. We're supposed to, er, bond with all of the alphas. It's, like, a political decree."

We followed the guys past a door with squeaky hinges and

into a wider tunnel that was just as dark and dank. Aaron's light wavered over the curved walls of the long-unused subway route.

Kylie's eyebrows had shot up. "Wait. When you say *bond*, you mean in a fully bodily way, right?"

The flush in my cheeks deepened. "That's the idea. We haven't gotten *that* far yet."

I braced myself for shock or disgust, but Kylie just laughed. She held up her hand for a high five. "You go, girl. If I had a chance to handle four guys like this at the same time, you'd better believe I'd go for it. What a way to give up your V-card!"

In that moment, I wished I hadn't admitted to her that I'd never gone all the way with a guy. "I'm pretty sure it won't be all of them at the same time," I said. So far they'd only reached out to me one at a time. The thought of more than one of them kissing me, touching me, together sent a sudden warmth through my body.

Maybe I didn't entirely hate the idea. But this wasn't really the time to be exploring *that*.

Kylie's expression turned a shade more serious. "You *are* okay, aren't you? Are you sure you can trust everything they've been telling you?"

"Yeah. I remember enough that it all makes sense. It's overwhelming, but at the same time, I feel more like myself the more I find out." I paused. "*You* don't think it's totally crazy, do you? I mean, shifters and vampires and who the hell knows what else?"

"Please. Of course it's crazy. But that doesn't mean I can't believe it. I saw Hunk-and-a-Half turn into a bear with my very own eyes. And I know you've got a good head on your shoulders. That's why I need you around."

She looped her arm around me to give me a quick sideways hug. The gesture sent a pang through my chest. How much longer *would* I be around? When—if—I did manage to take on the full role of dragon shifter, I couldn't hang out in Brooklyn with Kylie all the time.

We could figure that out later. After we'd figured out whatever it was Mom had wanted me to understand.

Aaron's voice rang out. "It's here." He was pointing the flashlight at a spot on one of the walls. The rest of us picked our way closer over the cracked cement and abandoned tracks. The air shifted, sending a cool chill over my arms. I rubbed at the goose bumps.

The wall had been built out of interlocking stones. The circle of light illuminated a rectangular one that had been carved with a symbol like the one in my locket: an upside-down flame in the midst of a spiral. My heartbeat kicked up a notch.

"That's really it," I said.

I glanced around, as if Mom might step out of the shadows now that I was here. As if she could have been waiting down here all this time, or even just since my birthday.

No one stirred in the darkness except West's tense form. Then Marco and Nate prowled closer to the stone. Nate prodded it first before stepping back.

Marco tested its edges with his more lithe fingers. "It doesn't seem all that eager to offer up its secrets," he remarked.

"They're not secrets meant for you," I said. This was why I'd insisted on coming. I walked up to the wall, into the glow of the flashlight. Up close, the symbol sent a tingle through my body. It drew my hands to it. I raised my arms and pressed my palms to either side of the flame, the way it seemed to want.

The stone jolted toward me with a scraping sound, and my mind cracked apart. The sensations of the tunnel washed away in a wave of memories.

I was a little girl, dashing through the forest to find a hiding spot before one of my daddies finished counting. The lush green smells of late spring surrounded me. I ducked behind a tree and swallowed a giggle.

Me and my sisters danced around our mother in time with the pop song she'd started playing on her old boombox. She grasped each of our hands in turn, spinning us around. Our feet pattered over the wooden floor.

We sat in a row along the edge of a platform where Mama was holding audience. The edge was high enough and my legs short enough that I could swing my feet without touching the floor. The shifters approached our mother one by one. We whispered to each other, guessing each shifter's animal by scent and mannerisms. "That one's got to be a badger." "No, no, I'd say raccoon."

We were running down the hall, Mama urging us faster. My pulse thundered in my ears. We had to get outside, outside where Mama could shift and fight. An immense lioness sprang from a doorway, snapping her jaws around my sister's arm with a burst of bright red blood. A shriek broke from my throat.

And on and on. The fractured memories hit me as if from inside and out at the same time, bubbling up through my head and pouring into me from the stone. I was drowning in them.

Then they stuttered to a halt. My mind went blank. My mother's voice washed over me, soft and lilting.

I'm so sorry it had to be this way, Serenity. I did the best I could to keep you safe. Follow the crystal—

There was a sound like an intake of breath. It jerked me back to reality.

I was standing in front of the subway tunnel wall. My fingers clutched the cool stone slab the flame symbol was carved into. It had popped out of the wall, revealing a dark hollow. The alphas and Kylie still stood around me, waiting.

My legs wobbled. Aaron leapt to my side to place a steadying hand on my shoulder. I leaned into him, trying to make sense of my swirling thoughts.

"I remember," I said. But that wasn't totally true. My head felt stuffed full of the early childhood I'd just recovered, but the memories jostled against each other with ragged edges. They didn't entirely feel like mine yet. There were still gaps and fuzzy bits. Whatever Mom had done to suppress them, it hadn't been an exact magic.

"What's in there?" Kylie asked.

I focused my gaze on the hollow. Something pale and flat lay on the rough surface inside. I set the stone down and tugged the hidden object out, my fingertips sliding over a polished surface.

It was a clear circle, like glass but with a brighter sparkle, twice the width of my palm. A faint pattern of lines and dots was etched into its surface. I squinted at it, trying to make sense of them, but they didn't form letters or even definite shapes.

Follow the crystal, my mother's voice had said. I guessed this was the crystal. How the hell was I supposed to *follow* it?

I swiveled, turning it in my hands as if that might trigger some kind of pull, and a tapping sounded farther down the tunnel. My body froze. The guys whipped around to peer in the same direction.

Several figures approached us, materializing out of the shadows. They stopped at the edge of Aaron's light. Nine men and women, all slim with deep-set eyes. Their skin ranged from pale to darker brown, but all of them had a slightly sallow look to them, as if they'd been too long out of the sun.

Oh. Understanding prickled over me at the same time as their papery acidic smell reached my nose. I'd never met one of their kind before, but I knew exactly what I was looking at all the same.

It wasn't vampires who'd threatened my family before, but it sure as hell was now.

CHAPTER 13

Ren

ONE OF THE vampires opened his narrow mouth, tasting the air with a snake-like swipe of his tongue. Thin fangs glinted behind his lips. I repressed a shudder.

"Shifters," he said, wrinkling his nose in distaste. "You're far from home, aren't you? This is our territory. There are penalties for infringing on it, as you should well know."

Smarmy bastards, weren't they? I stepped back, closer to the wall, but my hackles had risen. If they were threatening my alphas, they were going to have to contend with me as well.

"We didn't think there was any harm in taking a little stroll," Marco tossed out. "Checking out the sights, enjoying a change in scenery."

A couple of the vampires glanced around as if seriously wondering whether shifters thought subway tunnels were scenic. The one who'd spoken to us sneered.

"We don't have time for games."

Marco shrugged. "Funny, I'd have thought being immortal meant you had all the time in the world."

"What are you doing here?" the vampire demanded. "You wouldn't have come this far into our domain without reason."

"That might be true." West said, folding his arms over his chest. It was nice to see his glower directed at people who deserved it for once—if you could call vampires "people." "But you can forget it if you think we're going to stand around and chat with you. Back off, and we'll go."

The vampires did the exact opposite of backing off. They slunk closer, more fangs gleaming in the crowd now. Nate edged closer to me, his muscles tensed, looking ready to jump in front of me if need be.

"Answer my questions, or we'll simply destroy you," the vampire said. "Then your purpose won't matter one way or another."

Aaron stepped forward, his hands raised. "We apologize for this intrusion into your territory," he said. "And I apologize for my friends' rudeness. We had an urgent matter that didn't leave us time to parlay with your leaders. I swear by the moon and earth we came with no ill intentions, and we would leave just as peacefully."

"It's too late for that," a woman near the back of the vampire pack hissed. "You came uninvited. You must pay the consequences for that."

"Holy shit," Kylie said to me out of the corner of her mouth. "This is a little freakier than I was prepared for."

Me too. I grabbed her hand, tugging her closer to me. I wasn't letting *her* get hurt, especially when she'd only come down here to help me. We should have just gotten the instructions from her and gone down on our own. But I'd selfishly wanted the chance to talk to her—the one person from my old life I *could* still talk to.

"Please," Aaron was saying. "There's no need for this to come to violence. We've finished our business here. It was a shifter matter, nothing to do with your kind. If you—"

"Enough talk," the first vampire snapped. His cold gaze settled on me. "Something about this one smells strange. Not like any beast I recognize." His eyes narrowed. "What *are* you?"

He snapped his fingers, and the vampire beside him darted toward me as if to haul me over. Nate pushed between us with a growl. He shoved the vampire back toward the group, so hard the young man fell on his ass.

"Don't you dare touch her."

The lead vampire grimaced. "This is our domain. We take what we want. If you refuse to obey, you will not remain."

Just like that, the vampires sprang at us in a single flickering motion. A yelp broke from my throat. I yanked Kylie back as the four alphas threw themselves forward to meet the vampire's charge.

They shifted as they ran. Nate's form bulged through his clothing, looming into the grizzly bear I'd met in Marco's sitting room yesterday. Only he was no teddy bear now. He lunged forward, smacking one vampire's head against the wall with a sickening thud, swiping his massive paw at another that tried to dodge past him.

A golden eagle swooped from a heap of clothes and dove with claws extended to catch one of the vampires in the face. Aaron's battle cry rang through the tunnel. The beam of the fallen flashlight sparked across the bright feathers of his huge wings.

A wolf kicked out of West's jeans, his ruddy silver-tipped fur gleaming in the wavering light. He clamped his jaws around one of the vampire's legs and heaved. The vampire tumbled to the tunnel floor with a crack of her head against one of the subway rails. The wolf whirled to charge at another attacker. Something gleamed starker red on his chest. Had she hurt him?

A large black jaguar pounced into the fray. Marco knocked another vampire onto the ground, pinning him. His sleek tail lashed back and forth as he slapped the vampire across the cheek. The crack of a broken neck echoed off the walls.

The violence was horrifying, but at the same time the strength and speed of my shifter mates took my breath away. These weren't just forms they put on like some kind of costume. They *were* those animals, down to the center of their being, and they moved like magic.

My hand squeezed tighter around Kylie's. My heart was thumping in the base of my throat. The guys had taken down some of the vampires, but the others were still fighting, swinging daggers and baring their fangs. I should be out there with my mates, doing my part. It was for me that all of us were down here.

But what could I do with this human body against those undead creatures? In the damp tunnel air, I suddenly felt more useless than I ever had in my life. I had no weapons, no claws except the ones scrabbling in my chest. If I threw myself in there and tried to fight, all I'd be doing was giving the vampires a chance to grab me and turn the tables on the alphas.

If I could shift... If I could join them as an equal, prove I was worthy of the risks they were taking for me...

I pushed Kylie toward the wall. "Stay there," I said. "No matter what. Don't get any closer to them."

She nodded, at a rare loss for words. I balled my hands, staring into the midst of the fight. I knew how the transformation was supposed to feel. I'd glimpsed the feeling in my memories. That stretching, unfurling sensation that would rip through my body. I wanted it now, so badly.

I reached inside to the frantic scraping of those internal claws. *Burst out. Break free. Let loose the dragon inside.* I *was* that dragon. I knew it, as much as I'd known my mother when I'd seen her scaled form flying overhead in my memory. I could taste the charring of fiery breath on my tongue.

But my body didn't comply. My form stayed completely human. The dragon remained locked inside me. I groaned, wrenching at myself with all my will, and it was still me just standing there.

My memories had been unlocked. Mom's magic had fallen away. Why was it still so hard for me to follow my true nature?

In front of me, a vampire slashed at Nate's side, drawing a dark red streak through his bear's chestnut fur. He bellowed and swung his paw, but his attacker darted away. Another bloodsucker was struggling on the ground with Marco. She sank her fangs deep into the jaguar's foreleg, and he let out a pained snarl.

The memory of the lioness sinking her teeth into my sister flashed through my mind. It shook loose other fragments, bits of the past I didn't want in my head right now. A warthog stabbing its tusks into the side of a great tawny mountain lion. *Daddy*. A polished floor streaked with blood. My mother's fingers clutching mine so tight a stabbing pain shot through my bones. A whimper fading into a gurgle with the slitting of a throat.

A hoarse rumbling chuckle that seemed to echo all around me, rising higher as the blood flowed faster.

My stomach flipped, threatening to spew my hasty lunch up my throat. I gripped the wall to keep my balance.

"Ren!" Kylie said. She hugged me from behind. I let myself sag into her just for a second, and then I pushed myself forward.

I had to help somehow. I couldn't stand back through another massacre.

I flailed for some kind of weapon. A length of bent pipe lay by the opposite wall. I snatched it up, spun around to look for a target to whack across the head—and stopped.

There was no one left to whack. While I'd been caught up in my memories, my alphas had finished the job. The wolf was just backing away from a vampire whose throat he'd gouged out. The grizzly slammed our last conscious attacker against the wall one more time, and the bloodsucker slumped onto the ground. Aaron and Marco had already shifted back into human form. Blood dappled Marco's arm and side, and Aaron limped a bit as he moved toward his discarded clothes, but otherwise they looked fine.

And I mean *fine*. Even with fighting adrenaline still rushing through my veins, I couldn't help appreciating the full view of their impressive physiques. The gods had really outdone themselves when they made this quartet of men.

Aaron's impressive, er, apparatus and equally spectacular ass disappeared into his boxers and then his jeans. Marco sauntered over to another of the fallen vampires, looking as if he didn't mind showing off all his equipment to anyone who felt like taking an eyeful. No, he definitely didn't mind at all. He shot me a glance over his well-muscled shoulder and winked at me. My face flushed.

"Ren," Nate said, man again. He strode toward me and then stopped as if realizing his big, brawny body plus nakedness might be a little overwhelming. I suspected his clothes hadn't survived his transformation. Aaron shoved his shirt into Nate's hands. Nate gave me a sheepish smile as he tied it around his waist for makeshift modesty. "Are you all right? They didn't get to you?"

I shook my head and looked over at Kylie. She was okay too,

but her knuckles were white where she'd balled her hands around the hem of her tank top. "Is it over?" I asked. "Did you... kill all of them?"

"They're not dead," Marco said, nudging one guy's leg with his toe. "Or, not any more dead than they already were. But they won't be bothering us anytime soon."

"When vampires are injured severely enough, they go into stasis while they heal," Aaron explained. "They'll be out for a few hours at least."

"They didn't bargain for running into a bunch of alphas," Marco said flippantly. "That'll teach them to be that cocky."

Aaron shot him a warning look. "We don't want to be cocky either. They may have backup on the way. They'll definitely be reporting the clash as soon as they've recovered. When they do, the local vampire lord isn't going to be happy with us. They *did* have the right to question and attack us after finding us on their territory."

Marco shrugged, but Nate's expression had darkened. "We need to get Ren out of here fast, then."

Aaron nodded. "I don't think it's a good idea to stay at Marco's house any longer either. That's the first place they'll come looking for shifters who've recently passed through. Are there any shifter settlements we can make it to today while still giving ourselves some distance?"

West sighed. My gaze jerked to him. I hadn't noticed him shifting back, and now he'd already gotten his clothes back on. He was just buttoning up his shirt, a patch of white that looked like a bandage disappearing under the fabric, along with a six pack that would have made most pro athletes cry with envy. Even if he was a jerk, I found I was a little disappointed to have missed the full view.

Then he started talking again. Unfortunately.

"My kin has a village just south of Morgantown, West Virginia," he said in a clearly reluctant tone. "Or do you want to cower even farther away than that?"

Aaron gave him a measured look. "I think that'll do." He turned to Kylie. "You don't have to come with us if you'd rather stay here, but I think you'd be better off spending a little while out of town. If the vampires caught your scent, you could become a target."

Kylie openly ogled his bare—and buff—chest and gave him a sly grin. "Oh, don't worry, I'd *much* rather hang out with you guys than those creeps." She held out her hand to me. "Road trip! Just like we always wanted."

I managed to smile as I twined my fingers with hers. This wasn't the road trip I'd been imagining I'd take with my bestie. For one, I'd have preferred to kick it off with fewer semi-dead bodies. And to go without the threat of vampire vengeance hanging over us along the way.

CHAPTER 14

Ren

For the third time in as many days, I woke up in an unfamiliar bed. With no air conditioning in this home that was more cabin than house, the heat of the late June morning hung thick in the air. I'd kicked off my blanket, and the sheet was twisted around my legs.

I sat up on the twin bed, taking in the room I'd only seen in semi-darkness when we'd arrived late last night. A few of West's canine shifter kin-folk had put us up for the time being.

Kylie was sprawled on the matching bed across from me, her face buried in the pillow. A faint snore drifted up from it. The only other furniture in the room was a well-worn rug, a cedar wardrobe that gave off a sweetly pungent scent, and a stool by the window. Daylight streamed in across the wooden floor.

I peeled off my sheet and poked around in the bag I'd packed before our rushed departure from the city. The guys had given Kylie and me the okay to stop by our apartment briefly, so I had a few sets of my own clothes, not Marco's fancy get-up. Since it seemed possible we might need to run—or fight—again, I grabbed a pair of sweats and a comfortable tee. Once I was dressed, I pulled the dark waves of my hair back into a braid.

Mom used to braid my hair, when I was little. The ghost of her fingers brushed over the nape of my neck as I twisted and wove. My throat tightened.

Follow the crystal, her voice had told me yesterday. I'd spent an awful lot of the drive to West Virginia staring at that crystal slab, and I still had no idea how I was supposed to follow it anywhere. If the pattern on it was supposed to tell me, I was still at a loss. It just looked like a random jumble of lines and dots to me.

Why did you have to go, Mom? I thought at her, wherever the hell she was. *Why couldn't you have stayed so we could do this together? Why didn't you explain anything before you left?*

I couldn't get any answer to those questions right now, of course. I sighed and eased open the door.

The house was either empty or other inhabitants were still sleeping. The spread on the kitchen table suggested *some*one had already come through. A rich sugary smell wafted off fresh-baked blueberry scones. I hesitated, but the table was obviously set in anticipation of guests. I grabbed one, slathered some butter on it, and walked toward the front door as I took a bite.

The crumbly pastry melted on my tongue. That was heaven, right there. I closed my eyes, savoring it. Then I peeked outside.

The village we'd stopped in was apparently entirely made up of shifters. Aaron had told me more about shifter culture during the drive down. From what he'd said, it was pretty common for shifters to set up communities of their own, keeping the illusion of being normal human beings to anyone who happened to pass by, but having a little more freedom to be themselves the rest of the time. "It's easier than constantly being on the alert, remembering you have to blend in."

Standing on the cabin's doorstep, looking across the packed earth of what appeared to be the village common, I could see the appeal. Most of the people ambling into the shops or chatting with friends looked like regular human beings. But over here a group of older teens were preening, a few of them experimenting with letting their canine ears protrude from their human hair. Over there, a couple of foxes who must have gone out for a morning run ducked into their house through a swinging back door. There was a sense of openness in the air that made it hard for yesterday's worries to follow me.

As I watched, a familiar figure came into view at the edge of the common. The morning sunlight caught on the silver mixed into West's light auburn hair, reminding me of the silver-tipped ruddy fur of his wolf form. He was walking beside an elderly woman who was gesturing as she talked. When she finished, he said something to her that made her face light up.

West took her hands in his and bowed his head to her. As he let go, she patted him affectionately on the cheek. Then she shuffled away, smiling.

A couple of the teens sauntered over. From their expressions, whatever they said was pretty cheeky. West gave the first boy a playful cuff to the ears. They feinted back and forth a bit, West clearly giving the boy space to try his strength. He let the younger guy get in a few taps of his fists before grabbing him in a quick flip and setting him down on his ass.

The boy shook his head with a rueful laugh, and West grinned—a real, relaxed grin, not the tense smiles that were the most I'd seen from him before now. An ache filled my chest as the bond between us tugged at me. That man over there, acting the alpha for his people... That was a man I could really fall for.

As if he'd sensed my gaze, West looked my way. Our eyes locked. A flicker of heat passed through me, speeding up my pulse.

I shouldn't just stand here and gawk, right? I pushed myself off the cabin's front step and ambled into the common.

The two teens standing with West peered at me as I approached. At first I thought it was just normal curiosity. But one of them waved to the rest of their group. Before I'd even reached West, I found myself surrounded. They looked me over from head to toe with subtle twitches of their noses.

"You're the dragon shifter," one of them said in an awed tone. "This is so cool! We're, like, the first people to meet you now that you're back."

"Oh," I said, feeling awkward. "Yeah, I guess so. It's good to meet you too?"

"I *have* to see you shift," one of the guys said. "It must be amazing."

"Er..."

"Kids!" a woman's voice rang out. A middle-aged couple had come up on our group. The woman shooed the teens back. She turned to me. "I'm so sorry. They don't know the proper respect, at their age, and it being so long... It's an honor to offer our hospitality to you."

"History in the making," her husband agreed. He squeezed my hand briefly with a pleased smile.

More people were emerging from their houses and the shops around us. My chest started to constrict. My fingers itched. I jerked them back toward my body—too late. A warm metal circle pressed against my palm. I'd snagged the woman's ring without even meaning to.

An embarrassed heat flooded my face. I ducked down and

pretended to pick it up off the ground. "I think you dropped this," I said, handing the ring to her.

"Oh! Thank you so much. I can't think of how that slipped off."

I bit my tongue. A larger crowd was congregating around me. Murmurs of "Dragon shifter!" passed from person to person. "I talked to her first!" one of the teen girls was bragging.

What did they expect me to do? I sure as hell hoped they weren't waiting for me to demonstrate my awesome—and completely non-existent—shifting powers.

West wove through the gathering crowd. For the first time since I'd met him, I had to say I was glad to see him. He gave me a terse smile, but his dark green eyes were softer than usual.

"I think we have a few things to discuss between the two of us," he said, loud enough for the villagers to hear. They hung back while he ushered me back toward the house where I'd spent the night. His hand brushed the back of my bare arm. Even as overwhelmed as I was, my awareness of his body, just inches from mine, tingled into sharper focus.

West stopped when we were out of hearing distance and stepped to the side to give me more space. I felt that separation, too, like a tearing inside me. Whatever I thought about the wolf alpha and his attitude, some part of me wanted him next to me very, very badly.

"They, um, really are enthusiastic," I said, hoping my longing wasn't obvious.

West rubbed his jaw, which was covered with a light shading of stubble that made his handsome face even more appealing. He looked back toward the village common. "They've been waiting for dragons to return for a long time. Seeing you here gives some of them hope they didn't have before."

"But not you," I couldn't resist prodding.

He shrugged. "I haven't made up my mind yet."

Why should he, when all I'd been able to do was cringe in a corner yesterday while all our lives were in danger? I swallowed a grimace and turned to follow his gaze. Several of the villagers were still clustered together, glancing our way. Speculating about me?

Something felt off as I looked around. It took me several more seconds before I put my finger on it. "There aren't any kids. Or is there some rule about when they're allowed out of the house?" I hadn't seen anyone who looked younger than their mid-teens.

West's stance tensed. "There've been no shifter children born in sixteen years. At least not within the kin-groups. Kin can't conceive in their mate-pairs unless their alpha is mated. It's a biological block, to make sure vulnerable young aren't born into extremely troubled times."

"Oh." My eyes widened. "Because I—" Because Mom and I had been hidden away in New York, all the shifters had gone childless all this time. I glanced at West. He was still gazing into the common, his eyes even darker than usual. "*Could* you have taken a different mate? I don't know how all this stuff works yet."

"Yes," he said. "I still could. I could forsake the existing bond in order to form a new one. But once that's done, a shifter can never be mated to the one they gave up. You can't go back on the decision."

My stomach dropped. So all this time, despite all the doubts he'd had, he'd waited for me. Even though he'd had to watch his kin go without children.

Maybe I shouldn't have accused him of lacking loyalty.

"It... hasn't seemed like you'd have a problem with that outcome," I said tentatively.

West's gaze jerked back to me. "I *said* I haven't made up my mind." He rubbed his thumb over his palm, the scar there identical to the one Aaron had shown me. The mark of the alpha. "I knew you were alive, even if I didn't know where you were. I didn't think you'd stay away forever. It doesn't seem smart to throw away something without knowing what it is."

"I guess you do at least think I'm worth keeping alive," I said, tipping my head as if considering. "You fought the vampires to stop them from coming at me yesterday. I should probably thank you for that. So, thanks. I mean it."

"It was nothing," West said, his voice going gruff again. "No vampire is going to manage to hurt me. You *have* been making an awful lot of trouble, though."

"Yeah. I noticed. I'm sorry about that. None of this was in my life plan, you know."

"Of course not." He studied my face, some of the tension leaving his. For a second I thought he was going to add something. My pulse fluttered with the intensity of his attention. But he stayed quiet.

When the silence started to gnaw at me, I had to break it. "Do you really think the old traditions, with the dragon shifters and the alphas, could be wrong?"

He looked away, toward the buildings around us. "I don't know. I don't like how fragile that system turned out to be. One savage attack, and we nearly fell into chaos. If the rogues had caught you and your mother... I'm not saying it's definitely wrong. I just don't want to assume it's right. I have to be sure I'm doing the right thing for my kin before I take any steps I can't take back."

Well, if he'd put it that way to begin with, maybe I wouldn't have spent so much of the last two days pissed off at him. "Okay," I said. "That makes sense. I can respect that."

He shot me a look I could only describe as startled. "What?"

I said, setting my hands on my hips. "You didn't think I was capable of basic human empathy?"

The corners of his mouth twitched. "To be fair, you aren't actually human."

"Basic shifter empathy, then. I've gotten the impression we have that too."

"Some of the time, anyway." He kept his gaze on me. The energy between us had shifted somehow, with an electric prickling over my skin. His hand rose. I half expected him to reach for me, to pull me closer—

He made a dismissive gesture and stepped farther away. "I have a few more people to talk with while we're here in town," he said. "Try not to get into any *more* trouble, all right, Sparks?"

"I'll do my best," I muttered. Was I imagining things, or had that nickname sounded just slightly affectionate for the first time? It was hard to tell when he put on that gruff, no-nonsense voice.

West stalked off down the street. He must have said something to the people lingering in the common, because the group that had been watching me scattered. I rubbed my arms, feeling restless in the rising summer heat. And the heat that had started to rise inside me, standing next to him.

"It's good," a weathered voice said from behind me. As I turned, an elderly woman with a puff of frizzy white hair came up beside me. She patted my hand. "Matilda. Pleased to meet you, dragon shifter."

Her demeanor was so matter-of-fact after the awe I'd gotten from the other villagers that I immediately relaxed. "Pleased to meet you too, Matilda."

She turned her pale hazel eyes the way West had gone. "I'm glad Westley has finally found you," she said. "I can tell you'll be good for him."

West*ley*, huh? I let out a short laugh. "I'm not so sure he'd agree with you there."

"Aw, don't let his temper put you off. He's a good boy, even if he's slow to trust sometimes."

How long had she known him? Since he was a kid—or, what, a pup? And now he was running the whole kin-group. "You all seem to have a lot of respect for him," I said.

"He's earned it," Matilda said, and hummed softly as if to agree with herself. "That boy has always put his kin above everything else, even the folks he cared about the most."

That sounded like a story I needed to hear. But before I could push for details, Nate walked over. He gave the elder shifter a respectful bob of his head and turned to me.

"After last night, we're thinking giving you some self defense training might be a good idea, Ren. If you're up for it."

Anything if it meant I wasn't standing around like a hopeless damsel next time we got into a fight, as much as I hoped there wasn't a next time.

"Sure," I said. "Hit me."

CHAPTER 15

Marco

My Princess of Flames wasn't going to be demolishing vampires by the end of the day, but it wasn't going to be long before she could hold her own either. She mimicked the motion of the punches Aaron demonstrated while Nate held up his broad hands as targets.

The bear shifter swept his leg toward her, and she nimbly leapt out of the way. Aaron caught her around the shoulders. She snapped his hold the way he'd taught her, grinning. The physical exertion had brought an incredibly appealing flush into her cheeks. I'd bet that whole lithe body of hers would be hot to the touch.

Kylie, West, and I formed an audience at the edge of the clearing on the outskirts of the village. Ren's human friend whistled and cheered. Wolf boy looked as if he'd eaten something sour, but that was pretty much his standard expression, so it was hard to read anything into it.

Ren had a ways to go yet, though. The guys were still being careful with her. I wasn't sure that was the best tact. Didn't they see what a firecracker that girl was? All that power in her just waiting to explode.

And when she got there, I'd be right at her side.

Aaron exchanged a couple of testing blows with Ren. She blocked and jabbed out with her fist, catching him in the ribs. "Good," he said. "Can you feel that fighting energy calling to your dragon? See if you can catch hold of the feeling and shift that form to the surface."

Ren nodded, her expression tightening with determination. Oh, princess, as if a shift was something you should have to force. She needed to make friends with her inner dragon, not battle it.

Nate stepped in, weaving back and forth with surprising speed for a guy that big. The bear wasn't all bulk. He pushed Ren backward until she ducked under one of his swings and darted around him. A fierce gleam lit in her eyes. Then she faltered. Her shoulders sagged, and she swiped her hand across her mouth.

"I'm trying," she said to Aaron. "I can feel it in there. I don't know why I'm so stuck still."

I ambled forward. "Maybe you need a different kind of provocation," I suggested.

She straightened up, the fire in her eyes coming back. "What did you have in mind?"

I rolled my shoulders, testing the limits of my shirt. The fabric had enough flexibility to stay comfortable. "Spar with me a bit, and you'll see."

Aaron gestured for me to go ahead and take over. "If you think you have a better idea, Marco..."

"Even if I don't, a little variety never hurt anyone." I shot him a grin and then turned it on Ren. "Let's go, princess."

We circled each other, Ren watching me warily. Waiting for me to make the first move so she could decide how to respond. Fine, I could play along. I feinted and took a controlled jab at her stomach. She dodged, smacking my arm to the side with a well-executed block. Then she dove at me, swinging her elbow at my ribs. I just barely leapt out of the way. Damn, the girl was fast when she wanted to be.

I moved closer, speeding up my own movements. A tap to the shoulder, a strike at her neck. And smaller gestures I gave enough concentration to that I could be sure they landed. A caress of her hip. A fleeting stroke of her side. I blocked her flying fist—and let my knuckles graze the peak of her breast.

Her breath caught, her cheeks flushing darker. She narrowed her eyes at me, as if to say she saw what I was doing. That was fine. I wanted her to feel it. To feel the desire that sparked hotter between us every time we touched.

If aggression didn't bring out her dragon, maybe passion would. And if it didn't, I was sure as hell enjoying trying.

It was probably obvious to our audience what I was doing by now, but I didn't care. She was my mate as much as any of the other alphas. They'd better get used to seeing her with me.

As she ducked low to block a kick, I took the opportunity to tease my fingertips over her cheek. She jerked up, throwing a punch. I bobbed out of the way and gave her ass a quick squeeze.

With a heated noise of frustration, she came at me swinging. I wove back and forth and then threw myself right back at her when she least expected it. She yelped as I tackled her to the ground. I pinned her on the grass, my body pressed against hers, my dick getting harder with each heave of her breath that shoved her breasts into my chest.

"Marco," she growled, glaring at me, but at the same time

her hips canting welcomingly toward mine. There was as much lust as frustration in her eyes.

"Yes, princess?" I said sweetly. Before she could answer, I caught her mouth with a kiss.

~

Ren

Marco's kiss was as hot as the look he'd been giving me a second before. A shiver of pleasure rippled through me. God, did I want this man. I couldn't do anything except kiss him back just as hard.

He let go of my arm to trail his fingers down my side to my hip, and my hand leapt up to tangle in his hair. I yanked his mouth even tighter against mine. Marco hummed approvingly, nudging my lips apart with his demanding tongue. Mine slicked over his, tasting his mouth.

I could feel his pulse thumping in his chest, smell the spicy coffee scent of him, feel every shift and flex of his muscles as if I were all around him. The claws in my chest spread wide, reaching. The flavor of ash tainted the back of my mouth, but somehow that made the kiss even sweeter.

I nipped his lower lip—and tasted blood. My heartbeat raced faster. I wasn't just some girl for him to make out with. I was a *dragon*, and we were here to fight. I couldn't let him make me forget that.

With a strength I hadn't known I had in me, I shoved Marco off. He stumbled right onto his feet. A laugh jolted out of him, startled and impressed. Then I was springing after him, my feet barely seeming to touch the ground.

Marco's eyebrows rose as I lashed my arm out at him. The wind whistled strangely through my fingers.

Or rather, my talons. Scales had formed over my fingertips and sprouted dagger-like claws. *Yes*. A smile stretched across my face. I dashed faster, feeling the sinewy energy snaking through me, ready to break free.

Shouts carried across the field. "All right, Ren! You're amazing!" "Beautiful. Just give yourself over to the shift." "You've got this, Ren!"

The voices rattled my thoughts. I didn't have it, not yet. I needed more—I needed to *be* that dragon—

Even as I groped after the serpentine sensation inside me, it whipped away from me. I stumbled on the grass. My hands hit the ground, fully human again. I stared at them, those weak pale digits. My vision blurred. I blinked hard.

No. I was not going to cry. Not in front of the guys. Even if I'd just proven myself an even bigger screw-up than before.

I'd been so fucking *close*.

I dug my fingers into the earth, clawing my disappointment into it the only way I could. A large form hunkered down beside me.

"It's fine," Nate said. "You're getting there. That was progress."

"He's right, princess," Marco said, standing a short distance away. "It'll take time to get full control over your powers, just like it'll take time for us to become full mates. And I promise I'm more impatient about the latter." He chuckled.

Nate shot him a frown and reached to rub my shoulder. "You should be proud of yourself."

Proud of myself? When I couldn't even manage to get halfway to what they all did so effortlessly?

I pulled away from him, scrambling to my feet. "I don't need coddling," I said. "I need to figure this out."

Aaron ambled over to join us. West and Kylie had hung back, my friend looking concerned but uncertain. This was one challenge she couldn't meet with me.

"I think you're pushing yourself too hard," Aaron said in his mild voice. The evenness of it, paired with that faint rasp, seemed to file down the sharp edges of my emotions. "I know some mental exercises that might help with that for the next time you try. You could take a break, and then—"

"No break," I interrupted. "If you've got something to teach me that might help, let's do it now."

He paused, but then he nodded. "All right." He glanced around at the others. "We'll need to be undisturbed for this."

Marco saluted him. "Enjoy your mind games, eagle boy."

Nate drew back, his expression worried. I didn't know what to say to him to make him feel better. My sense of failure jabbed deeper into my chest. I turned to Aaron. "Let's go."

He motioned for me to follow him. At the edge of the clearing, close to the village's nearest buildings, a circle of beech trees formed a small, sheltered glade. We squeezed between them. Aaron sat down cross-legged in their midst, so I copied him, sitting across from him.

"Is this some kind of mediation you want me to do?" I asked.

"Something like that. To begin with, you could focus on your breathing. Feel it traveling into and out of your lungs. Let it fill your chest fully before you expel it. Get a sense of control over it, and of how by moderating it, you can moderate your emotions."

Apparently he could tell that my emotions were in severe need of moderation. I sucked in a breath, shaky with frustration. My hands balled at my sides. No, that definitely didn't fit the exercise. I had to give this a real try.

Maybe there wasn't some artificial block inside me that was keeping me from my dragon. Maybe *I* was the one holding it in, holding myself too tight and tense around it.

I inhaled more slowly, letting the air flow into my lungs. My ribs expanded. The breath shuddered on the way out, and I gritted my teeth. Why couldn't I get even this right?

"Hey," Aaron said gently. "Come here?"

He beckoned me over. I swiveled and scooted backward so I could lean against his folded legs. He set his hands on my upper arms, his thumbs tracing light arcs over my biceps. The warmth of his presence soaked into my back, even though there was at least a foot between our bodies. That bond, that tug. The tie that marked us as mates. I wet my lips, trying to push aside the swell of desire.

"This isn't something anyone masters on their first try," Aaron said. "Relaxing is one of the hardest things someone like us has to do. Try again? In and out, slow and easy. Focus on the feeling of my hands, and try to let any other thoughts wisp right by you."

His thumbs continued their careful arc back and forth over my skin. The thoughts they were provoking were a totally different kind of frustration from before. But I followed his instructions, closing my eyes. In and out. Like the to and fro of his caress. Slow and even. Nothing else needed to matter except for that and the heat of his touch.

Another breath slipped from my lungs, and I realized I was doing it. The tension had seeped out of me. Disappointment no longer ached behind my sternum. I didn't know if this was going to help me bring forth my dragon, but it definitely hadn't hurt anything.

"Thanks," I said. "I guess I needed that."

I heard Aaron's smile in the shape of his voice. "Sometimes

we shifters can get too caught up in the animal side of our natures. I think it's important to remember we're so much more than that. Our minds matter too. As enjoyable as certain animalistic impulses might be."

A little mischief crept into his tone with that last sentence. I shot him a glance over my shoulder, and the slightly wicked smile he gave me then sent a wash of heat over me. So my Disney prince had a bit of an edge to him, did he?

The attraction burning between us loosened a memory—one from not that long ago. "Marco said something... He said in time we'd become 'full mates.' I thought we were already mates. Is there something else we need to *do*...?"

Aaron's smile turned wry. "There's no hurry," he said. "You shouldn't take that step until you're fully comfortable with the idea, with each of us. The mate-bond isn't confirmed until it's consummated—that is, until the mates—"

"—have sex," I filled in for him. "Ah." My cheeks flared. "Yeah, I'm not sure how long it's going to take before I'm ready for that. I... never have before."

Because that wrenching, clawing feeling had always gotten in the way before. But I didn't feel that with any of the alphas. I wanted to open myself up to them. At least, I thought I did. There'd been so many upheavals and revelations in the last couple days—how could I really be sure what I wanted? What was best for me?

What was best for *them*?

"You knew you were bonded without even understanding it," Aaron said. His hands smoothed over my shirt to lightly massage my back. "It's possible to be intimate with someone you're not bonded too, but part of you is always going to balk. I won't pretend I haven't had desires and pursued them, to some extent, but the same feeling always held me back. Being that close with anyone else just didn't feel right."

So it wasn't just me. The guys felt it too? I glanced back at him again, with a fluttering in my chest. I'd waited for them without knowing what I was doing. And he'd waited for me too.

"There really isn't any rush to make that commitment," he said, gazing back at me with those clear blue eyes. "We've only just found you. We can give you whatever time you need."

Not everyone felt that way. My thoughts darted to West's words earlier this morning. It must be the same for all of the kin-groups, including Aaron's. The longer I held out, leaving him without a mate, the longer the rest of his kin had to go barren.

"Are you sure?" I asked before I knew I was going to. "I mean, that waiting for me is the right decision? What if..."

My voice faltered. My doubts jumbled awkwardly inside me.

Aaron leaned forward and wrapped his arms around me, tipping his face next to mine. "I've never been more sure of anything, Serenity. You're everything I could have wanted in a mate."

My back tensed against his chest. He drew back a few inches. "You don't like people using your full name, do you?"

I grimaced. "It's not so much that as—I just got so used to pretending it wasn't my name. To feeling like saying it would be a dangerous thing."

"Just one more thing you need to reclaim," he murmured. "You are Serenity Drake. You are the last in the dragon shifter line. That heritage belongs to you and no one else. No one can take it from you."

He pressed a kiss to the sensitive spot just behind my ear. A bolt of desire shot through me, right to my sex. I pushed myself toward him, and he eased me onto his lap. When I raised my head, his lips were right there to meet mine.

We kissed until I started to lose my breath. Aaron edged his thumb under the hem of my tee. I mumbled encouragingly, and he slid his hand right up under, over my bare skin. He teased his knuckles over my breast, making my nipple pebble. I moaned, kissing him harder. A tight ball of need formed between my legs.

Carefully, he eased the strap of my bra over my shoulder to loosen it. Then he dipped his fingers inside the cup to fondle me skin to skin. I gasped as he rolled my nipple under his thumb, drawing it to an even sharper peak. He bent his head and nibbled his way down my neck.

Every nerve in my body hummed at his touch. I was getting carried away again, but it didn't feel quite so scary. I could do this. I could take this pleasure. And if I wanted to stop, I knew all I had to do was say so.

I shoved my hands up under Aaron's shirt, needing to feel the hot, firm planes of his chest. All that coiled strength. I traced the lines of those muscles all the way down to the waist of his pants. Aaron groaned, squeezing my breast. His erection pressed against my thigh. So big and so *hard*, all for me.

The thought sent a flare of hunger through me, but it came with an icy splinter of panic.

I could have him. Tie him to me so he was mine for the rest of my life. If I said I was ready now, that I wanted all of him, he wouldn't hesitate. He'd give himself over just like that, for all time. To a shifter who couldn't even shift, a dragon who couldn't sprout her own wings.

I pulled back, my head dropping. Aaron's hand stilled. "Far enough?"

I dragged in a breath to steady myself. The hunger still gnawed at me. My lips ached to feel his against them.

"Far enough," I agreed. "But… we can stay here for a while."

He grinned and brought his mouth back to mine.

CHAPTER 16

Ren

"Wow," Kylie said, hugging my arm. "Shifters know how to eat, don't they?"

We were standing at one end of the huge table that had been set up in the village common. It stretched across the entire space, and even then it wasn't enough for all the villagers to sit down. Many were filling their plates from the bowls and platters set all down the middle and ambling off to find a spot on the ground or the extra chairs scattered around the common.

Delicious smells assaulted my nose: roasted meat and stewed veggies and fresh bread. I wasn't drooling, but it was a near thing. Between working out and making out, I'd developed a healthy appetite for dinner. I grabbed one of the plates.

"I don't think they do this all the time," I said.

"Obviously." Kylie rolled her eyes. "It's all for you. You're a celebrity!"

She said it teasingly, but the fact was it was kind of true.

Every shifter we passed gave me a longer look than they aimed at anyone else. Several of the cooks dashed over to encourage me to try this casserole or those ribs. When we made for a couple of chairs off to the side, a middle-aged man stopped us and motioned us back to the table.

"No, no, you have a spot here, of course," he said, dipping his head. "There's always room for you at our table."

I looked for my alphas, hoping one of them might step in and tell everyone to stop fussing, I wasn't that big a deal. But then, they kind of thought I was a big deal too, didn't they? West was busy stalking through the crowd, offering a greeting here and a friendly slap to the shoulder there. Marco was chatting with a few rather roguish-looking guys. Nate and Aaron had paused to talk down by the other end of the table. No help from any of them.

More of the villagers came around as I ate. As soon as I'd tried one thing off my plate, someone had brought me two more tidbits. They watched me eagerly, so I did my best to try everything, but before too long my stomach was protesting from being stuffed and from the pressure.

"What do you say we take a little stroll and walk off some of this feast?" I said to Kylie.

She nodded. "Yeah, I can see a breather might be a good idea. Being famous is hard."

She elbowed me playfully as we stood up, but she cleared the way through the crowd, giving our excuses. "Just taking a little walk. We'll be back soon!"

We ducked between a couple of shops that had closed for the evening, hurried past a short line of houses, and rambled out along the edge of the tree-spotted hills that surrounded most of the town. As soon as the sounds of the feast had faded behind me, I exhaled in relief. Kylie linked her arm around mine.

"It's weird, yeah?" she said.

"*So* weird." I laughed, glad there was one person here who understood that. I might be a shifter by birth, but after all those years in the city, living like and believing I was only human, I didn't belong here. Not really.

"But hey, at least that weirdness comes with four super-devoted and extra-super-hot guys."

I gave her a little shove. "Three devoted guys and one who's not sure I deserve the time of day."

She snickered. "Oh, no. I've seen the way the Big Bad Wolf looks at you."

"We're still bonded," I muttered. "He can't help feeling something. That doesn't mean he wants it to stay that way."

"Oh, so you might only have three super-hot mates? I guess you'll survive somehow. When you're queen of all shifters, maybe you can find some extras to send my way?"

"You'd really want that?" Kylie hooked up with guys now and then when she was in the mood, but she'd never seemed all that boy crazy.

She shrugged. "Why not? If they look like that and worship the ground I walk on, I don't see how it could go wrong."

"I don't know. You could find out that the entire future of the shifters depends on you. I was only just getting used to the responsibility of having rent to pay." I glanced back toward the common, hidden beyond the houses. "All those people think I'm going to *save* them somehow."

"Okay, I can see how that would be a bit much." Kylie dropped her hand to squeeze mine. "You don't *have* to do it, right? I mean, your wolfman is always going on about having a choice and making his own decisions. You get to do that too. If you really don't think you're up for the whole shifter queen gig, couldn't you tell them you're out, that they should go find some other mate?"

I paused. I hadn't really considered that possibility before. "I guess so. But then the kin-groups will be on their own, nothing uniting them. From what they've said, it's always been the dragon shifter doing that. And I'm the only one around." Maybe the only one at all.

What would have happened if my older sisters had survived? Would I have taken on this role at all, or just watched from the sidelines? I hadn't thought to ask that before, but now the question itched at me. I'd have to ask the guys the next time I had the chance.

Kylie waved her free hand in the air. "I'm just saying, you didn't sign up for this. It's your life too. Maybe when you find your mom, she'll be able to help you figure things out."

"*If* I find my mom. I still have no idea why she sent me down into that subway tunnel." I dipped my hand into my purse and tugged out the crystal slab. It was the closest thing I had to a connection to Mom, so I'd been keeping it with me. But looking at its glossy surface only made me more annoyed. "Why couldn't she at least have left me a note or something telling me what the hell I'm supposed to do with this?"

Had she meant to tell me more? Thinking back to the voice I'd heard in my head, she'd stopped so abruptly... Because that'd been all she had to say, or because she'd been interrupted? Maybe she'd had to tangle with vampires down there too.

Maybe she hadn't made it past them, without a squad of alphas to fight beside her.

No. I couldn't think like that.

I turned the circle, watching the light play off its faintly etched surface. "Let me see?" Kylie said. I handed it to her, and she held it up over her head as if examining the sky through it.

She wrinkled her nose and passed it back to me. "Nope. Still not getting it. It's a really nice piece of abstract art, though." She waggled her fingers over it. "Maybe you need a little voodoo to activate—"

I registered the moving shadow from the corner of my eye only an instant before a black-furred wolf leapt out of it. That instant saved my life. The wolf lunged straight for my throat, and my reflexes kicked in just soon enough to spin sideways.

The beast hit my shoulder instead, teeth raking my flesh though my shirt sleeve, paws pummeling me to the ground. Pain splintered through my arm. With a gasp, I lashed out with the only thing close to a weapon I had on me—the crystal slab in my hand. I smacked it into the wolf's skull.

The creature jerked back a few inches, blood dribbling from its mouth. With a snarl, it smashed its paw against the slab. The thick crystal didn't break, but it jolted from my clutching fingers and tumbled across the grass.

A blur of motion whipped past me. Kylie shrieked. I caught a glimpse of flailing arms and two gray-furred bodies looming over her. Then the wolf snapped at me again. I kicked at its heavy body, slammed my elbow into its jaw, and screamed with all the panic and pain rushing through me.

"Help! Somebody help us!"

The wolf cuffed me across the temple, growling. My head spun. I jabbed out with all my limbs. As long as I kept moving, as long as I kept fighting back, I had a chance. It sank its teeth into my blocking forearm, and a sharper pain radiated through my flesh. A whimper broke from my throat. I kneed at the creature's belly, but I couldn't budge it. It scraped its claws across my abdomen with another sear of agony.

Where were those goddamned talons I'd managed to sprout this morning? If I could just shift into the scaled, fire-breathing animal I knew I had in me, I'd show this beast what real hurting was.

But the scrabbling inside me felt more desperate than determined. Every time I tried to reach for the power inside me, the wolf wrenched at my arm or gouged its claws into me again. I couldn't focus on anything through the haze of pain.

Shouts rang out. The wolf flinched. It took one last bite at my throat, but I managed to knock its muzzle to the side with my throbbing arm. The stink of its rasping breath flooded my nose as its fangs nicked my chin. Then it was springing away.

A thunder of rushing paws echoed around me. A whole pack of wolves shot past me, snarling and snapping at the fleeing animals.

My whole body was on fire—and not the enjoyable kind. I rolled onto my side, toward Kylie. My shredded shirt tugged at my wounds, tacky with blood. More streaked down the hand I reached toward my best friend.

Kylie was sprawled in the grass, her face turned away from me, her arm twisted at an unnatural angle behind her. Her pink pixie-cut was streaked with red.

My fault. I hadn't protected her. I hadn't even been able to protect myself.

A few of the running bodies shifted back into human form around us. Nate's warm hand pressed against my side. "Ren! Quick, we've got to stop the bleeding."

Aaron pressed a folded shirt to my side. The sting expanded, and I shuddered. "You'll be okay," he said. "You're already healing. Dragons heal fast." But even his mild voice came out ragged.

"Kylie," I said. Marco dropped onto his knees beside me and clasped my hand to stop me from moving my arm any more than I already had. Four women had clustered around my friend.

One scratched her own wrist with her teeth and dribbled blood over Kylie's wounds. The others pressed bandages over them.

"She's alive," one of them said, catching my gaze. "We'll make sure she stays that way. No rogue will take a life on our watch. I'll empty my own body of blood before I let that happen."

Alive. Kylie was alive. A small shiver of relief passed through me. Not enough to dislodge the knot of guilt in my stomach, but I finally let myself sag into the grass.

Aaron was right. A splintering heat was crawling up to my skin from inside me now, knitting my flesh back together. At least that part of my shifter powers didn't need me to coax it into working.

The sensation hurt almost as bad as getting the wounds in the first place. My eyelids drooped as exhaustion rolled through me with it.

"What did they do to her?" a voice said from over me. Was that West? I'd never heard *him* sound so pained.

"Bit and scratched her up, but nothing too deep for her to heal on her own," Aaron said. "They were clearly trying to do a lot worse. Did you catch any of them?"

"Not exactly." West spat out the words. "A few of the others pounced on one of the coyotes, but they didn't stop to ask questions. And he's never going to be answering any now. The others took off too fast. Rogues."

"They all looked like canine-kin," Nate remarked.

"They *aren't* my kin," West snapped. "No matter what they look like."

"Of course the rogue group would send canines for an attack here," Aaron said. "They'd have been hoping you wouldn't smell them approaching, since they'd blend in with the locals." He smoothed his hand over my hair. I opened my eyes, and he gave me a tight smile. "Good thing we started on the self-defense lessons."

"I couldn't get it off me," I murmured, my throat hoarse. "I tried—I couldn't stop them—"

"Hey," Nate said. "You stopped them from *killing* you. That's all that matters."

Marco straightened up. "So they already know we're here. That's a pity. We'll have to assume they're following our movements from now on."

Were we going to move? I didn't want to go anywhere. I didn't want the guys to go. If they left...

My thoughts jumbled in my head. I ached too much to set them straight. I tipped my head, and my gaze caught on the crystal slab.

It was sitting in the grass, leaning against a rock where it had fallen. A splash of blood had splattered across its clear face. Splattered and seeped darker into the lines and dots of the etching. I stared at it, my vision doubling and steadying again as my body throbbed. A memory rippled past my eyes.

Mom, perched at our dining room table. Poring over a map on her tablet. I'd glanced over her shoulder as I'd walked by, and she'd tapped the app closed.

What are you looking at? I'd asked her, and she'd said, *Nothing for you to worry about.* And two days later, she'd vanished.

The lines and speckles—I hadn't seen their exact pattern before, but I'd seen patterns like them. They were laid out like a map's roads, rivers, and towns. They'd looked so random before, but now, at that angle, with them drawn so starkly in my blood, the full picture swam into focus.

Follow the crystal. The damned thing was literally a map.

CHAPTER 17

Ren

"ARE you sure that's the right place?" West said, frowning at my phone. I'd set it in the middle of the table between the five of us with the map app open.

"Look at it," I said, motioning between it and the crystal slab. "They're practically identical. I pored over the entire country, and that's the only place that's even close."

Aaron eased the phone a little closer to him to study it. "Sunridge, Wyoming. Do you have any idea why your mother would have wanted you to go there?"

"Or why there'd be a lovely picture of it imprinted on a crystal in the first place?" Marco remarked.

I shook my head. The muscles in my shoulder stung at the movement. I'd kept healing as I slept last night, but ruddy marks still streaked my arm, chest, and abdomen where the wolf had sliced me up. The pain hadn't completely eased either.

"I've never heard of it," I said. "Mom never mentioned it.

But why would she send me to find the crystal if she didn't want me to go to the place it shows?"

"We can make the drive," Nate said. "Even stopping for the night, we'd get there tomorrow. We can figure out the rest once we see what's there."

"As much as I enjoy a good adventure," Marco said, "I'm feeling weary of surprises at the moment. I say we don't leave until wolf boy's people are finished their patrol."

He glanced at West, who gave him a short nod. "They're still surveying the area around the village for any further signs of rogue activity. I expect them to report back within the next couple hours."

"So we're sticking around here until then?" I said. "In that case, I want to get in some more defense training."

Aaron's eyebrows rose slightly. "You're still recovering. You shouldn't strain your body too much."

I pushed back my chair. "I'm not saying we go all out. But I need to be able to handle myself better in a fight. These guys are obviously still after me. That attack won't be the last one. I want to know I can get through the next time on more than just luck."

"Ren," Nate started, but West glowered at him.

"She wants to train. She says she can handle it. Is she a dragon or not?"

Good question. My gaze darted to the ceiling. Kylie was lying in one of the bedrooms upstairs, resting from injuries she didn't have the supernatural ability to quickly heal. It wasn't just my own life at stake.

"I guess I'll just fight West if none of the rest of you wants to come," I said. West narrowed his eyes at me when I shot him a challenging smile.

In the end, all five of us tramped back into the clearing where we'd practiced yesterday morning. A few of the villagers trailed after us, but to my relief West spoke to them and they drifted away. I shifted my weight from one foot to the other, jitters running through my muscles.

I was way too wound up. That hadn't helped me any yesterday. Thinking back to my little interlude with Aaron—the part before I'd gotten distracted by his hands and his lips—I inhaled slowly and felt my lungs expand. In and out. Steady and even. I'd spent so much time hiding myself away, not even knowing why, but now it was safe for me to let my dragon out. Now I *needed* to.

Those rogue shifters who'd attacked me last night, they hadn't cared that I couldn't fully access my powers yet. They'd seen me as a threat anyway. Anger stirred in my chest at the thought, along with a shudder of energy like the flap of powerful wings. I could be that threat. I had it in me—I knew I did.

"When you're attacked by someone stronger than you, there's no shame in taking every advantage you can get," Aaron said. He pointed to his own body. "We all have weak spots where one quick hit can do a lot of damage. Eyes. Throat. Groin. If you can get a strike in any of those places, go for it."

"But maybe not while you're sparring with us," Marco piped up. "I'd personally like to keep the family jewels unsmashed."

Nate rolled his eyes at the jaguar shifter. "Not helpful, Marco." He glanced at Aaron. "Maybe we could find her a weapon she can get comfortable with, for the time being."

"And break shifter law?" West shook his head. "Are you out of your mind? I thought the whole point of bringing her back into the fold was to settle everyone down, not rile them up even more."

"There's a law against us using weapons?" I said.

Aaron nodded. "The kin-groups decided together that no shifter should attack another with anything but their own strength. Our strength we inherit and earn; winning that kind of fight is a fair measure of victory. It also means most of the time no one has to die over a scuffle."

"But she can't use all of her strength yet," Nate said. "If there's ever been a time to make an exception—"

"No," I said quickly. I didn't want any more exceptions made for me. "I've got to learn to do this the shifter way. Come on. Who's going to try me?"

Marco stepped forward with his crooked grin. I waved a finger at him. "No funny business this time."

"I don't know if I'd have called what we were getting up to yesterday *funny*," he drawled. Amusement and heat mixed in his gaze. The memory of our kiss stirred the embers of desire inside me. I swallowed and raised my hands defensively.

That desire had worked in my favor yesterday. If there was some way I could combine that with Aaron's clear-headedness and my anger at last night's attackers...

Marco came at me with a quick feint and a swing of his fist. I dodged to the side and managed to land a kick to his knee. "Oh, you're not getting away with that," he said, his indigo eyes gleaming, and caught me around the waist. I managed to yank out of his arms, spinning around, my heart beating faster.

As he circled me, I reached back to last night's assault. The searing of the rogue wolf's teeth and claws slashing into my flesh. They couldn't have sliced into scales. I could have towered over him, set him aflame.

Next time I would. Next time.

I held onto that thought, whipping a fist toward Marco and darting out of his reach. Tension started to tighten my chest, but I breathed into it, willing it to release. I wasn't going to force my dragon. I was going to let it come over me naturally. Because it was who I was. Because those beasts had threatened me and the people I cared about, and I was *not* going to let that stand.

From the corner of my eye, I saw Aaron motion to Nate. "Let's mix things up a bit." Nate shucked off his clothes in a couple of smooth movements. Before I'd quite processed what was happening, he was loping toward me in bear form. Marco veered to the side, chuckling under his breath.

Nate bared his teeth at me, but his grizzly face managed to look apologetic at the same time. "It's fine," I said to him. "Come and get me."

He bounded closer and loomed over me on his rear legs. One enormous paw swung at my head.

I ducked under it, my pulse racing through my veins. The gleam of claws and the massive animalistic presence brought back more flashes of last night. And more of last night's terror. The sealed cuts on my arms and torso prickled.

I was stronger than that. I *was*. I threw myself at Nate's furred legs, trying to tip him off-balance. He swayed and dropped down over me, but I rolled to the side just in time. My feet seemed to bite into the ground as I shoved myself upright. Power coiled through my thighs. An ashen taste crept up my throat.

Yes. He lunged at me, and I leapt to the side, faster than before. My haunches were bunching and expanding, unused muscles unfurling their strength. The armor of scales tingled over my skin from knees to waist. An itch formed in the middle of my back where my wings should form.

Let it come. Let it come. But as the sensation swept higher, my lungs expanding, a jolt of panic shot through me.

What was I doing? I couldn't control it, couldn't feel where it would stop.

I'd lost so goddamn much. I couldn't lose myself too.

The thoughts didn't make much sense, but they jarred against my shift. I stumbled and fell to my knees. Knees that were pale and human, peeking through the tears in my sweatpants.

I *had* started to shift. My pants were hanging right off me where my legs had swelled to closer to dragon size. I grasped the tatters, peering at the skin beneath as if I could will the scales to return.

I'd gotten closer. So close I could still taste the fire in the back of my mouth.

"You know, Sparks, I'm starting to think *you* want this to work less than anyone," West said from the edge of the clearing. My head jerked up, my cheeks flaming.

Nate growled, shifting back into human form as he strode toward West. "Could you shut up for once?" he snapped. "I'd like to see how well you handled the shift if you'd gone sixteen years without the chance to try."

"Nate," Aaron said, and the bigger guy halted. The eagle-shifter turned to West. "I agree with him, though. If you're going to just stand there griping, we don't need you here."

West scowled. The tension in the air wrenched at me. This was my fault too, the clashing between the alphas. Because I couldn't do the thing I'd been born to do. Damn it!

Marco cocked his head. "Company arriving," he said. "Come here, princess."

He offered his hand to help me up. I clutched at my ruined pants, holding the larger scraps of fabric over my crotch. Marco smirked, leaning in for a second as I stood. "Nothing I won't see soon enough." His sly voice sent a shiver of anticipation through me despite my churning emotions.

A squad of shifters appeared at the edge of the clearing. West's people—I was learning to read the signs. Canine shifters tended toward the lean and lanky, cool and wary. The red-headed one who looked like she was barely twenty-one herself I'd bet was a fox.

West stalked over to meet them. "Report?" he said.

"No sign of the rogues in a twenty-mile radius," the man at the fore of the group said. "We didn't even scent them. However they got here, they're gone now."

"Not too far gone, I'm sure," West muttered. He turned back toward the rest of us. "If we're going, we should get out of here while we know the immediate area is clear. Less chance that they'll be watching closely enough to see where we're headed. I want to hear the details, and then I'll be ready to go. Sparks, get some new pants in the meantime."

My bag packed and my legs re-covered by pants I hadn't mangled, I went in to see Kylie alone.

She was sitting up on the bed, her back propped against a pillow, skimming her thumb over her phone's screen. Thick bandages lay across her neck and her right arm, and those were only the ones I could see. A purple bruise marked her forehead. Our shifter hosts had washed the blood from her hair, but the pink tufts still lay more limply than usual. But she smiled when she saw me and set down the phone.

"Time to go?" she said.

"Yeah." I hesitated. "I don't want to just leave you here with a bunch of strangers, but we don't know if the rogues will attack again when we're—"

"Oh, Ren." She held out her arms, beckoning me over. I walked into her embrace. I hugged her carefully, worried about her injuries, but she squeezed me with all her strength. "Don't worry about me. These people are looking after me just fine.

You've got your stuff to do. I'll hang out a while longer, and Aaron said it should be okay for me to go back to the city by the time I'm all fixed up. You just have to promise you'll come visit me even if you get all busy with shifter queen business, you hear?"

A pained smile tugged at my lips. "Of course. You're still my best friend."

"That's right. Besties for life." She let go of me to raise her hand, and we tapped knuckles. "Don't get too distracted by all those yummy men either, okay? But you'd better indulge at least a little."

A blush tickled up the back of my neck. "I think I've already got that covered."

"Oh ho! Something else I'm going to need to hear all about." She gave my arm one last pat and waved me off. "Focus on finding your mom. I want to hear all about the end of that mystery too."

"I hope it's a good one," I said with total honesty. What was waiting for us in Sunridge, Wyoming? Another clue to another branch of this weird scavenger hunt Mom had sent us on, or some actual answers this time?

Was *Mom* waiting there? I didn't know what I'd say if I finally saw her again, but God, I wanted to so badly.

"Go," Kylie said, outright shooing me now. "Don't let me hold you back."

The guys were standing around the eight-seater SUV West had commandeered, as I guessed you could do when you were an alpha. The idea was that we could sleep in it overnight rather than going through the hassle of finding a hotel. And I suspected the guys liked having the extra space rather than being squashed into a regular car.

I tossed my bag in the trunk, and Nate yanked the hatch

shut. Without any debate—or maybe I'd missed one—West climbed into the driver's seat. Aaron got in beside him. He'd been studying the maps.

As Marco nabbed a spot in the middle row, Nate closed his solid, warm hand around mine. It was funny: Even though I'd seen him in his animal form more often than any of the other guys, and even though that form was the most menacing of the four, his presence wasn't anything but comforting. Well, and maybe a little exciting. My gaze lingered on the muscles that filled out his thin tee, and a headier warmth pooled low in my belly.

He tugged me with him toward the backseat, and I came without argument. When we sat down on the soft leather, he wrapped his arm around me and tipped me against his brawny torso. I breathed in the musky, peppery smell of him. So fucking delicious. There were a lot of things screwed up about the situation I'd found myself in, but having these four guys by my side... at least, the three of them who definitely wanted to be there... might make up for the rest.

The car's engine rumbled. Its vibration hummed faintly through the seats as West turned us toward the road out of town. I let my head lean against Nate's broad shoulder.

I didn't want to think right now—not about Kylie's injuries or having to leave her behind, not about the rogues who'd tracked me down to kill me just two days after I'd found out who I really was, not about the quest my mother had sent me on. Drowning in Nate's scent and the feel of his body sounded like heaven. If I lifted my face just a couple inches, I could have pressed my lips to the base of his collarbone just above the neck of his shirt and tasted him too.

But I held myself back. The other guys were right *there*. Obviously they had to know I felt this connection to all of them, but I wasn't the biggest fan of PDAs. And anyway, I wasn't sure I deserved to indulge after yet another failure this morning.

Nate's hand rubbed up and down my arm. "You're tense," he murmured. "Is there anything you want to talk about?"

"No," I said automatically, but maybe there was. "I just—I hate that I seem to have that block when it comes to shifting. If I could have shifted last night, I'd have destroyed those rogue shifters."

He smiled. "You absolutely would have, Ren. But you don't have to worry about that. You've got all of us. We're not going to let anyone get that close to you again. We should have been more careful to begin with—I didn't realize they'd be brazen enough to attack you that close to a kin settlement."

Shit, he'd better not be feeling guilty. "It's not your fault," I said. "And I know you all want to protect me. But *I* want to be able to defend myself, like I should be able to."

"And you will." He brushed his lips against the top of my head. The contact sent a tingle over my scalp. "You're comparing yourself to the four of us, and we've had decades to grow into our powers. I'm *impressed* by how quickly you're discovering yourself."

"Oh." He sounded like he meant it. Was I being too hard on myself? I found it difficult to believe, but the knot of guilt inside me loosened just a little.

I nestled closer to him. He lifted my legs onto his lap so I was completely cuddled against him. My great teddy bear of a man. His other hand kept up its caresses up and down my arm—and reached a little farther to graze the side of my breast. I swallowed a gasp, arching into the contact instinctively. Correction, my great *hot* bear of a man.

Nate ducked his head to nip my earlobe. My heart skipped

giddily. "I think you deserve a reward for all your hard work," he said under his breath, a playful note slipping into his voice.

"What do you have in mind?" I whispered back.

"You seem to be enjoying this." He traced his fingertips over the curve of my breast again, catching the peak this time. I clamped my mouth shut against a whimper.

"The other guys..."

"Won't mind at all. We belong to you, Ren. Whatever you need. Whatever you want."

His answer brought back Kylie's comment in the subway tunnel, about being with the guys at the same time. Nate kissed the side of my neck with a teasing swipe of tongue, and suddenly I was wondering what it would be like to have one of my other alpha's hands on me at the same time. Stirring up even more of these heady sensations. Driving me wild.

The thought dampened my panties. Nate cupped my breast, his thumb easing back and forth over my hardened nipple. Shivers of pleasure raced through me. There wasn't anything in the world I wanted more in that moment than to keep feeling what I was feeling right now. One last hesitation held me from completely giving in.

"I don't think I'm ready yet. I mean, to—"

"Ren," Nate murmured. My name in his low, longing baritone sent a flush over my skin. "You don't need to do anything. Let me just do this for you."

His free hand traveled up my thigh. He eased it up and down, still caressing my breast while he did, until the heat building inside me had me ready to melt. I flexed my hips, and he dipped his fingers between my legs to meet the spot so desperate for contact.

My whole body caught fire as he stroked my core. He teased his fingers over every sensitive part of me as if he knew exactly what I was hungry to feel. Pleasure sparked through my veins. I gripped his shirt, my breath growing shaky. I was melting together and coming apart all at once.

Nate flicked his thumb over my clit. I barely managed to bite back a moan. My hips moved to match his rhythm. "That's right," he said softly. "I've got you."

Oh, he did. He angled his mouth to capture mine, drinking in my whimper as his hand slid up to delve right under my clothes. He slicked a finger over my opening. The heel of his hand swiveled against my clit. A wave of bliss swelled inside me, tingling through my body from head to toe. I kissed him back as if I were starving for it, my fingers curling tighter into his shirt.

He pumped his hand gently. Then his rhythm started to speed up. I shuddered against him, so close to the edge, and he hooked his finger right up inside me.

The dam broke. Pleasure rushed through me like a flash fire, consuming my bones and leaving my muscles quivering.

Nate kept stroking me until the last waves of my orgasm had faded. He kissed me again, sweet but demanding, and tucked me against him as if I was meant to fit right there in his arms. I held onto him, momentarily sated.

Wondering how on earth I could possibly deserve this much devotion.

CHAPTER 18

West

ONE DEER'S trail smelled a little fresher than the others. That one had fallen behind the herd. From its scent, it was full-grown but young. Probably injured then. Some stumble that had lamed it and made it easier prey.

I stalked after it, the leaves of the forest underbrush rippling over my fur. Everything I needed for hunting was sharper in my wolf form: my nose, my claws, my teeth. It felt good to flex those muscles after all that time cooped up in the car. No living thing should spend an entire day on the road in one of those metal boxes.

As I wove through the forest, I tasted the air for other scents. The world was full of pungent sap and loamy moss. But what I was really watching for was the cloying sugary sweetness of the fae.

I hadn't caught a trace of it so far, but you couldn't be too careful when you ventured into the wilderness. The untamed stretches of countryside were as much fae territory as the human cities belonged to the bloodsuckers. The magic-burned scar on my upper chest prickled at the thought.

The only sweetness in the air now was a faint wisp from back at our camp. The tart honeyed scent that belonged to Ren. It tugged at me, even from that distance. Reminding me I was meant to be there with her. As if hunting for dinner wasn't a suitably mately duty. But that tug wouldn't ease off until I claimed her.

Or disowned her.

That thought brought back the expression on her face yesterday morning, when I'd told her how easily I could cast aside our bond if I decided to. It'd hurt her, hearing that, if just for a moment. But she'd still been able to tell me she respected my position. She hadn't pleaded or argued. She'd believed that I would do what I felt to be right, and that it was my right to do so.

Maybe I'd been too harsh with her, the last few days. *She* hadn't really run. And it definitely hadn't been her choice to hide. If I was going to be angry with anyone for the situation we found ourselves in, it should be her mother.

I didn't enjoy causing Ren pain. And when I remembered her agonized breath as she'd lain bloody in the grass last night—

My chest tightened. That was exactly why she needed someone to be harsh. She had to learn to withstand whatever got thrown at her. Because our enemies were going to be so much harsher than I'd ever stoop to.

The deer's scent grew thicker. I was almost on it. I slowed to a prowl, my ears perked. Hooves pattered in the brush. Unevenly, one leg holding it back with a limp. Just as I'd guessed.

My muscles bunched. I bolted forward and sprang. My jaws clamped around the deer's sleek neck.

With one snap, I severed its throat. A hot gush of fresh blood filled my mouth. The deer squealed, but its body was already sagging. By the time its head hit the ground, the poor beast had slumped completely, all the life gone from it.

My wolfish heart thumped with glee and the longing to dig in. But I wasn't hunting just for me. It'd be easier to carry the kill back to camp in human form.

I shifted, reveling in the smooth transition of muscle and bone from one form to the other. I was never more sure of myself and who I was meant to be than in those moments. With the back of my hand, I wiped the lingering blood from my mouth. Not a great look in man form. I lifted the deer, let the worst of the flow drain from its neck, and then hefted the slack body over my shoulder.

I'd left my clothes in a heap just beyond the grove at the side of the road, where we'd parked the van. I set down the deer and pulled them on before moving to join the others. I had nothing to hide, but I didn't want to have to explain the strange scar to Ren. And she wasn't exactly used to having people stroll around naked in front of her yet. The heat in her eyes whenever one of us did made that perfectly clear.

I didn't want that heat directed at me. It stirred up too much desire of my own.

"One deer, ready for dinner," I announced, stepping out into the grove. The other guys had already gotten a large fire crackling. Aaron was just finishing setting up a makeshift spit.

Nate grinned and moved to take the deer from me. Ren, sitting on a stone a few feet from the fire pit, wrinkled her nose. I didn't like the discomfort I saw in her eyes now either. Maybe I *should* have come out naked.

"So you just went out there and hunted it down?" she said.

I wasn't going to let myself feel ashamed about something

this basic. "What, like an animal? In case you've forgotten, I am one. I did a lot worse to those vampires a couple days ago."

"Yeah, but they attacked us first." Her gaze followed the deer as Nate set it on a log to skin it. As the knife cut into the hide, she winced and looked away.

"We need to eat. We're all predators here, Sparks. This is the way of the wild." I motioned toward the deer. "I picked off one that was already lame. It wasn't fit to survive anyway. So just enjoy your meal. You can thank me after."

~

Ren

I drew my legs closer to my stone perch and balanced my phone on my knees. *It's like he constantly has to be taking me down a peg*, I texted to Kylie. *He treats me like I'm an idiot.*

Boys pulling pigtails, she wrote back with a winking emoji. *He's got it for you bad.*

I glanced across the grove to where West was helping Nate arrange the deer carcass on the spit Aaron had fashioned. The firelight caught on the red and silver in his hair and the angular planes of his handsome face.

Way too handsome. Even when I was irritated with him, I couldn't squash the longing to see a real smile cross that face, directed at me.

He's twenty-seven, I replied. *I think he's past the preschool stage of flirting.*

You'd be surprised. Some guys never grow out of it. I say you march right up to him and plant one on him. And then write back to tell me all about the amazing sex you two get up to.

I shook my head at the screen. *Ha ha. Not likely.*

Oh, hey, dinner's here. Catch you again soon!

I tucked the phone into my pocket and watched the guys set the roasting stick holding *our* dinner over the fire. The flames sizzled as a few drops of blood dripped off the skinned flesh. The mass of pink and red muscle made me think of the claw marks that still hadn't quite faded from my skin. The blood in Kylie's hair last night. I rubbed my arms.

What had West said about that deer? That it'd been weak. Not fit to survive. Did he think the same thing when he looked at me? I wasn't even coming close to keeping up with my supposed mates. Marco had said a dragon shifter would put the rest of them to shame. I'd hardly been living up to that expectation.

A stick snapped in the forest behind me. I flinched and jerked around, my heart thudding. It was only Marco himself, coming back from a patrol of our campsite. He dipped his head to me with his slanted smirk. "Nothing to worry about, princess. All clear."

The thickening darkness behind him looked anything but clear. The rogue shifters might not be close enough for him to sense, but they could be tracking us. Who knew how quickly they could move? Most of the ones that had attacked me and Kylie had outrun West's kin.

Apprehension prickled over me. I hugged myself and turned back to the fire.

Marco sauntered past me and cocked his head, eyeing the spit. "Now that's a fine sight. I'm glad the rest of you are so domestic."

West snorted. Nate let out a disgruntled huff of breath. "I'd hate to see what your kills look like when you're done playing with them," he said.

Marco chuckled. "I'm a jaguar, not a house cat. And I'd bet I could have taken down a deer twice that size."

"Twice as long to cook, and more meat than we'd have time to eat. Sounds like a brilliant plan." West motioned toward the trees. "Go ahead and take a stab at it, if you've got that much to prove."

"Ah, why bother when you've already done the work for me?" The jaguar shifter lowered himself onto a log and stretched his legs out as if perfectly relaxed.

A thump from the other side of the van made me startle again. "That's Aaron coming back," Nate said, noticing. Right. The eagle shifter had been taking a turn over the landscape from above before it got too dark to spot our enemies.

He emerged from behind the van a moment later, buttoning up his shirt as he came. I couldn't help feeling a little sorry to see those sculpted muscles disappearing behind the fabric.

"See anything interesting, bird boy?" Marco asked him. He poked at the fire idly with a stick.

"Nothing worthy of immediate concern," Aaron said. "But we shouldn't lower our guards."

"No chance of that with the bunch of you."

Nate grimaced at him. "Why don't you make yourself useful and turn the damn spit, Marco?"

"Hmm, I think this side needs a little longer."

"Give me that." West grabbed the stick from him. "You're going to put out the fire at that rate." He prodded two of the logs Marco had jostled closer together. A flicker of a memory passed through my head—a brief squabble with my sisters, tug-of-war over a toy. A lump rose in my throat.

The question that had occurred to me earlier prodded me again. This seemed as good a time to ask as any.

"There are only four alphas at any time, right?" I said.

Marco gave me an amused look. "Aren't we enough for you, princess?"

I rolled my eyes at him. "I didn't mean it like that. I just meant… A dragon shifter is supposed to take the alphas as mates. So what if there's more than one dragon shifter? My sisters weren't *supposed* to die."

Aaron dipped his head. "No," he said. "And it's common for each dragon shifter to give birth to more than one daughter, in case of a tragedy. Generally speaking, your parents would have chosen which of you seemed best suited for the responsibility, and the others would have supported her. They could take mates as well, but their line wouldn't pass on."

"Oh. I guess that makes sense." So if the rogues hadn't carried out their bloody assault, it might have been one of my sisters bonded to these four now. The thought sent an uncomfortable prickling over my skin. I turned my gaze back to the fire.

The flames danced higher, nearly grazing the deer's flesh. It was starting to brown. The sizzles that reached my ears now were drips of fat, not blood. The smell of roasted venison was trickling through the air.

My mouth started to water. Maybe I didn't like the idea of killing a deer, but I wasn't too squeamish to eat it now that it was already dead. I guessed that kind of did make me a hypocrite.

The flickering light and the wavering warmth started to lull my nerves. I let my gaze sink into the fire. The flames darted up and back down, orange tinged with a darker red around the edges. Yellow-white at their core. Beautiful, the way they flared to life. Almost like—

The fragment of memory rushed up so fast it rocked me on my seat. For an instant, I was a little girl again, clutching my mother's scaled leg as the ground fell away beneath us. The swoop of her wings warbled through the air. Sharp cracks rang out below us. What was that sound? I'd never heard it before, but it terrified me.

Mama opened her dragon mouth and spewed a stream of flame at our attackers. My arm was throbbing. Blood seeped from a gouge just above my elbow. Tears streaked down my cheeks. Another burst of flame filled my vision, and—

I caught myself before I tipped right over, planting my feet hard on the ground. The heat of the campfire washed over me, sharper than before. My hand rose to my arm, to the phantom pain of that long ago wound. I rubbed the skin there even though I didn't have a scar to show it had been real.

"Ren?" Nate said from across the grove. "Are you okay?"

"I'm fine." I pushed myself to my feet. I couldn't be that little girl anymore, clinging helplessly while someone else did all the fighting. It didn't matter which of my sisters Mom and my dads would have chosen to lead. I was the only one left, and I had the ferocity in me... somewhere.

My gaze traveled up one of the tall birch trees near the edge of the grove. Its white bark shone against the darkness. Without letting myself second-guess the impulse, I strode over to it and grasped the lowest branches.

"What are you up to, princess?" Marco asked.

"Just need to stretch my legs a bit," I said. "Don't mind me."

I clambered upward from branch to branch, steadying myself when I needed to against the trunk. The papery bark rustled under my groping hands. The smells of the roasting meat and the fire fell away, leaving only the tangy scent of sap.

I stopped when the trunk had narrowed a little too much for comfort and peered down. West was turning the meat. The other guys were peering up at me, watching my progress. The firelight danced off their faces.

I was about as high up as I'd been in the pine a few days ago. A jump I knew I could make. But I didn't want to land. I wanted those wings to unfurl from my back and carry me back toward the sky.

The urge to fly had been with me my whole life. Maybe I could draw it all the way out if my body believed shifting was the only way to protect me from the fall?

I dragged in a breath. Then I launched myself out into the air.

Normally I'd have moved right into my landing pose: feet braced, knees bent, body properly aligned. But I had to believe I'd hurt myself if I hit the ground. I let my limbs scatter, a gasp slipping from my mouth as my hair whipped up behind me. I could break a leg or worse like this. If I didn't shift and glide out of the fall.

A fluttering sensation raced through my chest, but my body stayed totally human. My body careened on down. The ground looked far too close. Shit. Biting back a curse, I yanked my feet under me at the last second.

I hit the ground slightly off balance, but managed to roll out of the fall with at least a bit of grace. My left foot had taken too much of my weight. It throbbed when I straightened up. I gritted my teeth and managed to march back to my stone seat without limping.

"If you're looking for thrills, there are plenty of other activities I could suggest," Marco said, arching his eyebrows.

In what wasn't my greatest show of maturity, I stuck my tongue out at him. He laughed. He didn't seem fazed by my jump, but when my gaze traveled around the fire, I realized Aaron and West were both watching me. Aaron looked thoughtful. West's eyes had narrowed. My skin itched with the suspicion that neither of them totally bought my story about "stretching my legs."

Thankfully, Nate stepped in then to distract both them and me from my continuing failure to be an actual shifter. He carved a hunk of venison off the roasting deer and offered it to me on a paper plate. "You should eat something," he said. "We're all going to need our strength."

Yeah. I dug in, closing my eyes as the smoky juices filled my mouth. Delicious. When had I ever had meat this fresh in my life?

But it couldn't quite erase the twisting in my stomach. One more attempt to shift gone down in flames—or rather, gone down *without* flames. How many more tries was I going to get?

CHAPTER 19

Ren

I'D SLEPT in a lot worse places than the seat of a fairly luxurious SUV. In corners of vacant buildings surrounded by druggies. Under ratty blankets that smelled like cat piss tucked away in an alley. On the hard concrete floor of the church basement Fisher operated out of, with a hard lump of guilt filling my stomach over the previous day's thefts and the ones I'd have to commit tomorrow.

But tonight I couldn't settle. I pulled the wool blanket West had shoved at me higher over my shoulders and squirmed against the seat back. My body refused to relax into the soft leather.

In the backseat, behind me, the low, steady murmur of Marco's breaths told me he'd had no trouble passing out. Nate was sprawled in the driver's seat, which he'd tipped back to just above my feet, his rugged face soft with sleep. West and Aaron were somewhere out in the woods on first watch.

I was surrounded by my alphas. Perfectly safe. But maybe the idea of their protection nagged at me more than it comforted me.

I closed my eyes and tried to let my mind drift away. Crickets chirped outside the window. A breeze hissed through the trees branches. The taste of roast venison lingered in my mouth. It was starting to go sour. No toothbrushes out here in the wild. I groped for the bottle of water I'd left on the car floor.

Just after I'd set it back down, a faint humming emanated from Nate's seat. He stirred and reached to his pocket to switch off the alert he must have set on his phone. As he sat up, my restlessness gripped me even harder. I couldn't stand to spend one more second shut away in the SUV, not right now.

He glanced over at me when I sat up. "I'm just going to switch off with Aaron," he said quietly. "He'll be back here in a few minutes."

"I can't sleep," I said. "I think a little walk might burn off some energy."

The corners of his eyes crinkled with concern, but he didn't try to stop me. He slipped out the driver's side door, and I eased open the back one.

The sky was clear, the stars gleaming bright against the black. I couldn't remember the last time I'd seen the constellations that clearly. In New York City, the haze of city lights always blotted out all but the most insistent stars.

I followed Nate into the woods in silence, wondering whether he and Aaron had arranged a meeting spot or if he was just locating the eagle shifter by scent. The summer night breeze tickled past me, still pleasantly warm. We'd walked for several minutes, weaving between the trees, before a streak of moonlight caught on Aaron's golden-blond hair up ahead. He turned to greet Nate. His gaze halted on me.

"No activity so far," he said to Nate, and then to me, "I thought you'd gone to sleep."

There was no judgment in his tone, or even anything like Nate's almost suffocating concern. Just curiosity. My shoulders edged down from the argument I'd been braced for. "I tried," I said with a weak smile. "It didn't stick. I was hoping the walk would help."

"I can keep you company for that." He nodded to Nate and offered his hand to me. I took it, loving the feel of his strong fingers closing around mine.

"So has the walking helped?" he asked as we ambled back toward our campsite.

I bit my lip. I felt a little more settled with him there beside me, but that restless twitch was still nibbling at my nerves. "I don't know. Not as much as I hoped."

He ran his thumb over the back of my hand. "Do you want to talk about what's on your mind?"

"How do you know something is on my mind?"

"You can't sleep, and so you're wandering in the woods in the middle of the night. I figured it was a pretty safe guess."

I made a face at him, and he gave me an even smile. Well, it wasn't as if he was wrong. "I'm not sure talking will help either."

"It's worth a try, right?" He paused, turning me toward him. "What's bothering you?"

I looked at the ground. "I just... You've all been great. Well, West—let's not go there. The rest of you have been. And all the people in that village. Everyone is so eager to welcome me as a shifter. As the most important shifter there is. But I still can't even shift."

"It's only been a few days," Aaron said. "You're getting there."

"Maybe. It's not just that. I don't know how I can be even half of the things I'm supposed to be. What if... What if I'm ruined, because of all those years when I didn't know who I was, growing up the wrong way, without any idea about any of this? What if I *can't* ever be a full shifter?"

"Oh, Serenity." He opened his arms, and I stepped closer to him automatically. That pull, that need to be near each of the guys was getting harder to deny. He cupped my face, and I tilted my head to meet his kiss. The heat of his lips coursed through me. It didn't take away my doubts, but it was an awfully nice distraction.

After the kiss, he eased me back slightly, keeping his hands on either side of my face. His head bowed until the fringe of his hair brushed my forehead. "I'll tell you something," he said. "Something I've never really talked about with anyone. I spent most of my life wondering if I wasn't exactly what a shifter was meant to be too."

"What?" I pulled back far enough to stare into his eyes. "How could *you* think that? You're not just a shifter—you're the one chosen to be your whole kin-group's alpha."

"By a man who might have changed his mind if he'd been alive long enough to see me through to adulthood, for all I knew," Aaron said. "There are always cracks where doubt can creep in, no matter how secure your position seems. And mine never felt all that secure. The avian shifters... We're not always considered equal to the other groups. Most of the canine and feline kin see us as something lesser."

"That's ridiculous," I said. "If anything, they should be jealous. You can *fly*."

He chuckled. "Of course you'd appreciate that. But it is what it is. And even among my own people—I've told you how important it is to me to lead with my mind more than my animal side. That's not a common attitude among shifters of any kin-group. Some of my kin have been wary of my interest in learning and history. There've been more than a few who thought it meant I was making up for a lack of the 'real' strength an alpha needs to lead."

I gave him a look up and down, knowing my appreciation of his sculpted body must show in my expression. "So, those people must have been blind, I'm guessing."

Aaron's smile grew into a grin. "It's easy for people to distrust what they don't understand. But I've proven myself by now, more than once. When push came to shove, and I had the opportunity to let go—to let the alpha role pass to someone else—I knew I couldn't. That I wanted this. That I was meant for it. And here I still am."

I hesitated, remembering what he'd told me before about how another shifter could become the alpha. "You had to fight. People challenged you?"

"Yeah." The good humor in his expression faded for a moment. He glanced away, toward the trees, recalling events I could tell he didn't enjoy thinking about. "The worst was one of my advisors. He got used to having the extra authority. When I turned twenty-one and was meant to take over my full role as alpha, he attacked me. I hated having to fight him. He'd been like an uncle to me. But I was smarter and faster, and that can beat brutality if you know how to use it."

"And here you still are," I said, repeating his words back to him.

"Here I am." He drew his gaze back to me. Right then it was so intense I almost forgot how to breathe. My heart thumped faster.

He wasn't just strong and overwhelmingly sexy. He was *good*. Thoughtful and brave and compassionate. The kind of man I'd never been sure I'd be able to have in my life. The kind of man I could fall in love with.

Not just could. I was already falling. Right into those clear blue eyes.

"Well, as far as I'm concerned, anyone who thinks you're anything less than those other guys is an idiot," I said, for something to say. "As well as being blind."

"Probably," Aaron said agreeably. "I don't worry about it anymore. And I find it equally hard to believe that anyone could be around you and think you're anything less than a true shifter. It's in your blood. That's all that matters. The rest will fall into place."

My fingers had curled into the front of his shirt without my even noticing. I tugged, and he came to me.

He kissed me hard this time, nudging me a step backward so I could lean against the trunk of a tree. So I didn't even have to think about staying upright, only about the heat of his body against me and the slide of his mouth against mine. His hand traveled down my side to my thigh and back up to my shoulder, as if he wasn't sure what part of me he wanted to touch most.

Everywhere. I wanted him everywhere.

His hips brushed mine, and an ache started to form between my legs. Where Nate had gotten me off so skillfully less than a day ago. I whimpered as Aaron stroked my breast through another kiss, but one last thread of uncertainty held me back.

I grasped the side of Aaron's face. He eased back to meet my gaze. His was full of desire, so hot every nerve inside me caught fire.

My voice came out ragged. "You don't mind, do you, that it's not just you? That I'm supposed to be with the other guys too?" That I had been, in ways he'd witnessed or at least sensed.

Aaron bumped his nose against mine in an affectionate nuzzle. "Not at all," he murmured. "You deserve nothing less. It takes more than one man to satisfy a dragon." His fingers teased up under my shirt. I arched my back off the tree trunk to give him room to unclasp my bra. He circled my nipple with his thumb before flicking right over it with a speed that made me gasp.

"You deserve every bit of pleasure they can give you," he went on, moving to caress my other breast. He kissed the corner of my jaw, the sensitive skin of my throat. His words spilled out with his heated breath. "Anything that fulfills you, whoever it's with, fulfills me too. The flush in your cheeks after you've been kissed. The sound you make when you come."

So he had heard Nate and me in the back of the car. My face outright flared. But, God, Aaron was turning me on so much with every graze of his lips, every stroke of his fingers.

"I'm looking forward to someday seeing how much pleasure we can bring you together," he said. "But for now..."

His hands slid down my body. I whimpered, my hips canting toward his. Seeking every inch of contact I could get.

"I need to see you," he muttered. He yanked my shirt up. I raised my arms so he could pull it off in one smooth movement. My bra slid from my shoulders to fall to the ground by our feet. Aaron took me in, my smallish breasts with the nipples pebbled from his attentions, the flush creeping down between them. Then he ducked his head to suck one of those peaks into his mouth.

I moaned, pleasure racing over my skin. His steady tongue slicked over my breast with the slightest graze of his teeth, until I was trembling against him, my fingers tangled in his hair. He gave the nipple one last lick before attending to my other breast with equal enthusiasm.

It wasn't nearly enough for the hunger inside me. I grasped the hem of his shirt. "Off," I gasped. "Now."

He wrenched it over his head faster than I'd have thought

possible, with the snap of at least one button. Somehow that turned me on even more. I seemed to have no limit when it came to these guys.

He claimed my mouth again with an urgent fervor. The press of his bare chest against mine drew another moan out of me. My fingernails sketched lines up the muscles of his back. He hefted me as if I weighed nothing at all, bracing me higher against the tree with one hand supporting my ass and my legs splayed. I gripped my thighs around his. The hard length of him pressed against my core, and I whimpered.

Aaron rocked against me as he leaned in for another, even deeper kiss. I could feel the strength coiled all through him, holding me up, but also braced to withdraw the second I told him to stop. Pleasure rushed through me, but suddenly the sweep of it didn't feel unnerving at all.

I was exactly where I wanted to be. I belonged here, with this man, in every way he wanted to be with me.

Giving in to my desires wasn't letting go of control. It was taking it. Grasping hold of the destiny I'd never imagined and claiming it as *mine*.

The second I made the decision, a hum of power rose up inside me, stronger than I'd ever felt before. I linked my arms behind Aaron's neck and dipped my head between one kiss and the next.

"I want this," I said, breathless, "I want *you*."

He hesitated, searching my eyes, a wildness in his. "Do you mean—"

"Aaron," I said, as clearly as I could manage. "Be my mate?"

A strangled laugh burst out of him, as if he couldn't quite believe what I'd said. He crushed his mouth against mine, kissing me until I was dizzy. I fumbled with the button of his slacks. My hand brushed over his erection, and he groaned.

"I think we'd better take this to the ground," he said, guiding me away from the tree. He grabbed his shirt and stretched it over the dirt before he laid me down in it. "For our first time, anyway."

"Lots of time to experiment later," I said, and his eyes flashed even hotter. He kicked off his pants. I couldn't wait to touch his cock. The huge, hard length of him pulsed against my palm through his boxers.

Aaron bowed his head, exhaling with a stutter. Holding himself over me with one arm, he dipped the other hand down between my legs. A mewing sound escaped me as he stroked me there. My breath broke into panting as he slipped his fingers under the band of my sweatpants. My sex was already slick with my arousal. He trailed his hand over that wetness and muffled another groan in my hair.

"Please," I said. He didn't need me to beg more than that. He jerked off my pants and panties together and wrenched off his boxers. My hips arched up as he settled between my legs. The head of his cock rubbed over my opening. I pulled his mouth back to mine.

He kissed me and eased inside at the same time. His hardness filled me with a burning sensation, but it was oh so good. I was filled, completely, and it was everything I needed.

"You feel amazing, Serenity," he murmured between kisses. He lifted my hips higher and thrust into me with a steadily building rhythm. I clung on to him as the swell of pleasure carried me higher. Up and up, until it shuddered through my whole body. Until I barely felt the ground beneath me.

We were flying. Soaring up and away on a haze of bliss. No leap or fall had come close to comparing to this exhilaration.

His cock nudged against the sweetest spot inside me, and the bliss shattered apart. It radiated through my entire body, tossing me even higher. I gasped, digging my fingernails into his shoulders. Sparks flared behind my fluttering eyelids. The pull between us solidified into a solid glow that bound us together. It lit me up like a flare from the inside.

Aaron's thrusts turned erratic. He pumped into me a few more times and moaned as he followed me over the edge. His body settled over mine, resting against me but not pinning me down. Every inch of his naked skin aligned with mine.

I traced my fingers back up his neck and into his sweat-damp hair to draw him down for one last kiss. My muscles trembled with release—and happiness.

I had him. My eagle shifter. My alpha.

My mate.

CHAPTER 20

Ren

I WOKE up cuddled against Aaron on the middle seat of the SUV. Daylight was streaming through the windows. My head still felt fuzzy from not quite enough sleep, and various parts of my body ached, but in an enjoyable way. I had no desire at all to get up.

I buried my head into the crook of Aaron's neck. The wonderful salty fresh smell of his skin filled my nose. We'd gotten dressed before we'd finally made it the rest of the way back to the car, but I hadn't been quite ready to let go of him yet. It was a tight fit, our legs intertwined and him half on top of me, and yet I felt totally at home tangled there with him.

My mate. The knowledge thrummed through my veins. Only the first, if I fulfilled my role completely, but right now one was plenty.

Knuckles rapped against the window over my head. I blinked

and peered up at it. Aaron brushed a kiss to my temple before raising his head.

Marco looked in at us, his eyebrows arched. He opened the door a few inches to talk. "Wolf boy found us some eggs. You'd better get up if you want to grab them before our resident bear eats them all."

"I'm leaving plenty for the rest of you," Nate said from somewhere behind him. Marco dipped his head and shut the door again.

Did his expression look a little tighter than usual? Something about his stance had felt off. *He* wasn't upset seeing me with Aaron, was he? He knew how this was supposed to work just as well as the others did.

Probably it was my insecurities messing with my head. Out of the four guys, Marco seemed the *least* likely to get possessive. The way he carried himself, the way he talked, I was pretty sure he hadn't let a little discomfort stop him from enjoying all the pleasures of the body with other women while he'd waited those sixteen years for me.

Aaron straightened up, tugging me with him. He slid his fingers into my hair and kissed me again, on the lips this time. His mouth lingered against mine just long enough for me to start wishing we could launch into a sequel to last night's activities right now. Then he pulled back with a sheepish smile. His blond hair was delightfully rumpled. I couldn't resist ruffling it a little more for good measure.

He laughed. "I guess we really should get some breakfast. We don't know what's waiting for us in Sunridge."

Right. My giddiness faded as nervous anticipation coiled around my gut. I clambered out of the van. Nate looked up from where he was scraping at fried eggs on a metal sheet over the fire, the corners of his lips curling up when he caught my eye. Oh, he knew what I'd gotten up to with Aaron last night, all right. And from the slant of West's eyebrows as he very definitely *didn't* meet my eyes, it was obvious the wolf shifter did too.

Well, we hadn't exactly tried to hide our new intimacy. What else did I expect? It was only going to get weirder as I accepted each of the others as mates too... whenever I felt ready to do that.

I had plenty of other bigger concerns to tackle first. "How far off are we from Sunridge?" I asked the camp at large.

Aaron got out his phone to check the map, but West spoke up first. "About two hours, depending on the roads. Are you in a hurry, Sparks?"

I gave him a pointed look. "I've been wanting to know what happened to my mother for seven years, *Wolfie*. So yeah, I might be a little impatient."

Marco snickered at the nickname, and Nate covered a guffaw. West glowered at me. "I guess you'd better get eating then."

Nate handed me a plate, and I gulped down the flame-cooked eggs with one of the rolls the villagers had sent us off with. We piled into the SUV, West and Aaron taking their original places up front. "Come join me, Princess of Flames," Marco said, patting the middle seat beside him, so I did. As Nate climbed into the back and West started the ignition, the jaguar shifter squeezed my knee briefly—just long enough to send a spark of heat up my leg.

Marco grinned at me, looking more relaxed now. I smiled back, but the view beyond the windshield pulled my gaze away. Down the road, where the forest thinned, tall mountains rose. A faint dusting of snow gleamed on the highest of the dark gray peaks. Sunridge lay just beyond that first range.

"Have you remembered anything that might explain why your mom sent us on this little road trip?" Marco asked.

I shook my head. "I don't think she ever mentioned Wyoming. Are there any important shifter communities nearby?"

"Not that I'm aware of. But I'm sure the dragon shifters kept a few secrets to themselves."

He took my hand as we drove on, idly trailing his fingers back and forth over my palm, but he didn't push for any more contact than that. As much as I enjoyed the warmth of his touch, I was too distracted to *want* more.

Two hours, and I might finally get some answers. I might even see Mom again. The jitters of anticipation returned, fluttering around my stomach.

West eased on the gas as the road narrowed. It veered up, winding along a pass between two of the mountains. Stray rocks rattled against the SUV's undercarriage. The sunlight dimmed, hidden behind the southern peak.

"There's someone on the road," Aaron said. West slowed the car even more. He hit the button to lower his window and inhaled to scent the air. I leaned forward, peering between the front seats. A figure was standing in our lane a few hundred feet ahead of us—a young guy who didn't look much past his teens.

"He's one of us," West said. "Feline from the smell of him." He glanced back at Marco. "Do you know him?"

"Right," Marco drawled. "Because all us feline-kin must know each other." He narrowed his eyes. "No, he doesn't look familiar, but that doesn't mean much."

"Can you tell if he's one of the rogues?" I asked. "How do you know who's kin and who isn't?"

"Kin take a mark of loyalty, like our alpha mark, on their palms," Aaron said. "If someone once kin goes rogue, the mark fades. We'll need to get closer to know."

"I don't like this," Nate said from behind me. "It's too much of a coincidence."

"I don't like it either," West said. "But some of my kin back in the village knew where we were headed. They might have passed on word if there was bad news from another group. I can't just run the guy over without knowing."

"Well, you could," Marco said. "If he's anyone's kin, he's mine. You have my full permission to plow right into him. If he's got half a survival instinct, he'll jump out of the way in time."

"Right," West said with an obvious edge of sarcasm. "That'll really improve kin-group relations."

Marco dragged in a breath. "Whatever you want, wolf boy. He's just a bobcat. I'm sure between the four of us we can take him if we need to."

But could we take whatever allies the stranger might have lurking nearby? My body tensed as we came up on the guy, the SUV rolling to a stop. I scanned the mountainside along the road. Nothing moved, but there were way too many crags and boulders that could be concealing an enemy.

The guy started ambling toward the car. West glanced back at Marco. "As you pointed out, *jaguar boy*, he'd be your kin. You go talk to him. If something goes wrong, I'm sure you can jump right back in the car as we speed out of here."

His voice was dry, but a thread of tension ran through it. He'd left one hand on the steering wheel, gripping it tightly. Aaron eyed the guy through the windshield. In the back seat, Nate undid his seatbelt. Preparing in case he needed to shift, I guessed. We were all on high alert.

Marco muttered something about "ungrateful canines," but he got up and slid open the door. "Stay right there, princess," he told me. He hopped out and sauntered up the road to meet the stranger. "Kin mark?" he asked.

The guy started to raise his hand—and two sharp *cracks* split the air. The same sharp, echoing sound I'd heard in my memory of my mother's desperate flight with me from our old home.

The SUV hitched, with a sputtering sound from one of the tires. Marco's shoulder jerked. He stumbled sideways, clutching his chest just below his collarbone. Blood bloomed beneath his fingers.

My heart stopped. Gunshots. That's what that sound was.

The rogues didn't care about shifter law, obviously. They'd brought guns to this fight—and to that one long ago.

"Marco!" West hollered. He pressed on the gas pedal, but the deflated tire thumped weakly against the pavement. "Shit. I'll get him. Stay low."

He threw himself out of the driver's seat before anyone could protest. Another bullet struck the window across from me. The glass cracked. I flinched down, ducking beside the seat. Nate growled. Aaron wrenched off his shirt.

"You're going to shift?" I said, panic jolting through me. "They'll shoot you out there." Two more *cracks* rang out, with a *thunk* against the side of the SUV—and a snarl on the road outside. Where was West? Had he gotten to Marco? How many rogues were in on this ambush?

"It's a lot harder to hit a moving target," Aaron said. He shot me a quick look, his bright eyes intent. "Stay down. We'll take care of this."

He leapt out, slamming the door behind him. A flash of golden feathers rocketed past the window an instant later.

A hiss and a yelp carried from down the road. My alphas or the rogues? I didn't dare raise my head high enough to peek out the window.

"And it takes more than a few bullets to stop a bear," Nate growled. He shoved open the back hatch, shifting as he went. His immense furry body charged past my window into the fray.

Another shot crackled. I winced, my fingernails digging into the leather seat. My heart thudded so fast the beats blended together.

A voice, thick and guttural, called out from somewhere above. "Give up the dragon shifter, kin-bound, and you'll live to keep bossing your people around."

The words struck a chord of recognition deep down in the animal core of me. I'd never heard that voice speak before, but it jolted me back to the first rogue attack, the snarls and growls of the black wolf that had tried to gouge open my neck. The skin there stung in memory.

I swallowed hard. He must be the one leading this group. But my alphas obviously weren't interested in bargaining my life away. The snaps and cries from down the road were getting louder.

A high keening filled the air—Aaron's battle cry—and cut off abruptly. My throat constricted.

The rogues had killed four alphas once before. My fathers. They'd murdered my sisters too. Slaughtered almost all of the people who'd mattered most to me. And now they were trying to take away my mates too, to get at me.

No. Rage bubbled up inside me. My fingers curled tighter, forming fists. I dragged in a breath, slow and steady the way Aaron had taught me, and the anger streamed through me in a white hot glow. As powerful as the connection that had solidified between him and me when I'd claimed him as mine last night. When I'd grasped the role I was meant for with both hands.

The energy rippled through all my limbs. I was not going to let this happen again. Not here. Not now. I would not *stay*. My alphas deserved a mate who could protect them as much as they protected me.

And damn it, they had one.

I dashed forward to grasp the door handle. Yanking the side door open, I flung myself out of the car. Out and *up*.

The shift rippled through my muscles, stretching, burning. My body expanded, sleek and sinewy. Talons ripped from my arched fingers. Wings burst from my back. They flapped with an instinctive heft, and I careened through the air. My eyes sharpened. The wind warbled over the smooth scales covering my skin. Fire smoldered all through my extended neck.

I'd done it. I was a dragon. And it felt *amazing.*

I beat my wings, soaring higher. Testing every inch of my newfound body. But I didn't have time to savor the sensations. My shadow streaked over the ground, twice as large as the SUV, and my gaze caught on a woman crouched by a boulder thirty feet up the mountainside. A pistol was braced in her hands. She raised it toward me.

A fiery confidence blazed through me. Oh, no. She could forget that. She was going to regret ever messing with me and mine.

I dove toward her. She pulled the trigger. A splinter of pain lanced through one of my wings, but I didn't care. I opened my jaws and let loose the fire searing through me.

The woman screamed as the flames engulfed her. I swooped over her hiding spot and whipped around, seeking out her companions. There'd been two guns firing. Where was the other coward hiding behind a pistol?

There. A gray-haired man hunkered down in a crevice on the other side of the road, not a pistol but a rifle poised against the dark rock. I swung toward him.

He proved himself an even bigger coward. Dropping the gun, he shifted into a black-and-gray-speckled weasel and darted away up the mountain.

I sped after the weasel shifter, but he dove into a deeper

crevice. I blasted it with fire and then spun around. My gaze narrowed on a man with shaggy black hair who was leaping to snatch up the rifle.

"Keep at them, keep at them!" he hollered down the slope in the same guttural voice I'd heard demanding that my alphas hand me over. His scent laced the air with a wolfish tang. It was him. The rogue who'd left me marked all over with the slashes of his claws. Who'd led his followers to savage Kylie too.

Anger surged up inside me. I was never letting him get a chance like that again.

The wolf shifter swung toward me, yanking the rifle upward, as if he thought he might catch me by surprise. A hot, heavy blast of dragon-fire was already searing up my throat. I opened my jaws and let it flow.

My fury blasted over the rogue's leader, leaving nothing but a charred heap and the molten lump of the rifle where he'd been. A twist of brutal satisfaction filled my chest.

I wheeled toward the road. A few of the other rogues were already fleeing, racing up the mountainside the way they'd come. The young man who'd stopped our SUV sprawled on the pavement, his chest torn and his throat gashed open. My wolf and my eagle had pinned a black bear to the ground between them. My grizzly was cuffing a mountain lion across the head. It bolted away as my shadow swept over them. I couldn't see Marco.

I turned again, meaning to give chase, and a prickling sensation raced through my muscles. They were clenching, condensing, the effort of the shift catching up with me. I strained to hold my shape, but exhaustion gripped me.

It was my first time. I had no stored endurance.

Gritting my teeth, I plummeted to the ground.

CHAPTER 21

Aaron

Serenity!

The shout echoed in my head as I saw her brilliant body fall from the sky. My eagle's throat couldn't form the name. My talons loosened where I gripped the bear's shoulder, the urge to fly to her rushing through me.

The black bear had gone limp in my and West's grasp, but now it lashed out its paw in one last desperate smack. Its claws raked across one of my wings. A lance of pain joined the other aches already radiating through my body.

I bobbed to the side and slashed at the bear, torn between two duties. Nate lumbered over, baring his teeth threateningly at the rogue that could have been his kin. He swung his head toward me as if to say, *Go on.*

My wounded wing faltered as I pushed myself backward. I landed awkwardly on my clawed feet and shifted back into human form. Bleeding claw marks scored my right arm, and a burning gash ran across my ribs. Clenching my jaw against the discomfort, I pushed myself toward my mate.

Serenity had hit the pavement on her hands and knees, somewhere between human and dragon form. The dragon side of her had saved her from the worst of the impact. She was slumped a few feet from the SUV when my eyes found her, and my pulse lurched.

Before I'd even dashed two steps, she raised her head. A bullet wound was leaking blood down her forearm and a scrape marked her chin from the impact, but her amber eyes glinted with a deeper fire than I'd ever seen before. It took my breath away.

I dropped to my knees beside her and pulled her to me. She sagged into my embrace, her cheek against my collarbone. Her chest was still heaving with ragged breaths.

"You were fantastic," I said, stroking my hand over her dark hair. "The most spectacular thing I've ever seen." My heart swelled with the memory of her bright red scales flashing against the sky.

My mate. My dragon shifter. And she'd accepted me as her own last night. The awe of it filled my throat.

Serenity's hand brushed over my wounded arm and stilled. She pushed herself upright. Her eyes widened. "You're hurt. We have to get you bandaged up. Is everyone else okay?"

"We all survived," I said. "And I'll heal." But she was right. I'd lost more than enough blood already. I heaved myself to my feet, reluctant to leave her. Moving to the car, I grabbed my pants and tossed my shirt to her, since her own had ripped apart with her transformation. The shreds of it lay on the road by the open door.

There was a roll of sterile gauze in the glove compartment for exactly this eventuality. I wrapped up my arm and knelt beside Serenity to tend to her own wound. She winced as I covered it.

"Fucking bullets. That's how they came after my family before. I heard the shots in one of my memories, just didn't realize what they were until now."

The set of my mouth hardened. "It's a stark line for them to cross. Any shifter who's broken that law, used a weapon against their own kind, can never join a kin-group in future."

"I get the impression that lot is more interested in tearing apart our groups than joining them," Marco said, propping himself against the hood of the car. He'd balled his own shirt against the bullet hole on his upper chest. The wound hadn't stopped him from shifting into jaguar form and taking care of the bobcat shifter who'd tricked us and then attacked him. Nate had shoved him toward the shelter of the SUV after that.

"Rogues don't usually like to completely throw away their other options," I muttered. Serenity moved to stand, and I straightened up with her.

West and Nate had both shifted back. So had the black bear shifter, who was now a woman sprawled limply on the road. The blankness of her half-open eyes dampened my relief. "She's dead." Damn.

"She took one of the bullets meant for us," West said, nodding to a bloody mark on her chest. "Managed to fight like she wasn't dying for long enough despite it." Bloody scores marked his chest, just below the glowing splatter of a scar I knew had been left by fae magic. He hurried to the SUV to grab his clothes, shooting me a pained look as he passed. "I was hoping we'd get some answers too."

Our dragon shifter was staring at the woman. She bit her lip.

She'd taken lives with her dragon-fire a few minutes ago, but seeing a dead body up close wasn't something Serenity was used to.

"I got their leader," she said, jerking her gaze away. "The wolf shifter who attacked me in the village. He's a pile of ashes up there now." She jabbed her hand toward the mountain slope. "I tried to catch the ones that were running too..."

Nate's eyes darkened. "You did everything you could, Ren. I've never seen any other shifter hold their form that long the first time they made a full transition."

"Oh." She blinked. Then a small smile crossed her lips.

Nate followed West to the car. We had to get moving before any humans showed up. The road wasn't frequently traveled and we'd left the last town several miles behind, but that didn't mean there hadn't been anyone around to hear the gunshots.

Serenity pulled my shirt closer around her shoulders. "They still wanted me dead," she said.

"Apparently sixteen years of chaos wasn't enough for them," West muttered.

Marco's lips curled. "You put them right in their place, though, princess. Blasted them all to cinders."

We couldn't know what other rogues might be out there who were just as set on destruction, but I didn't want to say that. Not as I watched Serenity draw her back a little straighter. She glanced around at us as the others returned, looking every bit a princess in that moment. Every bit a queen. This was a victory, and it belonged to her. I felt, in the hum of energy passing between us, my alpha equals responding to her power.

We were all in this, all the way. None of us were backing down, not even West. It felt good. It felt *right.*

"Then let's get on with whatever the rogues were trying to

stop us from doing here," Serenity said. "There's just one thing I need to do first."

She turned to me and reached to cup my jaw, pulling me into a kiss I was more than happy to return. I kissed her back with all the passion and reverence I had in me, until a tremble passed through her body. Everything—the danger, the wounds just starting to heal across my body—was worth it for this.

~

Ren

I eased back from Aaron, breathless, but I wasn't done yet. I reached for Marco next. My jaguar shifter came easily, sliding his arm around my waist as he tipped his face to mine. He kissed me long and deep, with a teasing caress of his tongue. Of course Marco would slip that in.

Nate was there waiting for me when I stepped back from Marco. I joined my hands behind the bear shifter's neck, and he pulled me up to meet him with his broad arms. His kiss was firm but sweet, with a lingering brush of his lips over mine before he let me go.

Last I turned to my wolf shifter. West's stance had tensed. He eyed me warily, but heat smoldered inside his gaze. He wanted me, despite himself. We all felt the same pull.

I held out my hand to him. "It's just a kiss, not a contract. I need to know you're with me at least that much."

He wet his lips. The gesture sent a flicker of desire through me. "All right, Sparks," he said. "You can have your kiss."

After that, I expected him to give me nothing but the briefest of pecks. He stepped closer, bringing the smells of the forest with him, rich earth and sharp pine. My heart beat a little faster. He bowed his head, and I bobbed up on my toes to tentatively press my mouth to his.

A hungry sound reverberated in his chest. His hand found my waist, hot as a brand as he yanked me to him. He kissed me so fiercely that my head spun. For an instant, there was nothing but the heat of him and the demanding pressure of his lips.

West released me just as abruptly. He backed up, folding his arms over his chest in a familiar standoffish pose. "Let's go then," he said gruffly, holding my gaze for a moment before jerking his away.

The sharp taste of him lingered on my lips. I let out my breath, feeling as if I'd finally fully settled into my body. The body of a dragon shifter, surrounded by the four alphas who'd be my mates. "Yes," I said. "Let's."

After a brief delay while Nate and West swapped out the shot tire with the spare from the back, we set off down the road again. The mountains pulled back around a wide valley with a glittering river down its center. Sunridge lay on the south bank, a small town of a few thousand inhabitants. I peered out the window as we cruised down the main street, waiting for something to hit me.

Aaron glanced at me expectantly. I shook my head. "Nothing."

"They've got a town historical museum," Nate said, pointing. "That seems like a good place to start."

West parked outside the repurposed house. The woman at the front desk looked at us curiously as we walked in. Her badge marked her as a volunteer for the Sunridge Historical Society. How much history could a town this size have?

We wandered between the displays: weathered newspaper articles, old black and white photos, pieces of clothing belonging to some particularly exceptional mayor who as far as I could tell had simply built a new bridge over the river. Not exactly gripping stuff. I was about to call it quits when my gaze caught on a painting that filled one corner of the back wall.

My pulse stuttered. I walked up to it, a strange feeling of recognition prickling through me. I'd never seen the image before, but somehow I felt as if I knew it.

It was a simple design showing the sprawl of the snowcapped mountains. But in the center, between two of the ridges, a spark shot up like a flame toward the sky. I reached for it, catching myself just short of touching the canvas.

"Do you like that?" the historical volunteer asked, coming up behind me. She gave me a soft smile. "It's an interpretation of a larger piece in the town square, if you want to see the original."

"Yes," I said, so enthusiastically her eyebrows twitched up. "Where's that?"

"It's a quick walk from here," she said. "Just take a left when you go out, walk two blocks, then another left and you'll see the square."

"Thanks!" I rushed for the door. The guys fell in behind me.

"Did you find something?" Nate asked.

"I think so. Come on."

I hurried down the street along the route the woman had given me. We stepped into a tiny cobblestone square with only a few buildings on each side and an inn at the far end. In the middle of the square stood a dark gray stone obelisk, twinkling with specks of mica. It towered at least half again as tall as me.

The same image from the painting was carved into its flat surface.

It drew me to it until I was close enough to touch. This time I let myself lay my hand on the cool stone surface. It seemed to tremble beneath my palm.

A crash of memory swept the world away.

No, not memory. Because the image of my mother that rose before my eyes wasn't one I'd ever seen before. She was standing in front of that obelisk, her brown hair shining in the sun, wearing the same dress she'd had on the last time I'd seen her. My chest squeezed.

She'd left this message for me seven years ago, when she'd stood in this exact same spot.

"Serenity," she said, her bright voice wavering from right inside my ears. "I wish I had more time to say everything I should, but I don't know how far ahead of them I've managed to stay. So all I can tell you is this: I want to give you everything you need to survive the many challenges I know are ahead of you. Our people left a power in this place centuries ago. If I haven't returned to bring it to you, there's still a chance you can retrieve it yourself. For you to have made it this far, you must be so strong already."

She touched the image of the flame between the mountains. "Here is where you'll find it. Your dragon nature will help you follow the path." Then she gazed straight into my eyes. "I love you. Never forget that."

The image wisped away. I found myself braced against the stone, my eyes swimming with tears.

"Ren?" Nate said tentatively.

I inhaled shakily and swiped at my eyes. "I'm okay," I said. "I know what we need to do. I know why my mother sent us here.

There's something here I need if we're going to fix all the damage the rogues have caused."

I backed up, looking at the picture and then the mountain ranges around us. There. I stopped when my gaze settled on a matching pair of peaks. The sun was high above them now, but it would gleam between them like a flame when it was first rising. I raised my hand.

"We're going up that mountain."

DRAGON'S TEARS

THE DRAGON SHIFTER'S MATES #2

CHAPTER 1

Ren

If someone had told me a week ago that soon I'd be shopping for camping gear with the four hottest guys in existence, I'd have called up the loony bin to collect them. But there I was, in a little shop in a town I'd never heard of until two days ago, doing my best not to melt as one of those gorgeous guys helped me into a down-filled jacket. His fingers skimmed my chest, sending a pleasant shiver over my skin.

It wasn't just Aaron's touch that had me on the verge of puddle-dom. The late June sun was shining brightly through the shop's windows, and the still air between the racks of outdoor clothes, backpacks, and other gear was thick with warmth. I squirmed inside the jacket.

"Are you sure I need to be *this* suited up?"

Aaron smiled at me with a mischievous glint in his bright blue eyes. Between those baby-blues and his golden-blond hair, he could have passed for a Disney prince. Although I wasn't sure

I'd ever seen a Disney hero quite that buff. I'd definitely never seen one who could make me tingle between my legs with just a glance.

"You said you're not sure how far into the mountains we'll need to go," he said, with the faint rasp that gave a little flavor to his even voice. "It'll be a lot colder at the higher altitudes."

"And we wouldn't want our Princess of Flames getting frozen," Marco drawled, leaning against a rack with his usual crooked grin. It fit the rakish playboy vibe he already had going on with his spiky black hair, the little scar through his arched eyebrow, and his refusal to take any situation completely seriously. His indigo gaze swept over my body, sending a fresh wave of heat through me. His grin widened. "As sad as I am to see you covered up, of course."

I glowered at him as I shrugged the jacket off. "I'm sure you'll survive without a view of my cleavage for a few days."

Marco chuckled. "I do have the rest of my life to appreciate it after that."

Oh, yeah. That was the detail I'd have found hardest to swallow before *my* life turned upside down about a week ago. The four guys doing their shopping with me were all shifters—and not any old shifters, but the alphas of their respective kin-groups. Marco could turn into a sleek black jaguar. He ruled over the feline kin. As leader of the avian shifters, Aaron's animal side was an impressive golden eagle.

And me? I'd discovered I was a dragon shifter. One of only two left in the world, if my mother was still alive. If she wasn't, then I was the very last. And my job was to unite shifter kind by taking all four alphas as my mates. No pressure or anything.

There were worse things than being expected to hook up with four completely smokin' guys, don't get me wrong. But for a girl who'd never gotten past second base in the first twenty-one years of her life—and who'd had no idea shifters even existed—all that attention could feel a little overwhelming.

I slung the jacket over my arm. "It fits and it's comfortable. And I want to get going. I'll take this one."

It had been seven years since my mother had passed through Sunridge, Wyoming and left her message for me with an enchantment on the town monument, but I didn't want to wait a second longer than I had to before I found out what had happened to her after.

Nate ambled over, a couple of rolled sleeping bags tucked under his brawny arms. His bear side came through in his tall, well-built body and his chestnut brown hair. But his expression when he looked at me was all gentle warmth. He might be a grizzly when we were under attack, but with me he was a total teddy bear.

"Do you figure we'll be up there over at least one night, Ren?" he said. His rich baritone voice never failed to warm me up too.

"I'm... not really sure," I admitted. We'd ended up here in Sunridge after following a trail of clues my mother had left me. When I'd touched the obelisk in the town square, I'd gotten a vision of her telling me there was something I needed to find up one particular mountain. Some kind of power she'd gone to retrieve seven years ago.

She'd never come back. I'd spent all those years with no idea where she'd gone or what had become of her. Really, getting some answers about that mattered more to me than any special powers. I could transform into a dragon—a big, fast, fire-breathing dragon. Wasn't that enough?

The thought sent an anxious tremor up my arm. Before I'd quite realized what I was doing, my hand had snatched a metal karabiner out of a basket and tucked it into my sleeve. Damned pickpocket instincts. They always kicked in when I was nervous. I pulled it out and set it back in the basket with a flush of embarrassment, but thankfully none of the guys commented on my slip.

"It'll be better for us to bring more supplies than we need than not enough," Aaron said to Nate. He was the most practical of my guys, which I appreciated a heck of a lot when I had so much still to learn about shifter abilities—and limitations. "Sleeping bags will be a lot more comfortable than just the blankets we've got in the SUV." He turned, looking toward the fourth member of my alpha squad. "Didn't you say there's a tent in the trunk, West?"

The wolf shifter nodded where he was lurking near the shop's front door. The sunlight streaming in caught on the silver strands mixed with his light auburn hair. Like his animal, he was all lean muscle, on display now with his arms crossed over his firm chest.

West was frowning, but that didn't mean much. He frowned at pretty much everything, especially if it had anything to do with me. He'd made it very clear that he wasn't on board with this whole "destined to mate with the dragon shifter" idea just yet. I guessed I couldn't exactly blame him, considering the chaos that shifter tradition had apparently thrown the kin-groups into when my mother had disappeared from the community with me sixteen years ago.

I wouldn't have minded him remembering that *I'd* had nothing to do with the decision to leave before he turned his gruffness on me, though.

"I'm not sure the tent we have is big enough for the five of us, but with the trouble we've had getting here, we'll probably want a couple of us on watch at any given time anyway," West said. "There's nothing to carry it with, though. We'll need to grab some packs. I'm assuming we're not going to be able to drive right up to this dragon shifter treasure." His dark green eyes slid to me with that last sentence.

"I don't know," I said. "This trek wasn't *my* idea. Believe me, I wish my mother had given us more detailed instructions too."

"We're all following you in this, Sparks," he muttered. "Keep that in mind."

"I think it's a safe assumption that we'll have to go part of the way on foot," Aaron broke in, calmly. His practical side made him a good peacemaker too. "And we'll want to pick up food for the trip, since we can't be sure of the hunting."

"I saw a decent-sized grocery store on our way into town," Nate said.

"Perfect." I carried my jacket over to the counter. "I hope you all have good credit." Especially since I didn't even own a credit card. I'd only just gotten off the streets a couple months ago.

Marco chuckled. "Don't worry, princess. Money is not an object for any of us."

He paid for our new gear, which thankfully Sunridge had in large supply, being so close to prime hiking and camping ground. Then we drove over to the grocery store. I stayed in my seat as the guys started to clamber out.

"Grab me some spicy beef jerky and Doritos if they have them," I said. "Otherwise I trust your judgment. I want to give Kylie a heads up before we're potentially out of cell tower range."

Nate's head snapped around. "You shouldn't hang back alone. I'll stay in the car with you."

I was tempted to tell him I'd be fine, but the fact was I might not be. We'd already been attacked by a group of rogue shifters on our way into town—presumably the same group that had killed my fathers and my sisters all those years ago. That was what had sent my mother on the run with me. You couldn't really blame her, considering the circumstances.

I'd managed to complete my shift into a dragon for the first time to fend off today's attack, and I'd totally fried their apparent leader, but a few of them had gotten away. And we didn't know for sure how many others there might be around.

The rogues didn't play by shifter rules. They were willing to use weapons on their own kind, even guns, which the alphas had told me was strictly forbidden. Shifters healed quickly, but the sealed wound on my arm where I'd caught a bullet still ached.

So I smiled at Nate and said, "Sure. Just don't be offended if I'm giving all my attention to my phone."

Nate reached over the back of the seat to squeeze my shoulder. "I wouldn't get in the way of you talking to your friend."

The bear shifter stayed behind me while the other guys headed into the store. I pulled out my phone. *Hey, Ky. How are you feeling?*

My best friend had been with us a couple days ago during the first attempt the rogue shifters had made on my life. They'd nearly killed her. Which was why I'd insisted she head home to Brooklyn once she'd healed up instead of coming along with us.

She texted back almost immediately. *I'm doing good! I'd say 95% at this point.* She added a winking emoji. *Should be 100% by tomorrow. What have you been up to? Did you make it to Sunridge? What did you find there? I need answers!!!*

I had to smile. Kylie's hyper energy came through clearly even in text form. I could picture her so easily, lounging on one of the porch chairs in the shifter village where she'd been recovering, grinning as bright as her neon pink pixie cut.

As I tried to decide what to say, my smile faded. I didn't really want to worry my bestie by telling her about the second attack, especially when she was too far away to do anything. She'd already come running to my rescue once. Right now she needed to focus on making sure *she* stayed okay. But there was one thing I had to share.

I managed a full shift this morning. You're talking to a bona fide dragon now!

Holy shit! That's amazing, Ren. I so cannot wait for you to demonstrate for me.

First thing when I get back. But we might be gone for a while longer. My mom left another message for me here. There's this stone with a picture on it that seems to be tied to the dragon shifters somehow... Another trail for us to follow.

Any sign of your mom herself? Kylie asked.

I bit my lip. *No. It doesn't really look good. The way she talked in the message she left... It sounded like someone was after her. And that she planned on coming back to me if she could. So since she didn't...*

I'm so sorry, Ren. But maybe it's not as bad as it looks.

I wanted to think that, so badly. That Mom was imprisoned or forced into deeper hiding or something else that had stopped her from returning to New York City—something other than her being dead. But the farther we came without finding any recent trace of her presence, the harder it got.

I'll keep hoping until I know for sure, I wrote. *But anyway, we might be out of service range for a few days. So don't worry if you don't hear from me! Just keep looking after yourself.*

I'm on it. You take care of you too. Although it's hard to be too worried when I know you've got those four hunks of manliness chomping to defend you. And get it on with you. Any progress in that area? Devil emoji.

I rolled my eyes, but my cheeks had flushed at the same time. There had been, actually. I'd taken my first major step toward claiming my destiny as leader of the shifters last night—by officially claiming Aaron as my mate.

In other words, we'd had sex. Really, really good sex, that still sent a giddy quiver through me when I thought back to it.

But talking about my first time via text just felt wrong. That kind of girl talk, I wanted to have face-to-face with my bestie.

More on that when I get back, I wrote.

Aw, way to leave a girl hanging! I want all the deets the second I see you.

I promise.

There might be a lot more details by the time I got to hang out with Kylie again. To take on my full role as dragon shifter, I was supposed to be getting fully intimate with all four of the guys. And Marco and Nate, at least, had shown plenty of enthusiasm in that area. But just losing my V-card had been a big step. As much as I was drawn toward all of the guys—even West—I wasn't about to jump in the sack with all of them at once just like that.

As appealing as that image suddenly was. Exactly how many guys *could* you get it on with at the same time?

I was feeling a little hotter than I could blame on the sun when the other three alphas returned with their haul. They tossed the grocery bags in the back with the rest of the gear and piled in. I'd taken the front passenger spot since I was the one with the best idea where we were going—as shaky as even that was. Aaron, who'd spent the most time eyeballing the maps, took the wheel.

"The road goes about a quarter of the way up the mountain before taking a sideways route around it," he said. "Let me know if you sense anything along the way that tells us which direction we should take, or where we should stop."

I nodded. All thoughts of bedroom-type activities faded into the back of my mind behind a jittering of anticipation. I didn't know what was waiting for us in the mountains, but based on the way Mom had talked in the vision she'd left for me, I was sure this was the end of the path. I'd have my answers soon.

Aaron turned the car toward the mountain with the dual peaks, the one that matched the carving on the obelisk. The carving had shown a flame between those peaks as well. I guessed that was how the sun must look as it rose and flared between them. And maybe the image hinted at the power Mom had said was hidden there.

"You've done all that reading into shifter history," I said to Aaron. "Do you have any idea what kind of 'power' my mother could have been talking about?"

He shook his head. "The dragon shifters have always kept some things to themselves. It's such a close bond, from mother to daughters over the centuries, just that one line that all of shifter-kind revolves around. It makes sense that they'd have their secrets."

Such a close bond. Mom and I had always been close, for sure. We'd only had each other the nine years we'd lived in hiding together in New York City.

But we hadn't bonded over our dragon shifter natures. She'd locked all my memories of that part of our lives away, along with my powers. They were only just starting to trickle back in. I had to assume she'd only been trying to protect me, but now that I needed my powers, I couldn't help wishing she'd found another way.

A nagging sensation crept over my skin as the road rose to follow the slope of the mountain. It was more than anticipation now. A faint pull tugged me toward the slope, urging me upward. As if I were being called by someone who knew me and wanted to welcome me back.

"Dragon shifters do seem to have excellent taste in dramatic scenery," Marco remarked behind me. The high mountain range that surrounded Sunridge spilled out all around us, starkly majestic.

The road wove back and forth as it climbed the mountain, and then veered sharply to the left. We'd only driven a few seconds longer when the faint pull I'd felt turned into a pinching tug.

"Stop," I said. Aaron glanced over at me and hit the brake.

"Did you see something?" he said

"Not yet, but there's something here. I can *feel* it."

He pulled onto the shoulder a short distance along the road, where a low fence surrounded an overlook. I hopped out of the SUV the second it had stopped moving. My sneakers thudded against the pavement as I hurried across the road. I followed the steep rock face on the other side back to the sharp left we'd taken.

Here. The pull urged me upward. I gripped the uneven surface of the rock and hauled myself up the steep slope. I might not have full command of my shifting abilities yet, but I'd had a shifter's strength and agility with me my entire life.

After what would be a quick scramble up the rock face, the slope evened out. A shallow hollow ran through the stone, slanting slightly upward. The second my gaze rested on that hollow, the nagging sensation crept deeper, into my lungs.

That was our path. I knew it down to my bones.

My alphas had gathered at the edge of the road beneath me. I jumped back down. The exhilaration of the leap wasn't quite as thrilling now that I'd experienced actual flight. Damn, I couldn't wait to get back into dragon form. It was too bad I'd only been able to hold it for a few minutes that first time. I'd have to work on my endurance.

"We need to go that way," I said, pointing. "Farther up the mountain."

West eyed the slope and grimaced. "Good thing we're only bringing the one tent."

Marco gave him a light punch to the shoulder. "Quit grumbling and help me pack up, wolf boy."

My heart sank a bit as they sauntered back to the SUV. All four of them were following this path for me, because I said it was important. But I really didn't have a clue what was waiting for us up there.

"I don't know how far we'll have to go," I said. "It could be a long trek."

"We're prepared for that," Aaron said with a reassuring smile. "Your mother led us here for a reason."

Nate squeezed my shoulder. "We all believe in you, Ren. Even West, no matter how grouchy he's being about it. Your instincts won't lead us wrong."

I turned toward the tallest of my alphas, drawn to the solid heat of his body. Nate seemed to know exactly what I needed. He wrapped his brawny arms around me in a hug, ducking his head next to mine.

The brush of his cheek against my temple set a flare of a completely different kind of need through me. I eased back just enough to raise my head and bring my lips to his.

Nate leaned into the kiss, returning it firmly but tenderly. The heat of him washed right through my entire body. Oh, yes, a very large part of me was looking forward to getting *completely* acquainted with all of my guys.

But now was obviously not the time for that. I kissed him one more time, hard enough that he rumbled with pleasure deep in his chest, and then I made myself step back. My cheeks were flushed, but I suddenly felt twice as steady.

"Let's get our gear and get going."

CHAPTER 2

Ren

Several hours up the trail, I was starting to wonder if we'd really needed to bring quite so much stuff. I could survive without a sleeping bag, right? Who needed changes of clothes? What good was food? I *knew* the guys had given me the lightest pack, and it still felt like there was a ton of bricks weighing on my shoulders.

Apparently I needed to work on that endurance thing in more than just the shifting department. I hadn't had the opportunity to get a whole lot of practice mountain-trekking in NYC.

I didn't want to look like a wimp when my alphas were striding along like the effort was nothing, so I gritted my teeth and kept walking. But I couldn't say I was upset when Aaron paused and touched one of the walls of rock that had gradually been rising on either side of us. They loomed over the path now, not so high they blocked out the sinking sun, but enough that there was no hope of taking a shortcut out.

"There've been fae up here," Aaron said.

"What?" West pushed past Nate to stride over. Aaron pointed to a mark in the smooth rock—a couple of intersecting lines with a glow so faint I wouldn't have noticed it if he hadn't drawn my attention. West's shoulders tensed. The rest of us drew closer.

"It looks old," Marco said. "They haven't charged that any time recently."

"Charged?" I repeated.

"With magic." He waved his hand toward the lines. "The fae are big fans of making things shiny."

"So by fae, we're talking... fairies, right?" I guessed if shifters and vampires were real, there was no reason Tinkerbell shouldn't be too.

West cut his gaze toward me. "Just like we're a far cry from werewolves, the fae aren't anything like your fairy tales. They're nothing you want to mess with."

"They've had kind of a chip on their shoulder since human beings started taking over so much of their territory," Marco elaborated. "They do love their privacy."

"But mountains aren't exactly their usual type of wilderness. They usually prefer places where things *grow*." Aaron studied the path ahead with a thoughtful expression.

Nate set his hands on my shoulders. "We've got to keep going either way. The sooner we find what we're looking for, the sooner we can leave and not have to worry about dealing with the fae at all."

No one could argue with that. We started tramping along again, but we were all eyeing the stone walls a lot more carefully now. The path was maybe seven feet wide, not a whole lot of room to maneuver if we had to fight. Which West, at least, seemed to think was a possibility. But Marco had said it was humans the fae took issue with.

"How do the fae feel about shifters?" I asked.

West made a sound somewhere between a grunt and a wordless muttering, as if he thought the question was ridiculous. Aaron ignored him. "We used to have decent relations with them," he said. "Our interests and needs are pretty different, but we share an appreciation for wild, open spaces and privacy from humans. Unfortunately we've had some... clashes in the last several decades."

"As humans expand their cities and towns, we end up having to move around too," Nate put in. "And the fae are getting more protective of their territory. I've heard they used to be okay with us sharing ground when we needed to shift and let off some steam."

"And now they're as likely to try to barbeque us," Marco said. "But those tensions might get better once you're established in your role, princess. It's harder to maintain good relations when we're a little fractured even amongst ourselves."

Had Mom ever talked about that, when I'd been little? I reached back into my fragmented memories, the ones she'd buried with her magic after we'd fled. They hadn't come back easy, and it was still hard to piece anything very coherent together. I slipped my hand into my pocket at the same time, closing my fingers around the locket she'd given me before she left that last time. The one that had drawn my alphas to me. I'd had to stop wearing it around my neck to make sure the chain didn't snap during an unexpected shift.

I could feel a hint of the magic in the warm metal now, whispering against my palm. It helped center my mind on those distant memories.

An image swam up of Mom standing at the edge of a forest, talking with a tall, slender man whose skin was so pale it looked almost blue. He had a faint sheen to him too, that lit up where the sun touched him. I was crouched in the grass, watching, my heart hammering. Both nervous and excited.

"Who *was* that?" I'd asked Mom later.

"One of the fae," she'd said. "I need to negotiate with them from time to time, on behalf of our community. You won't see them very often, though." She'd paused, her expression going distant. "I suppose it's a little sad, how little we interact and how formally. My grandmother told me that long ago the fae and the dragon shifters shared a special connection. But that's faded now."

Then she'd kissed my forehead and ushered me to the dining room for our dinner.

A lump rose in my throat. I hadn't known her properly in the last sixteen years, because she hadn't let me know her. And now that I knew who we were, I might never see her again in anything but a memory or a vision.

A warmth brushed my skin, like the feeling of her presence when we'd sat shoulder to shoulder on our couch. At first I thought it was just because of my reminiscing. Then my gaze fell on a small swath of parallel scratches dug into the rock wall just ahead.

My pulse stuttered. I stopped as I reached them, running my fingers over the narrow crevices. A stronger sense of my mother's presence rippled over me. I could almost smell her, like lilies and honey.

"My mother was definitely here," I said when I could manage to speak. "She must have shifted—she made these marks. I can feel her in them."

"That's pretty dainty work for dragon talons," Marco remarked.

"She probably meant for you to see them," Nate said. "To know that she's with you here, one way or another."

Right. And there was a chance whatever lay ahead would lead me the rest of the way to her. I squared my shoulders under the straps of my pack and strode on.

Aaron made a humming noise. "That doesn't look good."

My head jerked up. "What?"

The question had hardly fallen from my mouth when I saw it. Down the path, a jumble of boulders had tumbled down to fill the gap between the walls. There must have been a rockslide. Just what we needed—more climbing.

But as we hurried closer, I realized our situation was more complicated than that. The highest boulders had fallen at an angle, jutting out over the lower ones. There was no way to climb that heap unless we could turn off gravity. Which as far as I knew was not a skill any shifter was gifted with.

We stopped at the edge of the landslide's shadow and peered up at it. Aaron rubbed his square jaw. Marco stalked from one side of the path to the other, looking very much the jaguar in that moment. Nate moved to test one of the boulders within reach, as if he thought he could dig his way through, and West made a warning noise.

"Don't bring the whole damn pile down on our heads."

"We've got to get past it somehow," Nate said.

"I can fly," Aaron said. "But I wouldn't be able to carry more than my pack in eagle form."

He wasn't the only one who could fly. "I can carry a lot more than that," I said. "Hell, in dragon form I could blast that pile right down so we don't have to deal with it on the way back." The sun was waning, and we hadn't seen another person since we'd left the road. I didn't think any humans would spot my dragon form all the way up here.

Nate frowned. "You only shifted for the first time this morning. You might not have recovered enough energy yet."

I shrugged off my pack and reached for the hem of my shirt. Shifting and clothes didn't get along so well, especially when you shifted into as large a creature as I did. "Can't hurt to try, can it?"

Marco leaned against the rock wall with an amused smile. "I, for one, am going to enjoy watching that."

"Here," Aaron said. He found the padded jacket I'd bought and brought it over as I tugged off my shirt and bra. "You won't be able to concentrate on shifting if you're freezing. Just keep it on your shoulders so it'll fall off when you make the transformation."

"Thanks." I tugged the jacket over me like a cape, thankful for both the warmth and the little bit of modesty. These guys had been stripping down whenever they needed to shift, regardless of who was around, all their lives. It was going to take a little while for me to get used to the casual nudity side of shifter-dom.

I kicked off my pants and undies and knelt down so the jacket hung around most of my body. I'd barely noticed the cooling mountain air on our hike up. It'd been warm when we'd started, and then *I'd* been warm from the hiking. Now the chilly air seeped over my bare skin.

I wouldn't mind it so much when I had scales. How could I bring them out? I'd shifted in the heat of battle before, desperate to protect my alphas before they died protecting *me*. We didn't face a threat anywhere near that urgent right now. How much could I even control that power?

The doubts wriggled through my mind. I closed my eyes and inhaled deeply, trying to will them away. I knew the dragon inside me now. I knew what it felt like to expand into that body, to spread those wings. All I had to do was get back there.

I thought back to the sensation of stretching muscles, of scales forming over my softer skin. But the memory didn't come alone. The *crack* of the gunshots echoed through my mind. Cries of pain. All the awful sounds of the rogue's ambush. My back went rigid.

No, that was no good. I had to let go of that stuff. I *was* a dragon. I had to just *be* one.

"If you can't manage it, we'll find another way," Nate said. "Don't push yourself too hard."

A spark of annoyance lit in my chest. Why shouldn't I push myself? Weren't all of them pushing themselves on my behalf all the time? I wasn't some weakling who needed to be coddled. I was a fucking *dragon*.

That flare of determination shot through my body. Yes, that was what I needed. I held onto it and dove headfirst into the searing sensation racing over my skin. Into it and through and out and up, limbs expanding, neck extending, every part of me stretching free. My head lengthened into jaws lined with sharp teeth, a smoky flavor trickling on my tongue. Fire danced in my lungs.

I launched myself up toward the sky, giddy. The shift pinched at my joints, but I didn't mind that little bit of strain. I'd done it. This was who I was.

The wind buffeted me as I swooped around. I drank in the pleasure of flight for a moment, and then I dipped back down. I didn't know how long I'd be able to hold this form. I couldn't forget the whole reason I'd taken it on right now.

The heap of boulders looked like pebbles to my dragon self. I dropped down over the highest one and grasped it between my hind feet. My talons closed around it and wrenched it off the pile. With a few flaps of my wings, I deposited it away from the path on the mountainside.

One down, a dozen or so more to go.

I tossed another boulder aside, and another, and another. The pinching I'd noticed earlier started to creep through my wings and chest. I'd already held the shift longer than last time. My body was getting worn out. Damn it, I wasn't done yet.

But I'd handled the worst of it. I eyeballed the remaining pile, only half as high as when I'd started. My alphas had backed up to give me room. If I just took a good running start at it...

I flew down the path the way we'd come. As I swung around, a flicker of movement caught my eye. I hesitated, peering down, but I couldn't see anything except shadows in the path below me. It'd probably been the motion of my own shadow I'd seen.

Gathering my strength, I raced toward the heap as fast as my wings could flap. The air whistled past me. My expanded heart thudded with glee. My dragon lips parted in what must have been a dragon-ish grin.

At the last second, I heaved my hind legs down and forward. I crashed into the pile feet first. The impact radiated through my body, but I hopped upright before I could fall on my back. The remaining boulders tumbled down the path with a rattling thunder, spreading out so we'd be able to walk between them.

Not a second too soon. That bone-deep exhaustion was rolling over me again. I sank down on the ground, hunching my back, shrinking into myself. The scales contracted back into my skin. In a moment, all that remained of my dragon form was the taste of smoke in the back of my mouth.

My human body felt tired too, but not enough to dampen my sense of victory. "I did it!" I said, springing up. "There you go, path cleared, dragon shifter at your service." I gave a little bow.

"Nicely done," Aaron said with a chuckle. Marco grinned and clapped his hands in a round of applause. Nate smiled proudly. And West—

West's eyes were fixed on my body, which in my enthusiasm I'd forgotten was now completely uncovered. At my glance, his gaze jerked back to my face. In that first instant as we stared at each other, hunger lingered in his expression, too intense for him to completely rein in. Despite the cool air, a wave of heat washed over me.

He turned with a snap, taking that heat with him.

CHAPTER 3

Aaron

WHEN I DUCKED into the tent, Serenity was sitting cross-legged on her sleeping bag in the middle, grimacing at her phone.

I sank down onto my own sleeping bag at her right. "Is something the matter?"

"Oh, I knew there probably wouldn't be much reception up here, but I was hoping I'd be able to update Kylie at least one more time before we lost it completely." She sighed and tucked the phone into her pack's outer pocket. "I guess I'd run out of charge before too long anyway. No handy electrical sockets up here!"

"We've made good time," I said, sensing the distress under her joke. I'd seen her with her friend enough to know how much they'd relied on each other. Serenity could rely on the four of us, her alphas, now, but of course it'd take time for her to adjust to that. She'd only just found enough trust to welcome me fully as her mate.

That thought drew me closer to her. I leaned in, and an answering spark of attraction lit in her amber eyes. She lifted her head to meet my kiss eagerly.

When I'd first met our dragon shifter, I'd wondered if the unshakeable pull I felt toward her—to be near her, to touch her, to bring her pleasure—would ease off once our mate-bond was consummated. It seemed the answer was no. Since last night, my desire for her hadn't eased off at all. I'd managed to keep my equipment in my pants for twenty-seven years, and now it was agonizing to imagine going even one night without hearing her moaning beneath me.

She made a sound that was almost a moan now as I teased my tongue into her mouth. Her fingers trailed up my neck to tangle in my hair. She tugged me even closer. Sparks of pleasure raced over my scalp. I cupped her jaw, kissing her harder. Then I let my hand slip down over her shirt to caress her breast. The nipple peaked beneath my palm.

A whimper crept from her throat. She arched into my touch encouragingly. Her curves were so soft under my fingers, but I could still feel the strength all through her body. The combination thrilled me. What a woman my mate was.

I edged up the hem of her shirt to touch her skin to skin. Serenity let out a gasp against my mouth when my fingertips grazed the tip of her breast through her bra. Her fingers curled against my shoulders. Then she tensed.

I eased back to see her face. "Are you all right?"

Her mouth twisted. Desire still burned in her eyes. "I want to keep going. But... West is supposed to be sleeping in the tent the first half of the night too, isn't he? He might come in while we're..." She gestured between us with a crooked smile.

Ah. It was going to take time for her to adjust to that aspect of our relationship too. I stroked her cheek and the side of her neck.

"You know if all goes well between the group of us, there'll be moments in the future when the other alphas aren't just seeing you with me… they'll be joining in as well."

She drew her legs up to her chest. "I know. It's still a little hard to wrap my head around. It's not like I've ever tried a *three*some before, let alone a… five-some?"

If Serenity had grown up among the shifters, seeing her mother with her four fathers, she wouldn't feel this hesitation. And that was the fault of the rogues who'd ripped her family apart with their bloodshed.

My jaw clenched for a second before I forced it to relax. The past was gone, as horrific as it had been. All we could do was move forward from there. And make sure none of the rogues who remained got another chance at harming the dragon shifter we still had.

Serenity didn't deserve to be rushed, but it wouldn't be right for me to encourage her to see me as her only mate either. I pressed a gentle kiss to her lips. "We can give you time. Don't feel you have to rush things. And I'm here for you, however you need me. But I think it'll be good for you to try to keep your mind open. Dragon shifters aren't meant for only one mate. I won't be enough to satisfy you on my own."

The glint in her eyes turned mischievous. "You're doing an awfully good job so far." She kissed me again, long and slow. Then she scooted her sleeping bag as close to mine as she could get. "Hold me until I fall asleep?"

I lay down next to her and wrapped my arm around her waist, tipping my face next to hers. "Until then and after, Serenity."

Ren

My toe caught on a ridge in the path, and I stumbled forward. A curse fell from my mouth, but I caught my balance before Nate's helping hand reached me. "I'm okay, I'm okay."

"Whoever picked this route obviously wasn't too concerned about ease of travel," Marco said, raising his eyebrows as he took in our surroundings. "A little redecorating might be in order."

I couldn't argue. If I'd thought yesterday's hike had been difficult, today's was downright brutal. The path had veered sharply upward through the morning, and just after we'd stopped for a quick lunch, the walls above slanted together to form a ceiling overhead. We were walking through a cave now. A cave with a really uneven floor and only dim light from the occasional gaps in the ceiling. Our steps echoed faintly through the cavernous passage.

The temperature had dropped at the same time. A damp chill brushed my face as I trudged on. I was very glad for that down jacket now. But the tug inside me kept urging me onward, more insistently now than before. Whatever we were heading toward, we were definitely getting closer.

"Have you gotten any clearer sense of what we're looking for or how far ahead it might be?" Aaron asked me.

I shook my head. "The feeling I have is still just a vague pull. But I know we're going the right way." If that feeling hadn't been enough to confirm it, just an hour ago I'd spotted another score mark where Mom's energy had lingered. She'd entered this cave too, seven or so years ago. Entered it and left her mark for me to find.

We'd also spotted a couple slivers of fae magic etched in the walls, although nothing the guys had thought was recent.

Something split the hazy gray tunnel ahead of us. I squinted at it. After several more steps, I made out what it was—a seam of rock. The cave was splitting into two passages.

"I'm not much of a fan of mazes," West muttered.

Neither was I, but as we reached the branching, the pull inside me tugged to the left clearly enough. "We go that way," I said, pointing. "No problem."

"I trust your instincts," Aaron said, "but I don't like the additional possibilities for an ambush when there are multiple passages to move between. I think we should quickly scout out both sides—check for any signs of potential enemies."

"Fine," West said, stalking toward the passage to the right. "Let's just get on with it."

"Fifteen minutes, and if you haven't seen any reason to worry by then, meet back up," Aaron called after him. He headed down the left passage, leaving me with Marco and Nate.

The big bear shifter crossed his arms over his chest, looming over me as if there were some immediate threat I needed to be defended from. I appreciated that he wanted to look out for me, but sometimes his protectiveness felt a little smothering.

"I'm pretty sure there's nothing around here except for rocks," I said. "Unless there are some rock demons or something you guys haven't bothered to tell me exist, we should be fine."

"No rock demons," Marco said with a grin. "As much as I might enjoy a little break. Hiking, hiking, hiking does get monotonous."

"We've seen those signs that the fae have been through here," Nate said. "It's better to be cautious than to put you at risk."

I couldn't say I exactly minded this kind of break. I set down my pack and rolled my shoulders. They throbbed with the motion.

"Need a little help with those?" Marco said in a suggestive tone.

I rolled my eyes at him, and his grin widened. But I actually wouldn't mind a little assistance working out the kinks in my muscles. "Give them everything you've got," I said, shrugging my jacket down to give him better access.

Marco's lithe hands settled on my shoulders over the fabric of my shirt. He dug his thumbs into my muscles with the perfect amount of pressure. I groaned at the burn spreading through my shoulders, and he chuckled. Suddenly the cave's air felt a whole lot warmer.

A pattering sound carried from the other end of the cave, back the way we'd come. Nate's back went rigid. He turned toward it, his bulky arms flexing. No other sounds followed, but he didn't relax.

"It's probably nothing," I said. "Just a pebble falling off the ceiling."

"I should take a look to make sure," Nate said. Then he hesitated, his gaze moving to Marco. "You'll watch out for Ren?"

"Of course," Marco said, sounding amused. "Anyway, there's one of the rest of you in any direction an enemy could come at us from. If you start screaming, we'll know to get moving."

Nate glowered at the jaguar shifter and headed down the cave. Marco resumed my shoulder massage. It didn't take long before the bear shifter's brawny form disappeared into the darkness. Marco leaned closer, letting his fingers dip down to my collarbone.

"Finally we're alone," he murmured in my ear.

A shiver of anticipation ran through me even as I smiled. "And what exactly are you assuming will happen now that we are?"

"I make no assumptions. Only offers. How would you like to

spend the rest of our wait in a way we'll both enjoy very much?"

"You think so highly of your abilities," I teased. Then his hands dipped right under my bra, tracing the sensitive skin just above the tips of my breasts, and my breath caught. My body moved of its own accord. I leaned back against him, tilting my head as he pressed his mouth to the side of my neck.

"For good reason," Marco said, his breath hot against my skin. It was so hard to resist the passionate need flaring up from my core. And why should I resist it? Like Aaron had said last night, all four of these guys were my mates. I needed to get more comfortable with all of them. To open myself up to the experience.

I turned in Marco's embrace and yanked his mouth to mine. He kissed me, a hungry sound reverberating from his chest. His hands slipped up my back under my shirt and nimbly unhooked my bra. As the cups loosened, he reached for my breasts again, swiveling his thumbs around my nipples and then flicking over them until I gasped.

My hips canted toward his. He dropped one hand to grasp my waist and spun us around so he could lean me against the stone wall. His touch teased over my hips and thighs. I kissed him hard, not caring about the rough surface behind me, just wanting to feel more.

Marco's lips moved away from mine to nibble a tingling line along my jaw. "Oh, my Princess of Flames," he said between nips. "You're amazing. There's no other word for it. I couldn't have imagined a better mate."

I mumbled something inarticulate and encouraging, lost in the haze of pleasure. My eyelids fluttered. The light in the cave behind Marco seemed to flutter with them—and to solidify into a humanoid form.

We weren't alone anymore.

CHAPTER 4

Ren

A YELP BROKE from my throat. I jerked away from Marco and the figure beyond him, smacking the back of my head on the wall of the cave. Marco whirled to place himself between me and the figure in one smooth movement. What must have been an instinctive shout of warning burst out of him, but his shoulders came down when he set eyes on the strange woman. He drew himself up straighter.

"You know, I really thought the fae had better manners," he said.

The fae. Yes, the woman standing at the other side of the passage was as slim and pale as the man I remembered Mom talking to. Her skin, hair, and filmy dress had the same bluish shine, a little dampened here in the dimness of the cave.

I fumbled to fix my bra, my face flushing. This wasn't exactly how I'd have wanted my first meeting with fae-kind to go down, not when I was supposed to represent the entire shifter community.

The woman didn't look at all distressed or apologetic about the make-out she'd interrupted. Her expression was blandly blank.

"I have a matter of some importance to relate to you," she said in a thin, shimmering voice.

Footsteps were thudding over the stone floor on either side of us. Nate appeared first, then Aaron and West, all of them slowing to a halt when they saw our visitor. Marco waved them all over, but I saw his jaw was still set a bit tight. He wasn't completely at ease, no matter how nonchalant he liked to appear.

How had the fae woman gotten past all of the alphas? Was there some other passage we'd missed—or had it been some kind of magic? It didn't seem wise to ask the guys right in front of her. I didn't need her knowing just how ignorant I was about all things supernatural.

West's lips had drawn back over his teeth in a wolfish snarl. His stance was completely tensed. "What are you doing here?" he gritted out.

Nate stepped closer, towering over the slip of a woman. I could tell from his pose that he was braced to shift into his grizzly form the instant he felt he needed to. Aaron set a hand on his arm, but the eagle shifter's eyes gleamed with a determined light. He might not want to rush into a confrontation, but he was ready for it.

"Apparently she has some important info to pass on," Marco said, and nodded to the fae woman. "So go on."

She cocked her head consideringly, taking in my alphas. "I come with the intention to help. There is no need to be defensive."

"We'll judge that for ourselves," West said.

Aaron stepped forward, making a brisk motion toward the wolf shifter as if asking him to stand down. "We're listening," he said, his voice even but not friendly. "What is it you wanted to tell us?"

"We discovered one of your kind sneaking after you in the caves, carrying a weapon," the fae woman said. "One with no ties to any of your kin-groups. Clearly he had ill intentions."

A rogue. My back stiffened. "Where is he?"

"You don't need to worry about him any longer. We disposed of him in an appropriate manner."

She moved her hand in an arc through the air and conjured an image like a hazy video recording, floating in mid-air. A weasel scuttled along the wall of the cave. It had a small knife clamped in its jaws. A chill ran down my spine.

I recognized that animal. One of the rogues who'd ambushed us in the mountain pass had transformed into a weasel to flee. I was sure that animal was the same one. So he'd been tailing us through the cave, carrying yet another forbidden weapon. The moment we'd all had our guards down, even for a moment, I had no doubt he'd have tried to finish the job the group of rogues had attempted before.

Killing me.

In the conjured image, a fae man appeared in front of the weasel. His mouth moved, but the conjured display contained no sound. The weasel flinched and darted for a crevice. The man threw a bolt of searing light toward it. The bolt struck the weasel —and consumed it in a brief blaze. When the light faded, nothing of our enemy remained.

The fae woman gestured again, and the image vanished. She spread her arms as if to say, *There you have it.*

"We would rather have had him captured alive so we could have questioned him," Aaron said. He managed to keep his tone even, but his rasp had become more pronounced. And why shouldn't he be upset? The weasel shifter might have been our enemy, but the fae couldn't have been sure of his intentions. He'd been *our* business to deal with as we saw fit. And they'd just slaughtered him with a single swipe of magic.

What if they decided we deserved the same treatment?

"He was not inclined to cooperate, as you could see," the fae woman said. "My companion could feel the murderous intent in him. We believed we were doing you a kindness." She paused, and her filmy eyes glittered in a way that set my nerves on edge. "You are the alphas of the shifter-kin, are you not? And the long-missed dragon shifter."

I liked the way her gaze settled on me even less. Apparently the guys all had the same feeling, because they drew closer around me at the same moment.

"We are," Marco said. I guessed she must have been able to sense their status, maybe through the oath-scars on their hands. "And she is. And as far as we knew, no one has made a direct claim on this mountain. I hope we aren't intruding."

"Not at all," the fae woman said, but I thought her sheen jittered a little. "We venture into the mountains from time to time, but we don't consider them truly part of our home. There is room enough for both."

"So this is basically a vacation spot for you," Marco said. He raised his eyebrows at the cave around us. "You have interesting tastes."

"The landscape has qualities that appeal in their own way. I suppose you've noticed other signs of our presence on your travels."

"We didn't think you'd been here recently," Nate put in. "Otherwise we'd have reached out to you."

"Did you pass on word to your people elsewhere?" the fae woman asked. She gave us a demure smile. "I know we've had our disagreements in the past. If there will be more shifters arriving, it would be best for us to know they're here on your request. To avoid any awkward encounters."

Like a fae deciding to incinerate another shifter?

"We aren't expecting anyone to join us," Aaron said. "But please, if you come across another rogue lurking around, bring the matter up with us before taking any action."

The fae woman bowed her head in a way that didn't look all that apologetic to me. My skin prickled. Maybe the dragon shifters and the fae had worked together long ago, but right now I didn't trust them at all.

"Is there any particular reason you're here right *now*?" West asked, his voice tight. He obviously shared my sentiments.

"We were simply passing by and noticed you doing the same." The fae woman tipped her head. "All four of the alphas and their long-lost mate up here together—*you* must be making this trip on a matter of some importance."

She said it as a statement, but the question was clearly implied. My hands clenched. She claimed she was helping us, but every sense I had screamed that she had other intentions. I had no interest in sharing my mother's story with her.

"Serenity is still adjusting to her new role," Aaron said. He was the only one who called me by my full name, the name my mother had urged me to keep secret the entire time we'd been in hiding, and sometimes it still felt as if he were talking about a stranger. Right now, faced with the fae, I appreciated the formality of it. "There aren't many places a dragon shifter can exercise her powers without needing to worry about discretion."

"I suppose your people must at least know you've traveled up here," the fae woman said. "They'll be awaiting your return."

"We'll be back soon enough," Marco said. I restrained a frown. What was she getting at?

Maybe it was time we started asking more of the questions. I didn't want to tell her much about Mom, but she might know things I didn't.

"My mother came up here at least once in the last several years," I said. "She liked to visit the mountains too. I don't suppose you 'passed by' her then?"

The fae woman pursed her lips. "I can't recall the last time I saw any dragon shifter in these heights. I can ask my companions if they have more knowledge."

That was an incredibly vague answer. And if she could tell the alphas were alphas just by sensing it, surely she'd picked up on the marks Mom had left behind on the walls. Maybe she just assumed we'd already seen those?

"It sounds as though you're more familiar with this mountain than we are in general," Aaron said. "Is there anything we should know for safe passage from here on?"

The fae woman's mouth curled into another smile, but this one looked even chillier than the last. "You're the five most powerful shifters alive. I'm sure there's nothing on this mountain that could threaten you. I suppose I shouldn't delay you in your journey any longer. We are moving on now, so I doubt our paths will cross again."

"Thank you for your rogue-cleanup services," Marco said.

"Our pleasure," the fae woman replied without any hint of irony. She stepped backward to where a thin stream of sunlight penetrated the cave ceiling. With a quick leap, her form wavered and vanished into the glow.

"Should we be... worried?" I asked, staring up toward the

sliver of daylight. Was she still here, only invisible, or could we assume she'd completely left? I didn't want to talk too freely in case it was the former.

"We'll just have to wait and see," Aaron said, a little grimly. "Let's keep moving while we have the light."

CHAPTER 5

Ren

SOMEONE'S MOUTH was moving over my bare skin. Searing it with hot breath and the graze of his teeth. My breath was already coming in sharp pants.

He kissed his way down my throat, between my breasts, and over my belly. His tongue scorched me everywhere it touched. His fingers trailed down my sides, even hotter than his mouth. They came to rest on my hips just as his face hovered over my sex.

A thrill of anticipation and need tingled through me. I arched up encouragingly, and he took me in his mouth.

His tongue slicked over my clit, sending sparks of bliss all through my body. I whimpered as he suckled harder. He was devouring my core as if he meant to swallow me whole, and I was all for it. I moaned, weaving my fingers into the soft, smooth strands of his hair. A deeper need swelled inside me. An ache to feel him inside me, all of him. To know he was mine and I was his, now and forever.

"Please," I murmured. "Please." I tugged at his hair, and he raised his head. West's dark green eyes gleamed. His lips curled with a satisfied smile, and—

I jerked awake, my heart thudding. The chilly mountain air cooled my flushed face. The weight of the thick sleeping bag enveloped me. I was completely covered up and completely alone. It'd only been a dream.

But fuck, what a dream. My panties were sopping beneath the leggings I'd worn to bed. The ache of need lingered deep in my belly. I had the urge to reach down and take care of things myself, but I wasn't *actually* alone in the tent. Marco lay on one side of me, with a murmur of breath that reminded me of the little meows sleeping cats made. And West, the real West—

I turned my head to look at him instinctively, as if to confirm he was definitely still the grouchy, standoffish guy I'd had to badger into even kissing me the other day. Although it'd been quite a kiss when he'd given in. My eyes found his form in the darkness, lying on his side a couple feet away from me.

But not asleep. Just enough of the light from the campfire outside seeped through the tent wall for me to make out his features. To see him staring right back at me.

My pulse skipped again as our gazes met. I expected him to pull his away, to roll over and shut me out. Instead his eyes stayed locked with mine. They didn't hold the same lustful warmth as in my dream, but a tingle crept over my skin all the same. His expression was tense, but I also saw the same hunger I had when he'd looked at me naked after my shift. As if he were just a hair's breadth from reaching out and yanking me to him.

As if he'd woken up from the exact same dream I had. Suddenly I was sure that was what had happened. I could smell his arousal in the air, a waft of piney musk. But he was fighting it.

I wet my lips, and his gaze twitched down to my mouth. Before I could decide what to do about this weird but oh-so-tempting moment, Marco stirred at my other side. He scooted closer and nuzzled the back of my neck.

"Someone feeling the need for a little middle-of-the-night action?" he murmured in his languid voice. I guessed it wasn't just West's arousal scenting the air. My nerves hummed with anticipation. I needed *something*, that was for sure.

I arched into Marco encouragingly, and he kissed the crook of my jaw. The zipper of my sleeping bag hissed as he eased it down for better access.

I tipped back my head to offer more of my neck to him. Marco branded me with his hot mouth, drawing his body against mine. His hand traveled up under my shirt. He groaned when his fingers brushed over my unconfined breasts. He stroked them skillfully, tracing pleasure all through my chest, and I whimpered. My gaze slid back down to meet West's again.

He was still watching. His pupils had dilated, and I could hear the quickening of his breath in time with mine. My awareness of his desire turned me on even more. I gasped as Marco pinched one of my nipples.

"Tell me what you want, princess," he said huskily. "Anything at all. It's yours."

I didn't think I'd ever wanted anything more than for West to cross that gap between us and add his mouth and hands to the mix. Just the thought of it made me twice as wet between my legs. In that instant, my hormones overrode common sense. I reached out my arm toward West to beckon him over.

Before I'd even finished the gesture, West flinched. His gaze snapped away. "*Don't*," he said, his voice thick with strain. He shoved off his sleeping bag and threw himself onto his feet. With a slap of the tent flaps, he'd stalked out.

Marco chuckled under his breath. "He'll come around, princess. Especially after he sees how good the rest of us have it. But don't worry, I can make you see stars all by myself."

He rolled me toward him and caught my mouth with his. The heat of his kiss washed over me. It was hard to think much about West when I had this much man right in front of me.

I kissed Marco back, letting all my need and desire spill into the places where our bodies touched. He let his hands slip lower, teasing over my stomach and tracing the waist of my leggings. When I kissed him harder, he dipped his hand right under the fabric. He cupped my sex, grinning against my mouth as I moaned.

His mouth claimed mine again. His tongue tangled with mine. His fingers stroked over the sensitive folds between my legs with increasing pressure. I clutched him, shivering with pleasure, riding his hand.

"That's right, princess," Marco murmured. "That's my girl." He kept up his gentle caresses as he kissed his way down to my chest and tugged my shirt up with his other hand. His breath spilled over my bare skin. He swirled his tongue around my breast before sucking the nipple into his mouth.

A little cry of pleasure burst from my lips. I felt ready to explode.

"You taste so good. I need to taste you everywhere." Marco gave my breast one more swipe and then ducked lower. I whimpered in dismay when his hand left my sex, but it was only to ease my leggings down. A second later, he'd lowered his face between my legs.

Like West in my dream. Fragments of that imagined intimacy darted through my head as Marco swirled his tongue over my clit. I gasped, arching up, and he licked lower, teasing my opening. Carried on the rising wave of bliss, I almost felt as if both he and West were there, my dream and reality merging into one. The ache in my belly came back, twice as strong. My hips bucked, wanting more. Wanting everything.

I gripped Marco's hair, but he didn't release his claim on my pussy. He laved my clit until I was trembling. One finger, then two tested my wetness and then slid up inside me. I moaned again as the pleasure rose higher.

Marco nipped me, just hard enough to send a brief spark of pain through the pleasure, and that tipped me over. I came, shuddering against his mouth. The orgasm washed over me, and the stars Marco had promised flashed behind my eyes.

Marco smiled and kissed my sex again as my tremors subsided. He eased up beside me, pulling my body flush against his, and brushed his lips against mine. My tart flavor lingered in his mouth. I pressed closer to him, sated and yet still hungry. The hard length of him bulged against the fly of his pants. His hips rocked against me as his hands caressed my ass, sending fresh sparks all through my nerves.

It would be so easy to peel off his pants and open myself to him. To solidify our mate-bond and tie us together for life.

"Ren," Marco mumbled against my mouth. I heard the wanting in his voice. An awful lot of me wanted it too. But as we rolled with him on top of me now, my gaze dropped to West's empty sleeping bag.

This whole encounter had started with the wolf shifter. With him and that scorching dream. And here I was getting down and dirty with Marco instead.

Could I really know *what* I wanted right now, in the heat of the moment? The mate-bond, it was for life. When I accepted it with each of the guys, I wanted to be absolutely sure, no room for doubts. No misguided lust clouding my thoughts.

Marco adjusted himself over me so our bodies aligned perfectly. His erection pressed between my legs. I was drowning in the heat of him.

I touched his cheek and eased him back after another kiss. He grinned down at me, his eyes so bright with longing that guilt twisted my stomach. The grin faltered when he took in my expression.

"Princess?"

I drew in a shaky breath. "I'm sorry. I don't think I'm ready. Not quite yet."

He couldn't hide the disappointment that darted across his face before he schooled it into his usual cool nonchalance. He nuzzled my hand, his smile coming back. "Ren, I'm not going to push. But you understand why I want you so much, don't you? My lovely Princess of Flames. You have no idea how much you mean to me already."

The soft words brought a flutter into my chest. "You hardly know me," I couldn't help pointing out.

"I know you enough." He bent his head close to mine, not to kiss me but to whisper by my ear. The rich spicy-coffee scent of him filled my nose. My mouth practically watered.

"I know you're the most determined woman I've ever met," he said. "I know you'll do anything to defend the people you love. I know you've got a sharp enough tongue to rival mine sometimes. I've never cared about anyone as much as I care for you. You can take that as a promise."

The flow of his words against my ear left me tingling. He moved above me, and I almost whimpered at the feel of his cock, still hard against me. My fingers gripped his shoulders. He rocked against me gently, sending quivers through my core. It was getting hard to think again. So much of me was screaming for another release.

"And I hope you have at least a few positive feelings about me," Marco added lightly.

"I think that should be pretty obvious," I muttered, but that flippant answer didn't feel good enough. "It's not about you. This whole situation just—it still doesn't feel normal to me. I've never committed to anyone, let alone *four* guys in just a few days. You grew up knowing it'd be like this. I can't wrap my head around the idea that fast."

"I know, princess. I know." He stilled and kissed my cheek. "I'll wait. I just can't help wanting to start our lives together as quickly as possible now that I've found you."

My throat tightened a little at the emotion in those words. "I'll be ready soon," I said. "I'm getting there."

At least, I hoped I was. The feelings in my chest suddenly felt a lot more tangled. Lust was easy. Love... Was I really going to be able to handle giving my whole heart to all four of these guys, as drawn to all of them as I was?

CHAPTER 6

Marco

I'd been through plenty of pain in my life. You named it, I'd probably been there at least once. But I'd never experienced any torture quite as exquisite as waking up next to my mate who still wasn't entirely my mate.

Ren was still sleeping. Her expression was soft and her hair a mess of dark brown waves spilling from the top of the sleeping bag. I wanted to kiss her gently like the angel she looked like—and I also wanted to pull her to me and ravish her until she agreed to finishing what we'd started and come so close to ending last night.

My cock hardened just remembering the feel of her. Her smell flooding my nose, her taste filling my mouth, the little cry she'd made as she came. I could take her even higher than that. All I needed was for her to give me the chance.

It was going to take time for her to come around. That was understandable. What we'd all been waiting for across nearly two decades, she'd only had a few days to process. I was a feline, wasn't I? I knew how to give a person space.

As painful as that space might be.

I stretched on the hard ground, willing my erection to subside. That fae woman—thinking of her was a good mood killer. I'd bet if she touched my dick, it'd shrivel up like a fallen autumn leaf.

There, that did the trick. All cooled down below. I peeled off the sleeping bag and ducked out of the tent.

Nate had a pan sizzling over the fire. We'd brought a good stock of cured bacon, but even though it didn't need cooking, it tasted twice as good fried. The salty, meaty smell tickled into my nose. My stomach grumbled. I wasn't normally much of a hiker, and all this mountain climbing had left me ravenous.

If I couldn't devour Ren the way I wanted, at least I could have my way with breakfast.

"Where's our wolf and eagle?" I asked, sinking down by the fire and stretching out my legs. The smoke curled up toward a small gap in the cave ceiling above us. "And how long until you surrender some of that bacon?"

"You can have it now," Nate said with a hint of a smile. The bear looked more relaxed this morning, even though he'd been up the second half of the night on guard duty. He flipped a couple of strips off the pan with surprising grace and tossed them to me. I snatched them out of the air and dug in. The hot, crispy pork seared my tongue, but the sting was worth it.

"Biscuits," Nate added, tossing over the bag. The doughy lumps didn't appeal half as much as the meat, but they made for good energy at the start of the day. Nate dug into one of his own as he tossed a few more strips of bacon onto the pan. "Aaron and West are taking a quick survey of the area farther down the cave in both directions. Aaron didn't want to be careless after yesterday."

Because of the fae woman or because of the weasel? Both were reason for concern. I tore a biscuit in half and shoved the rest of my bacon inside to form a rough sandwich. In a minute, I'd gulped that down and was reaching for another. Nate gave me a bemused look when I started eyeing the pan again.

"We *all* need to eat," he said. "Ren is still sleeping?"

I nodded. "I figured the princess deserved her beauty rest."

Nate bristled slightly, as if he thought I'd meant that remark as an insult. "She's been holding up well."

"Of course she is," I said, waving him down. Ren had been even less prepared for this kind of physical strain than the rest of us. And she'd shifted into dragon form twice that first day. I'd have let her sleep until noon without judging if I could have. But we did need to get to the end of this journey soon. The biscuits were already getting a tad bitter with staleness.

"West was sleeping by the fire when I got back from sentry duty," Nate said, with a prodding tone. "Instead of in the tent."

I shrugged. "You know how wolf boy is. He's still got issues with our Princess of Flames being anywhere near his personal space."

The canine alpha was an idiot. The mate we'd all been waiting our entire lives for had been right there in front of him, practically begging him to come to her, and he'd turned tail in the opposite direction. He had to want her just as much as I did. I couldn't understand that kind of self-denial at all.

Footsteps sounded on the rocky ground. Aaron came into view, his thoughtful expression perking up at the smell of the food. He ambled over to the fire and grabbed a piece of bacon right out of the pan. Show-off.

I eyed the eagle shifter as he hunkered down by the fire.

What exactly had he done to make Ren choose him first? Choose him—and still hesitate about the rest of us. I was at least that bird-brain's equal.

"No reason for concern up ahead," he said. "At least not from what I saw."

"Not behind us either," West said, emerging from the shadows in the other direction. He flexed his neck with a crack of his joints. "Let's eat and get going. Where's Ren?"

"Coming, coming," a muttered voice carried from the tent. Our dragon shifter pushed past the flap, running her fingers through the rumpled waves of her hair. Even barely awake and dressed in wrinkled clothes, she was the most gorgeous specimen of womankind I'd ever seen. I took her in, enjoying the eyeful.

She lifted her head and sniffed. "Bacon again?"

"Take what you can get, Sparks," West said, his already gruff expression shuttering even more. Yeah, wolf boy had a few issues to work through. Too bad for him. That just left more room for me to make my moves.

Ren ambled over. "Oh, I'm not complaining. I'd eat nothing but bacon for the rest of my life if I wouldn't end up with scurvy." She sat down cross-legged between Aaron and me and hummed happily as Nate passed her a couple strips.

Even the way she crunched into the bacon was sexy enough to get me half hard again. Fuck, this mate-bond thing was brutal. In the most tantalizingly torturous way.

A much less pleasant sensation twisted in my gut. My body stilled. I frowned as my stomach gurgled and roiled. I didn't like the feel of that at all. What was going on with my innards all of a sudden?

"What's wrong, Marco?" Aaron asked, being Mr. Eagle-Eyes.

"Nothing," I said with a dismissive gesture. "Just a little—"

I'd been going to say it was just indigestion. But before I

could get the words out, a feverish flush washed through my body. My stomach outright lurched, heaving up toward my throat. There was nothing I could do but spin around before I vomited the food I'd just eaten onto the ground.

Ren

Marco knifed over with a sickly gurgle. I jumped to my feet, my pulse hiccupping. My fingers dug into the biscuit I'd just taken. The salty flavor of the bacon went sour in my mouth.

The other guys sprang up too. Aaron ran to Marco's side. "I'm fine," the jaguar shifter protested, right before he gagged again, clutching his stomach. West eyed him, his stance rigid. Nate took a step toward him and stopped, his hand falling to his abdomen. A sudden sweat gleamed on his forehead.

"He's not fine," he said. "And I don't think I am either."

"The food," West snapped. He dropped down by the pack we'd filled with our meal supplies, leaning close to take in a deep breath. He smelled the package of bacon, tossed it aside, and reached for the biscuits. As he pressed his nose to the bag's opening, his eyes narrowed. He inhaled again, slow and careful.

"They're tainted," he said.

I hardly had a chance to wonder how or what exactly that meant. Nate barged around the fire and smacked the biscuit I'd been holding from my fingers. I blinked at him, shaking my stinging hand.

"Sorry," he said, his mouth twisting. "I just— I couldn't let you—"

He staggered over to the cave wall and sank down. Aaron's head had jerked toward West.

"What is it? How serious?"

"Some kind of toxin," West said. He pulled out one of the biscuits and broke it open to take another careful sniff. "A natural substance, not artificial. Hard to pick up if you're not looking for it. Which obviously was the point."

"They've been *poisoned*?" I burst out. "What are we going to do?"

"How many of these did you eat?" West asked Marco.

"A couple," Marco muttered. He wiped his mouth, his dark hair slanting over his hooded eyes. He kept his face averted as if ashamed—as if he thought I'd feel anything other than concern and sympathy seeing my mates in this state. My hands balled at my sides.

"I only had one," Nate said by the wall, his voice strained. A shudder ran through his sprawled legs.

"They're not laced very heavily," West said. "To make it harder for us to notice. You're feeling the effects, obviously, but I'd be surprised if it's enough to kill you."

Marco snorted. "Oh, *that's* comforting."

If he could still manage sarcasm, he couldn't be in absolute agony. But he was clearly feeling pretty wretched. His arm was wrapped tight around his belly. I looked from him to Nate, wanting to be with both of them, comforting them, at once. "Who could have done it? Who would have *wanted* to do it? Do you think—that weasel yesterday..."

West grimaced. "There's a faint scent that says mustelid to me. They all have that oily thing going on. I'd say he's our culprit, definitely."

That answered the *why*, at least. The rogues had wanted to attack us any way they could. And we didn't have to worry about more harm from that quarter, because the fae had taken care of that enemy yesterday. But... "*When* could he have done it? We all ate biscuits yesterday morning, and we were fine. They've been in the pack since then, haven't they?"

Aaron nodded. "And it hasn't been out of our sight."

"There were times when we weren't paying a lot of attention to the supplies," Nate pointed out. "While we were packing up the tent. During the lunch stop."

"You'd think we'd have scented the weasel himself if he came that close." West set down the bag of biscuits, his eyes narrowing. "It's almost as if he snuck around us by magic, isn't it?"

Aaron gave him a sharp look. "We're better off not making accusations where we have no proof."

"No," West agreed, straightening up. "But it's something to keep in mind."

Magic. Did he think the fae had helped the weasel shifter get to us? But even if they'd wanted to hurt us, why would they have killed their ally afterward and pretended to be ours?

I wasn't sure if it was safe to ask. The fae woman had said her people were on their way off the mountain, but if they'd resort to poisoning, we obviously couldn't trust anything they'd said. And the way she'd appeared out of nowhere—how could I be sure they weren't listening to our conversation right now?

An eerie prickling ran over my skin.

Marco pushed himself back toward the fire, away from the puddle of sick. Like Nate, he was sweating, his face grayed beneath the gleam of perspiration. His arm wobbled as it supported his weight. But his eyes were mostly clear.

I knelt next to him, gripping his shoulder in a way I hoped showed how much *I* cared about him. "You should rest until you feel better." I glanced over at Nate. "You too. I don't want you making yourselves any *more* sick than you already are."

My gaze moved to Aaron. He was the one who'd spent the most time studying. Maybe he'd gone through some medical books in his reading. "Is there anything we can do to help them recover quickly?"

Aaron's bright blue eyes were solemn. "Every poison has an antidote, but we're pretty short on supplies up here. And we can't be sure of exactly what poison it is. West, we brought the first aid kit from the car, didn't we? Do you have activated charcoal in there?"

West's gloom momentarily lifted. "Probably. We've had issues with drugs among the teen shifters, so we like to keep that on hand in case of an overdose. Let me find it."

As he shuffled through the packs, I went to Nate's side. The bear shifter leaned his head toward me when I touched the side of his rugged face.

"I'll be all right," he said, a little hoarsely. "The poison will just have to run its course."

But we were so much weaker while two of my alphas could barely sit up. I nuzzled his arm, my helplessness tearing me up inside. My mates needed me, and there was nothing I could do. Even my dragon form couldn't burn the poison out of them. And of course Nate had to act all stoic, as if my worrying was a bigger problem than him being fucking *poisoned.*

I gritted my teeth. If that weasel shifter hadn't already been sizzled up by fae magic, I'd have been tracking him down right now. And I wouldn't have stopped to ask questions either. A nice little dragon snack, that's what he'd have turned into.

West hurried over, carrying a jar of black powder. He scooped some onto a small spoon and offered it to Nate. "It tastes like crap, but it'll help pull the poison out of your stomach."

Nate gulped down the powder and made a face. He started to try to push himself onto his feet, and I caught his arm.

"No way. Take it easy for once. I need you getting better, not running yourself into the ground."

He eased back down, but hesitantly. "We shouldn't stay here very long. There were other rogues that got away. They might still be following us."

"Or others who want to do us harm," West murmured darkly.

"And we just lost a significant portion of our food supply," Marco put in. He'd stretched out on his back, his muscled chest rising and falling with halting breaths. "Well, I guess this trek just got a lot more exciting."

CHAPTER 7

Ren

THE OPEN AIR tingled over my wings. I swooped across the mountainside, reveling in the glide of my dragon's body. After so long cooped up in the caves, the sense of freedom made me giddy. Part of me longed to flap those wings as hard as I could and soar all the way around the towering peaks, but I reined my impulses in. I wasn't out here to have fun.

My sharp dragon eyes scanned the rocky terrain again. Aaron had been right to doubt the hunting possibilities up here. I hadn't spotted anything living at this level of the mountain.

He was following me now in eagle form, conducting his own search while keeping me in view. Just in case I lost control of my shift. I didn't exactly *like* having a babysitter, but it was kind of comforting all the same. I hadn't gotten a lot of warning the last two times I'd run out of energy and had to shift back.

I swerved around to glide lower down the slope, to where a few sparse trees and shrubs managed to cling on to the rock. The deepening evening dark hid my immense, scaled form from anyone who might have glanced up from the town below. All I could see of Sunridge was a faintly speckled glow amid the shadowed landscape between the mountains.

While Marco and Nate had been recovering, West, who seemed to have the sharpest nose out of all of us, had gone through the rest of our food stores. Along with the biscuits, we'd had to chuck a bunch of beef jerky and a bag of apples. My precious Doritos were safe, but they weren't going to get us very far.

So while hunting wasn't proving very fruitful, we didn't have much choice but to try. Once we'd started walking again, slower to accommodate the weakened guys, we'd been lucky to find a gap in the ceiling wide enough for my dragon shape to fit through. It'd been a tight squeeze.

My attention jerked back to the present. A shadow had moved amid the sparse brush. A large hare, hopping tentatively from one shrub to the next. Not much of a meal for five, but I'd take what I could get at this point.

I swooped down, extending my forelegs. The hare froze at the sound of my descent. At the last second, it decided running might be a better strategy. Too late. My taloned foot snatched it up, one claw severing its neck to stop it from squirming.

Killing it had been easier than I'd expected. Some natural instinct had taken over. I remembered what West had said the other night after he'd killed a deer. *We're all predators here.* At the time I'd thought he was just talking about the alphas. But he could have meant me too.

I didn't ever want to be *used* to killing things.

My muscles were starting to twitch with the need to let go of this form. I'd held it for a while now, longer than the last two times, but I didn't want to push my luck. I shot up the mountainside toward the crevice I'd emerged through. Aaron circled around after me, a smaller rabbit in his own grasp.

The prickling dug deeper into my muscles. My dragon's jaw clenched. I had to hold on. If I transformed back into human form out here on the mountain slope, totally naked... If we were too far from the cave, even Aaron wouldn't be able to get me back in time before I froze to death. And then there would be no dragon shifters left at all.

I pushed my wings through the air. It no longer felt so exhilarating. I spotted my salvation up ahead. A thin stream of smoke trickled up into the cold evening air. I plunged toward it.

The rough rock edge scraped over my scales as I dove through. I transformed as I fell, hitting the ground on knees already partly human. The impact jarred my bones.

But I still had the hare, its thick fur soft between my clutching fingers.

Nate hustled over with my clothes. The bear shifter was still moving more sluggishly than usual, but he'd regained a healthier color as the day had gone on. The charcoal West had given him and Marco seemed to have helped a lot. I hated to think what might have happened if they'd eaten more of the biscuits. Or if we all had.

I let Nate drape my jacket over my shoulders to fend off the worse of the chill and then tugged the rest of my clothes on as quickly as I could. I was shivering before I was halfway done. I hurried over to the fire, where Nate had already brought the hare and Aaron's rabbit.

My eagle shifter was just pulling on his shirt. The glimpse of his well-muscled chest—seriously, was that an eight-pack?—disappearing under the fabric was enough to send a completely different sort of shiver through me. Okay, now I was warm.

Marco was lounging by the fire, looking a lot less pained now too. But I knew the poison had hit him harder than it had Nate, probably because he'd gotten a bigger dose of it. His mouth still twisted a little when he bent over to grab the granola bar West tossed to him. And his joking didn't have quite the same lightness as it usually did.

"Those rogues had better not mess with us again," he said flippantly. "I *really* have a bone to pick with them now. And a few I'd like to shove into various parts of their body. A nice sharp rib through the gut would be just the thing."

West rolled his eyes. He leaned over to poke at the fire. We were getting low on wood too, I knew. It'd been too heavy for us to carry very much, and we hadn't been able to scavenge any to replenish our supply since we'd entered the caves. Maybe I'd need to make a different sort of trip above ground tomorrow morning.

"They obviously didn't do that much damage to you," West said to Marco. "You're still shooting your mouth off just as much as always."

Marco gave him a baleful look. "It takes a lot more than a couple of tainted biscuits to take down the leader of all feline kin."

"We don't know what they'll try next." Nate dug a knife into the hare's pelt to skin it. "We'll have to stay extra alert on watch tonight."

"Do you really think we have to be worried about... people other than the rogues?" I ventured. I still wasn't sure how wise it was to mention the fae directly. West hadn't done more than insinuate that they might be involved this morning.

Aaron clearly realized what I meant. "There are treaties between all the major supernatural communities," he said. "Attacking the leaders from one community, unprovoked, would bring about major consequences. It would be a huge risk."

"If it could be proven who was involved," West muttered.

"Just make it easier for someone else to do the job, and you can get off scot-free."

"Have relations between the different communities been so bad they'd *want* to get rid of us?" I asked.

Aaron shook his head. "I wouldn't have thought so. It's possible, but West is jumping to the most dire explanation, not the most likely."

"Easy to say when you can just fly on out of here if the going gets that tough, eagle boy," Marco said.

His tone was teasing, but I saw Aaron's jaw twitch. He'd told me a few nights ago how the other kin-groups tended to see the avians as something lesser—and therefore to see him as the least important of the alphas. He didn't buy into that belief, but off-the-cuff comments like that must still carry a bit of a sting. I knew he'd never leave us behind no matter how tough the going got.

"Except he wouldn't," I said. "We're all doing the best we can."

"The best we can would be to get out of this mountain already," West said. "I don't suppose you have any idea how much longer *that* is going to take, Sparks?"

I grimaced at the nickname, but my gut knotted at the same time. I'd still been feeling the internal tug toward whatever was waiting for us—but I had no idea how much farther we had to go. If I could have just raced ahead on my own...

But that would be stupid. And exactly what anyone trying to get rid of me would want. These attacks had always been about the dragon shifters first. The rogues wanted my line eliminated. My alphas had only gotten hurt because they stood in the way.

"It can't be that much farther," I made myself say. "There can't be that much more *mountain*."

"And tomorrow Marco and I should be able to keep up the

usual pace," Nate said. He set the skinned carcasses over the fire. The flames licked up over the meat, sending a mouthwatering roasting scent into the air. "There's no point in stewing over things we can't know. We just prepare as well as we can, and we'll be ready for whatever happens."

I wished I could feel the same easy confidence. I couldn't even be sure of holding a shift for more than ten minutes at a time.

But even if West's question had been a little harsh, he wasn't wrong. The four of them were here because of me, because of this quest Mom had sent me on. If Marco or Nate had gotten more than just sick that would've been on me too.

My fingers itched with nothing around to pilfer. Everything around me was an unappealing target.

Because it was all too close to being mine, I realized. Somewhere during the last few days, my mind had completely adjusted to the idea that the four guys around me and I shared an inexplicable connection, one that made them part of my inner circle—which until now had included only me, my mom, and Kylie. There was no relief in stealing from the people I trusted to be on my side.

The unease stayed coiled in my belly all through dinner. My hunger had faded, but I forced a decent portion of rabbit down, followed by a granola bar, just to keep my energy up.

Marco and West took the first guard shift. I went to help Aaron set up the tent while Nate finished securing the campsite.

As my fingers grazed Aaron's here and there, as he brushed past me to fix one of the poles, another kind of hunger started to well up inside me. The need to feel that connection between us, to remind myself that it was right for them all to be here with me.

When we ducked inside, I took his hand and pulled him

down to sit on top of my sleeping bag with me. He gathered me in his arms and kissed me. In that moment, with his lips parting mine and the heat of his body against me, all my worries faded. I was here, where I was meant to be, with the men I was meant to be with.

I eased us down onto our sides on the padded surface, wanting to feel him against me from head to toe. He hooked his arm around me, his thumb teasing over the bare skin of my back just beneath my shirt. I quivered with pleasure and kissed him harder.

The tent flap rasped. I eased back from the kiss and glanced up. Nate had come in, his tall frame stooped to avoid toppling the tent. Heat flared in his dark brown eyes as he took us in, but he hesitated as if unsure whether to continue forward or head back out.

Suddenly just having Aaron with me didn't feel like enough. I needed more. I needed to be completely wrapped up in the bond of desire and affection that ran between all of us.

I'd almost given in to that urge with Marco and West yesterday. The guys thought it was normal. Why should I hold back?

I drew in a breath and held out my hand.

A smile split Nate's face. He hunkered down at my other side, pressing a kiss to the back of my neck. And just like that, I was surrounded by warmth.

The musky pepper of the bear shifter's scent mingled with the salty tang of my eagle. I inhaled it deeply and pulled Aaron into another kiss.

Two pairs of hands traveled over my body. Two sets of lips marked my skin. Aaron's tongue twined with mine as Nate nipped the crook of my shoulder. The bear shifter looped his arm over me to caress my breasts. Aaron's fingers traced over my waist and tugged my hips closer to his. The bulge of his erection pressed against me, tantalizingly hard. I arched into it with a whimper.

Nate eased up my shirt, and the eagle shifter pulled back to let the other alpha peel it right off of me. Then Aaron made quick work of my bra. I yanked at his own shirt, eager to see the hardened chest I'd only gotten a glimpse of an hour ago. He stripped it off, and Nate did the same with a chuckle behind me. When they both slid closer again, the heat between us, bare skin to bare skin, was outright burning.

Aaron claimed my mouth, cupping my bare breasts at the same time. The peaks pebbled with a single touch. Nate started kissing his way down my spine. Every press of his lips sent an urgent pang of bliss through me. I moaned and squirmed, the desperation for release—any kind, whatever I could get—building inside me.

Nate paused at the small of my back, flicking his tongue over the sensitive skin there. I whimpered encouragingly. Aaron teased my nipples into even stiffer peaks with a swivel of his thumbs. Every sweep of them across those tips stoked the flame of need inside me. Then Nate's hand slipped over my ass and between my legs.

I let out another moan, pressing into his touch. My panties felt soaked through. Could he feel how turned on I was even through my pants?

Aaron dipped his head to suck the tip of my breast into his mouth. Nate stroked my sex. A gasp slipped from my lips. The sensations of their combined attentions were overwhelming, but oh so good.

I rocked my hips, and my clit brushed Aaron's erection. All at once, I couldn't stand the longing anymore. I wrenched at his slacks, fumbling with the button. I yanked the pants partway down. Aaron groaned as I palmed his cock. The silky hard length of him pulsed against my hand.

"Serenity," he murmured. It sounded almost like a question. One I knew the perfect answer to.

"Inside me," I said around another whimper. "*Now.*"

The two guys tugged down my pants together. Aaron rolled me over so I was facing Nate. As the bear shifter leaned in to kiss me on the mouth, my eagle stroked me between the legs from behind as Nate had before. He hummed happily as his fingers tested the moisture there. He dipped them into the hot, slick center of me, and I gasped against Nate's mouth. Then the head of Aaron's cock rubbed over my opening. I shuddered with pleasure, on the verge of losing it already.

He eased inside me with a slow, steady thrust that sent a flare of pleasure through me. I'd never felt so complete as when he filled me. But Nate was still there with me too, kissing me through my moans, caressing my breasts and then reaching down to massage my clit.

Aaron plunged deeper into me from behind, holding my hips to steady them. The pleasure inside me swelled with each pump of his cock and each motion of Nate's hands, until it was almost unbearable. I had to give more of it back.

I groped for Nate's jeans. He undid the fly with one quick movement. His hips jerked toward me as I slipped my hand inside. My fingers closed around his cock, just as hard and even bigger than Aaron's to match the bear shifter's massive frame. I moaned just at the feel of it.

Gripping the silky skin tightly, I slid my hand up and down in time with Aaron's rhythm inside me. Precum beaded on the tip. I slicked it down over his length. Nate groaned and crushed his mouth against mine.

Aaron adjusted our angle so he filled me even more deeply.

His shaft brushed that special spot inside me, and I felt myself careening toward the edge of total bliss. I squeezed Nate even harder, pumping faster, and he bucked his hips toward me. His kisses turned ragged. So did my breath. He rubbed my clit one last time, and my orgasm burst inside me like a firework.

I came apart, clutching Nate's cock, and he followed me. A hot liquid spurt hit my stomach. Then Aaron was coming too, with a few last jerks of his hips. He bit my shoulder as he spilled himself inside me. That mingling of pain and pleasure was enough to send me right back over the edge.

We collapsed against each other, gasping and boneless. Nate brushed the sweat-damp hair from my forehead and pressed a kiss there. "Our dragon shifter," he said, so tenderly my heart started to ache.

Aaron grabbed his sleeping bag and pulled it over us like a blanket. I fell asleep like that, cuddled up between two of my mates, able to forget just for a little while that the hardest part of our journey might lie ahead of us.

CHAPTER 8

Ren

"I THINK WE'RE GETTING CLOSER," I said, and then winced at how stupid that comment sounded. Of course we were getting *closer*, or all this walking was for nothing. What I really wanted to say was that we were *close* now. Over the course of the morning's hike through the cave, the tug inside me had strengthened into a yank. But I wasn't sure enough of what *close* meant to want to risk saying it, in case I was wrong. I could already imagine the look West would give me.

"For a place the fae apparently use as a summer home, it could really use better lighting," Marco said dryly. We'd left the last of the crevices in the ceiling behind a couple hours ago. Now the only light glowing off the rough walls was the beam of the flashlight Aaron was carrying.

"Is that something the fae do a lot?" I asked. It seemed safe enough to ask general questions about them. "Move around between different homes?"

"Not unless they have specific business there," Aaron said. "Each of them usually has an affinity for one particular tree or pond, and their magic is weakened if they're away from it very long."

"If this mountain is special to the dragon shifters, it could have some meaning for the fae too," Nate pointed out.

I thought about that memory I'd had, talking about the fae with Mom. "Have you heard anything about the dragon shifters and the fae... working together, or associating with each other somehow?"

Aaron frowned. "I haven't come across anything referring to a collaboration in the research I've done into our history. But that doesn't mean it never happened. There's plenty the dragons have kept to themselves. Why?"

"Oh, I just remembered my mom saying something about that. But she didn't know any details either, from what she told me." When I wasn't even five yet. How much more might she have shared with me if I'd known the truth when I was older?

The pain of that loss returned with a dull ache. It'd been seven years since I last saw her, but following her trail had made me feel as if she'd only just slipped from my grasp.

"It doesn't matter what dragon shifters might have done once upon a time," West said darkly. "*You* should steer clear of them."

"If they come to the mountain regularly, one of them might have seen my mom while she was here," I pointed out. "Even talked to her."

He shook his head without meeting my gaze. In the dim light, his deep green eyes looked even more shadowed. "It doesn't matter. They won't tell us anything unless they can use it to their advantage over us. Trust me. The only fae I like is one that's at least a hundred miles away. Or dead."

There was a rough note in his voice, beneath the more

typical bitterness. I peered at him from the corner of my eye as we tramped on. He'd obviously had personal dealings with the fae in the past. Dealings that had caused *him* a lot of pain. I wanted to ask more, but I had the feeling he'd bite my head off for prying.

None of the other alphas had argued with him. Even if they didn't have the same hate for the fae, they mustn't have found his comments all that inaccurate either.

I shivered and rubbed my arms through the padded sleeves of my jacket. In that case, I hoped those shiny beings were now far, far away from here too.

"I guess I've got a lot of work ahead of me when we're done all this running around," I said.

Nate stepped closer and took my hand in his large one. The smile he gave me brought back the memories of what we'd gotten up to in the tent last night with a flush of warmth. "We'll be right there beside you, figuring things out together."

West made a wordless noise of dismissal. My temper flared. Why did he have to make it seem as if he was offended by even the slightest suggestion that I was worthy of the role I'd inherited? I'd been hiking up this mountain right along side him. Couldn't he cut me a little slack?

"So what exactly are you planning on doing if you throw away tradition and any hope of making this mate thing work, Mr. Wolf Man?" I demanded. "Split off the canine shifters from the rest of the shifter community? That doesn't sound like it's going to help anyone."

West finally turned his penetrating gaze on me. "I don't think you know enough about our community to have any idea what will help or not. When we're finished this ridiculous questing, maybe I'll get to see what you're really made of as a dragon shifter."

Maybe you should open your eyes, because I've shown you plenty already.

I bit back the snappy retort, swallowing hard. West wanted me to argue with him. Wanted me to give him excuses to keep antagonizing me. As if it were *my* fault that my mother hadn't taught me anything about the shifters. Or that the rogues had slaughtered my fathers and sisters to force us into going on the run in the first place.

Another memory, a fragment from long, long ago, rose up, so vivid the rest of the cave fell away. I was sitting on my mother's lap while she brushed my hair, which was knotted from a scramble through the woods with my sisters. She tsked her tongue as she worked through a tangle.

"You're lucky I believe in letting children run a bit wild. Otherwise we'd have rules about rolling down hillsides and dangling from trees."

My four-year-old self looked up at her with wide eyes. "You could do that, couldn't you? You get to make the rules for all the shifters."

Mom laughed gently. "Not exactly. Not all by myself. Your fathers and I decide what's best for the community together."

"Indeed we do," my mountain lion shifter father had said, sauntering into the room. My other dads followed him. They stood around my mother and me, enveloping both of us in an aura of familial love.

In the present, I blinked hard at the tears that had started to well in my eyes. My throat had tightened. So much the rogues had stolen from me. I'd barely gotten to know my fathers at all. How much would *they* have taught me?

But I knew how much they'd loved my mother. That was what the mate-bond between the alphas and their dragon shifter was meant to look like.

I raised my chin, pushing down the pang of loss. If West really believed I'd be a total disaster, he wouldn't still be here. He'd have forsaken me as his mate and taken off to find one he liked better. I just had to keep reminding myself of that.

Aaron's flashlight beam caught on a claw-shaped scar on the wall up ahead. A deeper scrape than Mom had left before. For a second I wasn't sure if this one had been made by her or something else, but as soon as I came up beside it, her energy tickled over my skin. The sense of her presence—and a thicker emotion. I let go of Nate's hand to touch the marks, and a jab of distress jolted through my body.

I paused, my fingers twitching toward my palm as if echoing the sweep of her talons. She'd been upset when she'd scratched this mark. In pain or afraid. What had happened to her here? How had anyone even known she'd come up this way? She'd been so good at covering her tracks...

Nate hovered behind me. "What's the matter, Ren?"

"My mother," I said. "When she came through this part of the cave, something was wrong. She was upset. But I can't feel why."

"I don't see how we can get much more careful than we already are," Marco said. "Whatever comes, we'll handle it, princess. She shouldn't have had to come up here alone."

No, she shouldn't have. I bit my lip, but I forced myself to keep walking. The sooner we got to the end of this journey, the sooner I'd know what had happened to her. At least, I sure hoped so. If all it led to was another clue to follow, my dragon fire might come out in frustration.

That end might be coming up even sooner than I'd guessed. The light caught on a bend in the passage. As we came around it, the tug inside me yanked even harder than before. I stumbled, losing my breath. The second I caught my balance, my feet darted forward across the uneven ground, as if pulled from my control. I knew I could rein them in if I'd wanted to—but I didn't really.

"We're almost there. It has to be close now," I said.

The guys picked up their pace too. Light twinkled above us. I glanced up, thinking we must have come under another crevice to the outside world. Instead I saw crystalline stalactites glinting overhead, reflecting the artificial glow. A faint vibration emanated off them, quivering into my skin. Making me even more energized.

Almost there. Almost there.

I adjusted my pack's straps on my shoulders and pushed myself into a lope. That pull was reeling me in as if I were a fish on a line, but I was totally okay with that. I was ready for this trek to be done.

So it was my fault, really, that I was at the head of our procession at that moment. My fault that it was my feet the ground trembled under. I slowed as an eerie creaking sound resounded through the cave. The rock beneath my feet felt suddenly insubstantial, as if I'd stepped out onto a thinly frozen lake.

And then it cracked, exactly like the ice I'd just been picturing.

The ground fractured and started to fall away. My shifter reflexes kicked in not a second too soon. I threw myself forward.

The creaking rose into a full-bodied groan that reverberated through the cave. The pack dragged at my shoulders. Each time my feet hit the ground, the rock kept crumbling. I scrambled on. There was nothing I could do but run and hope I found a solid spot before I fell too.

My foot slipped, and I nearly crashed onto my knees. With a yelp, I heaved my body through the air as far as I could manage.

I stumbled, caught my balance—and realized the ground had steadied.

"Ren!" someone shouted behind me, and someone else said, "She's okay, let her get her bearings." I turned cautiously, not quite trusting the stone beneath me yet. My jaw went slack.

Between me and my alphas, some ten feet of the cave floor had dropped away into a jagged chasm. I was standing just a couple feet from its edge.

I crept closer to peer into its depths. Nothing but darkness showed below. It was so deep I hadn't even heard the clatter of the crumbling rock hitting the bottom.

I'd almost hit that bottom. My stomach knotted. If I'd reacted any slower...

"Are you all right, Ren?" Nate called to me.

I nodded, still lost for words.

Marco gave an exasperated chuckle. "Because we really needed more excitement on this trip. All right, I'm not jumping that *with* luggage. Good thing we didn't pack anything breakable."

He shrugged off his pack and tossed it over the chasm. It landed with a thump. The other guys followed suit. I thought they might strip down to take the leap in their animals forms—possibly I was looking forward to that view—but I guessed shifter strength made the jump not too much of a challenge even in human bodies. Two at a time, they took a running start and sprang across the chasm.

Nate's brawny body hit the ground near me with a thud, and one last creak carried through the cave. The hairs on the back of my neck rose. I studied the edges of the chasm in the dim light as the guys dusted themselves off.

"How did that even happen?" I said. "It doesn't make sense.

A big gap like this wouldn't just *appear* with a tiny bit of rock over top. It's almost like it was..."

"A trap?" West filled in. "How long did it take you to figure that out, Sparks?"

I glared at him, but Aaron spoke up before my tongue got away from me. "It was definitely purposefully constructed. You said you could feel we're almost at the place your mother wanted you to reach, Serenity. A place that holds some kind of important power. It's possible there's magic protecting that place and the 'trap' was meant as a test of worthiness or determination."

"Or it's possible we've got some magical 'friends' unhappy we didn't die of poison," Marco said. "I'm starting to come around to wolf boy's point of view, as much as it pains me to admit that."

"Is there any way to tell what kind of magic was used?" I asked. Fae or otherwise.

Aaron shook his head. "It would have been beneath the layer of rock, holding it in place. So it fell away at the same time." He glanced at me. "But we made it past. You kept your head and got yourself out of there. Whatever power your mother wanted you to have, no one's going to stop you from getting to it, are they?"

"No," I said with a fresh burst of resolve. "So let's get a move on before we have to deal with anything worse."

CHAPTER 9

Nate

As I HEFTED my heavy pack from where I'd tossed it across the chasm, a splinter of pain shot through my chest down to my gut. I set my jaw, trying not to let the discomfort show on my face.

Even with all the rest I'd gotten yesterday and the slow pace we'd set after, the poison was still in my system. Still making me weaker than I should have been. I hated it. We might have gotten all the way to the end of this cave yesterday if we could have kept up our usual pace. Hell, if I'd noticed the off smell in the biscuits when I'd first grabbed one, I could have stopped Marco from eating them too.

I'd been complacent, and my mate was suffering because of it.

Ren was taking it all in stride. She adjusted her own pack against her back and smiled at me when she caught me looking at her. That quick gesture warmed me even with the twist of pain and guilt in my gut. Remembering her hands on me last night, her soft sighs of pleasure, the sweet taste of her skin...

Okay, that line of thinking wasn't going to help her either. Someone was out to sabotage our journey here—to kill us if they could. They'd literally torn the ground out from under us. I had to stay focused on the present, on defending Ren from our enemies. How could I be worthy of our mate-bond if I didn't?

If I'd waited all this time only to lose her now... I couldn't stand that thought. It made me feel sicker than the poison had.

Marco shot one last glance down the chasm and sauntered over. "I say we send bear boy ahead from here on," he said in his annoyingly jaunty tone. "If the floor holds under all that bulk, the rest of us won't need to worry."

West snorted. I glowered at Marco. "I'm happy to take the lead if you're a scaredy cat."

"Ooh," he said, grinning. "The bear got in a burn. Not bad, Nate."

Ren rolled her eyes. "Come on, guys. *I'll* take the lead if the rest of you are going to stand around debating it."

She moved to set off, and I strode ahead of her. For the first few steps, I wasn't aware of much except the need to assert my intentions and Marco's mocking chuckle. Then a faint scent reached my nose that didn't fit the cold rock around us.

I stopped, holding out my arm. "Stay back. Something's not right."

West came up beside me as I inhaled again. His wolf's nose was the strongest out of all of us, but I could hold my own in that area when I concentrated. A faintly musky smell lingered in the air—something living. Something animal.

And we hadn't seen a single animal since we'd descended into this cave, other than our glimpse of that weasel the fae had taken care of.

"You're right," West said with a frown. He stalked a little farther ahead, scanning the cave around us. I wasn't going to be left behind. I followed him, testing the air myself. If anything, the scent got fainter. I turned and paced back the way we'd come. Ren watched me, her brow knit with concern. My stomach twisted tighter, seeing her worry.

"It's strange," I said. "It's strongest right around here. Whatever animal left that smell, it must have stopped here for a while. But then where did it go? We didn't pass anything on our way here."

"There's nothing I can pick up farther this way," West said from the spot where I'd left him. "It's so faint I can't get a clear read on it. Maybe it's old."

He sounded doubtful, probably because it didn't smell stale to him any more than it did to me. The faintness was more as if it'd been washed over somehow to try to remove the scent, with just a few lingering traces remaining. And that would mean someone had tried to cover their scent trail on purpose, so we wouldn't catch on. My shoulders tensed. You couldn't get much more suspicious than that.

"Can you tell what kind of animal it was?" Aaron asked.

I shook my head. It didn't really matter. If even a little weasel could pose a threat, we couldn't trust anything.

"We should walk close together," I said, motioning the other alphas over. "All of us around Ren, so there's no way anyone can get at her without going through us. If the rogues are planning another ambush, we have to be ready."

"I don't need a human shield," Ren protested. "Why don't we just—"

With a snarl, a blur of fur shot through the air toward her from the wall above. A bellow of warning broke from my throat.

I leapt in front of my mate, pushing her backward and bracing myself to shift to meet the threat.

~

Ren

The force of Nate's shove sent me stumbling back toward the wall. I gritted my teeth, feeling my dragon wake up with a scrabble of claws in my chest. *No* one got to push me around, not even my mates.

What the hell was even happening? The flashlight had fallen after the snarl I'd heard. Its light rotated around the cave as it spun. It caught on Nate, already shifted into his grizzly bear form. He was trying to pin down a spotted wildcat that had come out of nowhere. It kept squirming out from under his paws. Aaron's eagle dove down to add his talons to the mix.

Across from them, West's wolf and Marco's jaguar were facing off with a big, black weasel-like creature my mind vaguely registered as a wolverine. It hissed and snapped at them with razor-sharp fangs.

Nate gave the wildcat a smack as it clawed at him. The impact sent it careening over the edge of the chasm. The last I heard was a feline shriek as it plummeted into the depths.

A harsh pant of breath behind me made me spin around. Not a second too soon. A coyote lunged at me, teeth snapping at my throat. I barely managed to dodge out of the way before it took a chunk out of me.

The coyote's lashing paws scraped across my arm, drawing blood through the sleeve of my jacket. It landed and whipped around with a gnash of its teeth. The flare of anger inside me grew hotter, and not just for myself. Back in the shifter village, two coyotes had savaged Kylie while their wolfish leader had attacked me. I had no doubt at all that this asshole was one of them.

I clasped hold of that fiery fury and wrenched it free. My body burst from its clothes, expanding into dragon form.

The coyote flinched back with a startled whine as I loomed over it. Fire bubbled up my throat. I opened my mouth to fry the attempted murderer back to kingdom come—

—and Nate charged between me and the coyote. The grizzly was only half as tall as my dragon's body, but he managed to block my aim completely.

I swung my sinewy neck, determined to take a snap at my attacker. Nate growled from deep in his chest and tackled the coyote first. They rolled, biting and swiping. I clenched my jaw, knowing I couldn't bring out the flames without roasting my bear alpha too.

Damn it. Why couldn't he let me handle one thing by myself?

I swung around to check on the other guys, my scaled shoulders brushing the cave wall. There wasn't much room for me to maneuver in here.

The wolverine was just making a dash between West and Marco. Marco cut it off at the last second, battering its eyes with both paws and heaving it onto its side. West leapt over with a snap of his teeth.

Aaron dove down, placing a threatening set of talons over the wolverine's neck. He meant to trap it in the hopes it would shift back into human state so they could question it, I had to guess. But the wolverine wasn't willing to face that consequence.

With a grunt, it wrenched its head up, stabbing the eagle's claws through its neck. Blood gushed out. Its furred body slumped. Aaron gave a cry and flapped away.

Nate pounded the coyote's head against the ground with one thick paw. The nimbler animal shuddered and scrambled away. I lunged toward it, smoke curling through my mouth.

My dragon's gaze locked with the coyote's. A totally human panic flashed through its eyes. I hesitated, wondering if there was some way I could restrain it without killing it. Before I could think of one, the coyote hurled itself over the edge of the chasm. It plummeted out of sight after its ally.

I stared at the gap, hot breath rasping in my throat. My hold over my dragon form trembled. I let myself collapse back into my human body.

The frigid air closed in around me again with a prickling ache. I scrambled for my jacket, the only thing I'd managed to cast off before I'd gotten far into the shift. The rest of the clothes I'd been wearing were shredded. I tugged the jacket around me, wincing as it brushed over the scratches on my arm. My shifter body would heal them quickly, but not *that* fast.

The guys were all shifting back too. My eyes caught on a blotch like a scar on West's leanly muscled chest that glowed with a faint reddish light. Then my gaze dropped to the limp body of a middle-aged man with a wiry beard that lay where the wolverine had died. Blood pooled around his head and shoulders.

Marco nudged the corpse's leg with his foot and grimaced. "So much for getting some answers out of these assholes."

My mind leapt back to the coyote flinging itself to its death. My stomach clenched. "They decided it was better to die than be caught. The rogues are pretty dedicated to their cause, aren't they?" Their cause, which was seeing me and any other dragon shifters that might be left dead.

Another thought struck me with a deeper horror. "They must have something to protect, then, right? There must be other rogues out there with other plans. Why else would it matter if we questioned them?"

"They could have been too ashamed of what they've gotten themselves involved with to want to face the consequences," Aaron said. "But you're probably right. We can't assume the rogue threat is finished." He glanced around. "I hope that's the last we see of them on this mountain, though."

"There weren't very many that survived the ambush," West said, already pulling his shirt over the strange scar I'd noticed. "What I want to know is where they came *from.* It looked like they practically fell from the ceiling."

I stepped closer to the wall, peering up at it. Aaron picked up the fallen flashlight and pointed it where I was staring. A slice of deeper shadow cut into the rock just below the ceiling.

"There's a ledge up there," I said. "They got up there somehow. Trying to stage another last ditch ambush." I guessed we were just lucky I'd melted all the guns this group had during their first attack.

"*Somehow,*" West repeated. "Yeah, I wonder about that. Maybe the same 'somehow' that created the trap in the floor?"

"It doesn't matter now," Nate said firmly. "What matters is getting to the power Ren's mother pointed us to, and then getting Ren out of here before anyone else comes after us."

He strode over to me, his head high as if he saw himself as some kind of knight in shining armor. The anger I'd felt earlier flickered back up.

"Getting us *all* out," I said. "I don't need special treatment. And I *really* don't need to be treated like a weakling."

Nate blinked "What are you talking about?"

I waved my hand toward the chasm. "You were so busy trying to 'protect' me a few minutes ago that you got in my way when I was about to blast that coyote to bits."

His expression tensed. "It's our job as your mates to—"

"No," I said, cutting him off. There was no room for argument here. Either he accepted my point or he didn't. "From what I've heard, it's your job to stand beside me. Not in front of me, like I'm some wimp who needs to be sheltered. I can shift now. I can shift into a freaking dragon." I pointed to the bite mark on his arm. "If you hadn't run in there, you wouldn't have had to get hurt. I could have handled it *better* than you did."

The stiffness left Nate's face, leaving only a stunned blankness. "Ren," he said, his voice quieting. "I didn't mean— Of course I know how strong you are."

My anger eased off. I knew he hadn't meant to offend me. "Okay," I said. "Then treat me like you know it. I'm not a china doll. Go ahead and look out for me—but let me look out for you too. That's how it's supposed to be, isn't it?"

He inclined his head, a faint flush of shame coloring his cheeks. Marco cleared his throat. "If we're done with the dressing down, deserved as it might be, can we get moving? I'm liking this vacation less and less with every new development."

"No kidding." I turned toward the passage ahead. A glimmer caught my eye, there and then gone. My heart leapt. "I think it's almost over."

CHAPTER 10

Ren

As MUCH AS I wanted to run through the cave toward the beckoning glimmer, I held my legs in check this time. I didn't want to be caught unprepared by another booby trap. But the tug dragged at my chest and that hint of light called to me, propelling me onward as fast as I'd let myself walk.

The light brightened as we got closer, but it didn't expand. I realized why soon enough. The passage ahead of us narrowed into a slit so thin Nate was going to have to walk sideways to squeeze through it. The light was emanating from beyond it.

As I stepped through the opening, the light flared so bright that my vision filled with white. It didn't sting my eyes, though, only filled them with a faintly tingle.

I blinked the brilliance away. I'd come into a large, round room where the stone walls and floor were completely smooth. A pedestal stood in the center of the room. A clear crystal nearly the size of my head rested in its rocky hold. The light and a faint warmth glowed from within the crystal. The glimmer danced like a flame as I stared at it.

The tug inside me had fallen away. This was where it'd been leading me to. This was where I was meant to be.

I eased forward with a few careful steps. Shapes were carved into the pedestal's base. I bent down to examine them, holding my breath in awe.

The etchings showed the forms of dragons and other figures that looked almost human. But not quite. They were a little too tall and a little too slim to look exactly right. Like the fae woman we'd met below in the caves—like the fae man I'd seen my mother talking to.

The dragons and the fae stood side by side, sometimes touching, sometimes facing one another. In one depiction, a fae figure sat astride on a dragon's back. There was little detail to the faces, but all of the pictures gave me a friendly vibe.

I brushed my fingers over the fine grooves in the stone. "I think this must be something the dragon shifters and the fae created together," I said. "And that must have been a very long time ago, if there's no record of them spending time together."

Aaron nodded, coming up behind me. I circled the pedestal to give him room, and my gaze fell on not just pictures but words carved into the other side.

Between fae and draco, a power we birth, to give the clearest sight. To be taken in a time when no other power can set the world right.

A shiver ran through me, reading the words. Above them, the images showed a figure lifting the crystal, then dropping it. In the last etching, a jagged flare exploded up from it over the figure.

That was what I had to do? *Smash* that crystal? I wasn't even sure what this power *was*. And the thought of even touching the glowing crystal made me nervous.

It had been waiting here for centuries. Was it really meant for *me*?

Mom had thought so. She'd made it almost this far. From what she'd said in her vision, she must have intended to bring the crystal back for me to take its power. All those trips away from home, I had to assume she'd been checking up on the shifter community. Seeing how they were getting by without us. What she'd seen, the disarray the alphas had told me about, had driven her here. To this desperate measure.

Maybe in a time when all the supernatural communities were in conflict, when rogue shifters had succeeded in nearly eliminating dragon-kind, we did need to turn to something greater.

It didn't matter what I was getting into. We'd come this far. I had to take this final step, or the whole journey had been for nothing.

West stalked around the room warily, but he didn't make any comment. Marco ambled over beside me to read the words for himself. Nate stayed by the door as if standing guard—and maybe also keeping a little distance from me after my outburst. I didn't regret anything I'd said, but I could feel his unhappiness from across the room. It pained me.

As soon as I got this over with, we could move on. And no one would be able to claim I wasn't powerful enough to hold my own.

I felt all of my alpha's eyes on me as I lifted the crystal from the pedestal. The faceted surface was glossy and hard as glass, but even warmer than the air around it. I gave in to the urge to hug it to my chest. The flickering heat licked over me, beckoning. Wanting to reach all the way into me.

My heart thumped. I raised the crystal to the level of my forehead. The light inside sparkled with a rainbow of colors. My chest tightened. I braced myself and dashed the crystal on the stone floor by my feet.

Light exploded up over me with an even sharper rush of heat. A searing energy rippled through my skin and into my bones. My pulse stuttered, and my mouth went dry. Hell, that was intense.

The energy flared right over my eyes from the inside out. The room around me faded into a gleaming haze. Through that haze, a silhouetted figure emerged.

"Greetings, worthy one," she said as the thrumming energy wrapped tighter and tighter around me. "The flame of truth is yours. Burn to destroy or burn away lies to get at what is real: The choice will be yours. Now go forward!"

She vanished into the light. The energy contracted into me with a jolt. Its burning ran all the way through my chest, prickling but not outright painful.

The haze in my eyes started to clear—but I couldn't see the guys standing around me. Within the fading light, another vision appeared.

My mother strode into the room. My heart leapt, but then I noticed that she looked just as she had in my other vision of her from seven years ago. The same clothes, the same age. This was the past, not the present.

Her hair was rumpled and her cheeks smudged, but her eyes gleamed with determination. Her gaze settled on the crystal—the image of it that had reappeared as part of this vision.

"There," she whispered, as if hesitant to disturb the peace of this space. She stepped toward the pedestal—toward the spot where I stood beyond it. I swallowed hard, clenching my hand against the impulse to reach out to her.

She couldn't see me. This had all already happened. But she seemed so close.

Mom extended her hands toward the crystal. Her fingers were just about to close around it when something made her head jerk around. I hadn't heard anything, but the vision didn't seem to contain any sound at all. Just the rush of energy pulsing past my ears.

All at once, a crowd of other figures poured into the room as if straight out of the walls. At least a dozen slim, shimmering fae. One of them rushed between Mom and the pedestal. He shoved her backward with a spark of magic. His lips moved, but I couldn't make out the words.

Mom said something back—something angry, from the flash in her eyes. One of the other fae shook his head. A fae woman stepped forward with a sweep of her arm toward the doorway.

My mother's jaw tightened. I felt her starting to shift before her body had even twitched with the beginnings of the transformation. But the fae felt it too. At the same time, several of them, all around her, hurled glinting blasts of magic at her.

The blasts hit Mom with a burst of sparks. She staggered, faltering in her attempt to shift. With her arms raised defensively, she whirled around, but the fae were already whipping more of their glittering magic toward her. It smacked into her body, driving her to her knees.

A cry caught in my throat. My legs burned to run to her, as if I could help. I tried to shift them, and my feet stuck to the floor. There was nothing I could do but stand here and watch this piece of history play out.

Mom wasn't beaten yet. She pushed herself to her feet and lunged at one of the fae. Her face started to transform, scales dappling her skin, a flicker of dragon fire darting from her mouth.

The fae woman winced, but there were too many others. Before Mom could shift any farther, they caught her in another crashing wave of magic.

She fell again, this time onto her side. Her chest shuddered as she tried to breathe. Her lips moved with more words I couldn't hear. Then the fae man who'd blocked her way to the pedestal stepped closer. He clapped his hands and threw a spike of shimmering energy straight at Mom's head.

She crumpled, her body slumping against the floor. I choked on a sob. The fae looked at each other, a resolved expression crossing all their faces. One by one, they raised their hands over Mom's form. One stream of light, and then another, and then another, poured down at her.

The edges of her body shimmered, and then slowly started to disintegrate. My stomach turned. I couldn't stand still any longer. It didn't matter that this horrible moment was already done and over, seven years past. I *had* to stop this.

The muscles in my legs bunched to wrench my feet from the floor with every shred of strength in me, to run to her—but my joints locked. A vise seemed to clamp around my lungs.

You must watch, a faint voice echoed in the back of my head. *Watch and witness.*

So I did. I watched, my eyes getting hotter and hotter, as the fae's magic ate away at my mother's body. I longed to look away, to not have to see this slow destruction, but at the same time it did feel as if it was my duty to witness it. To acknowledge what had become of my mother—and who had done it to her.

When her body had completely faded away, the fae stepped back. The man who seemed to lead them had his mouth set in a grim line, but he brushed his hands together as if this had been nothing more than a brief bit of work. They wisped away into the walls again.

The vision fell away from me. The room came back into focus. My legs wobbled, and I clutched at the pedestal to keep my balance.

Marco and Aaron, still close by, each clasped one of my shoulders. Their presence steadied me, but my eyes were already full of tears. I inhaled with a hitch.

"What happened?" Nate said, moving from the doorway. "For a few minutes there, you looked like you were in another world."

"I saw what happened here seven years ago," I said. My voice came out hoarse. I cleared my throat and forced out the rest of the words. "They killed her. The fae killed my mother."

CHAPTER 11

Ren

Aaron's eyes widened at my declaration. Marco squeezed my shoulder tighter, but I didn't want comfort right now. I wanted answers.

I pulled away from him, striding to the wall. One of the walls the fae had emerged from in my vision. I swiped my arm across my teary eyes and raised my voice in a ragged shout. "You! Fae! Where are you? Stop lurking around and come out of there. Own up to what you did, you fucking assholes. Don't you dare hide away and pretend you don't know—"

My voice cut off with a growl of frustration. I lashed out at the rock, my dragon's talons already protruding from my fingers. They gouged the wall, but I didn't get any satisfaction from that act of destruction. The fae hadn't emerged. Fucking cowards. More than a dozen of them ganging up on one woman, battering her until she couldn't even stand...

My jaw clenched. "Serenity," Aaron started, but I felt

anything but serene. I whipped around, tossing off my jacket. If the fae wouldn't come to me, I'd just have to track them down and *make* them pay.

My muscles twanged as my body shifted fully into dragon form. I filled nearly half of the room. The pedestal suddenly looked tiny. I stalked around it, my nostrils flaring.

There. A faint scent remained under the cold rock smell. Like cut grass mixed with sleet. I'd never noticed that odor before, but every instinct in me told me it was the fae. I inhaled deeply, trying to follow the trail, and paused.

I could tell it was fae—and I could also tell it was old. Stale. My dragon senses suggested the scent had been left days ago. Maybe the fae woman who'd told us about the weasel and her companions had passed through here.

I let myself shrink back to near human size to dash through the narrow entryway. Then I prowled down the length of the cave back in dragon form. I tasted the air on my tongue, dragged more into my massive lungs.

Not a hint of fresh fae scent reached me. They were nowhere around. The bastards really had just left.

With a growl of frustration, I collapsed back into my human self. The stone floor chilled my bare skin, but I didn't care. I pulled my knees up to my chest and pressed my face to them, holding in a sob. Tears drew frigid streaks down my legs.

Mom was gone. She'd been gone for seven years, and I'd known all that time she might be dead, but now it was completely real. There was no hoping for any other outcome.

I didn't want to accept it. She'd come here for me. Because she'd wanted to give me all the power she could, so I could take this role as leader of all shifter-kind. Because she hadn't wanted to put *me* in danger by bringing me with her. Maybe if we'd been together, if I'd known what I was then...

Footsteps scraped over the floor. One of the guys draped my jacket over my shoulders. They all gathered in a semi-circle around me.

"I knew we couldn't trust the fae," West muttered. "They helped the rogues, set us up every way they could."

"Quite the strategy," Marco said. "Make it look like we were taken down by our own kind so they couldn't get in trouble over breaking the treaty. Very sneaky. I'd almost admire their wiles if they hadn't been using them against me."

"I don't think this is the time for jokes," Nate said, with a frown I could hear.

Aaron knelt down in front of me. When I raised my head to meet my mate's eyes, he rested his hand over mine. His expression was solemn. "We won't let this stand," he said. "The fae committed a crime, and they'll answer for it."

"How?" I asked in a croak. My throat felt thick with unshed tears.

"When we come down from the mountain, the first thing we'd have done anyway is visit the centers of the shifter community to spread the word that you've been found and taken on your role as dragon shifter. We can start with the avian estate, since it's the closest to here and our mate-bond is already consummated—and because the monarch of the fae has her domain only a short distance away. We'll bring the matter straight to her."

"Isn't there something else we need to talk about first?" Marco said. "What happened with that crystal? Your mom came all the way up here for a reason, princess—what's this power she wanted you to have?"

I reached my awareness through the ache of grief inside me and the soreness of my overworked muscles. Nothing inside me felt all that different. *The flame of truth*, that strange figure had called it when I'd smashed the crystal. *Burn to destroy or burn away lies.*

My lungs tickled at the thought of breathing fire. Could I produce a different kind of flame now? I didn't think I could even manage to shift back into my dragon form after two transformations in such close succession. My endurance still had a ways to go.

"I'm not totally sure," I said. "It has something to do with my dragon fire and with finding the truth. The flame inside the crystal is what showed me what happened to my mother. Somehow I'm supposed to be able to use it to get at what is real? But it didn't come with an instruction manual or anything."

Wouldn't it have been nice if it had. I guessed, like everything else since my life had taken this crazy turn, I'd just have to figure it out as I went along.

"That sounds useful, given how things have been going," Nate said. "You'll be able to tell who to trust."

"Once I figure out how to use it." I gave my eyes another swipe and pushed myself onto my feet. My loss still weighed heavy on me, but I had my four alphas to protect now, even as they protected me. I had a whole community of shifters to look after.

And the fae who'd killed my mother were still out there, committing who knew what other crimes against us.

"All right," I said. "Let's get off this mountain, and then I want a meeting with the fae monarch."

I lifted my head at the smell of salt seeping into the SUV. We were coming up on the coast. Which meant coming up on the estate by the Pacific Ocean where Aaron oversaw the avian kin-group.

Today I was going to *meet* that kin-group as his mate and one of their leaders. My skin itched at the thought. I curled tighter into the back seat and looked at my phone again. Kylie had just replied to my last text.

I wish I could be there with you, Ren. You shouldn't have to deal with news like that without your bestie. I know how much your mom meant to you.

I wish you were here too, I wrote back. The one comfort of getting off the mountain had been getting my cell phone service back. Although there was still a lot I wasn't sure how to tell Kylie. It was easier to go back to joking around. *You're just sad you're missing out on all the eye candy.*

Hey, they're your mates! I don't mess around with taken guys. But you can't blame a girl for enjoying the view. She added a winking emoji. *Are you handling it okay? Is there anything you want me to send from here?*

I considered, but we'd only just moved into our apartment. I hadn't exactly accumulated a lot of possessions during my years living on the streets. Part of me longed to snuggle up under the crocheted blanket we'd spread on the back of the used couch we'd scored and feel that familiarity of home again. But I had other things to take care of first.

It wasn't just the avian estate up ahead. The fae monarch's domain lay nearby too.

I hadn't told Kylie about that part of this trip. Hadn't even told her what I'd seen of my mom's death, only that I'd seen it. If she knew I was about to go confront a bunch of murdering magical beings, she'd *really* freak out.

What was the point in worrying her when she was too far away to help?

"Are we there yet?" Marco called from the seat ahead of me with a mock-childish voice. I gently kicked the seatback, and he shot an amused smile my way.

Aaron chuckled where he was sitting at the front in his usual spot as navigator. "Almost. Why are cats always so restless?"

"Because we know we have so much to contribute to the world, and can't stand to be held back," Marco declared. He propped his feet against the driver's seat in front of him.

Nate, who was sitting in that seat, made a gruff sound of dismissal. "I don't remember you contributing a whole lot to *this* trip, other than picking out the most expensive dishes at the restaurant last night."

Marco waved him off. "I just spent a week on a mountain eating non-perishables. Including food that was outright poisoned. We *all* deserved a good meal after that."

No one looked at me as he said that, but I felt the shift in attention all the same. All of the guys except West had offered to keep me company in the back seat, but I'd told them I wanted a little time to myself to think and chat with Kylie. I knew they were still worried about my reaction to finding out about Mom's death. I hadn't wanted to eat a whole lot in the restaurant, true. I just wanted to get out here and see some justice done.

As if he'd picked up on that thought, Aaron directed his voice toward me. "As soon as we arrive, I'll send one of my people to arrange an audience with the fae monarch. It shouldn't take long for her to respond."

"And I'm sure they'll be so happy to entertain us," West grumbled where he was sitting beside Marco.

I ignored him. "Thank you," I said to Aaron.

The salt smell in the air thickened. The SUV pulled up to a wrought-iron gate set in a high stone wall. My pulse kicked up a notch. Instinctively, I slipped my hand into my pocket to squeeze Mom's locket. The solid metal made me feel slightly more grounded.

I think I'd better say my good-byes for the moment, I texted to Kylie. *It looks like I'm just about there.*

Go be the best dragon shifter queen they've ever seen! she replied.

I smiled, but as I put away my phone, I didn't feel at all queenly. I was wearing a tee and jeans and no make-up, my body was still sore from all that hiking up and down the mountain. I had no idea what to even expect from a shifter estate.

Aaron had explained that the kin-groups each had a sort of center of operations, the avians in the northwest, the canines in the northeast, the felines in the southeast, and the assorted group Nate ruled over in the southwest. The alphas traveled throughout the country as they needed to, but they met with their advisors and kept their records on the estate. Any shifter who needed help could always show up there and know they'd be taken care of.

The dragon shifters had an estate too—one that had been left vacant for sixteen years. Right smack in the middle of the country, so it didn't favor any of the kin groups over the others. That was where my entire family had been when the rogues had launched their first attack.

My gut twisted at the thought of going back to that place. I had happy childhood memories from my first five years, growing up there... but my last memories of the house and the grounds around it were full of violence and panic.

Trills of music filtered through the sides of the van. I peered out the window. A huge mansion had just come into view up ahead. All its windows shone with inner light amid the deepening evening. White marble columns framed the double doors, and sculptures of bird-like figures clustered along the eaves of the angled roof.

The trees lining the drive leading up to the mansion were

strung with sparkling lanterns. A massive courtyard lay between the forested grounds and the mansion's broad front steps. In that courtyard, a swarm of figures had gathered. They were whirling in time with the music, swinging lights of their own.

Then someone must have caught sight of the SUV. A cheer rose up. The dancers stilled to watch our arrival.

Aaron glanced back at me. "My kin are all looking forward to meeting you," he said. "They wanted to make your first visit here special."

I hugged myself, trying to contain my nerves. These shifters wanted to like me. I was their alpha's mate. But stepping out into this excited crowd was a far cry from being questioned and pawed over by a small group of villagers in the shifter town we'd stopped at on our way to the mountain. There had to be hundreds of people gathered together before us.

"I don't know what to say to them," I said. "Or what to do. Or—"

"Just be yourself. Be our Princess of Flames." Marco aimed his sly grin at me. "No one could ask for anything more than that."

I wasn't so sure about that. But as Nate drew the SUV to a stop at the edge of the courtyard, I pulled my back up straight.

This was it. This was the start of the whole rest of my life, as the dragon shifter who held the four shifter kin groups together. I'd fought to be here. And now I was going to damn well make as much of it as I could.

CHAPTER 12

West

A WOMAN who smelled like a sparrow bumped into me from behind. A second later, a sparrow shifter jostled me to the side with his elbow. Gritting my teeth, I wove toward the edge of the courtyard. Music seemed to be clanging from every direction, only slightly louder than the cacophony of voices. And there were a lot of voices. Avians always had an awful lot to say.

Wolves were pack animals, sure, but a proper pack was ten, maybe fifteen strong. We didn't enjoy *crowds*. No room to run, no room to maneuver. How anyone enjoyed them, I didn't have a clue. And no one here gave any deference to my status as alpha. All their attention was focused on *their* returning leader—and, of course, the mate at his side.

I glanced back over the bobbing heads. Aaron's kin had set up a platform in the middle of the courtyard so that he could stand there and show off Ren. The dragon shifter was smiling and shaking hands and accepting hugs, but her stance was just as uncertain as it'd been in that canine village when she'd been swarmed.

A twinge I didn't like ran through my chest. The impulse to go to her, to lend my presence as support. Was she really ready for this?

I set my jaw. If she wanted this role, she was going to have to be ready. This time I couldn't step in and usher her away to give her some breathing room. This was the eagle shifter's show. Anyway, she'd asked for this by consummating the mate-bond with Aaron. Let her have it.

I wrenched my eyes away and spotted Marco at the edge of the courtyard. I'd have expected the jaguar shifter to be right there in the middle of the festivities, given the way he usually chased after fun as if it were a particularly tasty mouse. But maybe he was having a private party of his own here. He'd gathered a group of shifters around him who didn't look at all avian. As I came up to them, I got a good whiff. Felines, all of them.

"What's with the cat convention over here?" I asked.

Marco's gaze slid to me. He flicked his fingers dismissively. "A kin delegation caught up with me here. The vampires back in New York are throwing a bit of a tantrum. Nothing we can't sort out by ourselves."

Vamps. I grimaced. "After that encounter on their territory, I can't blame them for being pissed off."

"Well, we didn't have much choice in tangling with them, did we? And now we get to tangle with the fae. Although to be fair, in that case the fae started it."

One of the other feline shifters tapped Marco's elbow. Marco leaned in to hear whatever comment the guy didn't want me listening in on. As if I were all that interested in their private chat. I was happy to leave the vamp-taming to them.

Of course, I'd rather be dealing with vamps than the fae. A prickle crept over my skin as I turned away.

Ren was so set on taking the fight to the monarch. She had no idea what she was getting into. No idea how fucking dangerous the fae could be. They'd killed her mother to stop her from getting to the mysterious power Ren now carried—which meant they'd see Ren as twice as much of a threat. Going to them, no matter how horrendous their past crimes were, was only asking for trouble.

But our dragon shifter didn't like hearing the word "no," did she? My eyes were drawn to her again where she stood on the platform. I couldn't deny that even in her plain human clothes there was something regal about her. Something majestic she was growing into.

Something I wanted to touch and taste and own.

A rush of desire flowed through my veins. I clamped down on it, pushing it away.

How could I know that feeling was really mine and not just a symptom of the mate-bond, which only existed because of what we were, not who we were? Every instinct was pushing me toward her, but that didn't mean it was the right decision. She had much more to learn—so much more discipline to develop...

I just had to stop myself from giving into the urge to be the one to teach her.

My people were counting on me to make the right choice here. To lead them in whatever direction would serve *them* best. Ren was getting the chance to show who she was as a shifter now. As the dragon shifter all these people had been waiting for. It wouldn't take much time to see if she'd shine or sputter out.

My gaze was still glued to her. Damn if she wasn't shining right now. She beamed at a woman who'd come up to the platform to pay her respects, and her face turned toward me. I ducked my head before she could catch me watching her.

She'd already seen far too much of the power she held over *me.* I had to keep my distance until I was sure.

~

Ren

Aaron touched the small of my back and leaned in so I could hear him over the noise of the crowd around us. "Doing okay?" he asked.

"Yeah," I said, with a smile I meant. My body swayed automatically to the music pealing out across the courtyard. The nervous energy I'd felt earlier had transformed into a more enjoyable exhilaration. "Doing good. I mean, it's a little overwhelming, but... Everyone's so nice. What could I complain about?"

He chuckled. "Glad to hear it. They've been waiting for this day for a long time."

And so had he. A little flare of pride sparked inside me. He'd led his people for so many years on his own, from when he was little more than a boy. And now I got to stand beside him.

I curled my fingers into the front of his shirt and pressed my lips to his. Aaron traced his thumb over my cheek, kissing me back gently but thoroughly, until I'd lost my breath. A jolt of desire shot through me. Suddenly I did mind the crowd around us quite a bit.

But they didn't mind our PDA. A cheer rose up around us. I pulled back, flushed and grinning. "Sorry."

Aaron outright laughed at my apology. "For what? They loved that." His smile turned roguish. "And so did I. Shifters aren't shy about showing affection any more than we're worried about showing our bodies. Look around."

He nodded to the crowd. I let my gaze travel over the mass of bodies around our little platform. The crowd stretched all across the massive courtyard to the ring of marble arches at its border and the stretch of trees beyond. Despite the lanterns scattered around the place, it was getting pretty dark. I hadn't noticed the behavior he was talking about until I peered harder.

Oh. All across the fringes of the courtyard, pressed up against the columns of the arches or right in the midst of their fellow revelers, couples were going at it. Kissing, heavy petting, the works. I saw one young couple who looked ready to seal the deal right there on a stone bench between two of the arches. A woman lolled her head in bliss as her partner stroked her breasts beneath her shirt. A group of three were taking turns devouring each other's mouths. Apparently dragon shifters weren't the only ones who enjoyed multiple mates.

The flush on my face trickled right down my body. "Wow. Okay, I guess if I should worry about anything, it's that your kin are going to think I'm a prude."

Aaron looped his arm around my waist. "You *shouldn't* worry about anything. They'll take you exactly as you are. And those activities might be a little more, er, extreme tonight than is usual in public even for us. People have a lot of time to make up for."

It took me a second to realize what he was talking about. West had told me that none of the shifter kin could have children while their alpha went un-mated. Now it was no holds barred in the baby-making department. I guessed there'd be an awful lot of new avians being born nine months from now.

An awful lot of all sorts of shifter babies, once I fully accepted all of my mates.

The thought gave me a strange twinge: giddy excitement and

anxious uncertainty mixed together. I shouldn't be neglecting the other guys, even now—I wouldn't ignore Aaron when we were at the other kin-group estates, after all.

I searched the crowd again, this time looking for the rest of my mates. I didn't spot Nate or West, although my innate sense of their presence told me they were nearby. Marco was standing near one of the arches, talking with a few other shifters.

And frowning, which was not an expression I saw on his face often. My stomach twisted. Was something wrong?

"Hey," I said to Aaron. "Is it all right if I circulate around a little, or am I supposed to stay up here the whole time?"

"Go right ahead," he said. "The estate should be completely safe. I have people checking everyone who's arrived for their kin sign."

I hopped off the platform and was immediately swept up in the bustle of the celebration. Aaron's kin grasped my arms with friendly squeezes, shouted joyful comments into my ears, and beamed at me as if... well, as if they'd been waiting sixteen years just to meet me. I smiled back until my face ached with it. My heart thumped fast, but I didn't want to leave this chaos yet.

This was the first time I'd been somewhere I completely belonged since I'd fled with my mother all those years ago.

I gradually wove through the crowd toward the arch where I'd seen Marco. When I reached it, at first I thought he was gone. Then I heard his voice carrying from the other side of the thick marble column.

"I don't see how that's any of your business."

"None of our business?" a guy retorted. "We're your kin. And the security of our kin-group depends on you getting off your ass and locking her in."

Locking her in. What were they talking about? I hesitated, suspecting that if I walked right into that conversation, it'd stop in an instant.

"I'm working on it," Marco said. "I'm sure it was a hell of a lot easier for the alphas whose mates knew what they were getting into more than a couple weeks in advance."

Someone else, this one a woman, snorted. "Where are those charms you always speak so highly of? You know how many there are who'd happily take your place if it looks like there's an opening. And until you've consummated that bond—"

"I *know*," Marco snapped. "Thank you so much for your concern, but I assure you I'll get the job done. And before wolf boy or our resident grizzly gets in there too."

His tone was so callous my hackles rose. I backed up, merging back with the crowd, suddenly hating the thought of any of them noticing I was there.

It was me they were talking about, obviously. They were hassling Marco about our uncertain bond. But he hadn't exactly defending me, had he? He'd made it sound as if... as if being my mate was some kind of competition. Or a *job*. That word he'd actually used.

My mind darted back to the way he'd talked to me the other night when we almost had consummated our relationship. He'd gone on about how much he cared about me, about the life we'd have together...

My stomach turned. Had he really meant any of that? Or had he just thought a bunch of sweet nothings was the best way to get me to give in to his "charms"?

More avian shifters greeted me, and I managed to smile, but a sliver of pain jabbed at my gut. I'd assumed if I could trust *any*one, it was my mates. Even West, despite his gruffness. What if I'd been wrong?

Without meaning to, I wandered back into the vicinity of

the platform. Aaron hopped down to meet me. He took in my expression and brought his hand to the side of my face. I leaned into his touch, taking as much comfort from it as I could.

"Is the celebration getting to be a bit much?" he said.

No. I wasn't going to let some stupid remarks stop me from making the most of this moment. I could decide how to deal with Marco later, when I could speak to him alone. Tonight was about celebrating what we'd gained.

I wrapped my fingers around Aaron's palm. "I'm fine. Want to dance?"

"I'll never turn down that request from you." He set his other hand on my waist and twirled me around, fast enough that a laugh jolted out of me despite myself. Then he pulled me close to him, both of us turning together with the melody spilling through the air.

"How soon can you reach out to the fae monarch?" I asked. I couldn't forget that reason for coming here either. I wasn't going to be able to feel right until I'd gotten some sort of justice for Mom.

"I already have," Aaron said. "I sent one of my people to her citadel about an hour ago. We should hear the answer by tomorrow." He squeezed my hand tighter. "And if she tries to refuse to hear us, believe me, I'll make sure she changes her tune."

CHAPTER 13

Ren

The sky had deepened to near-black over the garden, twinkling with a dusting of stars. I tipped my head to them, letting their faint light soak into me, as I meandered down the path.

The avian kin celebration was only just starting to wind down. Music and chatter still carried over the hedges from the courtyard. I'd finally slipped away through one of the arches into this quieter space a few minutes ago. Sometimes a girl needed room to breathe.

The warm, salty air was such a relief after all that time in the mountain's cold. I closed my eyes, drinking it in. A faint breeze rustled through the flowers and hedges around me. A sweet perfume rose up from the blossoms to mingle with the ocean scent. The crash of the waves sounded from the other side of the house, just barely audible to my shifter ears.

As I breathed in again, another scent reached my nose.

Something darker, earthier with a prickle of pine. I knew before I opened my eyes that I'd see West nearby.

The wolf shifter was standing by a wooden latticework. A flowering vine climbed across the interlaced slats over a stone bench like the ones around the courtyard. West was facing away from me, toward the far end of the garden and the top of the estate wall visible beyond it. His hands were slung in the pockets of his jeans, and his head was tipped to the side at a thoughtful angle.

I hesitated, the mate-bond urging me to go to him while what was probably common sense suggested I leave him be. If he'd wanted company, he wouldn't be all the way over here while the party was still happening. And it wasn't as if he'd ever acted all that excited to spend time with *me*.

But maybe that was exactly why I should go to him. He was a jerk to me some of the time—okay, a lot of the time—but I could understand why. I'd seen how much he cared about his kin. The shifters' dependence on the ties between dragon shifter and alphas *had* gone terribly wrong after my mother's disappearance.

He felt the same draw I did. Maybe being a jerk was the only way he knew how to fend that desire off while he made his decision.

He should know that I wanted to give him a chance, at least. That I would do everything I could for his kin as well as Aaron's and the other guys' if he met me halfway. If he decided to forsake the mate-bond and look to form a new one separate from tradition, it wasn't going to be because *I* pushed him away.

And maybe a little part of me was remembering that one kiss he'd given me, after the rogues' first ambush. The passion in it that had left my head spinning. And the way he'd looked at me the other night in the tent...

My skin flushed a little just at the memory.

I ambled around a clump of red and pink rose bushes and a magnolia tree. I wasn't trying to be quiet, and West could probably smell my presence just as well as I'd smelled his, but it still startled me a little when he spoke.

"Did being the center of attention get a little old, Sparks?" he said without turning around.

I rolled my eyes at his back, even though he couldn't see my expression. "I spent most of my life practicing *not* drawing attention. I think it'll be a while before stuff like this feels totally comfortable."

He made a non-committal sound. Well, he hadn't told me to take off. That was some kind of progress.

I walked up beside him, peering in the same direction he was looking. "Don't you trust Aaron's sentries to keep a close enough eye on things?"

"You can't be careful enough with the fae," West said. "I heard he's already sent someone to request the parlay. She has to know you're here, and where we were before now. She'll know what the request is about."

"Do you think she already knows some of her people killed my mother? Do you think it was her *idea*?" My chest tightened. If the ruler of the fae had ordered the murder of the ruler of the shifters... That would be an act of all-out war, wouldn't it? Why would they hate us enough to do that?

"It's unlikely," West admitted, to my relief. "The last thing the fae are is stupid. But the monarch will have set the tone of conversation that made her underlings think it was a good idea. And I have trouble believing seven years could have gone by without word getting back to her. But she's stayed quiet. No interest in filling us in."

"What will happen if they decide they want to start some

kind of war?" I asked. The image of the fae blasting Mom with their magic flashed through my mind. I shivered. "Can we really fight back?"

West's mouth curled into a grim smile. "Shifters are strong. It takes at least a few fae to tackle just one of us, weaklings like that weasel rogue aside. And there are a lot more of us than there are of them. We'd give them a good fight. But that doesn't mean we should be begging for one."

"I don't *want* to fight," I said. "I just want some answers. I want the fae who killed my mom to face some kind of consequences. I don't think that's asking a lot."

"You don't know the fae," West said.

In the pale moonlight, his handsome face looked suddenly haunted. Maybe I didn't know the fae yet, but it was clear he did. The pain I could sense echoing through him made my own heart squeeze. I swallowed thickly.

"What did they do to you?"

His gaze jerked toward me for the first time, his penetrating green eyes meeting mine. "What makes you think they did anything?"

I raised my eyebrows. "Other than the fact that it's written all over your face and in your voice? I'm a newbie shifter, not an idiot."

He turned, bringing his lean body that much closer to mine. Close enough that a rush of heat washed through me from head to toe. He cocked his head with an expression I couldn't quite read, somewhere between curiosity and anguish and defiance. His voice dropped, the clear throaty tone tingling into my ears.

"Do you really care? Or do you just think you should?"

I stared back at him. It had suddenly gotten very hard to think over the clang of desire ringing through my body. Thankfully that wasn't a very hard question to answer.

"I care. Of course I care. Do *you* really think I'd put up with half the shit-talking you do if I couldn't see there's a hell of a lot more to you than that—more that I want to know?"

"What makes you think the rest will be any different from what you've already seen, Sparks?"

My own voice dipped lower to match his, with a slightly teasing edge. "I don't know. But I've heard dragon shifters tend to be extra perceptive about these sorts of things. And by the way, I'm actually starting to like that nickname, so if the point of it is to annoy me, you'll have to find a new one."

"I'll give that some thought," he said with a twitch of his mouth. I couldn't tell if he'd suppressed a frown or a smile. I was too busy being distracted by how close his mouth was to mine. Not much more than a foot of space between us. Practically nothing at all. And then some genius part of my brain came up with the perfect excuse to touch him.

"That scar you've got. The one that almost *glows*. Is that from fighting with the fae?" I reached for his chest, holding my breath as I did.

West caught my hand an inch from grazing his pecs. His fingers closed around mine, firm and hot. There was so much heat radiating off him that for a second I thought I might melt.

"Are you sure that's what you want to do?" he said, so dark and low it was almost a whisper.

An ache had formed between my legs. I wet my lips. Fuck it. "No," I said. "I want *this*."

I tangled my other hand in his silvery auburn hair and pressed my mouth to his.

A groan reverberated from West's chest. He kissed me back hard, letting go of my hand to grip my waist and pull me flush against him. The heat of his body enveloped me, as if we weren't two people but two parts of one whole. Two parts desperate to meld back together.

I clutched his shirt, losing myself in the crush of his mouth and the demanding slide of his tongue. There was nothing I could imagine wanting more than this.

My hips arched against West's of their own accord. With a hungry growl, he lifted me off my feet and laid me on the stone bench without breaking the kiss. He braced himself over me, his body grazing mine tantalizingly. I whimpered and tugged him closer. The bulge in his jeans brushed my sex, and I rocked against him. He let out another groan and dropped his head to devour my neck with the hot slide of his tongue.

I gasped, groping him with an abandon that would have embarrassed me if he hadn't seemed just as frantic for release. My fingers found the hem of his shirt and trailed up under it over his bare back.

West grasped my hips, shifting them so his erection could hit my clit at an even better angle through our clothes. A moan slipped from my lips.

I didn't care that some other revelers might wander into the garden and see us, hear us. He was *mine* and I was his, and we were meant for this. From the moment I'd been born; from the moment he'd been named alpha. Before all the violence and the bitterness had wrenched us apart.

"Westley," I murmured, ducking my head to try to reclaim his mouth.

At the sound of his full name, West stiffened. He pushed off me so suddenly that for a few seconds all I could do was lie there blinking up at him, my body throbbing at the loss of contact.

He stared back at me. A tremble ran through him. His hands clenched at his sides. His mouth was still red from kissing me and his cock still hard against the fly of his jeans, but his eyes had gone abruptly cold.

"No," he said. "I'm not *Westley* to you, and don't pretend that I am."

I sat up, my breath coming in a rasp. What was he talking about? "I didn't mean anything— One of the shifters in your village called you that, and I remembered, and it just seemed..."

It had seemed natural, in the moment. But obviously not to him. I didn't know how to explain it. I'd just been following my instincts.

"You've been gone for sixteen years," he said flatly. "You don't know me, and I don't owe you anything. I don't *need* anything from you. I've held my position as alpha all that time, and I'll damn well keep being alpha whether I accept your terms or not."

"West," I started, but his expression shuttered even more. My voice faltered.

He stalked off, striding down the garden paths toward the courtyard. I gazed after him, feeling achingly horny and alone—and more bewildered than I liked to admit.

CHAPTER 14

Ren

After the festivities had carried on far into the night, I'd been escorted to rooms reserved for the dragon shifter. It was a relief to roll out of the elegant oak sleigh bed the next morning and amble into a private dining area where I didn't have to face even one more stranger. The wide, white-walled room was tucked away between the estate's dragon shifter quarters and those assigned to the alphas, and no one else got to use it.

When I slipped inside, Nate was already digging into a breakfast of poached eggs, bacon, toast, and fresh-cut fruit at the polished teak table. The mingling sweet and savory smells set my mouth watering. Aaron was standing by the broad window that overlooked the ocean, a cup of coffee nestled in his hands. He turned from the view of the crashing waves and smiled in greeting.

"Did you sleep all right, Serenity?"

"Looks like I've missed half the morning already, so I'd say yeah." I ambled over to the buffet where the spread of platters was laid out. Man, where to start? My stomach gurgled eagerly. "It's a nice place you've got here."

Aaron laughed. "I can't really take much credit for that. The estate has been passed from alpha to alpha for as long as anyone can remember. It's a nice perk to go with the responsibilities, though."

Nate patted the table beside him as I headed over with a heaping plate. "This side gives the best view of the ocean."

"Or are you just saying that to keep me close?" I teased.

To my relief, the bear shifter grinned. Things had felt a little awkward between us since I'd told him off for being over-protective, but I didn't want him to think I was holding some kind of grudge. And I sure hoped he wasn't either. The vibe I got from him as I sat down in the next chair was a little hesitant but warm.

"I can't say that isn't an extra benefit," he said. I let my leg rest next to his under the table, and his grin grew.

I wanted him to remember what I'd told him about how to treat me, but I still *wanted* him, too. He ran his hand over my thigh to squeeze my knee in a gesture that would have seemed playful if it hadn't also sent a bolt of desire to my core. Oh, I wanted him all right, and I had no doubt he felt the same way.

But Aaron's comment about the alpha line of succession stirred up thoughts of last night. Of the deeper awkwardness I'd felt with my other alphas. First there'd been that weird conversation I'd overheard between Marco and his kin. And then the interlude with West that had somehow gone completely wrong. I still didn't know exactly what he'd been so upset about. But that comment he'd made had stuck with me, especially after the stuff with Marco.

I'll damn well keep being alpha whether I accept your terms or not.

Aaron had talked before about having to fight to keep his position as alpha. More than once, other avian shifters who'd wanted a shot at the leadership had challenged him. I'd been too occupied with my mother's mystery to think much about how my reappearance would change the dynamics of ruling for all the guys.

I dipped the corner of my toast into the perfectly runny egg yolk and took a bite, but now my mind was churning. I couldn't turn it off. Why should I? *I* was supposed to be ruling the shifters too. I should understand the ins and outs of every aspect as well as I could.

Aaron came over to sit down across from me. I glanced at him. "Is it going to be easier for you to be... respected as the alpha now that I'm here? And we're officially mated? I mean, like, fewer people challenging you or whatever?"

He nodded, considering me with his bright blue eyes. "A lot of the turmoil in the shifter community has come down to not having a dragon shifter around to provide the usual balance. With people seeing that you're here and taking on that role, they'll be less restless." His tone turned wry. "And there are many who'll feel your accepting me is an additional mark in my favor."

"And that'll go for all of the kin-groups, I guess."

Nate raised his head, his expression concerned. "You don't need to worry about that, Ren. You're here. You're with us as much as you're comfortable being. No one should be rushing you. We can handle any challenges that can come our way."

Except Marco kind of had been rushing me, hadn't he? Even though he'd tried to tell me he wasn't. I speared a piece of bacon but didn't lift it from my plate.

"I know," I said. I didn't want to outright accuse the jaguar shifter of something to the other guys. How could I put it? "I heard Marco talking with some feline kin yesterday. It sounded like there are a lot of them who are restless. I was just wondering if he's had more trouble than the rest of you?"

Nate made a humming sound. "Cat temperaments don't do well with being ruled over in general. They're always squabbling."

"On top of that, I'd imagine Marco being the youngest of us didn't help," Aaron said. "He was only ten years old when the previous feline alpha died. And you've probably noticed his personality can be a little… provocative."

"He likes to run off his mouth," Nate muttered. "Everything's a big joke."

Aaron chuckled. "I think he cares more than he likes to show. But yes, that's what I meant."

Marco cared a lot about staying alpha, anyway. I chewed and swallowed, but the bacon had lost its taste. My stomach had gone tight.

"But Marco's handled himself all this time," Nate said, giving my knee another quick squeeze. "You don't need to worry about him either."

Before I could decide whether I wanted to say anything else about that, there was a knock on the door. "News from the fae, sir," a voice called in.

Aaron straightened up. "Come in," he said. "Whatever it is, everyone here can hear it."

A tall, gawky young man who brought to mind a heron came into the room. He gave his alpha a quick bob of a bow. "The monarch has granted your request of a parlay," he said. "She is willing to meet with you and your party tomorrow at noon on the neutral ground."

"Did she say anything else?" Aaron asked.

The heron shifter shook his head. "She didn't look surprised to be asked, though."

Because she'd already been expecting us, like West had suggested? My stomach knotted even more. My fingers curled around the fork with the sudden impulse to pocket the silverware, as if that would make the situation more under my control. I hadn't quite shaken my thieving past yet.

As the messenger ducked out, I turned back to Aaron. "Is that what you expected?"

"Delaying by a day isn't a surprise," he said. "She wouldn't want to seem overly accommodating. Other than that, it's pretty hard to read the fae on the best of days. I don't see any warning signs." His gaze turned more thoughtful. "Our wolf alpha has been making you nervous."

"He really doesn't trust the fae. I'd call it paranoia if I didn't get the feeling he's got a good reason to. Where is West, anyway?" I figured Marco was sleeping in like usual, but getting a late start wasn't like West.

Nate motioned to the window. "He was stalking out of here when I came in. He's probably patrolling the grounds right now."

Aaron shrugged. "If that's what makes him feel more at ease. The fae *are* difficult to deal with. But you'll have all of us with you to support you, Serenity."

With every time he said it, I got more used to hearing my full name used. It reminded me how much more I was than the teen living on the streets who'd had to resort to stealing to get by. I'd found a real place for myself here. And just like the alphas had with their positions, I was going to hold onto mine with everything I had in me.

I really wasn't feeling all that hungry anymore though. I forced down a few more bites of toast and stood up. "Is there anything I should know about that's planned for today? Or can I just explore?"

"Stay within the estate, unless one of us is with you," Aaron said. "There's a formal dinner arranged for tonight where you'll get to meet representatives from many of the powerful avian families. Until then, enjoy yourself however you'd like. I have a few admin-type concerns to take care of now that I'm back, but I'll look for you later."

The warmth in his gaze made me think of all the ways I'd enjoyed myself with him. I'd been too exhausted last night to think of using my bed for anything other than zonking out on. But there were so many other possibilities... The huge mattress was big enough that it could have held five of us easily.

"I look forward to that," I said with a twitch of my eyebrows. The warmth in his eyes went from gentle to smoldering in an instant. Oh yes, I was looking forward to it a lot.

I *was* also looking forward to taking in the rest of the estate. Last night I hadn't seen anything other than the courtyard and the garden, by darkness.

I slipped through my rooms and out into one of the mansion's main halls. The ocean breeze filled the whole place with that refreshingly salty smell and took the edge off the summer heat. The white washed walls, teak floors, and big windows all through the open concept space made me feel like I'd stepped into a massive—and exclusive—beach cottage. The perks of being alpha indeed.

I hadn't made it very far when Marco emerged into the hall up ahead of me. He gave me his usual sly smirk as he sauntered over.

"Good morning, princess."

I wanted to smile and say it back, to pretend nothing was wrong. But with his indigo eyes on me and all the questions that had been whirling in my head, I froze up. The jaguar shifter cocked his head at my hesitation. "Is everything all right, Ren?"

This wasn't the best place for a confrontation. But at the moment there was no one else in sight. And I didn't really want to go somewhere private with him, not until I had a few answers. I braced myself and raised my chin.

"I don't know," I said. "It seemed like maybe things aren't totally all right with your kin? You didn't look very happy talking with them yesterday."

"Oh, that." Marco waved off my concern with a flick of his lithe hand. "A little vampire trouble, soon to be taken care of. The bloodsuckers just like making a fuss. I sent the delegation off to deal with it before they could get the avians' feathers too ruffled."

"Ah," I said. Well, of course he wasn't going to come right out and admit to the other things they'd talked about. I paused and then forced myself to keep going. "I've been thinking about some of the things you said the other night. About how much I mean to you. How much you want to start our lives together."

An eager light lit in Marco's eyes. He stepped closer, his voice dropping lower. "And where did those thoughts lead you next?"

Part of my body still responded to him the way it always had. My fingers itched to tangle in his dark hair, my lips to feel his against them. But another part of me, tight around my heart, balked at his eagerness. Because what was he *really* eager for?

I drew in a breath, keeping my gaze fixed on him. "I was wondering whether you actually meant any of it, or if the only reason being with me matters to you is so you can make a better claim as alpha."

Marco's jaw twitched. The light in his eyes went out. He managed a chuckle, but I didn't need any supernatural sensitivity to tell it sounded stiff. He summoned his familiar jaunty tone. "Princess, if someone's been telling you stories—"

And here he was, still fucking lying to me. My temper flared, fueled by a burn of betrayal spreading through my chest. "I heard it straight from your mouth last night," I snapped. "Talking about me like I'm a job you need to finish, a prize you're going to grab before the others. So don't pretend you have no idea what I'm talking about."

For once, Marco seemed to have nothing at all to say. His lips parted and just stayed that way as he stared at me. I could read the panic and guilt in him as clearly as if it'd been written in capital letters on his face.

I clenched my teeth against the pain swelling inside me. So it was all true. He couldn't even start to explain himself.

"I'm not a cat toy," I said, "so forget about treating me like one."

Then I turned and hurried off in the opposite direction before my tears caught up with me.

CHAPTER 15

Aaron

THE LAST ROOM I took Serenity into was the library. She sucked in her breath as she took in the bookshelves built into every wall from floor to ceiling, the clusters of sofas and armchairs on the deep-pile rug, and the view of the ocean from the two tall windows.

I smiled with a rush of pride. I might not be able to take full credit for this house, but I'd taken care to make it as welcoming as possible.

"And let me guess," my dragon shifter said, gesturing to the packed shelves. "You've read every one of those."

I laughed. "Hardly. But I did spend a lot of time in here when I was growing into my role, in between meetings with my advisors. I didn't have a senior alpha to guide me directly, so I found as much direction as I could in the books the previous alphas have accumulated over the decades."

"I used to read a lot, when my mom was still around," she

said. "The library was an easy place to get out of the apartment for a while, where no one would bother you if you found a quiet little nook for yourself. But once she left, and I ended up on the street..."

A shadow crossed her face. I wished I could brush it away with a caress of my hand. She didn't like to talk much about those years after her mother had disappeared, but every time she mentioned them, she couldn't hide how deeply the experience had wounded her.

But she was healing on her own. With every strength she discovered in herself, with every bit she let us in, she was coming back to the woman she was meant to be.

"You can find a quiet little nook in here whenever you want," I said. "The house is yours as much as it's mine."

She ducked her head for a second, as if embarrassed. Then she smiled at me with the glow of confidence that was coming to her more and more often now. The rush of pride that filled my chest now was for her. Followed by the desire to show her exactly how much I adored her, in every possible way up against one of those shelves.

The clock on the fireplace mantle chimed. No time for that sort of diversion now. I took her hand, enjoying the way her slender fingers automatically closed around mine.

"We should go back to your rooms. You'll want to pick out a dress for the dinner. People will expect to see all of us a little decked out."

The corner of her mouth curled higher. "So a tee and jeans isn't going to cut it, is what you're saying? All right, all right. I've got nothing against dresses. Let's make me into a real princess."

But as we strolled back to the dragon shifter's quarters hand in hand, another hint of shadow crossed her expression. Her fingers tightened slightly around mine. When she didn't speak, I glanced over at her. "Is something bothering you? You can tell me anything, you know."

"I know." She smiled again, but crookedly this time. "You don't have to worry—it's got nothing to do with you, or your amazing house. But it's not something I really want to talk about right now. If I feel like I do later, you'd be the first person I'll go to."

I couldn't ask for more than that. "Fair enough." I ushered her through her sitting room and into the vast bedroom that had belonged to generations of dragon shifters when they visited the avian estate. A private bath off to the side, a bed big enough for dragon shifter and four alphas, and several huge teak wardrobes. I walked up to one and tugged it open.

"The dragon shifter line tends to be pretty consistent in size," I said. "Some of the clothes in here might be a tad too small or too large, but we can always have a piece tailored if need be."

Serenity came up behind me. Her eyes widened. She fingered the drifts of silk and satin in their array of colors, a giggle escaping her. "I feel like a kid who just discovered the world's best dress-up box."

I chuckled. "Take your time. You should go out there tonight feeling every bit the princess."

I stepped back as she pawed through the dresses. She pulled out a few and tossed them onto the end of the bed for further consideration. "You said I'm going to meet some of the prominent avians," she said. "So there are shifter families with more power than others?"

"Like in any community," I said. "Sometimes it's based on the families of past alphas, sometimes just who fought best or contributed the most in past times of trouble... They don't have any official authority, but the rest of my kin would listen to them above others. So I try to keep them happy, as long as that doesn't mean making everyone else unhappy. You'll meet some of my family tonight too. My sister should be getting here in time for the dinner."

She glanced over at me as she shut the wardrobe, the last of her selections draped over her arm. "You have a sister?"

"Alice. Two years younger. Twice as fierce." I grinned. "She made herself my unofficial bodyguard when we were growing up. And she's done enough martial arts training to have earned that title. I think you two will get along well. And she'll watch out for you as much as she does me."

"Well, I'm looking forward to meeting her, at least." She strode over to the bed and threw the last dress on with the others. "Now let's get on with the decking out."

~

Ren

I ran my hands over the smooth fabric of the dresses, trying to lose myself in the moment. It was hard. The guilty expression on Marco's face had been nagging at me all day.

I'd trusted him. I thought I could, because he was my mate, because of the bond we shared, even if it wasn't fully consummated. But apparently he didn't feel it the same way I did. I was just a means to an end, not a person he cared about.

Aaron put his hands on my shoulders and rubbed them up and down. His touch brought me back to the present. He didn't ask again what was wrong, even though he could probably tell I was thinking about it again.

At least I had him. He cared about me. He believed in me. I could lean on him while I figured out where the hell things were going with the rest of my mates.

"You want to help?" I asked, letting a little heat creep into my voice.

Aaron raised his eyebrows, an answering spark lighting in his eyes. "Now that's an invitation I can't imagine turning down," he murmured.

I lifted my arms, and he tugged my T-shirt off me. His hands settled on my bare waist. He leaned over my shoulder, his breath tickling over my collarbone. "So, which one should we start with?"

My nipples had pebbled inside my bra. I squashed the urge to forget the dresses and just have him on me. Instead, I studied the ones I'd picked out.

Now that I was considering them together, the black gown seemed overly stuffy. I didn't want to look like I thought I was attending a funeral. I picked up the silky lavender one that had caught my eye. "How about this?"

"I think it'll be lovely on you."

Aaron reached around to undo the button on my jeans. He tugged them down, and I stepped out of them. The tracing of his fingers over my skin left me a little breathless.

I eased up the dress over my body and waited as he zipped up the back. He came with me to the full-length mirror hanging on the wall between two of the wardrobes. The silver frame was almost as shiny as the glass.

I definitely didn't look like some girl off the streets now. That was a woman gazing back at me. The silk hugged my slim frame, rippling like water around my legs. The lavender did look lovely with my dark brown hair. But something about it didn't feel quite right.

I ambled back to the bed and shrugged that dress off. My hands fell on the gold one in the middle. The embroidered leaf pattern around the shoulders and bodice gave it a little more structure, and I liked the faint coordinating pattern marked into the satin fabric.

"Another excellent choice," Aaron said with a smile.

That dress had its zipper on the side, but he helped me with it anyway. As the fabric settled into place against my skin, a sense of certainty was already rising over me. I headed back to the mirror, the gown's small train whispering across the floor behind me.

My breath caught when I saw my reflection. The gold fabric brought out the amber in my eyes, making them look like little flames. The cut hugged my hips slightly before flowing over my thighs, giving my figure a little more curve. I looked regal. Powerful.

I didn't just look like a princess. I looked like a *queen*. Woe betide anyone who messes with this dragon shifter.

My chin rose instinctively. Aaron's smile grew. "This one?" he said.

I didn't need to try any of the others. "This one," I agreed.

He pulled me closer to him. The press of his hands over the soft, smooth fabric felt amazing. And so did the press of his lips when he brought them to mine.

We kissed long and deep. My arms rose to loop behind his neck. He angled his head to kiss me harder, and I hummed encouragingly against his mouth. With a groan, he slid his hands up my sides to skim the curve of my breasts.

"You look fantastic with this on," he muttered. "But the only thing I want to do now is take it off you."

"I'm not really seeing any problem with that plan."

He grimaced against my cheek. "I'm supposed to meet with my advisors in a few minutes, to talk over the latest developments before the dinner starts. And to come up with a plan for our parlay tomorrow."

Our parlay with the fae monarch. My desire cooled at that thought. I stepped back to peer into his eyes. "How dangerous do you think it's going to be, meeting them face to face?"

He cupped my cheek, teasing his thumb over my temple in a reassuring caress. "They didn't outright attack us on the mountain. We can't trust them, but they're bound by the word they've given, the treaties they've agreed to uphold—in a magical sense. We just have to watch that they don't find some loophole like they did by using the rogues to their benefit. The entire shifter community will know we went to the neutral ground to talk with them. They can't hurt us without bringing an awful lot of pain on themselves."

He didn't sound overly worried. And with the fae monarch's domain right next door, he should know just how much trouble they were likely to stir up.

I dragged in a breath, not sure whether I was more nervous about meeting these bigwig shifters tonight or about meeting the fae tomorrow.

"You've got this," Aaron added. "And we'll be right there with you, just like always."

I nodded, suddenly too choked up on emotion to speak. He drew me to him again. This kiss felt softer and somehow more passionate at the same time. As if he were offering up all the devotion he felt in the brush of his lips against mine. I kissed him back hungrily, wanting that feeling. Needing it. Needing to give the same back to him.

Could I really call this love after just a couple weeks? I didn't know how else to describe the glow of happiness that filled me, being there in my eagle shifter's arms.

Aaron eased back, his eyes shining as if he'd heard what I hadn't let myself say out loud. "I really do have to go. But I'll see you soon at the dinner. Why don't you— There's a terrace overlooking the ocean just past our private dining room. If you'd like, you could take a walk out there. I've always found it calming. I'll send someone for you when it's time."

The way my nerves were jumping, a calming stroll sounded like just what I needed. "Thanks," I said. "I'll do that."

CHAPTER 16

Ren

THE SUN WAS JUST STARTING to come down over the ocean. It lit up the water with drifts of sparkles.

I walked across the stone tiles to the railing that surrounded the private terrace, drinking in the aquatic scents carried by the breeze. It was hard to stay anxious with that gorgeous scenery in front of me and the soothing crash of the waves filling my ears. I was a dragon shifter. The last dragon shifter in existence. Anyone who tried to mess with me was making the worst decision of their life.

My fingers curled around the cool marble surface of the railing. I raised my head high. The breeze rippled through my hair and through the flowing skirt of my dress. I felt the power of my heritage rippling through me too. And the little flame of power Mom had led me to, still flickering in the depths of my chest. Where was that going to lead me?

I had the sudden, wild urge to leap over the railing and down toward the beach. I could do it. The sandy slope below looked a little uneven, but nothing I couldn't manage a good tumble on.

But even as the urge rose up, I knew that jump wouldn't give me the same rush all my leaps and falls before used to. I'd experienced what it was like to *really* fly now. Nothing could compare to that.

Someday I'd be able to hold my dragon form for hours on end. Just soar and soar as far as my wings could take me. That sounded awfully nice right now.

I'd carried my purse out with me. My phone buzzed with a text alert. I pulled it out, already knowing it had to be Kylie. My best friend was the only one who had the number. There wasn't anyone else in my life I'd trusted enough to want to stay in contact with... except for the guys, now, and I hadn't needed to be apart from them yet.

What would it be like once we had to split up? They'd have alpha duties to take care of. Sometimes they'd need to be off at different estates, and I wouldn't be able to stay with all of them at once. Even with all the uncertainties whirling around us, part of me ached to keep them close.

All these crazy feelings had to get easier to deal with once I'd had more time to get used to the situation, right?

What's up in royal shifter land? Kylie had texted. I smiled and leaned back against the railing as I typed my reply.

Big fancy dinner upcoming. You would not believe the dress I've got on.

Ren in a dress!!! OMG, I can't believe I'm missing this. Take a pic. That's an order.

I laughed and held the phone out to try to capture as much of the dress as possible in a selfie. When I sent it to her, Kylie replied with a selfie of her face with her eyes wide in shock.

You look spectacular, Ren. Those four alphas of yours are going to have their hands full fighting off the rest of the guys there.

I don't think people are coming to this dinner looking to hook up, I wrote back. *It sounds like there's a lot of Serious Political Business to discuss. Heads of major shifter families and stuff. I guess they want to make sure I'm really real and that Aaron didn't just make up that they finally found me?*

So you're that big a deal, huh?

Yeah. I paused, thinking about my conversation with Marco this morning with a twist in my gut. *It seems like having a dragon shifter around as their mate makes it a lot easier for the other shifters to accept them as alphas. I guess that's what they meant about me uniting all the kin-groups. Seems like a lot of responsibility.*

But they'll help you through it. You can handle it. You don't think you're still in danger, do you? Now that you took care of those rogue douchebags?

My gut twisted harder. I didn't want to tell her about that continuing threat—or about how wary I was of the meeting with the fae monarch tomorrow. *Not immediately, it doesn't seem like. I don't know what to expect going forward. I'm still getting used to BEING a shifter. There's been a lot of conflict in the kin-groups since my mom disappeared, I guess, and I don't know the half of it yet.*

Well, you look after yourself. It doesn't matter what they want from you. You've got to put yourself first. And if anyone argues with that, you send them to me and I'll set them straight.

I had to smile at that. I'd bet she would too. Kylie always had my back—even with all this supernatural chaos descending on us.

YOU'RE okay now, right? I asked. *You've totally recovered from the attack at the shifter village?*

Oh yeah, I'm in tiptop shape now. Whatever those shifters did looking after me, it made the cuts heal so fast, I'd hardly believe I got mauled if I hadn't been there. The scars might stick, but that's okay. Just makes me look even more badass.

Well, I'm glad nearly dying didn't put a cramp in your style.

Hey, it'll take more than some murderous werewolves to get me down.

It would. I pictured her beside me, with her perpetual smile and that petite frame topped by her blaring neon-pink pixie cut. A pang of homesickness hit me.

As soon as I can figure out a way to make it work, I'm coming back to visit. Or maybe I can arrange for you to visit me wherever I end up. These "estates" the alphas have are amazing.

Like I said before, if you want to set me up with a quartet of shifter dudes of my own—any time, feel free!

I'll keep that in mind.

She sent a kissy face emoji. *I've got to jet for work. Knock 'em dead at that dinner tonight. Just not literally, obviously, Miss Dragon.*

I tucked the phone away and turned back toward the ocean. So much of my life was up in the air right now, but it was nice imagining some future time when I could just hang out with my bestie in a place like this, no worrying about sudden rogue attacks or fae conspiracies.

The door to the terrace sighed open behind me. Nate's brawny form pushed past it. He was looking even more fine than usual in the formal suit he'd put on, which hugged his muscular body to incredible effect. My breath might have caught a little, taking him in.

His gaze settled on me, and he gave me a smile that looked almost shy. His eyes roved over my body as he walked up to me, but the glint in them was appreciative, not leering. Apparently I was having an effect too.

"That is some dress," he said. "Although it's got to be the woman in it who really makes it."

I smiled back, the compliment warming me. "I like it a lot too. Never been much for dressing up, but I'm starting to think maybe I could get used to it."

"I'd be totally fine with that." He propped himself against the railing next to me, his gaze turning searching. "Aaron told me I'd probably find you out here alone."

My hackles rose, just slightly. "You know you don't have to worry about me being on my own for a few minutes, right? Because I'm completely fine. Just enjoying the view."

Nate held up his hands. "That's not what I meant. I promise. I didn't come looking for you because I was worried. It's..." He ducked his head, the sunlight gleaming off his thick chestnut hair. He was so tall and powerfully built, it still amazed me how gentle he could come across.

"I realized, after what you said the other day when we were fighting off the rogues, that there's something I should probably tell you," he said after a moment, rubbing the back of his neck. "It doesn't *excuse* how I've acted, but I think it'll explain it a little. And... it's an important part of who I am. I'd like you to really know me."

The warmth I'd felt earlier spread through my entire body. I stepped closer, touching his elbow. "I'd like that too. Sorry if I got a bit snappish just now."

"It's fine. I understand why." His smile turned crooked. He took my hand in his, smoothing his thumb over my knuckles. The contact sent a pleasant shiver up my arm.

"You know that the tragedy with your mother and the former alphas happened when we were all pretty young," he said. "I mean, I was the oldest of the four of us, and I was only twelve.

And then there was a lot of uncertainty because we didn't know where your mother or you were, or what would happen to our usual way of life..."

"Yeah," I said softly. "That must have been tough. Having all that responsibility and no clear path."

He nodded. "I had good guidance from my advisors. My kin—we're a little scattered because we're the shifters who don't fit into any of the larger kin groups, but maybe it's because of that we've never been all that competitive. We mostly just want someone leading the way and letting everyone else mind their own business. So I haven't come under exactly the same pressure as the other guys to stay alpha. But I wasn't always sure what I should be doing as alpha either."

"Of course. That makes sense."

"Well... When I was seventeen, and starting to take on more and more of the alpha duties on my own, I got to know another bear shifter whose family worked for the estate. We got along well—she was someone I could just relax with when I had time to myself, someone I could talk to about the decisions I was having to make."

A prickle ran down my back at the "she." My sense of the mate-bond between us twinged. "And then?" I said, managing to keep my voice steady. I'd known not all of the alphas would have waited for me in body as well as in soul. But I wasn't sure I wanted to hear about any earlier diversions either.

Nate hesitated. He had to know how hard it was for me to even think about him with someone else. "For a few years, we weren't anything more than friends. Then after a while, I realized I was falling in love with her. And she admitted she felt the same way. I'd always thought I would wait for the dragon shifter I was meant to be with, but—"

Tears welled in my eyes before the emotion even hit me. I

choked on my breath, the thought of Nate—of *my* mate—choosing someone else wrenching through me.

West had mentioned the idea that he might forsake our mate-bond before, but only vaguely. The idea of this specific woman nearly tearing Nate away from me—I hadn't expected it to hit me this hard, but I could barely stand it.

"Ren!" Nate said. He brought his hands to my face, cupping it as he leaned close. I closed my eyes against the tears. "I'm sorry," he said, his voice low and ragged. "I'm *here*. I wouldn't have ever brought it up if I didn't think I had to for us to move forward. I was tempted, and I was unsure, but in the end I chose you. I stopped seeing her—I *haven't* seen her in seven years. I knew that no matter how right things felt with her, being with you would be even more right."

I inhaled sharply, trying to get my reaction under control. "I'm not upset," I managed. "Not on purpose, anyway. I just—the feelings just came over me—"

"It's okay. I can't imagine how I'd feel if *you* talked about wanting to leave us for some other guy." He stroked his hand over my hair and kissed my forehead. I leaned into him, soaking up the heat of his body and the strength of his arms as they came around me.

"The reason I wanted to tell you," he went on, "is to show you that you've always been my first priority. Even when I didn't know you yet, and I had temptation right in front of me. I am so incredibly happy to have finally found you that... I think I've been a little terrified of losing you before we even have the chance to really be together. And I let that fear talk me into being over-protective. I *know* you're strong. I *know* you've got more power in you than any of us. I have to trust in that and not let my worries get in the way."

I hugged him back, nestling my head against his shoulder.

"Thank you," I said. "I can see why you'd feel that way. As long as you're *trying* not to act on it..."

"I will. I can't promise that I'll never again give in to the instinct to leap to your defense when you don't really need it—but I'll be doing my best. And if I slip up and you ask me to back off, I'll listen. So don't be shy about telling me off."

A giggle slipped out of me. I swiped away the tears. The wrenching feeling had faded, but an ache remained. An ache for Nate and the years he'd spent alone when he could have had that bond of love already.

I raised my head and touched his cheek. Nate smiled, with so much affection shining in his dark brown eyes that I couldn't doubt for a second he felt he'd made the right choice. I bobbed up on my toes to press a kiss to his mouth.

He kissed me back, softly and then more hungrily. His hand slid down the skin the dress left bare on my back and over the satiny fabric clinging to my hips. A sharper ache settled between my legs. I wouldn't have believed it was possible to want one man this much, let alone four, but I did. God help me, I did.

The murmur of the opening door interrupted those thoughts. The heron shifter I'd seen earlier stepped out onto the terrace, clearing his throat. I stepped back from Nate, not even flushing. After the near-orgy I'd seen in the courtyard yesterday night, it was hard to think a little kissing was going to raise any eyebrows.

"Your presence is requested in the dining hall, Dragon Shifter, Alpha," the young man said with a respectful dip of his head.

"We're on our way," Nate replied. He wrapped his hand around mine and pushed away from the railing. We walked hand-in-hand to the door, not with him leading, but in stride together.

I'd have thought it was a perfect moment if not for the dinner ahead of us, which I knew was going to be anything but fun.

CHAPTER 17

Ren

WHEN I WALKED into the dining hall, at first I couldn't do anything but blink in awe. The room was so big I'd bet you could have fit a football field in there. Long teak tables set for twenty each stood in rows across the hardwood floor. Another of those tables, this one covered with a red silk tablecloth, stood on a dais at one end of the room. Five of the chairs on the far side of that table were carved in an ornate style, with the one in the middle the tallest and most elaborately sculpted.

I didn't need anyone to tell me that was the dragon shifter's chair.

My heart started thudding twice as hard. Other shifters were already moving around the room, talking with each other and greeting newcomers. I felt all those eyes move to me as Nate and I approached the high table. I must have talked to a lot of them last night at the welcome celebration, but somehow this felt different. Then everyone had been partying. Now we were down to more serious business.

Aaron appeared by the high table to meet us. Like Nate, he'd put on a suit for the occasion—a royal blue number that made his eyes look even more brilliant. Damn, I really had lucked out in the mates department, hadn't I?

A woman who looked a few years younger than Aaron, with the same golden-blond hair and bright blue eyes, stood by his side. She studied me with an expression that wasn't exactly unfriendly, but wasn't all that welcoming either. Her dress was a simple Grecian style gown in gray silk, and I could tell from the way she held herself that it wasn't her usual get-up.

Her arms, crossed over her slim chest, were solid muscle. Right. Aaron had said I'd be meeting his sister—the one who'd appointed herself as a sort of bodyguard. She definitely looked the part.

"Serenity," Aaron said, motioning me over. "This is my sister, Alice. Alice, meet Serenity, my mate."

"Hmm," Alice said. She held out her hand for me to shake and squeezed mine tightly as she pumped my arm. "So you're the one who's had my big brother running around all over the country. Glad you finally made it back here."

Her voice was so deadpan I'd have thought she was being snarky, but her lips curled into a playful but warm smile. I relaxed a little inside.

"It was a long trip getting here," I said. "But I did make sure he returned in one piece, as much as certain rogues might have preferred otherwise."

Her smile grew into a grin. "I'll give you that. And it's probably a good thing he's got someone dragging him out of that library every now and then."

Aaron gave her a baleful look. "The more time I spend

outside the library, the more you complain about all the potential danger I'm putting myself in."

"Only when you don't bring me along." She gave him an affectionate pat on the arm and shot me another smile. Okay, I liked this chick.

Aaron escorted me the rest of the way to my special chair, as if I needed help finding it. I guess the formality looked nice for our spectators. And it wasn't like I minded the reassuring squeeze of my shoulder as he took his seat beside me.

I was particularly glad that he and Nate had been the first ones here, because I had them sitting directly next to me on either side. I still wasn't sure what to say to Marco or West. They'd both avoided me all day.

Marco showed up first, sauntering to the chair beside Nate with his usual carefree expression. When our eyes met for a second, his were wary. I dragged my gaze away, my throat tightening. I didn't want to think about our earlier conversation or the revelations it had brought right now.

West arrived a few minutes later. He stalked to his chair without a word or a glance at me and sank into it abruptly.

Alice, who was sitting at his other side, leaned forward to catch my eye and raised her eyebrow. Okay, so that chill wasn't just in my imagination. Was he pissed off because he hadn't meant to make out with me last night? Or was something else going on in that inscrutable wolf shifter head of his?

The chairs across from us began to fill. Aaron introduced me to each figure as they sat down. The Cumberlands, Hubert and Isla. The Porters, Frankford and Tracy. And so on. I caught whiffs of their scent, my instincts and their forms helping me determine their animal side. Hubert and Isla were swans. Frankford and Tracy falcons. The couples around them included hawks, pelicans, and even a couple of geese. I had to bite back my amusement imagining their rounded bellies and long necks in bird form.

"Well," Hubert said to Aaron after a passing nod to me, "I hope the arrival of the dragon shifter means the community can move forward in a more orderly fashion from here on."

Tracy gave a harsh sigh. "It has been a stressful several years."

I'm sure your alpha has been doing his best, I wanted to say, but I bit my tongue. Aaron didn't look offended. And it would probably be a wise idea for me to make a good first impression.

"I've already observed a change in the tone of conversations," Aaron said smoothly. "Seeing the four of us alphas united around Serenity gives everyone the stability we've been needing."

Frankford peered at me over his hooked nose. "And this is the girl we've been waiting for all this time."

He didn't sound impressed. Had he expected me to come to the table in dragon form? "Here I am," I said, trying not to show how uncomfortable I was.

Servers started to come around with plates of food. Oh, good, at least I'd have something safe to do with my hands—and my mouth. I picked up my fork, jabbed it into a slice of steak... and realized everyone on the other side of the table was staring at me.

My shoulders stiffened. Nate leaned over and said gently by my ear, "At the formal dinners, the tradition is that the five of us don't start until everyone else is eating. It's a symbolic thing, or something."

"Oh." My face flushed hot. I set down my fork as if it had burned me. Great, now I already looked like a nitwit in front of all these bigwigs. The last seven years, mostly living on the streets, waiting to eat often meant someone else snatching your food out from under you. I guessed I was going to need a major attitude adjustment.

"I'm sorry," Aaron murmured. "I should have warned you."

I should have waited and followed their lead. Had West just shot a glower at me? Great, one more reason for him to think I couldn't cut it in this role.

I kept my hands folded in my lap until the servers had finished moving around the room. All around the tables, the estate's guests dug in. When my alphas picked up their silverware, I figured it was safe for me to start too.

Now that I could eat, I had to say the food was freaking delicious. Not that I'd expected anything else after spending a day in this place. I chewed blissfully, letting the rich, tender bites of steak overwhelm my embarrassment.

It wasn't enough to keep Isla occupied, though. She jabbed her fork toward Aaron. "As soon as possible, you need to do something about that feline kin bunch who've been running around in the Southend forestland area."

"I've already started discussing it with their alpha," Aaron said in the same even tone as before. He tipped his head toward Marco, who offered a narrow smile. "It's a big forest. We're all running out of room where we can exercise our animal natures in private. I think we can find a fair division."

I frowned. "Why *divide* it? The cats will mostly be using the ground and the birds the canopy, right? Can't you all use all of it without much hassle?"

Isla pursed her lips with a disgusted expression. Her husband cleared his throat. "There are boundaries in place," he said, shooting Aaron a look as if accusing him of misinforming me. "For good reason. The feline kin have a history of harassing avians. They agreed decades ago they would not intrude on our kin's spaces."

So this was a Sylvester and Tweety sort of conflict? I'd have laughed if it weren't for all those disgruntled looks. I'd put my foot in it again. Shit.

"Oh," I said. "Okay. I didn't realize."

Was that *pity* they were looking at me with now? The back of my neck prickled. Hell, I'd only been preparing for this gig for two weeks, a significant amount of which I'd been busy simply keeping myself and my mates *alive*. Couldn't these people cut a girl a break?

Maybe I should just not talk. That was a surefire way not to sound like a total dumbass.

The talk turned to some event the Cumberlands wanted to organize for the kin group, and then a couple of business concerns I couldn't follow. I cleared my plate, sated but definitely still with room for dessert. Just sitting there, listening to conversation that was going over my head, made me restless. How could I be a proper mate to any of the alphas when every other shifter in the room could see how clueless I was?

Then Frankford started ranting about humans. "We should have bought up that plot of land when we had the chance. Now those people will be right on our doorstep. Making their stupid human assumptions, offering their stupid human advice. So wretchedly unaware."

"But can you imagine the stir if they did know?" Tracy twittered. "The poor creatures couldn't wrap their heads around the power we have."

I couldn't just sit quiet then. "Not all humans are jerks," I said. "My best friend has stuck with me through everything."

Isla gave me another of those pitying looks. "But would she if she found out what you are? I think not."

A flicker of anger shot up inside me. "Well, you'd be wrong. Because she already knows, and she's still got my back."

If I'd thought the shifter bigwigs had looked horrified before, now they looked absolutely aghast. The color drained from Isla's face. Hubert's mouth twisted into a grimace.

"You revealed yourself to a *human*?" Tracy spat out.

Aaron raised his hand for calm. "There were extenuating circumstances," he said. "We made a judgment call. It worked in our favor. Serenity's friend did prove to be a valuable ally."

"To expose not just shifter affairs, but those of our alphas..." Frankford shook his head.

I gritted my teeth. That wasn't enough to contain the rising flare of my frustration.

"Look," I said tartly, "I'm the dragon shifter around here. I'm the only one you've got. If *I* can't make a call about who can know what, who else exactly is qualified to do that?"

Someone down the table muttered something under their breath. Most of it was too low for me to catch, but I heard enough. "...so long away from her own kind..."

My hands clenched under the table. "Does anyone here need a demonstration?" I asked, raising my voice slightly. "To make sure I'm dragon enough for you? I could bring down the ceiling. I could set the whole place up in flames. The shifting part is covered. The rest of the details I'm learning as fast as I can." I eased open my fingers to grasp Aaron's hand, setting it on the table between us. He gripped mine in return, the corner of his mouth twitching up.

"And there's no one I'd rather have by my side while I'm learning than your alpha," I added. "He followed me when I needed his help, and I'll follow him anywhere he needs me to go. Anywhere all of you need us to go, to keep the community strong. So I'd appreciate it if you'd give me a little credit."

Silence hung all around the table for a moment. The shifters across from us lowered their eyes. Fuck, had I made an embarrassment of myself all over again?

Before I could make any more mistakes, dessert arrived. Perfect portions of strawberry cheesecake for me to drown my sorrows. I kept my mouth shut and watched and listened.

When the meal was over, Aaron stood up, tugging me with him.

"It's an honor to stand before you with my fellow alphas and, of course, my new mate," he said to our audience, pitching his voice to carry through the room. "Thank you all for how welcoming you've been to Serenity. You won't find a more devoted advocate or tenacious fighter for our people."

My face warmed. He said a few more things about how great I was, and I gave a wave to the crowd, but inside I felt unsteady.

The farewells to the guests passed in a blur. Aaron walked me back to my rooms. I let him in and collapsed face-first on my bed with a groan.

"You didn't have to pile on the compliments like that. I'm so sorry for running my mouth. I will never speak again."

Aaron chuckled. "What are you talking about? You *were* great."

I turned my head to raise a skeptical eyebrow at him. "What are *you* talking about? I made a total fool of myself at least five times."

"Not at all." He sat down on the bed beside me, smiling. "You showed them you'd follow our traditions when you knew what those were. That you were willing to take new information into consideration. That you're devoted to the people you care about. And that you've given that loyalty to me. I couldn't have asked for more."

Was he serious? He sounded like he meant it. I couldn't quite believe it, but a little of the tension around my heart fell away.

I pushed myself upright and leaned in to kiss him. Aaron slid his fingers into my hair as he kissed me back. I tried to channel every bit of love and gratitude I was feeling into the meeting of our lips.

My hand rested on his thigh. As I scooted closer to deepen the kiss, my palm slipped. My thumb grazed the hard bulge that had already come to attention in Aaron's dress pants.

Aaron hummed in pleasure, and a different sort of heat washed through me. Suddenly I knew exactly what I wanted to do with this wonderful, gorgeous man.

I trailed kisses along the edge of his jaw as I eased down his fly. When I tugged at his pants, he let me slide them down, watching me with eyes gone heavy-lidded with lust. The sight of it only stoked the fire inside me.

"Stay right there," I murmured, and knelt in front of him.

I flicked my tongue over the head of his cock. Aaron groaned. I grasped the base of his erection, and his hips canted toward me of their own accord. "Serenity," he started, as if to tell me I didn't have to, but I already knew that. I was dying to do it, for me as much as for him.

The man in front of me ruled over a quarter of all the shifter kin with even temper and measured words. But I had the power to make him lose his cool with a simple touch. And there were some parts of him I hadn't fully claimed yet.

I tipped my head, taking his cock into my mouth. The taste of him, even saltier than the ocean air, laced my tongue. I swiveled it around his shaft, loving the way it twitched at the motion. He leaned back on the bed, his hands fisting the covers. His breath was already rough.

I pumped my hand, gradually building speed, as I sucked him down and released him. Over and over, until his body was trembling and his breath coming in hoarse pants. I closed my lips around him even more tightly, and another moan carried into the air.

"Serenity," he said, "I'm going to come. If you keep going..."

Good. That was exactly what I wanted. A tingling grew between my legs as I slicked my lips up and down him. His cock twitched again. His breath stuttered. Then his hips jerked up as his release hit the back of my mouth.

"Serenity," he muttered. "Serenity." His hand stroked over my head. And just for that moment, nothing else mattered—not betrayals or lies or scheming rogues and fae. There wasn't a single thing in the world that could hold me down.

CHAPTER 18

Marco

It was hard to say what the most terrible moment in my life had been, but it had definitely happened in the last twenty-four hours. Maybe at the top of the list I'd put hearing the pain and anger in my princess's voice when she'd accused me of treating her like a cat toy yesterday. Maybe these few seconds now, knocking on the door to her rooms at eight in the morning and wondering if she'll even answer.

Soft footsteps padded over the rugs on the other side. My back tensed. Ren eased open the door.

No, this was the most terrible moment right here. Having to watch my Princess of Flames flinch at the sight of me, the wound I'd dealt her still blazing clear in her eyes. It cut me from heart to gut with a sharp, searing burn that I absolutely deserved.

Why the fuck hadn't I kept my mouth shut for once in my life? Why had I let those idiot kin of mine rile me up?

Why had I let myself start thinking about my mate like a

means to an end, even a little? I knew *she* deserved better. I could give her better. If she ever gave me another chance.

But I wasn't going to grovel and moan. The pain I was feeling was my own fault and mine to deal with. I'd be twice as much an ass if I tried to lay that on her too, as if she should comfort me through my epic screw-up.

"Princess," I said with a dip of my head. "May I come in?"

She hesitated, and that just about killed me. Less than a week ago I'd tasted her most intimate places, and now she wasn't sure she even wanted me in the same room. It was going to be a long, hard climb back.

But she was worth it. I just had to make her believe I believed that.

I forced a self-deprecating smile. "I can make my apologies here in the hall if you'd rather. But I promise I'm not planning on imposing for very long."

"No," she said. "All right. Come in."

She must already have been up for a while. I could smell the traces of soap mingling with the sweet scent of her freshly washed skin. She'd picked out another dress: dusty rose-pink silk, simpler than the one she'd worn to the formal dinner last night but no less regal. It clung to her slim curves in a way that provoked a flash of desire all through my body.

She hadn't chosen it for breakfast with her mates, though, I'd guess. That was her armor for meeting the fae monarch.

"You'll put her fairy highness to shame," I said, nodding to the dress.

Ren brushed her hands over the flowing fabric, looking briefly awkward. Then she drew her posture straighter again. "I just want her to know she's dealing with a different kind of monarch," she said. "What was it you wanted to talk about?"

As if she couldn't guess. It was hard to hold her gaze while I pulled together the words, but I didn't want her to think I was shying away from responsibility. "Like I said, I need to apologize," I said. "You're right to be angry with me. I should never have talked about you that way, to anyone. I can't tell you how much I wish I hadn't. And I hate even more that you had to hear it."

"So why *did* you say those things?" she asked, crossing her arms over her chest.

God, how to say it. The words tasted bitter as I formed them. "There's a certain... air of confidence I've found I need to show when talking to my kin. Especially the ones who might have an eye on my position as alpha. If they think nothing much affects me, they don't find any weaknesses to exploit. But I shouldn't have let that extend to you. I owe you so much more respect than that."

Ren's eyes studied me steadily, giving away nothing. "Do you owe me it?" she said. "So you're telling me nothing you said to your kin reflected your real feelings, even a little?"

I couldn't lie faced with her dragon shifter sensibilities. She'd know, and that would only dig me deeper into this hole.

"I meant what I told you in the caves, princess," I said. "I care about you. I want to spend my life with you. But I can't pretend I'm not also aware that my position will be more secure once our bond is consummated. I may have pushed too much. I'm even more sorry for that."

There was so much more I could have said to try to explain, but I could read her too. And with the avian upper class sniping at her and this fae parlay looming, she clearly was in no mood for excuses.

The excuses were beneath me anyway. I'd screwed up. I owned that. What really mattered now wasn't what had happened in the past, but what I did from here on.

"I understand it'll take time to get your trust back," I added. "But I will, however long it takes. I may talk a lot, but I don't give my word lightly. I promise you I'll earn that trust back honestly."

Ren nodded. I couldn't tell whether she accepted the promise or just wanted me out of her sight. "Thank you for the apology," she said carefully. "I guess we'll just have to see how it goes. I'll need some space, so I can think."

Of course. When we were close to each other, our mate-bond still pulled her toward me as much as me to her. I could be grateful for that much.

I dipped my head. "Until our field trip into the fairy realm, then."

She didn't say another word as she saw me out. The door clicked shut behind me, and I couldn't say my heart felt any less heavy.

~

Ren

My head was so full of questions and worries about the upcoming parlay that I barely had room in there to decide how I felt about Marco's apology. I hardly had room to even pay attention to where I was going.

I followed the smell of eggs and sausage down the hall to the private dining room. My stomach was tight with anxiety, but I was going to need energy for this meeting with the fae monarch. I had no doubt about that.

How was she going to react when I told her what I know her people had done? How was *I* going to react if she tried to brush it aside or deny it? Aaron's people would be *really* unimpressed if

I managed to bring the shifters to the brink of a supernatural war less than a month after I'd shown up to take my spot as dragon shifter.

A woman came out of the dining room and headed toward me. I distantly registered her scent (owl), the tray she was holding (must have been bringing or clearing food), and the thin gloves covering her hands (was it colder than usual today?). Then my mind went back to mulling over the day ahead of me.

I wasn't paying her any attention at all when she dropped the tray at my feet and rammed a carving knife toward my stomach.

My shifter reflexes kicked in before I'd even processed that I was under attack. I leapt to the side, smacking out with my arm at the same moment. The knife only nicked my belly.

The woman gave a little cry and threw herself at me. I grabbed her wrist before she could take another slash. Scales rippled over my body as I started to shift defensively. I loomed over her, my haunches growing, my claws extending, fire rippling in my throat.

"Ren!" Nate's voice carried from behind me.

Another distraction was *not* what I needed right now. "Stay back," I shouted, my voice gone hoarse with the partial transformation. "I'm handling this."

The woman squirmed in my grasp. She aimed a kick at my hip, but it glanced off the thickly scaled skin that had formed there. She jabbed at my eyes with her free hand. I jerked away, and my grip on her wrist loosened. She broke free and took another stab at me.

With a growl, I knocked her to the floor. The knife sliced across my shoulder. I swiped at it with a taloned hand, sending it flying into the wall. The woman stared up at me, her eyes wide with what now looked like panic. I pinned both her arms to the floor, staring at her as I caught my breath.

The gloves suddenly made sense. She had to be hiding her lack of a kin mark.

I had her trapped. I'd stopped her, and now she couldn't get away. We could finally talk to one of these rogues—whatever good that might do us.

Nate's footsteps sounded behind me. He'd hung back like I'd asked him to. I shot him a quick, fierce smile over my shoulder. "Thank you. What do you say we find out what she knows?"

"You've got this," he said, coming to stand beside me. "Let me know if you need me."

But now that I had the rogue, I wasn't sure what to say. "Why did you attack me?" I asked, fixing my stare on her again. "Are you on your own, or are there other rogues here?"

"I'm not going to tell you anything," she gasped out, and set her lips in a firm line.

"Are you part of the group that came after my mother before—that murdered my fathers and sisters? How did you even get into the estate?"

She looked back at me without a word. Frustration boiled up inside me. The heat collected in my throat, and my mind leapt back to the words I'd heard as I'd accepted the crystal's flame in the mountain.

Burn away lies to get at what is real.

The urge to breathe fire tickled in the back of my mouth. I could do it—I could shift all the way, spill my fiery breath over this woman. But I'd never tried to use this new power before. What if I used it wrong, and all I did was burn her alive?

I'd hurt people while fighting them in self-defense before, but this rogue was already subdued. And being set on fire—that wasn't defense, that was torture. Every bone in my body balked at the thought.

That wasn't how I wanted to start my reign over the shifters. The rogues were the cruel ones, not me.

"Serenity?" Aaron had come out of the dining room. He stiffened at the scene in the hall. The rasp in his voice thickened. "What happened?"

"She attacked me with a knife—looks like one from the kitchens," I said. "But she's refusing to talk."

How did you make someone talk if you *didn't* resort to torture? I peered into her eyes, trying to find an answer there. She blinked, and a strange impression came over me.

The way she was gazing up at me... it wasn't angry. It wasn't even entirely afraid anymore.

She was in awe of me. I felt it, like a rush of warm air. And under it, a tight knot of sorrow. The pieces clicked together in my head.

"You didn't really want to do this, did you?" I said, letting my voice soften.

The woman's jaw twitched. A shadow of that sadness crossed her face. I'd hit the mark.

The door at the far end of the hall murmured open, but I didn't look back to see who was joining us. All my awareness stayed focused on the rogue.

"They forced you to help them," I said gently. "Did they threaten you? Or someone you care about?"

Her composure broke. A little sob fell from her lips. Her eyes had filled with tears.

Aaron knelt down at my other side. "I swear you will not be punished for crimes you were coerced into. By my oath as alpha." He held up his hand with the oath scar etched in the palm. A pulse of power tingled over me.

The rogue must have felt it too. A few of her tears spilled

down the sides of her face. "They have my son. He's only seventeen. He's all I have. If they find out I told you..."

"They won't," Aaron said firmly.

"And we'll stop them. We'll get your son back." I glanced at Aaron, and he nodded his approval. "Where are the rogues who took him?"

"I don't know," the owl shifter said in a thin voice. "Everything is passed through messages. I never see them face-to-face."

"Are they planning anything else? Do they have anyone else working for them on the estate?"

She shook her head. "I don't know. They only told me that if I managed to— If I—" She couldn't seem to spit out the words.

"If you killed me," I prompted.

"Yes. Then they'd return my son. That's all I know."

I bit my lip. I wanted to help her. I wanted to take down every one of the rogues who'd forced someone like her to take the fall for their schemes. But we couldn't when this was all she knew.

"We'll do what we can for you," I said, "but we'll need you to help us too. Find out more about them, where they are, what else they're doing. Who's involved. Anything, so that we can track them down. We won't reveal that we caught you. You can pretend you're still waiting for your chance, but that you want to do more for them. Act like you've decided you agree with them so they'll trust you. Can you do that?"

"If it gets my son back, I'll do anything." She dragged in a breath. "Thank you for your mercy."

I pushed off her, watching her as I stood. She sat up, no sudden movements, no sign she meant to try another attack. She might have bruises on her wrists from my grip tomorrow, but I couldn't help that. From the expression on her face, she wouldn't blame me for them.

"I'll make arrangements for you to get word to me, wherever I am, when you have any news," Aaron said.

"And of course we'll be keeping our own eyes out for your not-kin," West said in a brittle voice. Marco stood just behind him. Some relaxing breakfast this was turning out to be.

Aaron helped the owl shifter to her feet and ushered her off to the side to talk with her further. I sighed, leaning my hand against the wall.

The rush of adrenaline was fading, leaving me shaky. The lovely dress I'd picked out in the hopes of impressing the fae monarch at least a little was now torn around my legs from my partial shift. The skin on my belly stung where the carving knife had pricked it. The cut on my shoulder was only seeping a little blood now, but it still ached.

Nate slid his arm around my shoulders. "Let's go back to your rooms and patch you up." He shot a glance at his fellow alphas. "Have one of the servers bring a plate for her."

West glowered as if he resented the order, but Marco accepted it with a quick nod. "Not a problem." He looked toward the rogue woman, and his lips curled into a grimace. "And might I suggest you keep the door locked until the food gets there?"

CHAPTER 19

Ren

By the time Nate and I made it to my rooms, my legs were done. I wobbled over to the sofa in the sitting room and sank onto it.

Nate ducked into the bathroom. He came back with a small silver case that turned out to hold pretty normal-looking first aid supplies.

I winced as he dabbed antiseptic cream on my cuts. He smoothed a thin adhesive bandage onto my shoulder and considered my stomach.

"I guess I should take this off," I said, reaching for the straps of the torn dress. "Being a shifter does seem to be hard on one's clothing supply."

Nate chuckled. "We always make sure to have lots of spares on hand."

I stripped the silky fabric from my body, leaving me in only my bra and panties. It was impossible not to see the heat kindling in Nate's gaze as he watched. An answering dampness formed between my legs. I swallowed hard and held out my hand for the other bandage.

He stood back while I attached it. I still didn't feel ready to stand up. I held out my hand to him, and he sat down beside me, collecting me against him—my bare legs across his lap, his arm around my shoulders, loosely so I had room to move away if I wanted to.

What I wanted was closer. I nestled against his solid body, letting the warm and strength in it soothe me. I didn't know the question was coming until it fell out of my mouth.

"Are they ever going to stop? The rogues—are they ever going to just leave me alone? I never did *anything* to them... They don't even know me!"

"I know," Nate said in his low baritone. He tucked his chin over my head and rubbed the side of my arm. "I don't even understand what they did sixteen years ago. To carry around that much hate, to want to hurt people that much... They're sick. Their minds are twisted. That's the only thing I can think."

"Then they won't stop. They'll just keep at it until they kill me—or we kill all of them."

"Maybe they'll be able to change their minds once they do get to know you." He pressed a kiss to my forehead. "You're already becoming a part of our community. Most of the kin are welcoming you—you've seen that, haven't you?"

My mind went to the iciness of the bigwigs last night, but the truth was they were just a small portion of the shifters, even if they were powerful. Most of the kin I'd met—the avians here, the canines in that other village—had thought more of me than I even did.

"Yeah," I said. "They've been wonderful, actually. I'm not sure I deserve it yet."

"Of course you do. By fighting back against the rogues, which you've done more than once already, you're fighting for all of us. For the security of all kin. And what you did just now, with that owl shifter... You proved you're trying to do the right thing for all shifters, even the rogues. People will see that. Word will be passed on. And the ones who aren't so twisted might realize they're wrong."

I wasn't sure whether I believed that was likely, but it was a nice thought all the same.

A knock sounded on the door. I couldn't help wincing. Nate gave my arm a reassuring squeeze and went up to answer it. He came back with a plate of breakfast foods that set my stomach grumbling.

For a few minutes, my hunger shoved our conversation to the wayside. I dug into the scrambled eggs, sausage, and hash browns as if I hadn't eaten in days. Shifting sure gave a person an appetite. Or maybe it was the adrenaline. Either way, I polished off the food like my life depended on it.

"Better?" Nate asked with an amused smile.

"Much." I set the plate aside and snuggled closer to him, wrapping my arm around his brawny chest. We still had a couple hours before we needed to leave for the parlay. And being with him, holding him and being held by him, was the best salve I could think of for my nerves right now.

What had the shifter who'd delivered my breakfast thought of this situation—of my hiding away in my room? That question brought my thoughts back to Nate's earlier comments.

"No one here really knows me yet," I had to point out. "Not even the people who like me. They're still waiting to see exactly what I'm going to do."

Nate hummed in agreement. "Maybe, but they're hoping it'll be good. They want to be on your side."

That was true, wasn't it? I'd felt that hope in every shifter I'd spoken to during the celebration. And with each step forward, I could give them a little more to justify their faith in me.

It wasn't just the ordinary shifters who had faith. My alphas had stood by me from the start, from when I'd been a total stranger to them, too. No matter how skeptical they might have been.

And Nate hadn't wavered once. He might have gotten over-enthusiastic with the heroics, but he'd never talked to me or acted in any other way like he doubted me.

I tipped my face back and touched his cheek. Nate didn't need me to tell him what I was looking for now. He bent his head, capturing my lips with a soft but eager kiss. His hands skimmed over my body, grazing every inch of bare skin. I slid my hand up under his shirt as I kissed him harder, wanting to feel him too. To explore every plane of that firmly muscled chest.

To really make him mine.

The thought swam up in my head through the haze of longing. No hesitation rose to counter it. The idea just felt *right.*

I tugged at Nate's shirt. He peeled it right off and leaned in for another kiss. Every spot his bare skin touched mine left me burning with even more desire. He stroked his hand up my back and worked the clasp of my bra free. As he trailed his kisses down to my collarbone, he cupped my breast with his strong, able fingers. His thumb swiveled over my nipple, sending a jolt of pleasure through me. I moaned, arching up on his lap.

He tipped my breast up to his mouth and teased the nipple even tighter with his tongue. My fingers dug into his shoulders. Pleasure coursed from my chest down to my core as he laved one breast and then the other. His hand followed his mouth, flicking and caressing until both nipples stood at stiff peaks and the rest of me was trembling.

"I love seeing how good I can make you feel," Nate murmured, nuzzling the side of my neck. "I love that I can take care of you this way. I've never wanted *anyone* like this, Ren. My heart always knew you were the one I needed."

A pang hit me, bittersweet. He'd taken such a chance, waiting for me. Giving up the happiness that had been right in front of him without ever knowing if I'd turn up.

I slid my hand around his neck and pulled him into a deeper kiss. My other hand rested on his lap beside my legs. On the hard length of his erection straining against his fly.

Nate groaned into my mouth. He eased his fingers up and down my hips, teasing the edge of my panties. Asking but not demanding. My tongue slipped into his mouth to tangle with his. For a long moment, I rode on the rush of pleasure that came from our mingling breaths. Then I pushed myself off his lap, pulling him with me. Toward the bed.

"I need you too," I said.

Nate gazed at me with a sudden intensity. He got up and stepped over to me, looming above me from his full height. But it was a reassuring loom. It made me feel larger that a man like this wanted me this much, not smaller. I hooked my fingers over the hem of his pants. His breath caught.

"Ren," he said, wonderingly. He touched the side of my face, so much tenderness in that powerful hand.

"I want you to be my mate," I said, gazing back at him. "And I want to be yours. From now until always."

"Hell, yes," he said. He bent to crush his lips against mine again. I gripped his shoulders as he walked us back toward the bed. When my legs hit the foot of the frame, I reached for the button of his pants. He kicked them off, and his boxers too.

For a second I just gazed at the perfection of his body. Six-foot-something of solid muscle and soft skin, all for my taking. And his cock, thick and long and standing at attention for me. Growing even harder when I stroked it from base to head.

Nate rumbled low in his chest. He scooped me up and laid me on the massive bed, making quick work of my panties. But the impulse to take control came over me. I nudged him onto his back and knelt over him. He grinned up at me, resting his hands on my hips.

"Lead the way. I'll be right there with you."

A rush of affection flooded me. I lowered my lips to his, kissing him long and hard. But too much desire had built up between my legs for me to wait long. I rubbed my sex against his cock. We both moaned. Inhaling slowly, I lowered myself right onto him.

His cock filled me completely with a heady burn. I whimpered, rocking against him until he was all the way in. He reached up to fondle my breasts with one hand while the other stroked over my clit. The combined sensations set off a flood of bliss that swept every other thought from my head.

I rode him desperately, chasing my release. He pumped his hips up to meet me. His breath turned ragged. A sheen of sweat dampened his muscled chest as I braced my hands against it.

"I want to watch you come," he murmured, swirling his thumb over my clit. "Take everything you need, sweetheart."

Something about those words sent me over the edge. The glow of our bond flared between us. It flowed over me, surrounding me in the protection I knew Nate would always offer me, whenever I needed him.

I bucked against him a few more times, and pleasure burst through my body. I gasped, clutching him. He caressed me through the wave, his eyes bright with appreciation—and a deeper desire.

Even as my nerves sang out, I wanted more too. Harder, faster. I sagged against him and gave him a little tug to roll us over. He flipped us without slipping out of me. I raised my legs on either side of his hips to give him even deeper access.

"More," I said. "Take me higher."

He thrust inside me with a shudder. "You feel so good, Ren. So fucking good."

A moan broke from my lips. "So do you. Give me everything. I can take it. I want it. Don't you dare hold back."

With a sound halfway between a groan and a chuckle, he thrust faster. Our skin slid together, slick with sweat. Every muscle in his body felt coiled beneath my groping hands, driving his shaft into me with everything he had. Just the way I needed it.

The pleasure swelled and swelled until I was shaking with it. I arched up, taking him all the way to the hilt, and another orgasm swept through me. Nate jerked with a hot gush inside me. His head bowed over me as he rocked to a stop.

We lay there, panting, for a long moment. I traced my fingers over his cheek, and he beamed down at me, so brightly it sent a flutter through my chest.

"I don't know how I got so lucky," he said, "but I'm sure as hell going to make sure I deserve it."

"Mmm," I said, pulling him down to cuddle against me. "I think this was an *excellent* start."

I fit against his body perfectly. His heart thudded beneath my ear where it pressed against his hot skin. I pressed a kiss to it, wishing I could stay here like this for the rest of the day.

His fingers glided up and down my back. "We'll have to get you back into another dress soon."

"I know. But not yet." Five more minutes without thinking about the fae monarch and what she might have in store for us—that was all I asked.

I nestled my head against his shoulder, closing my eyes against the rest of the world and the worries that came with it.

CHAPTER 20

Ren

INSECTS HUMMED around us as we tramped along the narrow path through the woods. The mossy smell in the air was kind of pleasant, but the terrain? Not so much. I glowered at a jutting root I'd nearly stubbed my toe on.

So much for getting a break from hiking after that long trek up and down the mountain. We'd driven most of the way to the neutral ground that lay between the avian estate and the fae monarch's domain, but apparently the fae found any sort of man-made transportation distasteful. Arriving to meet them with a motorized vehicle would have been a grave insult. So we were walking.

Which, frankly, was a grave insult to my feet, but I wasn't in a position to make demands on that big a scale yet.

It'd have been easier if I could have at least *flown*, but I was still pretty much a newbie when it came to shifting. The last thing I wanted was to blow my wad of energy before we even got to this fairy queen. From everything I'd heard, I was going to need all my wits and power for that confrontation.

My alphas had stayed in human form—so they could talk to the monarch too, I guessed, and probably also to keep me company. But a few of Aaron's kin had joined us as their bird selves. Alice had squeezed my hand and told me to give the fae hell before taking off as an eagle nearly as large as her brother's. A shrike, a raven, and an albatross were soaring over the forest alongside us as well, watching for any suspicious fae activity.

Aaron strode along in the lead, scanning the forest with his watchful eyes. Marco sauntered after him with his feline grace. West was walking as far behind me as he could manage without running into Nate, who was guarding our flanks.

The bond between me and my eagle and bear glowed through me with a comforting heat. But I was just as aware of my other two mates and the nagging pull toward them, begging to be fulfilled. Especially West. Even though he was keeping his distance, my back kept tingling with the sense of his gaze on me. A sudden, more heady kind of heat: there, then jerked away, then there again.

I tugged at the skirt of my new dress to lift it out of the way of my shoes as we scrambled up a small rocky slope. This one was a crimson silk instead of the earlier pink, but I liked it too. It was a color that said I wasn't one to take any nonsense.

Which I wasn't, with fae or with my mates.

I slowed my pace until West had no choice but to let me fall back beside him. The path was just wide enough for us to walk side-by-side, though I had to make a conscious effort not to let my arm brush his. He looked straight ahead, his jaw tightening.

"Is this really how we're going to do this from now on?" I asked. "With you going around all day acting like I've gravely offended you somehow?"

"None of my responsibilities as alpha demand that I pander to you," he retorted.

"Oh, please. In the last two days you've been friendlier to the furniture than you've been to me. I'm not saying you've got to throw me a party. I just don't see why you've got to completely freeze me out."

I heard him swallow. "I think you know what the problem is, Sparks."

A flare of anger I hadn't expected shot through me. Because I didn't know. Because nothing about how he was acting seemed remotely reasonable to me.

I raised my chin. "I can think of a whole lot of things you might be pissed off about, but I honestly haven't got a clue why you seem to be pissed off at *me*. You want to be my mate and you also don't. Fine. Take all the time you want figuring that out. When have I ever said anything else? I'm not trying to push you into anything. The most I've ever asked you for is a kiss, two weeks ago. So be frustrated with yourself, or the situation, or, hell, even my mom for how she handled things. But I don't see how it's fair for you to take that out on me."

Silence hung between us for a minute. There was nothing but the rasp of our feet over the uneven ground. I started to wonder if I'd pissed him off even more. Then West inhaled sharply. His voice came out even throatier than usual.

"You're right. I haven't been completely fair. I'm sorry for that."

Some of the tension in me ebbed. "So... we can move to at least polite conversation?"

The corner of his mouth twitched. "Maybe some. That's not really my forte at the best of times. Don't push your luck."

He hadn't said much, but the space between us felt less fraught now. I was about to pick up my pace and give him the breathing room he obviously wanted when he added, "So I guess we're heading to the bear shifter's estate next."

There was an odd note in his voice that squeezed my heart even though I couldn't say exactly why. "What makes you say that?"

One of his eyebrows lifted. "The five of us are all bound together to some extent, Sparks. When you confirm that connection with one, you'd better believe the rest of us know it."

My cheeks warmed at the thought of the other guys sensing what Nate and I had been up to a couple hours ago.

But why shouldn't they know? Eventually, the way things were meant to be, it *would* be all of us.

I rubbed my mouth. "Ah. Well, yeah, I guess it would make sense to visit Nate's kin next. The way things are."

West made a noncommittal sound. I wasn't sure what to make of that. But the conversation seemed to be over, so I sped up. We had to be getting close to the meeting spot anyway. I couldn't afford to be distracted from that.

The path had swerved. Aaron was just disappearing from sight up ahead. I hurried even more, my nerves prickling—and a bright feathered shape swooped out of the sky in front of me.

Alice transformed as she plummeted, but with complete control. She landed on her feet with a thump, her hands already rising in a defensive stance. She'd kept her eagle talons protruding from her bare feet. They looked nearly as sharp as my dragon claws.

Before I could take another step, Alice's right arm shot out to motion me back. I halted. My ears perked, but I didn't hear anything ominous in the forest around us. "What's wrong?"

"That tree." She waved a fist at the broad juniper a few feet ahead of us by the end of the path. "Something's off about it. It got this... glint to it when you came close."

The tree? I cocked my head at it, but it still looked like a totally ordinary plant to me. Alice took a few steps closer, totally at ease in her nakedness. I'd been around shifters enough in the last few weeks that their casual nudity was starting to seem a lot less weird to me.

The muscles running through Alice's sturdy frame tensed. The guys had stopped, Aaron backtracking. "What's going on?" he said.

"I think there's a trap in this tree," Alice said, jabbing a taloned foot toward it. "But Serenity is the one it's set to activate for."

Marco sniffed the air. "There is a whiff of fae around here. I assumed it was from their arriving at the meeting place."

"It sounds like there's an easy way to find out," I said. "Why don't we see what the tree does if I come closer? Unless you don't think it's worth the risk." Alice clearly had a lot more experience in this kind of situation than I did.

Her mouth flattened, but she nodded. "Slowly. And be ready to retreat."

I edged one careful step and then another along the path. Nothing moved in or around the tree. Maybe she'd been wrong? I trusted her instincts, but we were also all a little on edge.

I eased my foot a few more inches forward—and all at once the entire tree lunged. Its trunk wrenched forward and its branches dove down as if to swallow me in their grasp.

I ducked, stumbling backward. Alice leapt to meet the tree. Her leg slashed through the air, talons severing one branch. Her elbow slammed into another to snap it. A shower of leaves rained down on me. I spun back toward it, a shift already prickling under my skin.

Alice stood panting, her lips curled in a fierce grin. Twigs and broken branches scattered the path. The battered tree had pulled back into its original pose as if it had never moved.

"What the hell was that?" I said.

"Alice was right," Aaron said. "There must be an enchantment on the tree. It was set to descend on you when you came by. As soon as you backed away, the effect lifted."

"A *fae* enchantment," West spat out. "What else could use magic like that?"

My heart thudded. "Do you think—the monarch—"

"She wouldn't *dare*," Nate rumbled in a low, dark voice. A grizzly's rage flashed in his eyes.

"She wouldn't," Marco agreed. "But we've already seen that her underlings don't mind finding ways to circumvent the treaties. A few bad apples, I'm sure she'd say."

West bared his teeth. "It doesn't matter. We take responsibility for the rogues. Every fae is hers to deal with."

"And we'll make sure she does," Aaron says. "When we meet her. It's almost time." He glanced at me. "If you give the tree a wide enough berth, the trap shouldn't activate again."

I nodded. With one last glare at the juniper, I picked my way through the brush on the other side of the path. The tree didn't stir. I let out my breath when I'd come around the bend, back onto the somewhat clearer ground.

"I'd better get back to the skies in case they've got more surprises for us," Alice said. Her legs flexed to spring into the air.

"Thank you," I said quickly, catching her gaze. "I've never seen anyone fight a tree before, but you were pretty amazing at it."

Her grin came back. "Nothing's ever gotten the better of me yet. I'll have your back, Serenity."

I appreciated the promise, but I approached the neutral meeting spot with my nerves even more on edge. I was finding it less and less easy to believe that the fae monarch was an ignorant bystander in all this. Whatever friendship there might have been between fae and dragon shifters before, something had gone very, very wrong.

The trees thinned and then fell away completely. We came out into a wide clearing, nothing but grass and a dabbling of little pink flowers from one end to the other. The sky was stark blue overhead. The warm breeze warbled faintly through the branches around us.

We'd only taken a few steps into the clearing when the fae delegation appeared on the other side. There had to be at least ten of the tall, emaciated-looking figures with their blue-white skin. The cloying smell of them made my nose wrinkle.

At the front of their procession strode a woman even taller than the others. The silvery blond waves of her hair streamed across her shoulders and down over her filmy dress all the way to her ankles. Her large eyes glittered like black diamonds. A faint shimmer rose off her hair and skin. A crown of living vine coiled around the top of her head, but even without that, I'd have known she was the monarch.

My back stiffened, but I kept my expression as calm as I could manage. We walked to meet the fae in the center of the clearing, Aaron and Nate drawing close by my sides, West and Marco flanking us. The other avian shifters circled in the air just overhead.

"Monarch," Aaron said, with a slight dip of his head. "We appreciate you coming out to speak with us."

The fae woman's gaze barely glanced off him. She looked me over, her face impassive. "So this is the new dragon shifter."

So this is the woman who killed the last one, I wanted to say, but I held my tongue. Direct accusations of murder weren't very diplomatic. "Here I am. It's good to meet you." *So I can finally get some answers.*

"And what is the reason for this parlay?" the monarch asked, her gaze sliding back to Aaron now. As if he were more worthy of her attention than me.

I couldn't help bristling a little. "*I* requested it," I said, "because I have questions about the fae presence in the mountain over Sunridge. And also, now that I'm here, about the enchantment placed on a certain tree along our path through the neutral ground."

The monarch frowned, her eyes carefully blank. "Sunridge? The name sounds vaguely familiar, but I can't say it's a place I've given much consideration. And I know nothing about any tree."

Yeah right, she didn't. "There was magic on it," I said. "An enchantment for it to attack me. No one except a fae could have done that."

"Are you sure? You haven't exactly had much exposure to our kind, have you? From what I understand, you haven't seen much even of your own people."

Okay, now my hackles were *really* up. Was that how she wanted to play this? Nate stirred, but I held out a hand for him to stand down. I didn't need him fighting this battle. I wasn't going to make it far as dragon shifter unless the fae monarch learned to respect *me*.

"I know enough," I said. "And I have my alphas when I need extra guidance. I didn't need any help at all to see what your people did to my mother on that mountain."

A flicker of something passed through the fae woman's face, so fast an ordinary human wouldn't have caught it. But I wasn't human.

"The last I heard of your mother, she'd run off from the kin groups many years ago," the monarch said, but she was lying. I felt it through every bone in my body.

I drew myself taller. Maybe not as tall as her, but I had a whole lot more meat on my bones, so I had to look a little intimidating. "There is a treaty between your people and mine. You will take responsibility for the crimes committed by yours. But if you really want to try me, go right ahead and lie to my face again."

Behind me, Marco smothered something that might have been a snicker. A chill glittered in the monarch's eyes. "*Are* these your people?" she said in a cutting voice. "From what I can see, you've barely accepted two of their leaders as your chosen mates. And you're speaking to me of responsibilities?"

My throat went abruptly hot, fire flickering at its base. My skin tingled with the itch to take on its scales. I kept the impulse to shift in control, just barely. "It's still my life. I will make my choices in my own time. I'd have been more ready for them if your people hadn't taken my mother from me. But I *am* ready to make you answer for those crimes."

Aaron took a slight step forward. His voice rang out. "As alpha of the avian kin, I stand with Serenity Drake completely."

Nate lifted his head. "As alpha of the disparate kin, I stand with Serenity Drake completely."

Marco moved to stand at Aaron's side. "As alpha of the feline kin, I stand with Serenity Drake completely. And I will for the rest of her life, wherever it takes her."

I'd never heard him sound so serious. A piece of the hurt I'd still been feeling fell away.

Before I could wonder if the wolf shifter would extend his loyalty that far, he appeared next to Nate. "As alpha of the canine kin, I stand with Serenity Drake completely. When she demands your respect, she speaks for *all* of us." He glowered at the monarch.

The fae woman made a faint sniffing sound. "I have told you what I know. I have seen no proof of the crimes you claim. If all you've called me here for is baseless accusations, I've given you enough of my time."

She swiveled on her heel. Her fae attendants parted around her to give her room to pass through.

She really was going to just walk away from me. As if I had no authority at all. As if she owed me *nothing*, after everything her people had taken from me.

No. She was going to learn right this moment what a mistake it was to dismiss this dragon shifter. It didn't matter how long I'd been gone or how some of the bigwigs might talk about me. I was here now with my alphas by my side, and I claimed this power as mine.

"Stay right there," I snapped, my voice already hoarsening. I had just enough wherewithal in my fury to tug off my silk dress as the shift came over me.

My muscles stretched and sang, the burn only pleasant now. Flames seared the back of my lengthening throat. I rose and loomed, flexing my massive wings.

The fae monarch whirled around. She didn't look so tall now, standing beneath my dragon's body. I peered at her with narrowed eyes. She gave me a cold smile. A crackle of magical energy glittered around her body.

"To attempt to harm me would be an act of war," she sneered.

But I didn't want to harm her. No, the sizzling in my throat was the fire of the crystal, the fire of that gift of truth. I'd been afraid to try to claim it before, but I shouldn't have been. It *was* mine, and I trusted myself. This woman needed to know exactly who she was dealing with.

I opened my mouth and breathed from deep down in my chest, where a ring of loss ached around my heart.

Flames poured down over the monarch. They shattered her protective shield. Her attendants shrieked. But the flames weren't the bright yellow and orange fire that would have burned her to a crisp. They flickered white and violet, surrounding the fae woman in sharp shards of light.

Burning through to the truth.

Her eyes widened. Her lips parted, her hands clutching at the base of her throat as if she were trying to hold back her voice. But it spilled out anyway, wavering through the flames.

"I heard of your mother's death," she said, sounding choked. "I knew a group of fae were responsible, but no one else did, so I let it be. I have not punished them. There are others I've heard speaking out against the shifters. I haven't encouraged them, but I haven't stopped them either. If one used magic against you today, I can easily guess who it was."

Her attendants fell back around her, gaping at her admission. Aaron fixed her with a stare of steel. "Why have you let those crimes slide?"

The monarch's lips twisted, but my flames still surrounded her. "It's been easier for us while the shifter community was disordered. We've been able to claim more territory, refuse more compromises. I was happy to let that situation continue."

I winced inside at the admission. A hotter fire tickled the base of my throat, wanting to punish *her* for all the hurt she'd allowed to happen. I held it at bay and sent another gust of the truthful flames over her. My dragon form was starting to quiver with the strain of this unfamiliar power.

"Will you accept Serenity's authority and ours from now on?" Nate asked.

"Yes," the fae woman gasped. "As much as I have to."

I didn't like the sound of that. But I couldn't produce another burst of flames. I let them peter out, just barely holding on to my dragon shape. I stayed there and glowered down at her.

The monarch rubbed her hands over her arms as if trying to dispel the fire that had already vanished. She stared up at me. For the first time, I saw fear in her eyes. Fear—and a hint of rage underneath it.

I'd gotten the better of her this time, but she wasn't going to forget it. Whatever conflict had been brewing between the fae and the shifters, it was far from done.

"These accusations don't seem so 'baseless' now that you've admitted they're true, monarch," Marco said archly. "Where do you say we go from here?"

She seemed to catch a scowl. "I will make reparations," she said. "The fae who have acted against the shifters in any way will be punished according to the treaty. So will others in future if I hear of it myself. You have my word."

That last sentence settled in the air with a supernatural finality. We could trust her at least that far. I guessed we couldn't exactly ask her to commit to *feeling* any particular way about the shifters.

I bowed my head, blinking at her, and a shiver passed through her skinny body. "Does that resolve our business here?" she asked.

"Other than one thing," Aaron said. "When you address your people who've acted against us, that should also include any who've helped rogue shifters make attacks on us or the rest of our community. Agreed?"

She nodded with a jerk. "Agreed."

She shot me one last look before she turned with a sweep of that flowing hair. A look that told me she was beaten for now, but not forever.

But as victories went? I'd take that.

When the fae had disappeared back into the forest, I released my dragon form. My body crumpled with a shudder. I gasped a breath down my suddenly sore throat. The power I'd been granted had felt amazing, but it'd left my body throbbing.

Nate offered me my dress. I slid it back on, regaining my balance. "All right," I said. "Let's go home."

CHAPTER 21

Nate

"I DON'T KNOW why I feel so shaken up," Ren said. "I already knew she was dead, and that the fae killed her."

She rubbed her hand over her face. We were standing in her bedroom in front of the mirror where she'd been combing the dark brown waves of her hair. They spilled smoothly over her shoulders and the neckline of the teal dress she'd chosen for tonight's farewell gala. Tomorrow we were moving on to my estate to the south.

I rested my hand on the small of her back, and she leaned into me automatically. Touching her had always made my heart leap, but nothing could compare to the steady heat of the connection that now thrummed between us. A bond that should last as long as we both lived.

"You didn't know how much approval those fae had from their monarch," I said. "You had to hear her talk as if your mother's murder meant nothing to her. Of course that bothered you."

"Yeah. I guess that makes sense." She drew in a long breath and squared her shoulders. "Back out into the fray."

I chuckled, taking her hand as we headed for the door. "Just remember that you did what you came here to do. We can't bring your mother back, but we are getting justice for her. And you got it using the power she always wanted you to have."

Ren nodded, her hand rising to the hollow of her throat.

The courtyard in front of the avian estate was already teaming with shifters, like it had been when we'd first shown up two nights ago. A band was playing a jaunty tune on the steps, and people everywhere were dancing. Ren swayed my arm in time with the music, but I had two left feet when it came to keeping a rhythm.

"I think I'd better hand you off to Aaron if you're in the mood for dancing," I said with a grin. The eagle shifter was already making his way over to us.

"I'll be back," Ren said, with a quick peck on my lips. I watched as Aaron swept her away, spinning her and dipping her. Our dragon shifter laughed, her eyes shining, and the warmth in my heart grew.

She was finding her home here with us, in spite of all the tragedy in her life before now.

"And we're staking our livelihoods on *that*," a voice muttered just behind me.

The grizzly in me bristled automatically. I glanced around and spotted one of the couples who'd been sitting across from Ren at last night's dinner—one of the ones who'd sniped at her for every minor mistake. The man was the one who'd spoken. The woman was shaking her head in dismay.

"I know. It's shameful."

I gritted my teeth against a roar. My fingers itched to sprout my claws and smack those two bird-brain heads together. My hands clenched—and then I remembered everything Ren had said to me before.

She wouldn't want me making a scene in the middle of this party on her behalf. I could defend her without going into full bear mode.

"You'd almost think—" the husband started, and I cleared my throat, turning all the way toward them.

"You'd almost think what?" I said, letting my voice drop just low enough to be mildly menacing.

The couple startled, their stances stiffening. The man's jaw tightened. "I'm allowed to have whatever opinions I happen to hold about the people ruling over us."

"True," I said. "But if you'd seen how Serenity brought the monarch of all the fae to her knees earlier today, I don't think you'd be complaining. Or do you think *you* could make the fae tremble at the sight of you?"

His mouth opened and then closed again as he struggled for words. Yeah, that's what I'd thought.

"Talk to the guards who came along with us if you don't trust your own alpha's word," I said. "They'll tell you just how powerful our dragon shifter is."

"I suppose we will," the woman said. She grasped her husband's elbow and tugged him away. Which was for the best, because if they'd tried to take another jab at Ren, I couldn't have promised I'd have kept my animal instincts in check any longer.

"Defending our dragon shifter's honor again?" West said dryly. He'd come up beside me while I'd been distracted.

I frowned at the wolf shifter. "If you're here to snark, I don't really want to hear it. After this afternoon, even *you* have to admit she's something special."

West's gaze slid past me to where Ren was still dancing with Aaron. Her hair flew out around her face as he whirled her around. Joy and love shone on her face. I couldn't figure how any of us could have seen that and not felt his heart melt.

And maybe none of us could. West's expression softened slightly. So did his voice. "Maybe I do," he said. "Watching the monarch turn tail and flee... That really was something, wasn't it?"

A glow of pride filled my chest. "That was our dragon shifter."

That was my mate.

~

Ren

A sudden hush fell over the crowd around Aaron and me. We'd just stopped to catch our breaths after dancing for three songs straight. I looked up, and my body tensed.

A thin, pale figure had appeared at the edge of the courtyard, gleaming against the darkness. A fae man. He held his hand up with a motion I instinctively knew was a truce gesture. He meant no harm here.

But that didn't make me happy to see him.

Aaron stepped forward to meet the fae man, and I followed. The man's searching gaze stilled when it landed on us. He held out his other hand, which was shining with a sharper light.

"The monarch wishes you to know her word has been kept," he said. He whipped his hand upward.

A scattering of tiny lights burst apart over our heads. The fragments glittered and faded into the cooling night air.

"What—" I started, but the fae man had already vanished.

Murmurs rose up through the crowd, startled and awed. I turned to Aaron. "What was that all about?"

He looked up at the sky where the lights had disappeared, his expression solemn. "The monarch followed the terms of the treaty, according to their laws. The fae who acted to harm us and your mother have had their lights snuffed out."

"Oh." My stomach balled. I followed his gaze, thinking of those lives wiped out.

Just like they'd destroyed my mother's life. Just like they'd treated the rogue the fae woman in the mountain had claimed they'd found stalking us. That was how the fae worked, apparently. Quick and brutal.

Not the kind of enemies I really wanted to keep.

"The conflict between us and them isn't over, is it?" I said.

Aaron's mouth set in a grim line. "No, I don't think it is. But we're better prepared for whatever they try next than we've ever been before. And now my kin have all seen the sway you hold over them too."

He looked at me and smiled. I couldn't help smiling back. Maybe it was okay to pretend, just for a little while, that all our problems were solved.

The celebration wound down as night thickened around us. My eyelids were heavy by the time I found myself meandering down the estate's hall toward my rooms with my four alphas in tow.

When I caught sight of my door up ahead, a longing squeezed tight around my heart. Some part of my mind tripped back seven years to the nights curled up in the otherwise-empty apartment that had been my mother's, waiting with less and less hope every time to hear her key in the door.

I never wanted to feel that alone again. I shouldn't, now that

I'd found my mates. But just knowing they'd be on the other side of those walls suddenly didn't feel like enough.

Nate moved to head to his own rooms, and I held out my hand. "No. Stay with me?" My gaze slid over my other mates: Aaron calm and steady, Marco amused but slightly uncertain, West as gruff as ever. "All of you. I want you to stay. Please? I'm not asking anything more than that. I just don't want to sleep alone."

I knew Aaron and Nate didn't really need to be asked. Marco gave me his sly smile and said, "As you wish, Princess of Flames." West looked as if he'd bit back a scowl, but he inclined his head, as if to say he'd go along with the request begrudgingly.

Apparently he decided he needed to actually say it too. I held the door while they all filed in, and he paused in front of me. "Look, Sparks, what I said in front of the fae monarch doesn't mean—"

I rolled my eyes. "Of course," I said. "No commitments assumed. Now come on. I'm exhausted—aren't you?"

I climbed into the middle of the massive bed and settled amid the spread of pillows. The guys surrounded me, Nate and Aaron cuddling right up to me on either side. Marco and West kept a little more distance, but I hadn't expected anything else. I could still feel our bond winding warm and solid around me. The five of us altogether, the way I knew down to my soul it was meant to be.

My nerves settled. My body relaxed into the bed. I drifted off into sleep, encased in the certainty that no matter what troubles lay ahead, I was exactly where I belonged.

~

A frantic knocking shook me awake. I blinked in the dark room as my mates stirred around me. With a huff of breath I recognized as West's, one of the guys pushed off the bed and stalked to the door. The rest of us sat up. I rubbed my bleary eyes, my heart hammering.

"What is it?" West muttered as he opened the door.

A quavering voice carried through the sitting room to the bed. "We've just gotten word. There's been an attack on the bear alpha's estate."

DRAGON'S DESIRE

THE DRAGON SHIFTER'S MATES #3

CHAPTER 1

Ren

Sometimes you get a moment so heavenly you can hardly believe this really is your life. Like falling asleep cuddled between four insanely hot alpha shifters who are destined to be your mates.

A few weeks ago, I hadn't even been dating anyone. I'd only just gotten myself an actual apartment. Now I was enveloped in protective affection—and let's not forget the hotness—on the biggest, softest bed I'd ever seen in an estate so impressive it took my breath away. Okay, so more than a few people had tried to kill me in the last several days, but as I'd drifted off to sleep I was feeling like on the whole I'd come out ahead.

But of course, those heavenly moments never last. Something always shatters them. This time? It was a knock on the door in the middle of the night and a quavering voice saying, "There's been an attack on the bear alpha's estate."

West, who'd answered the door, flicked on the light in the

sitting room. The wolf shifter's voice came out tight. "I think you'd better come in."

The rest of us were already clambering off the bed. I'd been so exhausted that night I hadn't bothered changing. My dress from the farewell party with the avian shifters hung on me in a mess of wrinkles. I gave the soft fabric a quick tug and rubbed my eyes as I hustled to the doorway.

Aaron, the alpha of the avian kin and current owner of this estate, strode ahead of me. The light glanced off his golden hair the same way the sun shone off his feathers in his majestic eagle form. I'd always thought of him as my Disney prince, but right now his blue eyes were sharp and his square jaw clenched. More warrior than royalty.

"What exactly happened?" he asked the attendant who'd come with the message.

Nate, my massive bear shifter, came up beside Aaron. His usual gentle presence had fallen away, aggressive tension radiating from his brawny body. "Is anyone hurt?" he demanded in his low baritone. "Who attacked my people?"

West leaned against the wall by the door, his arms crossed over his lean chest and his green eyes narrowed. Marco, the jaguar shifter who was alpha to the feline kin, stopped beside me and set his hand on my shoulder tentatively. He and I hadn't exactly been on the best of terms in the last couple days—his fault, for shooting off his mouth to his kin and talking about me like I was some kind of prize to compete over—but now we clearly had bigger concerns.

The attendant ducked his head, his hands clasped in front of him. "I only know that we received an urgent call. The staff on the estate hope that their alpha can return as quickly as possible. It appears a group of rogue shifters somehow managed to break into the estate and attempted a surprise attack on some of the advisors and their families."

A growl rumbled from Nate's chest. "I'll go now."

"We'll all go," I said. "We were going to head there in the morning anyway. That's probably why they picked your estate to attack."

We all knew that the attack had probably been more about me than any of my alphas or their kin. As the last dragon shifter alive, it was my role not just to take all four of the alphas as my mates but to unite the entire shifter community at the same time. Given that I hadn't even known shifters existed, let alone that I was one, until a few weeks ago, I had a lot of work ahead of me.

But I wasn't going to back down. Especially not when it came to the assholes who'd killed my fathers and sisters.

Nate gave me a quick nod, already hustling out the door. For a guy that big, he could move awfully fast when he needed to. The rest of us hurried out behind him.

"Find whatever pilot is most rested," Aaron instructed the attendant. "We'll take the jet."

"The jet?" I repeated. I'd missed that part of the estate, apparently.

"Each of the estates has a couple of private jets on hand in case we or our advisors need to take care of matters elsewhere in a hurry," he explained as we headed down the white-walled hall. "It's a lot more reliable than counting on human-arranged flights."

"It just seems a little strange. Here, anyway. I mean, all of you can fly already."

The corner of his mouth quirked up into a tense smile. "Not half as fast as an airplane, even on my best days."

Fair. I wasn't sure I could beat a jet even in my dragon form.

And I couldn't hold my dragon form for more than fifteen minutes so far, so that was kind of a moot point anyway.

We'd just burst through a side door into the warm summer night when another set of footsteps pattered behind us. Alice, Aaron's younger sister and self-appointed bodyguard, dashed to join us. Her golden-blond hair was pulled back in a sleek ponytail and her eyes were brightly alert. Did the girl ever sleep?

"I heard the news," she said. "This time I'm coming along."

"Alice," Aaron started.

She waved her finger at him. "Nope. No arguments this time. Last time you were just going on a little trip to maybe find a missing dragon shifter, and you ended up battling rogues and nearly getting poisoned by faeries. This time we *know* someone where you're going wants you dead. Who knows what the hell other trouble you'll all get into?"

Aaron didn't look convinced, but he also didn't look like he had the energy to argue. It was still completely dark out. We couldn't have slept for more than a couple hours. And yesterday had been a very long day.

"I want Alice with us," I piped up to make his agreement easier. "It'll be nice to have a little break from all the testosterone."

West muttered something under his breath, and Marco chuckled. A twinge of guilt pinched my stomach. It was my best friend Kylie, who was back in Brooklyn recovering from a rogue attack right now, I should have been counting on for girl talk. But our friendship had gotten a little more complicated with every strange and scary revelation I'd encountered.

Alice grabbed my hand and gave it a squeeze in thank you. And I guessed to reassure me, because then she leaned over and said, "It'll be okay. We've handled worse."

I wasn't sure if that actually made me feel better. The shifter community had faced an awful lot of problems in the years they'd gone without a dragon shifter. It wasn't my fault that my mom had gone on the run and decided to lock away my memories of what I was, but it was hard not to feel a little responsible for the mess she'd left behind. I was the only one left who could pull the pieces back together.

The salty breeze off the Pacific washed over us as we loped along a path between a stretch of trees. On the other side, a small plane waited on a grassy runway. We scrambled up the steps into the cabin.

The space was bigger than I'd have expected from the outside of the plane. The ceiling was high enough that even Nate didn't need to hunch. Five pairs of leather-cushioned seats lined one wall. Marco dropped into one, running his hand through his jagged black hair. Aaron went to talk to the pilot who'd come running over.

It was a good thing the ceiling could accommodate Nate, because he was pacing back and forth in the aisle. His jaw worked and his hands were balled at his sides. "When I find them," he said. "When I find the rogues who did this..."

"Hey." I touched his arm, and he stopped, turning toward me. I looked up at him, raising my hand to cup his cheek. "We *will* find them, and we'll make them regret any harm they've done. We're getting there as fast as we can."

"I know. I just—" He shook his head. Teasing his fingers into my hair, he bent to kiss me. The tender press of his lips gave me the same shiver of pleasure as always, but I could still feel the frustration coiled through his body. He wasn't going to be able to relax until we got to his estate.

"This might help," Aaron said, returning. He tossed a cell phone to Nate and passed two others to West and Marco. "One of my assistants grabbed them from your rooms. The pilot is just checking the systems. We should be ready to go in a minute."

Nate grasped the phone with a relieved exhale and dialed a number. He went back to pacing as he brought the phone to his ear. I wavered on my feet, not sure what to do now. Was there anything I *could* do? I hated feeling this useless.

The jet's engine thrummed on. A hand grasped my wrist. "I don't think you want to try takeoff standing up, Sparks," West said in his usual gruff tone. He tugged me toward the seat next to him. "That might be a little much even for you."

I rolled my eyes at him. "Thanks for your concern." But I did sit down. West and I currently had a... very complicated relationship. He insisted he still wasn't sure I was cut out for the dragon shifter's role—or the role of his mate. On the other hand, he'd seemed very enthusiastic about me when we'd made out the other night. The earth and pine smell of him next to me was enough to get me a little warm between the legs as I remembered that moment.

At least the last time we'd talked he'd been able to admit that his issues were mostly his, not mine. And every now and then I saw a softer side to him. He'd stood up for me when I needed it. Thrown himself into battle more than once to protect me. The rest I guessed we'd just have to take it as it came.

Even Nate had finally sat down now, although he was talking urgently into the phone. The rumble of the engine rose as the jet started to move. It hurtled forward with increasing speed. There was a quick jolt, and we lifted off the ground.

My stomach lurched, but I knew it wasn't just because of the acceleration. The rogues had already caused enough pain in my life. The last thing I was looking forward to was seeing the destruction they'd brought to Nate's estate.

CHAPTER 2

Ren

THE PLANE SHUDDERED, and my eyes popped open. I hadn't even realized I'd closed them, but they were so heavy I'd obviously been asleep for a while. There was a crick in my neck from having my head slumped over.

Slumped over against... someone's leanly muscled shoulder. A shoulder that held the faint scent of earthy pine.

Oh crap. I jerked back in my seat, my heart skipping. I'd been so tired from our late and then interrupted night that I'd fallen asleep on my neighbor. Who happened to be West.

Who was watching me with an unreadable expression now.

"Um, sorry about that," I said. "I promise I didn't do it on purpose. I would never mistake you for a pillow."

Maybe that wasn't the most solid apology ever? I could definitely read the wolf shifter's expression now: That, folks, was a glower.

"Somehow that didn't stop you from using me as one," he pointed out.

"Yeah, well, you know, unconscious and all, can't be held responsible for my actions." I gestured vaguely with my hands.

"I hope that's not an excuse you're planning on pulling out very often."

I rolled my eyes. Would it kill him to cut me a break for a minute here and there? "If it bothered you so much, you could always have woken me up and made me move."

Something shifted in West's eyes. Something that made my mind trip back to that moment in the garden the other night when he'd laid me beneath him on that bench, his mouth all over me. I'd swear the temperature between us rose by ten degrees in that one instant as he held my gaze now, but maybe it was only me feeling it.

He reached out and grazed his fingers over my cheek. Brushing an errant strand of my hair away from my eyes. My pulse hiccupped at the gentle touch. He was so close it would have been simple to tangle my fingers in his silver-streaked auburn hair and—

West sat back in his seat, turning his gaze toward the front of the plane. Away from me. "We're almost there. Better prepare yourself, Sparks. Your job is only going to get harder."

I mentally smacked myself. Even if West had been remotely receptive to some kind of come on, now wasn't the time to be thinking about getting it on with anyone. We had the rogue attack to deal with. I still didn't know how serious the assault had been.

It was just hard to ignore the unceasing tug of the bond inside me. I was pretty sure the pull was getting even more insistent when it came to the two guys I hadn't consummated our bond with yet. Apparently *it* didn't care that I had perfectly good reasons for taking my time with Marco and West.

I leaned to the other side of my seat. It was easy to spot Nate a couple rows up. His dark brown hair, thick as his grizzly bear pelt, showed over the back of his seat. He had at least a few inches on all the other guys, all of whom were far from short.

My hand dropped to my seatbelt. But before I could go over and ask what the bear shifter had found out with his phone calls, the plane jerked again. A calm voice filtered from the speaker on the ceiling.

"You all should remain seated for the next ten minutes. We're coming in for our landing now."

Okay, I guessed I wasn't going anywhere yet. I tried to relax in my seat, but my heart was thumping now, and that had nothing to do with West a few inches away beside me. A glance out the window showed a stretch of rocky, desert-like landscape bleeding into a dense forest in the thin light of the emerging dawn. Nate's estate—the center of operations for the disparate kin who didn't belong to the canine, feline, or avian groups—lay in one of the wilder parts of California.

And because they'd known I was coming there, the rogues had gone after his advisors. *And* their families. If any children had been hurt because of me...

My chest tightened, and my fingers curled around the armrests. No. I couldn't think like that. I was doing my best. Any violence committed was totally on the rogues. If they had such a big problem with dragon shifters, they could have brought it up peacefully.

I knew all that, but it didn't completely loosen the twist of guilt around my heart.

My ears had started to pop with the change in air pressure when my phone chimed with a text alert. I wriggled it out of the pocket of my jeans. It had to be Kylie. At least talking to my best friend would take my mind off whatever disaster was waiting for us down there while I couldn't do anything to fix it yet.

Hey, girl. Didn't hear from you yesterday, just wanted to make sure you survived that big to-do the other night. And that they survived your gorgeousness in that dress!!!

Shit, had I really not talked to her at all yesterday? Between an assassination attempt, a confrontation with the faerie monarch, and the farewell party, I'd hardly had a chance to breathe. But Kylie had no idea what might have been going on here. Whether I might have found myself in more trouble. I hadn't told her the more dire parts of my adventures, but she'd seen the danger that could come with my role before I'd insisted she stay behind. Along with the rogue attack that had left her clawed up, she'd witnessed a skirmish between my alphas and a bunch of vampires.

Now I had double the guilt weighing on me. I quickly typed an answer. *Sorry! Crazy day. Yes, everyone survived the dress, including me. We just left for Nate's estate in California.*

Oh, wow, Cali! You definitely have to invite me over there sometime once you've settled in. That's at the top of my States To Visit list.

I smiled. *Of course. Right now, though... Probably not the best time.* I hesitated, debating how much to tell her. *You know the guys who attacked us in the shifter village? Some other rogues from their group broke into the estate last night.*

Oh, shit. Is everyone down there okay?

I don't know yet. But I'm definitely glad you're back in Brooklyn away from all the chaos.

Kylie sent back an emoji blowing a kiss. *You know I'd have your back no matter what, no matter where, Ren. Just say the word, and I'm there.*

I did know that. That was exactly why I wasn't telling her about the recent attempt on my life. It meant a lot to me that Kylie cared about me that much—until I'd met my alphas, she'd been the only person other than my mom who had—but I didn't want to put her in any more danger than I already had.

I started to text back asking what she'd been up to when the plane took a sharper dip. My seat vibrated as the wheels hit the runway. Stones rattled against the jet's undercarriage. It slowed to a halt almost immediately.

My gut knotted. We were here.

Sorry, I wrote to Kylie. *I've got to go now. Shifter business. I'll catch up with you more later.*

Don't worry about me! she replied with a line of hearts. As if I could help worrying.

But for now I was definitely more worried about what was waiting for us on the estate. Seatbelts clicked open all through the plane. We hustled out of our seats and down the steps.

The dry, hard-packed earth of the runway was lined with tall redwoods. Their tangy smell washed over me along with the chirping of an insect chorus.

A contingent of shifters I assumed were Nate's kin had come out to meet us. They were definitely a varied bunch. A muddle of scents tickled my nose as we approached the group. My dragon senses identified them on instinct: black bear, stoat, mink, elk, armadillo, manatee.

Nervous energy wafted off them, easing slightly when they saw their alpha in our midst. Nate strode to the head of our group, his jaw set and his eyes dark. But his kin's gazes drifted away from him to settle on me. A prickle traveled over my skin.

When I'd met some of West's canine kin in one of their villages, and when I'd arrived at the avian estate, almost all of the shifters had been friendly. Not just friendly, actually—they'd seemed awed to be in my presence. Fawning over me, wanting to touch me and hear me speak. It'd been a little overwhelming.

I couldn't say I missed the pressure of that kind of welcome. But this one... I wasn't sure these shifters were even happy I was here. Their eyes seemed to evaluate me as I came to a stop beside my newly consummated mate. Nate rested a hand on my back in acknowledgement, but his attention was completely on his kin.

"You made it here quickly," said the black bear shifter, a shorter but equally burly man who looked to be around forty. His short black hair stood up in a high buzz-cut. "It's good to have you back."

"We came as soon as we heard," Nate said. "Anything new to report, Thomas?"

Thomas started to walk down a path that I assumed led farther into the estate. The rest of us followed. Alice fell into step between me and Aaron as if she were trying to maximize her chances of protecting both of us. Her sharp eyes roved the forest.

"The current count is nine kin with major injuries, four dead," the black bear shifter said, his voice rough as he gave the numbers. "How many with scratches and bruises, we didn't bother to count."

Nate rubbed his mouth, grimacing. "Who did we lose?"

"The rogues were clearly targeting the wing where the advisors reside. They broke into Yvonne's and Garret's rooms first, before there'd even been much time to sound the alarm. And they had weapons—a few guns, the other ones knives... All of us put up as good a fight as we could, but Garret fell, and Yvonne's mate. And two of the guards who intervened."

"How did they get in?" Marco piped up. "I've seen the walls you've got around this compound. And I assume some of the guards were guarding those."

Thomas's voice dropped to almost a growl. He didn't like

anyone but his alpha questioning him, I got the impression. "We're not sure yet how they got in. We *do* patrol the grounds carefully, especially after hearing about recent problems, but none of the guards saw the intruders until after they were already at the estate house."

"I'm sure everyone here was doing their job with their full ability," Nate said. "The rogues have been turning to tricks that no shifter should lower themselves to. What happened to the attackers?"

We emerged from the path into a tiled courtyard. Our feet rapped against the polished slabs of clay. A huge adobe mansion that I had to guess was the "estate house" Thomas had mentioned loomed at one end of the yard. Kneeling figures were scattered across its steps and in the hallway beyond its open, arched doorway.

"We killed most of them in the struggle," Thomas said. "The way they came at us, with no concern for themselves—they almost forced us to. It was a bloody night, I can tell you that much."

We came up to the steps, his last words rolling through my mind, and I realized what all those kneeling shifters were doing. They were scrubbing at the tiles and the walls with rags. Scrubbing at ruddy patches that dappled the clay and the pale brown adobe.

Blood. All that shifter blood spilled here last night...

Suddenly all the blood in my own body seemed to be rushing past my ears with the thudding of my heart. My vision swam.

There had been blood—blood everywhere. Blood splattering the walls painted in the delicate shade of yellow my mother had let my sisters and me pick out. Blood pooled under my wolf-father's slumped form. Blood gushing from the bullet wounds in my oldest sister's chest. The boom of more shots echoing down the hall. My mother's hand so tight around mine the bones pinched. The frantic patter of my feet down the hardwood floor.

The smell of it. Thick and metallic, saturating the air, mingling with the harsh smoky scent of the guns. It had trickled down my throat and filled my stomach, until my gut twisted and heaved—

No, heaving was happening now. I stumbled and bent down, clutching my belly. My pulse rattled painfully. The memories kept streaming through my head, the horrible smell sixteen years gone clogging my nose.

Temperance, my oldest sister, the one who'd always encouraged me to climb higher, run faster, even when I faltered. She'd shoved me out of the way as the rogues had opened fire through the doorway. And Verity, just two years older than me—Mom had tried to grab us both. That was when my eagle shifter father had thrown himself at the rogue with the rifle, talons gouging and wings shielding us. The bullets of a pistol had torn right through him, and she—and she—

"Ren," someone was saying. "Ren!" A strong arm had wrapped around my trembling back.

A sob caught in my throat. Nate's musky peppery smell followed it, chasing away the phantom scents from my past. I grasped his shirt, clinging on to him as if he were the only thing keeping me in place. At that moment, maybe he was.

I wasn't in the dragon shifter's estate. I wasn't five years old anymore. I focused on the clay tiles under my feet, the warm breeze, the quiet murmurs around us—

Shit. I shoved myself upright with a quick swipe at my eyes. Nate kept his arm around me, which was probably a good thing, because my legs wobbled for a second before I found my balance.

Aaron was standing at my other side, Alice right in front of me. She touched my shoulder, her tone light but her eyes concerned.

"Hey. Are you okay?"

"Yeah," I said, willing my voice to stay steady. "I'm sorry. I didn't expect— It just reminded me of the attack on my mother's —on my estate. When I was a kid. When—" My throat started to close up. Better not to go into any more detail than that. From the look on Alice's face, she already understood what I meant.

And beyond her, the delegation of Nate's kin who'd come out to meet us, the shifters working at washing away the mess of last night's attack, they were all watching me. Watching me make a total fool of myself. How the hell were they going to trust that I could deal with this threat when just seeing the aftermath sent me halfway to a breakdown? My hands clenched.

"I'm okay," I said firmly, squaring my shoulders.

"Your memories were suppressed for so long, it's understandable that you're not used to handling the more traumatic ones," Aaron said. I wondered how much that reassurance was for my benefit and how much for the other shifters.

"Well, I'll just have to get used to handling them," I said. "Right now we have to focus on the attack that happened *here*, and how we can make sure it doesn't happen again."

Thomas made a soft coughing sound. He directed his gaze at his alpha. "On that topic... I said we had to kill *most* of the rogues in the assault. But we did manage to capture one—and to stop him before he could end his own life. We had to subdue him with a tranquilizer for the time being, but we can wake him up when you're ready to question him."

CHAPTER 3

West

We kin groups had plenty of differences between us. There was no denying that. But at the core, in some vital ways, we were the same. A shifter kin funeral looked and sounded like a shifter kin funeral whether the dead being honored were canine or feline or avian—or something else, like today.

All the shifters who lived on the estate had gathered around the massive pyre. The sharp smell of fresh sap nearly overwhelmed the stink of death. Four bodies lay there to be laid to rest. Their loved ones had come forward to talk about the lives of the fallen. Now Nate was moving from one body to the next, flames hissing on the end of the torch he carried. His low baritone voice swept through the clearing.

"Brother of my heart, kin to your alpha. Your light has snuffed out, but now you will burn brighter. As we let you go, we swear to rise up stronger for you."

"We swear to rise up stronger," a chorus of voices rang out

around the pyre. I added mine to it. A few bodies down from me, Ren startled and managed to join in for the last few words.

Just one more thing our dragon shifter didn't know about her own kind.

She'd missed the funeral for her own fathers and sisters. The massive one kin from all across the country had arrived for. I'd only been eleven, but I remembered starkly the sight of the alpha before me, the man who'd mentored me for the past three years, lying limp and vacant on the heap of firewood. The bullet hole marring his skin had looked so unnatural, like some horrible disease and not a proper battle wound.

The rogues were fucking unnatural, the way they slaughtered their own kind for their selfish reasons. I gritted my teeth, thinking about the one Nate's guards had managed to capture. Wouldn't I like to be sinking those teeth into him right now. If we hadn't needed the information he could give us, I'd like to tear out his throat for what he'd done here. For what they'd done back then. For all of it, really.

"We swear to rise up stronger," we repeated for the fourth time. Nate bowed his head. Then he tossed his torch onto the pyre.

The flames crackled, sweeping over the heap of woods and the bodies lying on it in a wave. Smoke billowed up. It prickled into my eyes and down my throat, coating my tongue. And the memory that rose up then wasn't of my mentor.

How many bodies had we sent back to the light the day I'd said good-bye to my mother? Eight. Eight loyal kin felled. I'd had to order my people to build two pyres to hold them all. My throat had been hoarse by the time I'd finished the rounds. One of my advisors had offered to share the duty, seeing as I was fifteen and not yet fully of age, but I'd told him no. It'd been my battle. The deaths had been dealt because of my decisions.

I'd just had to believe we'd have seen more deaths if my decisions had been different.

Dad hadn't believed that. Or maybe he hadn't cared. The memory of his turned back, his shoulders stubbornly stiff, had stopped stinging over the years, even though he still hadn't said a word to me since. I was his alpha, but I wasn't his son anymore.

Today, it took a long time for the flames to burn down. We stood in silent witness the entire time, letting the smoke and the smell wash over us. Honoring to our dead.

Normally when the last flames flickered out amid the embers, we would see the ashes carried to their resting place and then be done. But when Nate stirred to move forward, Ren touched his arm. She stepped out from our ring toward the foot of the pyre.

Her face still looked a little paler than usual, making her dark eyes and hair gleam starkly in contrast. But I had to admire the strength with which she held herself, the steadiness of her posture. Whatever memories had rocked her when we'd arrived this morning, she'd wrestled them under control.

Her voice came out steady too—steady and clear.

"The rogues have gotten away with too much, for too long. I wish I could have been here sooner to fulfill my role as dragon shifter. But now that I am here, I swear to you that we will see justice for these deaths. And if I have my way, the rogues won't shed one more drop of kin blood."

She raised a fist in the air and snapped it back to her side. A solemn air still hung over the gathering, but several voices in the crowd rose up in agreement. "Not one more drop!"

I bit back a frown. I wished I could cheer too, but our dragon shifter wasn't in any position to be giving her word on that matter. Her mother hadn't been able to take on the rogues, and she'd been a dragon shifter with years of experience, who'd grown up into the role. The fact that Ren would even try to make that kind of promise just showed how much she still had to learn.

Maybe the times really had changed. Maybe there were things a dragon shifter couldn't set right anymore, even with new powers and the four of us by her side.

Well, I hadn't committed myself yet, as much as parts of me had wanted to. It wasn't her fault she was so far behind, but that didn't mean I had to sacrifice myself and my kin holding her up.

I told myself that, but at the same time the determination on her face tugged at my heart. That damned mate bond still nagging at me, stirring up my emotions. I had to keep a tighter leash on them. If one touch from her could sever all my self-control, how could I put my kin first?

Ren

The pungent scent of the fire's smoke followed me down into the basement of Nate's estate house. I rubbed at my bare arms and resisted the urge to clear my throat. Would that be some kind of sign of disrespect? There were so many shifter traditions and expectations I still didn't know.

And from the way West had narrowed his eyes at me as we'd left the funeral clearing, he was keeping a careful tally of them.

Thankfully my other three alphas and Alice weren't looking for excuses to dismiss me. We had a rogue to interrogate—one who hopefully knew more than the avian woman who'd attacked me on Aaron's estate had. She'd been forced to cooperate. This one had joined the fight right alongside the others.

The guard who'd led us down to the short row of holding

cells nodded to one room. On the other side of the door's small window, a skinny man with scruffy light brown hair was slumped on a bench. His wrists and ankles were chained to opposite ends, so he couldn't hurt us—or himself. As long as he was in human form, at least.

I stepped back from the window. "How do we know he won't shift to get out of the shackles?"

"The tranquilizer we use in situations like this suppresses the ability to shift," Aaron said, ready as ever with explanations. "The guards will have lowered the dose so he's conscious enough to talk to us, but his bodily control is still inhibited."

"He should be awake enough now," the guard said. He unlocked the door for us.

Nate strode in first, anger radiating off him. Marco slipped in ahead of me. As I passed through the doorway, my nose caught the rogue's scent. He was canine—some sort of dog. I wasn't surprised. He had the look of a mutt.

West's teeth bared when he came in. For once his glare was turned on someone other than me. This guy would have been his kin if the dog shifter hadn't turned to murder instead.

Aaron stayed in the doorway, Alice right behind him. She stood tensed, as if she didn't totally believe the precautions taken would be enough to protect us.

"You," Nate growled. "Let's start with the easy questions. What's your name?"

The dog shifter's gaze slid up toward Nate's face, but his thin lips stayed clamped tight. He swayed slightly where he sat, his shoulders hunched.

Nate loomed even higher over him. "I don't want to hurt anyone," he said. "But I've just come back from sending off four of my kin, whose deaths *you* had a hand in. I've got nine others still recovering. So I'm not feeling very forgiving at the moment. We can do this the painful way if you want."

"I have nothing to say to you," the rogue spat out. His voice was slightly slurred, I guessed because of the tranquilizer.

My back stiffened. If he'd attacked us, I'd have had no problem seeing Nate savage him. And there was no question in my mind that he deserved payback. But if what we wanted was answers, I wasn't sure torture was going to get us any. We'd watched rogues throw themselves to their deaths, impale themselves on our claws, just to avoid talking. They didn't seem to value their own lives much compared to their cause.

"I'll ask you again," Nate said, his tone turning even darker. He raised his hand, and it shifted into a giant grizzly bear paw. "Just tell us your name."

The rogue stared back with a wavering but defiant gaze. Words tumbled from my mouth before I'd even thought them through.

"There's another way we can get him talking. I can use the truth-seeking flames. It worked on the fae monarch."

Nate turned to me. "Are you sure you're up for that, Ren?"

I shrugged. Now that I'd volunteered, I'd better be. "I've had a day to get my energy back. And it'll be a lot faster than anything else we could try. You know what the rogues are like."

"Yes." He eyed the dog shifter. The rogue stayed where he was with the same hunched posture, but I thought a little of the remaining color in his yellowed face might have drained away. He might not know what I was talking about, but he knew it probably wasn't good for him.

That settled things. "Let's do it. Now, while the tranquilizer is still affecting him. We'll need to bring him to a bigger space so I have room to shift."

"That can be arranged." Nate motioned to the guard.

The rest of us backed out of the room. "You'll have to ask most of the questions," I said to the other alphas. "I can't carry on much of a conversation while I'm busy spewing flames."

"I think we can handle that, Princess," Marco said with a grim smile. He brought his hands together, one clapping over the other in a fist. "There are an awful lot of things I'd like to find out from that asshole."

Nate and his guard marched the rogue out of the cell, Nate holding the chains for the prisoner's left arm and leg and the guard those for the right. The dog shifter walked sluggishly. He glanced over his shoulder at me with a flash of the whites of his eyes. Nervous.

We tramped back up the stairs. Just as we reached the hall, the rogue wrenched at his arms. He threw himself forward and around, putting all his strength into breaking his captors' hold.

Fortunately for us, Nate and his guard had plenty of strength on their side, and the rogue's was muted by the drug. Nate wrestled the dog shifter still with a quick jerk of the chains. Alice stepped closer, her hands fisted.

"You can walk, or we can carry you," Nate said. "Your choice."

The rogue grimaced at him. Then he started walking again.

Our strange procession took a sharp turn and ended up out behind the estate house in a small yard of hard-packed earth and tufts of grass. "This field is usually for outdoor sports and training," Nate told me over his shoulder. "We'll have plenty of room. And we can make use of this."

He hauled the rogue over to a rectangle of metal jutting out of the earth. A mini-sized football goal, I realized after a moment.

Nate and the guard attached the chains to the sturdy posts. The rogue tugged at his bindings, but only feebly. Then he shrank down as close to the ground as he could get in a cringing pose. I guessed he'd given up.

I walked up to him until I was just a few feet away. He just looked at the ground.

"I won't be doing this to torture you, but I don't get the impression it feels all that great either," I said. "If you want to skip that part, you could start answering questions now. Tell us why you and your 'friends' attacked this estate."

Not a peep.

Fine. We'd do this the dragon way.

I backed up a couple steps to make sure I didn't trample him as I shifted. With a nonchalance that was becoming easier every time I had to do this, I pulled off my shirt and kicked off my pants. I'd already ruined enough clothes with impromptu shifts over the last few weeks. The warm evening air washed over my bare skin. I leaned forward and let myself fall into the shift.

Reaching down and bringing forth the dragon side of me was coming easier every time too. I didn't have to struggle at all now. The scales and talons were waiting just on the other side of my skin, itching to break free. I opened myself up to them, and, with an exhilarating tingling, my dragon shape expanded through my body.

Literally. My neck extended, my eyes sharpening, my teeth rising into points. My limbs steadied beneath my lengthening torso. A barbed tail lashed out behind me, and vast wings sprouted from my back. I stretched them over me, taking a little of the edge off the urge to soar up into the sky. I wasn't needed up there right now. My business was right here on the ground.

Flames tickled the base of my throat. A deeper heat filled my dragon lungs. I dragged in a breath, sensing the difference between the two flames I could cast down. The scorching destructive burn of my usual dragon fire—and the bright, crisp blaze that could cut through to the truth. As much as part of me wanted to unleash the first for what the dog shifter had done here, it was the second I drew into my mouth.

With a hot gush, I let those violet flames pour down over the rogue.

A yelp broke from his throat. He thrashed at his chains, an incoherent mumbling spilling past his lips.

For a second I thought my power hadn't worked. That somehow this mangy shifter had enough will to resist where even the queen of the fae hadn't. Then his mouth burst wide open to answer my earlier request.

"We knew the dragon shifter was coming here with all of the alphas," the rogue gasped out. "The kin-groups are starting to rally. We had to show that even with the alphas united, we rogues have more power. We can destroy you if we want. The alphas no longer get to call all the shots. They have to bend to *our* will."

Yeah, we'd see about that. As my flames streamed on down, Nate stepped forward, his arms crossed over his brawny chest. "Are there more of your group nearby? Are they planning another attack?"

"There's a large bunch of us gathering in the south. I don't know exactly where. I wasn't told, so that I couldn't tell you. And we'll keep attacking until the alphas and the dragon shifters no longer control shifter kind."

"What exactly do you think is going to be so great about *that* situation?" Marco put in.

A whine crept into the dog shifter's voice. "I don't know. I haven't really thought about it much. But I don't like that we all have to kowtow to your rules, and everyone who doesn't is kept on the outside. If there were no alphas, we'd all be the same, making our own rules."

Somehow I didn't think it'd happen exactly like that. Whoever was in charge of the rogue group, they must be awfully persuasive.

An uncomfortable prickling was starting to fill my lungs. I couldn't sustain these flames for much longer. I scraped my talons against the ground in what I hoped the alphas would realize was a warning.

"How many of you are there still?" Aaron asked quickly.

"Maybe twenty that I've met. Dozens of rogues throughout the country. We recruit more of them every day." The dog shifter clutched his head, shaking it but unable to stay silent.

"What do you have planned as your next moves?" West said.

"I don't know. We don't know our instructions until right before we act."

My chest was outright aching now. I aimed one final blast of violet fire at the rogue, and Nate got in one last question.

"How did you get past the guards to break into the estate?"

The rogue chuckled. Actually *chuckled*, as if the question was funny. "Oh," he said. "We didn't have any trouble there. We had someone happy to help us. A raccoon shifter named Keith—one of the guards. He let us right in, your precious kin did."

CHAPTER 4

Ren

THE TRUTH-SEEKING FLAMES drained me faster than any of my other shifter powers. I tried to hold on a few seconds longer, to give my alphas a chance to push the rogue for more answers, but my body crumpled. The fire snapped out. I collapsed in on myself, into my human form.

Aaron was at my side in an instant, handing me my clothes. His jaw was tight. As I reached for my shirt, Nate lunged past us. He shifted into his grizzly form, charging up to the rogue.

The dog shifter recoiled instinctively. But when Nate opened his jaws threateningly, he sagged into the hold of his chains.

"Go right ahead," he said, managing to sound both disdainful and resigned. "Chew my throat out. I don't care. What else are you going to do to me anyway?"

A good question. I glanced at the other alphas as I dressed. Marco's eyebrows were raised, his mouth slanted at a crooked angle. Frustration smoldered in West's eyes.

Nate let out a huff of breath and snapped at the rogue's neck. But he didn't let his teeth even graze the skin. He swung his massive form around, shifting back into a human.

"Take him away," he said to the guard with a jab of his hand. "I don't want him in my sight unless we need him again."

"What about the raccoon shifter he was talking about?" I said as the guard moved to drag the rogue out of the yard. Alice sprang to help him, since Nate was obviously too agitated to join in. "If someone here helped the rogues, shouldn't we—"

"It doesn't matter," West said flatly. "One of the guards who died was named Keith. Unless that's a particularly common name among the kin here, I'm going to assume the rogues made sure their 'ally' couldn't tell any tales."

"He got what he deserved, then," Nate rasped. He stalked back and forth across the yard as he tugged on his shirt. He'd destroyed his jeans in his hasty shift. If the situation hadn't been so tense, I might have enjoyed the view. "Traitor. Betraying his own people like that." He ended the sentence with an agonized growl. "One of *my* people."

Aaron turned to him. "Nate," my eagle shifter said.

Before he could continue, the other alpha shook his head with a jerk. "I need to think. We'll talk more in the morning. Give me the night to make some sense of this. If I can." His gaze found me. "I'm sorry, Ren. This isn't at all how I'd have wanted your first night here to go."

"I know," I said softly. It killed me, seeing him in so much pain. "If you need anything from me..."

"For now I'm not going to be good company to anyone."

He swiveled on his feet and strode toward the estate house.

~

My bed felt too empty when I woke up in my room. I rolled over and stretched my arms across the soft mattress, feeling the vast space on either side of me. Just like at the avian estate, the dragon shifter's bed was sized for five. For me and my mates. But none of those mates had spent the night this time.

The breeze drifting through my half-open window was warm, but I shivered as I sat up. The rogue dog shifter's chuckle echoed in my head. *He let us right in, your precious kin did.*

What could have compelled one of the shifter kin to help an attack against their own kind? And if one could be persuaded, who was to say others hadn't been?

No wonder Nate and the others had been so upset. I was only just starting to understand the bonds between kin and their alphas, and even I was horrified.

Hopefully Nate had calmed down and cleared his head by now. I might not understand the situation completely, but I knew enough to realize we had to talk and come up with some sort of plan of action around this new revelation.

Also like the avian estate, my suite and those assigned to the alphas were down a separate hall from the rest of the house, with a branch that led to a private common room. This one had a view into a stand of redwoods. A long oak table stood at one end next to a sideboard laid out with breakfast foods. At the other, closer to the window, was a cluster of armchairs and couches.

The smells of fried eggs and sausages turned sour in my mouth at the sight of my gathered alphas.

Nate was bent over in one of the armchairs, his head in his large hands. Marco was lounging in another, ever the casual cat, but I could see the tension wound all through his sleekly muscled body. Aaron stood behind one of the couches, his hands braced on the top, as if he couldn't bear to sit down. Alice shadowed him, standing by the window. And West stopped his pacing between the sitting area and the dining table to scowl at me.

"You're here," he said. "We can finally talk."

I could have protested that no one had bothered to wake me up to tell me they needed me, but I wasn't in the mood to bicker with him.

"I'm here," I agreed, walking over to the sitting area. "Do we know anything new?"

Nate shook his head. He raked his fingers through his dark hair and straightened up without quite meeting my eyes. "I still can't believe it. My kin don't turn on each other. We agree to work together to each other's benefit, despite our differences. That's the whole *basis* of being disparate kin."

"Clearly it's not," Marco said. He might have been aiming for a teasing tone, but it fell flat. Nate glared at him.

As the bear shifter opened his mouth, Aaron cut him off. "It isn't just the disparate kin," he said, the rasp in his dry voice more pronounced than usual. "The owl shifter who attacked Ren at my estate was kin too."

My jaw went slack. "What? But she—"

She'd had no kin mark, I meant to say. Then the memory snapped into focus in my head. The avian woman who'd attacked me had been wearing gloves. I'd thought it was odd at first, and then I'd been so distracted by the attack and her story afterward that I hadn't thought to question it.

But Aaron had talked to her more, after we'd found out she'd been coerced into going along with the rogue group through the threats against her son. He was her alpha. Of course he'd have known.

Everyone's gaze had shot to the eagle shifter. "And why is this the first we're hearing about *that*?" Marco asked.

Aaron's hands flexed against the top of the couch. "I was

hoping it was an isolated incident," he said thickly. "That the rogues had gotten lucky and manage to find one rare kin member they had the means to manipulate. Do you think I *wanted* to say my kin were untrustworthy? But now I have to think our kin aren't so difficult to manipulate after all."

My heart squeezed. The avian alpha had told me before that the other kin-groups often looked down on his people. Saw them as something lesser because of their forms. I wished he'd told me everything, but that attempt on my life *had* only happened yesterday. His reluctance made sense.

"It's not about kin being trustworthy or not," Alice jumped in, coming to stand beside him. "The rogues are still behind all of this. The rogues are still the ones we have to deal with."

"I don't know," West said with an edge in his voice. "When we stayed in *my* kin's village, the rogues didn't get any help from my people. So maybe we can make a few judgments about where to trust and where not to."

"This is the first time any of my kin has betrayed me in the sixteen years I've been alpha," Nate said, getting to his feet. He glared at the canine alpha. "And I never heard of it happening before my rule either. We'll see what happens on your estate, won't we? If we ever get there, and you canines don't throw the rest of us off to be anarchists or whatever you've got planned."

"I do what's best for my kin first," West snapped. "That's what pack loyalty is."

"Hey!" I broke in, raising my hands. I stepped between them, close enough to Nate to make him step back. I glowered at West. "We've got enough problems without you guys taking jabs at each other. From now on we have to be extra careful even among kin. Stay on guard. I don't think any of us should go off alone. It's mostly me they want to hurt, but they killed the alphas last time too. I want all of us safe. From the rogues, and from each other."

I shot Nate a look too. He dropped back into his chair, his mouth twisting. "You're right. I'll watch my temper."

West looked faintly chagrined, which was about as good as I could hope from him. "All right. What other brilliant plans do you have to share with us, Sparks?"

Oh, great. Another chance for him to judge me and find me wanting. I groped for a reasonable answer. "The rogue we questioned said a bunch of his group is assembling in the south, didn't he? We need to find them and take them down before they can launch some new surprise attack on us."

"Great. That's the what. The tricky part is the how. Got anything on that front?"

"Wolf boy," Marco said from his chair. "Heel. Unless *you've* got some genius master plan, I don't think you should be knocking our Princess of Flames's contributions." He gave me a hesitant smile.

"Before anything else, we need to know where the rogues are," Aaron said, cutting off any snarky remarks West might have added. "This is partly my fault for not warning the rest of you sooner that our kin might be worthy of suspicion. I'll go. I can survey the area quickly in eagle form while drawing relatively little attention. I'll be able to spot their movements without getting close enough for them to know I'm anything other than your average bird."

The corner of his mouth crooked slightly upward. His guilt shone in his clear blue eyes. I swallowed hard. "You shouldn't go on your own either. I can come with you."

"As a dragon?" he said gently. "You can't let people see you soaring around all over the place, Serenity. And you're still working on your endurance. It may take hours, even days, for me to locate them, if I do at all."

I frowned, but I couldn't argue with his logic. And even if neither of those points had been true, the rogues would scatter the second they saw a dragon swooping by. We needed them to think we weren't on to them so we could turn the tables on them. Create our own surprise to get the upper hand.

"*I* won't have either of those problems," Alice said. "You'll have some company."

Aaron turned to his sister. "I want you to stay here with Serenity. She needs protection more than I do."

"She's got these three lunkheads looking after her already," Alice protested, motioning to the other alphas. The insult didn't seem to bother Nate, but West's lip curled in distaste and Marco looked vaguely offended.

"Lunkheads who can't spend ten minutes together without arguing," Aaron said lightly. "I'm thinking she might want a break from the guys here and there. Please, Alice. I'm not planning on taking any unnecessary risks. I won't engage the rogues—not even if I see one alone. It's a simple reconnaissance mission."

"Can you at least come back for the night?" I put in. "Report back anything you've seen, even if it isn't much? You're going to have to sleep sometime anyway."

Aaron hesitated and then nodded. "That's fair. I'd rather not cause you more worry than I need to."

He came around the couch and walked up to me. When he touched my cheek, I raised my face instinctively to his. He kissed me fleetingly, but in the brief moment our lips met, all I wanted was to cling to him and refuse to let him go. His salty, ocean-breeze smell wafted over me, settling just some of my nerves.

"I'll see you tonight, Serenity," he said, looking me straight in the eyes. Hearing my full name in his measured voice still made my heart thump. It was only because he sounded so sure that I managed to let go of him.

Alice came up beside me as her brother headed out. She touched my shoulder. "I wanted to go with him because we'll be stronger together, not because I don't think he can handle himself. He'll deal with those rogues if he needs to."

"Yeah," I said. But what if the rogues in question had guns?

Aaron had promised he wouldn't engage them. If they never knew the eagle soaring overhead was a shifter, they wouldn't bother him, right?

I rubbed my temple. "Well, the rest of us can't just sit around waiting for him. What are we going to do in the meantime?"

"There's a welcome party already set up for tonight," Nate said quietly. "I didn't want to cancel it. We'll have to keep a close eye on who comes into the estate."

"All the more reason for me to stick to Serenity like glue," Alice said, sliding her hand around my elbow. Her grip was gentle but confident.

A chilling thought struck me. "It's the guards we'll be counting on to check who comes and goes, isn't it?" I said. "What if the raccoon shifter isn't the only one the rogues have gotten to?"

Nate's posture stiffened. "I chose the guards for this estate carefully. The people I knew I could count on."

"One of them already proved you wrong," West pointed out.

"If I find out any more of them..." Nate couldn't seem to finish the sentence. A frustrated rumble emanated from his chest.

"Why don't we at least talk to them?" I said. "I'm pretty sensitive to people's motivations. If we gather the rest of the guards together and I talk to each of them for a bit, then we know we don't have to worry about any more traitors."

Nate sighed. "You're right. I can call the ones who are off-duty in for a briefing, and you can talk to them during that. I'll get that round-up happening now."

He pushed to his feet and made for the door. As I moved to follow him, West exhaled with a mutter under his breath. "Well, this should be an interesting show."

I decided not to even dignify that comment with a glare.

CHAPTER 5

Ren

"LINE UP ALONG THE WALL," Nate ordered the group of guards. This new set, a couple dozen shifters, shuffled to spread out through the massive dining hall.

I waited until they'd settled in against the exposed tan brick. They'd just come off duty after I'd spoken to the guards who'd now relieved them. So far I hadn't seen any reason for concern. As far as I could tell, Nate had chosen his guards pretty darn well.

The other alphas had wandered off on their own business, but Alice had stuck around. She was sitting perched on the edge of one of the big pine tables. The way her sharp eyes scanned the line-up made her look every bit the eagle even in human form.

"This is our dragon shifter, Serenity Drake," Nate said, pitching his voice to carry through the room. He stumbled slightly over my full name, so used to using the nickname I was most comfortable with. "On her first visit here, she wanted a chance to meet and speak with all of you. As your alpha, I know you'll do your kin proud."

We weren't telling them the full reason for this gathering, but I knew word had passed on about my talk with the rogue. They knew this was more than just a friendly chat.

"Hi," I said to the first guard in the line, dipping my head slightly so he could catch my scent. He did the same in return—a ferret. He looked it. His dark eyes studied me warily from his pointy face. But he was tough, too, his arms ropey with muscle. "Like Nate said, I'm Serenity, but I really prefer if you call me 'Ren.'"

"Mitchell," he said. "It's an honor to meet you, dragon shifter."

He didn't totally mean it. I could taste his hesitation. But that wasn't new. I'd gotten the same impression from about half of the other group too, as if they weren't quite sure their kin were better off or worse with me around.

"What made you volunteer to serve as a guard here?" I asked.

His gaze slid to Nate, and I sensed nothing but warm devotion from him then. "It is the *greatest* honor to be at my alpha's service. If I save my kin even a little trouble on his behalf, I couldn't ask for more."

I caught a thread of what he didn't say in the dip of his voice. He blamed the trouble they'd just had here on me. Well, fair enough. The rogues wouldn't have launched their assault if they hadn't known I was on my way to the estate. I'd gotten the same vibe from the other doubters.

Of course, some of Nate's kin still gave off those wafts of dragon-shifter awe I was in the process of getting used to. A little farther down the line, a mountain goat shifter bobbed on her feet almost giddily as she bowed her head to me. Her eyes shone with excitement.

"I heard you got the truth out of that rogue with your dragon fire last night," she said after she'd answered my questions. "That he couldn't do a thing to stop you! It sure is a good thing having a dragon shifter around again."

"I'm glad you think so," I said with a smile. I just hoped I could live up to her expectations.

I'd spoken with about half of the guards when I reached a muskrat shifter who greeted me with a wide grin. It should have looked friendly, but there was something slightly twitchy about him that set my nerves humming.

I gave him the same greeting I had the others. His bow was a little jaunty. I'd have liked him if it wasn't for that aura of discomfort he was giving off.

"The name's Orion," he said. "Big name for a little guy. My mom had the idea it'd make me more impressive."

The corner of my mouth tugged into a smile despite myself. "You must be decently impressive if your alpha chose you for his guard."

"Ah, I do what I can. A little stealthy sneaking here, a little rat-jitsu there." He winked.

Again, I was struck by the sense that he wasn't anywhere near as at ease as the front he was putting on was meant to imply. He wanted me to laugh and move on. And the sooner I did, the happier he'd be. But the emotions roiling beneath his jaunty demeanor weren't annoyed or skeptical.

No, if anything he was *scared* of my attention. Hmm.

Well, I'd let him think he was getting what he wanted. "Keep up the good work, then," I said, and moved on.

None of the other guards rubbed me the wrong way. When I reached the end of the line, I could see several of them shuffling their feet, eager to be dismissed. They'd just finished a long shift on duty. With this scheme, I'd probably irritated all the ones who already weren't impressed by me.

I touched Nate's arm and leaned close to him. "They can all leave except Orion. I want to have a one-on-one chat with him."

Nate's eyes darkened. "You think he's in league with the rogues too?"

"I don't know yet," I said. "So don't go into full grizzly mode on him right away. There's just something off about him. Different from the ones who are just thinking I might be causing more problems than I'm solving."

Nate bristled. "If anyone says anything—" he started, and I patted his arm.

"It's fine. I don't blame them. Let's find out what's going on with the muskrat, all right?"

Subtlety might not have been Nate's strongest point, but he managed to single Orion out without being totally obvious about it. My bear shifter ambled over to the doorway before telling the guards they were dismissed. As they filed past him, stances relaxing, he caught the muskrat shifter and tugged him to the side.

"Just one more thing I wanted to go over with you," he said, as if it had nothing at all to do with me. A couple of the other guards looked over curiously. From across the room, I felt the tension clench through Orion's body.

No, he wasn't happy about this development at all.

Alice hopped off the table. "Should we go somewhere a little less... expansive? I feel better when I've got the walls closer at my back."

"Yes," Nate said. "I think a little privacy is in order for this talk."

"I... don't understand?" Orion said as Nate ushered him to a side door at the other end of the hall. "What's this about?" He carefully did not look at me.

"I think we'll figure that out once we've gotten to the talking part," Nate said. "Come on." He gave the muskrat shifter a light cuff to the head to nudge him onward. Maybe not that light, actually. The smaller guy winced.

Orion had done a good job playing the joker in the middle of the line, but as we tramped deeper into the palace, his nerves started to show. He raked his hand through his bristly black hair. His narrow jaw worked. When Nate opened a door down the hall and motioned him in, his legs balked for a second before he complied.

I followed, glancing around approvingly. Nate hadn't picked anything that resembled a chilly interrogation room. The room looked like a study: built-in bookcases stuffed with books and binders, a desk at one end and three leather chairs at the other. Alice, who seemed to enjoy a higher vantage point, hopped up to sit on the edge of the desk. The rest of us took the chairs.

Orion twisted his hands in his lap. His gaze darted to me and then settled back on his alpha.

"You have to know," he said in a strained voice, "I had no idea that attack was going to happen. I haven't done anything to threaten the security of the estate or my kin here. I *wouldn't*."

"I *thought* I knew that," Nate said in a low voice. "But after what happened the other night, I'm sure you can understand we need to be absolutely sure of all of you. If something is bothering you, you can tell us."

Orion's choice of words hadn't escaped me. He'd picked them very carefully. He hadn't known about the attack. He hadn't done anything to hurt his kin. That left a whole lot of other things he might have known or done—or that he might mean to.

"Orion," I said, as gently as I could manage, "you can

obviously tell we singled you out for a reason. *Something* is eating at you. Something that wasn't a problem for any of the other guards. I don't know if you realized, but one of a dragon shifter's abilities is a sensitivity to people's emotions and motives. I know you're scared of me. I just want to know what it is you're afraid I'm going to do."

He wet his lips. "Isn't it normal to be a little nervous of someone who can transform into a mythical creature a gazillion times bigger than me?"

Damn it, he had me smiling again. "My dragon form isn't quite that enormous. And actually, from what I've seen, your reaction isn't normal. Most of your kin and the other kin I've talked to know that my job as dragon shifter is to look out for all of you. I'm on your side. An ally, not an enemy. Unless you've been doing something you know would make you *my* enemy."

The muskrat shifter looked at his hands. His fingernails had ragged edges, as if maybe he'd been nibbling on them. His mouth twisted. "I haven't done anything," he said.

"But maybe you've been thinking about it?" I suggested. "I've got to assume that if the rogues got to Keith, they've tried feeling out some of the other guards too. Maybe you've talked to them. Maybe you've considered doing more."

His shoulders tensed. He didn't need to say anything. I could read his guilt as clearly as if it was printed on his shirt.

It radiated off him strongly enough that Nate picked up on it too. He stood up, looming over his guard. His voice came out in a growl.

"If you've had any contact with the rogues at all—"

I held up my hand, and Nate swallowed the rest of his threat with a rumble.

"Just tell us," I said to Orion. "We'll figure out the truth one way or another. If you really are loyal to your kin and your alpha, then after what the rogues did here today, you should know that helping them at all is going against everything you're supposed to stand for."

"I just wanted to hear what they had to say," Orion blurted out. "Some of the things they said, it sounded as if they had ideas that would make things better for all of us kin, not just them."

He snapped his mouth shut as if he hadn't meant to say even that much. His fingers dug into the seat cushion.

"Okay," I said. "Fine. Like what? I want things to get better for all the kin too."

Orion shot me a frantic glance. I felt the emotion in that too. "No," I added, "I'm probably not going to like your answer. But I still want to hear it. I swear on my blood as dragon shifter that I'm not going to punish you just for sharing your thoughts. All right?"

The forcefulness of my oath seemed to convince him to speak. "I'm still deciding what I agree with," he said. "I had to meet you first, I had to see— They've been saying things like maybe we shouldn't be ruled by a shifter who doesn't have any ties to any of our kind. That—" His eyes twitched toward Nate. "That maybe our alphas should be focused completely on us and not on trying to make all the other groups happy."

"Doesn't have any *ties*?" Nate said, his voice rising. "The woman you're looking at is the daughter of the alpha who ruled our kin before me. Hell, Orion, we don't even *have* a kind other than not being one of the other main kinds of shifters. And you were ready to see blood spilled—"

"No!" Orion protested with a squeak. "I told you, I didn't know—I never wanted—"

"Now look," Nate said, grabbing him by the front of his shirt. Energy rippled over him as if he were about to shift. I jumped up too. This wasn't how I'd wanted this talk to go.

I pushed Nate back with a hand on his shoulder. His anger rolled over me, but his expression softened when he met my eyes.

"It's okay," I told him. "I asked for those answers. I can handle it. Maybe you should wait outside for a few minutes? I think it might be better if I talked to Orion alone." Without an alpha's temper in the room with us.

Nate let go of Orion's shirt. The muskrat shifter cringed in his chair. Nate's hands closed into fists at his sides and opened again. "We can't trust him. I don't want to leave you alone with that traitor."

"He hasn't betrayed anyone yet," I pointed out. "And I can turn into a dragon, remember? I think I can handle one muskrat."

"I'd bet she can too," Alice put in. She strode over and motioned to Orion. "Stand up. I just need to make sure you haven't got any weapons on you."

He stood stiffly as she patted him down. She stepped back, setting her hands on her hips. "All clear. Come on, Mr. Grizzly. What's he going to do—batter her with books? We can wait right outside the door." She arched an eyebrow at me. "Scream if you need us."

Nate grumbled wordlessly, but followed her out. As the door shut with a thud behind them, Orion sank into his chair. I sat back down too. He peered at me with eyes that suddenly looked flat and hopeless.

"Are you going to fry me now?" he asked. "Like you did the rogue you caught?"

Ah. I guessed I knew what he was most scared of now.

I leaned forward. "I wasn't planning on it, but I will if I have to. It doesn't hurt—at least not much. Not enough to kill you." He didn't look all that comforted by those facts. Moving on... "I only used it because your rogue friend wouldn't talk to us at all.

What matters the most to me is protecting all the kin. I don't want one more person dying on my watch."

Orion rubbed his mouth. "He isn't my friend," he said. "I'd never associate with anyone who'd do what they did."

"But you're still not sure you want to turn your back on the rogues completely," I said, reading his body language. "You still think they might have a point. About me."

He sucked in a ragged breath. "We haven't had a dragon shifter since I was five years old. I only just met you half an hour ago. I don't know."

But he wanted to. I felt it underneath the uncertainty and the fear. He *wanted* me to convince him that he could believe in me. As much as he'd probably hoped the rogues would offer guidance he could believe in when he'd entertained their ideas.

I didn't know how to give him that. The best I could think of was to be honest.

"Can I tell you a secret, Orion?" I said.

His expression turned puzzled. "All right."

I dragged in a breath. My chest clenched before I forced it to release the words. "I've been worried about all the same things you have. Whether I can really help. Whether me being here is changing things for good or bad. And I'm still figuring that out. I didn't even know I was a dragon shifter a month ago. I didn't even know there was any such thing as shifters."

Orion stared at me as if he couldn't imagine not knowing. I guessed he probably couldn't. "But you're supposed to be leading all of us."

"Yeah," I said. "That's the sticking point, isn't it? But I can tell you this. I'm doing everything I can to learn and accept my role as quickly as possible. I know I *want* to be the dragon shifter you all need. I'll do whatever I can, whatever it takes, to see all of you happy and safe. And from everything I've seen, the rogues want the exact opposite of that. They'll be happy to tell you otherwise so they can use you, but look at how they treated your colleague. He helped them, and they killed him to protect themselves. Maybe you can't trust me yet, but you have to see you can't trust them."

He lowered his head. When he spoke, his voice was quiet. "So what do you want from me?"

Good question. I considered it. "I want to know anything you've found out about the rogues and their plans, so I can make sure what happened here yesterday doesn't happen again."

He nodded. "I can't tell you very much. They wouldn't tell me very much unless I proved I was allying with them. They approached us when we patrolled outside the estate walls, the times when we ended up on our own for a moment. I think they must have had people watching the area just for that—but maybe not anymore. The one I talked to was a fox shifter."

"How were you supposed to reach out to them if you decided to join their cause?"

"I'm not sure." He spread his hands. "They said they'd reach out to me. I don't know how."

"But if they did, you'd tell us now?"

He raised his head. "Yes," he said. "I'd come straight to my alpha."

I tasted the honesty in his words. He was still scared, still unsettled. But he was upset by what he'd seen the rogues do too. He truly hadn't done anything to hurt us yet.

Maybe to trust me, what he needed was for me to trust him.

CHAPTER 6

Nate

ORION'S VOICE bounced off the close walls of the holding cell. "But I cooperated!" my former guard protested as one of my current guards jabbed him with a tranquilizer. "I answered her questions. I didn't do anything wrong!"

"You talked with shifters you know are out to screw us over," I replied, just barely holding my anger in check. "You didn't tell me what was going on. You considered going along with them. Be glad that our dragon shifter is merciful, because believe me, I'd like to do a lot worse to you than this."

The muskrat shifter opened his mouth as if to argue more, but the drug was already taking effect. His chin wobbled, and then his body sagged. The guard holding him let him drop onto the bench in the holding room. She turned to me. "Should I chain him?"

I shook my head. "If he comes to enough to shift, those

things won't hold him. Just make sure he's kept tranquilized enough until I decide where he'll end up next."

She gave me a sharp nod and threw one last disdainful look at her former colleague. With a sniff, she stalked out of the room. Our would-be-traitor wasn't going anywhere anytime soon.

I stalked down the hall, my muscles itching. I wanted so badly to shift. To shift and rage, clawing the floor, battering the walls, letting out every bit of the frustration that had been boiling up inside me since last night.

But I wasn't just an animal. I knew turning into a raging bear wasn't going to help anyone.

"Are you all right, sir?" the guard asked me.

"Yes," I said. "Go on back to your regular duty. And thank you."

No, I wasn't all right, not at all. I'd misjudged my own kin. I'd brought my new mate, the mate I'd been waiting for from the moment I became alpha years ago, into the worst kind of danger. I couldn't even promise her she'd be safe within my estate's walls.

She should have been looking forward to a grand celebration tonight, one that would have rivaled the reception she'd gotten at the avian estate. Instead we were limiting the guests, checking them over for weapons, setting an atmosphere of anxiety. And everyone would have been anxious anyway after the other night's attack. Word about that would be all over the countryside now.

We needed to shut those rogues down for good. Maybe we should have before we'd even found Ren.

It'd become easy to ignore the problem over the years. In the aftermath of the previous alphas' murders, I'd been too busy learning my role to offer a counter-attack. Some of the old guard had tried to track down as many of the rogues as they could, but the perpetrators had gone into hiding. And they hadn't stirred up much trouble since then.

Because they thought they'd gotten what they wanted, I had to assume.

I prowled through the halls of my home, not entirely sure where I was going but needing to keep moving. I stopped when I spotted one of my attendants coming around a corner.

"Vernon," I said. "Is the avian alpha back yet? Aaron?"

The panda shifter blinked his big round eyes. "Not that I've heard, sir. I can ask in case I missed his arrival."

I waved that suggestion off. If the avian alpha had returned, I couldn't imagine he'd have been quiet with his news. "That's fine. Just come find me if you see him."

I stalked on, my feet carrying me without thinking to the wing that held my advisors' quarters. The place where the other night's attack had been the most brutal. My people had rushed to clean up as quickly as they could, but a bullet hole still marked one wall. There were scratches in the floorboards no buffing was going to erase.

My jaw clenched. I knocked on the first door at my right.

Yvonne opened it a moment later. The stately horse shifter had been one of the first of the former alpha's advisors to really take me under her wing when I'd been hardly more than a boy. Now, her silver hair was slicked back from her face in its usual braid, but her eyes looked wearier than usual. Heavy with grief.

"My alpha," she said with a dip of her head. "What brings you here?"

"I just wanted to check in on you. See how you're doing."

"Well, about the same. Do you want to come in?"

I accepted the invitation. Yvonne wouldn't have offered it if she'd wanted to be alone, even when it came to her alpha.

The sitting room at the front of her quarters smelled the

same as it had since I was a boy, like clover and sunlight. The coffee table that had used to sit between the two low couches was gone, though. I realized with a lurch of my stomach why. It must have broken in the skirmish.

"If you wanted to change rooms, there are a couple of suites unoccupied," I said.

Yvonne shook her head. "We lived in these rooms for thirty years, and I'll remain until you no longer have any use for me as advisor."

"Well, that day is never going to come." I gave her a halting smile. It reassured me a little that she managed to return it. I groped for another topic of conversation. "What do you think of our dragon shifter?"

"Oh, she's a fiery one, isn't she?" Her smile grew, but it looked bittersweet. "Saying she'll put an end to the rogues. Is she really prepared for the battle ahead?"

As much as I valued Yvonne, my hackles rose at the question. "Ren has faced more troubles in the last few weeks than most of us have to deal with in a lifetime. I'd say she's handled herself well."

"There now." The horse shifter patted my arm. "I didn't mean anything by it. Of course you'll stand by your mate. I simply meant that it seems the pressure on her is only going to keep growing. She's had no training, no time to even ready her mind for what's ahead. I hope she can stay steady, but it would be hard for any of us."

"Exactly," I said. A little heat crept into my tone, remembering some of the standoffish reactions my guards had given Ren. "It isn't fair to her, being brought into our world when the community is in more chaos than it's ever been. But we'll figure it out, the five of us, together. It's what the rest of us trained for. No one should question that."

Yvonne looked up at me with her clear, sad eyes. "Sometimes I think we have human minds just so that we can question things. Even the people trying to show us the way."

Ren

"Your guests are starting to arrive," Alice announced. "Do you want to go check them out?"

I paused where I'd been wandering my sitting room, trying to think if there was anything I'd missed with Orion, some way I could have better won him over.

Some way to feel completely confident I'd won him over at all.

The view out the window told me the sun was still over the trees. "I thought the welcoming party was happening tonight."

Alice shrugged. "Apparently the disparate kin also have a disparate sense of time." Her lips curled up at the joke. "I just figured maybe you could use a distraction."

Yeah, I probably could. I sighed and rolled my shoulders, not sure meeting a bunch more strangers—stranger shifters who weren't half as impressed by me as the other kin-groups I'd met—was the kind of distraction I wanted. But it was the kind I had.

"I guess I'd better change into something a little fancier," I said, looking at the jeans and tee I'd pulled on this morning. I'd already checked out all the wardrobes in the dragon shifter suite. There'd been one with casual clothes, thank God, but most were full of the posh formal wear the regular kin apparently liked to see me and their alphas decked out in.

I'd had my eye on one dress already: an ankle-length satin gown in an indigo shade so deep it was almost black. This didn't seem like the right time for anything flashy. I pawed through the hangers for it and chucked off my clothes to put it on.

"Any news from Aaron?" I asked his sister as I adjusted the fall of the fabric. Even if Nate's kin didn't totally buy into me as leader of the shifters yet, they'd have to admit I at least looked the part.

Alice grimaced. "Nothing so far. But he's got a few hours left before I'll be ready to bite his head off. He should have let me go too. Not that I mind hanging out with you, but from what I've seen you can handle yourself around here just fine."

"Hey, I agree with you," I said. "I guess *two* golden eagles soaring around together might have looked a little conspicuous, though."

Alice grinned. "Not half as conspicuous as if he'd had a dragon keeping pace with him."

"Okay, okay, that was a dumb idea. I fully admit it. But I have a much better one now." I sniffed the air. "Someone's roasting chicken. Really, really tasty chicken. What do you say we go find some of that?"

"I'm in."

My heart started thumping a little faster as we headed toward the house's main doors. I wanted to peek outside before I walked right out, just to see what I was getting into, but that didn't seem leaderly at all. Squaring my shoulders, I pushed open the door and strode down to the courtyard as if nothing about the people down there could faze me.

Alice had been right. Several dozen shifters were already gathered on the clay tiles of the courtyard, most of them ones I didn't think I'd seen in the estate earlier. And all their heads turned toward me as I came down the steps. Quite a few faces brightened up. That made up for the ones that only looked thoughtful.

The atmosphere didn't feel all that celebratory, I had to say. I guessed it was hard to really party when four deaths and several injuries hung over the estate.

"Hi," I said, going up to a small cluster of bear shifters who appeared to be happy to see me. "I'm Ren. Um, I think this whole get-together is for you to meet me, so... here I am!"

One of the women touched my arm. Her hand trembled a little. "You've been through a lot to make it here," she said. "I'm glad we could make it here to greet you properly."

The guy beside her leaned close as if to share a secret. "People are saying you have more fire than the dragons before. A different kind."

"That's true," I started to say. Another of the women laughed with pleasure.

"We can burn all those rogues back to the darkness where they belong," she crowed.

Okay, that was a more violent turn than I really wanted this conversation to take. "I'll deal with them as well as I can," I said, and swiveled to look for someone else to introduce myself to.

By the time Alice and I made it to the refreshments table, I'd endured a multitude of questions about my special fire-breathing, more skeptical looks than I could count, and a few outright glowers. At least I had lots of practice with those thanks to West. I didn't feel all that hungry anymore, but I grabbed a glass of wine.

Where were my alphas anyway? Nate probably had more estate business to tend to, and Aaron was off on his reconnaissance mission, but the other two should be around somewhere.

It didn't really matter. I just wanted an excuse to take a breather. I meandered off around the side of the house with Alice in tow.

The gardens on the disparate estate were mostly prickly hedges dotted with flowers interspersed with even pricklier cacti. The vegetation was pretty in its own right, with a pungent perfume, but I was careful not to touch any of it.

"Not the friendliest flowers, are they?" Alice remarked, jabbing the chicken leg she'd grabbed toward one cactus.

"At least people know better than to mess with them," I said.

Voices carried across the grounds from up ahead. I slowed, my ears perking.

A wall of the same adobe bricks that made up the house stretched partway into the gardens. The voices were coming from beyond its arched doorway. I crept over and peeked inside.

The doorway led into a smaller courtyard with a gazebo surrounded by a moat of burbling water. Marco was leaning against one of the marble posts by the moat, a glass dangling from his hand, his eyelids lowered in a typical languid expression. A few other shifters—ones I recognized from Nate's guard—stood in a semi-circle around him. Their postures were full of bravado.

"Is that all you've got to say for yourself, cat?" one of the guards said. "Look at you. You still think you're better than us, don't you?"

"I have total respect for all kin," Marco said mildly. "Excluding those who align themselves with the rogues, of course."

One of the others took a step closer to him. "Your kind always turns your nose up at us. We've seen it. But the dragon shifter has turned her nose up at you, hasn't she? Picked our alpha to confirm as her mate without a second glance at you."

I bristled at the jab, both that she'd made it at all and at the thought of how Marco might respond. When his own people had hassled him about his status with me, he'd put them off with a bunch of blustering about how easily he was going to work his charms on me and finish the "job."

I almost stepped through the doorway to put an end to the confrontation before I had to hear anything like that again. But Marco's calm voice stopped me.

"Serenity makes her choices as she sees fit. I'm not so arrogant to think I know better than a dragon." He gave his harassers a thin smile.

"Aw, look at the kitty cat," the first guy said. "Completely pussy-whipped and not even fully mated yet."

Marco chuckled. "I'd rather be whipped by her than left with whatever dregs you court."

The guy's face flushed red. "Now listen, you—"

"Hey," the guard next to him said. "We've hassled him enough. Our alpha will be checking in soon. Let's leave this one to 'enjoy' his solitude."

The first guy let out a huff, but the three of them rambled off in the other direction. Marco rolled his eyes at their retreating backs.

He didn't even look upset. He'd taken all those comments in stride, even though they must have stung his pride. Instead he'd just sounded proud of *me*.

I swallowed hard, turning back to face Alice. "Give me a few minutes? I'll be with one of my alphas, so I should be safe."

"Sure," Alice said. "If you need me later, just give me a shout."

She drifted back toward the party, and I slipped through the doorway. Marco straightened up when he saw me. His eyes, their indigo irises almost the same color as my dress, glittered as he took me in.

"Aren't you a sight?" he said with a crooked grin. "Shouldn't you be out hobnobbing with your adoring public?"

I made a dismissive sound. "They're not all that adoring. Which is fine. The adoring ones are exhausting too. I'm just pacing myself."

"A wise decision." He held my gaze with that hint of hesitation I'd felt from him before. "Is there anything you needed from me, Princess of Flames?"

"Can we… talk?" I said.

His grin softened. "I think that could be arranged. Look, we've got this handy gazebo right here."

He offered his hand and led me up the steps. When he sat on one of the benches inside, I took the spot next to him. His presence didn't set me on edge the same way it had a couple days ago. We still had a lot of ground to cover, and he obviously knew that. But he was trying to make up for the mistakes he'd made. Even when he didn't have any idea I'd know how he was behaving.

And when I wasn't on edge, it was impossible to ignore the warmth of his body beside me. The bond drawing me even closer. I curled my fingers around the edge of the bench.

"I wanted to ask… The things you said, that I overheard—the way you talked about me— You said you've had to learn not to show any weaknesses around your kin. What has it been like since you've been alpha? Before I came into the picture, I mean."

Marco inhaled sharply. "Princess, you don't need to hear about that. And I'm not going to insult you by trying to justify what I said."

His hand was still cupped over mine. I turned mine over to intertwine my fingers with his and squeezed. "I'm asking because I want to know. You're not justifying. You're just letting me in on things I wasn't there to see."

"Well." He was silent for a moment. "You know the sort of temperament cats have. It carries on to cat shifters. We've always had issues with authority. So being alpha requires a certain attitude… of detachment, and confidence. You have to put on a show. I think I've gotten fairly good at that, and I've still faced over a dozen challenges since I came of age. It'd have been a lot more if I'd had a weaker disposition."

"Oh." I said. That had been how many years? Five? And he'd had to fight to hold onto his position more than twelve times already. "That seems like a lot already." My gaze went to the scar that notched his eyebrow. I raised my other hand to trace the pale line. "Is one of those fights how you got this?"

"The only one I almost lost." His mouth tightened, but he shrugged. "Dealing with challenges wasn't fun. But it's the way it is. I've gotten into the habit of turning on that cocky attitude when faced with any criticism. That's not an excuse for insulting you, though."

I glanced up at him. "No. But the fact that I haven't fully taken you as my mate… That makes your kin question you. They can't even have kids until we're together." My stomach twinged with a pinch of guilt. None of the shifters could produce children until their alpha was fully mated. The longer I delayed with Marco and West, the longer their people stayed barren. "I could understand if you were upset that I hadn't been willing to consummate with you yet."

Marco blinked at me with what looked like honest surprise. "What? No." His voice dropped. "I mean, I very much look forward to that time coming… assuming it does. But I've always known I'll have to be worthy of that bond. And clearly I haven't been yet."

"But when it could make such a difference—"

"*No,*" he said firmly. He turned more toward me, letting go of my hand to touch my cheek as he held my gaze. "Ren, do you know what I've been realizing the past two days? Feeling this distance from you, watching you come into your own… If I could give the damned alpha position to someone else and just have you, I'd take that deal in a heartbeat. I've never wanted the authority as much as I want to earn my place at your side. I wish I could give you more than just words to prove it."

My heart was pounding, but not with nervousness now. I felt his fingers against my cheek through every inch of my body. The warmth of them loosened my tongue.

"You could show me," I said. "Show me how much you want me."

Lust flared in his eyes. "Princess," he murmured, with so much longing it set my skin on fire. He bent his head and pressed his lips to mine.

The kiss started out slow and gentle. His mouth was sweet against mine, the spicy smell of him surrounding me. It wasn't halfway enough to satisfy me. I gripped the front of his dress shirt and pulled him closer.

With a groan, he kissed me harder. My lips parted, welcoming, and his tongue swept in to tease me. His free hand slid up the side of my dress. His thumb stroked in soft circles closer and closer to my sheathed breasts as one kiss bled into another.

It felt so good. So fucking good the rush of pleasure started to carry me away. The careening sensation made my breath catch. I hadn't intended to—did I really want to—

Marco pushed away from me with a rough gasp. He kept his hands on me, one at the crook of my jaw now, the other beside my breast, as he gazed into my eyes.

"You're not ready," he said. "Not really. It'll take more for me to show I deserve you in every possible way. But I will. I promise you I will."

My hand was still caught in his shirt. I dropped it. "Marco, I—"

"It's all right, princess." He kissed me again, just a brush of his lips against mine. "I'm not going to beg. I'm certainly not going to blame you. When I've earned my place, when you're sure of me, you can come to me."

CHAPTER 7

Ren

So WHAT ARE *you waiting for exactly?* Kylie's latest text said. *Just grab those hunks and have your way with them already!*

I shook my head with a smile she couldn't see. I sure wished it felt as easy as she made it sound. *I've been making progress. I've got two official mates now.*

Woohoo! Now we're talking. Was the second one Nate or Marco? Or did you manage to thaw out the chilly wolf?

I outright laughed at that, flopping back on my bed. The chilly wolf. Yeah, that was an appropriate description for West. Other than the rare occasions when he suddenly turned scorching.

Nate, I replied. *Things are still a little tense with the other two.* Although less so with Marco after this afternoon's conversation. It wasn't enough to completely make up for the callous way he'd talked about me, but it got us partway there. I wasn't sure I'd be able to completely trust him—and my body's reactions to him—until I'd seen how he acted when we were among his kin.

And how was it? Don't kiss and tell doesn't apply to besties, you know that.

Not in Kylie's book, anyway. But there was only so much I was willing to commit to written record.

It was good. Really good. I think I'm getting the hang of this mate thing.

Oh, my little Ren, all grown up.

I wrinkled my nose at the phone, but the comment was fair. I hadn't gone all the way with any guys in the entire time I'd known Kylie before now. Even when I hadn't known I was a dragon shifter, something inside me had felt that bond to my destined mates. Something that had gotten out its claws anytime I got too hot and heavy with a guy.

But that was fine. I'd take even West over any of the boys and men I'd met before now.

A knock sounded on the door. Nate's rich baritone carried through. "Ready to go, Ren?"

"Pretty much," I called back, shoving myself upright. "You can come in." *It's party time,* I wrote to Kylie. *More later.*

I met Nate in the sitting room. It was hard not to stare at his impressive form packed into that formal suit. I was still wearing the same gown from this afternoon. After a brief escape from the growing crowd, I felt ready to face the official celebration. Everything before this had just been a warm-up.

Desire kindled in Nate's gaze as he took me in. He wrapped a brawny arm around my shoulders to pull me close to him. I closed my eyes and leaned into his kiss. He felt more relaxed now. Less rage simmering beneath the gentle exterior. But I knew if anyone ever threatened me again, the grizzly would be back in an instant.

"Orion is locked away and on the tranquilizer," he told me when he pulled back. "The guards have been carefully monitoring everyone else who's arrived. I don't think you need to worry."

"I know you're taking every step you can," I told him. My stomach twisted. "Is it really necessary to lock Orion away? I mean, he hadn't done anything really wrong *yet*. Maybe he never would have."

"He tried to lie to us," Nate said. "He let the rogues' ideas get into his head. We can't trust him. And I'm not wasting one of the guards I *can* trust following his every move."

"Fair enough," I said. But it still didn't sit right with me, treating someone like a criminal for just thinking about taking the wrong path. Not much I could do about it right now, though. "And has Aaron turned up?"

Nate shook his head with a frown. "His idea of 'night' might be different from mine. I'm expecting him to show up soon."

The twist in my stomach tightened. "If something happened to him—"

"Hey." Nate tipped my face toward his and kissed my forehead. "You don't need to worry about that either. I don't know where he is, but I know if he were really hurt, *you'd* know it. You're his mate. That connection will take time to grow, but if anything were really wrong, you'd feel it."

Great. I could assume Aaron wasn't on the verge of death, but there were so many ways his expedition could have gone just somewhat wrong.

I bit back my frustration and took Nate's hand. "I guess we'd better get out there."

Dinner was being served in the courtyard—a much less formal affair than the banquet at Aaron's estate. I sat with Nate at a table at the head of the yard, Marco at my other side and West beside him. The empty chair where Aaron should have been sitting niggled at me. Alice caught my gaze from the other side of it and frowned in sympathy.

As attendants brought us plates of food, the other revelers moved from serving table to serving table. They stacked their own plates and then started eating standing up or sitting on the benches scattered around the fringes of the yard.

There were at least twice as many people as when I'd been out here before, but the atmosphere still felt subdued. The music playing had a slightly mournful sound to it even though the melody should have been lively. I guessed we all had too much on our minds.

While we ate, the other shifters also drifted past our table to make their greetings. A lot of them smiled more brightly at Nate than at me. Well, they'd known him a hell of a lot longer.

One elderly badger leaned his chubby hands on the edge of the table and fixed me with a beady stare. "Word is you've got special powers beyond compare," he said. "Going to sort out all those rogues right quick, are you?"

Maybe I'd been a little hasty making that speech at the funeral yesterday. "I'm going to do my best," I said.

"We won't have any peace here until that poison is rooted out and destroyed," he said with a firm nod.

The "poison" the entire rest of the shifter community had failed to destroy for the last sixteen years? Yeah, no pressure there.

The next group, a gaggle of lady voles, squealed over me and asked me to do a little shift for them to see. I brought my talons out of my fingers, and they cheered. I was feeling more welcome after they moved on—at least until a sharp-faced bear shifter ambled over.

"I hear one of our kin is in a prison cell right now," she said, glancing from me to Nate and back again, as if she figured the offense had to be my fault. "What's that about? We're locking each other away now?"

Nate cleared his throat. His voice came out low and firm. "We've always used the holding rooms under the estate to deal with kin who break our laws, Mildred. You know that."

She sniffed. "And what law has this one broken?"

Nate glowered at her. "That's not a matter for public discussion."

"It seems like a lot has changed since we had a dragon back in town."

My back stiffened as she flounced away from us. "Ignore her," Nate muttered. "She's always been a difficult one."

It was true that most of his kin were friendly to me. I spent another hour, at the table and then circulating through the crowd, smiling and laughing at jokes and telling a few of the less traumatic stories from my life among humans. But even when the shifters were smiling back, I wasn't sure how much to believe in their warmth. Did they really trust me, or were they just better at hiding their uneasiness than some of the others?

Alice came up beside me. "Time for another breather?"

"Yeah," I said with relief. "What did you have in mind?"

"It seems to me there's no reason we shouldn't help restock the wine table," she said with a grin.

We meandered into the estate house and down to the wine cellar. And a massive wine cellar it was. I didn't think I'd seen so many bottles in my life, even in a liquor store. I stopped and stared at them.

"I don't know where to start."

"Ah, we can always just hang out here for a bit and then let the attendants pick. That's their job anyway." She propped herself against a crate and cocked her head at me. "I'm guessing the life you had before my brother and the other alphas found you was pretty different from this, huh?"

"Uh, yeah, that would be the understatement of the year."

"Tell me about it. I've always wondered what it's like on the human side of things."

I let out my breath. Where to start? "Well, I'm not sure my 'human' life was all that normal. When my mom was still around, we always lived pretty simply. Her first concern was making sure we didn't draw attention to ourselves. And then after she left... I ended up having to leave the apartment and live on the streets. I didn't have a real home for more than five years. Let alone a home like this." I waved to indicate the entire estate.

"That must have been rough," Alice said, her tone going serious. "You don't let it show, when you're out there talking to the kin."

I shrugged. "That's not the side of me they want to see, right? The side that's human. Weak."

Alice grimaced. "I wouldn't call surviving the lowest rungs of the human world with no support and no powers *weak*, not by a long shot. You know, I can't say I've had to experience anything like that, but I have needed to spend a lot of time keeping up a strong front. It wears you out. The more you can be your real self, the easier it'll be on you in the long run."

"I guess that makes sense." I looked down at my hands. "It's just hard to know what anyone expects. There's still so much I have to get used to."

"This place is a bit of a change from the avian estate, isn't it? The different kin-groups have their own attitudes. Or attitude problems." She gave me half a smile. "We avians usually get along best with the canine crew. We both believe in strong bonds and keeping a united front. The felines and the disparate community, it's a bit more of a free-for-all. Everyone for themselves."

Okay, so maybe it wasn't that Nate's kin resented me for the attack. Maybe this was just the way they always were. That possibility was weirdly reassuring.

"Everyone wants so many different things," I said. "It's kind of... overwhelming. I don't know how I'm going to make them all happy."

Alice knuckled my arm. "Probably you won't. But I guess the best you can do is listen to everyone, and your alphas, and don't forget what's in here too." She tapped her head. "And you find whatever balance seems to be the best fit. See, simple! I have all the answers."

I had to laugh. "Right. I guess I'm all set then."

Her gaze drifted toward the door, and I abruptly realized that the flexing of her muscles wasn't just her usual bodyguard-like readiness. She was feeling edgy too. I didn't need any special senses to figure out why.

"You're worried about Aaron," I said.

She rubbed her mouth. "He's a big boy. He can take care of himself. As he likes to remind me on the regular. But... I thought from what he said that he'd be back by now."

If even Alice was worried enough to admit it, my anxiety wasn't just me being over cautious. I hesitated. Why shouldn't I change her orders? Technically I had at least as much authority over the shifter kin as Aaron did.

"You know what?" I said. "We've waited long enough. I want you to go looking for him. And if he has a problem with that when you find him, you can tell him to take it up with me."

Alice blinked at me. "Really?"

"Absolutely. That's a direct command from your dragon shifter."

Her mouth stretched into a real grin. "Now I'm *really* glad we've got you back."

We grabbed a couple bottles of wine somewhat at random so it'd look like we'd done more than just disappear. But when we emerged into the courtyard, it occurred to me that there were other orders given that I didn't totally agree with. I wasn't going to go against Nate's authority—but I could try to temper his harshness with a gesture of my own.

I picked up a new plate and snatched a little of this and a little of that off the tables. The kin watching were probably speculating about a dragon shifter's appetite. Let them wonder.

I carried the plate into the house and down the stairs into a different part of the basement. The part where we'd confronted the rogue just yesterday. I caught sight of Orion through the second window I glanced into.

The former guard was hunched over on his bench, his head in his hands. My heart wrenched.

The guard on duty walked over. "Dragon shifter," he said with a respectful bow. "What do you need?"

I held up the plate. "I'd like to bring this in to him."

The guard paused. "I wasn't told—"

I fixed him with a firm stare. "I'm your alpha's mate and dragon shifter. All I want to do is bring the prisoner a little dinner. He's too drugged up to shift, isn't he? He doesn't look like he's going to be any threat."

"Yes. Yes, he should be subdued. My apologies."

The guard pulled out a key and unlocked the door. I stepped inside tentatively.

Orion raised his head. The muskrat shifter's eyes were glazed. A dribble of drool shone at the corner of his mouth. He was at least aware enough to notice it and swipe it away when the back of his hand when he saw me.

"Dragon shifter," he said in a dazed voice. "What are you doing here?"

"Bringing you some food from the celebration out there, since you're not allowed to get it for yourself."

I offered him the plate. He stared at the spread of food for a few seconds before he reached for it. Then he just set the plate in his lap. He gazed at the meal for a moment longer and then peered up at me, squinting.

"Why would you bring me this? What does it matter to you what I eat? I'm a traitor."

I crouched down so my eyes were level with his where he sat on the bench. "I don't think you are," I said. "I don't think you'd decided one way or the other yet. And I think that matters. I know how hard it is to figure out the right thing to do when you're being pulled in different directions. What you choose in the end, that's who you are."

He wet his lips. His fingers clutched the edges of the plate. "Thank you," he said hoarsely. I couldn't tell if he meant the meal or the sentiment. Maybe both.

My heart felt a little lighter as I headed back to the party. So naturally I had to run into West right then.

He paused in the hall as I stepped out of the stairwell. His eyes narrowed. "What were you doing down by the holding cells?"

"Trying to make sure we don't turn another kin into our enemy," I said. "Is that all right with you?"

He held my gaze for a moment. Then he sighed and turned away. "I just hope you know what you're doing, Sparks."

So did I. He had no idea how much I did.

CHAPTER 8

Ren

I WATCHED the last of the guests drift out of the courtyard, and a weight settled in my gut.

It was just past midnight. The attendants were clearing the tables. The courtyard was quiet. No one was left except the shifters who lived on the estate.

And Aaron still hadn't returned. Alice hadn't either. She wouldn't have known exactly where to look for him, so I guessed her absence shouldn't be surprising. But he'd said he'd be back for the night. He couldn't have denied that it was absolutely, one hundred percent nighttime now.

Nate came up behind me, touching the small of my back. "Let's go inside," he said. "If he turns up, we'll hear about it."

I nodded, but my feet dragged as we headed back to our section of the estate house. Marco and West caught up with us.

"Nightcap, anyone?" Marco said. "If we're all going to fret

about eagle boy, we might as well enjoy ourselves at the same time."

We made our way down the narrow hall to our private common room. West stalked across to the far windows as Marco went to the liquor cabinet to mix the drinks. Nate sank down onto one of the couches. I paced from one end of the room to the other and back again as if I could outrun my anxiety. So far the motion was only making me feel more tense.

Marco handed me a shot glass. I tossed it back in one gulp. The alcohol burned down my throat and spread warmth through my chest. But it only took a slight edge off my worries. Several more might have done the trick, but I didn't think drinking myself into a stupor was a wise idea.

"You should try to get some sleep, Ren," Nate said. "We all should. If something has gone wrong, we'll need all our strength."

I rubbed my arms. "I don't think I *can* sleep." I was too wound up. Wondering about all the things that could have happened to Aaron that wouldn't trigger our mate-bond. He could be captured by the rogues. Too injured to fly home but not quite badly enough for the pain to tug at me.

I wanted him *here*, plain and simple. Someday I was going to have to get used to being apart from my mates, but I didn't think it was supposed to happen this soon after we'd consummated. It didn't feel right. This was the first night any of them had been this far away, and the distance gnawed at me.

"Come here," Nate said gently. He patted the couch cushion next to him.

I bit my lip, but I went to him. As I dropped down next to my bear shifter, he reached for my shoulders. His strong thumbs rubbed in steady circles over the tensed muscles there. They dug in, and the tension started to release.

"Okay, that's good," I said, my eyelids drooping. "Keep on doing that."

I heard his smile in his inhale. He eased his hands farther down my mostly bare back, kneading the muscles along my shoulder blades and spine. With each press, the tightness melted a little more.

And as it melted, a different sensation started to tingle through my body. His hands against my bare skin sparked a heat I should have expected, considering those hands belonged to one of my mates.

The heat shot straight to my core. My panties dampened. Oh, there were a hell of a lot of other parts of me I'd like those hands on.

My rising desire must have scented the air. Nate paused with his hands just below the base of my neck. He leaned closer, his breath spilling hot over my skin. "Maybe there's a little more I could do to distract you? Let out some of that tension?"

My body ached with longing. Fuck, yes. With all the turmoil since we'd arrived, I'd barely had time to feel anything good. But it seemed like far too long since I'd lost myself in the bond between me and my mate.

My *mates*. My eyelids fluttered open. I leaned back into Nate's touch instinctively, encouragingly, but at the same time my gaze sought out the other alphas.

Marco set down his empty glass, his eyes intent on me and Nate. A gleam of lust danced in them. West had turned, his stance tensed, but I could feel the hunger radiating off him.

Nate slid his hands around to cup my breasts. A gasp slipped out of me as he teased his fingers over the peaks, my nipples pebbling. Marco licked his lips. He moved as if to step toward us and then seemed to catch himself.

Waiting for me to give him the go-ahead.

I wanted all of them. All of them there with me, being with me in every way, taking my mind off the one who wasn't here for at least a little while. If even one more of them left my side—

The thought made my throat close up. I set my hands over Nate's to still them. The hot flush of desire coursed beneath my skin. I stood, pulling him with me.

"I think we should take this to my bed," I said, my fingers twined with Nate's. My gaze locked with Marco's and then West's to make it clear that my "we" included all of us.

A brilliant smile spread across Marco's face. "There's nothing I'd like better than to serve you however it pleases you," he said in a heated tone.

West wavered on his feet, looking torn. I held my other hand out to him. "I won't ask for anything you can't walk away from. I just want you all with me. How much is up to you."

I heard him swallow. Then he stepped toward us. "All right," he said, even more gruff than usual.

We slipped down the hall to my chambers. When we reached the end of my bed, I turned to face my mates. With a yank, I unzipped my dress. It crumpled into a heap at my feet, leaving me all but naked.

The heat in the room must have risen by ten degrees. I shivered with it, giddy—but suddenly uncertain. I'd been with Aaron and Nate at the same time before, but three guys... I needed them, but I wasn't exactly sure how.

"Just tell us what you want, Ren," Nate said, his voice slightly ragged. "We're right here with you."

I looked at each of them, my breath catching. "Shirts off. Pants too." Might as well spread the nakedness around a little.

Marco smirked as his hands darted to unbutton his shirt. West stripped down more hesitantly. A faint glow emanated from around the bandage he wore just below his left shoulder. A fae magic wound, I was pretty sure, though he'd avoided talking with me about it. In the midst of my rising lust, I made a mental note to be careful of it. Mess with that and he might never touch *me* again.

Nate discarded his clothes with a few jerks and the snap of a button. He was ready to get started, clearly. He stepped closer to me, his chest brushing mine, and claimed my mouth.

I moaned against his lips, reveling in the force of his kiss. He gripped my waist. A third hand grazed over my back to undo the clasp of my bra, a hot presence at my left side. Nate released my mouth to swipe his tongue across the crook of my jaw. I tipped my head to the side to give him full access to my neck, and Marco was right there to meet me.

As my bear shifter nibbled his way across all the sensitive spots on my throat, my jaguar shifter caught my mouth with his. He stroked his hand over my breast, tweaking the nipple until I whimpered.

Nate dipped his head to lave my other nipple into an even stiffer peak. Marco trailed his lips across my cheek to nip my earlobe. I shivered with pleasure, awash with sensation. Every part of my body was tingling.

But my mouth was being neglected again. I gasped as Nate's hand dipped between my legs, and my gaze flew up to find West's.

My wolf shifter was standing a few feet away, his hunger blatant on his face and coiled all through his stance. I met his dark green eyes. Nate's thumb stroked over my clit. I let out a whimper and mumbled, almost a plea, "West."

His jaw twitched. His eyes flashed. "Fuck," he said, and then he was striding toward me. He gripped my head as Marco brought his mouth to my collarbone. My heart skipped, ready for West to devour me. But as his fingers curled into my hair, he first pressed the softest of kisses to my forehead. The bridge of my nose. My cheek. My lips parted, wanting, waiting. The path he was tracing was the sweetest torture.

He finally brought his mouth to mine just as Nate tugged my panties down and slipped his fingers between my folds. Marco swiped his tongue around my nipple. I moaned into West's mouth, and the tender control he'd been keeping snapped.

His kiss ravished me, his tongue sweeping in to tangle with mine, his teeth grazing my lips. I kissed him back just as hard, wanting to plunder and be plundered. Marco was suckling my breast and Nate was kissing his way down my belly and oh, God, if I literally exploded from all this bliss, which seemed like a real possibility, I hoped the cleaning staff wouldn't hate me too much.

Nate eased me back on the bed. He knelt between my legs. I sucked in a breath as he swirled his tongue over my clit. Then Marco was kissing me again, his spicy coffee smell filling my senses. West licked one breast and fondled the other. Every nerve in my body was humming with fulfilled desire.

But I had even more desires that needed fulfilling. Nate pumped his fingers in time with the movements of his mouth, and I cried out at the jolt of pleasure. My whole body felt like a harp string being plucked harder and faster to reach a crescendo. When I shattered with it, I wanted to bring my mates with me.

I eased my mouth away from Marco's, panting. "Nate, inside me, please."

He didn't need more than my mumbled request to understand. His mouth left me for a few aching seconds before the hard length of his cock replaced it, tracing over my core from my clit to my opening.

I moaned hungrily and arched my hips. Nate gripped them, holding them off the bed and sliding into me with a groan of his own. The feel of him filling me sent an eager shudder through me.

"My Princess of Flames," Marco murmured beside me. "You really are on fire."

"Mmm," was all I managed to answer. I wanted to set him on fire too. I ran my hand down his chest to the cock jutting from between his legs, slimmer than Nate's and almost elegant. Marco practically purred as my fingers curled around it.

I tugged him gently forward. The heat in his eyes turned blazing as he caught on. He eased himself down on the bed so I could bring his cock to my mouth. It twitched as I licked the tip.

Nate thrust into me, sending a fresh wave of pleasure through me. I rode on it right down Marco's shaft, curling my tongue around his silky hardness, tasting the salty musk of his arousal.

"Fuck, princess, I'm not going to last long like that," Marco said around a groan. Good. Let him come apart right here with me.

My other hand had fisted in the duvet. As my body rocked with Nate's thrusts and the pump of my mouth over Marco, my knuckles brushed smooth skin over lean muscle.

I hadn't forgotten my other alpha. West was testing the edge of his teeth against my nipple now. With an instinct that must have come with being a dragon shifter, being meant for moments like this, I reached down and knew exactly where to close my hand around his cock.

West's breath stuttered against my breast. "Ren," he rasped. I stilled my fingers, sucking Marco down again, tipping my hips to meet Nate's next plunge into me. Ecstasy flooded me from every direction, but I wasn't going to take what West wasn't ready to give.

The wolf shifter lay there rigid for a moment. Then with a groan he pushed himself closer to me, welcoming my touch.

I slid my hand up and down his shaft in time with my mouth on Marco's, in time with Nate's inside me. A sense of bliss continued swelling not just from between my legs but my lips and fingers as well. From all of us together in this circle of pleasure.

Marco broke first. "Princess," he cried with a rough jerk of his hips. He moved as if to pull back from me, but I closed my lips around him tight.

His release spurted against the back of my mouth. I sucked it all in until he sagged beside me. He withdrew, kissed me on the lips for one long, aching moment, and then eased his hand down my body.

His lithe fingers found that bundle of nerves just above the spot where Nate and I were joined. They circled my clit, and the wave crested inside me. I gasped, squeezing West's cock. With a grunt he muffled in my hair, he spilled over. I followed, stars sparking behind my eyes, my whole body shaking with the force of my orgasm. As I clenched around Nate, he made a strangled sound and joined us in release.

We were probably quite the sight, the four of us sprawled together on the bed, limp and sated. But as Nate gathered me up and nestled into the pillows with me, the other guys joining us on either side, being with all of them felt like the most natural thing in the world. The best thing in the world.

Aaron's absence still gnawed at me, but it was a more distant pain now. Snuggling among my mates, I managed to drift off to sleep.

CHAPTER 9

Marco

THERE REALLY WAS nothing like waking up next to my mate. Her sweet smell laced the air, and the taste of her skin still lingered on my lips. Her body lay close enough to mine that its warmth traveled to me under the sheet.

My Princess of Flames was cuddled up next to Nate, who was lying opposite her. The glossy dark brown waves of her hair spilled over the brawny arm she was using as a pillow. Her head was tucked against the bear shifter's broad chest.

Some distant part of my brain suggested that I should feel jealous, but the only emotion rising through me was a swell of affection.

She looked content. Peaceful. It had been days since she'd been able to really relax, and she needed it after all the challenges she'd tackled—and tackled so well. Thinking back on how she'd faced down the fae monarch still gave me a flush of pride. Our dragon shifter was coming into her own by leaps and bounds. I'd already admired her when she'd stood up to me, confused but defiant, before she'd even known what she was. Now… She was magnificent.

So I couldn't resent Nate for giving her this comfort, even if my heart and the threads of the bond inside me throbbed with the longing for her to be just as much mine.

Really, it was pretty hard to resent anything at all with the memory of her mouth around my cock still fresh in my mind.

A couple days ago, I hadn't been sure when I'd even get to kiss her again. Me and *my* mouth—my stupid, stupid mouth. But last night we'd moved together like we were meant to bring each other pleasure. Maybe we were building a sort of peace between us now.

With a grunt, our other companion in the bed sat up. West raked a hand through his hair and shot a disgruntled look Nate's way. "Last time I sleep next to the bear shifter," he grumbled. But as he pushed himself off the bed, I didn't miss the way his gaze paused on Ren with a flare of desire.

Wolf boy's self-denial was reaching ridiculous levels. He could blame it on the mate bond and try to put up all the walls he wanted, but it was obvious every other part of him wanted her too. Ah, well. As long as he was denying himself, our dragon shifter had more attention for the rest of us.

As West grabbed his clothes and stalked out of the room, I eased a little closer to Ren. A joint cuddle didn't seem out of bounds. I pressed a kiss to the back of her neck and wrapped my arm around her waist.

Ren made a pleased sounding murmur and rested her arm over mine, squeezing my hand. "'Morning," she mumbled, her eyes still closed.

I traced my thumb in a slow circle over her soft skin. The feel of her against me combined with last night's memories had already gotten me hard. And that made me more daring. "Should we make it a particularly good one?" I asked.

"Mmm. You could try."

Well, that was a challenge I wasn't going to turn down. I trailed my hand up from her belly to the curve of her breasts. As I traced my fingers across the undersides of those soft peaks, she started to squirm. Her firm ass brushed my hard-on. I had to grit my teeth to clamp back a groan. But fuck, being with her like this was the most enjoyable torture I'd ever experienced.

I teased my fingers up, up the pert curves, and then flicked my thumb over one already hardened nipple. Ren gasped, her eyes popping open. I stilled my hand. She'd been half asleep. The last thing I wanted to do was overstep and lose what little trust I'd regained.

"Too much?" I said against her shoulder.

"Not enough," she muttered back. "Don't you dare stop."

I chuckled with a wash of relief—and hunger. As I caressed her breast again, I nibbled along the slant of her shoulder to her neck. Ren sighed, arching back her head.

The bear shifter stirred at the movement. An eager sound thrummed from his chest. He dipped his head to kiss Ren on the mouth. His free hand swept over her hip and thigh to the mound between her legs.

Ren whimpered, rocking into his touch. I flicked my tongue along the crook of her jaw and drew out another gasp. Dear God, there wasn't any joy in the world that could rival the sound and taste of our dragon shifter's desire. I could live on it and nothing else for days.

I was about to ease her onto her back so I could attend to her breasts with both my mouth and my hands when the door to her chambers thumped open.

"Stop messing around and get out of bed," West snapped. "Aaron's back."

~

Ren

I walked into Aaron's suite with bedhead and a dress I'd picked up off the floor, but seeing my missing mate ASAP was a hell of a lot more important than prettying myself up. The other three alphas strode in behind me.

Aaron was sitting on the edge of his bed. The weariness on his face and in the set of his shoulders made my heart squeeze. I went straight to him, cupping his face with my hands. He gave me an exhausted smile and hugged me to him.

My fingers slid into his golden hair. I bent down to catch his lips with mine, needing that contact. As if his kiss were the only thing that could convince me he was really here, back where he belonged.

"I'm sorry," he said when I eased back. His voice was weary too, its rasp thickened. "I meant to be back sooner. I know how worried you must have been."

"It's all right," I said. "I'm just glad you're back now. And okay. What happened?"

"He got himself stuck," Alice said, her dry tone more solemn than usual. She was leaning against the wall across from the bed, her arms crossed over her chest, looking equally exhausted.

Aaron chuckled faintly. "That's a fairly accurate description. I spotted some shifter movement below just before I would have planned to head back. They've set up a little camp, a few trailers and tents... I dipped down to confirm they were rogues, heard them talking, and found a perch I could listen from. But I stayed too long. Before I had a chance to leave, a couple of avian rogues shifted and took their posts around the camp, one of them close enough to me that he'd have noticed me leaving and raised the alarm."

"Couldn't out fly a couple of lesser birdies?" Marco said, mildly teasing.

"There was a falcon there, and a vulture," Aaron said. "They could have done some damage. But I was more concerned that what I'd learned wouldn't do us any good if they knew I'd overheard it. They'd have changed their plans."

"So he just waited there until I turned up and distracted them," Alice put in. "You're lucky we've got our sibling bond, or Lord knows how long you'd have been waiting there."

Aaron rolled his shoulders. "You can believe I'm glad you got there as soon as you did." He raised his head to meet my eyes again. "Thank you for sending her. It was the right call."

"Remember that the next time you want to go off alone," I said. "So what *did* you learn? What were they talking about? How close are they? Do we have to start preparing?"

He raised his hand to slow me down. When I went quiet, he tugged my wrist to sit me on the bed next to him. I wrapped my arm around his, watching his face as he started to speak.

"It sounded as though we should be fine as long as we're here," he said. "Unless, I suppose, we stay longer than they're expecting. They're settled in about a three-hour eagle-flight from here. The plans I heard, they were talking about waiting until we were on the move again. It was clear they assumed that within the next few days we'll be leaving here and heading toward the feline estate."

"That is what would make the most sense," Nate said.

Aaron nodded. "They want to catch us along the way. Make an attack with the advantage of surprise, on terrain they feel will skew the odds even more in their favor." He glanced at me to add an explanation. "Normally we'd make it a road trip so we could stop and meet with a few of the more distant communities along the way. We save the jets for emergencies."

"We could make an exception in a case like this, couldn't we?" I said.

"But then we'd lose our chance of confronting them. As soon as we reach Marco's estate, they'll have to make different plans. They'll move into a new position."

"Well, where's this prime terrain they're hoping to catch us at?" West asked.

"I don't know," Aaron admitted. "Either they'd already decided and didn't see the need to mention it to each other, or they haven't decided yet and are waiting to see what actions we take first. I couldn't tell from the way they talked about it."

Marco brushed his hands together. "Well, it doesn't matter, does it? Now we know where they are. We'll go deal with them before they can set up their little surprise."

"I agree," Aaron said. "But the difficulty is how. They're monitoring the area around the estate. They'll know if we set off straight toward their camp and scatter before we get anywhere near them. I counted around forty of them there. From what the rogue prisoner said, that might be as much as half of their remaining number. If we strike, it needs to be in a way that ensures none of them escapes. Otherwise we'll just have to deal with them again later."

"I've definitely had enough of that," West muttered. "Enough with the constant fleeing and regrouping. As long as enough rogues are out there to stir up trouble, none of our kin are truly safe."

"*Ren* won't be safe," Nate said. He moved to stand beside me, putting his hand on my shoulder. "They've gotten away with too much already. It's about time they faced some consequences."

"An excellent sentiment," Marco said. "It still doesn't answer the question of how."

Aaron rubbed his mouth. He looked so tired I wanted to tell the others to leave, to let him rest, but I knew from the determination in his stance that he wanted this settled. He'd waited out the rogues and spent the rest of the night flying back just so we could have this discussion. So we could come up with a plan of our own. I didn't think he'd be willing to rest until he knew the information he'd brought back could be put to real use.

"We do have some advantage now," Nate said. "We know they'll be trying to spring something on us."

"The trek from here to Florida is pretty long," Marco said. "We can't be on full alert constantly. I'd like a way to completely turn the tables on them."

An idea tickled its way into my head. I straightened up next to Aaron. "You know what? I think we already have the answer right here."

CHAPTER 10

Ren

"I DON'T KNOW ABOUT THIS," Nate said as we tramped down the stairs toward the basement holding cells.

"We don't have a whole lot of options," I pointed out. "What are you going to do otherwise—leave him locked up and drugged for the rest of his life? How is he ever going to prove whose side he's on if he never gets the chance?"

"I'd rather he was proving it in a way that didn't potentially risk your life," my bear shifter muttered.

"We can protect ourselves, can't we? We'll have our own sentries. We can withdraw if we need to." I stopped at the foot of the stairs and turned to face him. "Do you actually think it's a bad plan, or are you just worrying about me?"

He frowned. "It's the best plan any of us came up with. I won't pretend it isn't. But you can't blame me for worrying."

I patted his chest affectionately. "All right, I won't. Just try to go easy on him. We want him to feel he can trust *us*, remember."

Outside Orion's door, Nate produced a key ring from his pocket. The guard on duty hung back as we stepped inside.

Orion jerked up at the movement of the door. He'd been sprawled on his back on the bench, his head lolling. The tranquilizer still glazed his eyes and dulled his reflexes. He swayed before managing to completely sit up. His gaze stayed on Nate, wary even though his narrow face stayed slack.

I could just imagine how his last conversation with his alpha had gone. But I didn't want any grizzly behavior in here today.

I grabbed a stool from the hall and sat down across from the former guard. Nate loomed behind me, as if to give everything I said the extra weight of his authority. We'd decided it was probably better if I did the talking. Mainly because he wasn't sure he could keep his temper.

"Orion," I said, and the muskrat shifter's eyes dropped to meet mine. "We might have a job for you. A way for you to redeem yourself with your alpha and your kin—to show where your loyalties really lie."

Despite the vagueness of his expression, a spark of hope lit deep in his gaze. "What is it?" he asked. "What do you want me to do?"

"You've talked to the rogues before," I said.

He nodded. "One of them."

"So if we sent you out to talk to them, there should be someone in the local group who'd know who you are?"

"Yeah." His eyes darted between me and Nate. "But I don't know where they are. I told you."

"That's all right," I said with a crooked smile. "*We* know where they are. You could just... happen to stumble into them after we pointed you in the right direction."

He focused back on me, his head tipping slightly to the left. A furrow had formed in his brow. "And then what would I do?"

"Well, if you're up for it... We'd pick a spot for you to lead them to. We'll have a story for you to give them, something like that we're going to be sneaking out of the estate and heading down a specific stretch of road, somewhere that looks good for an ambush. You'll pretend you decided to side with them and you're bringing this inside information to prove your worth. And then we'll be the ones to ambush them."

Orion was quiet for a long moment, just looking at me. "You want me to trick them."

"They're planning another attack on us right now," I said. "They've already killed how many kin over the years? They support the people who killed the last alphas—my fathers. My sisters, who were only seven and nine years old. If any of them surrender, I promise you I'll treat them fairly. But if they're going to insist on fighting us, we can either fight back or lay down and die. And I wouldn't ask anyone to do the second. Including you. That's why I wanted you to have this chance."

"Your dragon shifter is being incredibly generous," Nate put in, his voice just shy of a growl. "As am I as your alpha, letting her bring you the proposition in the first place. Are you going to stay with us or fight against us?"

I shot him a look, and he grimaced but shut his mouth. "Or stay here," I added, turning back to the muskrat shifter. "If you don't want to take the risk, I'd understand. Maybe there'll be another opportunity for you to show your loyalties. This is what we've got right now."

Orion sucked in a breath. "I—I could do it. I think it could work. I can't promise anything, but I—" He stopped and rubbed his forehead. His jaw worked. "I can't think straight right now. But I know that I regret not coming to you as soon as they approached me, alpha. And, Serenity..."

"Ren," I corrected him.

He looked up again, his eyes gone watery. "Thank you," he said. "For thinking of me. For trying to do right by all of us."

"Will you try too?" I asked gently.

"Yes," he said. "For my kin. For my alpha. And for you."

My throat tightened at the emotion in his voice. "Then I should be thanking you." I stood up. "We'll have to let the tranquilizer wear off," I said to Nate. "He can make a final decision then, when his mind isn't so fuzzy. I want him to go understanding exactly what he's agreed to."

Nate didn't look enthusiastic about it, but it wasn't as if we could send his former guard off to consort with the rogues in his current state anyway. When we'd shut the door, he turned to the guard on duty.

"No more shots," he said. "Let him come out of the daze. Keep a close eye on him. If he shifts or does anything suspicious, restrain him if you need to and call for me. When he's had time to totally recover, call for me then."

"Yes, sir," the guard replied.

"You have your dragon's sensitivity," Nate said to me as we headed back to the main floor. "Do you think Orion actually wants to help, or is he just looking for any way to get out of that holding room?"

I thought of the former guard's watery eyes and the wave of feeling that had coursed off of him at the end. "He really does regret what happened. He wants to be part of the kin again. I can't tell how well his nerve will stand up once he's out there with the rogues, of course."

"I guess there'd be no telling that with anyone." Nate sighed. "Well, we'll see how he feels to you when he's totally awake."

"How long will it take for the tranquilizer to wear off?"

"A few hours at least." He paused when we reached the top of the stairs. "So we have a little time. There's something I wanted to show you here. It might actually be a little familiar."

I perked up, my uncertainties about our plan momentarily pushed aside by a spark of curiosity. "What do you mean?"

He smiled. "You'll see."

Nate led me through a few hallways and up a broad staircase to the second floor. He opened a door to a large room in what was obviously one corner of the house. The first thing that caught my eyes was the sunlight streaming through two pairs of windows on the south and east walls.

I stepped inside, and my breath stopped in my throat.

It wasn't just that the room was beautiful, although it was. The walls around the door were painted in reds and golds and glossy greens: stylized animals frolicking through a forest here, an ocean there, and up here by the ceiling puffs of dancing clouds. The designs stretched all the way to the windows, where trees and waves curled around the frames. The floorboards beneath my feet were polished to a shine so soft I almost felt as if I were walking on silk carpet.

I walked into the middle of the room and turned around. A warm, sandy smell hung in the air, like the kind of rock perfect for sunning yourself on during a hot summer day... if you happened to be a dragon. Like the actual rock that lay on the floor beneath the windows. A few chairs with plump cushions and wooden arms scattered the rest of the space.

Yes, it was beautiful. And also deeply familiar. Tears had sprung into my eyes.

"When I imagined bringing you to my home for the first time, I pictured the visit being a little more relaxing," Nate said. "But at least before we go you can spend some time in here. It was your mother's favorite room in the estate." He took in my expression. "You remember it."

"Yes." I sank onto the stone slab. The sun-drenched warmth of its solid surface spread up through my hands. "She would bring me and my sisters in here when we complained about being bored. Sometimes my father—my bear shifter father—would come with us. What did she call it?"

"The inspiration room," Nate said with a smile. "The first time I met her, she called for me to meet her in here."

"Even though I couldn't shift yet, I loved lying on this rock." I eased myself down on my side, soaking up the stone's heat and the beams streaming through the windows. "Sometimes she'd curl up around me here. All four of us would squeeze in together, or five if Da was there..."

I swallowed hard. Nate's expression softened. "You don't talk about them very much—your fathers and your sisters. You can, you know. I mean, if it's too hard, you don't have to. But if you want to talk to someone who remembers... I trained with your bear shifter father for four years before the attack took him. I didn't know you or your sisters well, but I remember watching you playing in the courtyard when you were visiting."

Watching us and wondering which of us would become his mate? And now here I was. The only one of my entire family left.

I swiped at my eyes and pushed myself back into a sitting position. "It is hard. Not just because it hurts, but also because... The memories don't come easily. I don't think there's any magic suppressing them now, but when it's been so long since I've practiced remembering them—I don't know where to start unless I see or feel something that triggers them."

Like that embarrassing breakdown when we'd first arrived. My face still heated at that memory.

But this place provoked better ones. I found, with an ache in my throat, that I did want to share them. To make them more real by conjuring those dead and gone.

I pointed to one wall. "My oldest sister, Temperance—she used to make up stories about all the animals. One time she spent hours connecting every piece of the painting into one epic tale. I never knew where she'd go with it when she started. The story came out totally different every time."

My gaze fell on the chairs. "And my other sister—Mom always said she must have accidentally birthed a monkey when Verity came out. Verity couldn't sit still for more than a few minutes. In here she'd climb up on the chairs and make a game of leaping between them, seeing how long she could provoke her dragon wings out for."

"And Da..." I could picture him in my mind's eye. Big and brawny like Nate, but longer in the face and even darker haired. My chest clenched up. "I always wanted to see more from the windows. He'd sweep me up in his arms and hold me right by the top, and tell me about all the things we could spot from here to the horizon."

I felt the giddiness that had run through my little girl's body. The joy of having my father's attention focused all on me.

What would he, and my other dads, have thought of me if they could see me now? What would my life have been like if the rogues had never sent it brutally off course?

Nate ambled over and sat down beside me. I leaned against his shoulder. He took my hand, rubbing his thumb over the back. "You lost a lot," he said. "More than any of us can understand. We each lost one mentor. Your whole family is gone. I have no idea what that's like. But whenever you want to talk about it, you can come to me. To any of us. I think I can speak for the other alphas there."

"Thank you." Now that I had talked about my family, my heart felt a little lighter. "I actually think I'd like to spend a little time in here on my own before we go. If that's okay."

"Of course," Nate said. "I should take care of a few things around the estate before we move on. If you need me, one of the attendants will know where to find me."

He tipped my face toward his and kissed me softly. When he moved away my body was humming. I could feel his presence through our bond even after he'd left and shut the door behind him. While he was on the estate and that close to me, I didn't think I'd need anyone's help to find him.

I lay back down on the sunning stone and just drifted in and out of memories for a while. Weirdly, letting those fragments of my past rise up didn't increase the pain of my loss. If anything, they soothed it. It was a heck of a lot better remembering the happy times. Why should my only clear recollections of my family be my fathers' and sisters' last moments of panic and torment?

When I sat up again, my nerves felt more settled. I touched the edge of my phone in my pocket. I did have another kind of family that I wasn't going to leave behind completely. I'd promised Kylie I'd keep checking in. The last thing I wanted was her figuring I'd ditched her.

Hey, Ky, I texted to her. *Exciting times here. We're going to take the battle to the rogues. I came up with a brilliant plan... Well, we'll see how brilliant it is when we try it.*

Her response came a minute later. *Oh please. If you came up with it, of course it'll work. I can just imagine your dragon self smashing all those assholes.*

There was something pretty satisfying about that image. *I wish you were here to really see it. I guess we'll be near New York again before too long. We're heading to Marco's estate next, in Florida, and then West's is up in the Northeast somewhere.*

Oooh, Florida sun and fun! Where's his pad?

I smiled. *Apparently not far from Miami.*

That figures. He totally looks like the clubbing type. Make sure you keep him in line, you hear?

Before I could answer, someone knocked on the door. "Come in," I said.

An attendant peeked inside. "Dragon shifter," he said. "Nate requests your presence by the holding rooms."

Shit. It was already time to see just how brilliant my plan was. I sucked in a breath. Add another one to the many conversations with my bestie I was going to have to put off finishing.

"All right," I said. "I'm coming."

CHAPTER 11

Ren

IT FELT STRANGE, being the only one of the shifters around me still in human form. I set my feet down as quietly as I could, moving with the others up the wooded hillside we'd chosen for our ambush. A loamy smell filled my nose. Furred bodies wove through the trees around me.

My mates and Nate's kin who'd joined us had all shifted as soon as we'd left behind the vehicles, stashed off the road. It made sense, since in their animal bodies they could move faster and more stealthily, extend their senses farther, and just generally be more badass. Nate and Marco padded along on either side of me, West loping along ahead of us. Aaron soared overhead alongside Alice, watching for worrisome activity below.

I could have been a hell of a lot more badass as a dragon, but the one thing I wouldn't be was stealthy. Not to mention it wouldn't do us much good if I burned out my limited shifting energy tramping through the woods and then had to do the actual fighting as a human.

Orion should have reached the rogues' camp last night. The plan was for him to tell them that we'd be passing along this stretch of road this morning—that we'd planned to slip away during the wee hours to avoid notice. They'd think they were coming right down to the road to ambush us there. But they'd run right into *our* ambush before they had a chance to see they'd been misled.

At least, that was how it was supposed to go. Assuming Orion came through and didn't just throw in his lot with the rogues. He'd seemed determined to follow my plan when I'd talked to him before he left, but also a little browbeaten. Maybe once he'd gotten farther away from my and his alpha's authority, he'd decided to take his chances with people who hadn't locked him up and drugged him. Even if they were murderers.

I really hoped I'd been right about him, though.

West slowed at the top of the hill. He walked to the crest where the ground slanted down again and glanced back at us. This was where we'd planned to stop.

Aaron dove from the sky, leaving his sister on sentry duty. He shifted as he reached the ground and made a graceful landing on both human feet.

"There's movement a few miles off," he said. "I'd guess they'll be here in half an hour or so. We should spread out downwind so they don't catch our scent before we're ready to spring."

I nodded. The other animals drifted back into the trees. I followed, staying by Nate's side. I was going to have to hang farther back than the others, because my smell wouldn't blend into the natural landscape as well.

There might be a few downsides to being the rarest type of

shifter around. But I did mean to use my unique skills to my best advantage.

When Nate stopped, with a dip of his head toward me, I ran my fingers into his thick grizzly fur and pressed my face to his shoulder. He nuzzled me back.

Back on the estate, while we'd been making our final plans, Nate had tried to convince me I should sit the battle out. He'd made it through about half a sentence before I'd laughed and given him my best dragon stare. There'd been no arguments after that.

The kin who'd died had been my kin too. And I wasn't going to stand by while the rogues who'd destroyed their lives and my family's were still walking free.

I turned and reached for the tree we'd stopped beside. The best thing about being a dragon was flying. And I'd be damned if I was going to spend any time at all on the ground as soon as I could shift.

I scrambled up the trunk and clambered from branch to branch until I reached the ones too narrow to easily support my weight. Sitting with my back against the trunk, I scanned the forest. I wasn't quite high enough to see over the canopy, but I had a decent view between the branches around me.

There was Marco's black jaguar form crouching a few trees to our left. West's wolf had blended completely into the brush. Aaron made one last swoop through the sky and came to perch on an oak to my right.

A half an hour. We'd burned through at least ten minutes fanning out around the ambush point, I thought. It shouldn't be that much longer. But it felt like an eternity between every beat of my heart.

A branch cracked, and my pulse leapt, but it was only a

sparrow flitting away. Damn regular animals. I resisted the urge to shuffle my feet impatiently against the branch.

Orion knew exactly where we were going to be waiting. He was supposed to lead the rogues right over this hill. If he was keeping his end of the bargain. If not... Alice was still keeping watch. She'd notice if the rogues looked like they were spreading out to try to take us by surprise instead.

The breeze changed course, and new smells filled my nose. Animal smells—and not the familiar ones of the shifters I'd arrived with—mingling with notes of aggression and anticipation.

The rogues were almost here.

I leaned forward on the branch, bracing my hands and feet against the bark. We didn't want to spring the trap too soon. Let them barge right into the middle of our ring.

Bodies rustled through the underbrush. Faintly, covertly, but in the quiet my sharp ears could pick up the sounds. My muscles tensed.

A small furry form scurried into view below. A muskrat, leading the supposed charge. Our Orion. I sent a silent thank you down to him, and then several more animals emerged between the trees.

Below my perch, Nate let out a grizzly bellow. We all launched ourselves at the rogues.

I ran along the branch and vaulted out into open space. My scales rippled over my body with the rush of the air around me. My wings whipped out, catching that wind. I stretched and snapped my jaws with my emerging fangs, and hurtled down into the fray.

The forest floor was a mess of writhing bodies. A black bear I knew was Thomas was wrestling with a puma. A scarred silver wolf faced off against Marco's jaguar. Aaron clawed at a huge weasel that tried to smack him out of the sky. And more, all around—a blur of fur and teeth and splashes of blood.

I let a dragon's roar rip from my throat. The rogues startled, giving my kin their openings. The puma whirled to make a run for it, and I dove, smacking it into a tree trunk with one taloned paw. A coyote stumbled backward and shifted into human form. He made a grab for the gun he'd been carrying wrapped around his narrow waist.

The echoes of long ago shots fired in my family home rang in my ears. Anger flared through me. Oh, no, he didn't.

I sucked in a breath and spewed out flame—the hot, searing, destructive kind. The coyote shifter yelped. Then he was nothing more than a charred body with a melted lump of metal in his hands.

There'd be others who were carrying weapons they'd meant to bring to their own assault. I swung around, scanning the fray. I had to pick any rogue off who'd come armed. They could hurt us too quickly. My alphas and my kin were too honorable to break their law about using man-made weapons, even when their enemies didn't care to play fair.

The click of a safety disengaging made my gut lurch. I swiveled and blasted the figure standing amid the trees before I had time to register anything more than her blond hair and the pistol in her hand. A guy who'd sprung into human form nearby fumbled with his own handgun. Before he could aim it, I turned him into charcoal too.

My muscles tingled as I swooped in the other direction. Another human form moved between the foliage at the other end of the clearing— No, wait, that was Orion. I guessed he figured he could defend himself better with size on his side instead of his muskrat teeth and claws. Naked, his hands clenched into fists, he punched a rogue fox shifter that came at him in the muzzle and then leapt out of the way of its snapping teeth.

I slashed my talons downward to knock the fox shifter to the side. As I dropped down to pin her to the ground, another human figure ran at Orion. A human figure clutching a gleaming dagger.

A rasp of protest broke from my throat. Orion spun around, but not quickly enough. The rogue slammed the dagger into his gut, all the way to the hilt.

Orion's lips parted. His body sagged. Blood gushed down from the wound.

No. Panic spiked through my veins, sharp and cold. I swiped at the guy with the knife, ripping the dagger from his hand and the skin from his arm. But in my distress, I lost my hold on my shift. My dragon's body crumpled back into my human one.

I stumbled toward Orion. He'd sunk onto his knees and was reeling backward. I caught his shoulders just before his head smacked the ground.

"Hey," I said. "Hey. Stay with me." Shifters could heal from a lot. I'd had my chest gouged by a rogue wolf and survived. If the dagger hadn't been that well aimed—if I could stop the bleeding—

Reddish flecks were already dappling the former guard's lips. Shit, shit, shit. I clamped my hand around the hilt of the dagger, suppressing the flow of blood there, as if that surface wound was really the problem and not the cuts he'd taken on the inside.

Orion shivered and groaned. "Dragon shifter," he murmured.

"That's me," I said brilliantly. "I'm right here. You did good. You did your kin and your alpha proud. You're a fucking hero, you hear that. So you'd better live long enough to celebrate that with us."

He gave me a sickly smile. "I'm doing my best. But I don't

think—" He coughed and gasped at the wrench of the blade with the movement of his chest.

"*No*," I said, with all the authority I could summon. "As your dragon shifter, I forbid you from dying right now."

He tried to chuckle, but it came out more like a gurgle. Oh, God, there really wasn't anything I could do, was there?

"There's something... didn't tell you..." His voice was fading.

"It's okay," I said. "Just—just rest."

"No. You need... There's a feline kin. Someone... someone high up in the families. Calling the shots. Allied... with the rogues. They listen to him. The rest of the group—every rogue remaining… Ready to attack all together. You have to..."

His throat worked, and his body spasmed. "Orion!" I cried out, but his eyes had already fogged. "No, no, damn it."

I could feel it, as much as I wanted to resist what my senses were telling me. He was gone.

I sat back on my heels, my shoulders slumped. Then I flinched around at a thud behind me.

West had just tackled the fox shifter. From their positions, she'd been about to leap at me. His wolf was twice as big as her form. She squirmed and clawed, but she didn't stand a chance.

And she clearly knew that too. Like so many of the rogues before, she wasn't letting herself be taken prisoner. West shifted one of his paws to get a better hold on her, and she rammed her neck into his claws.

He jerked back, but it was already too late. He'd severed her throat. With a snarl of disappointment, he sprang off her sagging body.

West looked around at the dwindling fray and shifted into human form. His gaze caught mine. He jerked his chin toward Orion.

"He's passed?"

I swallowed hard. "It was just—the cut was too deep—it happened so fast. I tried everything I could think of." My hands, tacky with the muskrat shifter's blood, clenched in my lap.

West's eyes dropped to them and rose back to my face. A shadow passed through his expression, from dark to light. "Yeah," he said quietly. "You did." He paused. "Ren—"

"We've got a prisoner!" someone shouted. A panting Thomas hunched over a sinewy body he'd managed to hold in place by the wrists. Alice had pinned the guy's ankles with her talons, still in eagle form.

"And I've got another," Marco announced, sauntering from amid the trees with a bobcat he held by the scruff of its neck and its restrained hind legs. His fingers tensed as the rogue struggled to break free. Nate shifted and moved to help him.

I pushed myself onto my feet. Too quickly. My legs wobbled, my stomach feeling as if I'd left it behind down by the ground.

West caught me by the shoulders. "Hey," he said, his voice somehow rough and gentle at the same time. He pulled me into a hug, tucking my head under his chin. We were both naked, but with the image of Orion's dead body lingering in my head, his blood staining my hands, there was nothing sensual about the embrace. I leaned into the heat of West's body seeking only comfort, from the mate I'd never expected to offer it.

He stroked his hand over my hair, and my hands slipped against his chest. Shit, I was getting blood all over him. I jerked back, not knowing where to put them. West looked down at himself, the smears of blood over the lean muscles, and shook his head.

"It's okay," he said. And then, in more the tone I'd have expected from him. "I expect you'll make plenty more messes than that before you're done, Sparks."

As I made a face at him, Aaron came up beside me. He

offered me a strip of moss to wipe my hands. "I think we'll need your help questioning the captives," he said. "They don't seem any more inclined to talk than the other rogues have been."

Of course. I dragged in a breath and took in the results of our ambush. At least a couple dozen bodies littered the forest floor—all of them, as far as I could tell, rogues, other than Orion. A couple of Nate's other people were sprawled, having their wounds tended to by their kin, but none of the rest of us had taken a fatal injury. There'd been more rogues in the attack party than I could see around me, though.

"Some of the others got away?" I said.

Nate nodded. "A few cowards ran when they saw the way the battle was going and moved too fast for any of us to catch them. But only a few."

Damn. I looked at the bobcat and then the rogue pinned on the ground. "You've got a choice. You can talk to us now or you can talk in my fire."

The man on the ground glared at me. The bobcat hissed. Well, I guess that answered that.

"Pour down the flames, and we'll toss them in," Marco suggested. "I don't think they'll be going anywhere once you're got them in the hot spot."

"All right." I glanced at him. "Orion told me there's an important feline shifter, one of your kin, who's been calling at least some of the shots. Making plans with the rogues."

Marco's eyes darkened. "Interesting," he said, an edge creeping into his voice. "Let's see what these two have to say about that, shall we?"

I closed my eyes, reaching back to my sense of my dragon self. The change came over me more slowly this time, lengthening and expanding, nerves twitching. I'd already exhausted a lot of my energy during the fight. But I had enough to make this interrogation count.

I loomed over the others in the middle of the small grove. My kin moved to clear a space. I focused on the burn tingling at the base of my dragon throat. On my anger at Orion's death and the other deaths the rogues had caused. On my need to know what else they might have in store for us.

Then I opened my jaws and let the violet flames stream down.

Marco threw the bobcat into the fire first. It shuddered and expanded into a woman's form, huddled in the midst of the flames. "Who among my kin have you been talking to?" Marco snapped immediately.

"I haven't spoken to anyone," the bobcat shifter said in a whimper. "No one tells me anything. I just did my best to help."

"Are you aware of any allies among the feline kin—or any other kin—that the other rogues have been talking to?" Aaron asked, phrasing his question carefully.

She shook her head. "No one except the one on the disparate kin's estate. And that one." She pointed toward Orion. "Much good as he did us."

"What were you going to do if your plan to ambush us here didn't work?" Nate said.

"I'm not sure."

West cleared his throat. "What do you know about the other rogues' plans?" he put in.

She shivered again, jerking her head away from the blast of my flames, but she couldn't resist their burn. "There were plans being made around the feline estate," she gasped out. "I don't know what. But they were preparing for something big if we failed here."

Something big. Orion has said the rest of the rogues were

prepared to launch a heavy assault. How many of them were left now?

I heaved another stream of flames over the bobcat shifter, ignoring the pinching sensation that was starting to work through my muscles.

"Specifics," Marco said. "Tell us everything you know about those plans."

"That *is* all I know." Her voice turned into a whimper.

Aaron made a gesture to Nate, maybe realizing that my strength was waning. The bear shifter grabbed the rogue woman and hauled her out of the truth-searing fire.

Thomas and Alice were ready with their captive. The gawky albatross shifter flinched beneath the flames, but he didn't have any more answers to the alpha's questions than the bobcat shifter had. My throat started to throb. I gestured to my mates, and West shot out one last inquiry.

"Your allies who ran away from this attack—where would they have gone?"

"I'm not sure," the guy said in a strained voice. "Maybe to meet up with the main group in Florida?"

My flames sputtered out. My shift sputtered out too. I shrank into my human body and immediately launched into a coughing fit. Very smooth.

When I got control of my lungs, Nate's people were already hauling the two captured rogues away. "What are you going to do with them?" I asked.

"Hold them, drugged, until we decide what punishment they should face." Nate sighed. "They were only lackeys. I'd banish them—but they were outside the kin already, and look what they got up to."

Our prisoners hadn't known enough. I'd gone all the way up a mountain to earn the power of those violet flames, the ones that burned through to the truth. No other dragon shifter before me had claimed Sunridge's secret. But it still hadn't been enough to win the day.

"It sounds like as far as they knew the group that's waiting in Florida, that's most of them," I pointed out. "The 'main group,' he said. That fits with what Orion told me."

"So if we can deal with the rogues there, we might have wiped up the rest of the problem," West filled in. "Which would sound a lot more hopeful if we knew where the hell in Florida they were."

"Are we still going there?"

"I think that's the best course of action we have," Aaron said. "The rogues don't know what we've found out. We should go on to the feline estate, act as if we don't suspect anything is wrong, and investigate from there."

"And when I find out which of my kin has been entertaining those lunatics, you'd better believe the fur is going to fly," Marco said, baring his teeth in a fierce grin.

Nate turned. His gaze fell on Orion's limp body. He looked to me, taking in the blood smeared over my skin. His jaw set.

"We'll deal with the rogues," he said in a voice that brooked no argument. "And the muskrat shifter will have a funeral with all the respect he's due."

CHAPTER 12

Aaron

Riding in an airplane never felt quite right. The whole time I was off the ground, my body never stopped itching with the awareness that I was meant to fly in other ways, not let some hunk of metal do the work for me. Given the choice, I'd almost always pick a land vehicle.

I stretched out in the leather seat, which I'd reclined as far back as it would go. I was still a little tired from spending the night before last awake and on edge, so I'd gone into the back room of the private jet on my own and drawn the curtain. So far I hadn't had a great deal of luck relaxing.

Considering the circumstances, getting to the feline estate as quickly as possible had seemed the best option. If we could deal with any rogues and their allies in Florida before they had time to finish preparing, so much the better. So I'd agreed when Nate had suggested he have one of his kin pick us up in a jet at an airfield near our ambush spot.

But even having the windows shut, the space was only shadowed, not really dark. With the thrum of the engine beneath me, I'd only been able to doze, not completely drift off. At least that had helped reduce my fatigue.

Now I was just mentally preparing myself for the events ahead of us. The feline kin and avians had never gotten on all that well, even without a traitor in the mix. Cats and birds—not a good mix.

Someone knocked against the wall outside the curtain. "Aaron?" Serenity said. "Do you mind if I join you?"

I straightened up, pushing the chair into its upright position. "Not at all. Please do."

My mate slipped past the curtain. She smiled at me, but I could see the worry and grief in her eyes. It tugged at my heart. I held my hand out to her, motioning for her to sit with me.

The seats in the back room were set up in pairs facing each other with a small table in between. Serenity sank into the one opposite me with a sigh and leaned her elbows onto the table. "Did you manage to get some rest?" she asked.

Concerned about me first, even with so much else on her mind. Every time I thought I couldn't love her more, she stole another piece of my heart. "I got enough," I said. "I think I'm ready to handle a gaggle of cats now."

Her smile twitched with amusement. "I guess they're not going to be super friendly to you, huh?"

"Doubtful. I've never actually visited the feline estate before. We've kept somewhat separate the last several years."

"Because you didn't have a dragon shifter pulling you together."

"Yes. But that time is over now." I cupped my hands around hers. "Something's bothering you. You wanted to talk to me about it?"

She bit her perfect pink lip, her amber eyes darkening. "I guess it's what you just said. The tensions between the different kin-groups. All this trouble with the rogues, and then finding out they're not just managing to sway a few of the regular kin to their side, they've got someone high up in the kin who's orchestrating attacks..."

"It's hard for all of us to accept that information," I said. "You know I didn't want to face the fact that they'd gotten to one of my kin."

She nodded. "But... you each deal with your own kin your own way. I'm supposed to somehow unite everyone. Make them all believe that, well, believing in me is the best way to go. But I hardly know them. I hardly know my own family!"

"That's not your fault. No one blames you for that."

"Well, I don't know about that," she said wryly. "I thought maybe I was getting by okay after how things went at your estate, but seeing how wary some of the disparate kin were of me—it was kind of hard to take. And I have the feeling the felines are going to be even more skeptical. They hardly trust *Marco* to lead them, and he's one of them."

I squeezed her hands, my heart squeezing too. "Look at how much you've already accomplished. You're rising to the situation better and faster than anyone could have asked, Serenity. There's more work ahead—I'm not going to pretend there isn't—but I know you can meet the challenge."

"I just..." Her gaze slid away from me. Her voice dropped. "What if trying to put things back the way they were *isn't* the best thing for all the kin? Obviously the way the rogues are trying to change things isn't right, but what if the time when dragon shifters could unify everyone is over now? Maybe it's been too long without one, and it's just causing more trouble trying to recreate the past."

"Do you really think that's true?" I asked.

"No," she said quietly. "I feel like this is where I'm meant to be. All the kin feel like my people. I want to be what all of them need. I just don't know if I can be that. And there's been so much blood shed since I came back, *because* I came back, already."

Oh, my darling mate. Taking so much responsibility onto her shoulders, more than ever should have been hers. "Come here?" I said, giving her hands a gentle tug.

She got up and sidled around the table. I eased her onto my lap, where I could look her straight in the eyes with barely any distance between us. The press of her thighs straddling mine sent a warm wash of hunger through me, but I ignored it. I brushed a lock of her hair back from her cheek. Serenity gazed down at me with affection and a little hunger of her own.

"I told you before that I've sometimes felt like an outsider, both among the alphas and among my own kin," I said. "I know what it feels like to wonder if you're really what your people need, because they're not entirely sure you are. But from what I've seen and been through, what matters most is simply that you *are* there, that you stand up for them in every way you can whenever you can. What all the kin need right now is something stable to hold on to. You can be that sure thing they look to."

"You say that like it's easy," she said.

I chuckled. "I know it's not. But you can do it. Stay steady. Find a balance between all the demands. You've got feline cunning running through your veins, as much as you've got avian grace and canine loyalty and a bear's strength. This is what you're made for."

~

Ren

I bent my head even closer to Aaron's. Emotions whirled inside me. "I don't know," I said. "I don't feel all that balanced."

"No?" he murmured, raising an eyebrow.

One particular emotion was rippling through me more insistently than the rest. I wet my lips. "No. In fact, all I seem to be able to think about right now is kissing you."

My mate hummed an approving sound. "I think there's a balance we can find there too."

He traced his fingers over my cheek and met me halfway to his mouth. If this was his demonstration, I was all for the lesson.

His tongue teased over mine and I slicked mine over his in return. My body settled lower on his lap. The bulge of his cock brushed my core through our clothes, and suddenly *that* was all I could think about.

I kissed Aaron harder, raking my fingers into his hair. He kissed me back as he gripped my waist. With a gentle tug, he fit us together perfectly.

A whimper crept from my throat. I couldn't help rocking against him, chasing the pleasure of that friction. Aaron groaned. He released my mouth to kiss a trail down my neck.

"Look at how easily we can fall into a rhythm," he murmured.

"You're my mate," I said around a hitch of breath. "We're meant for this."

He stopped and eased back to meet my eyes. "And they're your kin," he said. "All of them. They *are*. You're meant for them."

My throat choked up abruptly. I leaned my forehead against his. "I missed you so much," I said. "I know you were only gone for one night, but—"

"I know," he said, his voice thickening. "When I was stuck out there by the rogue camp, the main thing that kept me focused was thinking of you, of keeping you safe from them. I expect it'll be easier, after we've had more time together—"

"But not yet," I finished for him. "Right now, I want everything."

Desire darkened his clear blue eyes. "You can have it."

Our mouths collided again with a hot, heady kiss. Aaron's hands traveled up under my shirt to caress my breasts. I moaned into his mouth as he drew my nipples into harder peaks with each stroke of his fingers. My hips arched to meet his.

He pulled off my shirt and tossed aside my bra. Then it was his lips and his tongue teasing the tips of my breasts, one after the other.

Each nip and lick sent sparks of pleasure through me. I gasped, pressing into his embrace with a desperation I no longer felt embarrassed by. He experienced this need just as deeply as I did.

The pressure was building between my legs with a hot ache. I reached my hand between us to stroke it over his cock. Aaron's breath stuttered against my skin. He tilted his hips to give me better access.

With a jerk, I released the zipper on his slacks. My fingers slipped under the fabric of his boxers to grip him skin to skin.

"Too much clothing," I muttered.

Aaron gave a rough chuckle. "We could take care of that together too."

I lifted myself over him so he could yank my jeans and panties down my thighs. I wrenched his pants down in turn. His hand dipped between my legs, his thumb circling my clit. I gasped again, riding his fingers. But that wasn't what I really wanted to be riding.

I reached for his cock again. The way his expression softened with pleasure when I wrapped my fingers around it sent my own bliss spiraling even higher. I lowered myself onto him, moaning as he filled me.

"Serenity," Aaron whispered, like a prayer. He thrust up into me, sending a deeper wave of pleasure through me. I rocked in time with his rhythm, the ecstasy building as fast as I could follow it.

We matched each other's movements, setting the pace alongside each other. I didn't know if he was completely right about my greater role, but this? This passion couldn't have come more naturally to me.

My eagle shifter pulled me into another kiss. His hand returned to my breast, stroking it with each pump of his hips. I ran my hand down his chest as if I could grasp even more of the heat between us. The delicious burn inside me expanded, flooding all my senses.

I bucked faster, flying higher. Aaron thrust even deeper, and I plummeted over the edge into total bliss.

I kept riding him, my orgasm trembling through me, but it only took that sudden clenching to bring him past the point of no return too. He choked out a sound of release as he spent himself inside me.

I sagged against him, loving the feel of his hot, sweat-slick skin against mine. The salty, musky smell of him. He folded his arms around me, cradling me to him, and kissed my forehead.

"And any time you need another demonstration..." he said.

I laughed and hugged him tightly. I still wasn't sure I was ready for whatever waited for us up ahead, but at least I'd be facing it with my mates.

CHAPTER 13

Ren

I'D ALREADY DONE the arriving at an alpha's estate thing twice now. I shouldn't have felt so nervous. But as the private jet touched down on the fringes of the feline kin property just south of Miami, my stomach balled into one huge knot.

It wasn't just the new kin group I had to meet. It was the traitor we already knew was lurking among the prominent families. And maybe there was more than one. Orion hadn't been all that involved with the rogues. There had to be plenty they hadn't let him in on.

Marco had called a few of his estate's security people ahead of time to meet us at the airfield. "They'll give us the all clear when they've taken a thorough look around the perimeter," he said.

West leaned back in his chair, his shoulders tensed. "And you're sure we can trust *them*?"

Marco narrowed his eyes at the wolf shifter, but he smiled at the same time. "I trust that they're not *all* traitors, and the ones who aren't will catch anything that needs catching."

My phone's ringtone started playing, so unexpectedly I flinched in my seat. My mates all shot curious glances my way. No one had this number other than Kylie. I fumbled for the phone and answered it as quickly as I could.

"Kylie, what's up? Is something wrong?"

"Not at all!" her cheerful voice rang out on the other end. "Everything is spectacular. Especially because I just touched down in Miami. So how exactly do I get from the airport to this shifter estate of yours?"

I blinked, my mind going momentarily blank. "Um, what?"

"I flew down to see you! You said you were going to be near Miami, and there was a sale going on—the flight was *so* cheap. I couldn't resist."

I opened and closed my mouth a few times before I managed to produce more words. "Okay. Okay. Oh my God. Let me just... talk to the guys."

Who were all still watching me. Marco looked amused, Aaron curious, Nate concerned, and West—well, it was pretty hard to read West's expression at certain moments. I'd go with "grim" this time around.

Marco was the man to deal with logistics here, I guessed. I muffled the phone with my palm. "Kylie, uh, flew herself down here. She's at the Miami airport. Can we... bring her here? She wants to visit."

"I'm not sure now is the best time for that," Aaron pointed out.

Oh. Right. In my shock, I'd completely forgotten that even we weren't necessarily safe on the estate. And Kylie didn't have any shifter super powers to call on if the situation went south. A chill trickled through me. "She's already here. I don't know if she can even afford to change her ticket to go right back."

Marco was already waving his hand dismissively. "Don't even think about that. We can cover whatever you need."

I got back on the phone. "Actually, Kylie... We're in kind of a bad place right now. We found out that one of Marco's people has been helping the rogues, and it sounds like they're planning an attack while we're here. I don't want you getting hurt again, even though I do really, really want to see you."

There was a pause. "You're worried I'll be in the way," Kylie said. Sounding truly downcast was outside her vocal range, but I could hear her disappointment in the flattening of her enthusiasm.

"No!" I said. "I just know, if there's fighting or something, you can't defend yourself the same way."

Kylie sucked in a breath. "What if I'm okay with that?" she said. "I've survived a long time around people a lot bigger and tougher than me. I'm not going to be a liability, Ren. Maybe I'll even help! I found that first clue of your mom's for you." She paused again. "Unless you just don't want me there at all."

My heart wrenched. I did want to have her with me, to talk to her face to face instead of via a phone screen, so badly. Kylie *had* survived an awful lot in the city during the years we'd been on the streets. Maybe I was underestimating just how strong—and resourceful—a non-shifter could be.

"I do," I said quickly. "Believe me, I do. You're right. I'll get Marco to send somebody. When I know what the plan is, I'll text you any details you'll need."

As I hung up, Marco arched his eyebrow at me. I sagged in my seat. "She made a very compelling argument. And Kylie is the toughest person I know, even if she doesn't look it."

"It's up to you, princess," Marco said. "I can send someone."

I waited for one of the other alphas—probably West—to argue, but no one did. "Okay. When you send them off, let me know where Kylie should meet them."

Marco nodded. Then he swept his arm expansively toward the bunch of us. "We're good to go now. My staff have prepared an informal luncheon-slash-meet-and-greet. I'd tell you to behave yourselves, but my kin probably won't, so just do as you see fit."

Alice fell into step with me as we headed for the plane's door. "I'll keep an extra eye on your friend if you want."

My eyes widened. "If it's any trouble—"

"None," she said firmly. "Friends are important. Lord knows you're going to need as many as you can get, and I don't see any point in discriminating about who or what they are. If she's important to you, that's good enough for me."

I smiled at her, more touched than I knew how to say. Apparently I'd made at least one more solid friend during my time with the shifter kin.

Marco's estate was farther inland than Aaron's, but the salt in the breeze told me there was a brackish lake nearby. Otherwise the place felt totally different from either of the other estates I'd visited. Lush tropical vegetation grew all around the paths, palm trees shading us with their fronds overhead. The summer heat had a damp weight to it.

The house, when we reached it, was a massive colonial mansion, all peach except the ornate white trim around the windows and doors. A greenhouse almost the same size as the rest of the building, its glass tinted to prevent anyone from looking in, jutted from the northern wing.

Having stayed briefly in one of the feline alpha's guesthouses, I knew what to expect from the inside of the mansion: thick rugs, Victorian antique furnishings, and velvet basically everywhere. I felt underdressed the second I walked in the door.

Marco led the way to the expansive ballroom where his "informal luncheon" was taking place.

A few dozen feline shifters—the ones who lived on the estate grounds, I assumed—were already gathered there, snacking on tidbits from the platters set on tables along the walls. Most of them glanced our way, but no one hurried over to greet us.

Typical cat aloofness, I found myself thinking, and caught myself before I smirked. Yeah, the feline shifters certainly kept to the attitudes of their animal counterparts.

But one of the kin around me might be scheming right now to overthrow all of us. I studied each of them as Marco ushered me deeper into the room.

"Alpha," a woman in the first group we approached said, with the slightest bob of her head in deference. Her scent told me she was a lion. She turned her golden eyes on me. "And this is the dragon shifter." Her tone gave away no clear emotion, but I felt her sizing me up. I lifted my chin instinctively, wishing I'd insisted on changing into something more elegant than jeans and a T-shirt.

"This is the great Serenity herself," Marco said languidly but without any hint of irony. "I hope all of my kin will make her feel welcome."

"Naturally," the lion shifter said. She offered an elegant hand for me to shake. "Coreen of the Bushnells."

"A pleasure to meet you," I said, biting back any other comments I might have made about the warmth of her welcome—or lack thereof.

The other introductions went pretty much the same way. A cryptic remark, a once-over, a mild show of respect. The feline kin were definitely a lot different from the other shifters I'd met. I didn't get hostile vibes from any of them, but really, it was hard to tell who might have been simply unaffected and who outright dismissive.

"Are they always like this?" I murmured to Marco when we stopped by one of the tables for a moment alone. "Or are they insulting you—or me—or someone?"

He chuckled. "Princess, this is about as enthusiastic for leadership as my kin ever get. I'm actually impressed." His head turned, and he sighed. "Well, I was. Prepare yourself."

For what? I wanted to ask, but the problem he'd seen coming was already on us.

"*Well* then," purred the lynx shifter who'd sidled up at my right. I couldn't tell whether the flecks of silver in his tawny hair were part of his animal's coloring or a reflection of age, but if he was any more than thirty-five, he wore the years well. He gave me a sly grin as he considered me. "Aren't you the loveliest shifter I've ever seen walk in that door. No offense meant to my alpha."

He winked at Marco, who smiled indulgently. "None taken, Silvan. I know exactly how lovely I am without you buttering me up."

"Perhaps while you're busy with your duties, I could take this treasure on a tour of the estate." Silvan's attention came back to me. His voice practically dripped with flirtation. "There are so *many* things I could show you."

I'd bet there were. I clamped my jaw, not sure whether I was more likely to laugh or sputter in indignation. Was he seriously propositioning me right in front of my mate?

Marco didn't seem to care—but then, Marco made a habit of appearing not to care about anything. And maybe this guy thought he could get away with the flirtation because his alpha *wasn't* fully my mate yet.

Any good humor I'd been feeling about the encounter died. I gave the lynx shifter a firm stare. "I appreciate the offer, but I know Marco will look after me just fine." I tucked my hand around Marco's elbow at the same time. My jaguar shifter didn't say anything, but I felt a tremor of pleased energy travel through his posture.

Silvan seemed unfazed. "Well, if you should change your mind, I'm sure you can find me." He sauntered off.

"Wow," I said. "That was... something."

"I should probably warn you that you're likely to get at least three similar offers before the day is over," Marco said. His smile turned crooked.

A murmur rose up near the doorway at the far end of the ballroom. I glanced over, and my gaze caught in a shock of neon pink hair. My heart leapt.

"Kylie!"

I dashed across the room, suddenly glad I wasn't dressed up, because I could move a heck of a lot faster in sneakers than heels. My best friend squealed when she saw me. We threw our arms around each other, me being careful not to squeeze her *too* hard with my newfound dragon strength. Not that Kylie was any lightweight. She was small, yeah, but full of wiry toughness.

When I let her go, she looked around the room, her eyes sparkling. "This is freaking amazing, Ren. And I thought Marco's place in New York was posh. So this is, like, the capital of cat shifters?"

I grinned. "Something like that. I can't believe you're here! How long can you stay?"

"I'm supposed to be back at work on Tuesday, but I can always call in. I haven't used any sick days yet. Oh my God! I'm going to get to see you be a dragon." She grasped my hands, and we spun around in an excited little dance. "Where are those hunks of yours, anyway?"

I looked up and realized we'd become the center of attention.

The shifters all around the room were staring at me and my bestie—well, mostly at my bestie. One woman's nostril's flared.

"Why has a *human* been allowed into our estate?" she demanded.

I stepped closer to Kylie automatically, my hackles rising. Marco strode over with an air of authority I'd rarely seen him emit. But then, this was the first time I'd seen him among so many of his kin.

"The human is your dragon shifter's ally," he said, pitching his voice loud enough for the whole room to hear. "And you will treat her with the same respect you would a dragon. Any arguments?" He offered a sharp smile.

Several heads turned away. The other stares lowered. The woman who'd complained muttered something, and Marco said, in a soft, clear voice, "What was that, Livia?"

Her lips pressed flat, her face paling slightly. "Nothing, sir."

Marco didn't look convinced, but he let it slide. "A surprise visit, but a welcome one," he said to Kylie as he joined us.

Kylie's expression had gone a bit tight. "It's not going to be a big deal that I'm here, is it? Everyone seemed so chill in the other shifter village, I didn't think they'd get upset."

"They'll get over it. We felines are very adaptable." The smile he gave her was a lot warmer than the one he'd offered the crowd.

"Come on," I said, grabbing Kylie's arm. "You've got to be hungry. They've got *everything* to eat here." I kept my tone chipper even though my heart was thudding. Alice caught my eye from across the room, and I nodded. I was definitely going to want her to have my best friend's back around this bunch.

We'd only made it partway to the tables when a new voice boomed across the room. "Alpha! If you even deserve that title."

Bristling, I pivoted on my feet. A hulking tiger shifter was stalking toward Marco, his head high and eyes lit with menace. The guy must have had at least half a foot and fifty pounds on my jaguar shifter.

A prickle ran over my skin as my body instinctively readied to shift. I held myself back. It wasn't going to help Marco's case if his mate fought his battles for him.

"Julius," Marco said blandly. "What are you nattering about now?"

The tiger shifter came to a halt a few feet from his alpha and scowled. "I say you're not strong enough to lead us all. I say a real alpha would have consummated his bond with the dragon, not stepped aside while other kin's leaders did, leaving all of us still waiting. I say I could crush you with one blow of my paws."

My skin went cold. The other shifters had fallen completely silent, even more still than when Kylie had arrived. Marco folded his arms over his chest and cocked his head. "Is that a formal challenge, or just bluster?"

"Consider yourself challenged," Julius growled. "Tonight, unless you're going to try to weasel your way out of it."

"No weaseling necessary," Marco said lightly. "I'll be happy to settle this tonight. May the best kin win."

CHAPTER 14

Ren

KYLIE LOOPED her arm around mine as an attendant led us down the hall to our rooms. She pitched her voice low. "So… this whole challenge thing. What exactly does that mean for Marco?"

I swallowed hard. My pulse hadn't stopped racing since the tiger shifter had swaggered out of the ballroom. I wished I had a better idea what the challenge had meant myself.

"I'm not sure," I said. "The other guy wants the alpha position. I guess they fight it out. Tonight." In, what, just a few hours? Marco couldn't have been prepared for that.

Was *this* what being alpha had been like for him all along? Random challenges at every turn, not even being able to spend an hour back on his estate without some asshole confronting him? That would get old awfully quick. Suddenly I didn't find it hard to believe he'd meant the comment he'd made about giving up the position.

Only he couldn't do that and still be my mate. If he forfeited his position as alpha, my bond would shift to whoever was named in his place.

And the same if he lost this challenge.

"But he'll be fine, right?" Kylie said. "I mean, he's stayed on top this long."

"Yeah," I said. If only I felt totally confident of Marco's victory. In the back of my mind, I kept seeing the tiger shifter standing over him, taller and broader. Size wasn't everything—but it mattered a hell of a lot in a fight.

"Geez. I had no idea things would be this tense. I'm sorry if I made the situation any worse."

"Hey." I pulled Kylie around to face me as the attendant opened a door for her. "I'm glad you're here. Any trouble Marco's kin make is their fault, not yours. Thank you for coming. Just having you with me makes everything feel a little easier to handle."

My best friend beamed at me and pulled me into another hug. "That's why I'm here."

I hugged her back, and then stepped away. "I do still want you staying safe, though. Can you just, like hole up in your guest room for a little while. I think I should talk to Marco."

Kylie waved me off. "Of course, of course. Go tend to your 'mate.' I can already see I've got plenty of luxury in here to keep me occupied. But if you run into any handsome unoccupied shifters, feel free to send them my way too!"

I couldn't help laughing, even though my stomach was still tight. "I'll do that."

Marco's private rooms were just down the hall from mine. I knocked. "Marco?"

"Come in," he called from the other side. When I stepped in, he was standing by the chaise lounge in the sitting room. He shot me an amused glance. "You don't need to knock with me, princess. Consider these rooms as much yours as they are mine."

"I'll keep that in mind. Are you okay?"

Marco shrugged with a careless air, but I knew him well enough now to notice the angry glint in his indigo eyes. "Challenges happen. They have before and will again. It isn't how I would have hoped to spend my first evening here with you, but we'll just have to make tomorrow night even better to make up for it."

His grin looked a little tense too. I walked up to him. "It sounded like that Julius guy had been a pain in the ass before now."

Marco nodded. "He likes to hear himself talk, especially if it's to complain about how anyone else is doing things. Apparently he's decided to graduate from talking."

"Do you think he's the one allied with the rogues?" I asked.

"It could be. A challenge, if he succeeded, would be a fairly direct way to disrupt the status quo. But he's not going to succeed, so really it's a very bad plan, if it is one."

Julius had radiated aggressive disdain, but there was no way for me to tell whether that feeling was simply personal or whether he had a larger agenda. It didn't really matter anyway. It didn't change what I'd come here to do.

I touched Marco's face, tracing my fingers along the line of his angular jaw. "I guess we could enjoy ourselves before tomorrow evening too."

A different sort of light sparked in Marco's eyes. He dipped his head close to mine. "What exactly did you have in mind, my Princess of Flames?"

I kissed him in answer. He hummed low in his throat and

kissed me back, his hands rising to tangle in my hair. The graze of his fingers over my scalp left my whole body tingling in anticipation.

He tilted my head slightly to deepen the kiss. I pressed my mouth to his hungrily. The bond inside me thrummed with eagerness, urging me on.

Without breaking the kiss, I stepped backward through the doorway into the bedroom. Marco followed. His tongue teased into my mouth, and for one hot, heady moment it sparred with mine. Then I had to let go of him to hop up on the bed.

Marco prowled after me, nothing but longing in his gaze now. He bent over me on the bed and claimed my mouth again. His fingers brushed over my breasts with just enough pressure to pebble my nipples through my shirt and bra—but not half as much as I was dying for. I arched into his touch, and he chuckled breathlessly.

"All in good time," he murmured on his way into another kiss.

No. The more time we took, the more opportunity he had to question my motivations.

I grasped his shirt and tugged it up. Marco let me peel it off, staying poised over me for a few seconds as I drank in his lean chest. I ran my hands over the planes of solid muscle, and his eyelids dipped.

"Princess," he said in a hungry growl.

I pulled my shirt off too. Marco leaned in to kiss his way down the side of my neck and across my collarbone. I whimpered when he reached the boundary of my bra. To my relief, he made short work of that obstacle. With a quick gesture, he'd unhooked it and tossed it aside. Then he was slicking his tongue over one needy nipple.

I gasped at the rush of pleasure spreading through my chest. Yes, this was exactly what we both needed. One of my arms looped around Marco's shoulders. The other crept down my body to undo the fly of my jeans. I caught Marco's hand and guided it along the same path.

He groaned when his fingers reached the dampness on my panties. I shivered with longing, the ache between my legs only growing as he stroked me there.

"So determined," Marco said in a low, amused voice. He paused, his hand going still. His eyes sought out mine. His expression had turned abruptly serious. "Princess, what are you doing?"

Shit. "Seducing you?" I said with all the coyness I could manage, fluttering my eyelashes at him. "Is that a problem?"

He withdrew his hand completely. I almost moaned at the loss of contact. He set it on the other side of my body and lifted himself so he was staring down at me.

"Why now?"

"Does it matter? I want you, you want me..." I teased my fingers down his bare chest to the waist of his jeans.

Marco closed his eyes for a second as if gathering his self-control. When he looked at me again, his gaze was stark. "Ren. Please. Why *now*?"

I couldn't bear to lie to my mate, not when he asked me like that. I swallowed hard. "I do want you. But I also... Julius took a jab at you because our bond isn't consummated yet. I thought if it was, maybe he'd back down."

"Oh, princess." Marco let his head drop until his nose almost grazed mine. "Do you really think I'll lose to that sorry excuse for a tiger?"

"No," I said, mostly honestly. The images that had haunted

me since Julius had first spoken his challenge floated back into my head. All the ways I might find Marco after the battle, battered and bleeding. "I don't want to see how badly he might hurt you while you're winning. If I can save you from that..."

Marco sucked in a breath. "There was a time not long ago when I thought you might enjoy seeing me batted around some."

My back stiffened. The idea that I'd wish that kind of pain on him wrenched at me so hard tears sprang into my eyes. "No," I choked out. "I was angry at you, but I would never want—that's the last thing I—"

Marco's eyes had widened. He brushed his thumb over my lips, stopping my struggle for words. "I'm sorry," he said. "It was only a joke—a bad one, clearly. I... didn't realize my wellbeing meant so much to you."

"Of course it does, you idiot," I muttered. "You're my mate. You're obviously upset about the challenge. I just thought, this is the one thing I can do that might help..."

"Serenity." Marco lowered himself on his side next to me and tugged me against him. He kissed my forehead, his voice a little shaky. "You have no idea how much you've helped already, with everything you'd done so far. And I'm not upset about the challenge because I'm afraid of Julius. Confrontations like that—they just stir up memories I'd rather avoid."

I nestled my head against his shoulder. "Like what?"

He hesitated for a long moment. When he spoke again, his voice was even quieter. "You've asked me before how I got this scar." He touched the pale line that bisected his eyebrow. "I told you it was from a challenge. That particular challenge... came from a kin-member I'd considered a friend. One of my closest friends. We'd grown up together, played and trained together before I was even named next alpha-in-line. I'd have fought to the death for him."

My throat had gone tight. Oh, God. "But instead you had to fight to the death *against* him."

"Not to the death. Not in that moment. But I had to fight him, yes. I had to hear him tell me he didn't believe I deserved to be alpha, that I didn't deserve to even be kin, and then I had to beat him into submission." Marco paused with a hissed inhale. "It was him or me, and in the end I chose me."

"You did what you had to do."

"Yes. But when there's a challenge, the loser is banished. An alpha can't have someone who tried to undermine our authority just hanging around. And Devon didn't know what to do with himself once he was out on his own."

"What happened?" I asked. I could already tell from the weight in Marco's voice that it wasn't good.

"He ended up tangling with a bunch of vampires. They were *really* not pleased about whatever he said or did to them." Marco swallowed audibly. "When we found his body... it was obvious they'd tortured him for a while before they'd finished the job. So no, I didn't kill him. But I did send him to his death. And the worst death I can imagine."

I wrapped my arm around my mate, hugging him. "You didn't have a choice. You couldn't have known what would happen to him. It's not as if you made him mess with those vampires."

"I tell myself all that," Marco said. "But I still feel like I've been punched in the gut every time I hear the words of a challenge."

I drank in the smell of his skin, like spiced coffee. The stutter of his breath. The tension still wound through his muscles. He hadn't wanted to tell me that story. He'd avoided it for weeks. But he had, finally, so that I'd understand.

"That's why you were impatient to consummate," I said.

"Why it was so important to you to secure your position any way you could."

"I shouldn't have seen you that way," Marco said quickly. "I didn't *want* to think about you that way. But the thought was there. I let it get to me. You know how sorry I am for that."

"But now—" I started, moving my body against his.

Marco groaned, but he gripped my thigh to hold me still. "Ren, tell me the truth. Would you be offering right now if Julius *hadn't* challenged me?"

I wanted to say yes. The word caught in my throat. I couldn't know exactly what I'd have done if the luncheon had played out differently... but I could make a reasonable guess.

"That's what I thought," Marco said at my hesitation.

"Marco..."

He cupped my face, gazing into my eyes. "Princess, it's okay. The first time we go there, I want it to be only because you want it, not even slightly because circumstances are forcing your hand. I can beat Julius without breaking a sweat, and I can wait. It's the least I can do."

I choked up again, but for a completely different reason. The fact that he was saying no had dissolved the last of my doubts. I could have given myself over happily now, looming challenge or not.

But I'd already burned that bridge for the moment. I settled for kissing him, soft and sweet, as his hand stroked over the side of my face.

My body was still tingling with longing. Maybe Marco could feel that too. He drew back a couple of inches with a sly smile. "I would, however, be happy to enjoy you in another way."

Before I had to ask what he meant, he was easing down my body. His fingers hooked the hem of my panties as he brushed his lips over my breasts and belly. I gasped when his mouth closed over the bundle of nerves at my core. Every part of my brain that had been cycling through worries short-circuited, and for a brief moment in time, I was made of nothing but bliss.

CHAPTER 15

West

I NEVER FELT REALLY comfortable around feline shifters. Marco I could put up with, because at least he was dedicated to something. The rest of his kin—you never knew what was going on behind those shifty eyes.

At least, most of them read as shifty. The tiger shifter who'd challenged Marco a couple hours ago came across as a pretty straight-forward asshole. Or that's what I'd determined while I'd been keeping an eye on him. Right now he was playing pool with a couple of his kin in the estate's big entertainment room, bellowing victory whenever he hit a ball into a pocket. The sound made me wince inwardly even from across the room. I adjusted my position against the wall near the door.

I had my phone out, pretending I was mostly paying attention to that. I had actually checked in with a few of my lieutenants while Julius the Tiger had swaggered and blustered.

Now I was playing a very half-hearted game of Candy Crush while keeping my ears perked to the conversations around me.

I'd just cleared a level when Ren strode past me into the room. A whiff of her scent reached my nose: the usual sweetness mingled with a musk that got me half-hard in two seconds flat. I straightened up, resisting the urge to lick my lips. And ignoring the twist of jealousy in my chest. She'd just been with at least one of the other alphas—I knew that much. And that alpha had gotten her off, well.

One hint of the smell of arousal on her, and I was right back to the other night in her bed. My mouth on her skin, her hand around my cock—

Yeah, thinking about that right now wasn't going to take me anywhere useful. I dragged in a breath to steady the thump of my pulse.

Our dragon shifter wasn't here to see me. She marched right across the room and came to a stop by the pool table, her gaze fixed on Julius. Shit. What the hell was she up to now?

I shoved my phone into my pocket and ambled a little closer, trying to look casual, which wasn't easy when every feline shifter nearby glanced over at the scent of wolf. Julius turned and spotted Ren. He set his pool stick against the floor, grinning.

"Dragon shifter. Come to get an early start with your new mate?"

Ren's chin rose higher, her eyes flashing. She looked fucking gorgeous like that, but it also meant she was about to throw herself right in over her head. So damned determined to right every wrong even when she barely understood the threat she was facing. It wrenched at my heart, but that sense of justice wasn't going to do anyone any good if she got torn to pieces in the process. I tensed, ready to shift.

"No," Ren said, clear and loud enough that the whole room

had to hear. "I came to give you an out. Marco is going to win tonight. And even if he wasn't going to, I'd never accept *you* as my mate. I thought it was only fair to mention that ahead of time."

The tiger shifter's face darkened. His lips curled into more of a sneer. "Is that what our alpha is reduced to now? Sending you to protect him while he hides in his rooms?"

Ren rolled her eyes. "No. *He's* happy to put you in your place the regular way. But I'd rather not see any kin banished when they don't need to be. Consider it a courtesy. There's no point in pursuing a lost cause."

Julius rapped the end of his pool cue against the floor. His eyes had narrowed. "I don't think it's lost at all. And I think you'll find it a lot harder to say no when the bond passes to me."

Ren looked him up and down, letting every hint of her disdain show in her expression. Oh, Lord, she was aiming to get herself eviscerated, wasn't she?

"Believe me," she said flippantly. "I can't imagine even being tempted."

Julius bristled, baring his teeth. "We'll see if you change your tune after tonight, won't we? Or maybe you need to learn your place now."

"I know my place," Ren said. "And it happens to be very far over yours. But if that's how you're going to act, I'll enjoy watching you get your ass handed to you tonight."

She swiveled and headed back toward the doorway. Julius's arm jerked as if he meant to lunge after her, and I braced myself to leap between them. But he caught himself with a harsh inhale. His gaze tracked Ren to the door with an angry, predatory gleam.

I waited just long enough to make sure he was staying put, and then I strode after my mate.

~

Ren

My pulse was thudding as I walked out of the games room, but the second I crossed the threshold into the hall, my lips stretched into a smile. The *look* on Julius's face when I'd told him what was what—I was going to treasure that for a good long time.

I didn't get to savor my victory very long in the moment. I'd hardly made it two more steps when a hand closed around my forearm. A hint of pine laced the air. I knew my confronter was West before he spun me around to face him.

"What the hell were you trying to pull in there?" he snapped, his gaze in full glower mode. "That tiger shifter just about bit your head off."

I guffawed. "I'd have liked to see him try. He'd have been fried cat before he even got his teeth in."

"You're still learning control over your shifts. And you don't know these kin at all. You can't take risks like that."

"I don't know. Seems like I just did, and the world didn't end."

West let out a strangled sound. Suddenly his hand was on the side of my neck, his thumb tracing my jaw as he yanked me closer to him. His head bowed close to mine. His body was just inches away, so close it was almost an embrace. Every nerve in *my* body woke up in response. I breathed in his pine-forest scent and held myself back from turning my face that slight distance to kiss him. Let him make the first move here, when he figured out what he wanted.

His breath spilled hot and harsh over my cheek. His grip on my arm loosened. For a second, I thought he was going to grasp my waist and pull me flush against him. And whatever happened after that, I was pretty sure I'd be on board for.

Instead, his shoulders tensed. "Listen to me. Don't *ever* do anything that stupid again."

The rush of attraction faded. I gritted my teeth and shoved West back a step with my free hand. "I wasn't being *stupid*," I bit out, keeping my voice low. "But it's nice to know you still see me as an idiot. I was provoking Julius on purpose. I wanted to get a better sense of his emotions, and those of the other kin in the room, to figure out who might be allied with the rogues."

West's expression blanked. "What?"

"I can read people better when their emotions are on the surface," I said. "So I wanted to stir things up. He wasn't even close to trying to actually hurt me. I'd have felt it if he was."

"Oh." West deflated slightly. His fingers flexed around my arm. He looked down at them, into the space between us still narrow enough that I could feel the heat emanating from his body. "Are you so sure your senses work as well on shifters as the human beings you're used to, Sparks? Because you haven't really had much chance for practice."

"I can read you just fine," I muttered. "And right now you should be feeling a lot more embarrassed than you actually are, just FYI. Although I appreciate the not-wanting-me-to-get-hurt side of this whole outburst."

West grimaced. He raised his eyes again. There might have been a shadow of an apology in them, but he didn't bother to voice it. "Did you find out anything useful with all your 'stirring up'?"

"That depends on how you define useful. Julius has something motivating him other than just wanting the alpha position. I didn't get the sense he even considered backing down. Whether he wins or not, whether I accept him as a mate or not if he does win, the challenge is about more than that. Enough more that the rest doesn't matter."

"More as in he expects it to work into his plans with the rogues?"

"That would be my best guess." I frowned, thinking about the vibes I'd felt around me in the room. "I don't think anyone else who was in the room is involved. His kin were curious about what was going on, but none of them gave the impression of feeling at all threatened by me telling him off. Or angry. They just found it entertaining. Anyone who was in on a plot, I think they'd have cared more."

West nodded. "That reasoning seems sound." He raised an eyebrow. "Maybe your gambit gave us some results after all."

"Maybe next time you should ask me what I'm doing before assuming I'm being an idiot."

"Maybe you should stop coming up with plans that *look* idiotic."

I bit my lip, swallowing my frustration, and West's gaze dropped to my mouth. The heat between us flared in an instant. God almighty, why did he have to act like a jerk when I knew there was so much compassion—not to mention plain old passion—underneath that front?

Every muscle was urging me to just grab him and plant one on him. To draw out the desire I knew he was keeping locked down inside.

But we'd gone down that road already, and that blazing physical encounter hadn't made things any better. Actually, the moment we'd shared in the avian estate garden had only made me more on edge when I was with him, now that I knew how good the two of us could be together.

This game of snarking at each other and dancing around our

attraction was getting old. I was ready to be done with it, one way or the other.

I turned my hand, sliding it against his arm until my fingers could curl around his. "West," I said, "I think we should talk. *Really* talk. We're not getting anywhere like this. Whatever doubts you still have about me, you can just tell me about them. We'll hash them out. I know I'm still learning here. But I need to know what the problem is before I can fix it."

The sense I got from my wolf shifter then was completely bizarre, as if a rush of tangled emotions had blown open a door inside him—only to be yanked back in and the door slammed shut. And deadbolted for good measure.

West took another step back, his posture rigid. His hand slipped from mine. "I don't think this is exactly the time for chatting, Sparks," he said. "We've got a full-blown rebellion to stop."

And for some reason you're just as important to me as stopping it, you blockhead, I thought but didn't let myself say. I'd had my fill of verbal sparring for the day.

"Fine," I said. "When you get your head sorted out, you know where to find me." I turned and stalked away without a backward glance. Because I did have bigger things to think about up ahead. Like whether one of my other mates was going to come out of tonight's confrontation with all limbs and vital organs intact.

CHAPTER 16

Ren

THE GUEST SUITE Kylie had been given looked a lot like my set of rooms, other than her bed was only a regular king sized one and not wide enough to comfortably fit five. I guessed the shifter kin didn't expect anyone other than their dragon shifter to be calling multiple mates into their bed. Or else they expected those other people to squish.

"Is everything settled now?" Kylie asked me, bobbing on her feet. She'd only managed to sit on the elegant settee for about ten seconds before she'd bounced back up again with her irresistible energy.

"As settled as it can be," I said. "Marco still has to fight that guy. But he seems sure he can take him. I just hope he's prepared for anything. The rogues definitely don't mind fighting dirty."

"They haven't tried anything that big so far, though, right?" Kylie said. "I mean, there were the three that attacked us at

West's people's village, and then it sounded like you took on that bunch near Nate's estate no problem."

My heart sank with the weight of all the things I'd been avoiding telling her. I should have told her everything sooner. Maybe if she'd realized just how dangerous my life had gotten, she wouldn't have rushed down here on this visit.

On the other hand, maybe she'd just have rushed down sooner.

"There've been a couple of other... incidents," I said slowly. "When we were traveling to Sunridge, a bunch of them ambushed us. That was when I managed a full shift the first time. And the rogues who attacked Nate's estate—they killed four of the kin before the guards managed to stop them."

"Oh!" Kylie's eyes went wide. "The thing at Sunridge—that was weeks ago. Why didn't you tell me?"

I worried my lower lip with my teeth. My fingers shivered with an itch I hadn't felt in days—the urge to find some object to pilfer, to take control. I curled them into my palm instead. I wasn't that street rat thief anymore. I was a freaking dragon shifter now.

"I knew you'd be worried," I said. "We came out of the ambush fine, and the attack on the estate was over before I even got there."

Kylie was still looking at me with a hesitant expression. "I'd rather be worried and know what's really going on with you than be kept in the dark. You should know that, Ren."

I had. But I'd kept her in the dark anyway. There wasn't really any way I could justify it.

"I'm sorry," I said. "There was so much going on... Keeping quiet about it and focusing on the good stuff just felt like the best way of handling it at the time. But you see why *I'm* worried."

Kylie nodded. "I guess if those asshole rogues do turn up, you can go full dragon mode on their assess," she said, more of her usual cheerfulness coming back.

"That's the plan." I groped for a change in subject—to a subject that wouldn't make me want to pocket every valuable in the building. "Marco's people will be summoning us to dinner soon. I should put on something nicer. If there are rogues around, I want them remembering who's in charge here." I managed to grin. "You want to help me pick out a dress?"

"Want to?" Kylie said, clapping her hands. "I've been dying to since you sent me that photo of you at Aaron's place. All right, let's do this thing."

We ducked into the hall and passed a few doors to my rooms.

I opened one wardrobe and then another. Kylie made a squeeing sound as she pawed through the offerings. "Oh, this is amazing. You're going to look like a boss, all right. Forget princess—you're going to be the empress of all shifters."

I laughed and held out my arms to take the first dress she tossed to me. By the time she'd gone through all three wardrobes, my arms were aching and my face buried in silk and satin. I hefted the heap onto the bed. "Um, I think we need to do a little narrowing down here."

"Yes, yes." Kylie tapped her lips. She grabbed a couple out of the pile. "I don't know what I was thinking with this one. And now that I'm looking at them all, black is definitely too dour. The rest you'll just have to put on so I can ogle you."

She shot me a bright smile as she went to put back the discards. I shook my head and stripped out of my T-shirt and jeans. As I shimmied into one of the dresses from the top of the heap, a simple pale green silk number, Kylie sat down on the edge of the bed. She glanced across its width, her eyebrows arching in amusement. "Hmm, I can't imagine what you'd need a bed *this* big for… No, wait, actually I can."

My face flushed at her teasing. But when she turned back to me, a shadow had crossed her face.

"Is there anything else you decided not to tell me from the last few weeks?" she asked.

Shit. I looked at myself in the mirror, contemplating the green silk flowing over my body. Did I look like an ingénue or a girl who'd severely fucked up the best friendship she'd ever had? Neither was what I was going for. I reached to pull that one off.

"There might have been a few things," I admitted without meeting Kylie's eyes. "Not that I didn't want you to know. Just that would have been hard to talk about with only texts."

"You could have called me," Kylie pointed out.

"I couldn't see getting into it except face to face." Except now here we were, face to face, and I felt even more awkward. I grabbed a wine red gown out of the pile. "I told you my mom died on the mountain... I saw it. Like a vision. It was a bunch of fae who killed her. Murdered her. They were trying to stop her from getting that power she wanted me to have."

"The special fire that you can use to make people tell the truth," Kylie filled in.

"Yeah." At least I'd kept her up to speed that much.

"Why did the fae care about that?"

"I don't know," I said honestly. "Things have been tense between the shifters and the fae, but I'm still finding out the details there. Their attack wasn't, like, officially sanctioned, but the fae monarch hadn't discouraged it either. They must not have wanted any shifter to have that kind of power."

And to be fair, the first person I'd used it on was their own monarch. To be fair to *me*, I wouldn't have needed to use it on her if she'd been upfront with us in the first place.

Kylie rubbed her mouth. "Wow. So you have to worry about the fae coming after you too?"

"Not exactly. There's a treaty—and we confronted the fae monarch, and she swore to follow it. But I guess it's always possible they could decide to break their word."

That was an awful thought. I'd rather not go there while we had the rogue threat right in front of us.

"Damn." Kylie looked over at me, and her eyes lit up. Her smile looked a little stiff, but I'd take it. "And *damn*. Okay, forget all the other ones. That is The Dress."

My lips twitched. I glanced down at myself, smoothing my hands over the gleaming fabric. "Yeah?"

"Oh, yeah. Anyone who messes with you in that get-up is just asking to become dragon barbeque."

I laughed, and for a second, things between us felt almost okay. This was Kylie. My best friend, my one true friend. She'd always had my back. If I couldn't even live up to her expectations, I didn't have a hope in hell with the shifters.

"Holy cow," Kylie said when we stepped into the ballroom-turned-banquet hall. "And I thought this place couldn't get any fancier."

Marco, who was between us holding my hand, chuckled. "My kin are known for being easily distracted by shiny objects. I'm no exception."

"Well, you definitely went all out on the shiny," I said. Silver plates glinted at every seat; crystal wine glasses sparkled. Gold embroidery shimmered in a looping pattern along the edge of the gleaming white tablecloths. The crystal chandeliers overhead were all alight now, sending a sharp yellow glow over everything and everyone below.

I had a feeling it wasn't just those lights that made the feline kin look a tad jaundiced. Tension hummed through the room beneath the clamor of voices. This wasn't just a dinner. It wasn't even just their first formal dinner with their new dragon shifter in attendance. It was the dinner before their alpha's latest challenge. One that had even higher stakes than any of those before.

I nodded and smiled to the feline kin as Marco walked me up to the head table. The other alphas were already sitting in their spots around the two chairs reserved for us. I sat down with Marco at my left and Aaron at my right. Nate leaned past the eagle shifter to catch my eyes and offer a warm smile. But my pulse had already picked up again with a prickle of anxiety.

Kylie ended up at Nate's right, which was probably the best I could have hoped for when she couldn't sit right next to me. She grinned at the big bear shifter and immediately started gabbing away. I could only imagine how West would have reacted if he'd had to be her conversation partner through dinner instead of having stoic Alice on his other side. Kylie would have chattered my wolf shifter's ear off just like anyone else.

Actually, that might have been fun to watch.

Several more feline kin from the prominent families joined us at the head table. I found myself facing a cheetah pair, the wife rubbing her cheek with the back of her hand like a house cat washing its face. Next to them was a pair of lions that included the woman who'd greeted me so skeptically when I'd first arrived. Coreen—that was her name. My head was getting awfully crowded with those.

Thankfully, Julius was sitting nowhere near us. I spotted his hulking form at the far end of the room, where I guessed Marco had asked his attendants to put him. And I wasn't exactly disappointed to see Silvan stationed at a distant table too.

Marco's kin eyed him with darting glances as they dug into their meals. They ate like cats too, with swift delicate bites. Coreen dabbed at her mouth with her napkin after every forkful.

"Is the challenge arena already prepared?" she asked after a few minutes of strained silence. It was weird how a question that ominous could be said as if it was a polite inquiry. Her tone was the same as if she were asking what we were having for dessert.

But then, Marco acted equally unfazed. "My attendants are setting everything in order right now. I suppose you'll be there for the show."

"The more witnesses, the more worthy," Coreen's husband put in with a rumble of a voice.

"Interesting philosophy," West muttered.

Coreen shot him a hard look. Marco twitched under the table, and I suspected he'd just kicked the wolf shifter in the shin. His smile stayed pleasant.

"I'm glad the matter with the vampires up north was finally settled," the cheetah man put in. "There haven't been any more stirrings, have there?"

"Not of enough concern that my people up there have mentioned it to me," Marco said. "You know what the bloodsuckers are like. No attention span for anything unless it's actively bleeding."

The cheetah shifter woman snickered at that. My stomach had clenched tighter. "Was there a lot of trouble because of our confrontation with the vampires when we went into the city?"

Mom had left me a trail of clues leading to the mountain in Sunridge, and we'd had to go exploring the New York City subway system to find the first one. Right into vampire territory. They hadn't been real pleased about our intrusion.

Marco waved his hand. "Oh, just normal vamp mutterings. We sorted them out. They don't *really* want to tango with the shifters."

I wasn't sure how much that comment was the truth and how much was necessary bravado for his kin. Right now he probably needed to look strong and in control even more so than usual.

Aaron set his hand on my thigh under the table and squeezed reassuringly. He leaned close. "Tonight will be fine. Marco's been through this situation more than once. We all have. And we're still here."

I'd have felt more comforted if I hadn't sensed the worry underlying his words. He wasn't completely confident either. The rogue's involvement was a wild card none of my alphas had faced during a challenge before.

The talk all along the table quieted at the scrape of chair legs. A guy at the far end of the table had just stood up. He raised his hands with a smile that looked weirdly giddy. His hair, mixed with patches of dark brown and pale gray, poked up in tufts from his rounded head. I didn't remember being introduced to him earlier, but his appearance immediately made me think *snow leopard.*

"With all the commotion, I want to speak up and say how much I support our alpha," he said in a jovial voice that carried through the room. "Marco has kept us in line and seen us through troubled times no other alpha has had to address. I know he'll continue to do so."

He focused his gaze on his alpha and dipped into a low bow. Marco chuckled, smiling back, but the guy's demeanor made my skin tighten. He seemed *too* eager to speak. Praising Marco more to ingratiate himself than because he meant it.

Was this some kind of attempt to protect himself? Did he

think Marco would punish people who seemed at all in favor of Julius after he won? That didn't seem like the feline way of doing things.

Marco didn't appear bothered. "Thank you for your kind words, Phillipe," he said, holding up his glass as if to toast the leopard shifter. "I know it too. And in an hour, this whole room will know it."

CHAPTER 17

Ren

My heart started to thump harder the moment we reached the challenge area. It wasn't really anything more than a glade in the tropical forestland, a stretch of open grass maybe twenty feet in diameter surrounded by thick foliage. But Marco's people had clearly prepared it, as he'd said they would.

The grass was trampled flat as if the ground had been pounded as smooth as possible. A green smell like a fresh-mowed lawn hung in the air. A rope hung across the trees around the ring, separating the spectating area from the fighting turf. Lamps hung from a few of the branches, casting an eerie yellow glow over the space. The one near us emitted a soft electronic hum.

Marco walked ahead of me, right into the ring. Kylie and I drifted to the side, the other alphas and Alice surrounding us. Nate rested his hand on my shoulder. "If it's too hard for you to watch," he started.

I shook my head before he could continue. "I'm staying. I need to be here for Marco."

More feline shifters gathered all around the glade. It looked like everyone who'd been at the dinner had come. Why not? The leadership over their kin group might change tonight.

"Where's the tiger?" Kylie asked, craning her neck. "Maybe he chickened out at the last minute?"

Before I could even dare to hope, Julius came swaggering down the path. He sauntered into the ring across from Marco, flexing his bulky arms. Marco watched him calmly. With a casual ease, he pulled off his shirt, then his pants, folding his clothes one piece at a time on the ground at the edge of the glade. Julius bared his teeth and started undressing as well. Of course, they'd fight as animals.

I looked around the ring at all the faces I recognized. Coreen and her husband, the cheetah shifters from dinner, Silvan and the over-eager snow leopard Phillipe, others I'd met during the luncheon. None of them, not even Phillipe after his impassioned speech, looked all that concerned about what was going to happen. The vibe in the air now was swelling with anticipation.

Were they all sure Marco would win, or did they just not care that much either way who was ruling over them? From what I'd seen of the feline kin so far, I didn't have any trouble believing it might be the latter.

Kylie must have been thinking along the same lines. "Imagine having that musclehead as an alpha," she whispered to me. "I wouldn't trust him not to spend all day chasing his own tail."

My mouth twitched. I wasn't so tense that my bestie couldn't get a smile out of me. "No kidding. They'd be begging to have Marco back in no time."

Except he wouldn't be around for them to bring him back, would they? My pulse sped up even more.

I hadn't asked Marco what happened to *him* if he lost. I hadn't wanted to take the possibility that seriously. Would they banish him like they'd banish Julius? Or was the punishment of losing after you were already alpha more severe? The new alpha wouldn't want to risk you coming back to reclaim your position.

A chill trickled through me. Suddenly I was sure of it. If Marco lost, Julius would kill him. Maybe that was the only way Julius could win.

"The guards are still watching the edges of the estate, aren't they?" I said to my alphas.

Aaron nodded. "I was there when Marco gave the orders."

Alice gave me a meaningful look. "If you want the extra security, I could fly around and watch for any groups on the move heading this way."

A tiny bit of the tightness inside me released. "Yes," I said. "Please. And come back the second you see anything concerning."

She nodded and slipped away between the trees. Clothes rustled off, and her eagle form leapt up through the branches. I watched her disappear against the darkening sky.

"I don't know what they might have planned," West said. "But I haven't seen or scented any rogue presence nearby."

"Neither have I," Nate put in. "Maybe this *is* their plan. They're staking everything on Julius defeating Marco."

I frowned. "That doesn't make sense to me. They've never played by the rules before. There's got to be something more to it. But maybe the challenge is a separate part of the plan. Maybe Julius wanted to get that over with, to prove himself in front of his kin, before he has the rogues take on the rest of us."

Whatever happened, I needed to be ready. And I'd need to

protect Kylie too. I edged a little closer to her. "If things get crazy, you stay with me, all right?"

She saluted me. "Got it, dragon queen."

The smile tugged at my lips again. Then I looked into the ring, and any humor I'd been capable of feeling died.

One of the estate attendants had stepped into the middle of the glade between Marco and Julius. "A challenge for alpha has been called," she said in a ringing voice. "When my arm drops, the fight may begin."

She held her hand up as she backed up to the ring of rope. When her back hit it, her hand clenched. She jerked it down to her hip in one sharp movement.

Julius sprang with a growl that was half human, half animal. His body shifted into tiger form as he lunged through the air at Marco. But Marco was prepared. He shifted and dashed low under the larger cat, spinning to scratch at the tiger's belly as he slid out of reach. Julius roared. Four thin red lines formed against his fur.

"First blood!" someone in the audience hollered. Someone else let out a whoop. I assumed that was good for Marco. My hands had closed around the rope in front me, the coarse fibers digging into my skin.

"Wow," Kylie murmured. "They really aren't playing around."

No, they weren't. Not at all. Julius whirled around, still plenty fast despite his size. My gut sank, seeing just how much bigger he was than Marco now. The tiger had to be at least twice as brawny as the jaguar, taller and longer and more solidly built. If he pinned Marco even for a second...

That was obviously Julius's intention. He leapt at Marco again, swinging a paw as if to cuff his alpha. Marco dodged to the side, not quite in time. The tiger's claws raked over his haunch. He didn't make a sound, but I saw his lips curl back in pain. I gripped the rope tighter.

"So... how far exactly do they go?" Kylie said in a smaller voice than before. "How do we decide when someone's won?"

"When one of them can't get back up," West muttered.

I swallowed hard. Murmurs were rippling through the crowd again. Were they upset that Marco hadn't really fought back yet?

He must have been working up to it. Feeling out his opponent's style before he took the offensive. Before Julius could make another lunge, Marco dashed at him with a yowl. The tiger lurched forward to try to batter the jaguar into submission, but that was exactly what Marco had expected. At the last second, he darted around the bigger cat and lashed out at Julius's belly again.

The tiger was moving forward with too much momentum to dodge. Marco's claws opened a deep gash in Julius's side.

A nice bluff. Of course, if Marco was going to win here, he had to put on a front, prey on the larger shifter's confidence. That was the cunning his kin were supposed to be known for. And none so much as their alpha.

It wasn't so different from how he'd bluffed about his attitude toward me to his kin, put on a front of seeing me as nothing more than a means to an end. But I knew with every thud of my pulse that he'd used those words the same way he'd made that mad dash. A distraction, a show of force, to open up the way to what he really wanted. When this kind of hostility was what he'd had to face, month by month, I wasn't sure I could even blame him anymore.

Julius whipped around, his yellow eyes flashing. Marco sprang nimbly out of the way. But the tiger didn't seem slowed down by the gouge over his ribs. He hurtled after the jaguar like a Mack trunk, and Marco couldn't keep out of the way quite fast enough. The larger shifter bowled him over.

I flinched, my heart thumping so fast I thought it would explode from my chest. A scream caught in my chest. *No!* Not my alpha. Not my mate.

Nate set his hand over mine, squeezing my fingers, but the contact barely registered. I couldn't pull my eyes from the fight.

Marco rolled onto his back, all four sets of claws scraping at the tiger's hide. Julius smacked him in the head and snapped at his neck, but the jaguar twisted out of the way and the last second. He sank his teeth into the tiger's foreleg. When Julius flinched, Marco shot out from under him. He flung himself toward one of the trees, ricocheted off the trunk, and slammed into the tiger's side right where he'd clawed him before.

Julius let out a snarl that was as much pain as anger. He charged after Marco, clearly aiming to pummel him to the ground again. Marco slipped around him, but he wasn't moving quite as fast now. Blood dripped from where the bigger cat had clawed his shoulder and haunches.

"Geez," Kylie said, even more faintly. "They're really taking this to the end, aren't they?"

The fear in her voice wrenched at me, as much as seeing Marco battered and bloody did. Every nerve in my body was shrieking at me to intervene, to protect my mate. I held myself back by the barest of threads. If I stepped in, if I messed up this challenge somehow, the victory might go to Julius by default.

I wouldn't let him kill Marco. Not if it came to that. I knew that much right down to my bones.

Marco picked up his speed again despite his wounds. He raced around Julius, biting and clawing at the tiger's legs at every opening, leading the tiger in a whirling chase around the arena.

Julius pounded after him. With each turn, his orange and black fur darkened with more streaks of blood.

"All right! Let's end this!" someone hollered from the crowd. I didn't know which of the shifters he was supporting.

For a moment it seemed like Marco was gaining the upper hand. Then his pace started to lag. He nipped the tiger's hind leg and barely scrambled out of the way of Julius's smack. But the tiger kept coming, his lips curled back over his huge fangs. The jaguar stumbled, and Julius pounced. Marco tumbled under him.

A cry broke from my throat then. My hands flinched where I was gripping the rope. Aaron's arm came around me, holding me steady as Nate held onto me too.

Marco lay, his black-furred body limp, under the tiger's huge form. Julius raised his head with a victory roar—and the jaguar leapt up. Marco caught the tiger by the neck, sinking his teeth in deep around the most tender point of his opponent's throat. At the same time, he kicked out at one of Julius's legs.

All his scratches and bites and the strain of running around the arena must have weakened the tiger's muscles. The bigger cat toppled over, Marco rolling with him. The jaguar came to rest poised on Julius's vulnerable chest. He raked his claws over the paler fur there and yanked at the tiger's throat.

Julius's eyes rolled back. He heaved at the ground, but Marco held on tight, managing to keep him pinned.

My breath had stopped in my lungs. I let it out in a rush. A cheer rose up around the ring. "Marco! The alpha wins!"

Marco sank his teeth even deeper with a low growl of warning that was almost a question. The tiger's head swayed as if he couldn't quite find the will to keep it off the ground. Then Julius slumped down, his body sagging. The shift rippled through him. Marco sprang off as the tiger turned back into a man.

The cheers grew louder, the crowd whooping and clapping hands. A few of the waiting attendants darted into the arena to tend to the unconscious Julius's wounds. And to their alpha. Marco listed a bit to one side, blood smearing the grass under his paws—and plenty of it was his own. He pushed off the ground and shifted back into his human form, raising his hand in victory.

The tension in me broke, relief rolling through me. I raised my voice with a cheer of my own.

CHAPTER 18

Nate

"HOW LONG HAVE you been in league with the rogues?" I said, barely managing to keep the growl out of my voice.

Julius slumped silent in his chair in the small room, his neck still marked with red where Marco had bitten him yesterday night. The wounds had healed but left behind scars that wouldn't fade for months, if not years. The tiger shifter had resisted forfeiting the challenge until he'd been on the verge of dying.

Marco, standing next to me, had scars of his own. Even after a night's rest, his movements were still a little stiff. I'd volunteered to help him lead this interrogation after I'd seen him at breakfast. And I might have had ulterior motives as well.

Someone had sent the rogues to corrupt my kin. I wasn't leaving here without finding out how—and who else they might have turned.

"How long?" I repeated. The other alphas and Ren stirred where they were watching behind us. Julius swiped his hand across his mouth, the chain that linked his restraining cuffs clinking. He thought a lot of himself, all big and posturing, but he had nothing on me. I loomed over him, letting him think about what it'd be like to take on an animal more his own size.

"Since we got the news that the dragon shifter had been found," the traitor said in a reluctant voice. "Not long."

"So you admit that you've conspired with them?" Marco said.

The tiger shifter inclined his head slightly.

"You gave *them* orders? Was it your idea to send them to attack the disparate estate?"

"I thought it would be better if you were all dead," Julius said. "I might have given some advice about how they could manage that. I've been here on the estate the whole time, though."

"You sent them after *my* people," I snapped. "What did you tell them to say to my kin to persuade them to help? The rogues wouldn't have come up with any argument strong enough on their own—I know they couldn't."

"Oh, it wasn't that hard," Julius said with a twitch of his hand on his lap. He didn't look up at me. "Sweet talk them a little, give them the idea they'd be better off without some boss alpha running the show."

No. It had to be more than that. The answer set my teeth on edge. But maybe it was only because I didn't want to admit that my kin might be so easily swayed? Suddenly I was unsure of my judgment.

"You expect me to believe that's it?" I said, letting my voice rumble louder. "Exactly what were the rogues supposed to offer my kin that would be better than what they already have?"

Julius shrugged, his head still bowed. "What makes you think they have it so good right now?"

That wasn't an answer at all. I bristled and caught myself, taking a step back before I swung at him.

It wasn't an answer, and it also was. My kin *had* been swayed. Maybe the how didn't matter so much. They had their weaknesses, as much as I hated to admit it. But I had to admit it if I was going to address those weaknesses and help them get through whatever trouble lay ahead of us.

Because we were obviously far from done with that trouble.

"We know you had something planned with the rogues for our visit here," Marco said. "Care to share any details or should your dragon shifter burn the truth out of you?"

Ren came up beside me, wrapping her hand around my arm. She'd felt my distress. I didn't want to show any of my own weakness in front of our prisoner, but I did let myself quickly nuzzle her hair. The softly sweet smell of my mate steadied me.

"I just told them you were coming," Julius said. "That it would be a good time to get involved. That's all."

"Well, I definitely don't believe *that*," Marco said. He glanced at Ren. "Princess?"

Ren looked up at me as if asking my permission. As if she needed to. I could stand back for a moment. It might be better if I did. Instead of pushing for the answers I wanted, I needed to listen.

She'd gotten through to Orion. Maybe there was something redeemable in this wretched feline shifter too.

Ren

I came to stand directly in front of Julius. He kept his head low as if he thought he could worm his way out of telling the truth that way. Hadn't he heard the stories about my powers?

I wasn't going full dragon on him yet, though. He'd given me a strange vibe all through his questioning. I wanted to get a better sense of it.

"Look at me," I said. When he didn't move, I repeated the words with a hint of fire creeping into my voice. "*Look at me.*"

The tiger shifter startled, his head jerking out. He blinked as his gaze met mine. His light brown eyes looked oddly hazy. There was no reason for him to be spaced out. He'd been complying enough so far that Marco hadn't had him drugged. If he tried to shift, the chains that bound him would hold his tiger form even more tightly.

"Tell me exactly where you met with the rogues," I said. "If it's been different places, start from the first time."

"I—I've only talked to them in person once," he said. "Out beyond the glade. The other times, I had people speak for me."

I frowned. My senses told me he was telling the truth. But at the same time his whole demeanor, the vagueness of his answers, unsettled me.

"You could show us the spot?"

"I'm not sure I remember exactly where it was," he said. That seemed to be the truth too.

I ran my tongue over my teeth. "Who spoke for you the other times?"

"No one here. It was their idea. I couldn't tell you their names."

"We can make you tell us," Marco broke in. "And believe me, I'll very much enjoy watching you taken over by those flames."

I made a motion with my hand, and he stopped, his forehead furrowing. But Julius still gave every appearance that he was being truthful. My violet fire couldn't provoke more out of him than that.

If I got any clear answers, the most important questions were about what waited ahead, not what had already happened.

"Do the rogues plan to attack the feline estate?"

"I don't know," Julius said honestly. His lips curled slightly. I couldn't tell if he was on the verge of smiling or grimacing. A prickle ran down my back.

"Do they have anything planned for when we leave the estate?"

"I don't know."

"What *do* you know about what the rogues are planning to do next?"

The tiger shifter's head sagged back down. He let out a rough sigh. "I don't know anything about what they have planned next. As far as I'm concerned, they do a great job figuring out how to mess with you themselves."

"And what do you think they'd have done if you *had* managed to beat me?" Marco asked. "They're against the whole system of alphas. Did you really think they'd bow down to you after you'd become what they hate about the shifter kin?"

"I don't care," Julius said. "I just wanted *you* gone."

"Why?" Aaron asked from the back of the room. "What were you hoping to gain?"

Julius hesitated. Something about that question seemed to have thrown him off. His fingers curled over his knees. "Respect," he said. "Power. A better position than I have now."

All true. I bit my lip. Nothing he was telling us was any use, no matter how honest he was being.

I tipped my head toward the door. The alphas filed out, Marco lingering to shoot one last glare at his rival. I followed them. Marco closed the door behind us.

"Are we taking him outside so you can work your dragon magic on him?" West asked in his usual gruff voice.

I shook my head. "It wouldn't do any good. He's not lying to us. He's not being very clear, and there's something strange about the way he's answering, but the things he says he doesn't know... He really doesn't know them. Unless he's somehow strong enough to confuse my impressions when not even the four of you can manage that."

Marco smiled crookedly. "That hardly seems likely."

"It doesn't," I agreed. "But where do we go from there? He's admitted to working with the rogues, even if he doesn't seem to be half as involved as Orion thought. He seemed sure there was a feline calling a lot of the shots."

"Orion wasn't really in a position to give you many details," West pointed out.

"I don't like the idea of that one walking free," Nate said, jabbing his thumb toward the door. "If you simply banish him like a regular failed challenger, of course he'll go straight to the rogues. And who knows what plans he'll make with them then? He knows your estate; he knows your people. He'll tell them everything."

"There are other considerations," Aaron said.

"Like what?" the bear shifter demanded.

"Like how much I want to tell my kin about Julius's involvement with the rogues," Marco put in. "If I imprison him instead of banishing him, I'll have to explain it somehow. And they might not even believe it. For all they know, I'm making up an excuse after the fact to justify tormenting him further. Which won't exactly do wonders for morale around here."

Shit. I hadn't thought of that. I crossed my arms over my chest. "So what's our best option?"

Marco sighed. "I don't know. I can keep him confined a little longer without too many questions, but I'll need to make some kind of official move soon. Now would be an excellent time for my feline cleverness to kick in."

"We'll all think on it," Aaron said.

Unlike on Nate's estate, the holding cells on Marco's weren't in a basement but a separate building off to the side of the main mansion. When we stepped out, Kylie and Alice were waiting for us.

Kylie bounded to my side, but her face still looked a bit drawn. She'd been quieter since the challenge fight yesterday. That was part of the reason I'd wanted her to stay out here while we did the questioning.

"So what did you find out?" she asked, her gaze flicking back toward the building we'd left.

"Not much," I said. "We still have no idea whether the rogues are going to attack us here, and if they are, how."

"Was he really helping them?"

"It seems like it. He admitted to it."

Kylie cocked her head. "What happens to him now, then?"

I spread my hands. "From what the guys have told me, usually a failed challenger would be banished. His kin mark would be stricken, and they'd mark him on the forehead where anyone could see to show his new status." I gestured to my own forehead. "Any kin who saw him anywhere near kin territory would have license to kill him. And..."

My voice faltered when I noticed Kylie's expression. Her face had taken on a slightly sickly cast that clashed pretty awfully with her pink pixie cut. She glanced at me in my sudden silence and smiled, but her mouth wobbled.

Here I was talking about people getting killed like it was nothing. No wonder she was feeling ill.

"Are you okay?" I asked. "If you need anything..."

Kylie laughed awkwardly. "No, no. I think I've just had enough shifter brutality for a few days. I didn't sleep that well last night. Maybe I'll take a nap."

"I can see you back to your room," Alice offered. I was about to jump in and say I would, but I caught myself. Maybe it was me Kylie needed some distance from as well as the rest.

I looked around with a knot in my gut. My mates had ambled toward the mansion too. Marco had fallen a little behind the others, his expression uncharacteristically solemn. He didn't look worn down exactly, but his usual sly energy had dulled.

The challenge yesterday had clearly taken more out of him than he liked to admit.

I caught up with him, slipping my arm around his elbow. He brightened when he looked at me. "Hello, princess."

I tipped my head against his shoulder. Suddenly all I wanted to do was wrap myself up in his warmth. Revel in the fact that he was still here, living and breathing, not lying broken under that tiger shifter's paws.

"I feel like we both need a little more recovery time after last night," I said. "Is there somewhere on the estate we can at least pretend to relax? Maybe that's what you need to get those cleverness juices flowing."

The corner of Marco's mouth quirked up. "Actually, I know just the place."

CHAPTER 19

Ren

WITH ALL THE COMMOTION YESTERDAY, I hadn't gotten the chance to explore much of the house yet. When Marco opened the door into the vast greenhouse I'd only seen from outside, my breath caught.

"Wow." I stepped onto the stone path that wove into the thick tropical underbrush. Overhead, trees jutted limbs in an arching canopy. Artificial cliffs had been carved out of rock here and there along the walls, offering climbing ledges at various levels. The air was warm and humid but not stifling. A floral perfume drifted around me.

"It's like your jungle gym back at the New York house, only ten times bigger," I said.

"That's the idea." Marco took my hand, and we headed together down the path. "The climate might be warmer here in Florida, but the winters are still cooler than many of us prefer.

And this gives us space to exercise our feline natures without any worries about being observed. A wolf or a bear can get away with running around in the woods without too much caution. A jaguar or a lion? That'd draw some attention if any humans spotted us."

No kidding. "I don't suppose there's a *really* big one of these out at the dragon shifter estate?" I said. "Because if a big cat is noticeable..."

Marco chuckled. "Your home base is in an isolated enough spot that you can fly near there without any problems. The dragon shifters have accumulated a lot of property in the surrounding area to keep humans at a distance."

The temperature hadn't felt too warm when we'd first stepped in, but a sheen of sweat was forming on my skin now. I rubbed my arms. "Too bad you can't turn the temperature *down* if you need to."

"There are other ways to cool off," Marco said slyly. "Shedding clothes is always my favorite."

I shot him a mock glower. He grinned back, looking more like his usual self. At least that part of my plan was working.

"Actually," he said with a tug of my hand, "I think I have just the thing to convince you..."

We ducked through a passage formed by an arching bush and came out on the edge of a manufactured pond. Water burbled into it from a spout at one end. The walls and base were painted brown to look like soil and the vegetation grew right up to the edges, but the water was crystal clear. And it looked delightfully inviting.

"Hmm," I said. "You make a compelling case."

"I'm going in even if you're not," Marco replied, still grinning. He stripped off his shirt in a single movement and undid his pants. Damn. The casual air with which shifter guys got naked was starting to seem normal to me, but it was still fucking *hot*. In the best possible way.

And I was still hot, in a not-so-great way, standing here in my clothes. It wasn't as if Marco hadn't seen me naked a dozen times already.

I yanked off the cotton dress I'd managed to find among the fancier offerings in my wardrobes. Marco made an approving sound and leapt into the pool. A little of the spray dappled my skin as I wriggled out of my panties. The droplets felt so beautifully cool that I didn't stop to test the water. I just plunged right in after him.

The pond was deep enough that my head went under before my feet touched the bottom. I pushed myself back to the surface, reveling in the rush of the water against my skin. I'd never actually gone skinny-dipping before. Now I was thinking I'd need to make a habit of it.

I flipped my wet hair back from my face. Marco beamed at me, his own hair shining like black ink.

"There are ledges along the banks," he said. "If you get tired of treading water."

"I think my legs can handle a little treading."

"Hmm. Just be careful of the eels."

"What?" I jerked up, peering into the water below me.

Marco cracked up. "I'm teasing, Princess. I solemnly swear the entire estate is eel free."

"You..." I couldn't find the words to express what I thought of that joke, but that was fine. I had a whole pool of water to work with. I aimed a splash right at his face.

Marco's eyes gleamed. "Are you sure you want to go there? Don't start a battle you're not prepared to lose."

"Big talk from a wet cat," I retorted, and splashed him again for good measure.

He wiped his face with a playful growl. "You asked for it."

Instead of splashing me back, he sprang at me. I squealed and dove out of the way. I managed to get in one more splash before he caught me by the waist. With his other arm, he scooped up a heap of water and dropped it right over me.

I shook my head, sputtering a laugh, and squirmed out of his grasp. The kick of my legs sent a good spray back at him. Then Marco snatched my ankle. "Hey!" I protested as he reeled me in.

"Look what I caught," he teased. "A rare dragon fish."

In a stunning show of maturity, I stuck my tongue out at him and kicked up another wave with my other leg. Marco tugged my ankle past him, surging forward at the same moment to grab my wrists. He pinned them gently against the side of the pool. "That's enough of that."

My feet came to rest on one of those ledges he'd mentioned. "You're no fun," I told him.

"Oh," he said, his voice dipping lower as he eased closer, "you have no idea how much fun I can be."

I snapped into sudden awareness of the rest of his body, just inches from mine in the water. His very naked body. *My* very naked body ached with the longing for him to cross those last few inches. I held his gaze, warmed by the heat in his indigo eyes.

"I don't know," I said, my own voice dropping. "I think I've gotten a pretty good idea. But you're always welcome to give me another demonstration."

"A very tempting invitation," he murmured.

He bent his head, and I tipped mine to meet his kiss. His mouth was slick and hot, demanding enough to send a tremor of desire through me. I wanted to touch him, to run my hands over that sleekly muscled body and pull it against mine, but he held himself away from me and kept my wrists locked in place. All I could focus on was the kiss.

His tongue slid into my mouth, and mine rose to tangle with it. A needy whimper crept up my throat as the kiss deepened. I was drowning in it, in the faintly spicy taste of him, in the craving for more.

Marco released my mouth to trail his lips down my neck. My eyelids fluttered open. My gaze caught on a stark red mark that ran from behind his ear down the base of his scalp. I winced, my heart stuttering with an emotion that had nothing to do with arousal.

Marco pulled back. "What's the matter?" he asked, his eyes concerned. His grip on my wrists loosened.

I drew back one of my hands to touch the side of his neck. My thumb traced over the fresh scar. "I didn't realize Julius got you here." So close to his throat.

"It doesn't really matter, does it?" Marco said lightly. "I'm the one who got him in the end."

"I know." But the fear I'd felt during their fight echoed through me. "I hated watching the two of you," I said in a small voice. "Every time he hurt you, I felt it too. You have no idea how much I wanted to leap in there and go dragon ballistic on his ass."

I finished that sentence with a growl. Marco smiled. "That would have been a sight to see. Maybe you'll still get a chance, the way things are going."

I didn't want to think about that—about the rogues and the threat still looming over us. That huge problem would be right there waiting for us when we left the greenhouse. For now…

Lowering my head, I pressed my lips against the scar. Marco's breath hitched. His heart thumped under my hand where it rested against his chest. I kissed every inch of the ruddy line that had been just a hair's breadth from a fatal wound.

A light that was almost wild shimmered in Marco's eyes when I drew back. He leaned in, close enough that his nose brushed mine. His voice came out slow and almost choked.

"I meant what I said before. About wanting you more than I want to be alpha. When I was facing him, that was all I thought about. Beating him so I could stay your mate. Being able to kiss you again. Being able to laugh with you again." He paused, pulling back again so he could meet my gaze. "My Princess of Flames. My Serenity. My dragon shifter. No matter what else happens, there's never going to be anyone else for me. I love you, Ren."

My throat had gone tight. Emotion swelled in my chest, bright and heady. "I love you too," I said without even needing to think about it. It was almost a relief to say it. God, why hadn't I already, to all of the guys? I needed to, more. All of the time. Until they couldn't possibly forget it. Because it was true. In the midst of all the chaos, I'd fallen for them with every bit of my heart.

The same rush of feeling flowed back to me from everywhere Marco and I touched. He grinned at me, so brilliantly I almost lost my breath. He moved as if to kiss me again, but at the same moment voices carried from the other end of the greenhouse.

"What do you think, trees or ground?"

"Why not both? I could use a good run."

Shit. Of course, all the feline kin had free run of this place. I grimaced, and Marco shook his head, his smile turning wry. I was getting used to all the shifters seeing me unclothed, but I wasn't exactly keen to make this private moment with my mate suddenly public.

"When they see us together, they'll probably leave," Marco murmured.

A crazy idea lit in my head. One that would at least skip the seeing us part. And maybe would restore a little more of Marco's reputation with his kin. A mischievous smile crossed my lips. Marco raised his eyebrows, and I pressed a finger to his mouth to tell him to keep quiet. Then I raised my voice.

"Oh, Marco! Yes, just like that. Mmm, don't stop!"

The corners of Marco's eyes crinkled as he suppressed his amusement. The intruders' conversation fell silent. I threw in a loud moan for good measure. "Oh, yes. Give it to me hard! You're so good!"

There was a brief rustling, and then the thud of the door closing. Marco tipped his head next to mine, his shoulders quaking with muted laughter. A snicker slipped out of my mouth. We both burst into giggles.

I swiped the tears of amusement from my eyes. "How long do you think it'll be before they dare set foot in here again?"

"They'll probably wait until I'm halfway across the country," Marco said. "You're lucky they didn't happen to be eager voyeurs."

"Oh, I'm sure I could have come up with something else in that case."

His eyebrows shot back up. "Now I'm sorry I missed the opportunity to see that."

"Too bad for you." Or maybe not. His arm had come to rest just below my breasts. Our legs had intertwined on the ledge. My heart skipped, with nothing but desire now. "What do you think? Can you make me sound like that for real?"

Marco's gaze started to smolder. "I think I'm up to that challenge. Is that what you want, Princess?"

It was. In that moment, when he looked at me like that, there was nothing I wanted more.

"I want you," I said, low but clear. "All of you. Marco, will you take me as your mate?"

A guttural sound escaped him, and then he was kissing me again, with so much passion it set my body on fire. I gripped his shoulder with one hand, the other trailing down over the muscles I'd so longed to explore earlier. The water lapped around us as we claimed each other's mouths completely.

Marco brought his palms to my breasts, circling the heels of his hands against my nipples. The water teased them even harder between each of his caresses. I moaned against his mouth, arcing into his touch. He took the opportunity to tangle his tongue around mine. We dueled and devoured each other as his hands dipped. When he pinched my nipples between his thumb and forefinger, a spark of stark pleasure shot straight down to my core.

I gasped, my hips bucking against him. The hard length of his erection brushed my core, making me twice as hungry in an instant. He left my breasts to grip my thighs and pull me to him. His cock settled against my clit. I shuddered with pleasure as he rocked his hips, inflaming me more with every stroke.

"The answer is yes," he muttered. "In case there was any doubt about that." Then his mouth caught mine again. I floated on the bliss racing all through my body, but my sex throbbed with a deeper need.

I reached between us to curl my fingers around his cock. Marco hummed happily as I slid them up and down. I lifted my hips, offering myself to him, and his chest hitched again.

He pulled back from our kiss to meet my eyes. A question shone in his. As if I hadn't already made myself clear enough.

"Please," I said, drawing him forward.

He pressed me harder against the wall as he eased his cock into me inch by glorious inch. I clutched at him, resisting the urge to buck against him like a wild woman, no matter how much I wanted him all the way in, now. The thrilling burn radiated from my core through every nerve. He kissed the corner of my jaw as he plunged all the way to the hilt. His breath spilled hot down my neck.

"Oh, God, Princess," he groaned. "So fucking beautiful."

I panted, lost in my need for him. "Less talking, more fucking."

He chuckled roughly and started moving. With each thrust, my body trembled more, clamoring for release. Our bond flared between us with a rush of bliss that left me breathless. I pumped my hips in time with his rhythm, whimpering as he pushed even deeper.

"I don't have you screaming my name yet," he murmured. "That's what you asked for, isn't it?"

"This is good," I said raggedly. "This is—oh!"

He adjusted the angle of my hips with his next thrust. His cock pressed against that sensitive spot inside me with one long stroke. I quaked with the sensation, ecstasy blurring my vision.

Marco picked up his pace, hitting that spot with a heady caress every time. I moaned, my head falling back. "God. Right there. Don't stop."

His chuckle was lost in another groan. He plunged into me once, twice more, and that was enough to send me spinning over my peak. I cried out, loud enough that the whole room probably could have heard it if I hadn't already scared everyone else away.

Marco's lips collided with mine. I kissed him through the bursts of sparks going off behind my eyes. Then with a shudder he followed me over, spilling himself inside me.

He rocked to a stop, letting me ride out the aftershock. I

hugged him, shivering with bliss. "Now that's my princess," he said softly. His arms came around me, returning my embrace.

I tucked my head against his shoulder, overwhelmed by more feeling than I could blame on the sex. "And this is my mate," I whispered back.

He kissed my cheek, running his fingers over my hair. I nestled closer to him. How much longer could we stay here? It had become such a beautiful escape.

Marco tipped back my head to claim my lips again. The kiss started out gentle, but as I returned it, fresh desire stirred inside me. He made an approving sound as I kissed him more deeply.

I was just thinking we might go for a second round—to make up for lost time and all—when a clatter carried through the greenhouse walls.

We both froze, ears perking. For a second, there was nothing. Then the air split with the *boom* of a gunshot.

CHAPTER 20

Ren

Marco and I scrambled out of the pond. No time for clothes. No time to even try to dry off. Droplets trickled down my back and over my chest as we raced along the path toward the door. Any heat that had still been in me fled. All I felt was a chill piercing straight through the middle of my chest.

Another shot rang out, one that sounded as if it was coming from inside the mansion now. My muscles clenched. Memories flickered by in the back of my head. The clean pale halls of the dragon shifter home, splattered with blood. A sister, a father, another, sprawled on the floor. The click of a rifle being reloaded.

A coppery flavor rose in the back of my mouth. No. I wasn't going to witness another slaughter. The rogues wouldn't take my alphas from me. They wouldn't take any one of the kin here.

But the thud of my heart and the shots still reverberating in my ears told me they most likely already had. And to barge onto the estate in the middle of the day, guns blazing, they must have had help.

Not from Julius. We'd left him locked in that holding room.

I glanced at Marco as we reached the door. "There's another traitor among your kin," I said. "That must be why Julius was being so dodgy. He really didn't know that much. He was someone else's puppet."

Marco jerked open the door. "So it seems," he said, his voice tight. "Which just means someone else here needs to feel my fangs in their jugular before the hour is over."

If he could get close enough before he took a bullet. My lungs clenched. I grabbed his arm. "We'll hurry, but we can't go rushing right in there. They have weapons. We don't. We'll have to be smart."

Marco shot me a sharp smile. "I know how to fight smart, princess. Don't you worry about me. Didn't you see me last night?"

He took my hand, squeezing it tight, and we ran together down the hall. Voices clamored and a scream echoed from up ahead. My nerves twitched to shift, to rain a furious fire down over everyone who threatened my kin, but I didn't dare give in yet. I needed to save every bit of that energy for the actual fight.

Marco didn't have the same concerns, though. He gave my fingers another squeeze and then let go. A second later, he was leaping forward in jaguar form. Within a few bounds, he'd completely outpaced me.

I couldn't let him run into the fray alone. I pushed my legs harder, drawing on all the dragon strength I held even in my human body.

We turned a corner, and the main foyer with its expansive staircase came into view up ahead. A body was slumped at the base of the stairs. Three others ran past the hallway, their faces white with panic. A lion bounded forward and jerked to the side as one of the guns boomed. Blood boomed on his tawny shoulder.

"There's no point in fighting!" a vibrant voice called out. Something about it struck me with a twang of recognition. "We've got no quarrel with the regular kin. Bring forward the alphas and the dragon shifter, and the rest of you can go about your business as usual."

Another voice reached my ears from farther away: Nate's rich baritone. "Away into your rooms, feline kin," he was hollering. "Lock your doors. This is for us to deal with."

Were the other alphas already there too? My pulse stuttered. I threw myself forward even faster, the muscles in my legs burning. Marco dashed on ahead of me, his paws thumping against the heavy pile of the rug.

The lion charged again, even with its limp. The air crackled with gunfire. There was a thump out of my view, but I could imagine all too well what had happened: the great cat slumping and sinking back into his human form. Blood pooling under his slack body.

Another memory flashed through my mind, so sharp and stark I lost my sense of the hall around me. I was five, clutching my wolf father's arm. Sobbing so hard my stomach lurched. Hands tacky with blood. That click of the rifle. Then my mother's fingers snatching my arm and wrenching me to my feet.

Away. Away.

I stumbled, and suddenly the foyer was right there in front of me. The body I'd imagined lay just a short distance from my feet —Coreen's husband, his eyes unblinking. I jerked myself back against the wall.

Chaos reigned all around the staircase. The feline shifters hadn't listened to Nate's call, at least not most of them. Even in a crisis they apparently weren't willing to listen to a bear. Panthers and tigers, lions and lynxes, snarled and lunged at animal foes of all sorts beneath and on either side of the steps. Several other bodies were slumped in its shadow. I couldn't tell which were our people and which rogues. There seemed to be a hundred enemies battling us.

My alphas were in the middle of the fray, Nate's bear and West's wolf looking as though they were trying to urge the other shifters down the central hall while fending off the rogues, Aaron's eagle swooping around the stairs to tackle a weasel about to leap at the others from above.

Alice was there too—in human form, pushing Kylie behind her in one corner. My pulse hiccupped. I didn't know how they'd ended up in the room, but they were trapped now unless they ran through the fighting. My best friend braced her back against the wall, her arms hugged tight around herself. Her wide eyes were fixed on figures at the other end of the foyer.

Across the thick runner by the mansion's double doors, the rogues still in human form were standing. Two held pistols and three others rifles. They'd gathered more weapons than the other groups had carried for previous attacks. My gut twisted at the sight—and then twisted tighter when I spotted a familiar face in their midst as they marched forward.

I'd counted wrong. There were three pistols, but the guy holding the third wasn't a rogue. It was Phillipe, the patchy haired snow leopard shifter who'd made such a show of praising Marco last night.

As if he'd felt my gaze on him, his eyes darted to the side and found me. The woman beside him raised her rifle to take a shot at Aaron, clipping him in the wing. Phillipe smiled thinly and motioned to the others.

"There's our dragon shifter," he said, his jovial voice turned cruel. "Take her down."

Three of the guns snapped toward me. I threw myself back toward an open doorway down the hall. At the same moment, Marco hurtled forward.

The jaguar slammed into the nearest rogue, knocking her over just as she fired. The guy next to him flinched, his shot going wild. Phillipe swore and pointed his pistol at Marco.

"No!" I reeled forward again, pushing off the floor as I did. The shift ripped through me faster than it ever had before. My muscles screamed, and my skin stung. A stabbing pain shot through my bones. But I was there, with a draconic roar, plowing straight into Phillipe before he could pull the trigger.

Aaron dove at one of the other armed rogues. Nate came charging through the battleground to join us, West wheeling to follow. The rogue Marco had tackled slammed her gun against the side of his head and managed to roll out from under him. He caught her wrist with his jaws. With a yank and a cracking sound, she gasped. The pistol clattered to the floor.

Phillipe had toppled when I'd hit him. He shifted as he sprang away. I melted his gun with a blast of dragon fire and swung around to pursue him. Where was Kylie? I had to make sure she stayed okay. I had to try to keep *everyone* here okay.

The snow leopard crossed Nate's path, and the grizzly battered him to the side. All around us the battle raged on. One of the remaining human rogues fired a few more shots, one of them smacking Nate in the hip. Blood sprayed across the polished floorboards. Fur flew and animal voices shrieked. I could hardly tell which of the living bodies were my kin and which the rogues now.

In that glance, a hard certainty formed inside me. I didn't care if Nate's kin or Marco's had doubted my ability to lead them. I didn't care what the rogues might have offered them as an alternative. *This* was what the rogues brought. Violence, pain, mayhem. This was what they'd always brought.

Maybe I didn't know how good a leader I'd be, but I sure as hell could do better by my kin than this.

With the strength of that resolve coiled tight in my belly, I blasted the rogue who'd shot Nate with a spurt of flame. He screeched and crumpled. The rogue whose wrist Marco had snapped was struggling to grip her gun with her weaker hand. I charred her to cinders before she could get a handle on it.

West had charged at one of the guys who held a rifle. The wolf snapped at the rogue's legs while the guy tried to swivel far enough away to aim. He'd already gotten in one shot—a streak of starker red slashed through the ruddy silver fur on West's back where a bullet had clipped him, only just missing his spine.

Rage flashed behind my eyes. I couldn't fry the rogue without frying my mate at the same time. But I had teeth and claws too.

I bashed the guy's head with a swipe of my foreleg. In an instant, West was on him, his teeth at the rogue's throat. He kicked the rifle aside. I shot a bolt of white hot flame down on it, turning it into a bubbling mass of metal.

A sliver of a thought passed through my head: Mom would have made short work of the rogues that had attacked her family sixteen years ago, if she'd been able to fight like this. If she hadn't had three daughters who couldn't fully shift to try to protect.

The people we loved, the ones who were weaker than us—they made us vulnerable.

Panic washed over me. Kylie! I leapt over the staircase, searching for her. Searching for the snow leopard who'd managed to scramble through the fray.

I found both of them. Phillipe was facing off against Alice, still in her human form, but no less dangerous for it. He lunged at her, and she rammed her elbow into the side of his skull. The blow sent him staggering to the side. Kylie yelped. She groped toward a painting hanging just beside her. Heaving it off its hook, she hurled it at their attacker.

The corner of the heavy frame smacked Phillipe square in the head. I breathed a gust of fire toward the snow leopard, but he leapt out of the way at the last second. His cry of pain told me I'd at least singed him. He bolted away under the staircase.

With a roar, I barreled into the chaos of the fight. My talons picked off a jackal here, a rogue bear there, and another intruder, and another. The feline kin not too injured to keep fighting closed in around the dwindling number of remaining rogues. Which was a good thing, because the strain of the extended shift was catching up with me, with an even deeper pain than usual. Because I'd called my dragon form over me so quickly?

I'd have to ask Aaron about that, I thought vaguely as I tossed one last rogue against the wall. My muscles were contracting, no matter how hard I tried to hang on. I collapsed onto the floor. My human hands slammed into the floor, my human knees knocking the polished hardwood.

Sucking in a breath, I shoved myself to my feet. My gaze caught on a hunched form under the stairs.

Phillipe. The snow leopard sat curled in on himself. His left foreleg and most of that shoulder was burned black. His teeth were bared as he panted through the pain. Only the faintest shiver of sympathy touched me.

All of the blood spilled here was because of him. Why? So he didn't have to listen to someone else telling him what to do? Because he thought he'd get some kind of glory among the rogues?

It didn't fucking matter. The only thing that mattered was that he never did it again.

I strode over to him, slowing as I got closer. Phillipe snarled, but he clearly wasn't capable of putting up much of an actual fight.

One of the other feline shifters, a cougar, came up beside me. "Drag him out," I said to her. "Out where everyone can see."

The snow leopard growled, but he couldn't do more than squirm and wince as the cougar took him by the scruff of his neck. The larger cat dragged him out to where the noon sun streamed through the thrown open doors. I stalked after them. My jaw clenched.

The cougar let go of Phillipe and backed up a step. I loomed over the snow leopard, meeting his yellow-green gaze with a glare. From around the room, dozens of feline eyes fixed on me. And one pair of human eyes. Kylie gaped at me, her face still pale.

The thought of what she must think of me now sent a pang through my chest. But I couldn't let those worries distract me. What I did here mattered a hell of a lot.

So I'd better do it good.

"Phillipe," I said, pitching my voice loud. "You were kin, and you betrayed all the others you should have called kin. You brought all this destruction down on your alpha's estate, your shifter community." I swept my arm to indicate the entire foyer. "But I will give you a chance. Because *I* am not here to destroy if I can help it. So much of shifter kind has been broken by the rogues and kin like you. Will you help us rebuild it now? Or do you only care about wrecking things?"

Phillipe clung on to his feline form, his eyes narrowing. The muscles in his haunches bunched. I braced myself, feeling his intention. If that was how he wanted to end this, let them see him make the choice himself.

He threw himself off the floor with one final surge of strength, his jaws yawning as if to eat me whole.

My hand tingled as I drew a partial shift into my fingers. With the snow leopard's sour breath in my face, I slashed my dragon talons across his neck, severing his throat.

CHAPTER 21

Marco

THAT TRAITOR, Phillipe, crumpled at Ren's feet with a gush of blood down his chest. My dragon shifter dodged backward, shaking her hand to withdraw her talons. As the snow leopard shifted back into Phillipe's stringy human form, her head whipped around. Her gaze locked with mine. A sudden worry shimmered in her eyes.

Why? Because she'd killed one of my kin? Good riddance to that piece of excrement. She'd been fucking glorious.

I rose up out of my jaguar form, ignoring the aches and pangs where I'd have new scars tomorrow. Then I brought my hands together and started to clap.

Around the room, my kin and the other alphas were gradually shifting back. Most of them joined my applause. Ren's head swiveled as she took in our response, looking startled and then, with a lift of her chin that made my heart swell with affection, owning it. Not a princess of flames anymore. The woman before me was every inch a queen.

I walked up to her and took her hand. "He got what was coming to him," I said in a low voice. "You were amazing, Ren."

I leaned in to kiss her, and someone gave an exhausted but still joyful whoop in the crowd. All of my kin had to feel it now—that my bond with my mate had been consummated, that their own desires could bring them new feline children after all these years. But that wasn't the only reason to celebrate.

Ren kissed me back hard, as if replenishing her strength through the meeting of our lips. I was happy to give anything she needed to take. She touched my cheek, finding the claw mark just below my eye that hadn't yet sealed. I shook my head to tell her not to fret about that. The wound only stung a little while I stood here next to her.

Then I turned to face my kin and raised our joined hands in the air in a gesture of triumph. "The rogues and the traitors among our kin have been put down. This is the security a dragon shifter brings us. A new age for us is about to begin. An age when shifters will work together against our enemies, and live and love without the shadow of violence hanging over us."

"Here's to the dragon shifter!" someone—I thought Silvan—shouted from our audience.

"To the dragon shifter!" a bunch of voices joined in. Some wary, some limping, but all bright-eyed, several of my kin slunk over to show their respects to Ren, as if they'd only just met her.

Better late than never. A smile crept over my face as I watched them bob their heads and press their hands to hers, murmuring words of gratitude and encouragement. No one here had ever seen a battle like this on our home ground before. And no one here had seen a dragon fight like Ren just had.

Even a cat could appreciate the strength she'd shown—and

the mercy.

My gaze traveled away from her to those we'd lost despite my mate's courage and all of our best efforts. Coreen's husband, Raoul, had taken a fatal bullet to the chest. The rogues had dealt fatal blows to a few others in the fray. A couple of my attendants who'd rushed in to help had fallen and not gotten up. And there were many kin alive but too weakened from their wounds to stand.

Several more attendants had slipped into the room now that the chaos had settled. I motioned them over. "Bring our injured kin to the medical room, quickly. And we'll need to arrange a funeral for the dead." I paused. Not all of the dead. Phillipe had lost the right to that respect, and the rogues had never earned it to begin with. "The rogues we'll burn too, elsewhere."

They nodded and ran to follow my orders. Coreen had gone to kneel by her husband, resting her hand on his forehead, her shoulders slumped. "I'll help see to him," she said in a rough voice to the attendants who'd joined her. Her gaze found mine.

"I'm sorry," I said.

Her mouth twisted. "He fought well. He didn't know how to stand back. It wasn't his nature." She looked over my shoulder, toward Ren, and then back to me. "Thank you," she added. "Maybe we have gone too long without a dragon shifter."

"I have no intention of losing this one," I said, and she managed a hint of a smile.

I made my way back to Ren. Some of my kin were still clustered around her, fawning over her. She was holding herself straight, answering them all warmly, but I could sense the exhaustion in her. My mate had fought too many battles in the last few weeks.

I wrapped my arms around her from behind. Even with the pain of my healing wounds, the feel of her bare skin against mine was heaven. I pressed a kiss to her shoulder and murmured in her ear, "Shall I escort you back to your rooms? I can't imagine how big a break you need after all that."

Ren's lips twitched. She leaned into my embrace for a moment. But her eyes traveled across the room to where her human friend was standing.

"I think there are a few things I need to take care of before I get to do any resting," she said.

~

Ren

I walked over to Kylie tentatively, watching for any sign that I'd come close enough. She'd never seen my dragon form before, and her first time, all she'd seen me do was clobber rogues and fry them into cinders. And then I'd sliced open a guy's throat right in front of her.

She'd already been having trouble coping with the violence she'd been faced with. And now I was right in the middle of it. Maybe she'd just want to head right home and never speak to me again.

My best friend saw me coming and moving forward to meet me. I stopped, letting her set the pace. To my surprise, she strode right up to me and threw her arms around me, not seeming to care that I was naked and a little bloody.

"Oh my God, Ren," she said. "I was so scared for you. But you were such a badass! Holy shit, those rogues didn't know what hit them, did they? Fucking assholes."

I hugged her back with a halting laugh. "You were scared for *me*? I was freaking terrified one of them would hurt you."

"Aw, I had my eagle bodyguard fending them off. No

problems there. And I got in a couple hits of my own." A tremor ran through her body, but she sucked in a breath and kept her voice steady. "I mean it. You were amazing."

My heart felt as if it had cracked open. My own breath came in almost a sob. Kylie pulled back to stare at my face. "What's wrong?"

"I just— Maybe it was stupid. I've been so worried that this whole... well, everything would be too much for you." I waved to the remains of the battle around us. "It's not what the shifter community is usually like. At least, from what the guys have told me it isn't. But everything is such a mess right now. I don't want to have to fight, but I do have to. People are dying... You shouldn't have to deal with all that."

"Hey," my bestie said firmly. She gripped my shoulder until I met her eyes. "I don't have to. But I want to. The second F in BFF stands for forever, remember? How much shit did we get into and then back out of when we were in New York? So the stuff you're mixed up in now is a little scarier—fine. Maybe I need to take a step back sometimes, but I'm still in this with you." A grin broke over her face. "My best friend is a *dragon*. How many people can say that?"

I really laughed then, and squeezed her with another hug. "You're the best, Kylie. I'm sorry I was shutting you out."

"I get it," Kylie said gently. "Just don't do it again, you hear?"

When I let her go, we stepped to the end of the room. Kylie's gaze drifted over the wreckage. "So... we don't have to worry about any more of those jerks showing up, do we?"

"I don't think so. From what we heard, this was their last-ditch effort, all-in to take us down. Otherwise Phillipe wouldn't have shown his hand."

And we'd defeated them. The rogues were decimated now—the ones who'd wanted me and my alphas dead, at least.

My legs wobbled under me. I might have tipped back against the wall if a large hand hadn't caught my arm.

"Hey," Nate said, bending to kiss my temple. "The shift and the fighting took a lot out of you." He glanced at Kylie. "Do you mind if I borrow her and make her get some rest?"

"Please do," Kylie said with a sweeping gesture. She shot me a grin and a wink as the bear shifter ushered me away.

The other alphas were waiting in the hall. "What about the rest of your kin?" I said to Marco.

"Ah, they're pretty good at looking after themselves," he said in his usual languid tone. "I gave a nice little speech and passed out some orders. That should hold them over for at least a few hours." His expression turned more serious. "We'll have the funerals tomorrow."

"And luck willing, no more for a long time after that," Aaron remarked. He took my hand as we headed to my guest suite.

When we reached the door, the four guys followed me in. I crawled onto the bed, and they piled on around me. The morning's exhaustion was already catching up with me. I yawned and set my head on the pillow, surrounded by their warmth, and just like that, I was out.

I woke up, a little groggy and achy but feeling a lot more alive than before, to a streak of late afternoon sun drifting through the window. I stretched on the bed, and my mates stirred. Looking down at myself, I grimaced.

"Okay, I think a bath is in order before dinner."

Marco slid off the bed with a chuckle. "As much as I'd like to join you for that, I think I'd better touch base with my kin. But I *will* see you at dinner... and after?"

The lilt of his tone sent a flutter of desire through me. I pushed myself up to meet him, pulling him into a kiss. "Of course 'and after.'"

I'd already checked out the bathtub in the suite's bathroom. Like the bed, the circular tub was plenty big enough for five. Four should be a piece of cake. I turned the taps until the water was gushing out in a steamy stream. A handful of sea salt to make it nice and invigorating—perfect!

"I take it we're all invited?" Nate said, strolling in after me.

"The more the merrier. I'd like to think of it as a big, wet reset button in this visit. Good-bye, rogues! Hello, whatever the heck shifters usually do!"

"There's plenty of time for you to learn all of that," Aaron said. He slipped his arm around me and pressed his lips to my shoulder. "And I look forward to guiding you along the way."

"Hmm. Me too," I said with a suggestive waggle of my eyebrows that made him laugh.

As I plunged into the hot water, West finally emerged from the bedroom. He took in me already submerged and his fellow alphas climbing in after me, and shrugged. "Why not?"

Well, that was about as much enthusiasm as I could hope for from my wolf shifter.

The whisper of the water against my skin brought back the memory of the more pleasant activities I'd gotten up to this morning. My little interlude in the pond with Marco. All the fun that could be had while playing around in the water. I licked my lips, looking around at my mates. Then a deeper urge gripped my heart.

I could have lost any of them today. If one of them had been caught by the wrong bullet, like Coreen's husband had... Just the thought of it wrenched at me.

They needed to know just how much they meant to me.

I glided through the water over to Aaron. He smiled, reaching to cup my cheek. I settled on his lap and leaned in for a kiss. His other hand settled on my waist, his thumb stroking over my side as our mouths pressed together slickly. I was plenty hot and bothered already by the time I eased back. But I held myself a little away from him and gazed into his bright blue eyes.

"I love you," I said, the feeling of it rushing through me as if saying the words out loud had uncorked a whole new bottle of adoration.

Aaron's face lit up. He kissed me again, even more deeply this time. Then he said, with his lips just an inch from mine, "I love you, Serenity. Always."

I drifted from him to Nate beside him. The bear shifter welcomed me into his arms, already grinning. I snuggled into his embrace and kissed him hard, wanting him to feel how much this mattered to me. He rumbled in his chest, his fingers caressing my back. I touched the side of his face as I pulled away to meet his warm brown gaze.

"I love you."

"I love you too," he said. "Don't you ever doubt it."

I brushed my lips to his again. Then I turned. West watched me from the opposite corner of the tub. His body was tensed, but his dark green eyes looked softer than usual.

"Come here, Sparks," he said. "I might as well get my kiss."

Did he think he wasn't getting the rest? Well, maybe I wasn't totally sure either. It was a little hard to follow how I felt with all the push-pull between us. But if he was offering a kiss, he'd better believe I was going to take it.

I floated over to him, half expecting him to change his mind. Or to grab me and plant one on me so hungry it made my head spin.

He reached for me, easing his fingers around my wrist to tug me a little closer. He teased his other hand into my hair. We held each other's gazes for a moment, his strangely searching. A flutter passed through my chest. Then he drew me the rest of the way to him.

His mouth claimed mine with a tenderness I couldn't have been prepared for. His lips coaxed mine apart to deepen the kiss, and just like that, I was lost in him. Lost in the gentle passion of his embrace, lost in the smell that lingered on his skin as if he'd brought the forests of his home here with him.

This was the man I'd known my mate could be. The one I'd caught glimpses of in the rare moments when he let his guard down.

My head *was* spinning when he released me from that lip-lock. I stared at him for a second, catching my breath, my whole body aflame with both lust and a more heartfelt longing. I drew in a breath to say what I'd said to the others, what felt undeniably true now—and the door thumped in the other room.

As I swiveled around, Marco strode into the room. He was frowning, his eyes dark with concern.

"A few of the rogues escaped," he said. "Not so many that we'd need to worry about them on their own, but—my people's reports say they headed north. Straight toward a troop of vampires that just annexed my New York property and is now moving on from there. It looks like the rogues have even more allies than we realized. And they've just incited a full-scale paranormal war."

I groaned, tipping my head back against the cushion of the water. So much for resting. But the resolve I'd felt during the battle only hardened inside me.

"Fine," I said. "They've got no idea what they're getting into when they mess with a dragon. It's time to show *all* our enemies what a bad idea that is, once and for all."

DRAGON'S FATE

THE DRAGON SHIFTER'S MATES #4

CHAPTER 1

Ren

As THE PRIVATE jet soared down toward the canine shifter estate, resolve sat tight and heavy in my chest. I should have been arriving here to meet the last group of shifter-kin as the newly confirmed mate of their alpha. I should have been bringing good news. I was their dragon shifter—the last dragon shifter alive. By taking the four alphas of the kin-groups as my mates, I was supposed to unite all shifter kind and end the turmoil they'd all been through.

Instead I'd have to announce that we might be on the verge of a paranormal war. That was what Marco, the feline alpha I'd consummated my mate-bond with less than a day ago, had called it. And I hadn't consummated my bond with the canine alpha yet. Sitting in the seats closest to the jet's door, West looked even more grim and tense than usual.

We'd been through plenty of turmoil already, but this time it was worse. Before, it'd just been our own kind we'd had to fight, rogue shifters who wanted to disrupt the status quo. Now, the remaining members of the rogues' sort-of pack had fled to the vampires, and the vampires, for whatever reason, had decided to attack us.

All we knew for sure was that the bloodsuckers had taken over a house that Marco's feline kin used as a local base of operations near New York City. He'd told his kin who'd survived the attack to meet us here, at the closest shifter estate nearby.

My hands clenched as the plane bumped across the runway. The view of the majestic pines outside the window reminded me of our strength. I'd come through a hell of a lot in the last few weeks since my alphas had come to me and woken me up to my true role. I'd faced challenge after challenge and won. No undead creeps were going to get the better of us now.

The jet rumbled to a stop. Kylie reached across the armrest to grip my hand. My best friend, who was as human as I'd used to think I was, had come to visit me with even less of an idea of the shifter community's turmoil than I'd had, but she was still here. Still supporting me even though she'd seen me at my most vicious. Still giving me that brilliant smile as her neon pink pixie cut shone under the overhead lights.

I didn't know whether I was more worried or grateful that she was here. But I wasn't pushing her away anymore.

West stood up first to open the plane door. The wolf shifter's dark green eyes blazed with concern for his kin and anger at the people who'd put them in danger. Seeing him like that, my heart squeezed.

The rest of us got up to follow West. "How many of your kin were heading to the estate?" Aaron asked Marco. The eagle shifter, alpha to the avian kin, had a habit of focusing in on the facts. Hearing his calm, warm voice always settled my nerves at least a little.

"There were seven of them using the house," Marco said. "The last I heard, three of them were on the run—one of them injured. We'll get the whole story now. They should have made it here before us." The jaguar shifter's usual mischievous gaze had darkened. He raked an anxious hand through his jagged black hair as he stalked down the aisle toward the exit.

Nate, the last of my alphas, stood back to let Kylie and me go ahead of him. He rested his strong hand on my shoulder. Tall and brawny as the grizzly bear he could shift into, he'd always had my back. But he was a total softie when we weren't under threat.

The early morning breeze rushed over me as we clattered down the steps. It was cool and thick with the smell of the pines. A high stone wall bordered the runway. I headed in the other direction, along a winding path through the trees, and discovered a house that matched the wall at the other end.

To call it a "house" was really underselling it. Kylie sucked in an awed breath when she saw it. The place was a mansion, no doubt about it. Three expansive floors encased in solid stone blocks, with an arch of dark hardwood over the heavy door.

Several of West's kin had come out to meet us. If we'd been making our expected visit a day or two from now, there might have been a crowd. As it was, I couldn't help feeling grateful to see so few faces beaming at me in greeting. The canine shifters had always been welcoming to me—overwhelmingly so sometimes—but danger seemed to chase me wherever I went. I'd rather have fewer kin in the crossfire.

"Dragon shifter," they murmured first, with respectful bobs of their heads. The one who held himself with the most authority, one of West's lieutenants I guessed, turned to his alpha.

"Three feline kin arrived a couple hours ago. We offered them guest rooms, and the one who was wounded has been seen to."

Marco stepped up beside West. "Is she all right?"

The lieutenant—a coyote shifter by his scent—nodded quickly. "Her injuries were serious, but not fatal. She's sleeping now."

"And there's been no sign of vampires in this area—no word from any of the villages closer to New York City?" West asked.

"The settlement by the edge of New York City," the coyote shifter said with a grimace. "We got word that they'd scented vampires in the area not long after I last spoke with you. Then we lost contact. I sent a few of our people out there to check first hand."

West's jaw set. "You let me know as soon as you hear back."

One of the other canine kin, a fennec fox shifter with a narrow face and a shock of tawny hair, had zeroed his attention in on Kylie. "What's a *human* doing here?" he said in a needling voice.

I bristled. "She's my friend. Anywhere I go, she's welcome."

The fox shifter cocked his head. "I'm just saying, it seems like we've got major shifter business to take care of here, and I don't see—"

"*Felix*," West snapped. He pushed in front of us to glower at his underling, who stood a good half a foot shorter than the wolf shifter's lanky frame. West's teeth bared slightly. "As should be obvious, she's here with my permission."

The fox shifter's body had gone rigid. "Yes, sir. Of course. I wasn't thinking." He raised his chin high enough to show the pale length of his neck. I hadn't seen the gesture before, but there was something clearly apologetic about it.

Aaron had come up beside me. He leaned over to murmur by my ear. "Among canine shifters, exposing the throat is their most overt sign of submission."

West had already relaxed at the posturing. "All right," he said in his usual gruff voice. "Maybe try to do a little more thinking before you start shooting your mouth off next time? We *do* have a lot of important business to see to."

"And you'd better believe I'm going to help with that business," Kylie piped up. "Just wait. In a few days you'll be wondering why you don't have humans like me around all the time."

Felix raised a skeptical eyebrow, but he was smart enough not to say anything with his alpha watching over him.

"Let's go in," West said. "We should talk with Marco's kin, find out exactly what happened."

The outside of the mansion had looked kind of hard and cold, but warmth washed over us as soon as we stepped inside. The walls were painted a subdued gold tone and thick rugs covered the floors. The front hall opened into a great room with a massive stone-lined fireplace that must be incredibly cozy in the winter. A hint of fresh-baked bread in the air caught my attention, and my stomach rumbled.

"I'll summon the feline kin," West's coyote shifter lieutenant said. His gaze slid to two of the other attendants. "Bring the alphas and our dragon shifter—*and* her friend—some breakfast."

West gave him a thin but approving smile. I sank onto one of the wool sofas, the cushion immediately enveloping me. This place was a lot like its master, I observed with a tickle of amusement. Tough and apparently impenetrable on the outside, but with unexpected pleasures if you made your way past those walls.

West was the only one of the four alphas I hadn't yet consummated my mate bond with. We'd had a tumultuous run of it over the last few weeks. He'd been skeptical of me from the start, but I'd thought he was softening toward me lately, at least a little. It was so hard to tell with him. But the moments of passion he'd allowed himself with me… My skin heated just remembering them, even with everything else on my mind.

Kylie sat down on the sofa at my left and Nate at my right. The bear shifter gave my knee a reassuring touch. Aaron took an armchair across from us, his golden Disney-prince hair gleaming in the dawn sunlight streaking through the picture window. West and Marco stayed on their feet. West stood stiffly, his arms folded over his chest, while Marco paced.

"This never should have happened," he muttered. "We barely scuffed up those vamps the other day. We *settled* things with the king. Why is he going to listen to a few mangy rogues whining to him anyway?"

He fell silent when breakfast appeared, buttered bread and jam and slices of fried ham that made my mouth water despite myself. I put together a quick sandwich to ease the pangs in my stomach.

I'd only gotten in a few bites when Marco's kin appeared, one of the figures familiar: Leonard the lion shifter, one of Marco's lieutenants, his round face split by jutting cheekbones. We'd had kind of an unfortunate first meeting. That was, he'd kidnapped me, thinking that was the easiest way to get me to his alpha.

Now, he looked even more beaten down than when Marco had laid into him for that mistake. His eyes were hollowed and a slash of red ran across one of those high cheekbones where a wound was only just sealing. It looked like the scrape of a bullet. My gut clenched. I put my sandwich down on the coffee table.

"Look what the cat dragged in," Marco said, but he couldn't quite work a teasing lilt into his voice. He motioned Leonard and his companion, a stocky silver-hair woman who smelled like a lynx, to one of the other sofas. "Sit down before you talk. You've clearly done enough running for one night. We just need to know what happened at the house, and then you can get back to your napping."

Leonard dropped onto the sofa and leaned his head into his hands. He rubbed them up and down over his face.

"We had no idea they were coming," he said hoarsely. "We never keep watch that closely at the house—it's in the middle of the suburbs for Christ's sake. Not where you'd ever think… Right after sundown, they blasted down the door. At least ten of them, maybe fifteen. I couldn't have counted. They charged all through the place, spraying bullets. I barely pulled Lindy out of the way in time. Sandra and I carried her out to the car and got out of there. There wasn't anything else to do."

A chill ran over me. All of us around the great room had tensed. "Spraying bullets," I repeated. "They all had guns?" Some of the rogue shifters had fought us with pistols and rifles, going against one of the firmest shifter laws, but their resources when it came to human weaponry had seemed to be limited. I didn't know what restrictions vampires faced—or didn't.

Leonard shuddered. "They had *machine* guns, most of them. Pistol-sized, but still not anything I'd want to tangle with again. The bloodsuckers didn't even try to bite us. Knew they'd lose if it came to hand-to-hand fighting." His lips curled back. "Treaty-breakers *and* cowards."

Machine guns. Fucking hell. I saw the same horror echoed in

all the alphas' expressions. How could we fight against an army of undead stocked up with military grade firearms?

"And they'll be dealt with as the treaty-breakers they are," Marco said, his voice taut. "I don't suppose they offered any clue as to what this surprise assault was prompted by? Blasting up our homes isn't one of their usual hobbies."

Leonard shook his head. "They didn't say anything at all. Just opened fire. And the other four in the house—they'd fallen before I even realized what was happening."

He faltered, his face crumpling. Marco stepped toward him.

"It isn't your fault," he said firmly. "You couldn't have expected an attack like that. And believe me, the bloodsuckers are going to pay."

"Is there anything else you saw or heard that might be useful to us, for fighting back?" Aaron asked.

"I… I can't think of anything. It all happened so fast." Leonard rubbed his face again. He was obviously exhausted.

"Sandra?" Marco said.

The lynx shifter looked equally worn-out—and shell shocked. She swayed a little on her cushion. "I did hear one of the vamps say something to one of the others," she said. "That—that they'd been hoping the shifters would take each other out, but handling it themselves was more fun." She winced at that last word.

My hackles rose. If there'd been a vampire in the room with us right then, I don't think anything could have restrained me from shooting my dragon talons from my hand and slicing its head straight off.

"They know we're getting stronger," I said. "Because I'm here. Because there's a dragon shifter to bring the kin together again." I inhaled sharply. "And I am going to do that. What Marco said is right. The vampires are going to pay, any way I can make them."

It was almost painful seeing the hope light behind the anguish in the lynx shifter's eyes. I'd better fulfill that promise, even if I wasn't entirely sure how yet.

"All right, you two," Marco said with a shooing motion. "You did what you could. You got out of there alive, and saved Lindy too. Now get your rest. We might need you by nightfall."

"What happens at nightfall?" Kylie asked as Leonard and Sandra headed back to their rooms.

"Not all the legends about vampires are true," West said. "But sunlight does burn them to a crisp. They can stroll around in the subway tunnels all right, but they can't make any attacks above ground until the sun goes back down."

"So we've got some time to decide our next steps." Nate leaned forward, running his hand over his thick chestnut-brown hair. "We should find out if there's been vampire activity near any of the other city centers where they have their clans. New York is the biggest one—what else is there?"

"Los Angeles," Aaron said. "Las Vegas. Chicago. And Atlanta. But they've got smaller pockets scattered through the smaller cities too."

"I don't understand," I burst out. "Why would they suddenly attack us like this? I know shifters and vampires aren't, like, friendly, but this… the comment Sandra said she overheard… It sounds like they hate us."

Marco grimaced. "There's no love lost between vamps and shifters, that's for sure. We keep the peace with our treaty rather than any affection on either side—the same as with the fae. It's always been easier for both of our peoples to keep to our own territories rather than get into some kind of war. I don't know why they've changed their minds about that."

"But it is war. No one could argue that. With guns that powerful…" I swallowed hard.

"We have our advantages," Nate said. "We can prepare by daylight, but we know how to fight in the dark as well."

"We won't be easy targets when they can't take us by surprise," West added.

I swiped my hand across my mouth. "Okay. So sunlight burns them up. What else can we use to our advantage? What else are they weak against?"

Marco raised an eyebrow as he looked at me. "After sunlight? I'd say what they're most afraid of is fire."

CHAPTER 2

Ren

THE STONE WALL around the canine estate looked more than solid enough to keep out automatic gunfire. But of course that wouldn't help us if the vampires found their way over it. I bit my lip, considering it from where I stood in the front yard.

"What else do we have to worry about with vampires? They suck people's blood, they're stronger and faster than regular people—but not more than us—and it seems like they've got access to heavy artillery… Can they do the whole transforming into bats thing? Leap tall buildings with a single jump?"

Marco chuckled. "Shifters have the monopoly on animal transformations, princess, so no need to worry about that. And the bloodsuckers aren't Superman clones either. Their biggest advantage is that they're damned hard to kill, being already dead and all."

"Sunlight does the trick," West said, giving the sky a grim

look. The sun was nearly at its noon peak, pouring summer heat over us. "And fire. A clean beheading. Not much else."

"Wooden stakes?" Kylie suggested, making a sweeping gesture with her arm as if brandishing one.

"I don't know anyone who's tried that," Nate said with a thoughtful frown.

Aaron would probably know—but he'd gotten a phone call five minutes ago and walked off around the house to talk undisturbed.

"Well, it's not as if we're likely to get close enough to stake any of them if they've got their guns blasting anyway," I said. "Fire will do the trick."

But my dragon fire would only help the kin here on the canine estate. My thoughts leapt to the shifter village we'd spent a couple nights in after my alphas had first found me. All the kin there who'd been so awed to meet me, to know the dragon shifter had finally returned…

Those small settlements didn't have big stone walls to halt bullets—and they didn't have any dragons to pour flames down on their attackers either. Protecting my people would be a hell of a lot easier if there were more shifters like me.

Maybe someday there would be. The thought gave me a twinge low in my belly. Once upon a time there'd been four dragon shifters—my mother and my sisters and me. If I fulfilled my bond with all of my alphas, then we could start thinking about raising children of our own.

But not now. Not into a world like this. I could fight for the shifters with everything I had as long as I only had myself to protect. It was saving me, trying to save my sisters, that had held my mother back when the rogues had first attacked all those years ago. She'd only been able to save me, and only by leaving the rest of her people behind.

Aaron emerged from the shadows around the house, fallen pine needles rustling under his feet. One look at his expression was enough to tell me he had more bad news.

"They hit one of yours too?" Marco said as the eagle shifter joined us.

Aaron nodded, his mouth set at a pained angle. "A small settlement just up the coast from L.A. The vampires surrounded the village so they could shoot at anyone who tried to fly out. A few were able to make it, but most… It was a slaughter. Alice is seeing that the survivors are looked after." He'd sent his sister back to the avian estate on the coast when the rest of us had headed to West's, so he'd have someone he completely trusted overseeing his own people.

My stomach turned. We'd had similar reports from the village of canine shifters near New York, an enclave of feline shifters not far from Atlanta, and a collective of Nate's disparate kin a few hours outside Las Vegas. The vampires had made their bloody intentions crystal clear. But they hadn't made any demands.

"And we still don't have any real idea what the vampires want?" I said.

"They want us all dead," West muttered. "That's obvious."

"I know that," I said, resisting the urge to snap at him. "I mean *why*. If we knew why they've suddenly turned on us, we might be able to find some leverage we could use."

Nate made a discomforted sound. "As far as I can tell, the only 'leverage' the bloodsuckers are going to understand is being burned to a crisp. And I'm looking forward to seeing you teach them that lesson."

"If I were going to hazard a guess," Aaron said, "from what Marco's kin told us… They liked seeing us weakened without a dragon shifter. It reassured them when our kin started to pick at each other, new conflicts developing. They were hoping we'd keep heading down that road until we were right at each other's throats. But we've come back. As you said, we're getting stronger again, more unified."

He gave me a smile that was tight but genuine. "They may have realized this is their last chance to hit us before we're all the way to our former strength. And they got used to the idea that they might be rid of us. They didn't want to go back to how things were before, to having to work with us and make compromises."

"They can forget about compromising after the mess they've made of things around here," Marco said with a show of teeth.

But the vamps still had us at a disadvantage. I studied the wall again, thinking about all those villages that didn't have this kind of protection. "What exactly are the restrictions against shifters using weapons? Where do you draw the line?"

"We're not shooting back at them," West said.

"I *know*. Nothing that's intended as a weapon. But is there a law against using *anything* other than our bodies in a fight?"

"What are you thinking, Ren?" Nate asked.

I motioned to the field beyond the estate's gate. "We want to burn the vamps to a crisp. Am I the only one allowed to do that, or can your kin fight with fire too?"

Aaron's gaze turned distant with thought. "Anything we'd hold and attack someone directly with, like a torch, would be forbidden. But there are other ways we could use fire."

"We still have the whole afternoon to prepare," I said. "Could you have your kin lay down a ring of flammable material around their villages—around the other estates, too—that they could easily light up if the vampires showed up? It'd be mostly for protection… but if they happened to set it off while some of the vamps were walking by, and those vamps happened to catch on fire, that'd get a pass, right?"

Marco's lips curled into a smirk. "I'm liking the way you think more and more every day, princess."

"It would unsettle them too," Nate said. "Easier for us to pick them off in the confusion. A good shove into the flames…" He wiped his palms together with a satisfied expression.

"Our kin will need to clear the vegetation from the area," Aaron said. "We don't want to end up burning a whole forest down. But there's time for that. It could at least hold the vampires back." Nodding to himself, he pulled out his phone. "I've got some more calls to make."

Kylie clapped her hands. "Well, *I'm* not bound by any shifter laws, am I? I wonder if I can scrounge up some kind of flame-thrower. I can definitely put you in touch with people who'll supply fuel on the down-low."

I smiled at my best friend. If she had a superpower, it was managing to make a friend or at least an acquaintance out of everyone she met, which was a lot of people. With all her connections, she could obtain just about anything you could possibly need, at least in the regular human part of the world. Which my alphas had first discovered back in New York when she'd gotten a lead on a puzzle the rest of us had drawn a blank on.

"I'll take those names," Nate said to Kylie.

"There," she said, reaching for her own phone. "You tell that Felix guy I'm already making myself more useful than he's doing, West."

The wolf shifter smirked at that comment. "I might do that right now." He waved a hand toward the house.

Someone must have been watching, because a minute later, several of West's attendants hurried out. The tawny-haired fennec fox shifter was in their midst. He glanced at Kylie as he hustled past. His expression switched to a glower when she gave him a thumbs-up and a broad grin.

"We need a ring of ground cleared just beyond the estate wall, at least ten feet wide," the canine alpha told his kin. "Any brush that'd hold a flame, collect it for us to lay down the middle. We can douse it with gasoline for good measure."

"Hold on," I said as they headed for the gate. "You don't need that here. *I'm* here."

West gave me a baleful look. "You're just one dragon, Sparks, in case you forgot. A dragon who can only manage to stay a dragon maybe a half hour if you're lucky. If the vamps turn up here, we'll have to hold them off for the whole night."

"It's not going to take me the whole night to fry them," I retorted. "It's not like I'm going to toast one and then take a ten-minute whirl around the estate before I get around to the next."

"And if they come in waves? If you miss some before you run out of juice?"

I crossed my arm over my chest. "I can pace myself. And I've shifted twice in the same day before. Night shouldn't be any different."

He sighed. "Look, Sparks, it seems to me we're better off having the extra protection just in case one dragon isn't enough to save the day. These are my people here, and I'll be damned if I don't do everything I can to protect them. Unless you have some brilliant plan for destroying every vampire out there before the sun even goes down?"

He had a point. I knew he had a point. It was just that the way he made that point niggled at me. "No," I admitted. "I don't. Believe me, if I did, I wouldn't be keeping quiet about it."

"Oh, believe *me*, I know that," West said with a glint in his eyes. Before I could decide whether it was teasing or hostile, another thought struck me.

"*Could* we take the battle to the vampires?" I asked. "They're totally vulnerable during the day, right? If we found their hideouts and—"

Marco, who'd stayed near us, started shaking his head. "One compliment I'll willingly give the bloodsuckers—they're nothing if not painstaking when it comes to being careful with their daytime routines. They'll be behind about twenty locked doors in some deep dark basement—dozens of deep dark basements, all across those cities. And we don't even know which basements. I suppose if we burned the entire city to the ground…"

I exhaled sharply. "I get it. No luck there. Maybe we need to find ourselves some secret basements to hide out in too."

"If things get desperate, I get the impression your friend might have some ideas on that score," Marco said, looking amused.

Yeah, Kylie probably knew at least a handful of abandoned buildings we could hole up in for a while. But that would only help us until the vampires found us again. We needed to convince them it was too much trouble trying to exterminate us —or we needed to exterminate them while they tried.

The gate squeaked open again. Felix came in, holding up a young man so wobbly and bloody it looked like he'd have fallen over without the help. My heart leapt into my throat.

Marco's eyes widened. "Timothy," he said, striding over.

The injured shifter gave the feline alpha a hazy look.

"He just stumbled over to where we were working," Felix said. "He hasn't said anything. I'm not sure he even can."

"Get him inside," West said. "Quickly. He needs rest and someone to look at those wounds."

Marco took Timothy's other arm. He and Felix led the poor

guy into the estate house together. I hurried after them, my heart thudding. Had the vampires made another attack? Just now, in the middle of the day? That shouldn't even be possible.

Timothy's feet started to drag on the floor. Marco flinched at the sound and hefted him higher. "We've got you. Just a little farther."

"Over here," West said, opening a door just down the hall from the great room. An office, from the looks of it, with two walls of built-in bookshelves, a desk, an armchair—and a sofa, where Marco and Felix laid the feline shifter down.

Timothy shuddered and coughed. "Water!" Marco snapped. Felix went running. The jaguar shifter knelt beside his fallen kin.

Timothy hadn't been shot—or at least, if he had, those weren't the wounds currently bleeding. A deep gouge across the side of his ribs was slowly shrinking. A large chunk of hair had been scraped off his scalp. I cringed inside as I noted each injury. What had happened to him?

He obviously couldn't tell us yet.

"I can call one of my kin to—" West began.

Marco cut him off with a jerk of his hand. "I'll do it. He's my responsibility."

He flicked a jaguar claw from one index finger and dug it into the flesh of his wrist. I winced outright at the sudden stream of blood. Jaw clenched, Marco let some trickle over Timothy's side and then his head, combining the healing power of his healthy body with his underling's best efforts. Then he pressed his opposite palm to his wrist to encourage his own cut to heal.

Timothy murmured, his limbs relaxing into the couch. His eyelids fluttered. Felix reappeared clutching a glass of water. "Thank you," Marco said, accepting it. He returned to his kin and held the glass to Timothy's lips.

The feline shifter managed a couple of swallows. He exhaled

a relieved breath. Marco turned to set the glass on the side table, and Timothy's hand shot out to grasp the front of his alpha's shirt.

"Alpha," he rasped.

"Hey," Marco said, putting his hand over Timothy's. "You need to recover. It's a miracle you managed to escape them at all." He glanced up at me. "He's one of the missing four from my New York house."

He shouldn't know much more than Leonard and Sandra had, then. But Timothy yanked on Marco's shirt again. "No," he said. "Didn't escape. They sent me. I'm a message."

Beside me, West stiffened. Marco's gaze sharpened. "What's the message, Timothy?"

"Tonight," the injured shifter choked out. "The king will parlay with you tonight, at full-dark, by the Marveille crossroads."

CHAPTER 3

Nate

I ROUNDED a corner in the canine estate's halls a little too quickly and bumped shoulders with one of West's kin. The jackal shifter took one look at my face and cowered backward. His chin twitched upward with that instinctive reaction all the canines had to show their throats when avoiding a fight. "My apologies, alpha. I promise to be more careful."

Shit. I must look something fierce for him to react like that. I willed my expression as calm as I could manage—which probably wasn't all that much, consider the amount of the frustration churning inside me. "It's all right," I said. "I bumped into *you*. No offense taken."

He didn't look completely convinced. As he darted off, I forced myself to stay in place, leaning back against the wall. I swiped my hand over my face as if I could rub the tension out of it.

I'd been prowling the estate for the better part of an hour, and I didn't think I'd burnt off any of that frustrated energy. I'd already made all the calls I could to my lieutenants and other kin. Every settlement within half a night's drive of any vampire stronghold was already making preparations to fend off their gunfire with fire of our own.

Normally I'd have been flying out there to join them, to stand on the front lines. But Ren needed me. Our bond was only just solidified. She was still so new to her role as dragon shifter.

And even if she could have spared me for the night, we were meant to parlay with the vampire king just after nightfall not far from here.

Maybe this whole mess would be settled then. But after hearing about the mass murders the vamps had already committed against my kin and the other alphas'… I wasn't counting on it. I sure as hell wasn't in a compromising mood.

But lumbering around the house like a rampaging grizzly in a man's body obviously wasn't helping anything. I dragged in a breath and pushed myself off the wall. I should probably try to get in some sleep before it was time to head out. We might have a very long night ahead of us.

I headed toward the south end of the third floor, where the main bedrooms were, but my restless feet took me right past the door to my own suite. I stopped in front of Ren's. She'd gone up here after lunch to prepare herself for the night ahead. Maybe she'd appreciate the company.

I eased open the door and found myself looking at my mate's back where she was poised on the sitting room floor. She had her legs crossed and her hands resting on her knees, her head tipped slightly back, her dark brown hair cascading past her shoulders. I loomed high enough over her to see her eyes were closed.

Whatever zone she was trying to get into, I didn't want to

disturb her. I stepped backward, but the door hinges squeaked at my tug. Ren's eyes popped open with a jump of her shoulders.

"Sorry," I said, holding up my hands. "I didn't mean to interrupt."

She groaned and flopped down on her back. "It's okay. I'm not sure I was getting much of anywhere anyway."

She seemed to mean that as an invitation. I hunkered down on the floor beside my mate. "Where were you trying to get?"

Ren squirmed a little closer to me, and I was more than happy to loop my arm across her waist as she rested her head against my leg. Just that simple touch eased the tension in me so much more than anything else I'd tried. Maybe I hadn't come in here just for her comfort but for my own as well.

"I was hoping practicing some meditation might help me extend my shifting ability," she said. "I want to be able to hold the shift longer. Long enough to deal with every single vampire we need to fight."

"Hopefully we won't be fighting any of them, if we can settle things with the parlay."

She gave a dismissive-sounding snort, which was about the way I felt about that possibility too. "I have to be ready."

"You've been picking up the skill really quickly, you know," I said, stroking my thumb over her side. She was wearing the same T-shirt she'd had on this morning, but the warmth of her skin radiated through the soft fabric. "It's not exactly the same situation, but for kids, when they're first learning, it usually takes them a few years from when they can manage their first partial shift to reach a full shift. And then it's several more years before any of us gets to the point that we can hold our animal form nearly indefinitely. You got through the first stage in just a few days."

"Because I'm not a kid," Ren said. "Because I should have

been doing it all along. But the endurance part is taking a lot longer. I don't have several years. I don't even have several days. The vampires have already hurt us so much more than the rogues managed to."

"They're nasty, but they're smart," I said. "And organized, and disciplined. Things the rogues definitely weren't, or they wouldn't have rejected the kin groups in the first place. But we can still beat the bloodsuckers. You're doing everything you can. The vampires are *afraid* of you, you know. That's why they're attacking now. They know that with every day you're making the entire shifter community stronger and stronger."

"And I'm going to keep doing that," Ren said. I loved seeing that fiery determination light in her amber eyes.

Then she yawned, covering her face with her arm to try to hide it.

"Okay," I said. "I think both of us need some rest to be ready for tonight. You can meditate more in your sleep."

"I don't think it works like that," Ren muttered. I got up, sweeping her into my arms, and a squeak of protest slipped from her lips. "Nate! I can make it from here to the bed."

"But this is more fun," I said.

She muttered a little more, but she also nestled her head against my shoulder. I tucked my chin over her hair as I carried her to the bed. My mate was strong, yes, but it didn't hurt her to let the rest of us be strong for her every now and then.

I climbed onto the bed and lay down with her, sharing a pillow. Ren ruffled my hair. "My big strong bear," she said as if she'd read my thoughts, with so much affection my heart thumped happily. I bent my head to kiss her. She slid her arm behind my neck as she kissed me back, pulling me even closer against her, and suddenly sleep was the last thing on my mind.

My hand skimmed down her side to her hip and back up to

cup her breast. Ren's breath stuttered against my mouth. She kissed me harder as I drew her nipple to a stiff peak, a whimper working its way from her throat. When she drew back, her cheeks were flushed and her eyes sparkling.

"We should get that rest," she said. "But maybe if we're *really* quick, there's room for a little more fun first?"

I laughed. "I can't say no to that." Then I rolled right onto her, intent on turning that whimper into a moan.

Ren

Kylie was exactly where Aaron had told me he'd last seen her, in a small lounge room just off the main hall. She grinned when I came in, unfolding her petite body from her armchair. "Ren!" Then her expression turned abruptly serious. "Is it time for you to leave already?"

I shook my head, sitting down on the chair beside hers. "We've got about another hour. I've just been thinking..." I paused, trying to figure out the best way to approach this subject. The last thing I wanted was my best friend thinking I was trying to ditch her. But I wasn't going to feel okay unless we had this one last conversation.

"Thinking what?" Kylie prodded, watching me.

I met her gaze, hoping she could read the emotion in mine. "You know how much I appreciate having you here. How glad I've been to have you on my side for the whole time we've been friends. So I promise you I'm not saying this because of what I *want*. But because you matter so much to me, I have to ask, now that things have gotten even more dangerous—are you sure you want to stay here?"

Kylie gave me a wry smile. "Where else would I go?"

"Back to your old life, I guess," I said. "You have our apartment—I can keep paying my share of the rent, and hopefully I'll be able to visit lots. You have your job. The vampires won't hassle you there. But as long as you're here with the shifters… I don't think it'll matter that you're not one too. They're not being careful with their bullets."

"Okay," Kylie said. "I get why you're worried. I'm not exactly feeling super keen about taking on gun-toting vampires either. But can I ask you something, and you answer totally honestly?"

"Of course," I said.

She tipped her head, studying my expression even more carefully now. "If you could have your life be any way you wanted right now, just the most perfect possible situation, what would that look like?"

God, what a question. Just the idea of being able to shed all this conflict made my heart swell and ache at the same time. I let my mind drift into that imaginary scenario. What would it look like if I could have everything I wanted? I'd promised her total honesty.

"I'd be living with all four of the guys, everyone happy and getting along, no more doubts between us. Going from estate to estate and to different towns, I guess, helping solve whatever little squabbles came up. And you'd be there, of course. So we could hang out and have some girl time whenever I didn't have other stuff to take care of."

I focused on her again. "But I have no idea when—if—I'll get to that point. And that's just what *I'd* want. You've got a life too. I wouldn't want you sticking around if you'd be happier living a normal life. One where there weren't vampires taking shots at us and who knows what else in the future."

Kylie beamed back at me as if no possible future horror

could faze her at all. "What's so great about normal?" she said. "I just wanted to know where I'd fit in when you're not worrying about my safety. Because this is exactly where I want to be too. If you're happy to have me sticking around, if I can do some kind of job here instead of that crappy one back in NYC, I'm totally in. Sure, hanging out with shifters can be kind of scary, but it's also pretty amazing."

I swallowed hard, so much joy bubbling up inside me that I didn't know what to do with it. "You're sure?" I said. "Really, *really* sure?"

Kylie laughed. "I've had a lot of time to think about it in the last couple days, you know. And there really hasn't been even one moment where I wished I hadn't come out here. So you're meant to be queen of all shifters—I'm pretty sure I'm meant to be your right-hand girl. I might not have any paranormal destiny, but it feels fated to me."

The emotion overwhelmed me. Talking didn't seem like enough. I hopped up and grabbed my best friend in a hug. She squeezed me back. "There," she said. "I'm glad we got that settled. Once and for all? You really need to stop trying to protect me. I'm a big girl."

"I know," I said. "I promise, this is the last time I'll bring it up. I just wanted to be completely sure. If something happened to you and I thought you'd only been there for my sake…"

"Nope," Kylie said. "I'm one hundred percent in this for me too. I mean, just look at these digs." She gestured to the room around her with a mischievous glint in her eyes. But when she turned back to me she'd gone a bit serious again. "I know what I'm getting into here, Ren. And I'm ready for it."

I exhaled and gave her a crooked smile. "Good. I really hope that I am too. Come on, we'd better grab some dinner. I'd rather not be fighting vamps on an empty stomach."

CHAPTER 4

Ren

"DOES this crossroads give them any kind of an advantage if this comes down to a fight?" I asked West. I was sitting next to him in the jeep he'd picked from the assorted vehicles on his estate.

He'd driven quickly most of the way out here, but the last twenty miles we were taking slow and wary. The vibration of the engine thrummed through the seat beneath me. A matching rumble carried through the air from the cars ahead of and behind us.

"Immediately around the crossroads the terrain is pretty open," West said without taking his eyes off the road. "Not much shelter for us. I'd prefer surroundings like what we have right here if I had the choice."

He nodded to the pine forests looming on either side of the narrow highway. In the deepening night, the dark points of the treetops cut into the shadowy blue of the clouded sky. The moon still gleamed faintly through a thinner patch of haze.

One of his kin in the back had been in communication with the scouts West had sent ahead earlier. "Rayanne says there's at least fifty of the vamps gathered now," he said, a worried note in his voice.

West's jaw tightened. The other alphas had come too, of course, in other cars, and a few dozen of West's kin as well in case we needed back-up. But…

"If fifty vamps means fifty guns, we won't stand much of a chance," I said.

"No kidding, Sparks," West said. "Do you want to head back?"

I couldn't tell if he meant the question seriously or as a jab. "Is that really an option?" I said.

He gave a choked laugh. "I guess that depends on how much diplomacy matters to you."

"I'm not thinking about diplomacy. I'm thinking about not getting us killed."

"Believe me, that's at the top of my priority list too. Any brilliant suggestions for how to weight the odds?"

They might be calling us to this parlay to try to slaughter me and the alphas the way the rogues had failed to. Or they might honestly be willing to negotiate some kind of peace. Ha. On the other hand, if we *didn't* show up, we were pretty much ensuring that they'd immediately attack the shifter community again. Horrible situation or awful situation. I'll take neither, please!

Of course, *that* definitely wasn't an option. I sighed. "I didn't even know vampires existed a month ago. Shouldn't you have a better idea than I do?"

"I don't think you'd like the idea I'm having," West muttered.

What the hell was that supposed to mean?

Just then, the phone's alert went off again. The guy in the back made a disgruntled sound. "Another truck full of the bloodsuckers showed up. And they're fanning out around the crossroads. Blending into the darkness like they do, but our people can scent them. It looks like they're planning on having us surrounded after we arrive."

That didn't sound like preparation for an honest conversation. West and I exchanged a glance. His expression had gone even grimmer.

"We can't meet them like that," I said, braced for another snarky comment.

But the wolf shifter nodded. "No. There are risks and then there's insanity. Bertrand, is there anywhere decent to park between here and there?"

His lieutenant scanned the area on a phone map. "There's an old gas station a couple miles down the road. Out of business, so there won't be anyone there, and the lot looks a decent size."

"That's our place, then. Tell the other cars to convene there."

"And then what?" I asked.

West's smile was still grim. "Then we tell the vampires we've met them close enough to halfway, and if they want us, they can come to us, on ground *we* chose. And if they try any funny business while they're arriving, we deal with them then."

"The guns," one of the guys in the back said, and cut himself off with a swipe across his mouth as if worried he sounded too nervous.

"If the vamps start firing, we should get out of there," I said. "Everyone in the cars, head back to the estate. Tell them that too."

The second I stopped speaking, I wondered if I'd crossed a line, giving orders to West's kin. But he didn't comment. I guessed that meant he agreed with the plan. He'd pressed his foot to the gas, speeding up so we'd reach our new destination sooner. The sky was almost fully black now.

"I'll cover everyone," I added. "Lay down some fire of my own to hold them off while the rest of you are getting away."

West's gaze shot to me again. "Don't be stupid, Ren. You'll need to get out of there too. You're the last one we can afford to lose."

"I'm the most likely one to make sure we don't lose anyone," I said. "I can dodge a few bullets."

"You haven't faced guns like this before."

He wasn't entirely wrong. But my mind slid back to Fisher, the guy I'd stolen for in exchange for food and shelter alongside a bunch of other street kids when I'd been fending for myself after Mom had disappeared. To the revolver he'd always kept shoved in the back of his jeans. To the guns I'd caught glimpses of on some of his colleagues when they'd come to collect.

"You don't know what I've seen before this. I'd bet I've seen more guns than you have."

"That doesn't mean you should throw yourself at them," West snapped.

I tensed, but he looked immediately chagrined. Because he regretted saying that to me or he regretted saying it that way in front of his kin? Who knew? But I felt, underneath the tense anticipation coiled through his body, a quiver of concern.

Maybe he didn't want to put all his faith in me to save his kin. Maybe he didn't trust my ideas. But whatever the case, he was also at least a little bit worried about *me*.

The retort that had been on my tongue wisped away. "I'm not looking to get shot," I said, my voice softening. "I'll only do what I have to, to make sure we all get out. And all of us includes me."

"Well, I'm not leaving until you're leaving," West said—gruffly, but even though I wouldn't have expected anything else, hearing him say it brought a heady flutter into my chest. Like when he'd kissed me last night, with a new tenderness I hoped I'd get to experience again.

But not now, obviously. The arched beams of the gas station sign came into view up ahead. The truck and the sedan ahead of us turned in, and West followed them.

We parked along the edge of the abandoned lot. With a rev of an engine, any of the cars should be able to leap the shoulder back onto the road if we needed to make a hasty exit.

Dry leaves that must have been left over from last fall crunched under my feet when I stepped out. The sign overhead creaked as the wind swung it on its chains. The pumps must have been completely dry—not even the faintest tang of gasoline reached my sharp shifter nose. Only the pine scent of the forest, like back at West's estate, with an added edge of rusting metal.

"Give me the phone," West said, holding out his hand. His lieutenant handed it over. As the rest of our contingent spilled out of their vehicles, the canine alpha called up one of his scouts.

"Rayanne. Slight change of plans. The vamps can meet us at a gas station six miles down the highway from that crossroads. You tell them that from as far of a distance as you can manage, and then hop on that motorcycle of yours and come join us. I don't want them taking any 'disappointment' out on you."

The other alphas had ambled over to join us. "Let's see if they still want to play ball when we're wise to their tricks," Marco said with a fierce smirk.

"I'd imagine they'll realize why we're changing the plan," Aaron said. "If they believe they have anything to gain from coming to a compromise at all, they'll accept. If violence was their only goal…" His jaw set. He glanced down the highway as if we might see the vampires heading our way already.

They might still come then. With guns in hand, ready to open fire.

The scout called back in. West brought the phone to his ear, said a few encouraging words, and then glanced around at us.

"They appear to have agreed to meet us here. They're on the move now. Be ready."

"Where do you want all of us stationed, sir?" Bertrand asked.

"We don't want to give them a reason to think we're here anything but peacefully," Aaron said. "That'll end this parlay before it even starts."

"Even when they came out in full force against us already," Nate muttered. He stepped closer to me. "Let them just try to complain."

"No, the eagle shifter is right," West said. He nodded to his kin. "Spread out into the woods, but stay on our side of the lot. Just far enough back that they won't be able to see you. Vamps can't rely on smell. But I want you close enough to engage if you need to—or jump into those cars and get out of here if it comes to that. You know the signals."

Except for a few who continued to flank us, the rest of the canine shifters faded back into the forest beside the gas station.

Lights glowed in the distance down the highway. My shoulders tensed. Here were the bloodsuckers.

"I should shift now," I said. "So I'm ready. The second I see one gun, I'm blasting them all. If they actually negotiate, you guys have a better idea than I do what the treaty says anyway. Any arguments there?"

None of the alphas gave me one. "Just be careful," Aaron said.

Marco shot me a grin. "They're the ones who'll need to be careful with our Princess of Flames on the prowl."

They kept watching the road while I peeled off my clothes. When the first trucks were close enough that I could make out the shape of them behind their headlights, I knelt on the ground and beckoned the shift through my body.

It was a pleasure, getting to shift at a natural pace rather than rushing into it as quickly as I could force the change. My muscles stretched and tingled rather than aching. The scales rippled over my skin with a giddy shiver. My wings swept out from my back, sending a rush of anticipation through my nerves. I loomed over the cars, fire already prickling at the base of my dragon's throat.

I didn't think I'd have any use for my truth-seeking flames tonight. If the vampires who'd slaughtered our kin took one step wrong, I was turning them into instant barbeque. It wouldn't solve the problem of all the other vampire groups out there, but at least it'd knock down their numbers a little. And be plenty satisfying at the same time.

The trucks, small delivery ones with no windows on the bulky back compartments, slid into the lot, staying on the opposite side from us. I kept my dragon eyes trained on the windshields, the doors, for any hint of a figure raising a gun.

A slim, dapper-looking man stepped out of the cab of the middle truck. His hair was pure black and his eyes glinted with some semblance of life, but his skin was deathly pale. A sour smell reached my nostrils.

The stench of the undead, that only our sensitive shifter noses could pick up. Their human victims never realized.

This guy was clearly the king. He strode into the middle of the lot, past the vacant pumps, as if he wasn't worried for himself at all. His gaze didn't even flicker my way, even though there was no way he could have missed the massive dragon watching him. Nine of his people gathered behind him, standing guard. The others stayed in the trucks.

"We've come to your parlay," West said. He and the other shifters were poised by the first of our cars, ready to use it as a shield. "Maybe you'd like to explain why your people attacked so many of ours last night?"

The vampire king smiled thinly. "That was a demonstration. To provide context for this talk."

"That context meant more than a hundred deaths among our kin," Nate said, his voice almost a growl.

The king looked at him blandly. "And now you know how serious I am. But no one else *needs* to die."

"Wonderful," Marco said. "We're duly informed of your seriousness. How about you get on with the actual reason you're here?"

"This is entirely your fault," the vampire king said in a haughty tone. "We all know the space for the supernatural kind in the modern world is dwindling. We vampires have learned how to adapt, how to blend in among the humans so that they don't discover us. But you shifters." A sneer crept into his voice. "Like the animals you transform into, you let your baser instincts overcome common sense. You run around without control. You can't stick to a human form."

"We take care of any troubles caused by our own kind," Aaron said.

"Not well enough. You can't even control your own kind enough to stop them from turning against you. I've heard all about the chaos of your community from shifters who've already attacked you more than once and gotten away." He let out a faint huff. "You're careless, and eventually you're going to be found out. And then the humans will be on the hunt for the rest of us too. None of us is safe while you continue giving into those animal impulses."

"We need to shift just like you need to drink blood," West said tightly. "You don't see us trying to stop you from eating."

"We don't need to run around in the open with our fangs out

to eat," the king retorted. He slapped his hands together. "From my view, it would be better if we were rid of all of you. But I'm willing to consider an alternative. We have identified a few isolated areas of the country humans find so unpleasant they rarely travel there. You will stay there, and never cross those boundaries—and then you may live."

Did he really think we'd agree to that? Move the entire shifter community to some inhospitable zones—and what, with the vampires guarding us like refugee camps, making sure we never ventured out? I bared my teeth.

"You have to know that's a completely unreasonable suggestion," Aaron said.

Marco chuckled dryly. "We're not going to uproot all of our kin just so you can indulge your paranoia. What else have you got? We might be willing to work with you—if you're actually working *with* us and not just trying to herd us into a pen."

The king's posture shifted. I felt it from him then, before he'd even opened his mouth—he'd been playing the part of negotiating, but he'd never really expected us to accept. And he'd just checked out of the discussion completely.

Checked out to give himself over to the other purpose of this meeting.

A roar of warning broke from my throat just as a flood of vampires burst from the backs of the trucks.

CHAPTER 5

Ren

FIRE RUSHED up my throat after my roar. I'd have fried the vampire king into cinders just like that if he hadn't moved so fast. The boss bloodsucker leapt into the shadows around the old gas pumps and vanished. Apparently the vamps couldn't just blend into the darkness—they could disappear right into it too.

I didn't have time to figure out if I could chase him through the shadows. Dozens of vampire soldiers were charging forward to take his place, swinging the guns they must have had stashed in the trucks to aim at me and my alphas.

Fuck that. I spewed out the flames crackling at the back of my mouth with a sharp heave of breath. My dragon fire washed over the bloodsuckers in a wave. Every vampire body it touched burst into cinders.

Several shots rattled out over the hiss of the flames. A bullet caught my shoulder with a tiny burst of pain. Not enough to slow me down. With a whip of my head and a fresh spurt of fire, those guns turned into so much misshapen garbage.

I sprang forward into the heap of ashen dust I'd created, readying for another blast. A bunch of the vampires had gotten smart, racing for the tree line at the edge of the lot. My next outpouring of fire caught the stragglers, but more than I liked escaped into the shelter of the trees where I'd have to take them down one by one.

Shots rang out and snarls carried from the forest. The shifters who'd come as our defenders must be circling around the lot to hold off the vampire attackers.

"Into the cars!" Nate was shouting. "The parlay is done."

West's voice, harsh with anger, broke through the bear shifter's. "Everyone, let's get out of here, *now*. Do not engage unless you have to."

The vampires who'd walked to meet us with their king unarmed had run for their own trucks. To grab more guns, I'd bet. They could forget that—and forget driving the trucks as well. I wasn't letting them give chase once we got on the road.

I rained fire down on the fronts of the vehicles, melting the metal hoods and the engine workings underneath into twisted blobs. The windshields shattered with the heat. A few of the vampires around back ducked from behind the cargo areas, guns in hand. I leapt higher into the air, summoning another stream of fire.

I didn't catch one of them in time. The automatic gun thundered, its spray of bullets searing across my hind legs and thigh. I shrieked more in rage than pain and pelted the vamp with flames. In an instant, he and his gun were a molten lump.

More gunfire was still going off amid the trees. Ignoring the stinging ache radiating through my legs, I took off toward the forest. Some of the shifters were dashing to our cars, but others were still wrestling with the vampires, trying to cover their kin's escape.

A black wolf slashed open one vamp's neck, and the bloodsucker crumpled into a healing stasis. Two foxes, a red one and a tawny one with huge ears I guessed was Felix, sank their teeth into another vampire's legs at the same time and yanked. The vamp tumbled, and Felix was at his throat a second later.

The trees made it harder for the vamps to get a clear shot with their guns, but that didn't stop them from using their weapons. Bullets thunked into tree trunks and bark sprayed. A coyote stumbled and fell as the hail of bullets caught it across the chest. Marco's lion lieutenant, who'd joined us for the parlay, sprang at a bloodsucker and bashed the woman's head into a jutting root. Before he could wheel, another vamp had leapt from behind a tree and started shooting.

Blood burst from wounds down Leonard's side. I caught the vamp with a spurt of fire. A couple of canine shifters ran to grab the lion shifter as he crumpled, transforming back into human form. They hefted their injured ally up to carry him to the waiting cars.

I fried another two vampires. Between the pain spreading from my own wounds and the energy I'd expelled already, my dragon body was starting to prickle. I wasn't going to be able to hold the shift much longer.

Lights glowed across our end of the parking lot. Engines rumbled as the canine kin waited for the last few stragglers to make it to the vehicles. A couple cars had already pulled away. As the rest of the fighting shifters broke from the trees to make an escape, the remaining vampires pushed to the edge of the forest where they could more easily pick us off.

Not if I had anything to say about it. I dove, blazing a line of fire along the edge of the lot. In his wolf form, West wove among the fleeing shifters, urging them on toward the cars. Nate's bear charged at the vampires that were trying to dodge my flames. At the other end of the lot, Aaron and Marco had tackled the last of the vamps by the trucks.

My flames flickered out. I wrenched at my chest, trying to produce more, but my lungs stuttered. In that moment, one of the vampires sprang forward and pulled his trigger with his gun pointing straight at Nate's back.

West shoved the bear shifter to the side, but his wolf was barely big enough to jostle the much bigger animal. The bullets clipped the grizzly's head and streaked down his side. Nate groaned, spinning around but already swaying.

No! Panic knifed through me, twisting my gut. The fury that followed it blazed up so fast and hard my vision hazed white.

Not my mate. These undead monsters were *not* taking him from me.

More fire than I'd have thought I'd had in me—more fire than I'd have imagined I could ever have summoned—ripped up from my lungs. It scorched my throat and singed my own teeth. I expelled it all with a scream of anger.

The rush of flames crashed into the vampires at the edge of the forest, searing through all of them before they could so much as flinch. It seared up the trees too. Up the trunks, blackening the bark and biting into the wood beneath. Flickering into the leaves, filling the air with smoke. The rising wind whipped it into a fury to match my own.

A fury I couldn't control. The fire surged from tree to tree, burning the rest of the vampires up or sending them running into the shadows. But it didn't stop. It crackled on, devouring all the vegetation in its path.

I hit the ground. My human legs sagged as I shifted. Blood streaked down my pale skin from the bullets I'd taken.

Aaron rushed to my side. West and Marco had shifted back into human form too, hauling Nate into the back of one of our vans. The bear shifter's head drooped in West's grasp, his skin waxen. A dribble of blood spotted the pavement along their path.

"He's alive," Aaron said, but I thought I heard an unspoken *for now* in there. My raw throat squeezed shut. I stumbled upright at the eagle shifter's tug. He pulled my arm across his shoulders and looped his around my waist.

The fire blazed on through the forest, its heat wafting over us. A shudder passed through me.

"I started a whole forest fire."

"There's nothing we can do about it now," Aaron said. "As soon as we're on the road, I'll call the closest fire department. They'll know what steps to take."

He started to lead me to one of the other cars, but I shook my head. "I want to be with Nate. I *need* to be with Nate."

Aaron looked as if he might have argued, but then he changed his mind. "All right. But someone has to tend to you too."

I hobbled with him to the van. A couple of kin were already bent over Nate's prone body, sharing blood and digging out the bullets. "Ren," West said hoarsely, but Aaron waved him away.

"We should get back to our cars. Get everyone out of here before any more vamps show up."

"Right." West shook off his momentary hesitation and bellowed down the end of the lot. "Everyone! Move out!"

I half scrambled, half dragged myself onto the van bed next to Nate. Another canine shifter leapt to see to my wounds. I closed my eyes, tuning out his attentions and pressing my face to my mate's shoulder. The glimpse I'd gotten of Nate's torn-up torso was more than I ever wanted to see again.

Nate's chest still rose and fell with steady if shallow breaths. I longed to squirm closer, to hear the thump of his heart in his chest, but I was afraid to disturb the wounds that hadn't yet closed. Instead I nestled as close to him as I dared, willing with every shred of my soul for him to heal. For him to be okay.

The van's engine rumbled, but the roar of the forest fire carried over it. Flames danced behind my eyelids as the wheels lurched over the uneven ground to the highway.

Not all of the destruction here was the vampires' doing. In that moment when I'd seen my mate fall, I hadn't been thinking at all, only acting. A mindless animal, like the vampire king had said. It wasn't just Nate who might die because of this battle tonight. And if any innocent people did, those deaths would be on *my* conscience.

As we roared down the highway toward the canine estate, I wasn't sure which potential tragedy made my heart ache harder.

CHAPTER 6

Aaron

DAWN LIGHT WAS ONLY JUST STARTING to seep through the trees beyond my bedroom window when I pushed myself out of bed, but I wasn't getting much sleep there anyway. Bleary-eyed but with humming nerves, I found myself wandering down the hall to the healer's dormitory.

The room held several cots, but right now only two were occupied. The other shifters injured in last night's battle must have recovered enough to return to their own quarters.

Nate was still sprawled on his cot like he had been when I'd left the room a few hours ago. The healers who'd attended to my fellow alpha were leaving him be for now. They'd bandaged his wounds, and blood hadn't seeped through the white gauze, so I could assume at least that they weren't bleeding anymore. He was still breathing. He just hadn't woken up.

Serenity was curled up on top of the covers of the bed next to his, her eyes finally closed. Even asleep, her face looked tense.

She'd been afraid of disturbing Nate but unwilling to return to her own room last night, despite the healers' cajoling. Her own wounds had closed, only angry pink marks still dotting her pale legs. Soon they'd fade too, like all the other injuries she'd taken in her first few weeks as our dragon shifter.

What an introduction to the shifter community she'd had. Every time I thought the worst was over, the world upped the ante on us all over again.

I didn't want to wake her. There wasn't anything I could do for Nate. I'd at least seen he was still alive. But I couldn't quite convince my feet to carry me back to my own room. All that waited for me there was more restless dozing.

The door to the healer's dorm clicked open. Marco slunk in, looking as weary as I felt. He came to a stop beside me.

"No change?"

"Not for the worse, at least," I said.

"Small blessings." The jaguar shifter's lips curled as if he couldn't decide whether to smile or grimace and had ended up halfway in between. "What the hell are we going to do without the bear's strength?"

"We'd lose a lot more than that if we lost him."

"That's true," Marco agreed. The feline alpha must have sensed as much as I did that in a lot of ways Nate was the glue that had held our quartet of clashing personalities together—with his strength, but also that easy warmth he always seemed to radiate, unless you gave him a good reason to get angry. It was hard to squabble all that much when he was around.

We hadn't even come together properly yet, not with West still dangling the possibility of eschewing the mating alliance altogether. I'd thought the canine alpha was starting to come around, but what would happen if Nate died? How united would we be then? The young man he'd have been training to take the alpha position after him wouldn't be of age yet. Either the disparate kin would fall into fighting over the rulership, or Serenity would be left without another mate.

If we lost Nate, the vampires might have won already, without even one more drop of blood shed.

"Have you seen West this morning?" I asked Marco.

He nodded. "Wolf boy is prowling around the common rooms snapping at anyone he doesn't like the look of. So only slightly more annoying than usual."

"He feels responsible."

"We all knew we had to go to that parlay, no matter how much it looked like a trap." He glanced at me. "Any problems reported from any of your settlements?"

I shook my head. "It looks like the vamps elsewhere were holding back waiting to see how last night played out. I doubt we'll get another reprieve tonight."

We might have left the room then, our combined uselessness heavy enough to push us into motion, but Serenity stirred. She rubbed at her face and shoved herself upright on the bed. Her gaze rested on Nate for a moment, her mouth twisting, and then rose to us.

"What's happening?"

"Nothing," I said quickly. "He's still healing, just… slowly. We have to assume he is, at least. He hasn't taken any turns for the worse."

She got up and walked to the side of the Nate's bed, resting her hand on the bear shifter's arm. "But he hasn't woken up at all?"

"It's pretty normal for us to need a good long sleep when we've been severely injured, princess," Marco put in. "To make sure we don't go running around straining those internal organs all over again while they're still piecing themselves back together."

"I don't know. That just sounds like a coma to me. And sometimes people don't come out of those."

"Shifters aren't your regular sort of person," Marco said archly. "And alpha shifters least of all." But the tilt of his head was a little stiff. Nate wasn't out of the woods yet.

Our dragon shifter could clearly tell that too. Her expression held so much worry that I had to go to her. Marco shot us a look and then drifted away.

"Hey," I said, tugging Serenity to me. "He's hanging in there. The fact that he's still with us after the wounds he took last night is a very good sign. We've got centuries of history behind us. Shifters are a tough bunch. It's not all going to end just because some vampires got some ridiculous notions into their heads."

My mate gave me a pained smile. Then she bobbed up on her toes to kiss me. I leaned into it, reveling in the softness of her lips and the sweet scent of her skin. Wishing I could offer her more reassurance than I already had.

Ren

I finally peeled myself away from Nate's side when I realized it was past noon and I'd already lost half of the day. I didn't want to leave my mate, but the vampires were no doubt preparing for a full-out assault tonight. If there was anything I could do to protect the rest of my kin, I needed to be here to do it. They were counting on me.

Walking down the halls in a bit of a daze, little aches

shooting through my legs where my wounds weren't quite healed, it took me a minute before the change in atmosphere registered. There was a bustling sort of energy moving through the estate. And more kin than I remembered seeing before. A lot more.

When I emerged from the halls into the central common rooms, unfamiliar figures were scattered all over, filling the chairs and sofas, clustered around the tables and doorways. A hum of nervous chatter and a cacophony of shifter scents surrounded me.

Not all of those scents were canine. A group of avian shifters had collected in one corner. A haggard but alive Leonard had been joined by several other feline shifters where he sprawled in an armchair at the other side of the room.

I spotted West coming in from the front yard as I passed the main door. He was talking with Bertrand. I waited until he'd dismissed his lieutenant to go over.

"What's going on?" I asked, motioning to the crowded rooms.

He gave me a tight smile. "We're evacuating the shifter settlements closest to the main vampire hubs. As many as we can reasonably house on the estates. There'll be a lot of bed sharing and sleeping on the floor, but the fewer boundaries we have to defend, the better we can defend those that matter."

That made sense. And it made sense that the evacuated shifters would come to the estate closest to them, even if it wasn't the main center for their kin. I let out my breath. "And everything's ready around the estate? If we need more fire here?"

He nodded. "We've been ready since yesterday evening, but I had my people expand the barrier." His gaze slid down my body. I'd thrown on a simple shirt dress without much thought. The thin cotton only hung to my knees, exposing the scars below. The sting of last night's wounds prickled at me again.

"You should be resting, not walking around," West said. "You were hit pretty bad last night."

"*Nate* was hit bad," I said, with a sudden wrench of my heart. A fresh wave of anxiety passed through me, the image of his slumped body and slack face rising in the back of my mind. "Is there anything else your people can do to help him? They had Kylie up and walking around after she was torn up so bad before, and she's not even a shifter."

West's stance stiffened. "My kin have done everything they can," he said sharply. "He'd be dead if they hadn't. I look after my people, and that includes everyone under the protection of my estate."

I blinked at him, thrown by the sudden change in his temper. "I didn't mean—"

West was already shaking his head. "It doesn't matter, Sparks. You just get on with whatever you feel you need to be doing."

He stalked off before I could say anything else, leaving me feeling strangely adrift. What had just happened there? Had we even been having the same conversation?

"Still not getting along so well with Mr. Wolf?" Kylie said, tucking her hand around my elbow as she came up beside me.

"Apparently," I said. "I'm not even sure what was bothering him this time."

"Well, it's not exactly the most relaxing of days, is it?" My best friend tipped her head against my shoulder. "I heard about Nate. And about how the whole vampire thing went down. Seems like I made a very wise decision sitting that one out. Is he going to be okay?"

"No one's sure yet," I said, swallowing hard. "He looks like he's healing. But it's not like anyone's made me any promises, so I guess that's not a guarantee." And how long could healing from that many bullets take? One of them had only barely missed his heart. What if he *couldn't* heal completely?

"He's a tough guy," Kylie said. She squeezed my arm. "I'm sure if he's made it this far, he'll pull through."

"That's what I want to think."

A slim figure with tawny hair emerged from the bustle—Felix. He was carrying a plate with a few sandwiches and some sliced veggies. "Dragon shifter," he said with a bob of his head. "I wanted to thank you for having our backs last night. Those bloodsuckers got what they deserved. And also, have you had anything to eat? I know you've been with the bear alpha since we got back."

He hesitated, looking suddenly uncertain. "He fought well for us, too. I'm sorry I couldn't take down the vamp that got to him first."

My chin wobbled, but I managed to smile. "Me too. Thank you. I can't say I'm hungry, but it'd probably be better if I got some food in me."

I accepted the plate, picking up one of the sandwiches and then offering the spread to Kylie. She raised an eyebrow at Felix. "Is this for the dragon shifter only, or is her human friend allowed to chow down too?"

He made a face, but the lowering of his eyes was embarrassed rather than annoyed. "I saw the supplies you were able to arrange to have brought in. Pretty impressive. I think you've earned at least a sandwich."

"Hmm," Kylie said, grinning. "I wonder what I'd have to do to earn a prime steak. Or a nice big slice of chocolate cake."

Felix's eyes widened. "I don't think we have any cake at the moment."

Kylie laughed. "I'm kidding. It's okay. Thank you for the

sandwich. And no hard feelings. I'm used to being underestimated."

Felix looked a bit confused. Then he smiled back. "I'll make sure not to do it again."

Marco had slipped into the hall. Timothy, the lieutenant the vampires had roughed up before sending him to us with their message, was walking carefully but steadily beside him, nodding at something his alpha had said. This was the first time I'd seen him up and around since he'd staggered in here yesterday.

"Back to dragon shifter duty," I said to Kylie and Felix. I hurried over to the jaguar shifter and his companion.

"Princess," Marco said with a smile. He pressed a kiss to the side of my head. "My lieutenant was just telling me about what the dregs of the rogue group have been up to."

My eyebrows rose. I turned to Timothy. "Last night their king mentioned that the rogues had been talking with him. Did you see them?"

The lieutenant inclined his head. "Only a handful of them. From what I gathered, that's all that's left of the group they once had. At least, all who are still planning to keep fighting. But they know they don't stand a chance against you and our alphas. There was one grizzled old guy there—I didn't get close enough to scent him, but he looked canine. He seemed to be leading the stragglers. And he's led them right into the vampires' grasp."

I grimaced. "How can they ally with the vamps? Don't they know the king hates all shifters?"

Timothy shrugged. "They weren't acting very friendly with each other. The bloodsuckers were pushing them around some. But I guess to those few it mattered more to them to finish their fight than what happens to them after."

"Too much pride and not enough sense," Marco said,

wrinkling his nose. "Well, they'll learn their final lesson pretty soon, I'd be willing to bet." He patted his lieutenant on the arm. "You did a good job, Timothy. Keep focusing on your recovery for now."

"Have you checked in on Nate again?" I asked my mate as Timothy ambled off.

Marco nodded. "No change. Is there anything I can do to help out here?"

"I don't know," I said. *I* still had to find some way to help prepare for whatever the vamps had in store for us tonight. But thinking about my last interaction with West, the prospect of asking him for ideas felt pretty daunting.

Marco must have read some of that feeling in my expression. He touched my cheek. "Is something else wrong?"

"No. I just—" I bit my lip. "West seemed angry with me. I'm not sure if I did something wrong somehow last night—I *did* lose control of my fire—or… I mean, it's not like it's strange for him to be grouchy, this just seemed a little more extreme than usual."

Marco gave me a crooked grin. "I don't think that's about you, princess. Wolf boy—well, let's just say I'm sure recent events are stirring up a lot of uncomfortable emotions for him. And he does seem to have difficulty processing those emotions without getting them all over everyone around him."

I frowned. "What do you mean?" Obviously the vampire attack had upset all of us, but Marco sounded like he was hinting at more than that.

The jaguar shifter shrugged. "It's not really my place to talk about it. He'd probably bite my head off—maybe literally. But I don't mind pointing you in the right direction. Next time you have the chance, get him to talk about his mother."

CHAPTER 7

Ren

THE LATE AFTERNOON sun had already dipped to the tops of the trees, but it still managed to blaze against my dark hair. "Is that the last of it?" I asked, wiping sweat from my forehead.

The canine shifters glanced along the line of hastily chopped firewood we'd already heaped up just outside the estate wall. "I think we've done all we can," Bertrand said. "We'd be able to keep this fire going for a good long time. If we even need to, with your dragon fire on our side." He shot me a respectful smile.

At least West's kin figured I could hold my own.

"I think it's just about time for dinner," Felix said, licking his lips. The faint smell of roasting meat was drifting over the estate wall from the house. My own stomach gurgled.

We tramped across the cleared earth around the ring and through the gate. Bertrand shut the door with a thump and locked it. Then we all filed into the dining hall.

The canine estate wasn't quite as posh as some of the others, but the dining hall was still impressive. Huge oak beams crisscrossed the high ceiling all through the immense space. Heavy rugs overlapped each other under the matching oak tables, each of which was large enough to seat twenty. Light danced in sconces all along the walls, even though enough daylight streamed through the windows at the head of the room to make them unnecessary.

The roasting smell thickened as we stepped inside. My gaze snagged on the head table by those front windows, the one meant for me and my mates. Normally I'd have sat there with West by my side, for him to show me off the way the other alphas had. But since the estate was crowded with refugees, the tables were merely being used for serving now, with everyone eating on their feet as they circulated through the room.

I spotted Aaron and Marco at the far end of the space, but I couldn't see the canine alpha.

Would West even have wanted to show me off? We'd barely had a chance to really talk since we'd arrived. And I couldn't blame that on him, not really. The vampires had kept us plenty busy.

What did his kin make of the fact that he hadn't consummated our bond yet? They still seemed to treat me as if they considered me *their* dragon shifter.

All I knew was the uncertainty dragged at me—like a rough wind that washed over me every time I thought about that missing piece in my role as dragon shifter. In my *life*. I was meant to stand united with all four of the alphas, all four of my mates. And one of them continued to keep his distance. Another now lay on what could turn out to be his deathbed.

I was pretty sure this was not the future my mother had meant for me when she'd spent all that time trying to keep me safe. In fact, I'd be willing to bet this kind of danger and turmoil was exactly what she'd hoped to keep me out of.

At least my chances of surviving this situation were a lot better than they'd been when I was five. Small victories.

Bertrand moved to grab some pork tenderloin off one of the tables, and I made myself follow him. I couldn't afford to dwell on my worries right now. As far as I was concerned, every shifter in this room was my kin. They needed me girding myself for the battle ahead, not wallowing in whatever dire possibilities my imagination could come up with.

I chewed and smiled and chatted with the many canine kin —and a few avians—who came over to meet me. The canine shifters were as fawning as the ones I'd met before, but their eyes looked a little haunted. I found myself reassuring them again and again. "We won't let the vampires win. I'll see that they pay for what they've already done. The one thing they can't beat is dragon fire."

Even though I knew that wasn't entirely true. The vamps could shoot through the flames. And I couldn't promise I'd have enough, not when I hadn't shielded Nate quickly enough yesterday.

I'd eaten about as much as my stomach would take around the knots it'd tied itself in when I caught a glimpse of West near the doorway. He was just popping a last piece of flatbread into his mouth with a nod to the attendant he'd been talking to. Then he ducked out the door.

I didn't let myself think. I just hurried after him.

The wolf shifter was vanishing around the bend when I reached the hall. I jogged over in time to see him turning into another room just past the kitchens. What the heck was he doing over there?

When I reached that door, I paused before easing it open. On the other side, West's head jerked up.

He was standing in what appeared to be a storage room. Several metal tanks were stacked against one wall. They gave off a dull yellow shine in the dim light of the overhead bulb. A sour tang tickled my nose.

"Kerosene," West said, noticing my puzzled stare. "We keep a stock of it to hold us over in case there's a problem with the natural gas line. We're pretty isolated out here. In the winter… Anyway, I was thinking we might want to have them more readily at hand. In case we need extra fuel."

"Oh. That could be a good idea." I took a step inside, letting the door swing shut behind me. My skin twitched with an increased awareness of how small the room was. How little distance remained between me and my wolf shifter.

West rubbed his temple and ran his fingers back through his hair, the silver strands glinting amid the light auburn. He looked at me, his mouth flat, his eyes unreadable.

"I'm sorry about how I talked to you earlier," he said in a tone brisk but not quite dismissive. "I've got too much on my mind. Too much to keep track of. Is there something you needed?"

It wasn't the most effusive apology I'd ever gotten, but I could see the strain in him so clearly that any hurt I'd held on to melted. "No," I said, and then reconsidered. When would we get another chance to talk like this? That was why I'd followed him, wasn't it?

I sucked in a breath. "Actually, there is. I just—I want to understand. This war, or whatever it is, with the vampires… It's weighing on you more than the other alphas."

West let out a hoarse chuckle. "We're on my territory here.

This is my estate. The difference between host and guests, Sparks."

I fixed him with an insistent look. "It's more than that." Because he'd been more on edge, more worried about possible consequences of any conflict we faced, from before we'd had any idea the vampires might attack. From the moment he'd met me. And, hell, maybe even before, for all I could know about that. "Marco said I should ask you about your mother."

West muttered something under his breath that sounded like it contained several curse words and the word "cat." He shook his head, moving to brush past me to the door. "You don't want to hear that story."

I grabbed his arm, just above the elbow, with enough strength to halt him. To remind him that he might be alpha, but he was talking to a dragon.

"Yes," I said. "I do."

West met my eyes straight on for the first time since I'd come into the room. I felt suddenly hot, standing that close to him, my bare hand against the solid curve of his bicep. But I held his gaze. I wasn't backing down, not this time.

"Fine," he said, stepping away from the door and from me in the same movement. Just like that, I could breathe again.

The wolf shifter turned his head as if inspecting the tanks. "There isn't much to it. There's a major fae habitation not far from here. We had a clash with them when I was fifteen. They'd told earlier alphas we could settle on a part of their territory they were no longer using themselves. Then they changed their minds. Some of the younger shifters mouthed off at the fae who barged in to tell us to leave. I tried to make peace, but I'd only been alpha for four years."

"And you were only fifteen," I said. My heart was already sinking with the sense of where this story was going.

"Old enough to know my responsibilities," West said. "They thought we were weak, that they had an excuse to root us out and grab some of our domain to add to theirs at the same time. They hit the village by the border of those grounds. We all went out to fight, all of us able-bodied."

He hesitated. When he spoke again, his voice was rigidly even. "The fae were coming at us from all over. I was alpha. I was giving the orders. My parents had come to fight too. My mother was practically beside me. One of the fae came at her out of nowhere, knocked her over with a blast.

"I could have jumped in. I might have saved her life. But at the same time a whole charge of fae rushed at us from the front lines, where most of the fighting was, and my kin there started to falter…"

He stopped. The silence hung for a long moment. "I raced to the front," he said. "As fast as I could. Called everyone to me. Took down three of the glowy bastards myself. If I hadn't, it would have been a slaughter. We'd have lost at least a dozen more lives. We might have lost the whole village. Instead we pushed them back."

A lump had filled my throat. "But your mother died."

"Yes," he said harshly. "That's what real loyalty is, Sparks. I swore to serve my kin as much as they serve me. I could have been selfish and put one person I cared about over the good of the pack, but then I'd have been a wretch of an alpha. I have to put them first, always. Every time they show their throats to me, they're telling me they know I don't take *their* loyalty lightly. I won't let them down."

"And everyone knows about the choice you made." Marco had known about it, and the canine and feline kin weren't exactly buddy-buddy.

West shrugged stiffly. "There was a lot of talk, at the time.

Mostly because my father didn't agree with that choice. He saw what happened, but he was too far away to help my mother himself. He hasn't spoken to me since that battle."

I stared at him. When West was fifteen—his father had held that decision over him, a decision that had saved so many lives, for twelve *years*? "You were practically still a kid."

"I was alpha," West said, his gaze coming back to me as if daring me to blame him too.

But I didn't. I wouldn't have blamed him if he had saved his mom in that moment, but he'd made a sacrifice instead. One life to save several more, to protect a village, to turn the tide of the battle. I couldn't imagine it. If it'd been *my* mom—

The realization hit me then, like a smack in the face. It took me a few seconds to even form the words.

"You must have hated my mother," I said. "For what she did. For leaving all of you, for all that time. Just to protect me." By his standards, she'd been so terribly weak.

I didn't expect to see West's expression soften. "Ren…" he said. "I did. For a long time. But I don't know what it's like, being in those shoes. Having all the additional responsibilities that come with being dragon shifter. Maybe running and saving you was the best thing she could have done for us. It certainly could have gone a hell of a lot worse."

We could all have died, and the dragon shifter line could have died out completely. Was he saying he was sure now that his kin were better off with me than each kin-group fending for themselves?

"Anyway," West went on, "As a fellow alpha, Nate might as well be my kin too. If I'd gotten in there a little faster last night, before that vampire pulled the trigger…" He exhaled raggedly. "I carry *that* responsibility. All of us alphas need to stay strong.

United. I'd hate to see what the bloodsuckers do to us if we fall apart."

And what about after the vampires were dealt with? Did he see us staying united then?

My pulse had sped up, thumping hard in my chest. "West," I said, "if you—"

A wordless shout of alarm rang down the hall. Both of us whirled toward the door.

"They're here!" someone called out. "The vampires are outside the walls."

CHAPTER 8

Ren

"AWAY FROM THE DOORS!" West shouted as we dashed through the jostling crowd to the front doors. "If you've got an assigned task, join me outside. Everyone else, stay in the house. You're safest behind these walls. That's an order!"

I could taste the fear in the air, like an acrid chill. Uneasy murmurs traveled all around us. My heart thudded. Evacuating all these kin to this estate meant fewer walls to defend, but it also meant a whole lot more depended on us holding these particular walls. We couldn't let even one vampire break through.

I burst past the door with a bunch of West's guards and other kin who were joining the battle. Sandra, the wolf shifter he'd sent scouting this afternoon, fell into step beside us. Her face was flushed, her breath short. "I headed back as soon as I saw the trucks. I can't have gotten more than a few minutes lead on them. They'll be here any—"

The growl of engines sounded on the other side of the walls.

And here they were. West swung his arm. "To your assigned positions. Everyone, ready. We'll take them down just like we discussed."

I knew my role in all of this. I wanted to say something to West, to show how much I appreciated him opening up to me, but our enemies were right outside. I couldn't waste a second.

And after the story he'd just told me, I knew he wouldn't want me to anyway.

I yanked off my dress as I hurried down the front steps and launched myself into the air. My wings snapped from my frame, expanding as the rest of my body did too. No relaxed shift this time. My muscles screamed and my nerves twanged. But I was up in the sky, scaled and soaring, before the first vampires had even emerged.

Truck doors slammed. Feet crunched into the brush. Guns clicked, ready to fire. Was the king himself out there?

After the way he'd ducked out of the battle last night, I doubted it. Here was West leading our defense on the front lines, and the leader of our enemies couldn't even be bothered to show up to watch the results of his orders.

I gritted my teeth, my dragon fangs rasping against each other. If I ever saw the vampire king again, I wasn't giving him the chance to barter for his life. He'd be a crispy cinder before he'd so much as blinked.

The bloodsuckers moved through the forest along the edge of the ring we'd cleared. Their pale forms blended in and out of the shadows. They were spreading out, circling the estate, as we'd expected. And not venturing too close to the cleared area with its heaped line of firewood. I guessed the purpose of that defense was pretty obvious.

But we didn't want to light it until we needed to. That wood would have to last us the whole night, until the sun drove any remaining vampires away.

West's people spread out too, taking their positions along the walls. Ready to leap over and light the fire if they needed to—or to fend off any vampires who tried to scale those walls. As I swooped over the front yard, Kylie emerged from one of the equipment sheds carrying the flame-thrower she'd had one of her contacts fashion. Felix's head jerked around in a double-take when she passed him. Oh yeah, he definitely wasn't underestimating her now.

But I didn't want any of my companions to have to leave the protection of these walls. If I could turn all the vamps to cinders before they breached the estate—and before my shift started to falter—there'd be no more kin joining Nate in the healer room tonight.

Gunfire rattled by the far end of the estate. I swung around to pinpoint the sound, and the vampires near the gate moved forward. Oh no, they weren't getting away with that. I banked sharply to the left, gathering flames in my throat.

My blast crackled over three of the bloodsuckers. Shots boomed from deeper between the trees. Bullets tore through the lower edge of my wings with a sharp stinging.

I swept upward, out of the guns' range, and then dove back down. One undead figure, and another, and another, was visible here and there between the trees. I caught two of them before they wrenched their guns up. The third opened fire.

I managed to yank myself to the side just in time to avoid the worst of the onslaught of bullets. A fresh stinging radiated through my right wing.

Below me, farther down the wall, a group of vamps had made a run at the estate. They leapt at the wall, flinging themselves higher than any living human could have jumped, heaving their guns with them to get in some early shots.

I careened toward them, withheld fire searing the back of my mouth. The shifter guard on the platform inside the wall bashed one of the intruder's skulls against the stone blocks. Kylie scrambled up to join him and took out another vamp with a spurt of her flame-thrower. They both ducked back down as guns crackled from the edge of the forest.

Then I was on the vamps. I breathed a scorching line of fire over the rest of the group clambering over the wall and whipped myself around to blast the ones hiding in the trees.

I couldn't tell how many I caught amid the blackened tree trunks. They were keeping too far back, just close enough to have a clear line of fire with their guns. The forest was too dense for me to pick them off easily, not without setting it all up in flames.

More gunfire rang out from the far end of the estate. I wheeled, flapping my wings harder. Even here, I couldn't be everywhere at once. But I had to take out more of the bloodsuckers before I pulled back and let that protective ring do the fiery work for me. There were too many still out there. If our ring burned out before dawn, if even a few vamps got past the walls, this battle would turn into a bloodbath.

I rained fire down on another group of vampires that had run at the wall. Two of the shifters were grappling with one who'd managed to scramble over. I swooped toward him. He got a couple shots off before the guards wrenched the gun away from him. Blood bloomed on one of the guard's shoulders. He slashed the vampire's throat.

As the undead body slumped into stasis, the guards jumped back, looking to me. Oh, I could finish the job, all right. I breathed a spear of flames down at the vampire, my lips curling into a dragonish smile as he burst into ashes.

My smile didn't last long. I wheeled back toward the forest, and a cacophony of shots split the air. All of them aimed at me. The vampires knew who the biggest threat to them was. I spewed flames across the edge of the forest, not quite quickly enough. The hail of bullets had been aimed at my wings again, where the scales were softest and the flesh thinnest.

I flapped my wings, pushing myself higher. The air coursed through the dappling of wounds, sparking pain with every movement. More shots echoed up from beneath me. More bullets tore through the tender flesh. I poured down more fire, but the guns kept booming. Each bullet bit through my body with a sharp throbbing. My thoughts started to splinter.

I had to keep going. Had to stop all of them. But there were too many, and my wings could barely hold me up now. Every brush of air against them was agony.

My focus narrowed through the haze of pain. I couldn't fall outside the walls. My kin would come to try to rescue me, and the vampires would slaughter them. But I could give my shifters one last gesture of protection. If I set our ring on fire, none of them would have to venture beyond the walls for that purpose either.

My wings wavered. Another hail of bullets sprayed over me, some tearing more holes in my wings, some glancing off my thicker scales, a few digging into my side. I sputtered up one last gush of flames aimed at the circle of chopped wood.

The logs and branches hissed. Flames leapt up all along the ring in a rippling dance. With a relieved smile, I hurled my plummeting body toward the wall.

My knee glanced off the stones, but I tumbled over the side into the estate. Voices were hollering and footsteps pounding toward me before I even hit the ground, already human again.

The impact sent a fresh wave of agony through my shoulders

and down my back. I cried out, flinching against ground now slick with my blood. Then the pain hazed my mind completely, and the world went black.

My body came back into awareness gradually. First the dull prickling of pain running all down my back and sides, where my dragon wings had crumpled back into my human form. A deeper ache searing through my ribs when I tried to roll over. A soft sheet was draped over me. Warring smells of blood and a sweet, clean perfume drifting through the air to my nose.

I managed to blink my eyes open.

"Ren!" Kylie said. She was standing over me at the edge of the bed, her hands fisted where they rested on the mattress. The pink tufts of her pixie cut were drooping and dark smudges underlined her eyes, but she gave me her most brilliant smile. "How do you feel? Should I call the healers?"

Of course. I was back here in the healer room again. Holding my body still, I took in my surroundings. Pale light was shining through the windows. Good, that meant we'd gotten to the morning without losing the estate. More forms were slumped under sheets around the room, but the rasps of sleeping breaths carried to my ears. They were all alive still.

Everyone in here, at least.

"Sore, but okay other than that," I said, meeting Kylie's gaze again. "I don't think I need any help. What happened last night? Is everyone else okay?"

"We held the vamps off," she said. "Some of the shifters were injured, but all of us survived."

That should have been amazing news, but her smile had faltered. I pushed myself into a sitting position, wincing as I went. My back throbbed, but I needed to know. "What's wrong? Something's bothering you."

"You are way too good at picking those things up," my best friend said, waggling a finger at me. "And you should really stay lying down until someone checks you out again, I think."

When I didn't budge, Kylie let out a huff of breath. "I don't know what's wrong. But the vamps pulled back after the fire had been going a couple hours. They took off and didn't come back, but they didn't send any message about giving up the fight or anything. Your guys figure they're making some new plan now that they've seen our strategy."

Of course they were. I suppressed a groan. "Great. Well, I guess we can be glad we've got all day to prepare for whatever it is."

"And for you to recover," Kylie said, giving me a gentle shove. "You were really beat up, Ren. Just because you're a dragon doesn't mean you're immortal, you know."

"Believe me, I've never been more aware of that than right now." I stretched one arm and then the other, bracing myself against the twanging aches that shot through my muscles.

"I should go tell the guys. They'll want to know you're awake. They were hanging around looking worried for a really long while, you know, but then they had to get on with whatever alpha business needs taking care of. Maybe you'll listen to them about getting your rest even if you won't listen to me."

She wrinkled her nose at me, and I cracked a smile. Then a low rumble of a voice reached my ears from the bed behind me.

"You don't have to go far to tell me."

"Nate!" I threw myself around on the bed, so fast the pain sliced right through me. But seeing those warm brown eyes gazing back at me was worth the extra helping of agony. I scrambled right off the mattress and clambered onto his cot, slowing as I eased myself down beside him. If my body was aching this much after last night's wounds, I couldn't imagine how he must be feeling after the beating he'd taken.

My mate wrapped his brawny arm around my waist and tugged me even closer to him. I cuddled up to him, breathing in his musky, peppery scent. My heart swelled with joy. "I was so worried about you. You've been out a whole *day*, you know."

Nate let out a hoarse chuckle. "Looks like I should have been worried about you too. Throwing yourself into the middle of the battle like usual?"

"Someone's got to bring the firepower," I said. "Anyway, after that fight in the gas station, I don't think you're anyone to talk."

"Hmm. I'm definitely not looking to repeat that experience."

Kylie made an amused sound. "Well, I guess it doesn't matter which bed you're lying in as long as you're lying down. Don't get too frisky, is all I'm saying. I'll see if I can track down the other guys."

"Thank you," I called after her. I tipped my head back to kiss Nate and looped my arm around his back. The faint dimpling of his wounds made me hesitate. "I'm not hurting you, am I?"

"Ren," Nate murmured, "there is absolutely nowhere I want you to be except right here. So don't you dare budge an inch."

He pressed a kiss to my forehead and adjusted his body so we fit together even more perfectly. I nestled in his warmth, letting my eyelids slide shut. We both deserved a little reprieve before we had to face whatever the vampires were going to throw at us next, didn't we?

CHAPTER 9

West

I STUDIED my scar in the mirror as I readied a fresh bandage. This morning, the pulse of the old wound was still threaded with angry red, but mostly its glow shone yellow. A sickly yellow like the twist of anxiety that wound through my chest.

I scowled at the patch of color before I pressed the bandage over it. Damned fae. Trust them to come up with a kind of injury that'd haunt you more than a decade later.

Granted, at the moment I was feeling even less pleased with the vampires. My scowl deepened as I shrugged on a clean shirt to replace the one I'd been too busy to change since sometime yesterday. I had my kin running around doing everything I could think of to be ready for tonight… but who the hell knew what tonight was going to bring? The bloodsuckers clearly weren't going to be happy until they'd slaughtered the lot of us.

Like they'd almost slaughtered Ren last night.

My pulse hitched at the memory of her falling, bullet-riddled body. I clenched my jaw and turned toward the door.

Just as the woman in question burst past it into my rooms.

My dragon shifter's eyes were bright with excitement, her face split with a beaming smile. But I could tell from her slight hesitation as she nudged the door shut behind her that she was still in some pain. She had to be. The last time I'd seen her, she'd been slumped unconscious on that healer room bed while her flesh knit itself back together.

"Nate's awake!" she said. "He's okay. Still a little weak from all the wounds, but okay."

Her scent reached me then, that fiery sweetness mixed with the bear shifter's musk. Because of course they'd been all over each other the second he'd come to.

A twinge of jealousy I knew was ridiculous shivered through me. She *should* have gone right to him. He was her mate, and he'd almost died. I clamped down on the twinge and shoved it aside, along with the half a dozen other emotions I was trying not to feel.

"And you should be back there in the healer room too, not running around to tell me," I said. "You're not fully recovered yet either."

"I *walked*," Ren said. "And I thought you'd want to know, after everything you said yesterday. Kylie found Marco and Aaron, but you must have been off hiding somewhere."

"I just got back from making additional preparations farther down the highway," I said shortly. "I'd have found out soon enough. You should be more concerned about looking after yourself."

Was that a wince she'd stifled as she set her hands on her hips? For fuck's sake, she shouldn't be walking, or standing, or anything other than lying down right now.

"I'm fine," she said, in her usual stubborn way. "It was a tough fight, but we all got through it. You don't have to treat me like a weakling."

Did she not realize how close *she'd* come to dying? My temper escaped me. "I wouldn't if you'd finally learn you can't do everything. You practically got yourself killed out there, but we did still need that back-up fire last night, didn't we?"

Ren definitely flinched then. But not because of any injury. Because of my retort.

In a flash, I saw how her face had fallen, the joyful light gone out of her eyes. She'd come in here brimming with happiness she'd had every reason to feel, and I'd managed to crush it in less than a minute. My heart wrenched.

"I don't know…" Ren's voice wavered. She waved her arm vaguely, blinking as if trying to hold back tears. "I don't know what I'm doing wrong. But if after all this time you still don't think I'm enough, why don't you just tell the rest of us to leave so you can do whatever it is you think you're going to do without a dragon shifter?"

Her words tore through me. Did she really believe—

She was already spinning around, shoulders tensed, swiping at her eyes. I couldn't let her leave like that. Fuck plans, fuck principles, fuck good intentions. If this was where they'd gotten me, they obviously weren't worth much.

"Ren." I caught her elbow as she stepped toward the door. She turned back, her expression wary.

Suddenly I didn't know what to do with myself. I'd led hundreds of kin since I was a kid. Why was talking to this one woman so damned hard? She was meant for me.

And I was meant for her.

I rested my other hand against the wall beside her, leaning just close enough that I could feel the warmth emanating from her body. Not so close that she couldn't break my grasp and move away if that's what she wanted.

But she stayed there, gazing back at me. I swallowed thickly.

"I'm sorry," I said, forcing myself to keep looking back at her. If seeing the pain on her face hurt me too, well, that was my own damn fault. "You're more than enough. You're fucking spectacular, Ren. I'm sorry I ever made you feel otherwise. I don't know if *I'm* ever going to be worthy of *you*. But I'm going to try. I promise you that."

"West..." Her expression had turned puzzled. "But you— I thought— You've been acting like you're still not sure."

"That's not what I was aiming for. There just hasn't been a good time..." I didn't even know how to explain it. "I'm sure. I've been sure."

She blinked. "Since when?"

That one thing I could tell her. I could pinpoint the exact moment my heart had flipped over and I'd realized what an idiot I'd been. I could still see her in that instant in my memory, naked and blood-streaked at the edge of the clearing, her eyes shining with grief.

"When we ambushed the rogues with the disparate kin. The way you tried to save that guard of Nate's. How upset you were when you couldn't. If you could care that much about a muskrat shifter who'd considered betraying us... I couldn't ask anything more for all our kin than compassion like that."

"That was—that was *days* ago, West. Why the hell haven't you said anything?"

I opened my mouth and closed it again, trying to find the words. My reasoning had all made a lot more sense when I'd only had to work it out in my own head.

"There was so much going on," I said. "The rogues and Marco's challenge and now the bloodsuckers wreaking havoc... I know I have a lot to make up to you, for how I treated you before. I didn't want to put any pressure on you to forgive me while you were dealing with everything else. When things have calmed down, when you have room to breathe—you can take your time deciding whether you can be sure of me. I can prove to you that I'll be a good mate. I—"

"Oh, West," Ren interrupted, so softly my pulse stuttered. She rested her hand against my chest. "You don't need to prove anything. I already know who you are. I want you. Now, if I can have you."

Now. That sounded like a very, very good idea. I stared at her, and all I could see in her eyes now was the same longing coursing through me.

She wanted me. She wanted *me*, even now, in spite of everything.

The dam cracked open inside me, releasing a surge of desire more powerful than I'd even known I was bottling up. I bridged the last short inches between us and captured Ren's mouth with mine.

My dragon shifter kissed me back just as hard. Her fingers curled into my shirt, tugging my body to hers, as her other hand rose to tease into my hair. I pressed her up against the wall, with just enough self-control to be careful of her injuries. She tasted and felt like heaven. Why had I denied myself this bliss for so goddamned long?

It didn't matter. I had her now. Had her arching against me as I gripped her thigh, had her whimpering at the sweep of my tongue over hers. The possessive impulse I'd tried to bury earlier rose up, and I didn't have the will left to rein it in.

I jerked her hips tight against mine, tipping her head so I could claim her mouth even more deeply. Her hands clasped behind my neck. She hummed eagerly, with a gasp as I released her lips to trail my tongue and teeth along her jaw.

"Mine," I muttered. "Mine." I hadn't really believed it until this moment. I wasn't sure I totally believed it even now.

"Yours," Ren agreed with a happy sigh. "And you're mine."

Something about those three simple words made my throat close up. I pulled back just enough to meet her eyes.

"I am. I've been yours since the first second I saw you, even if I was too bullheaded to accept it."

"Wolf-headed," she murmured with a breathless giggle, and I was lost again. I fell back into her, the heat of her mouth, the rocking of her body against mine, setting all of me on fire in a way I was all too happy to burn. My hand rose to cup her breast. I was stroking its peak harder through the thin cotton of her dress, marking my territory down the other side of her jaw with the graze of my teeth, when she lifted her chin.

In that first instant, I didn't catch the meaning of the gesture. Then she raised her head even higher, not just giving easier access but blatantly offering the entire pale expanse of her throat.

My breath stopped. For a second, all I could do was ogle the vulnerable skin she'd displayed for me so easily. The highest show of trust any of my kin could give another. An act of total submission, placing her life at my discretion.

How had I become worthy of an honor that great?

I'd better *be* worthy of it. I dipped my head, pressing the most tender kiss I had in me to the center of my mate's throat. I couldn't bring myself to do more than that.

"Oh, Sparks," I said, my voice hoarse. "You should never have to submit yourself to me."

Ren lowered her head to meet my eyes. The corner of her mouth quirked up. "I figured we could take turns. Keep things fair."

A rough chuckle broke from my mouth, and all I could do was kiss her again. Firmly, hungrily, with all the passion I'd spent the last few weeks denying.

~

Ren

My lips slid against West's, and I reveled in the heat radiating off him. My nerves were already trembling with the bliss of having him here, like this, giving himself and taking me without restraint. But who was I kidding? I wanted more, so much more. I wanted everything.

My hands trailed down his chest to grip the hem of his shirt. I tugged it upward. With a hungry growl, West broke the kiss to tug the shirt off, capturing my mouth again an instant later. His fingers teased over my body until they found the zipper beneath my arm. One sharp yank, and the soft fabric of my dress was falling off me.

I hadn't bothered with a bra in my hasty departure from the healer room. My nipples pebbled as they grazed my mate's bare chest. I let out a whimper, kissing him harder, but a prickle of discomfort crept through the haze of pleasure. I *wasn't* completely healed, and my muscles were starting to protest about staying upright so long.

Well, I had no particular interest in staying upright any longer. I pushed West backward, toward the bed, careful of the bandage that covered his scar. He glanced behind him, and his lips curved into an eager grin. With a flash of his dark green eyes, he swept me off my feet. In a few swift strides, he'd thrown both of us onto the bed, him bending over me. Then his lips were pressed against mine again.

"Sparks," he murmured as he stroked my breasts. The nickname didn't sound like anything less than a reverent compliment now. His thumbs flicked over my nipples, and I moaned. My hips canted toward his of their own accord, wanting to feel him pressed against me there too. His hardness against my core.

He flipped us over in an easy motion, leaving me gazing down at him. Rising up on one elbow, he wove his fingers into my hair and claimed another kiss. I rocked against him, unable to help myself. The feel of that bulge beneath his jeans made me giddy.

West groaned. He eased back for a second, holding my gaze. Then, very deliberately, he tipped back his head to expose his whole throat to me.

My heart skipped a beat, or maybe two. I'd be willing to bet this man—this *alpha*—had never offered his throat to anyone except the alpha who'd come before him, years and years ago. I'd already believed everything he'd said when he'd told me how he felt, but seeing him volunteer that vulnerability to me made the truth of it hit me even harder.

I was his. And he was mine. All mine.

A little choked up, I eased down to kiss a gentle path from his jaw down the hollow of his throat, past his Adam's apple. Then I kept going. Down across the planes of chest, over his solid abs, to the buckle of his jeans. I could make short work of those. My knuckles brushed his erection as I tugged the zipper down. West sucked in a breath.

Before I could make good on my intentions, he grasped my shoulders and pulled me up the bed, rolling back on top of me in the same motion. His voice came out even more throaty than usual.

"If I'm going to be inside any part of you, there's only one place I want to be."

A flood of heat washed through my sex, as if he were already there. "So get on with it already," I said. "Do you have any idea how long I've been waiting to properly call you my mate?"

West made a rough sound. Then his mouth crashed down on mine as if he were desperate to taste me again. We wrenched his jeans off together, and somewhere in there my panties disappeared. His hands teased over my thighs as the hard length of his cock rubbed against my clit. I whimpered, clutching at him and raising my legs by his waist to urge him on.

A tremor ran through West's entire body. Then he was plunging into me, all the way to the hilt in one thrust. A moan burst from my lips.

"Ren," West murmured in time with his strokes. "Ren." Like he was laying claim and saying a prayer at the same time. The glow of our bond radiated through me, so bright my vision hazed. Bright and completely solid for the first time, as that rush of warmth joined the rest of the ties to my four alphas inside my chest.

I had my mates, all of them, exactly as it was meant to be.

West drove into me, filling me, completing me with that giddy burn. I caressed my hands over every inch of his skin that I could reach, the muscles coiling in his shoulders and down his chest. I bucked to meet his strokes. My breath broke into pants. With each pump of his hips he sent me higher, a wave of pleasure building and building until I was trembling with it.

He arched, bending to slick his tongue over one of my nipples. His cock surged inside me at a tighter angle, and my orgasm crackled through me like a firework. I gasped, clenching around him. His breath hitched too. "Fuck," he muttered, bucking harder. His muscles twitched beneath my gripping fingers. With a groan, he followed me into release.

We rocked to a stop, our skin damp with sweat where our bodies pressed together. A pleased sounding hum reverberated from my mate's chest. He lowered himself beside me, tucking his arm around my waist, his nose brushing my cheek.

"Mine," he murmured one last time.

I smiled and squirmed over to hug him back. "Mine."

CHAPTER 10

Ren

I DOZED FOR A FEW MINUTES, until a strange light hazing my eyelids brought me back to sharper awareness. I blinked, nuzzling closer to West and breathing the smell of his skin, like rich earth and the pines outside.

Somewhere in the midst of our coming together, his bandage had fallen off. The glow I'd noticed was emanating from his scar. I'd never seen it this close before: a slight indent in his skin with ragged edges marking the boundaries of a magical blast.

I raised my fingers to it tentatively. The surface of the scar was smooth, harder than the rest of his skin but just as warm. When West didn't pull away, I lay my palm right against it.

"It changed color," I said.

"It does that," West said. "What were you expecting?"

"I think it's always been red when I've seen it before." Now it was beaming a vibrant pink. Not a color I'd have expected West to sport, but I guessed he didn't have a whole lot of choice in the matter.

"That would make sense. You've probably only seen it when I was throwing myself into some kind of skirmish. Angry."

It took a moment for that information to sink in. I looked up at him. "It shows your emotions?"

He shrugged. I could tell from the slight tensing of his shoulders that he didn't enjoy discussing this topic, but he held my gaze anyway. "Fae magic works in strange ways."

"No wonder you keep it covered up." Imagine going around alpha-ing with all your kin being able to read anything you were feeling from the glow through your shirt. Wearing your heart on your sleeve pretty much literally. "You got it during that fight when your…"

"When they killed my mother," he filled in when I faltered. "Yes. It was red for a pretty long time after that."

I ran my thumb along the edge where the scar met the softer skin over his leanly muscled chest. "So what does pink mean?"

West chuckled. "Do you really need to ask that, Sparks?"

He tipped my chin up to bring my mouth to his. The kiss was so long and tender it left me feeling as if my heart were glowing too. Our lips parted, our faces still close enough to brush noses.

"I love you, Ren," he said, low and rough.

My pulse skipped. I looped my arm around his neck, tugging all of me closer to him. "I love you too."

"Lord only knows how I got that lucky."

I laughed. "You didn't exactly make it easy when we got started." But there were some things I didn't totally understand about how he'd reacted to me. "You were worried I was going to take off on your kin—all the kin—when the going got tough, like my mother did?"

He shrugged. "That was some of the problem. I wanted to be sure we could count on you before I put their lives in your hands. And also, especially later on… I wanted you. I didn't know how much to trust my judgment. I have to put what my kin need over what I want, so when my instincts seem to be telling me what they need just happens to be something I'd very much enjoy, I have trouble not being skeptical."

"Maybe you're a little too hard on yourself," I suggested.

"Maybe." He exhaled a ragged breath. "Ever since that battle, and losing my mother— It might not make total sense, but I've always had this feeling hanging over me that if I make a selfish choice for something else, I'm saying she didn't matter enough. If I was willing to sacrifice her and not something else."

My throat tightened. I nuzzled his cheek. "You're definitely too hard on yourself. I guess I can forgive you for being hard on me too."

He gave a hoarse guffaw. "You have no idea how much it's been killing me watching you throw yourself into harm's way, again and again…"

"That's my job," I said. "Just like it's yours."

"I know. That's why I don't stop you."

"You just mutter about it like a jerk."

"Hey." He bumped his nose against mine. "You *have* been known to place heroics a little too far over your own safety from time to time."

I smiled. "Hmm. Well, if we're comparing irrational behavior, where do we put 'making up for being a jerk by acting like an even bigger jerk' on that scale?"

"I'm not sure if 'bigger jerk' is a fair assessment. I was trying to ease off on you."

"Funny how easing off included an awful lot of snarking.

And, you know, there was always the option of saying how you actually felt."

"Before or after you were done getting yourself almost killed, *again*?"

"Either would have been fine." I poked him in the sternum, peering up at him through my eyelashes. "Of course, given your usual fluency at sharing feelings, I might have ended up thinking you were telling me to jump off a cliff instead."

West caught my hand. With a growl, he rolled on top of me, pinning both my wrists above my head. "I think I can make my intentions a little more clear than that," he said, the gleam in his eyes both amused and heated.

I squirmed beneath him, the playful hold getting me all kinds of heated up too. My breath caught at the hardness I felt pressed against my thigh. In an instant, I was twice as wet. "Already up and at 'em again?" I said, wriggling a little more to the side so his cock could settle against my core.

The contact made us both groan. West grinned down at me. "I do have a few impressive qualities."

"Mmhm?" An ache of need was already spreading up from low in my belly. "Then by all means, go ahead and make full use of them."

The heat in his eyes turned blazing. "Oh, believe me, I will."

He bent to kiss me as he slid back inside me, and we gave ourselves over to pleasure for just a little while longer.

After a quick detour back to my rooms to find a dress that didn't look as if it'd recently been torn off in the throes of passion, I headed back through the mansion's halls to see where I was needed. I couldn't keep drifting along in the bliss of having finally consummated all of my mate-bonds for the rest of the day. The vampire threat hadn't gone away just because West and I had gotten it on.

West's kin and the others who'd taken shelter here were already hard at work laying down more firewood in the protective ring. Others had ventured farther away to scout out where the vampires might be holing up during the day. If they'd found temporary shelter somewhere, maybe we could turn the tables on them before night fell again.

If only it would be that easy. Somehow I doubted the bloodsuckers would have suddenly turned that careless.

I was just veering toward the common areas when the outline of a closed door snagged my attention from the corner of my eye. A jolt of anticipation I couldn't explain shot through me. I turned

The hall around me faded away.

I was standing in front of a simple door, this one painted the same pale moss green as the walls on either side of it. A circle of dimples marked its surface just above my eye level. It had no knob, no handle. A faint ringing filled my ears, and the certainty rose up in my mind that I could open that door if I wanted to. That it was meant for me to open—for me and my kind.

A familiar smell, like sweet clover and sunbaked stone, wrapped around me. *Home*. Then the vision washed away.

I stumbled backward, my still-sore back hitting the opposite wall.

The door I was looking at now, here in the canine estate, was light yellow-gold. It had a perfectly ordinary knob where a knob should be. But it had stirred something up in my memory—or maybe not my memory, but something deeper, that ran down through my dragon-shifter spirit. Excitement jittered through my nerves.

I'd come fully into my role. I was bonded with all four of my alphas, and through them with their kin. Maybe there'd been a lot more that came with being a dragon waiting for me than I'd ever even realized.

Maybe enough to stop the vampires attacks for good.

I spun away from the door and hurried the rest of the way into the common rooms. My gaze halted on the first attendant I saw. I caught her arm. "Can you find all the alphas and ask them to meet in our lounge? I need to see them immediately."

She bobbed her head. "Right away, dragon shifter."

I knew Nate was already in the lounge area that was just for me and my alphas to share. He'd left his healer room cot so he could make some calls to his kin without disturbing the other injured shifters.

When I burst into the room, he looked up from the armchair where he was sitting. His eyebrows rose. "Is everything okay, Ren?"

"I think so," I said. "I think I might know where we can find some answers. Are you well enough to travel?"

Nate pushed himself slowly but steadily to his feet. "I am if that's what we need to do. What happened?"

"I'm… not completely sure yet."

Marco sauntered into the room, his stance casual but his indigo eyes sharply alert. West stalked in a moment later with Aaron close behind him.

As they all came to a halt around me, a tremor passed through the air. It quivered over my skin, stealing my breath just for a second. This was the first time my alphas and I had all been in the same space with our bonds confirmed. The power of it hummed between us, almost electric.

I obviously wasn't the only one who could feel it. Marco

smirked and cut his gaze toward West. "I take it you finally figured out how to remove your head from your ass."

The wolf shifter bared his teeth a sliver, but he couldn't seem to help smiling when his eyes rested on me. So this was what it really felt like, being the dragon shifter. Being the hub that held the shifter community together. The sensation was exhilarating and a little frightening at the same time.

"What's going on, Serenity?" Aaron asked.

I groped after the impression that had made me call for them. "The dragon shifter estate. You've been there at some point, haven't you? What color are the walls inside?"

My mates looked puzzled. "From what I can remember, they're green," Nate said. "Most of them, anyway. Why?"

"This feeling came over me just a few minutes ago," I said. "Like the visions my mother left for me—or the one I had of how she died. I saw a door in what I think was the dragon shifter's estate. It felt like home. And the color matches."

"A door," West repeated, giving me space to go on.

"I got the impression I'm meant to open it. Now that… Now that I'm completely bonded with all of you. That there's something on the other side I need, something intended for every dragon shifter. What if it's something that could help us against the vampires?"

The guys exchanged a glance. "That estate does hold secrets only the dragon shifters have ever understood," Aaron said. "When I visited with the alpha who mentored me, there was a whole section of the house we weren't allowed into. The records we have of the dragon shifter line have always been tenuous."

"What are you suggesting, princess?" Marco said. "Time for a field trip?"

I nodded. "I have to go, to find out what's there. The rest of you…"

"We're coming," West said firmly. "My lieutenants can keep our preparations going here, and lead our defenses if need be. Leaving you unguarded could be exactly what the vampires are waiting for. There's a jet here. We can be at your estate by the early afternoon."

That was all I'd needed to hear. I let out my breath. "Then let's get on that plane."

CHAPTER 11

Ren

Kylie draped herself across her seat on the private jet with a pleased sigh. "I could totally get used to this kind of luxury. Forget flying coach ever again."

I laughed. "I think most of the time we'll drive places. But the shifter cars I've been in have been pretty nice too. The jets are for emergencies."

"Very, very comfortable emergencies," my best friend declared, snuggling deeper into the smooth leather. "I've got no idea what those vampires could have been complaining about. Shifters know how to live right."

There'd been no way I was leaving Kylie behind again, not with another vampire attack on the horizon. And it wasn't as if she'd have let me anyway. I'd barely managed to tell her I'd decided I needed to visit the dragon shifter estate before she'd been grabbing the suitcase she'd brought from New York and announcing she was ready to go.

I thought she might even have convinced the attendants to haul that flame-thrower of hers into the cargo hold. But Aaron had looked over everything, and if he didn't think it was likely to blow us up, I guessed I shouldn't worry.

"There are some benefits to being in with the shifters, huh?" Felix said with a light grin. West had brought a few of his kin along for the ride to help set my former home in order after all those years of disuse. The fennec fox had settled himself into one of the seats across from us. At first I'd assumed his choice was a coincidence, but seeing the way his eyes gleamed watching Kylie, I wasn't so sure anymore.

"Oh, I can think of lots of reasons to stick around," Kylie said, grinning back. She ticked off her fingers. "Lots of feasts. Super comfy guest rooms. The company of my best friend, of course. And let's not forget all the amazing eye candy."

Had my bestie just… fluttered her eyelashes a little at Felix? And was he *blushing*? A hint of red had definitely colored the fox shifter's cheeks. He swept back his tawny hair, playing casual. "Sounds like you're exactly where you need to be, then."

"Oh, I'm sure of that."

"We have a lot more fun when there aren't vamps trying to massacre us. You should come back to the estate after we've crushed them."

"And you'll show me a good time?" Kylie said, her grin widening. Oh, she was absolutely flirting with him. I'd know that *come get me* smile anywhere.

"Felix, come here a second," West called from closer to the front of the plane. The fox shifter made an apologetic grimace and hustled to see what his alpha wanted. I followed his path automatically, my gaze rising to meet West's. My mate's expression had been serious, but his eyes softened just a bit as he gave me a quick smile. And fuck if that wasn't enough to make my heart flutter.

"Hmm," Kylie said, waggling her eyebrows. "Is it just me, or is there more of a glow around you today? Any secrets you're ready to share?"

Now *I* was blushing. I ducked my head as heat washed over my face. But I couldn't stop a grin of my own from splitting my face.

An awful lot of things in our lives sucked right now—uh, some of them literally. But there wasn't a bloodsucker in the world that could take away the joy of having all my mates around me. Knowing we were all here for each other.

"Later," I said. "When we've got a little more privacy to chat." No doubt West's kin had already sensed the shift in atmosphere. It was kind of hard to tell if they were being more effusive toward me now when they'd been incredibly fawning from the start. But I'd caught a new sparkle in several eyes as we'd made our way through the mansion on our way out.

I was going to guess there'd be a whole lot of new canine kids running around about nine months from now, vampires or no. That didn't mean I wanted to be talking about my encounter with West where any of them could hear me with those sharp shifter ears.

"Oooh. I knew it!" Kylie said. "You're on fire, Ren. I mean, in a totally metaphorical, not at all dangerous sort of way."

The flutter came back into my chest, like a flickering of flames. "It does kind of feel like that," I had to admit.

"It's about time. No more being jerked around. Just love, love, love."

She said it in such a goofy singsong voice that I had to laugh again. That was why I loved *her*. For a few minutes, talking with her, I could forget all the other crap we still had to deal with.

At least, until Marco sank into the seat Felix had vacated, tucking his phone into his pocket. His mouth was set in his usual crooked smile, but his eyes were shadowed. Nate turned where he was sitting one seat over to see what the jaguar shifter had to say.

"A few of my people followed the vamps that came at my estate last night," he said. He'd been talking to one of his lieutenants in Florida. "It appears they've holed up in a smaller city that's closer to our territory than their usual haunt. Faster access for their next attack."

"Can your kin take the attack to them?" I asked. "Use daylight to our advantage?"

Marco shook his head. "The building they've taken over is too secure. Every nook and cranny sealed, every door unmovable, even the garage section where they keep their vehicles. Either the vamps lucked out, or they've been planning for the possibility of taking on the shifter estates for long enough to do a custom job on the place."

Aaron came over and leaned against the back of Marco's seat. "My kin have seen something similar near the avian estate. The vampires are prepared for a long fight. And they know the estates are the key to winning."

My pulse hiccupped. "So we can't let them break through any of those walls. We'll need all the firewood the kin can prepare, every shifter who's able to fight ready to tackle any who make it to the walls… Can we get bulletproof vests for the guards to wear? Other safety equipment? Maybe we can't use weapons ourselves, but there's no law against protecting against them, right?"

Nate frowned. "That'll only work when we stay in human form. But it couldn't hurt to have that kind of gear on hand."

Kylie perked up. "I've got an acquaintance whose brother works for a security supplies depot. He can totally hook us up."

I shook my head with a wash of relief. "Of course you know someone."

She wiggled her fingers. "I'm the most connected gal in NYC. You'd better believe it!"

All of these strategies were only stalling measures, though. "At least the vampires can't hold a real siege. We'll always have the option to scatter if the situation gets too dire, during the day when they won't know where we've gone."

"I don't think we'll keep morale very long if we abandon the estates," Aaron said. "And I can't imagine the vampires will leave a single building on them standing if we give them free access. But yes, if it comes to that…"

"And then what?" Marco said. "We scurry around through the wild as if we really are animals? We could get by like that, but it'd only be surviving. We *aren't* just animals. We need to put down roots, to have our community. And our comforts." He ran his hand over the padded arm of his seat.

"You're right. I shouldn't have suggested that." It wouldn't be the kind of victory a dragon shifter should be able to offer. I raked my fingers into my hair, my mouth twisting. "They rely on those trucks. I should have burned up some of the ones they had by the estate last night."

"Ren." Nate reached across the aisle to take my hand. He squeezed it gently, his warm brown eyes seeking out mine. "You did lots last night. So much more than any of the rest of us could manage on our own. You can't beat yourself up for that. There were too many of the vamps, and they're smart."

"But we'll find a way to beat them," Marco said. "They're contending with a fully-fledged dragon shifter and all four of her mates now." His lips curled with what looked like a genuine smile. "You've got this, princess. And we've got your back."

"We'll need to give my kin a chance to set the house in order," West said as we stepped out into the landing field. "A bunch from the closest canine settlement got here about an hour ago to get started, but it's a big job."

The underlings he'd brought along on the plane were already hustling down the path. Only a sliver of the house's roof was visible from here. Enormous oaks and silver maples loomed between the building and our landing place.

"How long has it been since anyone's come here?" I asked. Everywhere I looked struck a new chord of recognition in me: the long stretch of the landing field, the rustling leaves of the trees, the craggy peaks of the mountains to the north that spilled down into rolling green hills that surrounded the rest of the estate. All my nerves were twanging, even though it'd only been a minute since I'd stepped off the plane.

I sucked in a breath. The breeze held the delicate floral smell of clover. That was familiar too.

"We've taken turns sending kin by to do basic upkeep over the years," Aaron said. "We didn't want the place to fall into disrepair." He rested his hand on the small of my back. "We trusted you'd be back. But it won't feel all that homey yet. They'll need to uncover the furniture, stock the kitchen, do a more thorough cleaning, all that."

I stepped toward the trees. The hiss of the breeze moving through them sent a prickle down my back. Calling to my wings.

This was where I'd first learned about being a dragon. Where

I'd first seen a dragon fly. My mother, gleaming bronze against the sky. My throat choked up.

"It doesn't need any of that to feel like home," I said. "It just *is*."

I strode down the path the way the other shifters had gone. My mates drew up close behind me. I felt each of their presences by me: calm, eager, proud, and wary. And all of them here for me, trusting that I'd been right to bring us here.

I'd better make sure I justified that trust.

When we emerged from the short stretch of trees onto the plains of tall grass that surrounded the house, my breath caught in my throat. Kylie came to a halt beside me.

"Holy shit, Ren. That's some house."

It hardly even looked like a house. It was a castle, twin turrets on either side of the broad arched door, a parapet wall in between, the stones that constructed it painted stark white with red and gold trim around the door and window frames.

My mother's voice trickled up through my memory, bright with amusement. *A regular medieval fortress. Keeping us dragons safe instead of keeping the royalty safe from dragons. Our ancestor who commissioned this place had quite the sense of humor.*

These fields, I'd run through with my sisters. Ducking low to let the grass cover us, springing up to surprise each other with a mock growl. Our dads would join in the games, slinking beneath the cover of the waving blades in their animal forms, waiting to make a gentle pounce. Only my bear shifter father had been too big to really hide. We'd clamber onto his back and send him lumbering after the others.

My gaze drifted to the thicker forest behind the house. Pines and cedars mingled with oaks and maples there. The shadows streaked darker between their trunks.

But not as dark as the night when we'd fled. The air sharp in my lungs, the branches whipping against my arms, pebbles rattling away under my scrambling feet. My mother's hand clamped so tight around my fingers—

I yanked my eyes away. My heart was thudding.

"Ren?" West said, watching me. How much did he see? It hadn't occurred to me that I might not get away with quite so much around those watchful green eyes now that he was no longer trying to convince himself he didn't care.

I dragged in another breath, letting the clover smell and the summer warmth relax me. Focus on the present. Focus on the happy times before. Anything but that one night.

"I'm all right," I said. "Come on, let's get inside."

The front hall was fine. The front hall was *gorgeous*. The pale moss-green walls I'd seen in my vision now snapped into clarity. A crystal globe dangled from the ceiling, that I knew could beam with light when darkness started to fall outside. The swooping doorways opened into wide, airy rooms with huge windows that would be letting the sunlight pour in.

My feet carried me farther into the house as if of their own accord. And maybe that was my mistake. Not bracing myself. Not watching for the first hint of horror so I could pull myself back.

Or maybe there was no way I could have avoided it.

My ballet flats squeaked on the polished floor, and my stomach lurched. Like the squeak of my sisters' feet as we'd dashed this way—like the strangled squeal that had burst from Verity's throat as the rogue's jaws clamped down on her.

I whirled, trying to pull myself away from the memories, but my gaze stuck on a spot on the wall. A perfectly even green spot —they'd washed it and painted over. But I could see clear as anything where the splotch of blood had been, just beyond that door. Where it had dribbled across the floorboards to where my wolf father had slumped.

My lungs seized up. I threw myself down the hall faster. "Ren!" Kylie called out. Like my mother, in my memories. *Faster. We can't let them catch us. Oh, please, Ren, stay with me.*

A sob had choked her throat. A moan had carried behind us. One of the rogues had stepped into the hall behind us with his rifle. It all rushed at me, faster and faster: the click as he reloaded. His mocking chuckle bouncing off the walls. Another puddle of blood. The smear of fingerprints across the baseboard.

I spun again—and crashed into a broad, solid chest. Nate's arms came around me. "Ren," he murmured, dipping his head low. "I'm here. We're here. All that is over now."

I pressed my face into his shirt, but my pulse rattled on. More memories bubbled up and burst in my head. My mind was spinning. I couldn't think. I couldn't breathe.

"Let's get her to her room," West said, somewhere behind me. "There wasn't any fighting there."

"Hey." Aaron's voice, always so measured even with its faint rasp. "Here we go, Serenity. You just need a little time to settle in. You were right. This is still your home. Hold on to that."

Was it? How could this place be mine when the rogues had painted it with my family's blood?

CHAPTER 12

Marco

I KNOCKED on Ren's door softly, not wanting to wake her if she'd fallen asleep. When we'd brought her to the master bedroom a little more than an hour ago, she'd been shaking, her skin turned sallow. It had wrenched at me to see her so affected by this house's past, but when she'd ordered us to leave so she could collect her thoughts, she hadn't offered any room for argument.

I hoped she'd been able to let her awful memories of the attack here fade rather than falling deeper into them.

"Come in," my mate said without asking who it was. Well, she must be able to sense my presence as well as I could sense hers through the bond between us. It had only strengthened when she'd finally made that last connection with West. Good to know wolf boy wasn't completely hopeless.

Ren's voice sounded steady enough. When I eased open the door and slipped inside, she was sitting up on her bed, on top of the covers. Her back was straight, but her face still looked paler than usual, stark in contrast with her dark brown hair. The light in her amber-brown eyes didn't hold quite the fire I'd have liked to see.

She smiled at me with just half of her mouth. I understood her well enough by now to read what she was feeling then. She was embarrassed by how she'd broken down. As if any of us who'd been with her when she'd gotten overwhelmed would judge her for it.

I ambled over to the bed as if nothing at all were amiss and sat down at the foot, reaching to take her hand. "How is my Princess of Flames?"

She scooted closer. "Not feeling very regal," she muttered. "I'm not going to accomplish whatever I'm supposed to do here if I can't walk down the hall without getting buried in memories."

"They'll fade," I said, stroking my thumb over the back of her hand. "It's your first time back here. Of course they hit you hard. I have no doubt you'll be back to your usual regal ass-kicking self in no time."

She gave me a fuller smile at that remark, but her eyes still looked a little weary.

"Is something else bothering you, princess?" I asked.

She leaned her head against my shoulder. My whole body lit up in an instant, with desire and affection. A week ago, she might have hesitated to get even this close with me. The fact that she was now my mate in every possible way felt almost miraculous.

I was very much looking forward to experiencing that miracle again and again.

For now, I suspected affection was going to be more what she needed than desire. I slipped my arm around her waist, and she sighed.

"The way the memories hit me, how much they shook me up… I'm just worrying about all the kin waiting for us back on the other estates," she said. "I thought I was going to find answers here. What if the past has clouded my mind too much to see where I have to go?"

"There are only so many doors in this place, big as it is," I pointed out. "I'm sure we can manage to find the one."

"The vampires could attack again in just a few hours. We don't have much time."

I pulled her closer to me. "Our kin fended them off before. The strategy you came up with is sound—and it worked just fine in the places that didn't have a dragon shifter on hand last night."

She rubbed her mouth, frowning. "It won't be enough if the vampires keep at us. There are ways of getting past regular fire, putting it out… I wish I could be everywhere at once. Burn them all up. Just *end* this."

Oh, my dear mate. I dipped my head to kiss her temple. "It's been a long, hard journey here, hasn't it? You deserved a much more peaceful welcome."

"Maybe I didn't. There was nothing peaceful about how I left." Her laugh sounded a bit choked. She twined her fingers with mine, looking down at our joined hands. Her voice dropped. "It felt so good for a little while there. Having my bond confirmed with all of you. Like everything had fallen into exactly the right place. But now I can't help thinking about how easily I could lose all of that."

The last four alphas had fallen here too. This was where her mother had lost her mates and Ren her fathers.

Ren's other hand drifted to her belly, so instinctively I wondered if she even noticed the motion. How much of her fear was the echo of the little girl she'd been—and how much the connection to the dragon shifter who'd come before her, who'd lost children and mates? Who'd lost *everything* to save Ren.

Some of both, I thought. All tangled up together. Maybe my mate needed more than affection after all. She needed to feel every bit of her power—the power she held inside her, and the power we generated between us.

I tugged her onto her feet. A full-length mirror, the glass bright within its ornate gold frame, stood against the wall across from her wardrobes. I guided her over to it. She raised an eyebrow at me.

"Trying to distract me with the horror of my bedhead?"

I chuckled. "No. Just look at yourself."

I stood behind her as she gazed into the mirror, my hands resting on her waist. Her hair wasn't actually all that mussed, falling in its loose waves halfway down her back. The casual dress she'd picked hugged her curves gently, but no less appealingly than if it'd been a silk gown.

"That's not just a princess looking back at you," I said, holding her gaze in the mirror from over her shoulder. "That's a queen. A queen who's taken every bit of bullshit anyone's thrown at her and soared above it all."

"Yeah?" she said.

"Oh, yeah. Look at those eyes. I've loved the fire in them since the first moment I saw you. That was all I needed for me to know you had it in you to take on whatever the world threw at you." I swept the fall of her hair to the side so I could kiss the crook of her jaw. "And that stubborn mouth. Never letting anyone off the hook—unless they deserve a second chance. Because a queen knows when to be merciful too."

I brushed my thumb over her soft lips. Ren's eyes glimmered.

She let her lips part, teasing the edge of her teeth against my thumb. Just like that, I was hard.

I ran my fingers over her arms next, down to the sensitive skin inside her elbows. "The strength in you, anyone can see it. Never backing down from a challenge. Always ready to defend your kin."

My hands slipped beneath her arms and up her torso to trace the undersides of her breasts. Ren's breath hitched, her eyelids dipping. "And I haven't even mentioned how fucking gorgeous you are. I could look at nothing but you for days and still be enjoying the view."

"Go on," she said, her voice roughening. The color was coming back into her cheeks, a lovely rosy flush. I kissed my way down the side of her neck to her shoulder. My hands rose to completely cup her breasts. She leaned back against me as I stroked the peaks, making her nipples pebble against the fabric of her dress. Heat radiated between us.

"We both know how much passion you've got in this beautiful body," I murmured by her ear. "Keep watching. See what a woman you are."

Ren

I shivered with pleasure as Marco continued to caress my breasts. Each flick over my nipples sent a fresh quiver of electric bliss through my body. And somehow seeing it in the mirror—the rising flush in my cheeks and neck, his lithe fingers working over my curves through the dress—turned me on even more.

I watched him lower his head a second before his mouth found my earlobe. He gave it a light nip that made me gasp.

When his eye met mine again, they were hooded and dark with his own passion.

Marco's hand trailed down my side to the hem of my dress, just past my thighs. I pressed back into him instinctively, my ass brushing his cock, already at attention in his slacks. An even deeper tremor ran through me—and a knock sounded on my door.

Aaron's voice carried through. "Serenity?"

My mind was so muddled with desire an answer popped out automatically. "Come in."

Marco arched his eyebrows at me in the mirror. Oh. Er... But Aaron was already stepping inside.

He stopped on the threshold of the bedroom, the door thudding shut behind him. His bright gaze took in the scene: Marco and me standing together in front of the mirror, my cheeks pink and nipples poking against the fabric of my dress, one of the feline alpha's hands still molded over my breast. I could almost feel the thump of Aaron's heart speeding up, the heat emanating from his skin at the sight of us.

"If I'm interrupting something..." the eagle shifter said, his tone mild even though his eyes had lit with interest.

Marco shifted a little to one side, dipping to kiss the other side of my neck, as if to indicate there was plenty of room to share. My pulse raced a little faster. Of course it didn't matter if another of my mates saw us. He could join us.

"Definitely not," I said, a little breathless. "At least not if you want to stay."

The eager sound he made in his throat seemed to answer that question. Aaron crossed the space between us in an instant, sliding his arm around my waist.

I turned my head to kiss him. As the avian alpha captured my mouth, Marco slicked his tongue up my neck. Heat flooded me from both sides. Aaron teased his thumb over one breast as Marco continued to fondle the other. My panties had already dampened, but I had the feeling they were soaking now.

I reached up to curl my fingers into both of their shirts. No, that wasn't what I wanted to be feeling. I jerked at the collars. Aaron smiled against my mouth. He gave me one last kiss, tilting his head to deepen it. Then he eased back just enough to pull his thin polo over his head.

Marco followed suit, undoing the first two buttons of his linen dress shirt and then yanking the whole thing off, rumpling his jagged black hair. I glanced over at him, wanting to see him beside me and not just in the mirror. My fingers traced over the fading scars in his tan skin where the tiger shifter who'd challenged him had wounded him. I kissed one mark on his shoulder, another on his jaw, then brought his mouth to mine.

Marco kissed me hard and hungry. His eyes gleamed when he pulled back. His fingers gripped the hem of my dress insistently. Aaron grasped the other side, and they pulled the cotton sundress off together.

The avian alpha immediately bent to suck my bare nipple into his mouth. His steady hand caressed the curve of my ass. Marco claimed my lips again, his hand slipping between us. I trembled as his fingers glided over my sex to the nub of my clit. Pleasure sparked from my core. I moaned against his mouth.

Marco's thumb swiveled over my clit, drawing another whimper from me. Then he yanked my panties down and slid his fingers down over my hot, slick opening. My hips canted toward him of their own accord. Yes. Yes, *please*. I clutched the hem of his slacks with a determined tug. He chuckled and eased back to chuck them off.

Aaron took the opportunity to trail his lips down my body until he reached my sex. I gasped as he pressed his mouth to my core. The tips of his teeth grazed over my clit, and a full-out cry broke from my throat. I rocked into his touch, needing more.

Marco brought his body up against mine from behind again. His hands slipped over my hips. The hard length of his cock rubbed over my ass and between my legs. I edged my feet apart to give him better access, tipping forward to rest my hands on the mirror's frame.

Aaron kissed the planes of my stomach as the jaguar shifter nudged my opening with the head of his cock. Marco pressed forward, and I whimpered as the solid length of him penetrated me. "Fuck, princess," he muttered, his fingers tightening around my hips. "You're the best thing I've ever felt."

He drew back and plunged in even deeper, sending a rush of bliss through my nerves. Aaron ducked back down to lave my clit. My body swayed with each of Marco's thrusts, pressing my mound to Aaron's mouth. He rocked with us, gripping my thigh, his tongue swirling over my nub until I was outright shaking with the rising pleasure.

"Look," Marco murmured, leaning over me as he adjusted his angle. I moaned, bucking faster to meet his pace, chasing that peak of bliss I'd almost reached. At the same time, I lifted my gaze.

My reflection looked back at me, flushed and wild. I'd never seen my eyes so bright with emotion before. Emotion and power. I had one man groaning against my shoulder as his hips jerked to meet me, another devouring my sex from the outside. Aaron's golden head didn't miss a beat as he unzipped his jeans to stroke his cock in time with our love-making.

He nipped my clit, and Marco thrust even harder. Ecstasy swept through me. I shattered between them with a sharp cry, my hand dropping to squeeze Aaron's shoulder. Marco's breath shuddered against my skin as my pussy squeezed tight around his cock. He spilled himself into me. Aaron groaned at the same time, giving me one last swipe of his tongue as he spent himself in his hand.

I stayed there between my mates as the crash of pleasure ebbed, my legs shaking. Aaron let me hold onto him. He pressed a tender kiss to my inner thigh. Marco hummed happily as he softened inside me, and nuzzled my shoulder.

I looked at the wild, sated woman in the mirror—a woman who had claimed her four mates. A woman who'd overcome rogues and fae. Yes, that was who I was now. The tragedies of years ago didn't matter, not when it came to fulfilling my role.

I wasn't that little girl anymore. I was a woman. I was the dragon shifter. And I *would* unearth whatever secrets my estate was keeping hidden.

CHAPTER 13

Ren

A COUPLE of West's kin had already gotten to work in the kitchens, which was a good thing. None of us had eaten anything resembling lunch, just a few snacks that'd been stashed on the plane. Feeling a lot more grounded than I had when I'd first walked into the house, I ambled into the dining area, found a platter of stuffed rolls ready and waiting, and grabbed one to chow down on while I wandered farther.

My memories hadn't faded completely. Now and then my eyes twitched to a doorway a rogue had left from, a spot where I'd heard an agonized cry. But my mind didn't spin off into the past like it had before. I focused on the firm floor behind my feet and the heady warmth of the bonds between my mates and me. It seemed to have grown even more solid during that interlude with Marco and Aaron.

The strength in this body and the strength of those bonds held me here in the present. I had so much more to do here.

Maybe a victory against the vampires wouldn't make up for what had happened in the past, but I could hope that victory would send us toward a much brighter future.

The rooms in the east wing were all familiar. I'd spent most of my time in those when we'd been living here—when I wasn't roaming around outside. When I entered the west side of the house, a prickle ran down my back.

Mom had taken me this way a couple times to show me something she was working on. But mostly we'd steered clear. It had been her domain as the ruling dragon shifter.

I swallowed the rest of the sandwich and treaded farther down that hall. *I* was the ruling dragon shifter now.

I wasn't expecting to hear a patter of footsteps coming toward me. Kylie hustled around a bend, her face lighting up when she saw me. "Ren!" She twisted her hands in front of her with a slightly guilty expression. "I know you're exploring this place on your own, but I couldn't help being curious… I found a door like the one you described, the one from your vision. Do you want to, like, find it on your own or is it okay for me to show you?"

Trust Kylie to have already scoped the whole place out.

"It's fine," I said with a grin. "Lead the way."

Whatever I found here, I didn't know if I was meant to face it alone. I'd rather have my mates by my side. As Kylie beckoned me down the hall she'd emerged from, I focused on the warm pulse of the bond inside me. I knew where each of my alphas were, approximately. And I discovered, testing the feel of our connection, that I could give them all a tug. *Come here.*

That was handy. I'd have to remember that trick. Nate had told me that eventually I'd be able to sense whenever he or the others were in pain, even across a long distance. Being able to give them a nudge in my direction must be part of that increased awareness.

The hall Kylie had explored took us around to the back corner of the house. She stopped in front of the door. And it was The Door. They were all the same moss green, but this one had that circle of dimples just above my line of sight. And no handle, no knob. But just like in my vision, I knew, looking at it, I could open it easily.

Heavier footsteps sounded down the hall. All four of my mates came into view. They must have caught up with each other on the way over.

"This is it?" Aaron asked, inspecting the door as they joined me.

I nodded. "I haven't tried to open it yet."

"Well, what are you waiting for, Sparks?" West said. His tone was more teasing than gruff. "This is what we came all this way for."

Nate eased closer as if to offer his help, but I could feel down to my bones that this task was only mine. I drew in my breath and stepped up to the door. My hands rose as if summoned to rest on either side of the dimpled circle.

A shiver of energy raced down my arms. A burning sensation crept up my throat, as if I were kindling dragon fire in my human form. I paused, and then exhaled in a steady stream against the circle.

No fire burst from my lips, only a rush of air. But the door twitched and swung open, away from my hands.

On the other side, a straight, narrow staircase led down into a basement room. A soft glow crept into the space below as I watched. I hadn't realized this house even had a basement. I stared at the staircase for a second, anticipation tingling over my skin.

"You've got this, princess," Marco said.

I did. I moved forward, down one step and the next, my fingers trailing along the smooth wall. The tingling sensation washed over me even more deeply, with one very clear impression.

Whatever was waiting for me below, it was only for me.

"I don't think you can come with me," I said to the guys and Kylie behind me.

"Nope," Marco agreed. "Couldn't even if we tried. That place doesn't want us at all."

"I've never felt anything like that before," Aaron murmured, mostly to himself, with awed curiosity.

"You just holler if you need us, then," Kylie said.

I walked further, down into the room. The door clicked shut behind me. The air pressure thickened, as if to embrace me. My feet hit the tiled floor at the bottom, and a fresh breath rushed into my lungs with a cool, powdery smell.

I was here.

And where was *here*, exactly? I rotated slowly, taking in the whole room.

The space was lined with shelves, and each of them held a row of glinting slabs. I stepped closer. They were crystal tablets, like the one Mom had left for me in the abandoned subway tunnel that had led us to Sunridge—and to my new fiery power to get at the truth.

The room was packed with them, all of them etched with one or more symbols, many of which didn't mean anything to me. The only other objects the room contained were an armchair with a high arched back and a small rosewood side table.

The place felt like a library, if you could read crystals instead of books. But then, Mom had managed to leave me a message in that first crystal. The truth-seeking flames and a vision of my mother's murder had been contained in a larger crystal. Who knew what any of these might hold?

I had no idea where to start, so I grabbed one at random. A quiver of energy raced across my palms. The etching on this one showed what looked vaguely like a bear standing on its hind legs between a horse and a weasel. Interesting.

I sank into the chair. Instinct told me to press the crystal tablet to my chest. An odd warmth bled from its smooth surface into my skin. Then a clear, even voice started speaking in my head.

"Dragon shifter Matilde, May 2, 1876. I record this history of a conflict resolved among the disparate kin."

As the long-gone dragon shifter's words rolled into my mind, a vision formed before my eyes, like the glimpse I'd gotten of my mother's death. But I got the sense this one was more symbolic than any literal event. A tall woman with sleek black hair stood with a burly man next to her, in a yard I vaguely recognized from the disparate estate. Several shifters in animal form prowled on either side of the pair.

"For five years, my alphas and I have seen a growing hostility between the meat-eating and plant-eating members of the disparate kin. Accusations of wrongdoing have been thrown from both sides. A few skirmishes have resulted in many injured and four dead. The primary point of contention appeared to be—"

I pulled the crystal away from my chest and set it on the side table, breaking the vision and the voice. With a couple of slow breaths, I settled back into the present. My gaze skimmed the shelves again.

So these were histories? Records committed to the crystals by the dragon shifters before me—reports they hoped later dragon shifters would find useful?

I hadn't seen any conflicts among the disparate kin while I'd been there, and Nate hadn't mentioned any. That record might be worthwhile to listen to later, but for now, it wasn't what I needed.

I stood up, slid that crystal back onto its shelf, and considered the others. There were hundreds in this room. Which one would give me something I could use against the vampires?

No way to find out but through trial and error.

The tablets clinked softly as I flipped through several on the shelf at head height, peering at the images etched on them. Those clearly gave some idea as to the contents. How would you draw a vampire? A stick figure with little triangles jutting from its mouth?

An artist I was not. God, would I be recording the trials I'd experienced over the last few weeks on one of these crystals when all this trouble was over?

I pushed that thought aside and bent to look through the next shelf. My hand stilled over a tablet with a few sketchy human-ish figures on left and a wolf, lion, and eagle on the right. Those first figures could be vampires, maybe?

Worth a try. I picked it up and got comfy on the armchair again.

The voice that spilled into my head when I held this tablet close was huskier, more abrupt. "Dragon shifter Geraldine, November 14, 1937. I chronicle the current state of shifter-human interactions. I've been watching this problem get worse since I was a little girl. The humans keep breeding, and more of them keep pouring in from across the ocean. Their cities are expanding. They set down new roots anywhere they please. Sometimes far too close to our shifter territories than is really comfortable."

The image that swam up before my eyes showed a group of shifters watching houses being erected up the hillside from their village. It morphed into a scene of the same shifters loading up cars with boxes from their houses, then driving off down a winding road, deeper into the wilderness.

"We have preserved the lands around our estates for centuries, but those who want to live elsewhere are finding their options increasingly limited by the number and distribution of human communities. I'll now go into detail about some of the strategies we've used to limit exposure between—"

I removed the tablet and gave my head a quick shake to clear it. The information my ancestor had been relating there was stuff I'd definitely want to come back to—but not right now, when vampires were causing us a hell of a lot more trouble than any humans.

A couple of the shelves were empty, I guessed to make room for future contributions. I left the human occupation tablet on one of those so I could find it again easily when I had time to really pay attention.

A glance into a closed cabinet revealed stacks of blank crystals that must have been for my or later dragon shifter's use. Hopefully there was an instruction manual around here somewhere. I returned to pawing through the other records.

Partway through the next row, an etching caught my eye with a pang of recognition. I pulled out that tablet.

On closer examination, the image wasn't exactly the same as the one I'd remembered. It showed dragons and humanoid figures a little too tall and slim to be really human. The fae. I'd seen carvings like this on the pedestal in the mountain caves, where I'd found the truth-seeking flames that fae and shifter magic had created together.

Dragons and fae stood together in the picture on the tablet too. One fae figure had its hand resting on the shoulder of the dragon beside it. Two others stood with their heads bent toward each other, a shape like a flame between them.

It didn't look like this one would say anything about vampires, but then, maybe our relations with the other dominant paranormal community would give me some insight. And I couldn't deny I was curious how we and those wispy, shimmering beings had ever gotten along.

I took my spot on the chair again and clasped the tablet to my chest.

"Dragon shifter Charlotte, 1842. I would like to record a joint project I've embarked on with our fae companions, and to detail the current state of our alliance."

An alliance, huh? That had obviously fallen apart a long time ago.

I managed not to tense up as this tablet's vision spilled out before my eyes. Tall, slim, shining fae were flitting through an open forest amid a pack of wolves. A dragon, emerald green, soared by overhead.

The fae weren't fleeing the shifters or chasing them. I could tell from the flashes of smiles and the way they wove between each other's groups that they were… *enjoying* sharing the woods. Not an image I'd ever expected to see.

But then, the only time I'd seen more than one fae at a time was in the vision that had showed a bunch of them killing my mother with their magic.

"I suppose it makes sense that we shifters and the fae can understand each other better than either of us relates to the vampires," the former dragon shifter's sweet voice continued. "Unlike them, we are both drawn to life more so than death. While some of us may enjoy a night-time run, every shifter I've ever met enjoys a good lie-about in the sun, which the fae worship. And my dragon fire has so much in common with fae magic, they assure me we can link the two together, their power sharing mine. I'm excited by the possibilities."

The image whirled around to show the emerald dragon breathing fire toward a fae woman—who was encompassing it in a stream of her own blue-ish magic. My breath caught, watching it. I eased the tablet away from me to get my bearings.

Blue and red, mingling together. To create the violet of my truth-seeking flames? Had this dragon shifter been the one to create the power I'd stumbled on nearly two centuries later?

If we'd managed to create *that* power with the fae, what else might we be capable of together?

As soon as the question passed through my head, my throat tightened. Maybe the dragon shifters had been able to work alongside the fae in the distant past, but a lot had changed since then. How had we come to the point where the fae monarch would look the other way while her people slaughtered my mother?

How the hell could we ever trust them again?

I didn't know what had gone wrong, but I couldn't answer any of those questions without knowing more. Inhaling deeply, I brought the tablet back to my chest to see what else my long-ago ancestor could tell me.

CHAPTER 14

Ren

My NAME REACHED me as if from a huge distance away, across an ocean maybe. At first I almost didn't hear it. Then it penetrated my focus even more insistently.

"Ren! Princess, if you don't say something soon, I'm going to have to start clanging the sirens."

I jerked the tablet I'd been clutching away from my chest. My head spun. My stomach pinched, deep into the hollow it had formed in my belly.

How long had I been down here in the basement archive? I rubbed my forehead as if that would clear the mugginess around my thoughts and finally found the wherewithal to answer Marco. "I'm here! Sorry. I just got… really absorbed."

His chuckled carried, muted, down the stairs. "You might want to consider getting unabsorbed for a bit. I'm thinking it's about time you ate something. And while *I* have full confidence in your ability to look after yourself, some of your other mates may be wearing holes in the carpet with their pacing up here."

I had been down here longer than I realized, then. That pinching in my stomach was a reminder that yes, at some point I should have dinner.

I pushed myself off the armchair. The muscles in my back twanged from so much time spent sitting. Sitting and gazing into visions of times past.

But I still hadn't found what I was looking for. Not the reason we'd fallen out with the fae. Not a reason to think we could ever count on them again. I bit my lip, nibbling at it in my frustration, as I climbed back up to the main floor.

Marco had stepped back from the doorway to let me through. "There's my dragon shifter," he said lightly. "Did you find anything useful?"

"I don't know," I said. The climb had left me dizzy. This belly needed food ASAP. "It'd probably be better if I talk about it with all of you at once."

"I can summon a little patience."

He paused, giving me a once-over. I guess I looked about as rough as I felt. The feline alpha's expression softened. He cupped my face, cradling my jaw, and pressed a butterfly of a kiss to the middle of my forehead. "If you're not there yet, you will be soon, princess. I'm sure of that."

Good. Someone really should be, and it sure as hell wasn't me.

The hearty smell of freshly grilled steaks reached my nose. By the time we arrived at the dining room, my mouth was full of saliva.

"Look what the cat dragged in," Marco announced with a smirk as the other alphas glanced up where they were standing around the table.

Kylie was there too. She bounded over first. "So what's the big secret? Can you even tell us what's down there? What have you been doing all afternoon?"

Everyone's eyes trained on me. Waiting to hear that this trip had been worthwhile. My gut knotted. "It's… kind of hard to explain."

Marco rested his hands on my shoulder. "I think our Princess of Flames needs to get some nourishment into her. Where's that dinner?"

As if on cue, a couple of the kin emerged from the kitchen then, carrying plates. Nate motioned for them to give the first one to me. I dropped into the nearest chair and grabbed the waiting cutlery.

It only took a couple of bites before my head started to clear. I gulped water from the glass someone had brought me and looked around the table. My alphas and Kylie were all eating, the rest of the kin having left us some privacy.

But their attention was still on me. As soon as my hands stilled, West looked up, catching my gaze with a question in his. Aaron raised his head, his own eyes glinting with enthusiasm. He must have been dying to know what dragon shifter secrets I'd discovered.

Nothing down in that archive felt all that top secret. I had the feeling no one except the dragon shifters was meant to go down there and handle the tablets directly, but nothing about them told me I shouldn't share the information I'd learned.

The hard part was figuring out how to explain all that information without the helpful murmur of a voice in my ear and mental images for illustration.

"I haven't found out anything specific about the vampires," I said slowly. "There's—it's basically a records room. Pieces of history past dragon shifters saved for the ones who came later, about what happened in the past. I ended up spending most of the time on records about the fae."

West's eyes narrowed. "How do they fit in? Do you think they're helping the vampires?"

"No, not at all," I said, waving my hand as if that gesture would dispel any wrong impressions I'd given. "One thing I know from what I've heard is there's *no* way the fae would ever ally with the vampires. They're pretty much opposites. But I guess you all already know that."

I rubbed my face. In so many areas, I was still just catching up to basic paranormal knowledge. There was one thing they didn't know much about, though. "I was more interested in the ways they used to work with the shifters."

"So the records talked more about that association?" Aaron leaned forward. "I don't know why our own histories are so sparse on that subject."

"It seems like the fae leaders mostly preferred to deal with the dragon shifters," I said. "Something about… feeling the closest kinship with us, because they're all about light and energy, and that's kind of the same as our fire? So I don't get the impression they interacted with the other shifters a whole lot even back then."

"And better for us that they didn't," West muttered.

I hesitated. I knew better than maybe anyone here what a sensitive subject this was for him. "They were *good* allies, at least in some ways, back then," I had to say. "It's thanks to them and one of the past dragon shifters that I've been able to draw the truth out of our enemies. They created that power so it would be ready when there was a time of great need… It took them *years* to perfect it and contain it. The fae didn't get anything out of that effort except knowing they'd given us a new strength."

"That and a handy way to tempt shifters up the mountain where they could pick us off," Marco pointed out.

I glowered at him. "That obviously wasn't the original plan."

"What was the plan?" Nate asked in his low baritone. "Why did they think someone would need that power? Why not give it to the dragon shifter already there?"

"I guess that dragon shifter didn't need it. The impression I get is that it was, like, an ace for us to have up our sleeve. Seeing how quickly the world was starting to change, how much territory humans were claiming here… Little did they know it'd be partly our own people causing the chaos." I grimaced. "But that's not the point."

"Something about this alliance seems meaningful to you right now," Aaron prompted, his gaze intent on me. "Why did you focus on that thread of our history?"

"Partly I just happened to stumble on it. And after that… I get the sense that it's all tied together somehow. The relationships between the different paranormal communities. The way we've clashed. I can't pin it down yet, but I feel like there's *something* important in all those past events that might help us see what to do." I paused and sighed. "And also I haven't come across many records about vampires at all. It seems like we've mostly steered clear of each other."

"That sounds accurate," Marco said. "If only they'd keep steering clear."

"If there's anything to learn about the fae, it's that they're backstabbing bastards," West broke in. "Maybe they pretended to ally with us before, but everything they've done since…" He swept his arm through the air in a violent motion that made me think of his mottled scar. "You follow whatever paths you want, Sparks, but I can't see us gaining anything from the fae we're dealing with now."

The twist of his mouth echoed how I felt, thinking about the fae. They'd taken both of our mothers from us, hadn't they? I swallowed hard and reached across the table to touch his hand.

A day or two ago, I'd have expected him to jerk his arm away. Funny how much one conversation—and, er, other activities following said conversation—could change things. He turned his hand so I could twine my fingers through his.

"I know," I said. "Believe me, I don't trust them either." But even as I said those words, a deeper discomfort echoed through me. The way that past dragon shifter had talked about the fae, warmly, almost admiring…

Had she really been completely deceived, or was there more to the fae than I'd been able to see in my own experiences?

"What do we do now?" Kylie asked.

I frowned. "I don't know." My gaze slid to the window. It had darkened into evening outside. "Has there been any word from the estates or any of the other communities?"

Nate shook his head. "I gave my kin instructions to contact me as soon as there was any news. I'll be keeping my phone right by me."

"Same as all of us," Marco said. "And when we hear anything, you'll be the first to know, Ren."

Were the vampires really going to hold off on us tonight? I found that hard to believe. Some part of me had felt I needed to come here. I *had* to figure out why.

I gave West's hand a quick squeeze before letting go and reaching for my fork. "I guess the best plan I have is to get some more dinner in me, and then go back to the records room. There's got to be something useful down there."

~

The soft glow of the crystals was starting to sting my eyes. I leaned against the side of the armchair and rubbed them. The meal had revived my energy for a few hours, but I could feel myself flagging again. The last few tablets I'd taken out, more out of desperation than any clear sign they'd be useful, hadn't given me any real guidance.

There had to be something more about the fae. How could we have fallen apart to the point of becoming almost enemies without any dragon shifter recording those events? They'd reported on the freaking crop growth patterns, for fuck's sake.

I'd just straightened up to roll the cricks out of my shoulders when my gaze snagged on a glinting corner just barely protruding between two of the shelving units. Kneeling beside them, I slid my hand in and tugged. One, and then another, and then another tablet tumbled out. They must have fallen through a gap in the partly open sides of the shelves and gotten wedged back there.

As I examined my new finds, my pulse fluttered. One of them showed a fae figure and a dragon on either side of a jagged line. I didn't need to be a psychoanalyst to take a stab at what that might mean.

I shoved the other two tablets onto a shelf and dropped into the chair. Time to find out what the hell had gone wrong between us and the fae.

"Dragon shifter Mirabel," a weary voice said. "1908. It is with sad heart that I report the dissolution of our friendly relations with fae kind. An accident was made on our part, I'll admit that, but they've proven completely unwilling to listen to reason."

The images rose up and faded from one to another before my eyes. Humans settling near one of the shifter villages. One of them killing a partridge shifter who'd gone out to stretch her wings. The shifters gathering their things and moving deeper into the nearby wilderness. "Fae territory," Mirabel said. "But they had shared with us before. And my kin had little choice of where to go."

But the scene before me went wrong. The shifters hustled the carts packed with their belongings along through the sparsely wooded plains and sent them careening down a hill without seeing the small group of fae who'd been relaxing below. The fae shrieked and scattered, but one didn't leap up quite in time. A cart's wheel slammed right over his leg.

I flinched, watching. The fae boy scrambled away, dragging his wounded leg, his face twisted with agony. One of his companions gave a shout and hurled a bolt of magic at the cart. It split in two with a sizzle, half the cargo bursting into shimmers of light.

Precious belongings, all the shifters had left from their own home. My long-ago kin let out a wail. One of them lunged at the fae who'd cast the magic, knocking her to the ground with a slash of talons. Then the image faded.

"So naturally I was called in to resolve the conflict," the dragon shifter said. "I went to see the fae monarch to resolve the situation peacefully. But she was not happy to see only me. She wished for my kin to be brought before her for her judgment. As if she didn't trust my own. I couldn't leave my kin to that potential vengeance. But she took my refusal as a horrific insult. Wouldn't hear any talk of compensation for *my* kin's losses."

The fae queen in the vision spun on her heel, a cloud of magic gusting between her and Mirabel. The dragon shifter strode off in the other direction.

"They've been cold to us ever since," she said in my mind. "Driving us from lands we once shared. Refusing assistance to kin in need. The way they're behaving, I can't help but wonder if they've been simply waiting for a moment such as this as an excuse to set themselves apart from us. My mother said they once tried to steal her fire. Maybe they've realized we'll never permit that, and we're no longer of any use to them. Good riddance, in that case."

Her voice faded away. I came back to the records room, clutching the tablet. My heart was thudding.

Was that really how the animosity between our peoples had started? With a simple accident and a kneejerk act of retaliation. But I guessed tensions had been building for some time underneath, if the previous dragon shifter had suspected the fae… of trying to *steal* her fire? What the hell did that even mean?

And how did you get from there to outright murder?

CHAPTER 15

Nate

I DIDN'T KNOW what time it was, but the moon was stark against the black sky outside my window. I shoved myself out of bed and checked the phone on my room's desk again, as if I'd have missed it if someone had called or texted. No alerts, of course.

I grimaced at the screen and walked into the ensuite bathroom. Tiny aches still nibbled at my muscles here and there if I moved at any speed. I could pretend to be totally recovered, but inside the holes the bullets had dug weren't quite finished healing.

My body had better hurry up and stitch itself whole. There was too much fighting still ahead of us.

The brief walk didn't leave me any more ready to sleep. My head was muggy, but the rest of me was on high alert. Any moment, that call announcing disaster might come. Any moment, Ren might need me.

I tossed myself back into bed anyway, burrowing my face in the pillow. I'd be a lot more useful to all of them if I wasn't a zombie from exhaustion.

The blanket cocooned me in warmth. Crickets chirped beyond the window. The aches faded from my muscles. But I still couldn't quite drift off.

The door to my rooms eased open, a faint click and a whisper of air. Quiet footsteps padded across the floor. I caught my mate's familiar scent before she'd made it halfway across the bedroom. My eyes opened, and she shot me a soft smile. I pushed myself over on the bed to make more room for her.

She clambered right up and slid under the covers, wrapping her arm around me. I slept in nothing but boxers. The feel of her bare skin against mine set my nerves on alert in a much more gratifying way.

"Finished your researching?" I asked.

"For now, anyway." Ren nestled her head under my chin and pressed a kiss to my shoulder. "Everyone else is already asleep. I wanted someone to cuddle up with. And I thought you might be feeling a little neglected."

I snorted. "I'm sure you were giving me plenty of attention while I was out of commission. It's not your fault I wasn't conscious enough to enjoy it."

She made a humming sound and squirmed even closer. I definitely wasn't going to complain about the attention now.

"How are you feeling now?" she asked. "Still sore?"

I didn't want her fretting about me, but I wasn't going to lie to her. "A little. When you're injured that badly, it takes a while for everything to sort itself out. But I'm almost there." I ran my hand over her hair. "You must still be feeling that attack last night."

She shrugged. "It's not so bad. I've spent most of the day

sitting in one chair or another. Plenty of rest." She tipped her head back to look me in the eyes. "I'm sure you need *your* rest. You came out of that coma less than a day ago. I hope I didn't wake you up."

"No, I've been doing a good job of keeping myself awake all by myself," I said with a half-smile.

Her brow knit. "Worrying about your kin?"

"Mostly. It's hard not to. But I think I'll have an easier time letting go of those thoughts with you here."

"Hmm." She teased her hand up my neck and urged my head down. I met her lips with a long, gentle kiss. My body reacted instantly, heat washing through me, my cock thickening. By the time our mouths slipped apart, I was painfully hard and not minding it at all.

"You know," Ren said, a mischievous note coming into her voice, "I remember a time not all that long ago when I was all tensed up with worries, and you found the perfect way to relax me."

An eager quiver ran through me. "I'm all for that."

I moved to cover her body with mine, but she held me back with a light press of her hand. "No," she murmured, letting her fingers slip down my chest and abdomen to the waist of my boxers. "I was thinking of that first time, in the van… I don't want you straining anything that's not quite healed. You just relax and let me take care of you."

Dear God, when she said it like that, looking at me through her eyelashes so coyly, I just about came apart from that alone.

Ren pulled me into another kiss, this one more intense, while her hand ventured under my boxers. I groaned as her fingers closed around my erection. She stroked me loosely at first, and then with firming grip, her thumb flicking over the head of my cock. Pleasure shot through my veins.

I kissed her harder, but that wasn't enough. Even if she wouldn't let me respond with all the passion I wanted to give her, I could still share this bliss. As I rocked into her grasp, I reached up under her dress and tucked my hand between her legs.

Ren whimpered. Our kisses turned sloppier as we both began to pant. I rubbed the heel of my hand against her clit, my fingers testing and then dipping inside her opening. She slicked precum down my length and pumped me faster.

I was soaring on pleasure now. Was this how it felt when she shifted into that magnificent dragon form and sailed up into the sky?

The pressure building in my balls was the most amazing torture, but I wanted to see her through first. I hooked my fingers higher into the tight, hot center of her. She gasped. My thumb pressed down on her nub, and her sex clenched around me. She shuddered with a broken sound of ecstasy, but her hold on me didn't falter. Two more steady strokes, and I was spilling over with her.

We sagged deeper into the mattress, our breaths falling back into an easier rhythm together. Ren kissed me one more time, so perfectly sweet. And perfectly right. As she snuggled against me again, my body finally let go of the last of its tensions, and I drifted into sleep.

Ren

When I woke up next to Nate, my eyelids protested, too heavy to comfortably lift. I blinked blearily at the dark room. It was still night outside the window.

But a tremor of unease had passed over me. My pulse was thumping faster.

Something was wrong. My mates were upset.

I tried to slip out from under the blanket without waking Nate, but he stirred as soon as I moved. "Ren?" he murmured.

"I just want to make sure everything's all right," I said. "You can stay right there."

Fat chance of that. The bear shifter shoved back the blankets to join me. He grabbed a housecoat from a hook on his wardrobe. My dress was wrinkled, but I didn't really care. Everyone in this house had seen me looking a lot worse.

We came out into the hall to find West striding toward us. He stopped, taking in the two of us with a twitch of amusement at the corner of his mouth. Otherwise his expression was grim. My stomach balled tighter.

"I was just coming to get both of you," he said. "Looks like it's an easy job."

He turned to head back the way he'd come with a motion for us to follow. I caught up with him. "What's going on?" I said. "Have the vampires made another attack?"

"Of course they have," he muttered, his voice as grim as his face. "They've been experimenting with different tactics to counteract the fires. Water tanks with hoses to spray them down, mostly. Around the estates our kin added extra gasoline to the wood so it wouldn't burn out so easily, but there were a couple of villages hit that hadn't evacuated… They weren't prepared enough."

My heart sank. "Did anyone make it out?"

He shook his head, his jaw clenched. Behind me, Nate swore. "None of my lieutenants have contacted me."

"They might still be busy fighting the vamps off," I pointed out. And no matter what was happening out there, there was nothing he or the rest of us could do about it right now. By the time we made it to any village, it'd be morning, the vampires gone—and whatever wreckage they'd left behind already settled.

"That's not all," West said as we strode into the private common room meant for just the five of us. "I had a couple of my people watching the only highway that comes close to this estate. A truck stinking of vamps passed by not long ago, heading our way. Maybe they're hoping they'll catch us by surprise, coming this deep into our territory, like the rogues did before. The speed they were going, they'll be here in the next half hour."

My pulse stuttered. "We haven't put up any defenses." The dragon shifter estate boasted a stone wall around its inner boundaries much like the one at the canine estate, but that wouldn't stop the vampires by itself. We hadn't brought enough kin with us to fully defend it. We hadn't laid down wood for a fire. We'd assumed the vampires wouldn't be prepared to venture this far—and wouldn't see any reason to. "How do they even know we're here? We left in the middle of the day."

"They might not," Aaron said. He was standing at the end of the dining table, looking at a map he'd spread out there. "They might just want to do whatever damage they can to the property—as a show of force, to lower our general morale. It doesn't sound as if there are a lot of them on their way here."

Marco folded his arms where he was leaning against the table's edge. "Or one of those last few rogues who've thrown in with the bloodsuckers decided to play spy. They might have heard something from outside the walls of the canine estate, the kin there talking about our trip, or simply guessed from the direction the jet headed in."

I gritted my teeth at the thought of those traitors. What had the vampires offered them to make them think they were better off siding with creatures who wanted to exterminate the rest of us? Or did they think the vamps would be satisfied once they'd taken out me and my alphas and leave the rest of us alone? Hadn't they *seen* what those monsters were doing?

Of course, from what Timothy had reported… maybe they weren't thinking very much at all. Sixteen years was a long time to be carrying that much rage. I'd bet some of the losers from the battle at Marco's estate had faded back into the wilderness to live their lives apart from us in peace. The ones who'd run to the vampires—they were too far gone to reason with.

"So what's the plan?" I said.

Aaron tapped the map. I came over to stand beside him. "There's only one road that can support a truck that comes into the lands around the estate," he said. "Here, between two of the lower hills. So we know where they'll be coming from."

Looking at the lines on the paper, it all seemed very clear. "I go out there and blast them to bits, then."

Marco's lips curled up. "Sounds simple enough."

West, on the other hand, frowned. "You're tired, Ren. How late were you up in that records room?" I pressed my mouth flat against an honest answer, and he glowered at me. "That's what I thought. I don't like the idea of you going out there alone. What if there are more of them than we expect? If they shoot you down, you might be too far from the estate to make it back."

"We have a few vehicles in the garage," Nate started.

I could read the answer to that suggestion in Aaron's eyes. "None of them is solid enough to withstand automatic gunfire, though, right?" I said. "You guys are a lot more vulnerable out there than I am. And they'll be just as happy to kill you." My hands clenched. "Look, I'll just fly up and keep watch. If I see them stopping and getting ready to come out with the guns, I'll fry them before they have the chance. Otherwise I'll wait them out here. Okay? We can't do *nothing*."

West didn't look happy, but he didn't argue either. Aaron nodded. "That sounds like the best we can make of the situation."

"Then I'd better get out there before it's too late to stop them anyway."

We loped together through the halls to the main entrance. I glanced toward the guest wing, but I didn't want to wake up Kylie for this. I had the feeling there'd be plenty more fighting where she could pitch in.

On the front steps, I undressed and shifted as smoothly as if I'd been doing this my entire life. My body expanded up into the air. With a heave of my taloned hind feet, I was swooping up toward the sky.

I kept my word. As the alphas and a few of the guards West had brought along gathered in the courtyard, I hovered above the estate with vast, steady flaps of my dragon wings. Fire itched to unfurl up my throat. I couldn't help remembering that past dragon shifter's comment about the fae trying to steal those flames from her mother.

I didn't have time to puzzle over that idea further. Movement caught my eye in the distance between the rolling hills.

The vampires had left their headlights off, having perfectly good night vision and no interest in giving us any warning. But the moon was bright enough for my shifter vision to pick out the shape of the vehicle cruising toward us down the road.

It must also have been bright enough for the vampires to see me, waiting against the starry sky. The truck had only crossed about a quarter of the distance between the hills and the estate buildings when it started to slow.

I braced myself, my muscles bunching. With a few broad flaps of my wings, I soared closer. The second the vamps stopped or showed any sign of disembarking, I had to dive. I had to burn them up before they could turn their guns on me.

The truck didn't stop, though. At my movement, it swerved around in a U-turn. As soon as the vehicle was pointing away from me, they hit the gas. The truck shot down the road the way it'd come.

I hurtled after it, tucking my wings tight as the wind warbled over my scales. The itch in my throat deepened into a furious burn. In the back of my mind the echo of gunshots rose up, the jabs of the bullets' impact, Nate's body as he'd crumpled the other night.

The vampires were stretching the distance between us. Almost at the pass between the hills already. No, I couldn't let them escape. I smacked my wings through the air, fangs scraping together in frustration.

A tickle of sensation broke through my rage. A tug. I tried to shake it off, but it wrapped all through my awareness. Abruptly, the meaning of it hit me.

My mates were calling me home.

My muscles twitched, rejecting the idea of retreat. I could keep going, fly harder, farther. I could feel it.

But that wasn't the point, was it? I'd promised them. And the last time I'd gotten carried away with vengeance, I'd burned most of a forest down. As soon as the truck veered out of sight into the pass, the vamps could stop and get ready for me with their guns.

That might even be what they wanted—for me to keep chasing them.

An ache formed in my chest. I didn't want to let them just leave. I wanted them all burned into cinders. But I forced myself to bank on the wind and wheel around.

The smell of clover filled my nostrils again as I glided over the property I'd inherited with my role and landed in the estate's grassy yard. I let myself shift back when my feet touched the ground. The grass pressed soft and cool against my tender human skin. Then an arm slid around my shoulders, pulling me into a tight, pine-tinged embrace.

West. The last of my anger fled as I buried my face in his shoulder. He'd never been the one to come to me after a shift before. But everything was different now.

Everything was different.

He helped me up, keeping his arm around me. I didn't need his support to stand, but it felt kind of nice having him there anyway. And I liked being able to see up close the faint embarrassed flush that had crept up his neck.

My other mates had gathered around us. "The vamps left," I said. "They saw me and they took off. For now."

The last words fell from my lips with an ominous weight. We all knew they'd be back tomorrow, with larger numbers or a more thorough plan.

"Then we get ready for them," Nate said, but I heard the thread of worry in his voice. It wasn't just this estate but so many other kin all across the country we needed to protect.

It was too much for one dragon alone. I could admit that. Maybe it was too much for even me and my alphas and all the kin who stood with us.

If we could summon powers beyond our own kind, I had to find that out.

I took a deep breath and raised my chin. "As soon as it's light, I want to talk to the fae."

CHAPTER 16

Ren

"I DON'T KNOW about this, Sparks," West said as we pushed through the brush in the dense forest. Twigs crackled under our feet. My alphas and I were making our way through the woods on the other side of one of my hills, not far beyond the property that belonged to the dragon shifter estate, toward a pocket of fae land. The sky had clouded, but a few streaks of sunlight pierced through, bringing the summer heat with them even this early in the morning.

"For any reason other than the hundred or so complaints you've already made?" I asked the wolf shifter.

West narrowed his eyes at me. Then his expression gentled as he wiped away a cool drop of dew that had dripped onto my cheek. "You haven't had many dealings with the fae yet. I've never seen a sign they have the slightest friendly feeling toward us. Even the history fanatic back there hasn't heard of any warm relations between our communities." He jabbed his thumb toward Aaron.

That sounded pretty similar to his earlier objections. "Okay, but I *know* they worked with the dragon shifters before. You all saw the carvings on that pedestal in the mountain. I listened to a dragon shifter from almost two hundred years ago talk about how great the fae are."

"Two hundred years is a pretty long time," Marco pointed out.

"I know," I said. "And obviously relations have gone pretty—incredibly—sour. But…" I touched West's arm with what I hoped was a reassuring caress. "We need allies. The vampires are almost overwhelming us. The fae used to be willing to stand by our side. I'm not saying we let them off the hook for the things they've done wrong. I just have to find out if there's anything I can do to mend that falling out—at least enough that they'll help us push back the bloodsuckers."

"You always want to see the good in people, don't you?" he said with a baleful look.

I raised my eyebrows at him. "A quality I think *you* should be particularly thankful for."

Nate gave a cough that might have been covering a laugh. West glanced back at the bear shifter with a growl, but it was more playful than menacing. He elbowed me. "Point taken. And I do think the fae probably hate the vampires at least as much as they hate us. Possibly more. If it's more, we might be able to work with that. I just don't want them anywhere near my kin."

"I'll keep that in mind."

"You really are an overachiever, Princess of Flames," Marco said teasingly. "A few weeks ago we grab you and tell you you've got to unite the kin-groups—surprise! And you've already moved on from that to uniting entire paranormal communities."

I smiled. "Well, I don't think I'm exactly *finished* uniting the kin-groups yet. And I don't know if I'm going to manage to unite anything at all with the fae. We'll just have to see."

"West is right about one thing," Aaron said. "You can play to the idea of their own self-interest. The vampires could easily decide they want to exterminate the fae when they're done with us."

"Just that one thing?" West grumbled, cocking his head.

Aaron chuckled. "We'll see about the rest. I doubt Ren's ancestors recorded events that never happened. But I agree that the fae haven't shown much indication of friendliness in my lifetime."

Well, that seemed to be par for the course for me these days. Taking on the Impossible: The Serenity Drake story. Who would I want to play me in the movie version?

Nate paused, touching a mark on one of the tree trunks. "We're coming into the local fae leader's domain now. Maybe we should keep the negative comments quiet from here on?"

"Good plan," I said, with particular emphasis at West.

He held up his hands. "I'm not going to ruin your peacekeeping mission, Sparks! But I also don't promise I won't say 'I told you so' if this goes sideways."

I rolled my eyes at him. "As long as you say it while you're making better use of those hands, I promise I won't mind."

His gaze heated up in an instant. "I'll take that deal."

There, now I had him grinning. Maybe that thought would keep him in a better mood until we were finished with this mission.

The fae weren't expecting us like they had been when I'd met with their monarch not that long ago. I stopped a few steps down the rough path by the edge of their territory and propped myself against a tree to wait. The last thing I needed was to start this impromptu parlay off on the wrong foot by barging deep into their lands. I could show proper respect. I just wanted them to notice I was here.

It only took a few minutes. A slender, elongated figure slipped from between the trees. Her entire form shimmered with a glow that made it difficult to tell if she was even wearing clothing—or if she wasn't, how human her body was.

"Shifters," she said, with a slight bob of her head. "Dragon and alphas. These are our grounds."

I straightened up. "I know. I'd like to speak with the one who rules over you in this territory."

The fae woman's eyes gleamed with an even deeper sparkle, like a silver coin under sunlit water. "On what matter?"

I remembered Aaron's suggestion. "A major threat that could affect both our peoples."

The woman pursed her lips, but she bobbed her head again. "I will see if he is willing to meet with you. Stay here."

There was a slightly accusatory note to her last words, as if she thought we'd want to go gallivanting around fae territory the second we had the slightest opening. "That's fine," I said, leaning back against the tree.

"Oh, yeah," West said under his breath after she'd vanished into the woods. "I'm bowled over by that warm welcome."

I stuck my tongue out at him and then *really* hoped no fae were still watching us. "I haven't had a chance to make my case yet."

He sighed. "Well, if anyone can convince them, it's you."

That was the greatest vote of confidence I'd ever gotten from him. I'd take it.

"So the fae have leaders based on where they live?" I asked Aaron, figuring the eagle alpha was the one most likely to have in-depth knowledge on this sort of subject. "I guess there aren't different types of faeries like the shifter kin-groups."

He nodded. "The fae have a unique equilibrium with nature. When one is born, they come into being alongside a plant or natural spring or something of that sort. They sort of sprout up in colonies, with all their connected trees and so on nearby."

A chilling thought struck me. "What happens if they're forced to leave the place where their connected thing is? Like if humans move in?"

"I'm not sure," Aaron said. "Speculation is that they would wither away after a certain amount of time if they were forced away. We have a few reports of fae dying if their connected object is outright destroyed. The tie is very strong."

That meant human encroachment affected the fae even more than it did us. Shifters could get up and move, as long as there was empty land to move to. The fae didn't have that luxury.

A glossy whisper carried through the breeze, raising the hairs on the back of my neck. I pushed myself completely upright. A second later, a glinting fae man appeared in the middle of our glade.

He wasn't as impressive as the fae monarch I'd encountered near Aaron's estate, but I guess that was to be expected. He was just the local leadership. The fae man still shone brighter than the lesser fae who'd directed him to us. He held himself with chin high and shoulders squared. Like all the fae, his body was tall and slim, but he was taller than most, that knobby chin of his nearly level with Nate's forehead. I'd have bet the bear shifter had a hundred pounds more muscle on him, though.

"My name is Cerimon," the fae man said. "I tend to this part of the woods. What is your business here, dragon shifter and alphas?"

He didn't bother with any sign of respect, but the fae

monarch hadn't bowed even slightly to us either. It didn't really matter to me. I'd rather just get down to business.

"I don't know how much you're aware of what's going on outside this part of the forest," I said. "But we shifters have come under attack by the vampires. They've already slaughtered everyone they could reach in several villages. They nearly killed one of my mates. They're using guns of the worst kind, and they seem determined to keep at us until they've destroyed all of us."

Cerimon made a tiny dip of his head. I couldn't tell whether it was acknowledgment that he'd heard of this happening or that he was hearing me now. "And how does this matter concern us?"

I suppressed the urge to grimace at him. "I've learned that the dragon shifters and the fae were once allied." I touched my throat. "I hold the power that my kind and yours created together. I know in the last century relations have been… strained between us, but I was hoping there might be room to at least talk about working together to tackle our enemy."

"*Your* enemy, it sounds like," the fae leader said.

"Likely to become the fae's too, if you stand by doing nothing," Aaron said evenly.

"Do you really think you could defend yourselves if the bloodsuckers took a mind to rid the country of fae too?" Marco asked.

I waved at my mates to stand down. Cerimon was frowning.

"You can say that," he said. "But we've had more troubles with your kind than with the vampires in recent years." His gaze slid to Nate. "What of the group of your kin that set up new homes at the edge of our territory in New Mexico and cut down one of our trees for firewood?"

A shiver ran down my back. Nate spread his hands. "The fae in that area hadn't appeared to my kin at all. They didn't realize the tree was special."

"It was marked," Cerimon snapped. "A life was lost."

"And we did everything we could to make reparations."

How did you make up for a life cut short? My stomach was starting to churn. The fae leader's gaze shot to Marco. "And your feline kin. I can't even count the mentions I've heard of your kind snapping branches and trampling bushes while they roam around, without concern for whose land they're venturing onto."

"Believe me," Marco said dryly. "I know just how frustrating my kin can be. I'd keep them on a shorter leash, but cats don't take well to leashes in the first place. I do what I can. And we've offered compensation as needed too. I promise you it was only carelessness, not malice. There was no intention to harm you."

"And you." Cerimon's attention moved to West. "Your people took over an entire stretch of forest that had been ours not far from your estate, and attacked us when the fae there tried to take it back."

West's lips drew back to bare his teeth. Uh oh. "The fae there tried to 'take it back' by blasting every shifter they saw with their magic," he said in what was close to a snarl. "And it was land that the last we'd heard you'd abandoned. If the fae had come to speak with me about it peacefully, I'd have seen the new village moved. Instead you killed eight of my kin."

"And how many of ours do you think we've lost to your 'mistakes' and your 'carelessness'?" the fae leader retorted. He turned back to me. "I know you are new to your position among the shifters. I will not blame you for what was done before you had any command over your kind. But I have every reason to feel you shifters can no longer be trusted."

"I'm sorry," I said, meaning it. I didn't know exactly what had happened in any of the situations he'd talked about… but I could see how it had looked bad to the fae. My alphas trusted that their kin had good intentions and that the fae must be at fault. How could I blame the fae for assuming the same thing? I was starting to suspect that if we looked at any of those incidents carefully, it'd turn out the truth was somewhere in the middle.

"All I can do is appeal to our history," I went on. "We've clashed, we've fought—but we also appreciate the same things, don't we? Life, roaming around in nature, lands where we can be ourselves away from human beings. From what I've seen, the vampires don't care about any of that. They probably *want* more cities, more people, so they have more victims to feed from."

Cerimon's jaw twitched. His eyes had clouded. No, he didn't like the vampires at all either.

I felt a brief burst of hope. Then the fae leader spun on his heel, giving me his back.

"This is what shifters do," he said over his shoulder as he moved to leave us. "They ask and they take and they take, but when do they ever give to us? If you want a compromise, any sort of collaboration, I can tell you one thing for certain. It's going to require more than talk for us to believe in you."

CHAPTER 17

Ren

"STUBBORN BASTARDS," West muttered as we headed down the hall of my estate to the main dining room. It was early for lunch, but we'd eaten breakfast at dawn, so I was more than ready to dig into whatever the cook had prepared. Even if my stomach seemed to be mostly made out of knots at the moment.

"There's a lot of history," I said. I didn't have to ask to know it was the fae he was still grumbling about. "Obviously a lot of the recent history has not been very good. I get why they don't trust us."

"He made it sound as if we've been running amuck, ruining everything for them. Of course he didn't mention all the times *they've* intruded on us or lashed out without any real provocation. That attack on the lands near my estate? They made a couple of huffy comments and then less than a day later came at us pouring down rage for not realizing they changed their minds."

"Hey." I tugged him back as the other alphas went ahead of

us into the dining hall. "You know I don't think your kin—*our* kin—deserved what happened to them there, right? I'm not saying the fae have always been right. They sure as hell should have left my mother alone. But of course the stories they pass on to each other always make them sound like the victims. Everything's a mess right now. But maybe if we untangle it, we can find a way to both be stronger for it."

West's mouth twisted. His frustration showed in every inch of his body, from the flare in his eyes to the tension in his limbs. But as I held his gaze, his shoulders came down. He swallowed audibly and leaned close to me, his cheek brushing mine.

"You know I don't mean any of this venting as an attack on you, don't you?" he said, his throaty voice going abruptly gentle. "I don't believe in the fae, but I believe in you."

"I know," I said. "And good. Because that's all I need."

I touched the side of his face, and he turned his head to kiss me. Just briefly, but with enough hunger to leave me wishing we didn't have a whole bunch of company waiting for us to join them for lunch. My mate tasted more delectable than any feast that could be waiting in there.

West made a frustrated sound as if he were thinking the same thing. "I didn't think I could want you more than I already did," he murmured. "But now that I can have you… You have no idea how much I'd love to carry you to my bed and keep you there for at least an entire day."

An eager shiver tingled through me. "That sounds like an excellent plan for after all this is done," I said.

He grinned. "I'm counting on it, then."

The other alphas were already grabbing food from the bowls and platters laid down the length of the long table. A tang in the air told me deviled eggs and beet salad were among the offerings. Kylie was sitting on the other side of the chair that had been reserved for me, next to the rest of the kin who'd joined us. Somehow I wasn't surprised to see Felix had claimed the spot across from her.

"Are you really going to eat all of that?" she was saying with wide eyes as I took my seat. Felix's plate was heaped with enough food to form a mountain.

The fox shifter brandished his fork and licked his lips. "You'd better believe it. Gotta fuel these muscles, you know." He flexed a lean bicep.

Kylie giggled—her flirty giggle, not her dismissive one. She leaned her chin onto her folded hands as she looked at him with lowered eyelids. "Well, I can't argue with the importance of that."

I raised an eyebrow at them as I reached for the eggs. "You two are getting along well."

"Felix made it very clear that he's sorry he ever doubted my awesomeness," Kylie said, smiling. "And it turns out he's come here to do maintenance on the house before, so he knows where *all* the fun stuff is."

"I hope you don't mind me giving your friend a little tour, dragon shifter," Felix said to me. "I've got to admit I'm getting a little addicted to spending time with her." He winked at Kylie.

"Better than having you at each other's throats," I said. Although I had the feeling maybe there had been a little necking going on, of the happier sort. It was good that Kylie was enjoying herself rather than stressing about missions I didn't think it was wise to bring her along for. Funny how she'd ended up getting that enjoyment from the one guy who'd doubted her when she first arrived.

Kylie's phone chimed. And chimed again. She fished it out of her pocket to check the messages, her brow knitting. After she'd typed in a couple of texts and read through the replies, she glanced over at me and the alphas.

"You know that brother of an acquaintance I have who works for the security equipment company? They had an order come through early this morning for a bunch of armored trucks. All different spots around the country—but including the cities you said the vampires have a major presence in. They're supposed to be delivered tonight. That seems like more than just a coincidence, don't you think?"

My shoulders tensed. "It does. An armored truck could drive through a bonfire, couldn't it?"

"Maybe even break through our gates," Nate said, his face darkening.

"What about your dragon fire?" Kylie said. "I've seen the way you can melt things. You could still take them down, right?"

"Only where I am. If they're coming at us in those from all over…" I set down my fork. A chill had flooded me, so intense I didn't think I could swallow another bite.

I might be able to protect one estate, but the others… We couldn't evacuate everyone. What would we tell the other kin? To just flee and hide wherever they could?

"We'll figure something out," Felix said, looking at Kylie rather than me. He couldn't have faked the worry—not just for us shifters, but also for her—that was shining in his eyes. "We've never let the bloodsuckers get the better of us before."

Kylie gave him a soft smile, reaching across the table to clasp his hand. I watched them, a slow warmth spreading through me, easing back the chill. It was amazing the way these two who'd spent their first encounter making evil eyes at each other were now taking comfort in each other's presence.

That was how things went sometimes, wasn't it? Look at how West and I had been cuddled together just a few minutes ago. He and I had hardly gotten off on the right foot either. And now the thought of him being taken from my side was physically painful. All that gruffness and criticism had softened as he'd seen who I was and who I could be.

So much angst and hurt could be avoided if you just took the chance to get to know someone.

That thought settled with an unexpected strength in my mind. Saving our kin wasn't all on me and the alphas. I hadn't given our other option everything I had. I *had* to try, before we lost everything. We couldn't understand how the fae saw us—and they couldn't understand why we feared them, or why I was willing to consider trusting them again. But maybe if I could let them know us, if I could show them…

I pushed my chair back. Everyone glanced up. "Ren?" Nate said.

I waved off their attention. "I just thought of something I need to do. I'm not leaving the house. I'll be back soon, I think."

I hurried from the dining hall to the far end of the house, to the door of the records room. The light glowed on as I scrambled down the steps. The two main crystal tablets I'd listened to lay on the table where I'd left them: the one that detailed how dragon shifters and fae had worked together, and the one that explained how we'd fallen apart, from our perspective.

A slanted perspective, I knew. Mirabel had sounded so certain that the fae were in the wrong. But she'd gone into her meeting with the monarch already expecting her suspicions to be justified. Maybe even wanting them to be. If I could show today's fae that I understood our history—

I couldn't bring them down here. I knew that much. If the room wouldn't even admit my alphas, non-shifters had to be out of the question. But maybe… Maybe I could bring that proof to the fae.

I could give instead of asking to take.

My arms trembled as I headed back up the steps, the tablets

clutched to my chest. For a second I thought the room might block me from leaving with them. But I stepped out into the thinner air of the hall without any restriction.

For all I knew the fae wouldn't be able to make any use of these anyway. They were precious historical records. If I was wrong to take them from the room, if they were lost somehow…

I looked down the hall. In my mind's eye I saw myself as a little girl, scampering through this house. Never thinking anyone would want to hurt me or my family. Never worrying about who might be coming down the road.

That was what I wanted for my children. They deserved to grow up without this fear hanging over them. If this was what it took to end the threats we faced once and for all, then I'd take that risk. For them, and all the other shifter children not yet born.

I carried the tablets down the hall to the dining room. When I reached the doorway, I cleared my throat. My mates and Kylie and the gathered kin stopped their tense conversations to look over at me.

"It wasn't enough to talk to the local fae," I said. "I need to speak with the monarch. Now, before the vampires have another chance to attack. The jet is still here. Can we fly to your estate, Aaron?"

The avian alpha stood up. "We can," he said. "Are you sure? We can lock this house up as tightly as possible, but the vampires who scouted the place out last night will probably be back."

My gut tightened, but I nodded anyway. "If they damage the property, we'll just have to rebuild when we're done with them. If they come back with help, it's probably better if we're not here anyway. There aren't enough of us to really defend the place."

Aaron's gaze settled on the tablets in my arms, but he didn't ask. West got up beside him, motioning to his kin.

"You heard the dragon shifter. Let's move!"

The sun was still high over the trees as the jet came into view of the avian estate. I watched the property expand beneath us, my face nearly pressed to the glass.

The last time we'd parlayed with the fae monarch, it had taken us a little more than an hour to reach the fae monarch's chosen meeting place, on neutral ground between her territory and Aaron's. Aaron had called one of his kin to reach out to her immediately as we'd packed up at the dragon shifter estate, but I didn't even know if she would agree to see me.

The last time we'd met, I'd spilled the truth-seeking flames her people had helped create down over her and forced her to admit a lot more than she'd have wanted to. All things we deserved to know, but I couldn't imagine she was feeling particularly happy with me or my alphas at the moment.

"We have time," Aaron assured me from the seat behind mine. "The sun won't set for hours yet."

"I don't know how long we'll have to wait for her," I said.

As soon as the words fell from my mouth, the wrongness of them stuck me. *We*. That didn't feel right.

A heavy certainty settled over me. I looked down at the tablets, the crystalline memories meant just for me. With etchings of fae and dragon. It had always been the dragon shifters the fae had dealt with when they'd made their alliance with our kind. They'd seen my mother as their greatest threat… but they'd also once seen the women like her as their greatest allies.

The plane touched down with a jolt and a rattling of its wheels. I was out of my seat the moment it jerked to a halt. "A car should already be waiting for us to take us most of the way there," Aaron said as we all hurried down the steps. "We can—"

"Wait." I raised my hand to hold him and the other alphas back. Kylie glanced at me curiously, but I motioned for her to go on with the rest of the kin. My mates gathered around me.

"What's up, princess?" Marco asked.

I dragged in a breath. "I think I need to go alone. Just me and the monarch. And if she brings reinforcements, fine. She has to see that I trust her. She needs to know how much I want this to work."

West bristled, as I'd known he would. "No. Sparks, it's too dangerous. She tried to have you *killed* the last time."

"Not her," I reminded him. "Some other fae, who acted without her knowing. Not discouraging something like that is different from giving an order. And she swore not to let anything like that happen again."

"I trust your judgment, Ren," Nate said. "But I don't like the sounds of this either. We could come along to the meeting place, but hang back from the actual spot, farther down the path."

I shook my head. "That'll look like an empty gesture. Aaron, I need one of your kin to drive me out there, and I'll make the rest of the trip alone. I'll fly, in my dragon form, from the road—they won't find it easy to lay any traps that way. If this attempt is going to work, I can tell this is how I need to do it."

Even Marco was frowning. West's face had completely clouded. It itched at me, seeing how worried they were. Feeling it in niggling threads through our mate bond. But my certainty rang deeper.

"I've come a long way since that first meeting," I added. "I can handle this. You all *know* I can."

West let out a sharp huff. "You have. And we do. Just…" He met my gaze searchingly, with so much concern and affection in his eyes it made my heart ache. "Be careful of the fae. And come back as quickly as you can."

If even West agreed, there wasn't much the other alphas could say. My hand clenched around the straps of the bag that held the tablets. "I will. I promise. Now where's that car?"

CHAPTER 18

Aaron

I RESTED my hands on the sun-warmed railing of the balcony and looked down over the courtyard. It was as crowded with my kin as it had been when I'd arrived with Serenity at my side just a couple of weeks ago. But now the energy around the estate was fraught, not celebratory.

Everyone knew the vampires would be back for another battle tonight. More firewood had been heaped on top of the ashes of last night's protective ring. My guards were stalking warily along the walls and wheeling overhead, keeping watch even well before the sun set.

We hadn't told anyone about the armored trucks yet. I didn't want to start a panic until I found out the results of Serenity's last-ditch plan.

Footsteps tapped against the floor behind me. My sister came up to the railing, leaning her elbows on it as she considered the crowd.

"We held our own the last two nights. They haven't won yet."

"No," I said. "But it's been a near thing. If they manage to gain one more advantage…"

Alice's mouth flattened. "Everyone who's able bodied is ready to defend the walls. The scouts along all the roads will alert us as soon as the bloodsuckers show their faces. We've got extra tanks of gasoline; everyone's carrying a lighter…" She paused. "But yeah. I don't know how long we can keep doing this. Especially if the vamps up the ante."

"Well, all we can hope for then is that we manage to up the ante right back at them."

"Yeah." She glanced in the direction Serenity had gone. "Do you really think the fae might agree to help us?"

A question I'd asked myself so many times in the last day. "I think Serenity will do everything she can to convince them. Maybe it'll be easier for her to see a way to mend the damage that's been done between us… She has information none of us had before, other than the past dragon shifters—and she's looking at the problem with fresh eyes, without decades of prejudices already built up."

"There are prejudices and then there's just sound judgment," Alice said. "I guess the more important question is, do you really think we can *trust* the fae if they do offer to lend a hand?"

That was a subject I'd been puzzling over too. I rubbed my mouth. "I don't know. Serenity has proven herself to be a good judge of character so far."

"But she's still learning."

"Yes. She is."

I didn't need to say more. I knew my sister could decipher the tangle of my emotions. Serenity was on her way out there right now to face the fae monarch, the strongest of those flighty but powerful beings, on her own. Our dragon shifter was so powerful, and becoming more so every day, but if the monarch found a way to break the treaty she'd sworn to… I didn't know if I'd ever see my mate again.

"Should we prepare for *them*?" Alice said cautiously. "The fae, I mean."

"How so?"

"Come here."

I followed her down through the house and into the dim garage out back. A truck had come in with several tanks of gasoline. A thick chemical odor rose off them. Alice tipped her head to it, folding her arms over her chest.

"We have more than enough," she said. "We could send these out with a few of our people if we thought they might be more useful… elsewhere."

I studied her expression. "Elsewhere like where?"

"The fae rely on their home ground to survive, right? On their chosen plants or whatever. We could have a team ready near the monarch's territory in case the situation looks like it's about to turn sour. Ready to burn that whole forest down if that's what it takes to give us some leverage."

That's what I'd suspected she was getting at. My chest tightened. Was that what we were going to be reduced to? Preparing to destroy people we were hoping would become our allies, before we'd even tried to work together?

Would it be stupid of me to say no and leave my own people that much more vulnerable?

"When did you become such a pessimist?" I asked, delaying the need to answer the real question.

Alice gave me a crooked smile. "When I realized there's no way in hell we're fending off an army of vampires and a contingent of fae at the same time."

Clearly. I eyed the truck, focusing on the rhythm of my

breath. Trying to find a solid path through all the uncertainty around me. I was the one who'd always advocated for listening to reason over our animal instincts, wasn't I? And this desire to defend against a threat that hadn't even arisen yet—that was all animal fear. I felt it with a sharp prickle down my spine.

That was my answer then.

"No," I said, my heart thumping a little harder as I said the word. "We can't enter a new alliance already on the verge of burning their homes to the ground."

"Aaron," my sister said, but I cut her off with a shake of my head.

"Serenity watched her own mother die at the fae's hands," I said. "She's still willing to give them a chance despite that. If she can be that generous, so can we."

~

Ren

The clearing where I'd met the fae monarch before looked so much smaller from high above. The little pink flowers nearly blended into the green of the grass.

There was no sign of the monarch or any other fae yet. My nostrils didn't pick up any scent that worried me, only the green smells of the wilderness with a faint floral sweetness.

I swept over the trees, the leaves rustling in my wake, and landed in the middle of the field. With a shake, my dragon's body constricted back into my human form. I'd dropped the leather bag I'd brought with me on the ground beside me. I pulled the dress I'd packed over my head and left the crystal tablets inside the bag. If I had to shift again to make a quick exit,

I wanted to be able to grab my cargo quickly with my dragon talons.

It was only a minute or two before the towering but spindly fae woman with her crown of living vine strode from the woods at the other end of the field. No delegation accompanied her this time.

I drew in a breath, testing the breeze. A cloying smell had trickled into the air, more than I could attribute to just her. I suspected she'd brought company but left them behind in the forest when she'd seen I was alone.

Well, fair enough. I couldn't blame her for being cautious. The fact that she was coming out here to meet me without any guards at her side, when I could transform into a dragon in a matter of seconds, was a gesture of trust in itself.

She stopped a few paces from me, shoulders back and head high. I'd almost forgotten those eyes, large and stark like black diamonds against her pale skin. The silver blond waves of her hair seemed to clothe her almost as much as her thin but elegant dress.

I supposed I looked a lot less elegant than I had before, with my hair wind-rumpled and this dress I'd picked for ease of changing rather than for looks. But I wasn't here to try to impress her this time. I just wanted her to listen.

"Thank you for coming," I said. "I know you didn't have to."

The monarch acknowledged my comment with a slow blink. "I assume you wouldn't make such an urgent request without good reason. Only a fool avoids information they might need."

Okay, so she wasn't any warmer in personality than she'd been last time, but I hadn't expected anything else.

"You know the vampires have been attacking us," I said. "They've said they want to wipe out shifters completely. They've been killing my kin in the cruelest ways, innocent people who've done nothing to them."

Her jaw tightened. "I have heard of this."

I couldn't read her expression. "You're not on their side, are you? I know we've had our conflicts, I know you've been willing to look the other way when your people have acted against us—but you don't agree with outright slaughter like this, do you?"

I couldn't mistake the twist of her lips and the flicker in her eyes now. It was horror. "Absolutely not," she said sharply. "We will protect our own as we need to, but senseless killing is completely abhorrent. The *vampires* are abhorrent. We have been willing to keep our peace with them only as they offer the same to us."

That was a step in the right direction. "And do you really think you can trust them to leave you in peace if you let them exterminate us without saying a peep? Once they've eliminated the shifters, what's to stop them from coming after you next?"

"That is a matter I have given much thought."

But had she drawn any conclusions? She obviously didn't want to make this conversation at all easy for me.

I bent to pick up my bag. "I think both our peoples will be better off if we can set aside our grievances with each other at least long enough to push back this threat. But I'm not coming just to ask you to offer help. I wanted to offer you something first. I want you to be able to see how relations between shifters and fae have looked through our eyes."

I pulled out the crystals. The monarch's eyes widened.

"My dragon shifter ancestors recorded pieces of our history into these tablets," I said. "Some of it relating to the fae. So that we could each learn from what's happened before. That's what I've tried to do. And I don't like being near-enemies with you when I know it could be different. No one has ever seen these before except the dragon shifters. But I think you deserve to."

I handed the more recent record to her. She looked down at the etchings. "What is this one?"

"A dragon shifter's account of the first major falling out between our people," I said. "Can you activate it?"

"I think…" She traced her long fingers over the image and nodded. Her eyes slid shut. A glow streamed up from the crystal, brightening the shimmer of her skin.

Did I light up like that when I was accessing those records, or was that only because of her magic?

She must have been able to absorb the account faster than I did. After just a few minutes, her eyelids stuttered open. A purplish flush had colored her cheeks. She thrust the tablet back into my hands.

"That isn't how it happened at all. Your dragon shifter then refused to even bring the responsible shifters with her so our monarch could talk to them directly. She wouldn't accept any compromise. And this talk about stealing your fire—we have never wanted to *steal* anything from you."

"Hey," I said, raising my hands. "I didn't think everything she said was completely accurate. I just wanted you to know what all the dragon shifters before me have had to go by. That's how that moment seemed to them. It's easier to blame the other person, isn't it?"

The monarch's eyes were still glittering with anger. "I didn't come here to be told—"

"Wait. Just wait. That isn't the only thing I wanted you to see." I fumbled for the second tablet and offered it to her. "This is the one that brought me here. This is the one that made me think we could do so much better."

She frowned, but she accepted the tablet. With a graze of her fingers, the glow flowed up her arms again. I waited, my stomach clenched with anticipation, as the more hopeful piece of our history washed over her.

This time, when the visions were finished, she lowered the tablet more gently, still holding on to it. A shadow of sorrow crossed her face. "It's hard to imagine," she said.

"I know. But that's how it was between us before. The power I hold inside me, your people and mine created together, for our mutual good. Because the fae once thought that what benefited the dragon shifters benefitted them as well. That we'd support each other."

"But much has happened since then."

I swallowed hard. "Yes. I heard some of the complaints one of the local fae leaders made, just from recent years. My kin have hurt your people. I hate that it happened, but I'm not going to deny it. Accidents *will* happen, but I think there must be ways to make sure they happen less. And to make sure we accept responsibility where it's due."

The monarch gazed at me for a long moment. She looked a little startled by my admission. "We have hurt your kind too," she admitted quietly. "We have let resentment grow. I have let cruelties go unpunished. We should have been better than that." She exhaled. "But it isn't so easy to turn back time. The wrongs done have already been done. Trust already broken."

"I know," I said. "And I'm willing to talk through anything we need to talk through. I don't expect that we're going to trust each other immediately. I just want us to hear each other more, to start with. And I'm hoping you'll help us defend ourselves from the vampires so we're still around to do that."

"You want us to throw ourselves into the line of fire on your behalf?"

"No!" I said quickly. "I, er, was actually thinking it might be possible for you to help us without even extending yourselves all that much. What the previous dragon shifters said, about stealing our fire—the way we worked together in the past, combining our strengths… Is there some way you can use *my* fire?"

She hesitated. Then she inclined her head. "Yes. We can connect our magic to your spirit. Channel that power through our own. That is how your flames of truth were made, with the power of that dragon shifter before."

I liked the sound of that. "How long can you hold onto that power? And from how far away?"

"For as long as you sustain it," the monarch said. "And for a short time longer, depending on how much we've gathered. One of us would need to be with you, accepting it. But that one could pass the flames on to the rest of our kind wherever they might be."

My heart skipped a beat. "So I could be in one place, and a bunch of you could be in other places, and we could rain down dragon fire on all those sets of vampires at the same time?"

Her eyes narrowed. "Yes. *If* we agreed to help you. If I thought it worth the risk."

This was exactly what we needed. How could I convince her I meant everything I'd said?

The second the question passed through my mind, a memory swam up: my violet flames streaming down over the fae woman in front of me. Forcing her to admit the truth. My heart skipped again, in a much more nervous way, but I forced myself to speak.

"If you could borrow my regular fire, then you could also use my truth-seeking flames, couldn't you?"

She considered me. "Yes."

"Then use them on me like I did on you, before." The corner of my mouth curled up in a slight smile. "It's only fair, right?"

For the second time in this meeting, she stared at me as if she couldn't quite believe what she was hearing. Then she collected herself. "You'll need to shift back into your human form for me to question you."

"Of course. Are you ready?"

She moved back a couple steps. I tugged off my dress, my pulse racing now. I was giving her the opportunity to ask me anything, and I'd have to answer honestly. Who knew what vulnerabilities I had that she might exploit, that I wasn't prepared for?

But I was asking a lot from her people. I had to give in return. And this was the best I could offer.

I was dragon shifter of the shifter kin, and I would not be afraid.

I shifted as quickly as I comfortably could. As always, the flames of my twin fires tickled the back of my dragon throat. I reached toward the violet ones and let them flow down my throat.

I didn't blast them at the monarch the way I had when she'd been trying to march away from me last time. Instead I let them drift down toward her gently. She'd already raised her hands as if to catch them. And that's what she did. As the violet haze reached her hands, she seemed to ball it between her palms, collecting it.

After a moment, she nodded. I closed my mouth and shifted back, bracing myself for the interrogation.

The monarch's shimmer flared brighter. She pushed her hands toward me, and the violet flames streamed from her grasp.

They shot up over me from foot to head with a tight, prickling pressure. Okay, this wasn't being burned alive, but it was pretty far from pleasant. Something to keep in mind when I decided who to apply these flames to in the future.

I couldn't move out of them, couldn't convince my body to

do anything except stand there, pinned. And to answer her questions as she asked them.

"Why have you come to me today?" she said.

My mouth opened automatically. The words spilled out, beyond my control. That was fine. I didn't fight the process.

"Because I'm afraid the vampires will destroy my people, and I think working with the fae is our best chance of survival. And because I would like to form a new alliance, with more trust and friendship between us, if that's possible."

"What will you do if we join you in fighting the vampires?"

"Offer whatever power I can for you to use where I can't be myself. And any other support you need to help us."

"And after the fighting is over, if we've defeated the vampires?"

"I want to talk about how we can move forward. How to heal the damage we've done to each other in the past. How to adapt to the ways our world has changed *together* instead of clashing with each other so much."

She paused. "Do you want revenge for your mother's death?"

My eyes heated at the thought of Mom's death, but the answer came immediately. "No."

"Why not?"

"Because you already punished the fae who murdered her. And I understand why you felt threatened by us, enough that you hadn't punished them before. And I know my kin have looked the other way when your kin have been killed by our carelessness. I'd rather find a way to move forward from all that. I think that's what my mother would have wanted too."

I hadn't even realized that last part, but it was true. I might not have known Mom as a dragon shifter for very long, but she'd always taught me to see all sides of a problem, to remember that my perspective wasn't the only one. To find ways to make something good out of any situation.

The monarch dropped her hands. The flames sputtered away into the air. I stumbled forward before catching my balance. A sweat had broken out on my forehead.

"Does that satisfy you?" I asked.

Her expression had gone unreadable again. "I asked everything I wanted to."

"And what you did there, you could do the same with my burning flames, aiming them at the vampires."

"Yes, as I said before." She brushed her hands together. "But I haven't said we will help you yet. Leave. I need time to think it through."

My heart sank. "If you're going to help, it'll need to be soon. They're coming at us again tonight."

She fixed me with a hard look. "I need time," she repeated. Then she turned and stalked away.

CHAPTER 19

Ren

I COULD TELL the two figures in the avian estate's hall were arguing before I could even hear them. Both of the middle-aged men stood with chests puffed and faces darkened.

Shit. With the threat of the vampires looming, the last thing we needed was to be fighting among ourselves. I hurried over.

"I told you, there isn't enough space," the guy in the guest bedroom doorway insisted.

"There are only four of you in there," the other man said in a growl of a voice. "Your alpha said each room could take ten."

"Why don't you find one with your own kin?"

"There *aren't* any other badger shifters here. My wife and I are the only ones."

The two shifters jerked back from each other when they saw me coming up on them. The guy who already held the room—a hawk shifter, I gathered from his scent—looked about ready to swallow his tongue. Too bad I couldn't make him actually do that.

"What seems to be the problem here?" I asked, setting my hands on my hips. "I think the instructions about the rooms were pretty clear."

The hawk shifter ducked his head. "My apologies, dragon shifter. I just thought… There are still more rooms with openings… This fellow might be happier with shifters more like him."

The badger shifter groaned. "This is the first room I've found that has space, and I'm tired of asking. I just want somewhere for my wife and I to rest. We traveled all day getting here. And we plan on helping defend *your* estate all night if we have to."

"Okay," I said. "We're all tense because we're all worried about tonight. I get it. But let's try not to take it out on each other, all right?" My gaze settled on the hawk shifter. "If you don't think you can share this room with anyone who's not an avian shifter without squabbling, the four of you can come with me and I'll find you spots in other rooms. It sounds as if this gentleman has been on his feet long enough."

The hawk shifter looked from me to the badger shifter as he weighed his options. His expression turned chagrined. "We'll appreciate your help in fighting off the vampires," he said to the other guy. "Come on, get your rest."

He didn't sound exactly happy about it, but the offer was genuine enough that I stepped back. The badger shifter smiled and motioned to a woman who'd just come into the hallway.

More kin were already gathering around the guest bedroom doors all down the hall. The estate was packed, and the refugees from various shifter communities hadn't stopped trickling in. Everyone had heard about the villages that had been decimated last night. No one wanted to risk being next to face that carnage.

We still hadn't gotten any word from the fae.

Well, if they didn't come through, we'd just have to make the best we could of the situation on our own. And that meant having a conversation I'd been dreading.

I continued out into the common rooms. Aaron was holding court with a few of his advisors and some of the newcomers. I caught his eye and tipped my head toward our private wing of the house. He nodded.

As he finished his conversation, I ducked out into the courtyard. Nate was showing a bunch of the young shifters the best way to quickly take down a vampire at close range. They copied his swipe through the air with their own hands. Marco was giving what looked like a stern talking-to to a couple of bobcat shifters who I was going to guess had been messing with the avian kin.

And West… I reached out through our bond and felt his presence near the wall at the side of the estate. At my gentle tug, I felt a tickle of acknowledgement. He was coming.

Marco had finished his dressing-down and was already strolling over. I gestured to Nate. "I need to talk to all of you."

The bear shifter cuffed one of his young students lightly on the shoulder. "Keep practicing," he told them, and ambled to join me.

"What's going on?" Kylie asked, getting up from where she, Felix, and some of the other shifters had been preparing a stack of torches with dry chunks of branches and gasoline.

"I think we need to make a small adjustment in our plans," I said. "You might as well come along too." I'd be telling her afterward anyway.

We slipped around the fringes of the crowded public areas to the hall where the alphas' private rooms lay. Aaron was already waiting in the small lounge area there. West came in a moment later.

"What's the matter?" he asked, his eyes immediately seeking out mine.

"Nothing exactly," I said. "But there's something I need to say before it's too late. I think, whether we hear from the fae or not—but especially if we don't—it'd be best if you all went to your own estates."

The last few words made my throat ache coming up. My whole body ached, thinking about it. Seeing the way my mates stared at me in response.

"You want us to *leave* you?" Nate said, as incredulously as if I'd suggested he should fly back to his estate with his arms instead of a jet.

"Well, I'd be leaving too," I said, willing my voice to stay steady. "I think I should be at the canine estate. It's been hit the hardest already, and the vampires from both New York and Chicago will be focused there. So if I can only protect one place, that seems like the one that'll need me the most. And your kin need you with them more than I do tonight. You can rally them, keep them hopeful."

I caught Nate's gaze, and then Marco's. "Most of yours haven't seen you since before this war started."

"Serenity," Aaron said softly. I realized I was trembling. I clenched my hands, drawing my shoulders back.

I'd never been apart from my mates, not by more than an hour or two's drive, since they'd found me. It'd wrenched at me having Aaron gone on a reconnaissance mission for less than a day.

But I'd have my fire whether they were all with me or not. I meant what I'd said. Their kin needed them more. I couldn't hold them back for my own comfort. Then the rogues really would be right about me distracting the alphas from their duty to the rest of their people.

"I'll be fine," I said. "I have to get used to it anyway, don't I? You all will have business on your estates and the other settlements after this is over. It's not like you're supposed to be with me 24-7."

"No," Aaron agreed. "But given the circumstances—how long you were apart from shifter society—ideally we'd have stayed with you until you were a little more settled in."

I laughed roughly. "Not much chance of really getting settled until we've dealt with the vampires, is there?"

"Well, wherever you're going, I'm going too," Kylie announced. "In case there was any doubt about that."

I smiled at her. "I was counting on it."

"Are you sure, Ren?" Marco asked. "I'd imagine my kin think they haven't much use for me at all."

"They think that, but we both know how much you do for them," I said.

The corner of his mouth quirked up, but he still looked sad. "I can't argue with that, princess."

Nate opened and closed his hands as if he didn't know what to do with them. "I don't like it," he said. "Leaving you with just one of us to defend you—no offense meant to you, West. Or to you, Ren. I know you can defend yourself. But if you're injured again…"

"Then West will be there, and all his kin too," I said, and touched the bear shifter's arm. My throat tightened. "I don't want to be apart from you either. Any of you. But my job is to make sure all our kin have what they need, isn't it? And I can't let what I want get in the way of that."

He sighed, bowing his head by mine. "I know."

"All right. Then we should all go, quickly, while we still have time to make it back before nightfall."

I bobbed up on my toes to press a quick but determined kiss to Nate's lips. Marco caught me next, teasing his fingers into my hair as he brought our mouths together. I turned to Aaron, and he kissed me gently before resting his forehead against mine.

"We'll be with you, either way," he said. "Part of us always will be."

The nervous jittering inside me calmed just slightly. "And part of me will be with you."

I wasn't going to let myself think about how this might be the last time I saw any of them.

West had stayed quiet through the whole conversation. There wasn't much for him to say, I guessed, when he was the one I'd be with. And I knew he had to want to get back to his own kin. But when I came up beside him as we all strode out toward the air strip, he looked almost haunted.

"You haven't even had all of us for a whole two days yet, Sparks," he said.

I managed to smile. "Oh, I don't know. I think I had you a lot longer than that."

He glanced at me with a flash of his eyes. His mouth twitched. "All right. I'll give you that."

"You'd better go round up the rest of your kin who came with us," I told him. "I think my best friend will be particularly disappointed if a certain fox shifter gets left behind."

West chuckled and loped off toward the courtyard. The best friend in question looped her arm around mine. "Always looking out for my best interests."

I nudged Kylie in the side with my elbow. "When you let me."

West's underlings caught up with us as we reached the field where the avian jets and the canine one we'd arrived in were waiting. I'd only made it two steps toward the latter when an eerie sensation rippled over my skin, raising the hairs on my arms.

An instant later, a pale slender form appeared as if out of the sunlight in front of me.

"Forgive the unexpected intrusion, dragon shifter, alphas," the fae man said in a cool voice. "My monarch wanted me to reach you as quickly as possible. I have just one question before I give you her answer: If we help you now, do you swear that you will come to our aid in a similar time of need?"

My heart skipped a beat. "Ren," West said beside me, cautioning.

Sure, the promise was vague—but how could I say no, considering how much I was asking of them? I didn't let myself second-guess my answer.

"Yes," I said. "Of course. I swear it."

The fae man gave me a slight bob of his head. "Then we will assist in your fight against the vampires."

Just like that? It took me a second to catch my breath. "Thank you. Tell your monarch thank you from me too. What do you need from us to make this work?"

"Tell us where you need us to be and where you will be," he said with a thin, shimmering smile. "We can handle the rest."

The sky deepened from pink to purple as the sun sank toward the horizon. The summer heat cooled in the breeze. I moved my weight from one foot to the other, trying to curb my restlessness.

Beside me, West set his hand on my shoulder. We watched the gate to his estate together, at least two hundred of our kin gathered around us and spread out all along the stone wall, as if we'd see the first sign of the vampires there.

Really, West would get a call on that phone in his pocket from one of the scouts down the road before we got our first glimpse. The vamps wouldn't be on us the second the sun set. They had to get out here from wherever they were holed up first. But we knew they'd been gathering forces—and their new armored trucks too.

It wasn't just our kin, and Kylie of course, with us. My gaze slid to one of the softly glowing figures standing near me in the courtyard.

A dozen fae had been waiting for us when we'd landed at the canine estate. Three of them were in my view now. The other nine had taken positions along the wall so there'd be one in range no matter where the vampires struck. The other alphas had reported similar numbers at the other estates. They'd also arrived at the towns I'd told them seemed most in danger.

West tensed, presumably noticing my glance. My stomach knotted. What if I'd made the wrong decision? The fae could decide to turn on us after all, to make sure the bloodsuckers wiped us out, so shifters wouldn't trouble them anymore either.

I'd invited them in. Offered our throats to them, in a way.

It was too late to take back that choice now. I just had to hope my instincts had been right.

My restlessness drew me away from West to the nearest fae. The woman was as tall and slender as all her kind, but I had the sense she was on the younger side, whatever that meant in fae terms. She gave me a faint smile when I joined her.

"Is there anything else I'll need to do?" I asked. "Or do I just have to stay near you and start breathing my fire?"

She nodded. "From what I understand and what my monarch said, that's all we'll need. I've already tapped into your energy with my magic. When you stir up that fire, I'll be able to channel it—for my own use, and to stream it through me to all the other fae who've come out."

"Even the ones across the country?"

"It isn't so far," she said, as if she were in the habit of taking a jaunt from one ocean to the other in her daily walk. "We are all connected, you know. We can reach each other without much effort at all. Otherwise it would be very lonely, needing to always stay close to our homes."

Oh. So they had some sort of telepathic communication? I guessed that made sense, when she put it that way. No wonder the fae leader near the dragon shifter estate had known about all the offenses the shifters had made in other fae territories.

The fae woman paused. "We fae live a long time, you know," she went on. "Longer than shifters. One of the elders in my domain spoke to me once of sharing fire with a dragon shifter. She said it was the most thrilling experience of her life. I'm saddened by the reason you needed our help—but I'm excited to be a part of it."

My eyebrows shot up. "Really?" I said. "I, ah, got the impression you were all pretty uncertain about having anything to do with shifters."

"Some of us, maybe," she said. "Some didn't have anyone to pass on those memories. There've been so many bad ones in between. But I don't think it makes sense for any of us to be *afraid* of you."

My stomach started to unclench. Afraid of us? Was that what it came down to? I guessed it did. All of us, afraid of how the other could hurt us, striking out to try to defend ourselves from offenses no one had even committed yet.

We should have been better than that, the monarch had said. We all should have. And maybe we could be, tonight.

"Or for us to be afraid of you," I suggested. Her smile grew a little, as if she understood exactly what I meant.

West had raised his phone to his ear. While I'd been talking to the fae woman, the sun had disappeared completely. The wolf shifter called over to me. "The trucks are on the move. They'll be here soon."

I breathed in and out deep and slow, readying myself for a shift. I'd need to hold it as long as I possibly could if we were going to push the vampires back all across the country. All we needed was for them to arrive and try to breach our walls, and we'd incinerate them inside those damned trucks they must have thought themselves so smart to obtain.

The other shifters stirred in their places around the courtyard. An owl hooted in the distance. Then my ears picked up the distant sounds of engines.

They grew from a hum into a rumble. Everyone along the walls went still, braced for action. The engine's growl rose even higher—and cut off as the trucks must have come to a stop.

I exhaled sharply in the sudden silence. A different sound reached my ears: a low, rolling chuckle that made every nerve in my body jangle in alarm.

"Oh, dragon shifter," a cajoling voice carried over the wall. "Won't you come out and play?"

West looked to me, frowning. My skin had turned clammy. Nausea swelled inside me.

"It's him," I said hoarsely, just loud enough for my mate to hear me. "The rogue who led the attack on my estate—the one who had my family killed."

CHAPTER 20

Ren

"Do you remember me?" the voice went on, lilting over the canine estate's stone wall with an amused tone that set my teeth on edge. "I remember you. Scared little girl scampering after her mother down the halls. Too bad we didn't paint them with your blood too that night."

I remembered. Oh, hell, did I remember. When he chuckled again, the tone of it took me back sixteen years to that panicked dash through the estate, adrenaline sour on my tongue and heart thudding at the base of my throat. To the blood the rogues *had* spilled all over my home. My dads'. My sisters'.

I'd assumed we'd caught the rogue who'd led that assault in one of our past battles with his group. I hadn't seen him clearly back then, didn't even know what kind of shifter he was, so there'd been no way to tell other than that chuckle. But charging into battle wasn't how he worked, was it? He led others to the fray and then stood back to watch the carnage.

To watch and laugh.

So he'd survived. Survived and gone running to the vampires with his last few rogue accomplices? Was he using them to get his revenge or were they using him?

Possibly both.

"Well, then, where are you?" the rogue called again. "Still too scared to stand your ground and face me?"

My jaw clenched. West gripped my arm. I hadn't even heard him coming to my side.

"Ignore him," my mate said in a low voice. "He's trying to get you worked up. To distract you. But he doesn't matter. When we take down the vampires, we'll take down any rogues with them too."

Bertrand jogged across the courtyard to us. "We've got eyes on four rogues. The vampires are staying back, but those traitors have come right out of the forest. Looks like the bloodsuckers have shared their guns."

If they were at the edge of the forest, then they were in my firing range.

As if triggered by my thought, a crackle of gunfire sounded near the gate. The guards along the wall jerked down. One yelped, clapping his hand to his head where a bullet had grazed his temple. A couple of his kin rushed to help.

I gritted my teeth. We couldn't just leave the rogues alone. With that weaponry, they were almost as big a threat as the vampires.

I yanked my arm away from West and strode to the wall. The urge to shift was already prickling through me. I could at least pick off these few, even if the vampires were still hiding in the shelter of the forest. A little warm-up. Show them how far from scared I was.

"Wow," the lead rogue said, his voice dripping with disdain.

"Still no sign of that fearsome dragon. I guess we don't have anything to worry about here after all. She can't even be bothered to protect her kin."

West followed me, catching my wrist again. "Don't," he said.

The rogue kept going. "Just like your mother, apparently. Running away instead of standing and fighting. Not that it did her any good. Did you hear your sisters crying out as we cut them down? And those pathetic alphas—I put the bullet in one of your fathers' heads myself, while he lay groaning."

Rage flared through my body. It pushed the talons from my fingers and the scales to the surface of my skin. A draconic roar rang from my throat as my muscles twisted and expanded. My wings unfurled, ready to cast me up in to the air, so I could incinerate them like so much barbeque. Wrench their lives from this world like they had my family's. Pay them back for every bit of pain they'd caused—

Flames scorched the base of my throat as I tensed to push myself off the ground—and a memory seared through my head. The wild rush of the fire over the trees when I'd lost control after our parlay with the vampire king.

I caught myself, regret twisting around my fury. Containing it, just barely.

No. This was what the rogues wanted. Why else would he be saying things that horrible? I had to keep a clear head. I had to keep my human reason, like Aaron always said.

It was our animal sides, the sides that wanted to lash out and bite back the second we were hurt, that had gotten us into so much trouble, wasn't it? That had split us apart from our alliance with the fae all those years ago.

I'd chosen differently. I could choose differently again.

A ragged breath released from my already constricting throat. I collapsed back into my human form. West was there waiting.

His arms went around me as I stumbled. I accepted his support for just a second as I got my bearings. Then I straightened up.

"We have to deal with them," I said. "But we make a plan first. What do they want? What are *they* planning?"

West's eyes were still worried, but he followed my cue. "They want to lure you out there, so they must think they'll have an advantage when they do. Four guns isn't enough to take you down before you fry them."

I nodded. "And the vampires are going along with whatever the rogues are doing. It might even be a plan *they* came up with. They want to get rid of me before they come at the rest of you." I ran my tongue over the edges of my teeth. "There must be a bunch of the vamps waiting with a good line of sight to where the rogues are. They'd shoot me while I'm occupied with the rogues."

"That would make the most sense, strategically," Bertrand said.

"So we turn the tables on them." I'd learned other things during that skirmish at the gas station. I glanced between West and his lieutenant. "The kin can take on the vampires while they're in the denser forest, right? The vamps won't be able to take long shots, and we have the advantage hand-to-hand. I can pretend I'm going after the rogues, and while they're focused on me, a bunch of your people can come at the vampires from the other side."

"Pretend?" West repeated. "I'm thinking that's going to look an awful lot like actually doing it."

I glowered at him. "I won't get too close. I'll swing around. Their range of fire can't be very wide through the trees. And if a few bullets clip me, well, I've survived that before. We get in there, take out as many as we can in the first minute of confusion, and then withdraw. Maybe that'll be enough to get them to stop lurking and come at us so I can really take them on with our fae friends."

West's jaw tightened at the mention of the fae, but he nodded. "Don't cut it too close," he told me gruffly.

"I know," I said, suddenly choked up.

He turned to Bertrand. "You heard her. Get a bunch of our people, the fastest fighters, ready to dash for the forest the second she goes over the wall."

His lieutenant gave a jerky bob of his head and rushed off. Within moments, he'd rounded up a pack near the gate. I marched the last few steps to the wall and pitched my voice to carry over it.

"Rogues!" I shouted. "And your vampire allies. This is your last chance to back down before I destroy all of you. Leave here and call off your forces around all our communities, and we can discuss a new treaty. Stay, and you're going to burn."

"Big words from a little girl hiding behind a wall, dragon shifter!" the rogue hollered. "I'd like to see you try. In the meantime, should I describe what we did to your fathers after you fled? We pissed on them, you know, and then we—"

I shut my eyes, shutting him out, clamping down hard on the rush of fury that surged through my chest again. "No movement from the vampires," one of the guards reported.

Fine. I hadn't really expected anything else.

"I'm going," I said to West. "I'll be back. I promise."

Then I launched myself off the ground.

The wind whipped over my expanding body. I flung myself high with a vast sweep of my wings.

My sharp eyes caught the cluster of four shifters just a step from the edge of the trees, twenty feet from our wall. A whiff of their scents reached my nostrils.

Jackal. The grizzled man with white streaked hair who was

hollering more insults at me even now was a jackal shifter. A scavenger, happy to desecrate the dead for his own gain. How fucking fitting.

I let out a furious shriek and dove. At the edge of my vision, I saw my kin slipping over the wall and darting across the cleared ring into the trees farther down the estate. The rogues raised their guns. *They* didn't need any special angle to get a shot at me. Bullets pinged off my wings and chest, the distance offsetting the damage they might have done. I careened faster, closer—

And whipped myself to the side before I came into full range. The rogues let out a shout of surprise.

Then a different sort of shouting echoed from within the forest. Shots crackled and bullets thudded into tree trunks. Bodies thumped to the ground. Snarls and the slicing of claws through undead flesh carried from below.

The rogues spun around, and so did I. My heart thumped hard in my chest. While the vampires were otherwise occupied, I could finish what I'd come out here wanting to do.

The jackal shifter looked up at the last second. He bared his teeth in a sneer and yanked up his gun. But I was already pouring flames from my throat.

In an instant, my dragon fire had swallowed up all four of the rogues. Their forms toppled into heaps of cinders. A small part of the clenching around my chest released.

They were gone. The last of them were gone.

But the vampires, our greatest threat, were still here. "Retreat!" one of the canine guards shouted. The kin who'd tackled the vampires amid the trees streamed back toward the walls.

I dove toward them, aiming a burst of flames at the vampires who charged after my kin. Gunfire echoed around me. A bullet tore through my foreleg; another, my shoulder. The truck's engines revved. Forget stealth. They were storming us now.

I aimed one last blast at the ring of firewood, as long as that might hold us, and flung myself toward the courtyard. These weren't the only vampires we needed to deal with. My kin were fighting all over this country.

And I would lend my flames to help them.

I hit the ground still in dragon form, right beside the fae woman. She didn't need any further prompting. I opened my jaws, and she held out her hands. With a heave of my lungs, all the firepower I had in me gushed out to meet her magic.

The heat and the light flowed away from me. I felt it go, in a strangely detached sensation. Felt it rush from me to the fae woman to all the fae around the estate. Felt the sizzle of the fire streaming from their hands to hit the trucks racing at the protective ring, at the vampires pouring out bullets from the edge of the forest.

And onward, from them to the fae to the south and the west. I could almost hear Marco calling commands to his lieutenants, Nate growling as he bashed the head of a bloodsucker who'd made it to his wall, Aaron commanding a legion of eagles, hawks, and falcons.

All my mates, with me even while they weren't. My fire reached them all. Them and the smaller towns and villages where more fae had gathered. More fire washing over the charges of vampires. Bloodsuckers bursting into ashes. Flaring on and on until the sensation of it made me dizzy.

Or maybe that lightheadedness was from the effort to keep producing so much fire. My whole dragon body was tingling. But I had so much more in me to give. So many kin I wanted to protect.

Even as I sensed the paths my flames traveled along, the

battle in front of me waged on too. West barked orders and sprang to help the guards by the gate. Kylie shouldered her flame-thrower and shot a blast into the chaos on the other side of the wall. My kin raced by all around me, gathering the injured, joining the defense, fighting with everything we had. All of us, together, bound by blood and history and a friendship with the glimmering figures among us that we were only just rediscovering.

"They're retreating!" someone hollered. Here, or at one of the other estates I was distantly connected to? Footsteps thundered. Fire crackled. My throat burned, but I expelled another long breath. The tingling had faded, leaving only the comfortable weight of my dragon form. Just as much mine as my human one.

I could do this. I could stand and fight all night if I needed to.

But I didn't need to. More shouts rang out, and at least some of them were definitely here. "That's the last of them! The ring is clear."

The fae woman lowered her hands. I let my flames flicker out. She beamed at me, as brightly lit as if the moon had shone a spotlight from her.

"It's done," she said.

I was done. I could shift back now, if I wanted. I stretched my dragon limbs and raised my head toward the sky, letting out a hoarse cry of victory. Only then, carefully and because I wanted to, did I pull back into my human self.

CHAPTER 21

West

IF SOMEONE HAD TOLD me a week ago—no, even a day ago—that I'd be entertaining the leader of the local fae on my estate grounds, I'd have laughed my head off. And then given whoever had said it a good cuff across the head for coming up with ridiculous stories.

But here I was. Walking the gardens to the east of the house in the thin dawn light with one of those gawky glowing figures.

To be honest, the sight of her still made my skin crawl. Too many sour memories. I could ignore that, though. I was man enough to admit when I'd been wrong. And to listen to someone else admit the same.

"We have a long way to go," the fae woman said. "On *both* our sides." She fixed me with a sharp look, as if to remind me that my kin had played a role in the tensions between us. I'd let that slide too, at least this once. "But I am ashamed of the violence that was born out of what should have been a simple misunderstanding. I hope that we can approach each other with an assumption of good faith… or at least neutral faith, from now on."

"I think we can offer that," I said. And then, because that statement didn't feel like enough. "And I would like us to go forward that way. With patience instead of suspicion. If we can."

All right, so we might both be hedging our bets a little when it came to agreeing to a truce. Old habits died hard. And there was still—

The fae's voice quieted. She stopped and turned toward me. "I must apologize, for the deaths when my people drove you from that grove twelve years ago. Killing is never our goal. I should have been there to temper the panic."

I gaped at her for a second before I found the wherewithal to snap my mouth shut. "Those lives can't be brought back by an apology," I said, but without as much anger as I might have if the apology hadn't sounded so heartfelt.

"They can't," the fae woman acknowledged with a bob of her head. "The best I can give is my promise that my people will not cross that line first in any conflict from here on."

I supposed if my kin started slaughtering fae sometime in the future, I couldn't really complain if they paid us back in kind. But I had no intention of stirring up violence on our end. No, I'd be much happier if we simply left each other alone unless absolutely necessary.

Hopefully my mate didn't have other plans she'd end up dragging me into.

The fae leader motioned to my chest—to the area just below my shoulder where my flesh prickled around the glow of my bandaged scar. "You were injured in that fight," she said. "Our magic left its mark. I could heal the scar, if you wanted. As a gesture of our good will."

I hadn't thought I could be more surprised by her, but it took all I had not to let my jaw go slack again. My hand rose to the scar instinctively. But I didn't need much time to find my answer.

"Thank you," I said, meaning it. "But no. It's a reminder I'd like to keep."

Her eyes hazed with momentary confusion. "A reminder?"

"Of the sacrifice I made that day," I said. And of my feelings, just in case I got too focused on burying them again.

"It is your choice," the fae woman said calmly. "I will take my leave of you. May our paths cross only in peace."

I turned back toward the house. I'd only just come around into the front courtyard when Bertrand came striding over to meet me.

"We've gotten word from the kin we sent to New York," he said. "Just before sunrise this morning, the vampires who survived last night converged on their king. Apparently they were pretty peeved about the catastrophic war he'd gotten them into, and not in any hurry to continue throwing themselves into the flames. The report is that they tore off his head and then tossed his body outside to meet the sun."

I grimaced. "Sounds fitting. So now they don't have a king."

"No, they agreed on a new one in a hurry." Bertrand's eyes glinted with amusement. "The new king has already reached out to the estate to talk about reparations and compromise."

A laugh burst out of me. Damn, when was the last time I'd felt like I could really laugh? I sucked in the dewy morning air, and the last of the tightness around my lungs released.

"Of course he is. Take on the fae and this dragon shifter along with all of our kin? After last night, he'd have to want to see his own people exterminated to make that order."

"Do you want to speak to him?" Bertrand asked.

I shook my head. "Tell the bloodsuckers we're thinking about what kind of 'compromise' we'd find acceptable. Let them stew a little. I've got other things I'd rather focus on right now. Speaking of which, where's our dragon shifter?"

"Still in her rooms, as far as I know, sir."

Ren had stayed up most of the night with me helping with the recovery efforts and making sure the vampires weren't going to return. I'd finally sent her off to bed a few hours ago. The fact that she'd barely protested gave me some indication of how exhausted she'd been.

I should probably get a little rest myself. But that could wait a little longer too. Right now, I wanted my mate.

No one answered when I knocked softly on the door to Ren's suite. I eased the door open. The corner of my mouth curved up.

My dragon shifter hadn't even made it to her bed. She'd curled up on the sitting room sofa, hugging one of the plump pillows, her face gentle with sleep. Her dark brown hair tumbled over her naked shoulder.

There was a lot to appreciate about the view, but my gaze stayed on her face, my heart squeezing. This woman. This goddamned woman. I'd almost let her go. And then I'd almost pushed her away. What the hell had I been thinking?

I couldn't imagine loving anyone else this much, now or ever.

I knelt down beside the sofa and rested my head against her side. I hadn't meant to wake her, not exactly, but when she murmured and reached to stroke her fingers over my hair, I couldn't say I was upset either.

"Is everything all right?" she asked, her eyes only half open. Fuck, she looked even more irresistible like that.

"You know what?" I said. "It is, and I think it might actually stay that way for more than an hour just this once."

She smiled then, so brilliantly I had to kiss her. She scooted forward into my embrace, raising her head to kiss me back harder.

Tired? Who was tired? I could stay awake another week if I was doing this.

Ren snuggled her head against my shoulder. "I want you," she said, her voice still dreamy. "But I want to see all my mates. Soon."

"That's what I came to tell you," I said. "The other alphas are heading to the dragon shifter estate now. I'll take you there to meet up with them. What do you say we catch up on a little more sleep on the plane?"

She hummed happily. "Sounds like the perfect plan. As long as you're right there beside me."

I couldn't restrain the smile that stretched across my face. "Forever and always, Sparks."

Ren

Aaron, Nate, and Marco were waiting at the edge of the runway when I got to the jet's open doorway. Suddenly my feet couldn't move fast enough. I scrambled down the steps and dashed into their arms.

All of their arms, all at the same time. With a low chuckle, Nate wrapped me up in an embrace. Aaron was there at the next second, then Marco, and finally West, nuzzling the back of my neck.

Somewhere beyond the boundaries of our group hug, Kylie coughed and said, "I think I'll leave the five of you alone for a while."

I grinned, snuggling deeper into my mates' embrace. Their

smells, salty and musky, spicy and piney, mingled together into the headiest perfume. Their warmth enveloped me. The love inside me swelled to meet it, filling every part of my body with its giddy glow.

It wasn't enough just to feel that love. It was time I did something with all that emotion.

"Last night was amazing," Aaron said. "The way your fire reached all the way to us."

"Well, I think it's the fae you can thank for that," I said.

"And whose idea was it again to reach out to the fae?" Marco said, amused.

Nate pressed a kiss to my forehead. "You kept the flames going for so long. The vampires didn't know what hit them when all that fire started flooding over them."

"She held the shift even after she was done with her fire-breathing," West said, the pride in his tone tingling over me. "I think we've got a fully-fledged dragon shifter on our hands now."

"About that…" I wet my lips, feeling abruptly shy.

"Serenity?" Aaron said gently.

I ducked my head. "I was thinking… Our kin have gone too long with only one dragon shifter around. Maybe it's time to see if we can add to that number?"

I'd thought maybe I'd need to be a little less coy before they'd get my meaning. Nope. A tremor of anticipation passed through the bodies around me with a collective intake of breath. "Ren," West said behind me, sounding incredulous and eager all at once.

Marco's lips curled up. "Our Princess of Flames wants to make a princess of her own. I think we can fulfill that request. To the lady's bedroom?"

We walked into the house together, the bond between us making me feel so light my feet hardly seemed to touch the ground. When we reached my bed, I paused at the foot of it.

Hunger thrummed through me, but underneath it a quiver of uncertainty passed through me.

"You decide how you want this to go," Aaron said. "We'll follow your lead."

I clambered onto the bed and sat down in the middle of the huge mattress. Then I patted the sheet. My mates moved to join me, settling in a ring around me.

I reached for Aaron first, pulling him into a kiss. His hand drifted over my belly. I leaned back to find Nate's mouth next, and the eagle shifter bent to nibble my shoulder, his hot breath spilling over my skin.

Nate kissed me deeply, easing down the strap of my dress as he did. I turned from him to Marco. The jaguar shifter's tongue teased my lips and slipped between them to tangle with mine.

Someone was easing my dress down to my waist now. Another hand was caressing my breasts. A tremor of pleasure rippled through my nerves. I whimpered against Marco's mouth.

Then there was West. My stubborn wolf. He pressed his lips to mine as if he meant to memorize the shape of them, to chart every curve of my mouth, every hitch of my breath. His fingers trailed over my hip, and the sense of how I wanted this to go swam up through the thickening haze of bliss. From the end to the beginning, back the way I'd come.

For the first several minutes, though, I just floated on that bliss. My mouth moved to meet one of my mates and another's and another's in turn, and then down to the heated skin of necks and chests. Four pairs of hands stripped my dress, my bra, and my panties off me. Somewhere in there I tugged off their clothes too.

Teasing fingers explored every inch of my body. A mouth closed over one nipple. A thumb flicked over the other. I gasped as one of my mates stroked between my legs. My eyelids fluttered shut.

But I knew exactly where West was when I wanted him. I reached out to cup his face. "Please," I said, breathless.

His eyes darkened with lust. He kissed me so thoroughly it left my head spinning. Then he eased between my legs. The head of his cock brushed over my clit, and I whimpered. My hands traced up the lean muscles of his chest to clasp behind his neck. "I love you," I whispered.

He exhaled shakily. "I love you too, Sparks. And I won't let you ever doubt it again."

An ecstatic burn spread through my body as he slid inside me. I clutched him and tilted my hips to welcome his thrusts. West groaned, his head bowing close to mine.

The other alphas had eased back just a little, but they continued their caresses, stroking my breasts, kissing my neck, until I felt as if I were made of nothing but pleasure.

West plunged even deeper into me, and I came with a cry. The sparks of his nickname for me danced behind my eyes. "Fuck," he muttered as I shuddered around him, his voice choked. I felt him spill himself inside me with a hot gush.

He withdrew, sinking beside me to press a trail of kisses down my arm. "Marco," I said with a gasp. I was too empty. We weren't halfway done here.

The feline alpha bent over me. He claimed my mouth with another searing kiss. His hips rocked with mine, his cock testing my opening. I moaned with need.

"My beautiful princess," he murmured.

I met his gaze with a soft smile. "My gorgeous mate. I love you."

He gave me that familiar crooked grin. "And I love you. Couldn't more."

He filled me with one quick thrust that shocked another moan from my throat. His hand slipped beneath my ass to urge me up to meet him. His cock stroked against the most sensitive spot inside me. Bliss raced through me. I was so close to coming again already.

"Oh, Ren," Marco muttered. "You have no idea how amazing you feel. If it was just us, I'd stretch this out forever, but I won't be selfish."

He sped up his rhythm. Someone pinched one of my nipples. My hips canted up with my whimper, my clit grazing the base of Marco's cock, and just like that I was gone. As the second rush of pleasure swept through me, Marco followed me over the edge with a few quirk jerks of his hips.

Marco sat back, dipping low to kiss my core with a smirk. As he scooted to one side, my hand closed around Nate's. The warmth in my bear shifter's eyes turned smoldering.

He flipped us over, pulling me on top of him. I gasped as my sex slid against his thick erection. When he touched my cheek to meet me for a kiss, other hands glided over my thighs, my back. Nate cupped my breasts, rolling my nipples against his palms until I shivered with pleasure.

"I love you," he said, before I rediscovered my capacity for words. "Standing beside you is the greatest honor of my life."

My throat tightened. I leaned down to kiss him again. "I love you too. And I'm honored to stand by *your* side."

He grasped my hips, and together we guided me down onto his cock. His thickness stretched me with a pressure that made every nerve in my body tingle.

I threw back my head, starting to ride him with all longing I had in me, chasing another release. Nate's hand slid down to stroke my clit. A tongue slicked over one nipple. Teeth teased another. One of my other mates kissed the small of my back. I braced my hands against Nate's broad chest, pumping against him, shivering as I started to shatter.

A long moan broke from my throat. The bear shifter caught me as I sagged over him, a groan slipping from his lips at the same time. He thrust up into me one last time and filled me with his release.

My thighs were wobbly as I eased off of Nate. Aaron was there waiting. He pulled me into his embrace, kissing the back of my neck. "Not tired out yet?" he asked with a slightly playful note in his raspy voice.

I laughed. No, the itch inside me wasn't quite scratched yet. I reached to close my fingers around the hard length of his cock. "Not any more than you are."

"Then what do you say we fly?"

I tugged him around to kiss him on the mouth. We toppled over on the bed together.

Aaron sank into me as if he was meant to be nowhere else—and in that moment, he wasn't. I ground against him with each thrust, my hips bucking faster. My skin was damp with sweat now, my breath lost in panting, but I'd never felt so lit with energy in my life.

Flying. Yes, that was the word for this.

"I love you," I mumbled before I lost my hold on my words again.

Aaron's breath stuttered against my cheek. "I love you too. My first and my last. One and only."

He thrust into me so deeply the final damn burst. I toppled over the edge of that last peak of ecstasy, shaking and gasping. My sex clenched hard around Aaron's cock. With a moan, he came apart too.

Finally, blissfully sated, I let my muscles go slack against the mattress. My four mates cuddled close around me, surrounding me in a wash of affection—and more than a little satisfaction.

"You know," Aaron said lightly, "coming together all at once—it's not guaranteed to work on the first try. Just so you're not disappointed."

A giddy giggle popped out of me. "That's okay," I said, tugging them all a little closer. "We'll just have to keep practicing until we get it right."

CHAPTER 22

Ren

Several months later

"It won't hurt them at all, right?" I said, standing at the edge of the boundary the fae woman had just laid down. Her magic shimmered faintly against the earth between the trees—and then faded from my sight completely. It left the slightest scent in the cool spring breeze, something faintly sweet under the crisp green scents of the forest just waking up from the winter.

The fae shook her head. "The humans won't even feel it. They'll simply find themselves completely uninterested in continuing in this direction." She gave me a small but bright smile. "And you shifters won't be affected at all."

A couple of her companions farther away raised their hands to us to indicate they were finished with their parts. The effort was one step in a plan the alphas and I had come up with after discussions with the fae leaders, to expand the shifter territories without encroaching on the fae. New settlements could be formed in areas of wilderness where we'd no longer need to worry about random hikers or curious tourists happening by.

"Thank you for helping us with this," I said. "I'm really hoping having more room to spread out in will make it easier for us all to get along." There'd still been a few spats between shifters and fae since we'd conquered the vampire threat, but at least they'd been minimal, nothing harmed but egos and feelings.

"I'd like to see us happily sharing more ground again someday," the fae said. "But it's hard to enjoy sharing when you're forced into it. I believe this will benefit both our people. Will we set down the next one near the avian estate next week?"

"That's the plan." I waved to them before heading across the boundary to where the car I'd come in was parked.

Kylie and Felix were waiting there, enjoying a little picnic in the meadow beside the road. The fae's magic *would* affect my best friend, but she didn't have any need to visit the smaller settlements anyway. These days she split her time pretty evenly between the dragon shifter estate and Felix's post in New York.

She jumped up when she saw me coming over. "It's done? That didn't take so long at all."

"Fae magic is powerful stuff," I said.

Felix stood too, gathering the remains of their meal into the basket. He shot me a grin. "The vampire king will be happy to hear about the progress we've been making. More precautions to stop humans from catching wind of us. They're still pretty paranoid about the whole keeping supernaturals secret thing."

The fox shifter was now our ambassador of sorts among the vampire community. Not that he lived right with the bloodsuckers or anything—I could only imagine what he'd say about that suggestion—but they'd given permission for one shifter to live right within New York City so that any disputes between vampires and shifters could be settled quickly.

And also so he could simply keep an eye on things. The new king might not be as eager for carnage as the last one, but I didn't think any of us trusted the vamps farther than we could spit.

"You can tell him all about it at that big party tonight," Kylie said, wrapping her hand around her boyfriend's elbow. Her face lit up almost as bright as her neon hair whenever she looked at Felix these days. I'd been a little worried that moving in together so soon after they'd met might bring out the clashing sides of their personalities again, but I'd never seen her happier.

"You've got to head back right now?" I said as we piled into the car.

"After we drop you off at the estate," Felix said. "Unless there's something else you needed first."

My heart pinched. It would have been nice if Kylie could have stuck around to hear my news right away… but this was definitely one case where my mates, not my bestie, should be the first to know. But I wouldn't have to wait very long.

"No, that's fine," I said.

Kylie gave me a playfully suspicious look. "Is there something going on that you're not telling me?"

I smiled back at her. "You'll just have to wait and see."

She waggled a finger at me. "I'm due back in a couple days, remember. I'll pry all your secrets out of you then."

When we reached my estate, one new car was already parked by the house. Marco was lounging on the front step. He leapt up with his easy grace as we pulled in.

I went to greet him, feeling my own face light up. I'd gotten used to spending days and sometimes even weeks apart from one or more of my mates, but I never felt quite as centered as when they were with me.

"Hello there, princess," Marco drawled. He brushed a strand of hair back from my cheek and leaned in to press his lips to mine. I gave myself over to the heat of the kiss for as long as I felt I could get away with when we had company.

"I've just got to say good-bye to Kylie," I said. "Then I'll be right back with you."

"Take your time," the feline alpha said. "I get to have you for the whole rest of the day."

I headed back to the car and gave Kylie a tight hug. "I expect you back in two days," I said. "Be on time."

She laughed. "I always am. Like I'd want to miss out on whatever adventures you get yourself mixed up in next."

"Keep up the good work with the vampires, Felix," I added to the fox shifter.

He saluted me with a twinkle in his sharp eyes. "I'm glad to serve."

As they drove off, I ambled back to Marco. "How have relations been going between the feline and avian settlements I talked to last week? No further conflicts?"

"They've managed to keep the peace so far. I think your talking-to—and the compromise—did the trick. Until they find something new to squabble about." He shook his head. "We also had another stray rogue turn up, one who was born on that side of the divide, wanting to make amends. The next time you can make it to Florida, I'll have you truth-fry him to make sure he's genuine.

"Happy to," I said. The kin had claimed a couple dozen former rogues since our war with the vampires—and the death of the last of the rogue's leaders. But I'd helped question them all thoroughly first, of course.

Marco slid his arm around my shoulders. "So do I get you all to myself, or is this going to be a bigger party?"

"The other guys should be on their way," I said. "I asked everyone to get here mid-afternoon-ish."

"Well, no reason we can't enjoy this alone time while we have it," he murmured.

I snuggled into his arms as he lowered his mouth to the side of my neck, but he hadn't gotten any farther than that when another engine sounded down the road. "Hmm," he said, raising his head to look. "We can always pick up where we left off later."

I laughed. "I'm sure we will."

West got out of his jeep with his usual gruff expression. It still gave me a little thrill seeing that serious look vanish behind a warm grin when our eyes met. He strode over and tipped my chin up for a kiss without bothering to detach me from Marco's arms.

"Too long," he said. He'd been off dealing with some issues in a few of the canine settlements while I'd been busy with the fae alliance, so we hadn't seen each other in nearly two weeks.

"We're almost done enclosing the new territories," I said. "Then you won't be able to get rid of me."

His grin stretched wider. "Believe me, I'm looking forward to that."

Aaron arrived next, in a sedan that sputtered when he brought it to a stop. A thin stream of smoke trickled from the hood. He made a face as he got out. "I'm not sure which I like less now—jets or cars."

"One of the kin on the estate is a mechanic," I said. "I'll get her to have a look."

Marco brushed his hands together. "Let me at it. I'm not totally hopeless with cars."

The other guys and I exchanged a skeptical look. The feline

shifter waved us off. "Just because I like extravagant things doesn't mean I'm afraid to get my hands dirty now and then."

We'd just gotten the hood propped up when Nate's pick-up truck pulled in. "Okay," I said as the bear shifter emerged. "Car maintenance can wait. Come on inside."

Nate fell into step with us on the way to the house, and that beautiful sense of completion wrapped around me. Here I was with all my mates. Everything as it should be. More than they even knew yet.

"What's going on, Ren?" Nate asked. "It sounded like this meeting was a little more urgent than usual."

"Not in a bad way," I assured him. "There's just something I wanted to talk to all of you about, that I figured it'd be best to do in person."

"I'm never going to object to spending time with you, any time I can," Aaron said. He raised my hand to kiss the back of it, his blue eyes gleaming with affection.

I led the way down the hall to my private quarters. In the sitting room, I stopped, motioning them closer. "Give me a hand. All of you."

Marco raised an eyebrow, but my alphas all held out one of their hands. I grasped them lightly with my fingers and guided their palms to my belly.

"Can you feel her?" I said softly. "Because I can." The new life I was carrying inside me touched my senses with a gentle energy like the flickering of a candle flame.

Nate's eyes widened. His hand left my belly to pull me into a fervent kiss. Then Aaron was kissing me, then West and Marco again, all of them closing around me in a ring of love.

"Here's to the next dragon shifter," Aaron murmured.

Motherhood was a whole new expanse of brand-new

territory waiting ahead of me, but I was ready for it. Especially with my mates by my side.

I rested my hand over that glimmer of life and smiled. "Here's to her and all of us, and the future we're building for her." A future that could now be lit with harmony and hope.

DRAGON'S JOY

THE DRAGON SHIFTER'S MATES CHRISTMAS NOVELLA

CHAPTER 1

Ren

Naturally, the string of Christmas lights I'd been unraveling and hooking along the hedge ended exactly five feet before the hedge did. I glowered at the string and at the hedge, as if that were going to convince one to grow or the other to shrink. Unfortunately, neither gave a damn what the leader of all shifter kind would have liked.

I stepped back into the courtyard of the avian estate and considered. Worse to leave a gap in my decorations or to have to go searching for another extension cord?

The damp chilly wind swept over my hair, flicking strands across my cheeks. It wasn't the biting cold I was used to from New York winters growing up, but at least in New York we'd have had a little chance of seeing snow. Aaron had told me it hadn't snowed in December here by the west coast in as long as he could remember.

Good thing I had three more Christmas celebrations after this to cover all the bases.

Footsteps tapped across the courtyard, and my avian alpha's sister, Alice, came to a halt beside me. She cocked her head at my handiwork.

"We do have estate staff who can handle this kind of thing for you, you know," she said in a slightly teasing tone. "There's no reason our dragon shifter should be out in the cold, hanging lights."

I made a face at her. "It's not really a strain stringing lights on a hedge. I'm staying off ladders as promised." The dampness in the air filled my lungs as I dragged in a long breath. "All these celebrations were my idea. I wanted to show how much I value the support I've gotten from the kin. I'm not sure that'll really come across if I sit back and make them do the work for me."

"I think they'd understand. You're eight and a half months pregnant. Which no one with eyes would be able to miss, even if all shifter kind hadn't been celebrating the news since you announced it."

I rested a hand on my rounded belly. As if in answer, my daughter prodded my bladder with an elbow or a heel—something knobby. She had an awful lot of knobby bits, I'd discovered over the last few months of squirming and kicking.

Not yet, I reminded her. *Sleep in there a little while longer.* Not that I wasn't looking forward to having all of her out where I could cuddle her without my internal organs getting bruised.

"I'm fine," I said, waving Alice's comment off and patting my belly. "We're a team effort. Believe me, I've already promised at least ten people that I'll put up my feet the second I start feeling worn out."

Alice gave me a skeptical look, but she didn't prod any further, just walked with me back to the front of the courtyard by the avian estate's massive house, where I'd left the last string of lights. Possibly I waddled more than walked. Even my dragon shifter reflexes couldn't completely offset the extra weight in front of me. It wasn't a struggle to carry my growing child, but it did require a bit of a balancing act.

"Have you decided on a name?" Alice asked. "Not much time left."

My daughter squirmed again, and I smiled. "I've thought about it," I said. It was hard not to, with all those months feeling her grow inside me. "But I don't think I'll know what's right until I've actually gotten to meet her."

"Fair enough. But you know all the kin will be waiting with ears perked for that announcement."

The wind settled down as we moved along the last hedge. We'd just positioned the last of the lights when a golden eagle soared by overhead.

My heart leapt at the sight of my mate. Aaron dipped down around the side of the house—probably to land on the balcony of his bedroom.

A few minutes later, the avian alpha strode out the mansion's front doors in slacks and a wool coat. I hurried over to meet him. A pleased light lit in his bright blue eyes as he leaned in to kiss me, his hand coming to rest over mine where my fingers had instinctively smoothed over my belly again.

"How are you?" he asked. Not exactly an unusual question, but I'd swear I'd been hearing it ten times more from the moment my pregnancy started showing.

"Ready to kick things off," I said. "Did you get everything set up out there?"

The corners of his eyes crinkled with his smile. "Following your precise instructions."

"All right then. I think we can start letting people in." I

turned to Alice. "You want to help me see about some wine?"

Aaron's sister grinned. "Absolutely. Especially if I get to drink for both of us."

As the kitchen staff helped set up the beverage tables, the avian kin who'd responded to my widespread invitation to our Christmas festivities trickled in. By the time Alice finally got to partake of her first glass, the courtyard was buzzing with eager voices.

I stepped back to survey the crowd. The faces of the assembled shifters were as bright as their voices. And more than a few bellies as big as mine showed in the crowd. A swell of sorrow-tinged happiness filled me at the sight.

For the sixteen years before my return, with their dragon shifter missing and their alphas unmated, none of my kin had been able to have children of their own. I hadn't seen any youngsters at all when I'd first toured the territories. They'd had to wait so long, but now there would be a whole lot of shifter children returning to our community alongside my own.

A pair of large hands came to rest on my waist. I leaned back into the familiar brawny form of the man who'd come up behind me, and my bear shifter mate's arms rose to encircle me just above my belly.

"Keeping warm enough?" Nate asked in his low rumble of a voice.

"I definitely am now," I said, resting my arms over his and hugging them to me.

"They really do get the best of all possible weather here, don't they?" Marco said, sauntering up beside us. The feline alpha ran a hand through his spiky black hair and gave a shudder to match his mildly sarcastic tone. "Cold *and* wet."

"Poor kitty," I said with an arch of my eyebrow, and he laughed.

"Just as long as none of it touches my darling princesses," he said more tenderly, giving my cheek a peck and my belly a brief caress.

West had ambled over at my other side, his lean arms loosely folded over his chest. "I think our dragon shifter can withstand a slight chill." The canine alpha's dark green eyes softened as he studied my face. "As long as you're comfortable?"

I swatted him. "I'm *fine*." But as irritating as the constant check-ins could be as the end of these nine months approached, I couldn't deny that the way my four mates had been doting on me brought a flutter of pleasure into my chest more often than not.

We didn't often get to spend this much time all together, rather than each handling his own kin's business while I traveled wherever I was needed most. For the next five days—the four leading up to Christmas and Christmas itself—they were all mine. Barring any emergencies, of course.

The wolf shifter's gaze traveled over the crowd of avian kin, the twinkling lights around us catching on the silver strands in his auburn hair. "Should we be heading out?"

"Soon," I said. "I think if you leave when we set off, you'll get there right in time to meet us."

Nate's embrace tightened. "Are you sure the flight won't be too much of a strain when—"

I turned to shoot him a look before he could even finish expressing that worry, and he hung his head apologetically. The alpha of the disparate kin still needed occasional reminders to rein in his over-protective nature. I rumpled his thick brown hair and bobbed up on my toes to press a kiss to his lips.

"I'm a dragon," I said gently. "I'm made to fly. And our daughter is too."

Aaron joined us, his pale cheeks and the tips of his ears

flushed from the cold. "That's everyone," he said. "The last stragglers just came in. Do you want to give the directions, Serenity?"

"Yes." I gave Marco and West a quick kiss for good measure. "I'll see you three in a bit."

Aaron's staff had set up a platform at the edge of the courtyard, similar to the one I'd stood on to meet this kin group when he'd first introduced me as his mate. A hush spread through the crowd as we climbed up on to it. The avian shifters turned to see what I would say.

"Joyful greetings to you all, avian kin!" I said, pitching my voice to carry. "It's been an honor to work with you and for you over the last year, and I think after all the challenges we've overcome, every one of you deserves a fantastic celebration. What's here is only the beginning. We're creatures of flight, and I'd like the chance to fly with you all. Please shift with me and follow my lead to the main site of the festivities. There are warm clothes waiting for you there."

Eyes glimmered with interest, and curious murmurs carried through the crowd. I shed my jacket and knelt down in the dress I'd picked precisely because I didn't care if it got ripped to shreds. My mates had raised a rather strong objection to the idea of me stripping down totally naked in this weather.

The shift flowed through me as naturally as breathing. My body expanded, my neck lengthened, and hard scales sprang to the surface of my skin beneath the scraps of falling fabric. Fire smoldered in my throat. Vast wings flared from my arched back. And deep in my now much larger belly, my daughter somehow seemed to snuggle even closer to me, as if eagerly anticipating the ride.

All across the courtyard, hawks and falcons, seagulls and pelicans, sparrows and doves emerged from crumpling clothing. I launched myself off the platform toward the darkened sky, and a flurry of wings followed me.

Aaron, his golden feathers gleaming as brightly as his hair did, soared up over the estate right beside me. I reveled for a moment in the sensation of the wind buffeting my wings. Then I swooped over the forests to the south with a vast flock of avian kin surrounding me. The sound of all those wing beats carried through the air around me like a sort of music, and a grin stretched my dragon lips.

The broad field I'd picked out lay just a few minutes' flight from the estate, still within the property that belonged to the avian alpha. As it came into view, my breath caught.

Aaron and the people he'd asked to help had set up the lights exactly as I'd sketched them—and they shone even more spectacularly than I'd imagined. Strands of them hung between posts set up across the field in interlocking lines, forming a pattern like a vast sparkling snowflake, one you could only fully appreciate from far above.

I glided over it and circled around, wanting to drink in the sight for as long as I could. The avian kin followed me, keeping up with my leisurely pace. Right now, we might as well be the same kind of being, united by this act of propelling ourselves through the air and the love of the feelings that came with flying.

My wings flapped easily against the damp air. These days, I could hold my dragon form for hours at a time without the faintest prickle of fatigue. But hundreds of bird shifters were wheeling over the field with me, and their feathered bodies didn't come with quite the same inner heat source.

I drifted through one last circuit of the field, and then I dove down to the grass at the end by the lodge.

That building's windows were already beaming with light. Stacks of clothes arranged by size stood on tables on either side of the door, which stood open wafting heat and the scents of the feast awaiting us.

My three mates whose animal forms didn't come with wings were waiting for me. I shifted as I dropped the last short distance, landing on the wooden boards of the porch with my human feet, and Marco wrapped a thick velvet dress around me. Nate was ready with a long wool coat to drape over that. West tugged a scarf around my neck and gave me a tender smile I'd never seen him offer to anyone but me.

"This is some light show, Sparks," he said.

The avian kin had descended all around us. After they'd dressed on the porch with the ease of people who had to make quick changes on a regular basis, we poured into the broad open room on the other side of the doorway. I scooped roast beef and mashed potatoes and carrots drenched in butter onto my plate and then headed back outside to eat under the lights.

The display was pretty spectacular even from below, if I did say so myself. I meandered deeper into the field, swiveling on my feet between bites and taking in the sparkling patterns all around me, even brighter against the stark black of the sky. The music Aaron had suggested was playing—the first lilting tune in an album recorded by a band composed of avian shifters. The speakers around the field pitched the spirited melody across the entire open space.

The avian kin explored the field around me, murmuring to each other with unrestrained awe. Another grin I couldn't contain crossed my lips.

I'd pulled it off—everything I'd wanted this celebration to be. And I could see the pleasure it had brought this group of my people reflected in every face.

But this was only the beginning. No getting cocky yet, not when I had three more epic revelries to pull off.

CHAPTER 2

Aaron

As THE STACKS of cleared plates along the edge of the porch grew, more and more of my fellow avian shifters got caught up in the rhythm of the music and started to dance. Watching them dip and spin under the arcs of glittering lights brought me back to the first celebration my kin had enjoyed with Serenity—one they'd organized for her instead of the other way around.

It was hard to believe that had happened less than a year and a half ago. We'd all come a long way since then.

I caught a glimpse of my mate whirling in the midst of the crowd, her dark brown hair streaming around her, one arm resting protectively over her belly. Beautiful, as always. I would have gone to join her if one of my attendants hadn't hurried over to me just then.

"She's here," he said, with a twitch of his head toward the far end of the field. "You wanted her to wait for you?"

My pulse skipped with both nerves and relief. "Yes. I'll go speak to her right now."

"Do you need company?" the attendant asked respectfully.

"Did she bring any?"

He shook his head.

"I think I'm well covered then," I said. My sister had already caught sight of us talking and was weaving her way through the crowd. Alice knew about the arrangements I'd made, and she did enjoy her role as bodyguard. I didn't want to give the impression of distrust, not when the trust we'd managed to build so far was still somewhat fragile. "Thank you."

I skirted the edge of the field, and Alice fell into step beside me.

"Do you think she's really going to go through with this?" she asked.

"I can't see why she'd have bothered coming at all if she changed her mind."

"The fae aren't exactly known for their transparent natures."

I had to laugh. "Fair enough. I suppose we'll just have to see, then."

My sister rubbed her bare hands together in the chilly air. She'd never liked wearing gloves, even when we were kids. "I'm surprised you went for this idea at all. Mysticism and secrets aren't usually your thing."

No, they weren't. And that was why my stomach was knotting as we made our way toward the stretch of forest beyond the lights. But I kept striding on regardless. Because…

"We can prepare in all sorts of practical ways as well. This mysticism served us awfully well last year. I can't see how it hurts to prepare that way too. And I think it'll mean a lot to Serenity."

Alice dipped her head. "That's true. You don't think we still need to be wary of the fae?"

"Oh, I doubt it'll ever be wise to trust them blindly. But they have proven themselves true allies since that battle with the vampires." I glanced at my sister. "I wouldn't be letting you join me if I didn't think it was best to err on the side of caution and have a bit of back-up along."

"I'd like to think I'm more than a *bit* of back-up," Alice said loftily, and bumped me with a playful elbow I returned with a chuckle.

The music fell away as we stepped from the field into the thicker darkness of the woods. I didn't need any more direction than my attendant had given me to find the woman we were looking for. A faint glow glimmered amid the trees up ahead.

The fae monarch gave the two of us a measured look as we approached. She stayed where she was in her formal silvery gown, a shimmer of light rising from the fabric and her pale skin and hair. Her crown of vines was nestled on the top of her head, the leaves a crisp golden brown they'd stay until the trees' first buds opened in spring.

"Monarch," I said, with a moderate bow that Alice echoed.

"Alpha of the avian kin," the monarch returned with a bob of her own. "Are you ready?"

"You've brought the crystal?"

She motioned to the thick folds of her dress. "Yes. You provided a temporary resting place?"

"Everything is set up," I said. "Will you join us, then?"

She stepped forward to walk with us back toward the field. When we reached the first ring of lights, she paused, her dark eyes widening with reflected sparkles. I shifted my weight uneasily at her stare, taking in the huge gathering of my people in revelry, but the expression that crossed her face after a moment looked only like awe.

Did the fae even have celebrations, or at least any that came close to this? There was still a lot I didn't know about our nearest neighbors. As the tension in my chest ebbed, I made a note to myself to rectify those gaps.

The more we knew, the more we wrote down for future generations to learn from, the less chance there was that we'd end up at each other's throats all over again.

Some of the dancers nearby glanced over, and their eyes widened in turn. They eased to the side to part a way for us through the crowd. As the path opened up and we walked along it, I spotted Serenity swaying with Nate by the center of the field.

The attendants I'd given advance warning to must have gotten word. The music turned off. My mate lifted her head in confusion and went still when she saw me and our guest approaching.

"Monarch," Serenity said, easing away from Nate. She bowed, only a little, as one head of their kind to another. Her gaze slid to me, and I gave her a reassuring smile.

"Dragon shifter," the fae woman said with equal respect. "I hope I can contribute to your celebration here. Your alpha made a suggestion that struck me as wise, given the strides our two peoples have made toward a long-term alliance."

She reached into the folds of her dress and drew out a crystal so large and clear it was my turn to stare in awe. The carved stone, which filled her entire hand, caught the lights overhead and bounced them back in every color of the rainbow.

I kept enough wherewithal to motion toward the low column set in the middle of the field. The slight indent on its top held the crystal perfectly when the monarch set it down. Serenity looked from it to me and back to the fae woman.

"Your presence is welcome," she said, not forgetting her role even in her confusion. "I'm pleased to take part in any activity that would strengthen the bond between our peoples."

The monarch gave her a thin smile that held about as much warmth as I ever saw any fae offer.

"It's to replace the one you smashed in the mountains," I said quietly. "Just in case, if there's ever a need in the future..."

Understanding dawned on the dragon shifter's face. When she spoke to the monarch again, her voice trembled, but her eyes had lit up. "We can do that? Recreate the magic that was in the other crystal, that will give another dragon shifter the flames of truth?"

"We can," the fae monarch said. "I believe the first crystal was put there for good reason—I believe you've proven that our ancestors were right to provide that option for times of need. If you would join with me in creating the power it will contain?"

"Of course. You'll just need to tell me what to do." Serenity's mouth formed a crooked grin. "I've never imbued anything with magic before."

The fae monarch motioned for Serenity to join her on the opposite side of the podium. All around us, my kin had fallen silent. Several breaths drew in around me with a quiver of anticipation. My heart was thumping fast, but it was all enthusiasm now. Yes, I'd made a good choice, arranging this ritual for tonight.

"The magic will come from me," the monarch said to Serenity. "You will contribute your flames. Let your usual dragon fire flow into the crystal, and I will shape it into the power to be claimed."

Serenity nodded. The crowd had stepped back enough to leave her room to shift. She shed her coat. I caught the eye of one of my attendants and signaled her to collect another change of clothes for our dragon shifter.

The sight of my mate taking on her animal form still filled my chest with wonder. The lovely woman rose and lengthened with a gleam of bright red scales and a fierce glint in her draconic eyes. She held her narrow head at a regal angle and looked toward the monarch. The fae woman stretched her hands toward the crystal as if to say, *Be my guest.*

There were shifters in the crowd who'd never seen Serenity let loose her flames. She hadn't had much reason to use her dragon fire since we'd fended off the vampire threat the summer before last. When she bared her curved teeth and sent forth the first burst of flame, a collective gasp ran through our audience. Everyone stayed completely still, transfixed.

Her regular dragon fire, streaked red and orange and yellow, coursed down over the crystal with a crackle and a wash of heat I could feel from where I was standing several feet away.

The fae monarch made a scooping gesture with her hands as if to encircle the crystal and Serenity's fire at the same time. A fizzing glow lit up around the top of the podium. A sudden wind gusted up, tossing the fae woman's long silver-blond waves. A thrum of energy washed over me that tickled my skin and made my ears pop.

The glow contracted around the crystal and seemed to pull Serenity's fire with it. She raised her head, letting the flow of flames ebb. The ones she'd brought forth danced within the sphere of magic as it closed in around the crystal and then seeped into its polished surface.

A sharper light beamed from inside the stone. It flickered and danced like a miniature flame contained within the gem. Which I supposed it was. A flame giving the power to uncover the truth and burn away to the heart of the matter, like the gift Serenity had earned for herself all those months ago.

The fae monarch smiled, looking pleased, and lifted the crystal. Serenity dropped back into her human form, and I hurried forward with the dress my attendant had handed me. My mate tugged it over her head with a swift practiced motion. Her gaze stayed on the fae monarch as she accepted her coat.

"Will you bring it up into the mountain?" she asked. "Or should we find a different place?"

"I think the place of the two peaks still serves well for this purpose," the fae monarch said. "None go there for any other reason. It will not be discovered unless another like you comes searching, seeking it out. That will be your legacy, to decide what guidance you leave behind. I will see this token conveyed there now."

"Thank you," Serenity said before the monarch could go. "This—it means a lot. I hope no dragon shifter ever needs to use it, especially for the reasons I had to, but I'm glad we can support each other enough now to ensure that power will be there if any reason arises again."

"I'm glad too," the fae monarch said, her tone unusually soft. She bowed to the dragon shifter a little more deeply than the first time. Serenity dipped in return, and the fae woman blinked out of sight like a flash of light, here and then not.

I blinked as a murmur of surprise carried through the crowd. I was never going to get used to the way the fae could travel like that when they chose to.

My mate turned on her feet to take in the revelers. "To our past, our present, and our future, and all the strength we'll carry with us!" she called out. "More eating, more dancing. This is a celebration, isn't it?"

A cheer rang out all around us. The music started again, leaping across the light-strung field. As my kin launched back into their rejoicing, Serenity stepped closer to me. I moved to meet her, looping my arm around hers and squeezing her hand.

"You didn't tell me you were planning that," she said, chiding but only lightly. Her face glowed like the crystal had.

"Christmas is a time of surprises, isn't it?" I said. "Consider it my first present to you."

She raised an eyebrow. "You've got *more* than that? I think that'll be hard to top."

I laughed. "I think my fellow alphas might give it a try. We'll have to wait and see." I leaned closer. "I thought you should know you haven't taken anything away from our people by claiming that power. You accepted the gift that was there, and now you've passed it on."

Her expression went momentarily serious. "Let's just hope our people don't need that gift again for a long long time, if ever."

"If that's our goal, I think we're well on our way." The melody swept around me, and I reached for her other hand. "May I have this dance?"

My mate's smile came back. "Please do."

CHAPTER 3

Ren

LOOKING at the table only half covered with platters, I couldn't restrain a groan. Nate ambled over with a frown. "What's wrong?"

"It looks strange. Maybe this was a bad idea." I turned to take in the rest of the disparate alpha's estate house dining hall: the polished wood tables dotted with tall candles, the exposed brick walls hung with evergreen boughs to add that Christmas-y smell to the air, the silky red and green streamers that crisscrossed the high ceiling. The dry breeze that traveled through the open windows was warm, because it was never going to *feel* like my kind of Christmas here in southern California, but I'd tried to recreate some of the atmosphere I loved.

"Are you sure they didn't think the request was weird?" I asked Nate.

He set his brawny hands on my shoulders. "It's fine, Ren. Everyone I talked to loved the idea. It's not as if you put them out. We gave them a stipend to cover ingredients or just buying something outright—and everyone who joined in volunteered. We didn't put them in any hardship."

"I just… I'm still figuring out the best way to relate to your kin." In some ways, Nate's people were the trickiest, because they were all the shifters who didn't fit into the neat little boxes of avian, feline, or canine. They'd come together not out of what they had in common with each other but what they *didn't* have in common with any of the other kin groups. That wasn't the best recipe for cohesion.

"I want to make sure I'm recognizing them for themselves," I added.

"And I think, like I thought when you first talked to me about it, that this was a perfect approach," the bear shifter said. He dipped his head and nuzzled my cheek with a brief kiss. "You're doing a lot this week, Ren. You've done a lot all year. None of our kin expects that the five of us will never make the slightest slip. Not that I can see any you need to worry about."

"Okay," I said, closing my eyes for a second and trying to convince my nerves to settle. "Do you have the list? I want to put out labels for each dish so they know where to put them—and so everyone else knows who to thank."

I'd just finished arranging—and rearranging, and re-rearranging—the labels when the first of the disparate kin Nate had reached out to arrived. A petite couple I recognized as rabbits from their scent set a sweet carrot-beet salad in the place I'd designated and gave me a shy bow. "Thank you!" I said. "It looks delicious."

Next came minks and then voles, grizzlies and then boars. All in all, thirty families representing thirty different shifter animals had volunteered to contribute to our sort-of potluck meal. From the way they all deferred to me, you'd have thought I was doing them a favor by letting them help feed the party, not the other way around.

More than one glance dropped to my belly. I'd been resting my hand on it again, just out of habit. My daughter kicked lightly against my fingers. Could she feel my touch already? The thought made me a little giddy.

"Best wishes and safe arrival," more than one of the kin murmured, as much to her as to me. A couple of the women were growing round themselves and shot me an extra knowing smile.

More and more of Nate's kin poured into the room. He must have told them they weren't supposed to eat yet, although I saw a few shooting longing glances toward the platters and serving bowls. I shifted anxiously on my feet.

To distract myself, I mingled, welcoming all of our guests and accepting their good wishes with a grin, making my way slowly to the table at the front of the room with just five place settings, reserved for my alphas and me. Aaron, Marco, and West were already waiting there, the eagle shifter and the jaguar shifter chatting about something that had Aaron looking amused and Marco sly, the wolf shifter standing a little stiffly at the other end. Nate turned up just as I reached them, with a nod to me. That was my cue.

I came around the table and picked up my glass to tap my spoon against it. Nate loomed beside me with a meaningfully cleared throat. The shifters milling around the tables closest to us picked seats and quieted, and then the ones just beyond them followed suit, until the whole room had fallen into a hush. Hundreds of eyes fixed on me.

"Disparate kin," I said in the queenly voice I'd had lots of chances in the last year and a half to practice. "It's wonderful to have you all here today as we celebrate the Christmas season and our first full year of peace since the long-ago tragedy that claimed my family."

Heads lowered respectfully at the mention of the attack that had left my alpha fathers and my two sisters dead, and my mother and me on the run. My alphas and I had taken down the leaders of the rogue group that had orchestrated that attack, and in the months since then, a steady trickle of their followers had come to rejoin the kin groups. Any others who still refused to live under an alpha's authority hadn't stirred up further trouble, which I'd take as a blessing.

"It's also to celebrate you and the way you show right here how different types of people can come together and create a beautiful harmony," I went on. "I wanted to honor all the many traditions that make up your kin group. So your alpha and I asked representatives from various families to bring a dish they feel showcases their unique sensibilities to add to our feast. You can find those dishes interspersed with the ones from the estate kitchens all around the room.

The guests craned their necks to peer at the serving tables with renewed interest before their gazes came back to me.

"We shifters have always come together despite our different animal natures," I went on, "and I think it's those differences that make us so strong together."

A shout of agreement carried through the crowd, followed by a few whoops. I had to grin. The anxious twitch in my gut finally settled.

"Now I'd like to give the families who contributed to our meal a chance to stand up and share with everyone the thoughts that went into their chosen dish. Only if you're not feeling too shy, of course. Who'd like to speak?"

A family of skunk shifters stood up and spoke for a minute about the history of their raspberry-glazed chicken. The brother and sister grizzlies followed, talking about the excitement of fishing their salmon out of the river near their home. Several more said their piece, until no one new stood up. My daughter squirmed, and my stomach rumbled.

"Thank you again, everyone, for making this feast even more memorable," I said. "Now let's eat!"

The kin held back as the alphas and I grabbed our plates and made our way to the serving tables along the edges of the room, but as soon as we'd started scooping up food, they streamed over to join us. The sight of so many different dishes, the mingling of all those delicious smells in the air, left me wishing that my daughter didn't seem to be lying on my stomach right now, squeezing it to half its usual size.

"Eat up, mother-to-be!" Nate said with a wink, nudging me toward a roast pig. I stuck out my tongue at him, but I kept heaping food into my plate. Our little one might move in ten minutes and then I'd be starving twice as much.

"Well," Marco said, cocking his head as he poked at a dish of shiny noodles mixed with seaweed and pumpkin seeds. "This experiment has certainly given us a wide variety of flavors, hasn't it?"

"I'm pretty sure there's enough food here that you can find something that suits you," I said.

"Or maybe *you* could experiment a little and open up that refined palate of yours," Aaron teased.

"I'll have you know that I'm perfectly capable of experimenting," Marco said loftily. His nose twitched as he caught a scent. "But not when there are seared tuna steaks to be had. If you'll excuse me…"

"He's really never going to get over himself, is he?" West said with what looked like a barely contained eye roll.

"You should be used to him by now," I said, bumping him

along with my hip. "And, I mean, considering the patience we give *you* and your grouchy moods…"

West glowered at me, but the heat in his eyes was far from irritation. "I don't recall any recent complaints."

"Oh, I think you got in at least ten years' worth of grumbling just in the first month I knew you," I said, with an affectionate quirk of my lips. "It's going to take a while to off-set that."

The wolf shifter made a faint growling sound in his throat, and then he was kissing me, quick but hard. He lowered his voice. "And every day I'm thankful for your patience then, believe me."

Marco had circled back around. "More eating dinner, less eating our princess?" he suggested in a wry tone as he brushed past us. West muttered something inaudible but clearly scathing under his breath, but he moved on.

When we returned to our table at the front, I sampled everything I'd managed to squeeze onto my plate and then dug back into my favorites. I'd heaped the plate high enough that I only made it through about half of the food before I had to sit back with my hand lower down on my belly, where my stomach was achingly full. My daughter wiggled as if eager to come out and enjoy the offerings firsthand.

Not yet, darling, I thought at her. *Your time's coming soon enough.*

I had enough time to settle down from aching to just very full, and then Nate's attendants started clearing the tables. I stood up again, holding up my arm for the attention of the gathered shifters.

"I think you were all told about the tree," I said. "I hope you've brought your own item to add to it. Everyone and everything is welcome! Please come join me in the back yard."

Evening had fallen while we were eating. In the fading light outside, the air had turned not cold but crisply cool. Close enough to winter that it wasn't too hard to picture the massive pine Nate had chosen for our purposes as a Christmas tree. The twinkling white lights that wound around it and the glittering star at its highest peak—courtesy of Aaron—made it all the more fitting.

The shifter kin gazed up at it with gasps and murmurs, and then after a few encouraging gestures from me, they started walking right up to it and picking spots to hang the decorations they'd brought to add to our grand Christmas tree: glinting balls painted with symbols or scenes, toys and figurines hung from loops of ribbon, here and there a candy or a candle. Soon the lower branches were dappled with delights.

"I think it's still missing something," Nate said, his voice playful, as he considered the tree. "There's not enough of our dragon shifter on there."

I shot him a puzzled look, and he drew something out of his pocket with a grin. It was a silver dragon figurine, rearing on its hindlegs, fire blazing from its mouth. A black cord looped from its back. "For your strength," my bear shifter said, and moved to add that ornament to the tree.

The other alphas were all pulling out figurines from their own coat pockets. Aaron held a dragon that was glossy white with two amber gems for eyes, its head tipped in an authoritative pose. "For your integrity," he said, and went to find a free spot to hang it.

The dragon in Marco's hand had been carved entirely out of a gleaming red gemstone, stretched out in flight with its wings spread. "For your passion," he murmured, stealing a swift kiss. He hooked its cord over the tip of the highest branch he could reach.

West's fingers tightened around his for a second before he

opened them, as if he were afraid his wouldn't live up to the others. The dragon he'd brought was whittled from a fine-grained wood, its body looping around on itself as if it were reaching toward something or someone behind it.

"For your *com*passion," he said, so quietly no one other than me might have heard it.

All of them in a row and that one at the end in particular left me choked up. "West," I said.

"You know how much I love you, Sparks," he said, holding my gaze for a beat before he went to place his ornament alongside the others.

"How much we all love you," Nate added, hugging me close with an arm around my shoulders.

I dug into the little purse I'd been carrying. My fingers closed around warm copper. "Great minds think alike?" I said, drawing it out.

I'd commissioned the piece, so I doubted there was any other quite like it in the whole world. A wolf, a bear, a jaguar, and an eagle leapt from the design in different directions, but they were joined together in the center by an etching like a flame.

"It's beautiful," Aaron said.

"It's *us*," Marco declared.

As West rejoined us, the four of them drew me into a combined embrace. I soaked in the heat of their bodies and their twining scents. I was aching again, but this time with gratitude for the path that had led me here, that had let me find the men I was meant to share this life with.

Please let me never lose them.

CHAPTER 4

Nate

I RAN my thumb over the book's cover, its new leather smell tickling my nose. It looked well bound to my unpracticed eyes, the pages inside crisp and the black text neat. Of course, the contents of that text were going to matter a hell of a lot more than how the type looked.

I turned to Aaron, who'd left the Christmas celebration outside to come with me to the office that had belonged to every disparate alpha before me. When I held the book out to him, he took it gingerly.

"Does it look well put together to you?" I asked. "You've got to have a much better eye for this sort of thing than I do." The eagle shifter had never made any secret of his fondness for books and the information he could glean from them.

Aaron flipped to the table of contents and then through several of the entries. "It's come together really well," he said, in a tone that was impressed enough that I relaxed. "She's going to love it, you know."

"I hope so." I swallowed down a twinge of worry as I took the book back from him.

"Why wouldn't she?"

I grimaced. "I just can't help wondering if it'll end up upsetting her more than anything else. All those reminders of the past…"

Aaron gave me a friendly pat on my arm. "Nothing in that book is about the painful parts of the past. Our dragon shifter lost a lot on the day of the attack, and every day after while she was forced into that secret life. This gift is going to take a large step toward replacing things she might never have expected to get back. I wouldn't be surprised if she cries, but I guarantee they'll be happy tears."

"I don't really want to make her cry at all," I muttered, and this time he gave me a playful cuffing instead of a pat.

"You definitely know how she feels about you trying to protect her."

"Hey! I learned my lesson. I've been very good about not overstepping." I tucked the book into a gift bag I'd set aside for this purpose—simple red paper printed with gold snowflakes, too pedestrian for what it contained? But it was too late to find anything else—and pushed away from my desk. "Thank you for all your help with the particulars. I might not have had anything to give at all without your advice."

I couldn't say organization was exactly my strong suit, and bringing this book together had required quite a lot, from tracking down the best contributors across each of the kin groups to working out the necessary timelines for receiving their submissions to presenting the stories they'd offered in a coherent way. The eagle shifter had cheered the project on and offered much-valued tips from the start.

"Oh, I'd imagine you'd have been fine," Aaron said. "But I was happy to help. I can't wait to see her face when she opens that up."

My feet hesitated before I reached the door. I glanced at my fellow alpha. "Do you think she's all right—just in general?"

Aaron raised his eyebrows. "What do you mean?"

"Just—all the effort she's been putting into these celebrations, running around, handling half the work on her own, trying to make each one of them spectacular… I know she's enjoying it, but at the same time, it seems a little much. Considering..." I motioned to my belly area.

Aaron chuckled. "You'd better not let her hear you suggest she should be taking it easy," he teased. Then his voice turned more serious. "One of my healers on staff looked her over yesterday morning and didn't raise any concerns. Hanging decorations isn't pushing herself all that hard."

"Not physically," I agreed. "And I suppose it makes sense that she wants to accomplish something major before she *has* to take it easy for a little while." Even our dragon shifter would have to take some time to settle into life as a mother. It was going to be an adjustment for all of us—but one I couldn't have been looking forward to more. The thought of finally getting to hold my infant daughter in my arms sent an eager quiver of excitement through me.

"Exactly." Aaron nudged me toward the hall. "Serenity knows her limitations. If she needs more from us than we'd naturally offer, we can trust that she'll ask. I think what she needs most right now is to have all of us there by her side, celebrating with her."

Which was all the more reason we should get back to the festivities.

We emerged into the back yard to the sound of voices raised and instruments blending together in harmony. As the final part of her celebration of our disparate natures, Ren had invited all those among my kin who performed music of one sort or another to play a song or two for everyone. Those watching the band of raccoon shifters playing now were swaying along in time with the melody. Ren stood near the front of the crowd, her face lit with pleasure as she took in the music.

During the Christmas before this one—Ren's first as dragon shifter—we'd still been so busy picking up the pieces and getting our domains back in order after dealing with fae and vampires and rogues that the holiday had passed with relatively little fanfare. I wasn't sure how much she'd celebrated her last few years before we'd found her, when she'd been scraping by mostly living on the streets. But she'd occasionally mentioned the private holiday moments she'd shared with her mother while they were still together: sparkling trees and colorful window displays, curling up together in their apartment watching classic movies over hot chocolate.

If the events she'd put together over this week filled even a little of that hole, I guessed I could understand why she'd put so much energy into them. My heart ached, in a good way, seeing the happiness in her expression right now.

Damn, I really hoped I wasn't about to break that.

I caught the eyes of a few of the book's contributors in the crowd and motioned them over. The white-haired badger shifter, the elegant horse shifter, and the wizened black bear shifter came to join me. Yvonne's eyes sparkled as she smoothed back a silver mane no less impressive than that of her animal form.

"It's time?"

"Seems like as good a moment as any," I said.

We let the raccoon shifters finish their song, and then I stepped forward with my hand raised for attention. "Ren," I said, beckoning her. "You've given us the gift of this incredible celebration. Now I and my kin have a gift for you."

"Nate," our dragon shifter said, glancing around as if checking that no unexpected figures were going to appear in the crowd like the fae monarch had yesterday night. She walked up to us and came to a stop in front of me with a curious expression. "I'm starting to get the impression there've been a lot of other preparations going on behind my back while I was busy with my own."

I couldn't help grinning at that comment. "You're not the only one who wants to honor the people you care about."

A flush colored her cheeks. Her gaze slid over the shifters who'd accompanied me. Yvonne spoke up in her clear smooth voice.

"We disparate kin have many different natures and perspectives, as you pointed out so well in the dining hall. One of the beliefs we—and all shifter kind—can unite under without hesitation is the certainty that your mother, our last dragon shifter, was a leader we're proud to have called our own. And we've been more than pleased to see how you've been following in her footsteps."

Ren blinked hard. "Thank you," she said, and was that a wobble in her voice? Damn it, Aaron might be right about the tears. Hopefully on both counts and not just the first.

"We can only imagine, as difficult as it was for us to lose an esteemed leader, how hard it was for you to be torn from your community and then to lose your mother as well," the bear shifter said in a gentle tone. "Which is why, when our alpha asked us to help bring her back to you in the only form we can, we were more than happy to."

I offered Ren the gift bag. She eased it open with trembling hands. When she pulled out the book, she just stared at the cover for a moment, reading the gilded lettering there. *A History of Haven Drake.*

"I asked kin from all across my people—and some from the other groups as well—who spent time with your mother while she ruled to share some of their memories from her time as our dragon shifter," I said. "So you can get to know that side of her in a way you didn't have the chance to before. Over a hundred of her people—and yours—sent me recollections."

Ren opened the book slowly, turning from the title page to the table of contents to the beginning of the first account, from an old wolf shifter who'd worked on Ren's mother's estate while Haven was growing up and who had helped organize the ceremony of her ascension. Aaron and I had decided to include the stories in chronological order, for lack of any better guiding principle.

Our dragon shifter ran her fingers over the first few lines. The tears the avian alpha had predicted glimmered in her eyes. But the smile that came with them reassured me that they hadn't been brought by pain.

"Thank you," she said again, nodding to the three shifters standing with me in turn. "I'll need to thank everyone who contributed. And… thank *you*." She threw her arms around me, still clutching the book, hugging me with all her dragon strength.

Applause broke out in the watching crowd. I hugged Ren back and bent over her when she eased away to claim a kiss. If I hadn't already been convinced, the enthusiastic press of her lips to mine would have told me I'd chosen my gift well.

I motioned for the next group of musicians to jump in with their performance. Ren stayed tucked close to me as she looked over the book again.

"The only problem is that now I want to abandon my own party so I can start reading," she said.

I kissed the top of her head, my heart swelling with so much love it threatened to burst through my chest. "I'm sure my kin can spare you for a little while."

She paused, and then she shook her head, tucking the book under her arm. "This week is about all of us celebrating together. And anyway, it'll probably be better if I take those memories in gradually so I completely appreciate each one."

"Whatever makes you happy," I said.

Her arm tightened around me. "I am happy," she said. "So much."

She did sound happy, but a faint tremor had crept into her voice as well, bringing me back to the concerns I'd mentioned to Aaron earlier. I didn't think our dragon shifter was going to appreciate me asking yet again whether she was all right in front of so many of our kin. So I settled for resting my palm on her belly next to her hand, encircling her and our unborn daughter in all the steady warmth I could offer.

CHAPTER 5

Ren

"WHAT ABOUT THE ORDER FROM FRANCE?" I said into the phone. "Has that shown up?"

The attendant of the feline kin estate gave a short sigh. "No, but the shipping company has promised it'll be here in the morning."

I adjusted my position in the plane's seat. The soft leather that covered most of the surfaces in the private jet that was carrying us from Nate's estate to Marco's was one of the most comfortable materials I'd ever sat on, but between my irritation and the weight of my daughter pressing down on me, I couldn't enjoy it.

"It'd better be there," I muttered. That was half of the drinks for the feline kin's Christmas celebration. "And that machinery I put in a rental order for?"

"It showed up this afternoon, but apparently the delivery

person realized there was a piece missing. He promised he'd get that to us tomorrow."

Great. I stifled a groan and tipped my head back in the seat. The plane had gone through a bit of turbulence earlier, but now it was cruising along smoothly with nothing but a faint vibration in the floor and the hum of the engine to match. Maybe I'd feel better if I got up and paced some of this frustration out.

"Okay," I said to the attendant, rubbing my eyes. My head was getting muggy from two busy days in a row. But we were only halfway through—and the feline kin had exacting standards. I couldn't screw up there. "Thank you for the update. I'll touch base with you in person in the morning."

"Happy to help!" the puma shifter said in that slightly flat tone the feline kin were so good at, that always left you wondering if they were actually being sarcastic no matter what they'd said.

I shoved my phone into my purse and clamped my jaw against a yawn.

"Hey," Aaron said, leaning over from the seat across the aisle from me. "Don't you think you've been working on this enough for one day? I don't think much is likely to change overnight."

"I guess," I said, and the yawn snuck out despite my best efforts, stretching my jaw. Well, that wasn't the most convincing show of alertness either.

Marco got up and held out his hand to me. "Why don't you come to the back room and really get some rest? We'll all join you."

I gave him an odd look. "It's just the five of us. It's not like we don't have plenty of privacy right here."

He shrugged with a sly smile. "One more door if the pilot happens to peek back from the cabin. And also, I may have arranged a bit of a renovation of the back room."

He did know how to appeal to my curiosity. I hefted myself out of the seat and let him guide me down the aisle to the inner door just past the bathroom.

When I'd come into the back section of any of the alphas' private jets before, I'd found nothing more than a smaller room with similar seating to the front. Tonight, the first thing I noticed as I pushed open the door was the lack of any seats at all along the closer wall. Then my gaze caught the end of a broad footboard.

The back room was set up as a bedroom. An oversized bed filled most of the space, two lamps glowing on the end tables at either side of it. A pearl gray duvet that looked deliciously airy stretched across the mattress.

"Okay," I said. "I see your point."

Marco laughed and nudged me toward the bed. I sat down on the edge and rolled my shoulders. The stress of the days ahead was still dragging at me. I wasn't sure I'd be able to fall asleep.

"I think our dragon shifter deserves to relax," Nate said, his rumble of a voice even lower than usual. He dropped down beside me and applied his strong hands to my shoulders. A contented sigh escaped me as he started to work over the tensed muscles of my neck and upper back with his insistent thumbs.

I sank into his touch, letting him support me while he continued his massage. Aaron and West climbed onto the bed, each taking one of my ankles and easing off my shoes. I hummed happily at the enjoyable burn of their careful fingers stretching the arches of my feet.

Marco settled next to me and started to stroke his hand lightly over my belly. It wasn't the same sort of release as the others were offering, but I wouldn't have wanted much pressure in that area anyway. His caress sent delightful shivers over my skin.

Nate worked his way down my back, and Aaron and West eased up from my feet to my calves. My eyes slid shut. I gave myself over to their ministrations, feeling every kink and knot smoothed away. For a few minutes, between the joint massage and the fluffy duvet beneath me, I could almost have believed I was floating.

As Nate's hands circled my waist so his thumbs could dig into the small of my back, a different sort of pressure formed between my legs. The heat flowed up to my chest and down my thighs. My heart thumped faster with it.

My hunger for my mates had never completely faded, but I couldn't say I'd felt all that much desire in the last month since my body had gotten increasingly unwieldy. But right now? Oh, hell, I *desired*. There were other kinds of knots inside me that only these men could release.

My arousal must have scented the air. When I glanced down the bed, a spark had already lit in West's eyes. He slid his hand up to my knee. "Can we do even more for you?" he asked, his voice so husky it made me shiver.

"Please," I said. "I want— Mmm, yes, that."

My wolf shifter had lowered his mouth to my leg, charting a course over the sensitive skin on the side of my knee. The stubble on his jaw in contrast with the tenderness of his kisses made the perfect mix of sharp and soft sensations.

With a pleased thrum in his chest, Nate scooted closer to me, pressing his lips to the crook of my neck. Marco eased up my dress to bare my panties and belly. He slipped his hand up under the fabric and flicked his thumb experimentally over the tip of my breast. At my eager gasp, he grinned.

Aaron kissed my hip as West continued his slow scorching path up my inner thigh. Nate cupped one of my breasts with a gentle squeeze while Marco teased the other nipple until it stood stiffly at attention. With all that pleasure coursing through me, the immense bulge of my belly didn't seem all that awkward. After all, our daughter was a result of moments of pleasure like this.

When West's mouth reached my core, my breath shuddered. I arched up toward him as much as my body would allow. He swiped his agile tongue over my clit, sending a bolt of bliss straight through me, and dipped lower to tease over my opening.

At the same moment, Marco lowered his lips to my breast and sucked the tip into the heat of his mouth. I moaned, every nerve quivering.

West went back to devouring my clit. Every flick of his tongue sent fresh quivers of pleasure all through my limbs. He slicked a finger over the liquid arousal on my folds and eased it inside me with careful pulses. Another moan escaped me. I tried to push into his hand, wanting more, wanting him deeper. Wanting everything my mates could offer me.

Nate trailed his fingers along my jaw and captured my lips with his. Marco tested the tips of his teeth against my nipple. Aaron was peppering kisses all along the side of my body. And West—West was summoning ecstasy with every stroke of his tongue and his fingers.

My hands balled in the duvet, my breath breaking into pants. I kissed Nate back hard until his tongue twined with mine. Marco reached to fondle my other breast while he continued to have his way with the first. Then West sucked hard on my clit with a swivel of his finger, and I shattered with a cry of pleasure. The release rolled over me in a shimmering wave.

The wolf shifter drew back with a grin. The heat flowing through me pooled again around my core. Some part of me wasn't quite satisfied yet.

"Aaron," I gasped out.

One look in my eyes, and my eagle shifter knew what I needed. He undid his pants with a jerk of his wrist, kicking them off to the side. His cock already jutted at stiff attention, so thick and hard my mouth watered at the sight and my sex dampened all over again.

"You're sure?" he murmured as he bent over me. Nate nuzzled my shoulder, still supporting part of my weight. I couldn't have asked for anything more delightful than the feeling of all my mates so close around me.

"Go gently," I said. "I'll be fine. She'll be fine." My hand drifted to my belly, just briefly.

Aaron slid his cock over my folds, and I whimpered. A ragged breath escaped him as he pushed inside. Oh, God, yes, this was what I'd been missing. That fantastic heady rush of being completely filled.

As the avian alpha moved in and out of me with measured thrusts, I realized I wanted to be filled even more. My mouth was still watering for the taste of my mates. I gripped Marco's shirt, and he met my gaze with a lifted eyebrow. My hand slipped down to the waist of his slacks. His erection strained against the fly.

"Oh, princess," he rasped. With a few quick movements, he'd freed himself. I flicked my tongue over the head of his cock, and he groaned.

Nate began stroking my breasts as I welcomed Marco into my mouth. He rocked into me with the same steady rhythm Aaron was setting between my legs. West swiped that sharp tongue of his across the recently massaged arch of my foot, sending a giddy tremor through me alongside all the other swells of bliss.

I bucked to meet Aaron as well as I could, urging him faster. He let out another groan and followed my cue. Marco's fingers closed around my hair as his hips jerked.

"I'm there," he warned in a shaky voice, so different from the feline alpha's usual self-possession that it turned me on even more. I squeezed my lips around him to encourage his release.

He came with a low guttural sound, a salty tang filling my mouth with a rush. Aaron clutched my thigh, torn between caution and desire, and I clamped my hand over his, rising to meet him even more deeply.

"I want you," I gasped out. "I want all of you."

He plunged into me again, and again. His cock penetrated me at just the right angle to hit that perfect place inside me, and my body exploded with pleasure. The sensation crashed through me, leaving me slack and trembling and smiling uncontrollably. Every inch of my body seemed to be singing with joy.

Aaron followed me a moment later with a bow of his head and a harsh inhale. Then he was easing himself out and down onto the bed beside me.

All four of my mates tucked themselves around me, so that every inch of me really was enveloped by the most joyful warmth I could imagine.

"I love you," I said with a sudden bubbling of emotion from the depths of my chest. "I love you so much."

"Oh, Sparks," West said, tucking his head against my waist. "It's an honor to be able to say I love you."

Nate brushed a stray strand of hair from my cheek. "You're everything I ever hoped to have in a mate and more."

"The only woman I've ever loved and ever will," Marco said, his voice almost a purr. "My Princess of Flames."

Aaron smiled. "Every time I think I couldn't love you more, the feeling keeps growing. I'm not sure there is a limit."

Surrounded there by my mates, I let my eyelids slide shut. Just for that moment, nothing at all weighed on me, nothing at all could penetrate the haze of happiness that contained us. And in that circle of peace, I drifted off too.

CHAPTER 6

Ren

"THIS ISN'T my kind of Christmas," Kylie said cheerfully as we tugged a satin tablecloth straight in the feline kin's banquet hall. "Give me paper streamers and dorky plastic Santas."

I shook my head at her with a smile. "I can only imagine the looks of horror I'd get from these shifters if I dared to disgrace their alpha's estate with anything even slightly tacky."

"Me too," Kylie said. "That's why I think it'd be worth it. Let them squirm." She winked at me and straightened up, brushing her hands together. She must have recently re-dyed the bright pink in her hair, because her pixie cut gleamed almost neon under the crystal chandeliers. "Okay, what's next?"

My best friend had flown down from New York to meet up with us here in Florida even though she'd also be joining us for the final celebration on West's estate, much closer to her home. "Why only have one Christmas with my bestie when I can have two?" she'd said. "Anyway, I *know* you. You're going to need someone jumping in to make sure you don't try to do everything yourself, mama-to-be."

I'd grumbled something about how I already had four alpha mates hovering over my every move, but I hadn't really protested the idea. I didn't get to see Kylie anywhere near as often as when we'd been making ends meet on the streets together. She was the one who'd really helped me get back on my feet after I'd fallen in with a bad crowd, stealing just for the privilege of getting to sleep on a concrete floor and share a little food. We'd finally gotten an apartment together, ready to build a new life, when my mates had found me.

Of course, I hadn't exactly left Kylie behind as I'd moved into my *new* new life as queen of the shifters. She'd fought alongside us in the battle against the vampires—and caught the interest of one of West's lieutenants, a fennec fox shifter named Felix. West had sent Felix to New York to act as liaison with the new vampire king, and as far as I could tell Kylie and him had been honeymooning it up together ever since.

"The candle sticks are in that box," I said, hustling over to it as I pointed. "I'm thinking four per table, spread out at equal distances."

"I don't think they're going to measure the spaces in between them," Kylie said.

"Have you met these people?" I said, only half joking. "Some of them totally will." The feline kin, like cats everywhere, didn't take all that well to authority—especially when the person calling the shots for them wasn't even feline. They gave Marco a hard enough time of it now and then, and he was one of them. They'd been skeptical of me and my questionable upbringing in human society from the moment I'd turned up. And calling them finicky would have been a huge understatement.

"They've been going a little easier on you, haven't they?"

Kylie said as she grabbed a few of the silver candlesticks from the box. "I mean, you've been kicking butt since you showed up. What could they possibly complain about?"

"Mostly I get the impression they're still reserving judgment," I said. "Which means, waiting until they find a moment that they *can* judge, when they'll happily jump all over me for making a mistake." Which was why I wanted this particular celebration to be absolutely perfect. Why wasn't the wine here yet?

But the tablecloths were almost as shiny as the chandeliers, and the wine that had arrived was an uber expensive Italian red that Marco had approved of, and the kitchen staff were whipping up all sorts of delicacies from rare ingredients I'd ordered in from around the world. The feline kin liked to feel they were a little superior—well, tonight I was going to cater to that sensibility completely. Other than the little surprise I had planned for the end, which I was hoping would appeal to a different side of their natures.

This night had better work out without a hitch.

As if echoing my anxiety, my daughter twitched restlessly inside me. I paused for a second with my hand braced against the table, the other rubbing the shape of her through my belly. *Hey there. Settle down. And can we try to keep those heels away from my liver?*

"Are you okay?" Kylie said, her eyes wide, immediately on high alert.

"Just a normal bit of kicking," I said, straightening up. "She's definitely a strong one—and she doesn't let me forget it."

"Hmm. Sounds like someone else I know." Kylie grinned, but her gaze lingered on the bulge of my belly, concern still shadowing her face.

"Hey," I said, giving her shoulder a squeeze. "I'm all right.

Really. I'm pretty sure it's the job of all babies to make their moms as uncomfortable as possible in the last few weeks so we'll be looking forward to the part where they come out more than dreading it."

Kylie laughed. "Okay, okay. You know, you're my first friend who's gone the mom route. I don't have any practice at the whole godmother thing yet."

"You'll get plenty," I promised, and then couldn't help waggling my eyebrows at her. "And maybe I should be watching for you to 'go the mom route' sometime soon? You and Felix just seem to get cozier and cozier."

Kylie laughed again, but she also blushed. Ah ha. A year and a half was by far the longest I'd ever known Kylie to be hooked on or hooking up with a guy—clearly they had something special. Not that I could picture her totally settling down any time soon.

"I was worried things might go off the rails when we moved in together," she admitted, her voice dropping. "But… it's actually been even better. Not that we never have little arguments or anything, but he gets me. And I get him. It's the first time I've ever had that. With a guy, anyway. Obviously he'll never replace you as bestie." She tapped me playfully with her elbow and went back for more candlesticks.

"You've been holding out on me," she called over her shoulder. "What's my god-daughter's name going to be, huh?"

"If I'm holding out on you, then I'm holding out on myself too," I said. "I don't know yet. I think I've got to see her before the right one will come to me."

Kylie made a disgruntled sound. "Since when are you indecisive? You'd better spill the beans as soon as you're ready."

"Of course," I said. My throat tightened a little. Maybe it

wasn't like me to waver over a decision for months. But my daughter would have her name for her whole life. She was the first person I'd ever given a name to. When I picked one, I wanted to be completely sure of it.

As I fished out the candles themselves, elegantly tapered cylinders of pure white that gave off a pleasantly warm waxy smell, a couple of feline kin passed the doorway and peered into the room. They only paused for a few seconds, but their vaguely impressed expressions as they took in the décor gave me a boost of confidence.

Maybe I could pull this off without any of Marco's prominent families making snarky remarks about my tastes or approach. They were so good at getting in those subtle jabs. It was a delicate political dance, setting them in their place without seeming fazed.

Who would have guessed that maneuvering cat shifters would end up becoming one of my main concerns in life?

Nate appeared a few minutes later holding a handful of forks. "Apparently each of these sets is equally fancy silverware," he said, fanning them for my inspection. "I didn't know which design you'd like more."

I blinked at them. "Of course the feline kin's kitchen would have five different sets for fine dining. Um… Let's go with this one." I tapped the one in the middle, simple and sleek. When in doubt, going with a less-is-more philosophy had served me well so far.

"Got it! I'll grab the rest. And I think Aaron and West have settled on the plates."

Kylie shot him an amused look as he left. "You've put all your men to work too, huh?"

"Oh, believe me, they insisted on pitching in however I'd let them. I had to give them jobs so that they weren't following me around offering to take everything I'm doing off my hands." But even as I said that, I smiled fondly. The whole parent thing was new to all of us. I couldn't blame them for being nervous when I, well—

I pushed that thought away before it could completely solidify in my head and hustled the candles over to the tables. By the time Kylie and I had one in every holder, Aaron and West had arrived with the plates. I glanced at them and gave a thumbs up before motioning for them to help us set them out.

One of Marco's attendants bustled into the room. "The French delivery is here!" she called. "Where do you want it?"

Oh, thank God. "Bring it here—no. Sorry. Have them take it to the kitchens." The serving staff would bring around the wine. The feline kin weren't much into buffet style dining.

The attendant nodded and darted away. I scanned the tables. "Glasses—we still need the glasses for putting that wine *in*."

"I think Marco was seeing about those," Aaron said.

"Well, where is he then?" I muttered. "The dinner is supposed to be starting in an hour."

West gave me a wry look. "I think an hour is plenty of time to set up a few glasses."

"More like two hundred," I said. "Oh, and I should check the sound system. Crap."

"Hey." Aaron came up behind me and rested his hands on my waist. "It's all coming together. You've thought of everything important. And if anyone suggests anything else, Marco will bite their head off."

My mouth twitched at the image that provoked. My shoulders came down as I exhaled slowly. "I know. But I want them to have a good time because I pulled it off, not because he bullied them into pretending to enjoy themselves."

"If they complain about this set-up, then I don't think even the queen of England could impress them," West said, making a face.

"Is anything else bothering you?" Aaron asked quietly. "Everything you've been doing this week—it is a lot."

I made a frustrated sound and turned to steal a quick kiss. "I just want everyone to have a great Christmas. Nothing so weird about that, is there? You don't have to worry about me—I say for the hundredth time."

Aaron wrapped his arms around me. "We want *you* to have a great Christmas too, you know."

"I am," I said firmly. "The last two days have been wonderful. So we're going to make the next two amazing too." And then the five of us could have our own little Christmas, before everything changed all over again.

I just had to make it through two more days without melting down from the stress along the way.

Marco came in at that moment with a few attendants in tow, all carrying platters of wine glasses. I gave a little cheer and jumped at the chance to get back to prep and away from conversations about my well-being.

The feline kin might have believed in being fashionable in most ways, but they weren't fashionably late. About fifteen minutes before the time on the invitations, the first guests started to drift in. I was crouched by the sound system, just finishing tweaking the volume. Faint strains of classical music drifted out into the air.

I left the speakers to stand at my and my alphas' table on the dais at the front of the room. As more and more feline kin arrived, I watched gleams of delight come into their eyes at the elegant styling. The highest families would get to sit with my mates and me at our table, but none of them had appeared yet.

They wanted to make an entrance when enough of their kin were here to see.

A smile crossed my lips as our guests took their seats amid the glinting candles and glossy tablecloths. My hand stroked over my belly. *This place will be part of your rule someday too*, I thought to my daughter. *Even if they like to act as if they don't need you. That's part of the reason why they do.*

CHAPTER 7

Marco

THE LIGHT from the chandeliers glimmered over Ren's dark hair as I spun her in a gentle circle in time with the music. All around us, my kin were dancing on the floor now cleared of dining tables, but I felt I could say without a doubt that not one of them compared to my mate.

I pulled her back to me and tucked my arm around her waist. We swayed with the graceful strains of violin and piano, the sort of refined classical piece that made even the snobbiest elitists among my kin perk up. Ren beamed at me, some of the strain I'd seen in her earlier gone from her face now.

She shouldn't have been worried. In the past year and a half, she'd gotten to know my people and their whims awfully well. Every element she'd chosen for tonight had been perfectly tailored to their tastes. I'd heard their exclamations as the staff had brought out each of the dinner's delicacies; I could see the pleasure they were taking in the party in every expression around me, even if some tried to keep a poker face.

Oh, my kin would be talking about the Christmas celebration that our dragon shifter had orchestrated for the whole rest of the year—while looking forward to the next one. It really couldn't have turned out better.

Her part of it, at least. Mine—that remained to be seen.

"It seems like the dinner has gone over well," Ren said.

I smiled, dipping and turning her, careful of her balance in her current front-heavy state. "Understatement of the year, princess. Anyone you hadn't won over before today I expect is ready to kiss your feet now."

She rolled her eyes at me, but they shone even brighter at the same time. "I can't imagine many felines ever lowering themselves to foot-kissing."

"Possibly I was speaking in metaphors," I allowed. "Don't argue about it. Tonight was a triumph, Ren. *Your* triumph."

"It's not over yet," she said, with a sudden glint of mischief. She'd kept quiet about whatever she'd been setting up with a few of my staff—sworn to secrecy—over in the immense greenhouse attached to the mansion, where anyone visiting the estate could blow off steam in their feline forms without worries of being spotted by humans in the wilds beyond.

"When do I get to hear about this secret plan of yours?" I asked, leaning close enough that my nose grazed hers.

Ren grinned, apparently unswayed by my powers of seduction, formidable as those generally proved to be. "You'll see when everyone else does. Don't you like surprises?"

"Not particularly," I said.

She tapped my chest. "Curiosity killed the cat, isn't that what they say?"

"Oh, if I have to wait, I suppose I'll survive the suspense."

She eased closer to me again, and as the song petered out, I closed my eyes and just enjoyed the feel of her body next to mine. Her body and that of our daughter so soon to come contained within it.

Straightening out affairs in the shifter realm after sixteen years without a dragon shifter and an interspecies war on top of that had taken a lot of work, with even more ahead of us. We didn't have many moments where we could simply be together without any pressing responsibilities nagging at us.

The melody of the next song swelled from the speakers, and a hand heavy enough that I knew who it belonged to before he spoke came to rest on my shoulder.

"You can't hog our dragon shifter the whole night, even if this is your estate," Nate said in a genial tone. "May I cut in?"

I let out a huff of breath as if offended, but grinned to show I didn't mean it. "I suppose I should share a little." I gave Ren a kiss, quick yet sweet enough to send a tingle down to my groin. "I'll be back to reclaim you later."

She laughed. "Not if I find you first."

I left her in the bear shifter's arms and wove through the crowd toward the tables bunched together at one end of the room. I did actually have one responsibility that still needed taking care of, even if it'd been a completely optional one. Our dragon shifter wasn't the only one who knew how to put together a surprise.

Stepping onto the dais that held the alphas' table, I peered around the room until I caught the eye of Coreen, lion shifter and matriarch of the most established lion family among the kin. At the tip of my head, she left the friends she'd been talking with and came to join me.

"I think this is as good a time as any to do the presentation," I said. "Can you assemble the others?"

"Of course," she said. Coreen had been skeptical of our new dragon shifter at first, but after she'd watched Ren put down her husband's murderer without hesitation, she'd been one of my mate's most loyal advocates. Trust was not a concept that came easily among my kin, but I'd have depended on her through dire circumstances if need be.

She slipped through the crowd, finding the other figures from families prominent enough to have gotten a seat at the alphas' table earlier tonight: husband and wife cheetah shifters, a broad-nosed tiger shifter, mother and daughter mountain lion shifters, and another couple made up of two leopards. At Coreen's gesture, they ducked out of the banquet hall and returned a few moments later each with a parcel wrapped in gold foil paper.

I supposed I shouldn't be surprised they'd decided to coordinate so their presents matched. That was the only way they could make sure none of them managed to top anyone else's in appearance. Saying feline kin were image conscious was something like saying fish enjoyed living in water.

My people weren't big on public spectacles, though, at least not ones done in an overt way that outright demanded their attention. As the next song wound down, I didn't make any big announcement. Instead, I found Ren in the crowd and peeled her away from the bear shifter. "Time for a little break from the dancing," I said with a grin.

Ren raised her eyebrows, but she followed me. I didn't have to say anything—my kin around me noted my passing and that of our dragon shifter, and their gazes automatically tracked us to the front of the room. Without my calling any direct attention to what was about to happen, the dancers had already stilled and gone quiet by the time we reached the dais where the eight waiting figures stood.

I wasn't sure I could say that everyone in this room respected all of them, being the finicky bunch our audience was, but certainly there shouldn't be anyone here who respected none.

"Dragon shifter," the male cheetah shifter said, pitching his voice loud enough to carry but not so loud it was obvious he wanted all eyes on him. "To pay tribute to you and your young one about to arrive, we hope that you will accept these gifts. Each was chosen with the most careful consideration."

His wife offered their wrapped box to Ren with a respectful bob of her head. Ren's hands closed around its glossy surface. She glanced to me as if for guidance, and I gave her a hint of a nod.

The paper peeled away with a jerk of Ren's thumb. She opened the box inside, and a delighted smile crossed her face. She held up a red woolen coat and pants, the same shade as her dragon scales.

"It's the finest lambs' wool you'll ever find," the cheetah woman said in an eager voice. "Soft for your daughter while she's still so delicate—and thick to keep her warm through the winter of her birth."

"Thank you," Ren said, running her fingers over the fabric with an expression of wonder. I wasn't sure whether she was more amazed by the quality of the gift or the fact that my people were gifting her anything that had taken much consideration in the first place.

I bundled the clothes back into the box and set it on the table so that Ren could receive her next gift. The tiger shifter gave his own small bow and held out his offering.

"Mine comes with much the same thought," he said. "My

whiskers tell me we have a cold winter coming—as cold as it ever gets down here. Our littlest dragon shifter will need protection from chills. And she can dream of her first flight in the meantime."

Ren unfolded a blanket more than half her height from the opened wrapping paper. "It's lovely," she said a little breathlessly. The blanket was velvet edged and made from the same soft wool as the coat and pants, woven with an image of a dragon in flight.

The mountain lion shifters stepped forward next. Ren unwrapped their present and lifted out a mobile of animal figures, each of them carved with the finest detail out of ebony and mahogany. They bobbed on their glittering strings as Ren turned it.

"To hang over her crib and keep her entertained," the mother said. "Because any dragon shifter child will have an active mind in need of stimulation."

Ren smiled, her gaze going distant for a second. "I know exactly where I can set it up. I'm sure she'll love it."

The leopard shifters handed over their box, the contents of which required a little more explanation. I could tell Ren was fighting a puzzled expression as she examined the silky rectangle of fabric with its loose strips on either side.

"It's so you can carry her with you wherever you'd like," the wife said quickly. "Light material so neither you nor her will get too hot and you won't be weighed down. I thought you might want to always have her close by, even when you're on the move. Let me show you."

With lithe fingers, she demonstrated to Ren how to arrange the carrier's straps over her shoulders and around her waist. Ren let out a pleased laugh. "I'll definitely be getting a lot of use out of this. It's wonderful."

Coreen was the last to offer her present. The box was small, but Ren's face lit up when she opened it. She drew out a silver rattle and mirror.

"Those belonged to my own son," Coreen said in her resonant voice. "They were his favorite things to play with when he was a baby."

Ren's eyes widened. "Coreen," she said. "Are you sure you don't want to keep them in your family?"

The lion shifter's lips stretched with a smile. "Your daughter will be part of my family—part of all of our families. It has been too long since a dragon shifter was born into our people. She will be our kin as much as you have proven yourself to be."

For the second time in as many days, my mate appeared to be on the verge of tears. She blinked hard as I slipped my arm around her.

"Thank you, so much," she said, and then turned to the watching crowd. "Thank all of you for being here today, and for working with me since I came back to you, even though you weren't sure of me yet. You know… We can have more time for dancing, if you'd all like, but first I'd like to show you something else. Would you all come with me to the greenhouse?"

I tucked my hand around hers as she led the way into the hall, my kin following us with murmurs of retrained excitement. I was a little excited myself to see what our dragon shifter had cooked up. A couple of my attendants darted ahead of us, I supposed to get some part of the surprise in order.

Ren bent her head toward me. "Be honest—did you tell them what presents to get, or was that all their own initiative?"

"I suggested it might be a worthy gesture to present you with something," I said. "The rest I left up to them. They did rather well, didn't they?"

"Yes. Yes, they did. I wouldn't have thought—" She stopped herself with a smile. "I guess we really have come a long way."

We spilled past the greenhouse doors into the vast treed space. I drank in the floral perfume from the vegetation all around us. The lynx shifter next to me eyed the rock ledges along the glass walls as if he were itching for a climbing session.

"I know Christmas in Florida isn't the same as the Christmases I grew up with up north," Ren said to the shifters assembled around her. "But I thought you might enjoy a little taste of my kind of Christmas too."

She motioned with her hand, and a whirring started from somewhere deep in the brush. A burst of glinting white dust shot out into the air over our heads—

No, I realized as the first few flakes hit my cheeks. Not dust. Snow. She'd brought us a white Christmas.

"Watch it, play with it—whatever you want," Ren said, grinning. "Let the celebrations continue!"

The lynx shifter at my side had already scrambled out of his clothes and leapt forward in his feline form. He swatted at the tumbling flakes and spun around in their midst like he was returning to his kittenhood.

The growing flurry had stirred something inside all of my kin. Some of them hesitated, but as the first few dashed deeper into the greenhouse as their furred selves, others shed their clothes and joined the romp. My own jaguar urges tugged at me to spring into the artificial snowfall.

Ren was looking my way. "Go ahead," she said, affection shining in her gaze. "It's for you too. I'll get plenty of snow to play with later."

A chuckle broke from my throat, and then I was shifting into my jaguar self, muscles lengthening, tail swishing behind me. I bounded across the now-slippery surface of the path and swiped my tongue at the falling flakes. A giddy sensation swept through me.

It was strange, wasn't it, to feel so childlike when I had a child of my own almost here? But maybe that was the real gift my mate had given me.

CHAPTER 8

Ren

"Do you think this is enough wood?" I asked Kylie, cocking my head as I studied the heap in the courtyard of the canine shifter estate. A pungent pine scent rose off the chopped logs.

My best friend laughed. "Ren, it's almost as tall as I am. Unless you're planning on roasting a giant on that thing, I think we're good. And maybe even then."

I mock-glowered at her. "I am going for epic here."

"Somehow I don't think West is going to appreciate it if you burn down his estate in the meantime."

"Not going to happen," Felix said easily, coming up beside Kylie and slinging his arm around her shoulders. "This place has seen lots of fire, most of it thanks to our dragon shifter here, and we all came out okay." He grinned at me.

I had to smile back at the fox shifter, but at the same time a twinge ran through my chest. Not *everyone* had come out okay. Shifters had died during our battles with the vampires and the rogues. Entire villages had been razed to the ground. Nate had almost died just a short drive from where we were standing right now. If we ever faced another war like that…

I shoved those thoughts aside and spun on my heel. "We should get the tokens and the pencils ready—Felix, do you know where those ended up?"

"I saw the boxes over in the storage shed," he said. "We can get 'em for you."

He gave Kylie a little tug, and she offered me a thumbs up before ambling off with him, tipping her head toward his shoulder. Funny to think that when she'd first shown up here, Felix had been skeptical of the idea of even having a human on the premises. Now I was sure he'd have been baring his teeth at anyone who suggested similar. I'd bet he'd gotten a bit of hassling from some of his kin over his choice in girlfriend, but I'd never seen him show the slightest doubt in that choice.

Which was good. I'd pulled Kylie into this dangerous world of supernatural creatures and unpredictable magic accidentally, and she didn't have dragon fire or claws to protect herself with. The rogues had already nearly killed *her* once. Even if I still felt a jab of worry every time we had to part ways, it was a relief knowing she had at least one shifter by her side most of the time.

I checked that everything else we needed for the bonfire was in place, tugging my coat tighter around me against the wind. The air had a touch of ice to it now, but there wasn't any sign of real snow yet. It'd be nice to get at least one properly white Christmas. The one I'd manufactured on Marco's estate didn't really count by my standards.

The smell of roasting meat and vegetables was starting to carry from the estate house. I hurried inside, following that smell to the kitchen and poking my head inside. The staff were bustling around, pots clattering and dishes clinking. The head chef caught sight of me and dipped into a quick bow.

"Dragon shifter. Did you need something?"

"No, I just wanted to make sure—we're on track to have dinner ready at six?"

She smiled. "Everything is on schedule. No one will go hungry, I can promise you that."

"Okay, great. Thank you." My own stomach rumbled, my mouth watering at the smells. How long had it been since I'd eaten lunch? *Had* I even eaten lunch? Suddenly I couldn't remember. I'd had too many other things on my mind since we'd touched down here.

Well, it'd be dinnertime soon anyway. I hustled from the kitchen to the dining room with its stone-lined walls and crackling fireplace.

West's home was the least posh of the estate houses, but I'd always found it comfortingly cozy. Most of my childhood memories came from the modest two-bedroom apartment my mother and I had shared in Manhattan, not the sprawling dragon shifter estate amid the mountains where I'd spent my first five years. Sometimes, even now, the fancy mansions that belonged to the alphas made me feel a little overwhelmed.

It might have been nice to drop into a chair by the fire and soak up that wafting heat for a few minutes. But our guests would be here soon, and I wasn't going to slack off on this final celebration. The canine kin deserved as great a party as much as the other kin groups had gotten.

The thick wooden tables were already set, but I'd known that, because I'd been here helping make that happen an hour ago. I bit my lip as I scanned the room. Was there anything I was missing? I couldn't ignore the itch nagging at me that there had to be something else I needed to get done.

"There you are." The canine alpha stalked into the room, slowing as he reached me. West wrapped his arms around me from behind and tucked his head close to mine. "It's getting hard for even a wolf to track you down, the way you're running all over this estate."

I made a face at my mate. "I just need to get everything ready. It's almost time for people to start coming in."

"I'm pretty sure everything is as ready as it can be, Sparks."

My pulse hiccupped as a sudden thought occurred to me. "Aaron and some of the staff set up the lights in the trees, but I didn't check to make sure they're working."

I started to pull out of West's arms, but he tightened them around me, holding me in place. "Hey," he said, his throaty voice as gentle as I'd ever heard it. "I can get one of my attendants to check. You don't need to do everything."

"It's not everything," I protested. "The celebrations were my idea—it's my responsibility if anything goes wrong."

"And what would be so horrifically wrong about a few lights not turning on?"

When I couldn't think of a good answer to that right away, he shook his head at me. "You know, I do enjoy a good meal and holiday cheer in the air, but I'm starting to be glad Christmas will be over soon."

I could tell from his tone that he was mostly joking, but a lump of emotion filled my throat anyway. "Do you really think — Has it been too much? Am I just being ridiculous?"

"What?" he scoffed. "You can be a lot of things, Sparks, but ridiculous isn't one of them. Why does all this matter so much to you?"

"It just—" I started, and the lump swelled, choking me. My eyes felt abruptly hot. I dragged in a breath, and it came ragged.

"Ren." West turned me toward him and cupped my cheek.

His dark green eyes searched mine. "What's wrong? You've been pushing yourself to the limit all week. These are just Christmas parties. People will have a good time—they aren't expecting perfection. So why are you? What's really going on?"

I swallowed hard. Tears I didn't want to let fall burned behind my eyelids when I blinked.

West had been the last of my mates to trust me, for the same reasons that made him the hardest to brush off when he wanted an answer. And now that I had his love and loyalty, I knew I had every shred of them he had to offer.

It couldn't hurt him to admit the things churning inside me. The real problem was I hadn't wanted to acknowledge them to myself. But I didn't think he was going to let me sweep this topic aside now.

My voice came out quiet. "Staying busy getting things ready for the celebrations—it's kept me distracted. So I don't have to think about—" My voice caught again.

"About what?" West said softly.

My hand went to my belly, to the shape of my daughter—our daughter—that I could feel in increasing detail through my own flesh. "I want to meet her. I'm so happy she's coming. But I'm also—I'm scared for her, West. The last year has gone really well: no major conflicts, everyone getting along reasonably well. But what if that doesn't last? I've never been able to count on keeping the things I care about. I don't want to take the happiness I feel right now for granted, and then have it be taken away."

"Oh, Sparks." My mate trailed his thumbs over my cheeks to ease away the few tears that had managed to seep out. I made myself meet his gaze again and saw nothing but love and compassion there.

"I don't think we should ever take our happiness for

granted," he said. "But I don't think you need to be scared either. The last year has gone well because of the work you've done, the decisions you've made. You're the best dragon shifter any of our kin could have hoped for." The corner of his mouth quirked up. "Hell, you even managed to win me over, so clearly you're doing something very right."

I couldn't help snorting in amusement. "The biggest challenge of my rule." The knot inside me hadn't entirely released, though. "There are so many things I don't know. I've never been a mother before. I haven't even been a dragon shifter, really, for all that long. What if I do end up screwing something up?"

"Then we'll set it right again. We all start somewhere. Look at how much we've figured out as we go already. Life's thrown a hell of a lot of challenges at us so far, and we've met them all." He bowed his head until his forehead touched mine. "You don't have to tell yourself there'll be nothing but happiness from here until forever. Just trust that whatever comes, we'll find our way through it. You can believe that, can't you?"

When he put it like that, his reassurance didn't seem so hard to accept. My next breath came a little easier. I raised my head, seeking out West's lips. He kissed me intently, as if he were pouring all the feeling he had in him into that embrace. I lost myself in it, in him, just for that minute.

"Better?" he asked afterward. "I know I'm not always the most elegant with my words. If you need to talk to the others too to feel more secure..."

I shook my head. "No," I said. "I think I'm good now. Maybe I'll want to talk to the others later, but you said just the right things." Or maybe it was also that *I'd* said the right things. My chest felt lighter with those worries no longer unspoken.

West smiled. "Come on, then," he said. "Someone told me there's some lights we really need to check."

I elbowed him, and he chuckled as we walked out of the dining hall.

An hour later, as I sat with West and the rest of my mates at our table, filling my hungry stomach and watching so many of my kin doing the same, a sense of satisfaction spread through me in a warm glow. Laughter and upbeat voices carried from all the tables. Kylie and Felix had scooted close together, him offering her a bite of something off his fork. There was nothing in the air right now except the enjoyment of good company and an excellent meal.

I had done well by my people—the people I hadn't even known were mine until eighteen months ago. My alphas and I had accomplished an awful lot in that time. And when I stopped worrying about the future and let myself just look at what was here in the present, all I could see was happiness.

Even if it didn't last forever, the fact that we had it now counted for something. And I'd do my damned best to see that we had it for as close to forever as I could manage. That was all anyone could really ask from me.

West leaned over when I'd taken my last bite. "Should I tell them to get the bonfire ready?"

I nodded and got to my feet. This part of the celebration that I'd planned specially for the canine kin felt even more appropriate now. Time for all of us to take a little weight off our chests.

"Everyone," I called out to our guests. "Please join us in the courtyard now for a special bonfire."

The crowd followed us out to the courtyard. Flames were already licking over the heaped wood, sending tangy pine smoke up toward the darkening sky. The breeze nipped at my ears as I stepped outside, but the blaze chased the chill away as soon as I got close. Its ruddy light wavered over the faces all around the fire.

"It's been a good year," I said over the crackling of the flames, turning to take in all of the kin gathered around me. "And I mostly want us to celebrate those good parts. But nothing good comes from sweeping over past hurts. Any of you who was here on this estate or in one of the settlements that came under siege last year had more than your share of pain. So tonight I thought we could let our old fears and angers go. Anything leftover that we don't need to hang on to, to free up that space in ourselves for the next year."

I motioned to the containers of tokens and pencils that Kylie and Felix had set out on one of the wooden benches. "You don't have to share it with anyone else—just write what you'd like to release on one of these wooden tokens and toss it into the fire."

I picked up one of the tokens myself, a sanded-smooth rectangle about half the size of my palm. As I stepped back from the bench where the containers were sitting, others gathered around. I printed carefully on the pale birch surface.

Doubting that I can be a good leader. Focusing on fear instead of joy.

I tossed mine into the fire. It disappeared into the red-hot depths in an instant, with a sizzle I felt as much as heard. A smile tugged at my lips.

Around the fire, more and more of my kin threw in their own tokens. Their faces glowed now with more than just the reflected firelight. In that relief, I saw all the proof I could have needed that I belonged here.

CHAPTER 9

West

My fellow alphas and I had all grabbed tokens of our own to join in the fiery ritual Ren had suggested. Aaron and Nate jotted down a few words quickly and let theirs fly. Marco smirked to himself as he scrawled something.

I stared at the blank surface of mine, the hot sharp smoke tickling my lungs. My fingers had tensed around the pencil.

"Having trouble thinking of anything to put?" Ren said teasingly.

I grimaced. "No. I know exactly what I most need to let go of. It's the doing it that's not easy."

But I'd committed to this course already, hadn't I, in a much more concrete way than writing a word on a scrap of wood? My body balked for a second longer, and then I scribbled the letters quickly.

Prejudice.

That covered it in a nutshell. I flicked the token into the flames to join the others.

I wasn't sure I felt all that much of a release. My gut was still tight when I left my mate and the other alphas to see where Felix had gotten to.

I'd been a little worried I'd find him literally wrapped up in *his* almost-mate, that friend of Ren's, but they were just chatting with a few of the staff near the fire. I caught the fox shifter's eye and motioned him off to the side.

"Should we head out to get him?" I asked.

Felix checked the time on his phone. "He's not supposed to meet us at the pick-up spot for another half an hour."

"It's a fifteen-minute drive," I said. "I want a bit of time in advance to scope out the lay of the land. He might be acting friendly, but he's still a bloodsucker."

Felix shrugged. He was my main liaison to the vampire community in New York, helping keep the peace with them since we'd overcome their attacks last year, but he didn't dispute my sense of caution. "We can go, then. You're the one who invited him."

I glowered at him, and his jaw twitched as he lowered his eyes apologetically. But it was true. I'd invited the bloodsucker. I'd probably have felt a lot better if this whole thing *hadn't* been my responsibility.

Kylie ambled over to us. "What are you two discussing all secretively?" she asked, setting her hands on her hips.

"Nothing anyone who doesn't already know needs to know yet," I said, and paused. "If Ren starts looking for me, tell her I'll be back soon."

"Oh, yeah, I'm sure she's going to be real happy with that answer," Kylie said, but she didn't push. "Make sure you bring my guy back in one piece, you hear?"

I shouldered Felix toward the garage. "I think that depends more on him than me."

Felix gave her a little wave before loping ahead of me to the garage around the side of the estate house. He was already in my favorite car, the engine just rumbling into action, when I came in.

"Are you sure it's a good idea making this a surprise?" he said as I dropped into the passenger seat.

"It's not going to be a surprise to the guards," I said. "They're all prepared. I'll handle the rest. I don't think anyone's going to be all that happy about the idea without the proper context."

I couldn't say for sure they'd be happy about it even with the context, but I guessed that was on me too. This plan had seemed like a good idea when I'd thought of it, after Ren had started on her Christmas obsession and Aaron had mentioned to the rest of us his bright idea of reaching out to the fae monarch.

Of course, the difference was that during last year's battle, the fae had stepped up and helped us survive. The vampires had been the ones trying to kill us.

Felix drove the car out through the side gate and along the road that rambled off farther to the northeast. The pines loomed on either side in pointed silhouettes.

We stopped at the crossroads I'd suggested as the meeting spot, pulling up on the gravel shoulder. No one else was nearby that I could see. I stepped out of the car and prowled around the intersection, drinking in the air. Not a hint of that sickly undead smell reached my nose.

No ambush. Everything was proceeding according to our agreement so far.

I was back at our car when headlights gleamed in the distance. A sleek sedan glided into view and parked on the opposite shoulder. The driver got out—I couldn't see anyone else in the car. We'd asked him to come alone, and it looked as though he actually had. The thump of my heart slowed just slightly.

The vamp who'd come was a tall skinny guy with the usual pale gauntness to his face. He smiled tightly at me, standing as if he wasn't completely sure he should leave his car.

"Alpha of the canine kin," he said in a thin but steady voice. "My name is Edwin. I come from the house of the king, and I can speak on his behalf."

"All right, Edwin," I said, trying and failing to erase my instinctive gruffness from my voice. "Come on over. We won't bite."

His jaw tensed, and I reminded myself that I was supposed to be aiming for diplomacy here. But the vampire envoy did cross the road and allowed me to usher him into the back of the car. I hesitated for a second there, torn between having to sit next to the bloodsucker or sitting up front knowing he was at my back.

A show of bravery and good faith seemed like the better option. I shut the door and took my seat next to Felix again.

"So, Edwin," I said as Felix started the engine. I studied the vampire through the rearview mirror. "Why did the king send you?"

"When your liaison extended the request, I volunteered," the vampire said from where he was sitting stiffly on the aged leather.

My eyebrows jumped up. "And why's that?" I wouldn't have thought any of the vamps would be in a hurry to throw themselves in with a crowd of shifters, but I managed to restrain myself from voicing that fact.

"I've been pushing for us to make a greater gesture of good will for some time," he said. "This seemed the ideal opportunity to put my money where my mouth is, as they say."

Ah. Well, that didn't sound particularly suspicious. And it was only fair that I gave him a warning. "A lot of my people were hurt during the attacks. Some of the kin who'll be there tonight lost friends or family. You'll have to be prepared that not everyone is going to be all that welcoming."

"I was never led to expect anything else," Edwin said dryly. He was silent for a moment, his gaze sliding to the dark landscape outside the car window. Then he added, "If it makes any difference to you, I was against those attacks from the start. I didn't participate in them because at the time they were going on, I was confined in one of the former king's prisons, awaiting trial for speaking against him."

Anyone could have said that to try to gain sympathy points, but his tone sounded genuine to me. I swiveled in my seat to look at him directly. "Thank you," I said, and found I meant it more than I'd expected to. "You put yourself on the line for us—whatever your reasons."

The tight smile came back. "And my people never should have put any of your lives on the line. But all we can do now is move forward. If anything, I should thank you. It's quite possible I owe my continued survival to your victory."

The lights of the estate came into view around the still dancing blaze of the bonfire. Felix moved to turn the wheel, and I shook my head. "The front gate this time."

"Whatever you say, boss," he said in a voice that was a tad tongue-in-cheek. I decided not to submit him to another glower. Felix had a mouth on him, but he'd done good work.

The guards at the gate tugged it open. We drove just inside, and I motioned for Felix to stop. If this went sideways, I wanted us to be able to escort Edwin off the premises as quickly as possible.

I got out first and stepped to the back door to escort the

vampire out. My kin around the bonfire had let their conversations trail off to peer over at us. Just barely in view beyond the flames, my mate was craning her neck to see. Aaron rested a hand on her shoulder, and all three of the other alphas started heading our way with her.

"My kin," I said. "We have a guest tonight who will be making only a brief appearance, who would like to take the opportunity during this celebration to make a gesture of trust and peace. He is here on my invitation, and I expect you to behave with that in mind. He has something to say to our dragon shifter."

I opened the door, and Edwin stepped out. I heard breaths drawn in sharply and a few rough mutters, but no one said anything loud enough that I could hear it.

Ren paused where she'd been skirting the fire. Edwin's gaze found her and then drifted to the wavering flames. His body went momentarily rigid at the sight.

Fire was one of the few things that could kill a vamp.

Before I had to say anything, he pushed himself forward, toward Ren and toward the bonfire. My kin had drawn back in the wake of the car, leaving him a clear path. I walked just behind him, scanning their faces, offering a show of confidence to reassure them.

"We should toss him into the fire and be done with him!" someone called out, and someone else laughed.

My head snapped toward those voices. "Insult my guest and you also insult me," I said with a growl.

There was only silence after that.

The fire crackled and snapped as Edwin approached my mate. Sparks drifted in the air near him. He winced, only a few feet away from those flames now. After another step, he sank down onto one knee with his head bowed before our dragon shifter. Aaron, Nate, and Marco stayed at her flanks, poised to protect her if need be.

But there was no need. "Dragon shifter," the vampire said in a strained voice, "I've come here tonight because I want to show how committed my people are to ensuring the peace between our kinds continues—and strengthens. We've kept our distance out of shame and reluctance for far too long. We *should* be the ones to come out and meet you on your ground, to prove your forgiveness matters enough that we will lay our lives in your hands for the opportunity to receive it. Knowing what I do about what happened here and elsewhere at my people's hands, I wouldn't have blamed you if you *had* ordered me tossed into that fire. I thank you for your mercy."

Ren stared at him, looking momentarily speechless. Then she drew up her chin. "Did you come all the way out here just to say that?"

It was haughty, but that was the attitude my kin needed to see. They needed to know she wasn't immediately softened by his words. Pride swelled in my chest. This woman had grown into her role so well, so quickly. With the firelight washing over her, she looked every inch a queen.

"No," Edwin said quietly. "I am merely an envoy. My king wishes to express that if you would have him, he would attend to you to make apologies in person and to discuss how we might proceed in greater harmony, in the place and at the time of your choosing."

Ren's eyes widened. Even I was a bit flabbergasted at that offer. The king of the vampires was lowering himself to being at the dragon shifter's beck and call? I couldn't think of when that had ever happened in any history I'd been taught.

But then, they'd never before had such a horrifying crime to atone for.

Ren's voice softened in turn as she gave her reply. "I thank you and him for that offer. I'll need some time to decide what would suit me best, but I will take him up on it. And thank you for coming to show there can be trust between us."

Edwin eased himself to his feet. "I'll take my leave of you, then," he said, "and convey your thanks to my king. I have no wish to disrupt your kin's celebration any more than I already have."

He slipped back to the car, and I nodded to Felix. Enough tension had left me that I could watch the fox shifter drive the vampire back to his sedan without any emotion other than relief.

When the gate had closed behind them, voices rose up again, most of them falling back into the same sort of chatter as before.

"Hey!" Marco called out. "Didn't I hear something about some glorious singing we were going to get to hear?"

A few nearby shifters laughed, and several carolers assembled by the fire. They launched into a rendition of "Silent Night," punctuated by howls from a couple of wolves who'd shifted. Ren sidled over to me and leaned against my chest when I tucked her into my embrace.

"Well, that was definitely an unexpected present," she said.

"But a good one, I hope?" I said.

"Yes. Very good. That is—" She looked up at me. "Do you think he really means it? The king?"

I thought about the way Edwin had talked in the car. The fact that he'd shown up here at all. "Yeah," I said. "I do."

A smile crossed her lips, so sweet and delicate I wished I could hold it and this moment close forever. Her hand dropped to her belly. For a minute, we just rocked gently from side to side in time with the singing. Then my mate's shoulder tensed against me.

"What?" I said, tensing in turn.

She gazed down at herself, her hand completely still. Her fingers twitched. Her eyes shot back to me.

"She's coming soon," she said with a faint tremble in her voice. "I can—I can feel it. We need to leave for the dragon estate *now*."

CHAPTER 10

Ren

West's healers checked my pulse and my belly and down below, despite my faint protests. "I'm not having contractions yet," I said. "It's not happening *right* now. I can just tell it'll start soon. If we leave now, we should be fine."

But I understood why they wanted to check first. It wasn't as if I had any desire to give birth on a plane in flight, as appropriate as that might have been in a metaphorical way. I really wasn't in labor, though. What I felt from my daughter was a sort of hum of energy, slowly heightening, that I recognized even if I hadn't known to expect it and didn't know how to put it into words. As if she were gearing up for her main appearance.

"Are you sure we should risk it?" Nate asked. All four of the alphas had gathered around me in the healers' room.

"It's only a two-hour flight," I said. "A couple of the healers can come along if you're worried." I glanced around into my mates' nervously excited faces. I couldn't keep a quaver from coming into my next words. "I want to be home when she comes."

I didn't know if it would sound silly to them. The dragon shifter estate had only been my home until I'd been five years old, and then for the last year and a half since I'd returned. And in that year and a half I'd spent more time traveling between my alphas' estates and to other shifter settlements than actually there. But it sounded less silly than the desire that was really ringing through me, which was, *I want my mother.*

I couldn't have her. I'd lost Mom years ago. But the dragon shifter estate was the only place we'd been together while we were really ourselves, no secrets, no suppressed memories. Fragments of her presence lingered in the halls and the rooms.

More than anything, I wanted that presence with me as I took this final step to becoming a mother myself.

My mates gazed back at me, their expressions softening. West looked at the others. "The jet here can leave almost immediately. The healers confirmed that she isn't in labor yet. If this is what she needs…"

Aaron nodded. Marco brushed his hand over my hair. "Then she should have it," he said.

Nate still looked worried, but he tipped his head in acceptance.

So a few minutes later, we hustled through the night to the landing strip. "Sleep on the plane, as much as you can," the healer who came with us told me. "Once you do get really started, you'll want to be as well-rested as possible."

In the jet's back room, I curled up on the bed with my arms cradling my belly and closed my eyes. My nerves were jumping with so much anticipation that I wasn't sure I'd managed to drift off at all when Aaron came to wake me for the landing.

Something in my heart brightened at the sight of my estate,

the windows all along the walls of that miniature castle gleaming in preparation for our arrival. One of my mates had called ahead for the staff to be ready, and they'd expected us in the morning anyway. The four alphas formed a shield against the cold wind as they ushered me into the house.

I'd just made it to my bedroom when the first contraction came, like a pinch expanding into an ache that spread across the base of my belly. My breath caught. I sat down on the edge of the massive bed.

"It's started, has it?" said one of the healers from my own estate—a wolf shifter named Lydia whose face was lined and whose hair was slate-gray streaked with white. She'd helped my mother deliver me and my sisters, and she guided me farther up the bed with a knowing look. "It'll take some time before we have any real work to do. Rest as well as you can until the pains start coming close together."

"What do you need from us?" Aaron asked me.

I swallowed hard, feeling abruptly uncertain with the unfamiliar sensations starting to rise through my body. "Just—stay with me."

"Of course."

They all climbed onto the bed around me, surrounding me so I could nestle between their forms. I breathed in their combined scents, my forehead resting on West's shoulder, one hand clasped around Nate's fingers while my other palm stayed on my belly, and right then I didn't feel nervous at all. My daughter was coming. My mates and I were here, ready to welcome her. I was simply going to do what every dragon shifter before me had done.

Bathed in that warmth and reassurance, I did doze for a while. When I woke to dawn light streaming through the bedroom windows, it was with a sharper pinch that radiated all through my abdomen. A shiver ran through me. I waited for the next contraction to come, just a few minutes later, but I was ready for it. I could feel it. She was on her way.

My mates stirred when I sat up. "Should I call for the healers?" Aaron asked, studying my face.

"Yes," I said. "I—" My voice hitched as I rode out another contraction. "I think it's time."

Marco brought me a glass of water and rubbed my lower back as I drank from it. Nate slipped out and returned in a few minutes with an orange and some toast with butter. The younger healer who'd already arrived in the room nodded approvingly.

"It'll probably be a long day," she told me. "Best to keep up your strength."

I gulped down the meal I didn't really feel hungry for as quickly as I could. In between swallows, I practiced the steady inhale-exhale the healers had taught me during the birth preparations over the last few months. A restless urge wriggled through me.

"I don't want to just sit here."

"Walk around," Lydia said. "Find a good rhythm. That often helps carry you through the earlier stages."

West had already been pacing the room. He fell into step with me as I wandered from one side of the room to the other, pausing here and there to brace myself against those deepening twinges.

"Don't look so fretful," I told him. "You're not the one about to propel an entire dragon shifter out of her body."

His tense expression broke with a chuckle. "I can't argue with that. I've never been good with waiting."

As another rush of pain shot through me, an idea sparked with it. "You can get the water running in the tub," I said. "I think I'm going to want that pretty soon."

He gave me a kiss and a grateful look before hurrying off to the en suite bathroom. Marco had started my phone playing the songs we'd picked out ahead of time—I'd almost forgotten about that. The sweet music of my mother's favorite folk singer filled the room. It brought a fresh inspiration.

"Her book," I said. "Where's my mother's book—the one Nate's kin gave me?"

The bear shifter grabbed it off the side table where I must have set it down last night. "Do you want to read it now?"

I pressed my hand to my belly as another contraction rocked me and then started walking again. "I don't know if I really can. I feel better if I keep moving. Can you read a few of the stories to me?"

He gave me that warm smile I loved and sat down on the edge of the bed, opening the book. His low voice washed over me as he read a mouse shifter's account of seeing my mother when she'd come to the disparate estate for the first time to officially claim the alpha as her mate and be welcomed by his kin. I could almost picture her there, a younger version of the woman I remembered, telling the assembled shifters how proud she was to be the one to serve them, already preparing an even-handed resolution for some dispute.

He was on to the fifth account, from a bobcat shifter, when my legs started to wobble with the intensity of the labor. "West!" I hollered. "Is that bath ready?"

"It has been for a while," he said from the other end of the room. I'd been so lost in the stories and keeping myself steady that I hadn't noticed him coming back in. "Let me make sure it's still hot enough."

I followed him in and paced on the tiled floor while he and then Lydia adjusted the water. With their help, I clambered into the tub. The warm water closed around my body in a liquid embrace that gave an immediate relief. I sighed, leaning against the polished side of the tub.

My mates took turns sitting by the edge, stroking my hair, rubbing my shoulders. After a while, the contractions blurred together so much that I wasn't aware of much except bracing myself for each new wave and gripping the hands that reached out to me. As the pressure inside built, my dragon's claws started to extend from my fingertips with each rush. Scales broke out on my sides.

"Partial shifting is normal during this stage," Lydia said, unperturbed. She made me sip some fruit juice. The other healer added more hot water to the tub. Then all at once my entire body seemed to clench from the waist down. Tears sprang to my eyes.

"I think she's ready to come now," I gasped out.

"We can do this in the water or out, however you feel most comfortable," Lydia said, her voice so calm and sure that the momentary flicker of panic wisped away.

I tested my arms against the water and grimaced. "I think out."

My mates had to support me on the way back to the bedroom, where the healers had set down sheets. The stool they'd brought looked suddenly appealing. I hunkered down on it, panting, and my mates circled me, all of them holding me up together.

The time after that was a total haze. I breathed and I pushed, and voices murmured encouragement all around me. My clawed fingers dug into the sides of the stool. A small puff of dragon fire slipped from my mouth. And then, with one last pang that echoed through every muscle, my daughter emerged into the world.

The healers fussed over her for a minute, cleaning her and

whispering softly to her as she started to wail. My gaze stayed glued to that tiny form as my body shifted completely back into its human state. My heart was already swelling with even more love than I'd already had in me for this life I'd helped create.

Lydia brought my daughter to me and laid her on my chest so her little infant mouth could find its way to my breast. I cradled her, tears in my eyes, as she drank her first meal. A sprinkling of dark hair covered her round head. Her skin was so soft I was almost afraid my embrace would break her. But I could already feel strength in her too.

She wasn't just a baby. She was a dragon shifter too. And she would be a great one. I'd be there to guide her, every step of the way.

"Have you decided on a name?" Lydia asked.

I almost laughed, hearing that question again. "Not yet. I think I want to get to know her a little bit first." Maybe just meeting her wasn't enough. It felt like an even bigger decision, looking at the little person I was cradling against me.

The sky had darkened outside the window. A whole day had passed while I'd been bringing this treasure into the world. With a sigh, I let my mates guide me to the bed. They settled around me again as I lay on my side, tucking our daughter close to me.

She blinked, peering around at us with squinty eyes. "Looks like she's got Marco's hair," Nate said, beaming.

"Lucky for her," Marco said, his voice just as bright. "And our eagle shifter's eyes, it appears?"

Aaron grazed his fingers over our daughter's back with a fond smile. "I think all babies' eyes are blue to start out with. But we can always hope it'll stick."

"Because there'd be something wrong with her ending up with green ones?" West put in wryly, kissing my shoulder.

I offered my other breast to our little girl, and she turned her head away with a grunting sound. Marco started to laugh. "Clearly she got wolf boy's attitude."

Despite my exhaustion, I started to giggle. "Hey!" West protested, but then we were all laughing. In the midst of that blissful sound, our daughter snuggled closer to me and shut her eyes. I slid my arm around her protectively and relaxed my head into the pillow, waiting for sleep to take me too.

The last thing I heard was Aaron's voice murmuring, "Merry Christmas."

CHAPTER 11

Ren

THE THIRD TIME my daughter woke me up to feed, the sun was up outside. I'd stirred awake before she'd made much of a sound to her delicate face nuzzling at my breast. My mates were all still sleeping.

I lay there quietly for a short while, letting her have her fill. A lot of my body was still achy, but my legs itched to move. I carefully eased myself off of the bed without disturbing the guys, holding our little one against me with one arm and then the other as I tugged on a night gown. My slippers were right there waiting for me to step into. Then I picked up a blanket that had been left folded on the dresser and wrapped that around both of us.

The gleam of the sunlight called to me. I shuffled over to the glass door that led to my chamber's balcony.

Chilly air washed over me as I eased it open. I cuddled my daughter even more carefully under the shelter of the blanket before I stepped outside. She let out a contented-sounding sigh. Her tiny hand traced over my collarbone.

My breath caught at the scene that met me. It must have snowed overnight. A white crust sparkled across the valley and the mountain slopes as far as I could see. Frost glittered on the balcony railing. We'd gotten our white Christmas after all.

My daughter tipped her head toward my other breast, and I helped her latch on. I gazed down at her for a moment before raising my head again.

"This is your home," I told her quietly. "It was mine too, when I was your age, and your grandmother's and your great grandmother's before me, going so far back I can't even count. No one will ever be able to take that away from you. I promise."

For the first time I could remember since the first moment I'd felt her growing inside me, a sense of certainty rose up inside me with those words. I could keep that promise. Whatever it took, whatever happened along the way. I knew that, down to my bones.

The rogues were gone. We'd made peace with the fae. The vampires were doing penance. The future that lay ahead of us could be a beautiful one.

When I looked down at her again, a smile stretched across my face that felt as brilliant as the gleam of the sun on the snow.

She was here. My daughter. And she'd woken up more love in me than I'd ever have imagined my body could contain.

The door rasped open behind me. My mates stepped out, one by one, to stand around me. West set his hand on the small of my back. Marco rested his on my shoulder. We stood there for a minute, taking in the snowy landscape in silence, one united family.

"Have you gotten to know her enough to decide her name?" Nate asked gently.

I brushed my thumb over our daughter's cheek, memorizing every detail of that perfect face. My mother had been Haven. My sisters, Temperance and Verity. Myself, Serenity. Running through those names in my head, reveling in the swell of emotion inside me, I found I was certain about one more thing.

"I have," I said, my smile stretching even wider. "Her name is Joy."

ABOUT THE AUTHOR

Eva Chase lives in Canada with her family. She loves stories both swoony and supernatural, and strong women and the men who appreciate them. Along with the Dragon Shifter's Mates series, she is the author of the Their Dark Valkyrie series, the Witch's Consorts series, the Demons of Fame Romance series, the Legends Reborn trilogy, and the Alpha Project Psychic Romance series.

Connect with Eva online:
www.evachase.com
eva@evachase.com

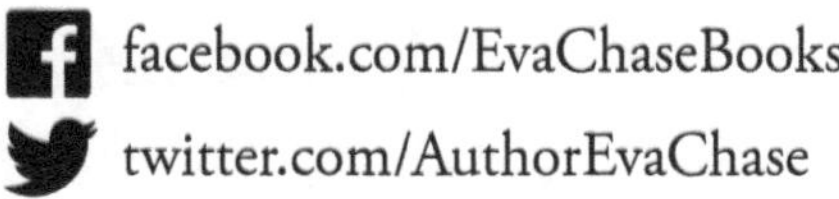

www.ingramcontent.com/pod-product-compliance
Lightning Source LLC
Chambersburg PA
CBHW020345310726
48979CB00015B/2514/J

* 9 7 8 1 9 8 9 0 9 6 9 7 0 *